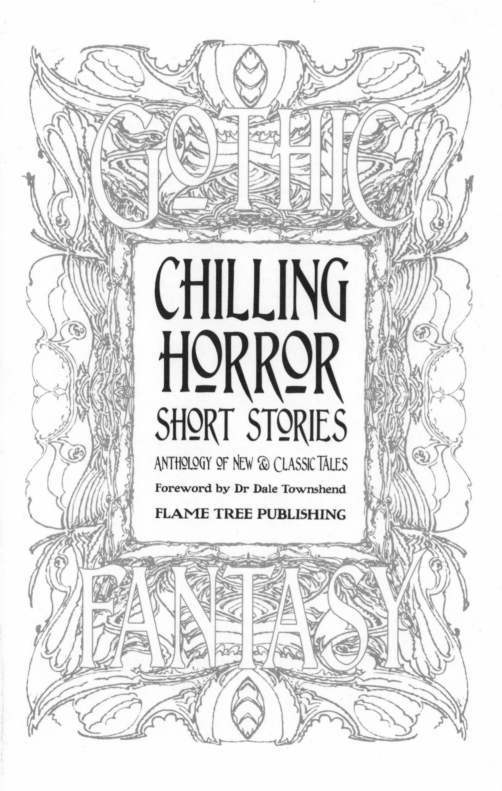

CHILLING HORROR

SHORT STORIES

ANTHOLOGY OF NEW & CLASSIC TALES

Foreword by Dr Dale Townshend

FLAME TREE PUBLISHING

This is a FLAME TREE Book

Publisher & Creative Director: Nick Wells
Project Editor: Laura Bulbeck
Editorial Board: Frances Bodiam, Josie Mitchell, Gillian Whitaker

With special thanks to Amanda Crook, Kaiti Porter

Publisher's Note: Due to the historical nature of the text, we're aware that there may be some language used which has the potential to cause offence to the modern reader. However, wishing overall to preserve the integrity of the text, rather than imposing contemporary sensibilities, we have left it unaltered.

FLAME TREE PUBLISHING
6 Melbray Mews, Fulham,
London SW6 3NS, United Kingdom
www.flametreepublishing.com

First published 2015

17 19 18
5 7 9 10 8 6 4

ISBN: 978-1-78361-374-8

The cover image is created by Flame Tree Studio based on artwork by Slava Gerj and Gabor Ruszkai.

A copy of the CIP data for this book is available from the British Library.

Printed and bound in Turkey

GOTHIC

CHILLING HORROR

SHORT STORIES

ANTHOLOGY OF NEW & CLASSIC TALES

Foreword by Dr Dale Townshend

FLAME TREE PUBLISHING

FANTASY

Contents

Foreword: Chilling Horror Stories

IN HER POSTHUMOUSLY PUBLISHED ESSAY 'On the Supernatural in Poetry' (1826), Ann Radcliffe, the most popular, successful and well-remunerated Gothic writer of the late eighteenth century, set out an extremely influential distinction between the aesthetics of terror and horror. 'Terror and horror are so far opposite', her fictional stand-in in the essay, Mr W_, observes, 'that the first expands the soul, and awakens the faculties to a high degree of life'. Horror, by contrast, 'contracts, freezes, and nearly annihilates them'. While, according to the principles that Edmund Burke had outlined in *A Philosophical Enquiry into the Origin of Our Ideas of the Sublime and Beautiful* (1757), the terror that Radcliffe's speaker finds in the work of Shakespeare and Milton is sublime, horror, the essay maintains, is lacking in the requisite sense of uncertainty that is central to the generation of sublime or awe-inspiring effects. It is on the principle of obscurity, then, that the distinction between horror and terror for Radcliffe ultimately depends: 'and where lies the great difference between horror and terror', her speaker rhetorically enquires, 'but in the uncertainty and obscurity, that accompany the first, respecting the dreaded evil?' If terror demands a lack of clarity, horror thrives on a sense of immediacy; while terror proceeds by means of hints, suggestions and subtle prompts, horror is always graphic in its rendition, leaving almost nothing to the work of the imagination. Terror is an aesthetic of economy, while horror is the writing of excess.

Though located very firmly in eighteenth-century debates, Ann Radcliffe's account remains central to the ways in which we conceptualize the aesthetics of horror today. Notable in this regard is the emphasis that her essay places upon horror's effects upon the physical body of the spectator: while the life-enhancing scenes of terror are said to 'expand' the 'soul', horror 'contracts, freezes and nearly annihilates' his or her faculties. The ghost's lines from Act I, scene v of Shakespeare's *Hamlet*, frequently cited in Gothic tales of terror and wonder, illustrate horror's corporeal effects particularly well: 'I could a tale unfold whose lightest word / Would harrow up thy soul, freeze thy young blood, / Make thy two eyes, like stars, start from their spheres, / Thy knotted and combined locks to part / And each particular hair to stand on end, / Like quills upon the fretful porpentine'. Freezing the blood, causing the eyes to leave their sockets, the hair to stand on end like the quills of a porcupine: horror demands of the reader's body a physical reaction. Indeed, perhaps its appeal today lies precisely in its ability to reawaken through its repulsive and shocking scenes the human bodies that have been elided and repressed by the screens and digital networks of cyberculture in the twenty-first century.

More than generating these effects in its participants, horror, from its eighteenth-century literary origins to the horror films of the present, is also internally characterised by a concern with corporeality, with bodies that splatter and bleed, decompose and decay, mutate and change form. While terror engages the mind of the reader in attitudes of mystery, tension and suspense, horror, invariably with a certain forcefulness, confronts us with bodies that are broken, violated, wretched and foreign indeed, with physical forms that may no longer be deemed 'human' at all. Such is the case in Ambrose Bierce's 'The Damned Thing' (1893), in which the invisible, superhuman force or 'thing' of the story's title violently destroys and eviscerates the body of Hugh Morgan in ways that suggest the activities of a mountain lion. When such forces of invisible horror assume physical shape and form, they are often monstrous, as they are in H. P. Lovecraft's 'The Dunwich Horror' (1929), in which the town and its people are menaced by an oozing, formless monster that is neither man nor beast nor fish. If the ghost is the cipher of terror, the monster, often spectacularly rendered, is horror's equivalent. These abject, monstrous figures characteristically engender feelings of dread, nausea and disgust in those who perceive them, three powerful impulses that are often recorded as protagonists' responses to monstrous objects within horror narratives themselves.

Here, the examples offered up in Matthew Lewis's seminal horror novel, *The Monk* (1796), are particularly illuminating: in each of the many scenes of horror that the novel contains are episodes that include the bloody dismemberment of an evil Prioress at the hands of an enraged crowd, and the live-burial of a young mother who, when she is discovered, is found still clinging to the maggot-eaten corpse of her baby. It is disgust that is the overwhelming response. Inducing repulsion, nausea and disgust, horror is an aesthetic of negative impulse, a characteristic clearly illustrated in the deranged narrator's responses to the screaming skull in F. Marion Crawford's story of 1911 of that name. As it does here, horror often involves the voluble articulation of the presence of death, either through the dead and mutilated bodies that litter so many horror fictions and films, or through foregrounding death's ubiquity even at the heart of life, perhaps no more so than in Edgar Allan Poe's 'The Masque of the Red Death' (1842). Continuously reminding us of the death-head beneath the mask, the skull beneath the skin, the grimace behind the smile; we're reminded of Radcliffe's observations that horror 'contracts, freezes and nearly annihilates' the human faculties. Herein, perhaps, lies the secret to the extraordinary popularity that the mode has enjoyed globally ever since it was first given literary expression in Britain at the end of the eighteenth century: though horror does not constitute for its devotees and fans a form of enjoyment in any simple sense, its appeal is no less gripping and powerful.

Dr Dale Townshend, 2015

Publisher's Note

THIS COLLECTION of *Gothic Fantasy* stories is part of a new anthology series, which includes sumptuous hardcover editions on Horror, Ghosts and Science Fiction. Each one carries a potent mix of classic tales and new fiction, forming a path from the origins of the gothic in the early 1800s, with the dystopian horror of Mary Shelley's 'The Mortal Immortal' to the chill of M.R. James's classic ghost stories, and the fine stories of the many modern writers featured in our new series. We have tried to mix some renowned classic stories (Edgar Allan Poe's 'The Black Cat'), with the less familiar (E.M. Forster's 'The Machine Stops'), and a healthy dose of previously unpublished modern stories from the best of those writing today.

Our 2015 call for new submissions was met by a tidal wave of entries, so the final selection was made to provide a wide and challenging range of tales for the discerning reader. Our editorial board of six members read each entry carefully, and it was difficult to turn down so many good stories, but inevitably those which made the final cut were deemed to be the best for our purpose, and we're delighted to be able to publish them here.

GOTHIC

CHILLING HORROR

SHORT STORIES

ANTHOLOGY OF NEW & CLASSIC TALES

Foreword by Dr Dale Townshend

FLAME TREE PUBLISHING

FANTASY

Ecdysis

Rebecca J. Allred

THE WAITING ROOM is empty, but it isn't quiet. Behind the door marked PRIVATE, a woman chokes out wet, anguished sobs. Dr. Allison's secretary pretends not to notice. She greets me with a practiced, professional smile that lacks even a hint of warmth and asks me to wait. Wait? For what? I'm the last patient of the week. Always have been. Always will be. It's not like there's a line.

I smile. Nod. Sure. I'll wait.

The secretary punches a few buttons, clicks the mouse once, twice, drags something across the screen, double clicks, and resumes typing. Once, I arrived early and caught her snooping through patient files. I could have turned her in – HIPAA violations are serious business – but frankly, I don't care, and even if I did, who'd believe a paranoid nutbag like me?

The secretary finishes checking her e-mail, or whatever's so important she couldn't check me in immediately, and asks for my name. She knows my name, but I give it to her anyway. She asks me to confirm my address. It hasn't changed since last week. Neither has my insurance. When she's done checking all her little boxes, I take a seat on a cream-colored sofa. The room smells like those little bars of soap shaped like sea shells, and an instrumental version of a song I almost recognize wafts from speakers I can't see. There is a coffee table made of black wood. Resting on its surface is a little Zen garden and the latest issues of half-a-dozen tabloid magazines. Behind the door, the crying has stopped.

My palms itch. I scratch them with nails jagged from daily dental manicures; they are barely long enough to register any measure of relief. One of my fingertips slides over a pair of fine, almost invisible, hairs.

In middle school, the kids said if you masturbated too much you'd get hairy palms.

I don't masturbate, and the hairs on my palm aren't really hairs.

Delusional Parasitosis, eponymously known as Ekbom's Syndrome (I read that in one of Dad's medical texts, back when I wanted to be a doctor, too) is the medical name for my particular brand of nutbaggery. Or it would be, if the bugs infesting my body were all in my head like Dr. Allison says. They *are* in my head; I can feel their antennae quiver as they poke through the skin on my face, masquerading as a beard, but they're other places, too.

I look back to Dr. Allison's secretary. She's working on the computer again, getting ready to go home for the long weekend. Mentally, she is already gone, and so she doesn't see me pinch the hairs, pluck a beetle from my palm, and toss it into the Zen garden on the table. It lands on its back, legs combing the air a few moments before it rights itself and burrows beneath the sand.

The door to Dr. Allison's office opens. A short woman with puffy eyes and dark hair pulled back into a tight ponytail exits. Her son is dead. Just like my mom. I know, because Dr. Allison's secretary isn't the only one who has been snooping in patient files.

Lately, I've been thinking about this woman. Every week, I think about stopping her as she passes me in the soap-scented waiting room, wrapping her in my arms, and allowing sorrow to flow freely between our wounded souls. We would share everything, she and I, and we would be made whole again. The woman's eyes never leave the floor as she moves across the room, her shoes whispering against the high-quality beige carpet and carrying her out of the building.

Dr. Allison lingers in the frame of the door marked PRIVATE. She invites me inside.

* * *

Dr. Allison isn't my first shrink, and she won't be my last. My first therapist was Dr. Carlson; he went to medical school with my dad. I went to see him when the bugs first showed up. Back then, they didn't call it Delusional Parasitosis – I know because Dad has copies of all my medical records up until age eighteen in a locked drawer in his office. They sit right on top of Mamma's.

Dr. Carlson was cool. He had red hair and a beard and smoked cigars (not during our sessions, but always when he came over to drink wine and "talk shop" with Dad). He told me the bugs were all in my head, too, but that it wasn't my fault, because Mamma had put them there. They were contagious, like the chicken pox, so Mamma had to go to the hospital for a while. When Mamma went away, so did the bugs.

Folie à deux is French for 'a madness shared by two.' The medical term is Shared Psychotic Disorder. That's what's written in my clinic notes from Dr. Carlson.

* * *

Dr. Allison's office doesn't smell like soap. It smells like lavender and tears. There is no music in here, only the soft, predictable tick of a clock counting down the minutes with malign diligence. The walls are lined with bookshelves, neatly organized. A desk with a computer, a stack of folders (patient files), a fountain pen, and a lead crystal paperweight is nestled in the corner. Near the center of the room are a high-back leather chair and a couch. She sits in the chair and gestures to the couch. Usually, I lie down. Today, I sit.

She comments on my beard, says she likes it (she's lying), and then asks how the last week has been. I tell her my roommate is mad at me because he thinks I killed his cat. She asks if I did, and I tell her I didn't (I'm lying, sort of), and she asks how that makes me feel.

I tell her I feel itchy.

* * *

The last time I saw Mamma alive, she was lying in an expensive hospital bed. The bugs hadn't bothered me in months, and both Dad and Dr. Carlson thought it would be okay for me to visit.

She looked different. Not like Mamma at all. Her soft yellow hair had been cut short. Dad said it was because she'd been pulling it out. The medical word for this is trichotillomania. There were little red sores all over her face and scalp, and she wore mittens that she couldn't take off.

Mamma just lay there, ignoring both me and my dad, murmuring over and over again that she was hungry. I begged Dad to get her something to eat. He patted me on the head, told me I was a good boy, and asked me to keep Mamma company while he stepped out to get some graham crackers.

As soon as he was gone, Mamma popped out of bed like some lunatic, termite-infested jack-in-the-box. She told me that the bugs were hungry. That if she didn't feed them soon, they would eat her instead. Tears welled up inside her eyes; tiny black specks swam in them. Mamma kissed me on the forehead and I felt something crawl out of her lips and up onto my scalp. I pulled back, running my hands thorough my hair, trying to dislodge the invader.

When I looked back at Mamma, she was standing very still, arms outstretched, staring at the ceiling. Her mouth was open wide, and a torrent of black vomit (not vomit, vomit doesn't writhe) spewed from it.

I screamed and screamed and screamed.

* * *

Dr. Allison asks if the new pills have been helping. At first I don't answer. I'm staring at the floor. One of the bugs has escaped. It's meandering across the nylon weave.

Formication is the medical term for the sensation of insects crawling in or under the skin. But it's the itching that really bothers me. The medical term for this is pruritis.

She asks again if the pills are helping.

I answer in the affirmative.

Dr. Allison follows my gaze, asks what I'm looking at.

I change the subject.

* * *

The last time I saw Mamma, she was lying in an expensive woden box. Her hair was long and soft again (a wig), and makeup covered most of the holes in her skin. Neither, however, could disguise how hollow she was. Dad said she'd gotten so skinny because she stopped eating.

The medical term for this is anorexia.

But I knew better. She hadn't stopped eating; she'd been eaten.

During the service, a procession of tiny insects filed out of the casket and onto the floor. They looked like ants, but they weren't; these were smaller. Harder. *Meaner.* They formed a quivering semi-circle around the coffin. Their soft hum was a nearly inaudible requiem. I pulled my feet up onto the pew and cried.

* * *

Dr. Allison is scribbling furiously on her yellow legal pad.

I've never spoken about my mother before.

* * *

The funeral was bad, but nowhere near as bad as what happened that night.

I was dreaming about Casey Nelson. In real life she was a redhead, but in my dream she had yellow hair like my mom, and her face was round and healthy, free from blemishes. Her eyes were lined by thick velvet lashes, and they glittered like geodes. Casey smiled as her lips whispered permission. I reached out and touched her, and she did the same, but where my hand closed around soft, pliable tissue, hers gripped flesh turned nearly to stone. I moaned and felt my crotch moisten.

Casey looked at me, but she wasn't smiling anymore, and her eyes had lost their mischievous sparkle. She released her grip and raised her hand to eye level. It had turned black. I shrank back in revulsion, only to realize it wasn't just her hand – my groin was black, too...

Necrosis is the medical term for premature tissue death.

At first I didn't think there could be anything worse than a lapful of necrotic penis, but as I reached a trembling hand down to examine my discolored genitals, I realized I was wrong. The stain didn't just cover my withering erection; it was coming from inside. And it was spreading. Little blebs of darkness separated from the primary mass, budding off like spores. They sprouted legs and antennae and—

I woke up, horrified to discover it wasn't just a dream.

The bugs were everywhere, clinging to my sheets, swarming over my thighs, marching up my belly toward my face and my silent, gaping mouth. I tumbled out of bed, knocking the lamp off the night stand; it clattered loudly but did not break. A few seconds later, the hallway light blinked on, and heavy, rapid footsteps climbed the stairs.

The light worked the insects into a frenzy. Desperate to get back inside, they filled my eyes. My ears. My nose. I gagged and choked as they fled down my throat.

That's how Dad found me: writhing on the floor, choking on my own nocturnal issue.

* * *

I tell Dr. Allison that it's my fault. That Mamma is dead because I couldn't help her. My beard quivers and I tug at it, dislodging a handful of beetles in the process.

Dr. Allison asks what I think I could have done to help Mamma. She doesn't notice the insects tumble from my fingers and scurry toward her.

I explain that the infestation is too much for a single person to accommodate. Mamma hadn't been trying to kill me that day in the hospital, as I'd thought at the time. We'd shared the burden before, and she'd desperately needed to share it again, but I had been too afraid. I hadn't understood.

She tells me that this is a major breakthrough. That the insects are just a representation of suppressed guilt. That all I have to do is learn to accept that I am blameless in my mother's death, and the bugs will go away.

The itch is almost unbearable now.

* * *

After that night, Dad and I didn't talk much. He assured me that what had happened was just a normal part of growing up, and that Mamma's death was responsible for transforming a normal, run-of-the-mill wet dream (the medical term is nocturnal emission) into the nightmare I had experienced. Whenever I tried to broach the subject of my affliction, Dad would just turn away and tell me to discuss it with Dr. Carlson. Then Dr. Leavett. Then Dr. Cotner. He was incapable of sharing the burden of my illness any further than financing its treatment.

If he suspected anything when the Girl Scout disappeared while selling cookies on our block, he never said a word. Maybe because after that, things got better, a *lot* better. For a while.

After nearly a decade of doctors and drugs, I stopped scratching and started sleeping again. That was the stretch where both Dad and I thought I was well enough to pursue a career in medicine after all. I moved out, enrolled in pre-med classes, and even took the MCAT. Scored damn well, too. I was out celebrating with some classmates who had also scored well when I felt the twinge.

I always got a little anxious when something itched – I couldn't help it, it was a conditioned response – but this was different. The tickle between my left index finger and thumb wasn't the usual pruritoceptive itch (that's the medical term for an itch originating in the skin) I'd learned to accept as part of normal human physiology. It was deeper, and as the weeks passed, it grew in both distribution and intensity.

* * *

I tell Dr. Allison that Mamma's isn't the only death I'm responsible for, and she frowns, the excitement of our "breakthrough" melting from her face. I tell her I lied about my roommate's cat. That it had been an experiment because I felt so badly about the homeless woman. And the Girl Scout, especially since she'd been an accident.

I stand and pull my shirt over my head, revealing constellations of angry red sores. I scratch at them, and Dr. Allison asks me to please return to my seat. Her face is calm, but her eyes are broadcasting an SOS to an empty ocean. She knows her secretary has gone home. There is nobody here to help her.

I am the last patient of the week. Always have been. Always will be.

* * *

It was Dad's birthday, and he invited me over for dinner. He'd been pressuring me about medical school applications, and that night, I finally mustered the courage to tell him what I'd known for the better part of the semester. That no matter what my MCAT scores had been, or how outstanding my letters of recommendation were, I would not be attending medical school the following fall. The only explanation necessary was for me to roll up my sleeves.

When Dad saw those old familiar craters, his face became an amalgam of disappointment and rage, and we spent the rest of the evening in silence. I thought he might never speak to me again, but as I was leaving, he told me to expect a call from Dr. Allison's office the following day.

Cruising past City Park on my way home, the itch flared so intensely that I couldn't resist the need to rub my shrieking eyeballs. If there had been anyone else on the road, I'd have caused an accident for sure. I piloted the vehicle into three parking spaces and rubbed and scratched until my eyelids were swollen and my cheeks were soaked with tears.

I opened the door and tumbled out of the car. The cool autumn air acted as a salve against my hot, prickling skin, and it chased away the rank aura of failure that had shrouded me since realizing a normal life was forever beyond my reach. I didn't dare get back in my car, so I walked, following the cement perimeter for about half a mile before the itch flared again.

I'd never entered the park after dark before, but the insanity burning just beneath my skin compelled me to abandon the sidewalk and venture into the wooded area. The pricking discomfort dulled, but did not abate, as I trudged deeper into the park. At the center was a playground. A pair of swings twirled lazily in the gentle breeze, inviting me to sample the careless freedom of childhood. As I approached, a shape broke free from the shadows.

I froze, fearful of what it might be, what it might *want*, but it was just a homeless woman. She asked if I had any spare change. I didn't. If I had, I'd have given it to her. Not because of some altruistic impulse, but because as soon as she spoke, my skin ignited once again, and I knew if I didn't put some distance between us it would be the end.

I told her I wasn't carrying any cash (no, not even a few cents for a cup of coffee) and brushed past her, my interest in the swings gone. Her next proposition stopped me in my tracks. She offered to blow me.

The medical term for this is fellatio.

In all my years, I'd never had a girlfriend, had not so much as kissed a girl, or a guy for that matter, opting instead to avoid any and all forms of sexual stimulation as if they might spell death – if not for me, then for the object of my desire. The only desire within me at that moment was to relieve the horrible itch. Despite my disgust, I knew that if it wasn't now, it would be later, and I really did feel badly about the Girl Scout. I even kept one of her MISSING posters folded between the pages of my dad's old Diagnostic and Statistical Manual, next to a copy of Mamma's death certificate.

With the flavor of bile creeping up my throat, I turned to face the woman and accepted.

* * *

I explain to Dr. Allison that what I really need is somebody to share this burden with me. Someone who understands my pain. A kindred spirit. A mother.

I'm crying, choked sobs of anguish and pain drowning out the indifferent tick of the clock. They're pouring out of me now, black perspiration streaming from my pores, infested tears squeezing from my eyes. Dr. Allison screams and leaps from her seat. Swatting away the first troops of the oncoming arthropod assault, she dives for the alarm switch under her desk. I snatch the paperweight and swing, striking her in the temple. There is a sound like a hard-boiled egg rolling over a granite countertop, and Dr. Allison crumples to the ground. The bugs on the carpet race toward her and disappear into an expanding pool of blood.

I remove the remainder of my clothing and move over Dr. Allison's unconscious form. I tell her I'm sorry, call her "Mamma" (the words materialize without a conscious thought), and then I descend, the swarm erupting, tearing through my skin, rising from my body like smoke above a raging fire. Sweet, blessed relief.

I call this cycle of agony and release ecdysis. This, however, is *not* a medical term, but an entomological one; there is no medical term for what I am.

When it's over, I flip through the stack of files on Dr. Allison's desk, searching until I find the one that belongs to the dark-haired woman with the dead son. All I need is the first page: the intake form with her name, address, and phone number.

I wipe the tears from my face and get dressed before taking one last look at the half-consumed pile of flesh that used to be my therapist. The sores on my skin are gone now, replaced by raw, healthy tissue, but the insects tumble over Dr. Allison like grains of black sand – humming, burrowing, feeding. By morning there will be nothing left. My stomach churns and I think I'll never eat again, though I know from experience it isn't true. I didn't want to hurt her, but Dr. Allison was no different than the Girl Scout, or the homeless woman, or my roommate's poor, stupid cat – all fit for consumption, but not for habitation. Despite her best efforts, she never could have helped me.

As I turn to leave, I glance down at the photograph in the bottom corner of the intake sheet clutched in my left hand and hope for both our sakes that next time will be different.

The Damned Thing

Ambrose Bierce

BY THE LIGHT of a tallow candle, which had been placed on one end of a rough table, a man was reading something written in a book. It was an old account book, greatly worn; and the writing was not, apparently, very legible, for the man sometimes held the page close to the flame of the candle to get a stronger light upon it. The shadow of the book would then throw into obscurity a half of the room, darkening a number of faces and figures; for besides the reader, eight other men were present. Seven of them sat against the rough log walls, silent and motionless, and, the room being small, not very far from the table. By extending an arm any one of them could have touched the eighth man, who lay on the table, face upward, partly covered by a sheet, his arms at his sides. He was dead.

The man with the book was not reading aloud, and no one spoke; all seemed to be waiting for something to occur; the dead man only was without expectation. From the blank darkness outside came in, through the aperture that served for a window, all the ever unfamiliar noises of night in the wilderness – the long, nameless note of a distant coyote; the stilly pulsing thrill of tireless insects in trees; strange cries of night birds, so different from those of the birds of day; the drone of great blundering beetles, and all that mysterious chorus of small sounds that seem always to have been but half heard when they have suddenly ceased, as if conscious of an indiscretion. But nothing of all this was noted in that company; its members were not overmuch addicted to idle interest in matters of no practical importance; that was obvious in every line of their rugged faces – obvious even in the dim light of the single candle. They were evidently men of the vicinity – farmers and woodmen.

The person reading was a trifle different; one would have said of him that he was of the world, worldly, albeit there was that in his attire which attested a certain fellowship with the organisms of his environment. His coat would hardly have passed muster in San Francisco: his footgear was not of urban origin, and the hat that lay by him on the floor (he was the only one uncovered) was such that if one had considered it as an article of mere personal adornment he would have missed its meaning. In countenance the man was rather prepossessing, with just a hint of sternness; though that he may have assumed or cultivated, as appropriate to one in authority. For he was a coroner. It was by virtue of his office that he had possession of the book in which he was reading; it had been found among the dead man's effects – in his cabin, where the inquest was now taking place.

When the coroner had finished reading he put the book into his breast pocket. At that moment the door was pushed open and a young man entered. He, clearly, was not of mountain birth and breeding: he was clad as those who dwell in cities. His clothing was dusty, however, as from travel. He had, in fact, been riding hard to attend the inquest.

The coroner nodded; no one else greeted him.

"We have waited for you," said the coroner. "It is necessary to have done with this business tonight."

The young man smiled. "I am sorry to have kept you," he said. "I went away, not to evade your summons, but to post to my newspaper an account of what I suppose I am called back to relate."

The coroner smiled.

"The account that you posted to your newspaper," he said, "differs probably from that which you will give here under oath."

"That," replied the other, rather hotly and with a visible flush, "is as you choose. I used manifold paper and have a copy of what I sent. It was not written as news, for it is incredible, but as fiction. It may go as a part of my testimony under oath."

"But you say it is incredible."

"That is nothing to you, sir, if I also swear that it is true."

The coroner was apparently not greatly affected by the young man's manifest resentment. He was silent for some moments, his eyes upon the floor. The men about the sides of the cabin talked in whispers, but seldom withdrew their gaze from the face of the corpse. Presently the coroner lifted his eyes and said: "We will resume the inquest."

The men removed their hats. The witness was sworn.

"What is your name?" the coroner asked.

"William Harker."

"Age?"

"Twenty-seven."

"You knew the deceased, Hugh Morgan?"

"Yes."

"You were with him when he died?"

"Near him."

"How did that happen – your presence, I mean?"

"I was visiting him at this place to shoot and fish. A part of my purpose, however, was to study him, and his odd, solitary way of life. He seemed a good model for a character in fiction. I sometimes write stories."

"I sometimes read them."

"Thank you."

"Stories in general – not yours."

Some of the jurors laughed. Against a sombre background humor shows high lights. Soldiers in the intervals of battle laugh easily, and a jest in the death chamber conquers by surprise.

"Relate the circumstances of this man's death," said the coroner. "You may use any notes or memoranda that you please."

The witness understood. Pulling a manuscript from his breast pocket he held it near the candle, and turning the leaves until he found the passage that he wanted, began to read.

"... The sun had hardly risen when we left the house. We were looking for quail, each with a shotgun, but we had only one dog. Morgan said that our best ground was beyond a certain ridge that he pointed out, and we crossed it by a trail through the *chaparral*. On the other side was comparatively level ground, thickly covered with wild oats. As we emerged from the *chaparral*, Morgan was but a few yards in advance. Suddenly, we heard, at a little distance to our right, and partly in front, a noise as of some animal thrashing about in the bushes, which we could see were violently agitated.

"'We've started a deer,' said. 'I wish we had brought a rifle.'

"Morgan, who had stopped and was intently watching the agitated chaparral, said nothing, but had cocked both barrels of his gun, and was holding it in readiness to aim. I thought him a trifle excited, which surprised me, for he had a reputation for exceptional coolness, even in moments of sudden and imminent peril.

"'O, come!' I said. 'You are not going to fill up a deer with quail-shot, are you?'

"Still he did not reply; but, catching a sight of his face as he turned it slightly toward me, I was struck by the pallor of it. Then I understood that we had serious business on hand, and my first conjecture was that we had 'jumped' a grizzly. I advanced to Morgan's side, cocking my piece as I moved.

"The bushes were now quiet, and the sounds had ceased, but Morgan was as attentive to the place as before.

"'What is it? What the devil is it?' I asked.

"'That Damned Thing!' he replied, without turning his head. His voice was husky and unnatural. He trembled visibly.

"I was about to speak further, when I observed the wild oats near the place of the disturbance moving in the most inexplicable way. I can hardly describe it. It seemed as if stirred by a streak of wind, which not only bent it, but pressed it down – crushed it so that it did not rise, and this movement was slowly prolonging itself directly toward us.

"Nothing that I had ever seen had affected me so strangely as this unfamiliar and unaccountable phenomenon, yet I am unable to recall any sense of fear. I remember – and tell it here because, singularly enough, I recollected it then – that once, in looking carelessly out of an open window, I momentarily mistook a small tree close at hand for one of a group of larger trees at a little distance away. It looked the same size as the others, but, being more distinctly and sharply defined in mass and detail, seemed out of harmony with them. It was a mere falsification of the law of aerial perspective, but it startled, almost terrified me. We so rely upon the orderly operation of familiar natural laws that any seeming suspension of them is noted as a menace to our safety, a warning of unthinkable calamity. So now the apparently causeless movement of the herbage, and the slow, undeviating approach of the line of disturbance were distinctly disquieting. My companion appeared actually frightened, and I could hardly credit my senses when I saw him suddenly throw his gun to his shoulders and fire both barrels at the agitated grass! Before the smoke of the discharge had cleared away I heard a loud savage cry – a scream like that of a wild animal – and, flinging his gun upon the ground, Morgan sprang away and ran swiftly from the spot. At the same instant I was thrown violently to the ground by the impact of something unseen in the smoke – some soft, heavy substance that seemed thrown against me with great force.

"Before I could get upon my feet and recover my gun, which seemed to have been struck from my hands, I heard Morgan crying out as if in mortal agony, and mingling with his cries were such hoarse savage sounds as one hears from fighting dogs. Inexpressibly terrified, I struggled to my feet and looked in the direction of Morgan's retreat; and may heaven in mercy spare me from another sight like that! At a distance of less than thirty yards was my friend, down upon one knee, his head thrown back at a frightful angle, hatless, his long hair in disorder and his whole body in violent movement from side to side, backward and forward. His right arm was lifted and seemed to lack the hand – at least, I could see none. The other arm was invisible. At times, as my memory now reports this extraordinary scene,

I could discern but a part of his body; it was as if he had been partly blotted out – I can not otherwise express it – then a shifting of his position would bring it all into view again.

"All this must have occurred within a few seconds, yet in that time Morgan assumed all the postures of a determined wrestler vanquished by superior weight and strength. I saw nothing but him, and him not always distinctly. During the entire incident his shouts and curses were heard, as if through an enveloping uproar of such sounds of rage and fury as I had never heard from the throat of man or brute!

"For a moment only I stood irresolute, then, throwing down my gun, I ran forward to my friend's assistance. I had a vague belief that he was suffering from a fit or some form of convulsion. Before I could reach his side he was down and quiet. All sounds had ceased, but, with a feeling of such terror as even these awful events had not inspired, I now saw the same mysterious movement of the wild oats prolonging itself from the trampled area about the prostrate man toward the edge of a wood. It was only when it had reached the wood that I was able to withdraw my eyes and look at my companion. He was dead."

The coroner rose from his seat and stood beside the dead man. Lifting an edge of the sheet he pulled it away, exposing the entire body, altogether naked and showing in the candle light a clay-like yellow. It had, however, broad maculations of bluish-black, obviously caused by extravasated blood from contusions. The chest and sides looked as if they had been beaten with a bludgeon. There were dreadful lacerations; the skin was torn in strips and shreds.

The coroner moved round to the end of the table and undid a silk handkerchief, which had been passed under the chin and knotted on the top of the head. When the handkerchief was drawn away it exposed what had been the throat. Some of the jurors who had risen to get a better view repented their curiosity, and turned away their faces. Witness Harker went to the open window and leaned out across the sill, faint and sick. Dropping the handkerchief upon the dead man's neck, the coroner stepped to an angle of the room, and from a pile of clothing produced one garment after another, each of which he held up a moment for inspection. All were torn, and stiff with blood. The jurors did not make a closer inspection. They seemed rather uninterested. They had, in truth, seen all this before; the only thing that was new to them being Harker's testimony.

"Gentlemen," the coroner said, "we have no more evidence, I think. Your duty has been already explained to you; if there is nothing you wish to ask you may go outside and consider your verdict."

The foreman rose – a tall, bearded man of sixty, coarsely clad.

"I should like to ask one question, Mr. Coroner," he said. "What asylum did this yer last witness escape from?"

"Mr. Harker," said the coroner, gravely and tranquilly, "from what asylum did you last escape?"

Harker flushed crimson again, but said nothing, and the seven jurors rose and solemnly filed out of the cabin.

"If you have done insulting me, sir," said Harker, as soon as he and the officer were left alone with the dead man, "I suppose I am at liberty to go?"

"Yes."

Harker started to leave, but paused, with his hand on the door latch. The habit of his profession was strong in him – stronger than his sense of personal dignity. He turned about and said:

"The book that you have there – I recognize it as Morgan's diary. You seemed greatly interested in it; you read in it while I was testifying. May I see it? The public would like – "

"The book will cut no figure in this matter," replied the official, slipping it into his coat pocket; "all the entries in it were made before the writer's death."

As Harker passed out of the house the jury reentered and stood about the table on which the now covered corpse showed under the sheet with sharp definition. The foreman seated himself near the candle, produced from his breast pocket a pencil and scrap of paper, and wrote rather laboriously the following verdict, which with various degrees of effort all signed:

"We, the jury, do find that the remains come to their death at the hands of a mountain lion, but some of us thinks, all the same, they had fits."

In the diary of the late Hugh Morgan are certain interesting entries having, possibly, a scientific value as suggestions. At the inquest upon his body the book was not put in evidence; possibly the coroner thought it not worth while to confuse the jury. The date of the first of the entries mentioned can not be ascertained; the upper part of the leaf is torn away; the part of the entry remaining is as follows:

"... *would run in a half circle, keeping his head turned always toward the centre and again he would stand still, barking furiously. At last he ran away into the brush as fast as he could go. I thought at first that he had gone mad, but on returning to the house found no other alteration in his manner than what was obviously due to fear of punishment.*

"*Can a dog see with his nose? Do odors impress some olfactory centre with images of the thing emitting them? ...*

"**Sept 2.** *– Looking at the stars last night as they rose above the crest of the ridge east of the house, I observed them successively disappear – from left to right. Each was eclipsed but an instant, and only a few at the same time, but along the entire length of the ridge all that were within a degree or two of the crest were blotted out. It was as if something had passed along between me and them; but I could not see it, and the stars were not thick enough to define its outline. Ugh! I don't like this.... .*"

Several weeks' entries are missing, three leaves being torn from the book.

"**Sept. 27.** *– It has been about here again – I find evidences of its presence every day. I watched again all of last night in the same cover, gun in hand, double-charged with buckshot. In the morning the fresh footprints were there, as before. Yet I would have sworn that I did not sleep – indeed, I hardly sleep at all. It is terrible, insupportable! If these amazing experiences are real I shall go mad; if they are fanciful I am mad already.*

"**Oct. 3.** *– I shall not go – it shall not drive me away. No, this is my house, my land. God hates a coward.... .*

"**Oct. 5.** *– I can stand it no longer; I have invited Harker to pass a few weeks with me – he has a level head. I can judge from his manner if he thinks me mad.*

"**Oct. 7.** *– I have the solution of the problem; it came to me last night – suddenly, as by revelation. How simple – how terribly simple!*

"*There are sounds that we can not hear. At either end of the scale are notes that stir no chord of that imperfect instrument, the human ear. They are too high or too grave. I have observed a flock of blackbirds occupying an entire treetop – the tops of several trees – and all in full song. Suddenly – in a moment – at absolutely the same instant – all spring into the air and fly away. How? They could not all see one another – whole treetops intervened. At no point could a leader have been visible to all. There must have been a signal of warning or command, high and shrill above the din, but by me unheard. I have observed, too, the same simultaneous flight when all were silent, among not only blackbirds, but other birds – quail, for example, widely separated by bushes – even on opposite sides of a hill.*

"It is known to seamen that a school of whales basking or sporting on the surface of the ocean, miles apart, with the convexity of the earth between them, will sometimes dive at the same instant – all gone out of sight in a moment. The signal has been sounded – too grave for the ear of the sailor at the masthead and his comrades on the deck – who nevertheless feel its vibrations in the ship as the stones of a cathedral are stirred by the bass of the organ.

"As with sounds, so with colors. At each end of the solar spectrum the chemist can detect the presence of what are known as 'actinic' rays. They represent colors – integral colors in the composition of light – which we are unable to discern. The human eye is an imperfect instrument; its range is but a few octaves of the real 'chromatic scale' I am not mad; there are colors that we can not see.

"And, God help me! the Damned Thing is of such a color!"

Beyond the Wall

Ambrose Bierce

MANY YEARS AGO, on my way from Hongkong to New York, I passed a week in San Francisco. A long time had gone by since I had been in that city, during which my ventures in the Orient had prospered beyond my hope; I was rich and could afford to revisit my own country to renew my friendship with such of the companions of my youth as still lived and remembered me with the old affection. Chief of these, I hoped, was Mohun Dampier, an old schoolmate with whom I had held a desultory correspondence which had long ceased, as is the way of correspondence between men. You may have observed that the indisposition to write a merely social letter is in the ratio of the square of the distance between you and your correspondent. It is a law.

I remembered Dampier as a handsome, strong young fellow of scholarly tastes, with an aversion to work and a marked indifference to many of the things that the world cares for, including wealth, of which, however, he had inherited enough to put him beyond the reach of want. In his family, one of the oldest and most aristocratic in the country, it was, I think, a matter of pride that no member of it had ever been in trade nor politics, nor suffered any kind of distinction. Mohan was a trifle sentimental, and had in him a singular element of superstition, which led him to the study of all manner of occult subjects, although his sane mental health safeguarded him against fantastic and perilous faiths. He made daring incursions into the realm of the unreal without renouncing his residence in the partly surveyed and charted region of what we are pleased to call certitude.

The night of my visit to him was stormy. The Californian winter was on, and the incessant rain splashed in the deserted streets, or, lifted by irregular gusts of wind, was hurled against the houses with incredible fury. With no small difficulty my cabman found the right place, away out toward the ocean beach, in a sparsely populated suburb.

The dwelling, a rather ugly one, apparently, stood in the center of its grounds, which as nearly as I could make out in the gloom were destitute of either flowers or grass. Three or four trees, writhing and moaning in the torment of the tempest, appeared to be trying to escape from their dismal environment and take the chance of finding a better one out at sea. The house was a two-story brick structure with a tower, a story higher, at one corner. In a window of that was the only visible light. Something in the appearance of the place made me shudder, a performance that may have been assisted by a rill of rainwater down my back as I scuttled to cover in the doorway.

In answer to my note apprising him of my wish to call, Dampier had written, "Don't ring – open the door and come up." I did so. The staircase was dimly lighted by a single gas-jet at the top of the second flight. I managed to reach the landing without disaster and entered by an open door into the lighted square room of the tower. Dampier came forward in gown and slippers to receive me, giving me the greeting that I wished, and if I had held a thought that it might more fitly have been accorded me at the front door the first look at him dispelled any sense of his inhospitality.

He was not the same. Hardly past middle age, he had gone gray and had acquired a pronounced stoop. His figure was thin and angular, his face deeply lined, his complexion dead-white, without a touch of color. His eyes, unnaturally large, glowed with a fire that was almost uncanny.

He seated me, proffered a cigar, and with grave and obvious sincerity assured me of the pleasure that it gave him to meet me. Some unimportant conversation followed, but all the while I was dominated by a melancholy sense of the great change in him. This he must have perceived, for he suddenly said with a bright enough smile, "You are disappointed in me – *non sum qualis eram*."

I hardly knew what to reply, but managed to say: "Why, really, I don't know: your Latin is about the same."

He brightened again. "No," he said, "being a dead language, it grows in appropriateness. But please have the patience to wait: where I am going there is perhaps a better tongue. Will you care to have a message in it?"

The smile faded as he spoke, and as he concluded he was looking into my eyes with a gravity that distressed me. Yet I would not surrender myself to his mood, nor permit him to see how deeply his prescience of death affected me.

"I fancy that it will be long," I said, "before human speech will cease to serve our need; and then the need, with its possibilities of service, will have passed."

He made no reply, and I too was silent, for the talk had taken a dispiriting turn, yet I knew not how to give it a more agreeable character. Suddenly, in a pause of the storm, when the dead silence was almost startling by contrast with the previous uproar, I heard a gentle tapping, which appeared to come from the wall behind my chair. The sound was such as might have been made by a human hand, not as upon a door by one asking admittance, but rather, I thought, as an agreed signal, an assurance of someone's presence in an adjoining room; most of us, I fancy, have had more experience of such communications than we should care to relate.

I glanced at Dampier. If possibly there was something of amusement in the look he did not observe it. He appeared to have forgotten my presence, and was staring at the wall behind me with an expression in his eyes that I am unable to name, although my memory of it is as vivid today as was my sense of it then. The situation was embarrassing! I rose to take my leave. At this he seemed to recover himself.

"Please be seated," he said; "it is nothing – no one is there."

But the tapping was repeated, and with the same gentle, slow insistence as before.

"Pardon me," I said, "it is late. May I call tomorrow?"

He smiled – a little mechanically, I thought. "It is very delicate of you," said he, "but quite needless. Really, this is the only room in the tower, and no one is there. At least–" He left the sentence incomplete, rose, and threw up a window, the only opening in the wall from which the sound seemed to come. "See."

Not clearly knowing what else to do I followed him to the window and looked out. A street-lamp some little distance away gave enough light through the murk of the rain that was again falling in torrents to make it entirely plain that "no one was there." In truth there was nothing but the sheer blank wall of the tower.

Dampier closed the window and signing me to my seat resumed his own.

The incident was not in itself particularly mysterious; any one of a dozen explanations was possible though none has occurred to me, yet it impressed me strangely, the more, perhaps, from my friend's effort to reassure me, which seemed to dignify it with a certain significance and importance. He had proved that no one was there, but in that fact lay all the interest; and he proffered no explanation. His silence was irritating and made me resentful.

"My good friend," I said, somewhat ironically, I fear, "I am not disposed to question your right to harbor as many spooks as you find agreeable to your taste and consistent with your notions of companionship; that is no business of mine. But being just a plain man of affairs, mostly of this world, I find spooks needless to my peace and comfort. I am going to my hotel, where my fellow-guests are still in the flesh."

It was not a very civil speech, but he manifested no feeling about it. "Kindly remain", he said. "I am grateful for your presence here. What you have heard tonight I believe myself to have heard twice before. Now I know it was no illusion. That is much to me – more than you know. Have a fresh cigar and a good stock of patience while I tell you the story."

The rain was now falling more steadily, with a low, monotonous susurration, interrupted at long intervals by the sudden slashing of the boughs of the trees as the wind rose and failed. The night was well advanced, but both sympathy and curiosity held me a willing listener to my friend's monologue, which I did not interrupt by a single word from beginning to end.

"Ten years ago," he said, "I occupied a ground-floor apartment in one of a row of houses, all alike, away at the other end of the town, on what we call Rincon Hill. This had been the best quarter of San Francisco, but had fallen into neglect and decay, partly because the primitive character of its domestic architecture no longer suited the maturing tastes of our wealthy citizens, partly because certain public improvements had made a wreck of it. The row of dwellings in one of which I lived stood a little way back from the street, each having a miniature garden, separated from its neighbors by low iron fences and bisected with mathematical precision by a box-bordered gravel walk from gate to door.

"One morning as I was leaving my lodging I observed a young girl entering the adjoining garden on the left. It was a warm day in June, and she was lightly gowned in white. From her shoulders hung a broad straw hat profusely decorated with flowers and wonderfully beribboned in the fashion of the time. My attention was not long held by the exquisite simplicity of her costume, for no one could look at her face and think of anything earthly. Do not fear; I shall not profane it by description; it was beautiful exceedingly. All that I had ever seen or dreamed of loveliness was in that matchless living picture by the hand of the Divine Artist. So deeply did it move me that, without a thought of the impropriety of the act, I unconsciously bared my head, as a devout Catholic or well-bred Protestant uncovers before an image of the Blessed Virgin.

The maiden showed no displeasure; she merely turned her glorious dark eyes upon me with a look that made me catch my breath, and without other recognition of my act passed into the house. For a moment I stood motionless, hat in hand, painfully conscious of my rudeness, yet so dominated by the emotion inspired by that vision of incomparable beauty that my penitence was less poignant than it should have been. Then I went my way, leaving my heart behind. In the natural course of things I should probably have remained away until nightfall, but by the middle of the afternoon I was back in the little garden, affecting an interest in the few foolish flowers that I had never before observed. My hope was vain; she did not appear.

"To a night of unrest succeeded a day of expectation and disappointment, but on the day after, as I wandered aimlessly about the neighborhood, I met her. Of course I did not repeat my folly of uncovering, nor venture by even so much as too long a look to manifest an interest in her; yet my heart was beating audibly. I trembled and consciously colored as she turned her big black eyes upon me with a look of obvious recognition entirely devoid of boldness or coquetry.

"I will not weary you with particulars; many times afterward I met the maiden, yet never either addressed her or sought to fix her attention. Nor did I take any action toward making her acquaintance. Perhaps my forbearance, requiring so supreme an effort of self-denial, will not be entirely clear to you. That I was heels over head in love is true, but who can overcome his habit of thought, or reconstruct his character?

"I was what some foolish persons are pleased to call, and others, more foolish, are pleased to be called – an aristocrat; and despite her beauty, her charms and graces, the girl was not of my class. I had learned her name – which it is needless to speak – and something of her family. She was an orphan, a dependent niece of the impossible elderly fat woman in whose lodging-house she lived. My income was small and I lacked the talent for marrying; it is perhaps a gift. An alliance with that family would condemn me to its manner of life, part me from my books and studies, and in a social sense reduce me to the ranks. It is easy to deprecate such considerations as these and I have not retained myself for the defense. Let judgment be entered against me, but in strict justice all my ancestors for generations should be made co-defendants and I be permitted to plead in mitigation of punishment the imperious mandate of heredity. To a mésalliance of that kind every globule of my ancestral blood spoke in opposition. In brief, my tastes, habits, instinct, with whatever of reason my love had left me – all fought against it. Moreover, I was an irreclaimable sentimentalist, and found a subtle charm in an impersonal and spiritual relation which acquaintance might vulgarize and marriage would certainly dispel. No woman, I argued, is what this lovely creature seems. Love is a delicious dream; why should I bring about my own awakening?

"The course dictated by all this sense and sentiment was obvious. Honor, pride, prudence, preservation of my ideals – all commanded me to go away, but for that I was too weak. The utmost that I could do by a mighty effort of will was to cease meeting the girl, and that I did. I even avoided the chance encounters of the garden, leaving my lodging only when I knew that she had gone to her music lessons, and returing after nightfall. Yet all the while I was as one in a trance, indulging the most fascinating fancies and ordering my entire intellectual life in accordance with my dream. Ah, my friend, as one whose actions have a traceable relation to reason, you cannot know the fool's paradise in which I lived.

"One evening the devil put it into my head to be an unspeakable idiot. By apparently careless and purposeless questioning I learned from my gossipy landlady that the young woman's bedroom adjoined my own, a partywall between. Yielding to a sudden and coarse impulse I gently rapped on the wall. There was no response, naturally, but I was in no mood to accept a rebuke. A madness was upon me and I repeated the folly, the offense, but again ineffectually, and I had the decency to desist.

"An hour later, while absorbed in some of my infernal studies, I heard, or thought I heard, my signal answered. Flinging down my books I sprang to the wall and as steadily as my beating heart would permit gave three slow taps upon it. This time the response was distinct, unmistakable: one, two, three – an exact repetition of my signal. That was all I could elicit, but it was enough – too much.

"The next evening, and for many evenings afterward, that folly went on, I always having "the last word". During the whole period I was deliriously happy, but with the perversity of my nature I persevered in my resolution not to see her. Then, as I should have expected, I got no further answers. "She is disgusted," I said to myself, "with what she thinks my timidity in making no more definite advances"; and I resolved to seek her and make her acquaintance and – what? I did not know, nor do I now know, what might have come of it. I know only that I passed days and days trying to meet her, and all in vain; she was invisible as well as inaudible. I haunted the streets where we had met, but she did not come. From my window I watched the garden in front of her house, but she passed neither in nor out. I fell into the deepest dejection, believing that she had gone away , yet took no steps to resolve my doubt by inquiry of my landlady, to whom, indeed, I had taken an unconquerable aversion from her having once spoken of the girl with less of reverence than I thought befitting.

"There came a fateful night. Worn out with emotion, irresolution and despondency, I had retired early and fallen into such sleep as was still possible to me. In the middle of the night something – some malign power bent upon the wrecking of my peace forever – caused me to open my eyes and sit up, wide awake and listening intently for I knew not what. Then I thought I heard a faint tapping on the wall – the mere ghost of the familiar signal. In a few moments it was repeated: one, two, three – no louder than before, but addressing a sense alert and strained to receive it. I was about to reply when the Adversary of Peace again intervened in my affairs with a rascally suggestion of retaliation. She had long and cruelly ignored me; now I would ignore her. Incredible fatuity – may God forgive it! All the rest of the night I lay awake, fortifying my obstinacy with shameless justifications and – listening.

"Late the next morning, as I was leaving the house, I met my landlady, entering.

"Good morning, Mr. Dampier," she said. "'Have you heard the news?'"

"I replied in words that I had heard no news; in manner, that I did not care to hear any. The manner escaped her observation.

"About the sick young lady next door," she babbled on. "What! you did not know? Why, she has been ill for weeks. And now – "

"I almost sprang upon her. "And now," I cried, "now what?'

"She is dead."

"That is not the whole story. In the middle of the night, as I learned later, the patient, awakening from a long stupor after a week of delirium, had asked – it was her last utterance– that her bed be moved to the opposite side of the room. Those in attendance had thought the request a vagary of her delirium, but had complied. And there the poor passing soul had exerted its failing will to restore a broken connection – a golden thread of sentiment between its innocence and a monstrous baseness owing a blind, brutal allegiance to the Law of Self.

"What reparation could I make? Are there masses that can be said for the repose of souls that are abroad such nights as this – spirits "blown about by the viewless winds" – coming in the storm and darkness with signs and portents, hints of memory and presages of doom?

"This is the third visitation. On the first occasion I was too skeptical to do more than verify by natural methods the character of the incident; on the second, I responded to the signal after it had been several times repeated, but without result. Tonight's recurrence completes the 'fatal triad' expounded by Parapelius Necromantius. There is no more to tell."

When Dampier had finished his story I could think of nothing relevant that I cared to say, and to question him would have been a hideous impertinence. I rose and bade him good night in a way to convey to him a sense of my sympathy, which he silently acknowledged by a pressure of the hand. That night, alone with his sorrow and remorse, he passed into the Unknown.

Mirror's Keeper

Michael Bondies

LYRIS KISTA eased the gate open, clutching the mirror against her chest like a shield. Rumors of human bones found in nearby creek beds flashed through her mind.

This is crazy, she thought. I should go home.

But she couldn't. Not yet.

Ahead of her, old Mrs. Griper's cottage loomed, partly silhouetted by the sinking late-afternoon sun like an ugly black toad. Ivy twisted over the roof, down the walls. A low-drooping willow banded the front porch with shadows.

Just get it over with, Lyris told herself. You're fifteen now. An adult. You can do this.

A breeze ruffled her unruly red hair. She tucked a few loose strands behind her ear and glanced behind her, hoping to see someone that might be able to hear her if she should need to call for help. But she saw no one.

As she stepped tentatively forward, she glanced down at the mirror. It was surprisingly light for its size. Despite an intricate web of cracks, the reflective side still gave a clear image. The bone handle, she thought, looked suspiciously like a human forearm – but she put that out of her mind.

The gate banged closed behind her and she jumped. A white starling fluttered out of the bushes, its wings a blur. The bird landed on Mrs. Griper's rooftop and perched there, watching Lyris with a squinted eye. For a moment, Lyris was comforted by the sight of it. But then she noticed a beetle hanging from the bird's beak. With a flick of its head, the bird tossed the twitching insect to the roof and picked at it, tearing off a leg. Then, as if deciding it needed more privacy, the bird scooped up its prize and flapped away.

Lyris took another few steps. She found herself thinking of all the terrible things she and her friends had said about Mrs. Griper over the years. She wasn't the only one, of course – but she had probably been worse than most; and never mind that she had never actually seen the old woman up close. She remembered getting into her adoptive mother's makeup box and doing herself up like an old hag, then running around the neighboring farms shouting: "A hex on you! I'm the Griper! I'll make you ugly! I'll make you ugly!" Her friends would run and scream, scattering like fireflies on a summer night as she laughed and chased after them.

Just yesterday, Lyris had discovered a notice posted on the community board at the edge of town – signed by Mrs. Griper – offering a generous reward for the return of a mirror with a gold butterfly etched into its handle. She never dreamed she might find it. Yet this morning, there it had been, right under the old evergreen tree where she and Akyn sometimes went to be alone.

With the reward money, she knew her parents would be able to buy food and hire additional help to save what was left of the harvest. At least, that's what she kept telling herself. Deep down, her thoughts returned to Akyn. All the fun they could have with the money. Not all of it. Just some of it. The rest, of course, she would give to her parents. The damage done by late summer storms had ruined nearly everything but the corn. Most of the neighboring farms had survived with minimal damage, but Lyris's adoptive family hadn't been so lucky.

I should have brought my dog, she thought. His warm muzzle against her hand would be a great comfort right now. All her friends had been too busy helping their own families with the harvest to accompany her and her parents had gone to the Dagenport market to sell what remained of last year's crop – they wouldn't be back for another two days.

She was on her own.

A chill tingled her skin as the first of the willow's shadows enveloped her. The steps to the cottage's front porch were cracked and overgrown with weeds. A curtained window to the living room offered no hint of what might lurk inside. Then, something – a shadow – moved behind the curtain.

Lyris froze. Her guts shriveled. A terrible urge to toss the mirror and run nearly overwhelmed her.

The door latch snicked back. The door creaked open. Candlelight leaked out. A hunched figure stood backlit in the doorway, waiting just inside. A floral shawl was draped across the figure's shoulders under a hint of grandmotherly curls.

Lyris cleared her throat. "I've ... brought this for the reward. I'll just put it here on the steps –"

"No, no," a sweet voice interrupted, dripping with honey. "I can't come out that far, dear. Please bring it inside."

Lyris's legs went to mush. She didn't want to go in there. She didn't want to see Mrs. Griper in the candlelight. But she willed herself forward. Moments from now, I'll be on my way home with my pockets full of gold.

The door creaked open the rest of the way.

Lyris went in.

The cottage stank like the dirty old well at the edge of town – like mushrooms and rot. Lyris kept her eyes on her boots and the mirror clutched to her chest. Mrs. Griper closed the door and waddled down a hallway with the help of a walking stick. "Bring it into the kitchen," she said. "It's right down this way. I'll get your reward."

Lyris's will melted. There was something commanding about Mrs. Griper's voice that quashed any thoughts of disobedience. She shuffled down the hallway behind the old woman.

In the kitchen, the windows were boarded up, so no fading sunlight – what little would have been left – was coming in. Flickering candles stood in a circular pattern on the table. A black pot simmered on the stove, emitting a sickly-sweet odor of mushrooms and rotten eggs.

Mrs. Griper stood stooped over her walking stick, back turned. Lyris noticed she was dressed all in black. Where had the floral shawl gone? Had Lyris imagined it?

"Put the mirror on the table," Mrs. Griper said.

Lyris set the mirror inside the ring of candles. The gold butterfly on the handle winked in the flickering light.

"I want to tell you a story before you go," Mrs. Griper said. "It won't take long."

The old woman turned, and –

"Oh," Lyris said. "Oh, I ..."

Mrs. Griper was beautiful. Old, yes, but her skin was radiant. Lips pink and full. Her eyes looked like luminous black pearls. Elegant gray hair framed her face, perfectly done. The old woman was watching Lyris, gauging her reaction. "I like your red hair. So curly."

The comment caught Lyris off guard. She faltered for a moment, then managed a quiet, "Thank you."

"You know, when I was your age, I looked just like you. The boys lined up. Back then, mine were neat and perky – just like yours."

A gasp escaped Lyris. She glanced down at her chest, cheeks burning.

"Oh, don't act so shocked," Mrs. Griper said. "I know about you, dear. I know what you do with that farm boy, Akyn."

Panic sprang up in Lyris's stomach. How could she know that? No one knew that! "I have to go –"

"Wait, wait, I haven't told you the story yet. It will only take a moment. You have a moment for a poor old woman, don't you? You wouldn't want me getting so lonely that I start leaving notes for the neighbors about what a certain young girl is doing with a certain farm boy, would you?"

Defeated, Lyris shook her head. Mrs. Griper pointed her walking stick at a chair that had been placed in front of a closet door. "Sit down."

Lyris tried to sit in the chair directly behind her but Mrs. Griper whacked her walking stick against the kitchen table. "No!" she said. Her voice was gravelly and wet with phlegm, as if she had overexerted herself. She wasn't looking nearly so attractive as she had a few moments ago. She jabbed the stick at the chair in front of the closet door. "That one there."

Lyris edged to the chair and sat down. The overpowering smells roiled her stomach. She glanced up at the boarded windows, dread creeping through her. She imagined the feel of the fresh autumn air on her face as she sprinted toward her farm as fast as her legs would take her.

Mrs. Griper reached into her pocket and removed a vial of red liquid. She uncorked it, tilted her head back and drank it down. Lyris cringed at the way the old woman's turkey neck worked as she gulped and swallowed.

Then, as Lyris watched, she thought she saw movement under the skin of Mrs. Griper's face. Like a ripple of water across a still pool. Had she imagined that too?

Mrs. Griper shoved the vial back into her pocket. "Energy tonic," she said. "You need it at my age." She hobbled to the table, picked up the mirror, looked it over admiringly, then returned her attention to Lyris.

"Now," the old woman said, "the story goes like this. Once, there was a beautiful young girl. But her beauty was stolen by an old witch who ran off and disappeared, leaving nothing behind but a mirror. Awful, yes?"

Lyris nodded, not knowing what else to do. She gripped the edges of the chair.

"Many years went by," Mrs. Griper continued, "but the beautiful girl – now ugly and old, of course – could not reverse the curse." She hobbled forward, eyes blazing. "Finally, though, after countless hours of searching, she discovered the witch's secret." A smile tugged the corners of Mrs. Griper's mouth. "Does any of this sound familiar, dear?"

Lyris shook her head, too frightened to speak.

"I thought not. You see, I've been watching you. And that's part of it. You forget." She tilted the mirror at Lyris, studying the reflected image. "But only those touched by the curse can be reflected in this mirror. That's how you know you have the right ... girl."

In a flash, Mrs. Griper's face drooped like melting candle wax. Her nose sagged and hooked. Ghastly brown teeth flashed through suddenly bluish lips and her perfectly quaffed hairdo sprouted shags of gray straw. Her walking stick clattered to the floor. With horrifying speed, she spread her arms and sailed through the air, black dress whipping her chubby legs as she reached for Lyris with a gnarled hand covered with purplish veins.

Lyris shrieked. The door behind her sprang open. She tried to dive out of the way but Mrs. Griper crashed into her and they both tumbled into the closet. The door swung shut, plunging them both into darkness.

Lyris flailed blindly. Hitting, screaming, clawing. She lurched to her feet. Reached for the doorknob. Found it. But it wouldn't turn. A hand gripped her shoulder. Something pricked her neck. She screamed.

"Shh," Mrs. Griper hissed. "It's too late for that. I know who you are. Remember! Remember what you did!"

Lyris fought a dizziness that had suddenly come upon her. She could barely support her weight now. Her knees began to buckle.

A fizzing burst of light, as if from a chemical reaction, briefly illuminated the closet and Lyris realized the mirror was in front of her. She could see Mrs. Griper's reflection now but the old hag was horrifically deformed: her left eye had popped its socket, dangling from a ropy pink cord. Bits of exposed skull gleamed through a gruesome mess of melted skin.

"Look in the mirror!" Mrs. Griper insisted. "Look and remember!"

Lyris felt another prick in her neck. This one more forceful, more painful. Images swam in the mirror's cracked surface: images of sneaking through an open window, of clutching a crude syringe with a wrinkled hand and laying the bone-handled mirror on a pillow beside the face of a beautiful young girl.

Could it be true?

As a child, Lyris had dreamed often, vividly, of being a fully-grown woman. But didn't everyone? This was impossible! Mrs. Griper was just tricking her – justifying what she was doing! The old hag was mad! The syringe had drugged her. It had shot poison into her neck and made her see things. She would never do anything like that! She was a good person! She knew who she was!

Lyris quickly backtracked in her mind, searching for anchor points. She remembered, clearly, the day she first arrived on the Krista's family farm. She remembered the smiles on her new parents' faces as they had welcomed her in. She had just come from ... from ... why couldn't she remember? It was the drug! It was confusing her! Or ... no! Of course she knew! Of course she did. She just –

"Time to sleep now," Mrs. Griper crooned.

Lyris collapsed.

After what seemed only a moment or two, Lyris regained consciousness. She was still in the closet, in the dark, but she was on the floor now. She felt heavy. Exhausted. Her back ached. She didn't feel Mrs. Griper's presence anymore, so she stood – with great effort, as her legs were wobbly – and tried the doorknob again. It turned.

She stumbled out of the closet and looked back. Empty. Mrs. Griper was gone.

It was quiet. The mirror, once more, lay in the center of the kitchen table. The ring of candles had burned down to nubs of wax. A dagger had been stabbed into the tabletop beside the mirror, its tip skewering a piece of paper. Lyris hobbled forward and stared at the paper. A message was scribbled in black ink:

It's your turn again.

Lyris blinked at the note. Then, hesitantly, she picked up the mirror.

And shrieked.

Mrs. Griper's face shrieked back at her, mouth agape, scattered with rotten brown teeth.

Lyris turned around and around, mirror held in front of her, eyes wide with horror. She clawed at her sagging face. She raked a vein-covered hand through her straw-like gray hair. She threw the mirror to the floor and it shattered, then instantly regretted it. Had she ruined it? Broken shards of mirror sparkled on the floor around her swollen feet as she stared at her drooping breasts and chubby legs. Revulsion coursed through her in a sickening wave.

She looked at the purplish veins in her wrists, and then at the dagger. On the hilt, the words "easy way out" had been scratched into the leather.

Somewhere, off in the distance, she could hear the sweet laughter of a young woman from the direction of Akyn's farm.

The Watcher by the Threshold

John Buchan

A CHILL EVENING in the early October of the year 189— found me driving in a dogcart through the belts of antique woodland which form the lowland limits of the hilly parish of More. The Highland express, which brought me from the north, took me no farther than Perth. Thence it had been a slow journey in a disjointed local train, till I emerged on the platform at Morefoot, with a bleak prospect of pot stalks, coal heaps, certain sour corn lands, and far to the west a line of moor where the sun was setting.

A neat groom and a respectable trap took the edge off my discomfort, and soon I had forgotten my sacrifice and found eyes for the darkening landscape. We were driving through a land of thick woods, cut at rare intervals by old long-frequented highways. The More, which at Morefoot is an open sewer, became a sullen woodland stream, where the brown leaves of the season drifted. At times we would pass an ancient lodge, and through a gap in the trees would come a glimpse of chipped crowstep gable. The names of such houses, as told me by my companion, were all famous. This one had been the home of a drunken Jacobite laird, and a king of north country Medmenham. Unholy revels had waked the old halls, and the devil had been toasted at many a hell-fire dinner. The next was the property of a great Scots law family, and there the old Lord of Session, who built the place, in his frouzy wig and carpet slippers, had laid down the canons of Taste for his day and society.

The whole country had the air of faded and bygone gentility. The mossy roadside walls had stood for two hundred years; the few wayside houses were toll bars or defunct hostelries. The names, too, were great: Scots baronial with a smack of France, – Chatelray and Riverslaw, Black Holm and Fountainblue. The place had a cunning charm, mystery dwelt in every, cranny, and yet it did not please me. The earth smelt heavy and raw; the roads were red underfoot; all was old, sorrowful, and uncanny. Compared with the fresh Highland glen I had left, where wind and sun and flying showers were never absent, all was chilly and dull and dead. Even when the sun sent a shiver of crimson over the crests of certain firs, I felt no delight in the prospect. I admitted shamefacedly to myself that I was in a very bad temper.

I had been staying at Glenaicill with the Clanroydens, and for a week had found the proper pleasure in life. You know the house with its old rooms and gardens, and the miles of heather which defend it from the world. The shooting had been extraordinary for a wild place late in the season; for there are few partridges, and the woodcock are notoriously late. I had done respectably in my stalking, more than respectably on the river, and creditably on the moors. Moreover, there were pleasant people in the house – and there were the Clanroydens. I had had a hard year's work, sustained to the last moment of term, and a fortnight in Norway had been disastrous. It was therefore with real comfort that I had settled myself down for another ten days in Glenaicill, when all my plans were shattered by Sibyl's letter. Sibyl is my cousin and my very good friend, and in old days when I was briefless I had fallen in love with her many times. But she very sensibly chose otherwise, and married a man Ladlaw – Robert John Ladlaw, who had been at school with me. He was a cheery, good-humoured fellow, a great sportsman, a justice of the peace, and deputy lieutenant for his county, and something of an antiquary in a mild way. He had a box in Leicestershire to which he went in the hunting season, but from February till October he lived in his moorland home. The place was called the House of More, and I had shot at it once or twice in recent years. I remembered its loneliness and its comfort, the charming diffident Sibyl, and Ladlaw's genial welcome. And my recollections set me puzzling again over the letter which that morning had broken into my comfort. "You promised us a visit this autumn," Sibyl had written, "and I wish you would come as soon as you can." So far common politeness. But she had gone on to reveal the fact that Ladlaw was ill; she did not know how, exactly, but something, she thought, about his heart. Then she had signed herself my affectionate cousin, and then had come a short, violent postscript, in which, as it were, the fences of convention had been laid low. "For Heaven's sake, come and see us," she scrawled below. "Bob is terribly ill, and I am crazy. Come at once." To cap it she finished with an afterthought: "Don't bother about bringing doctors. It is not their business."

She had assumed that I would come, and dutifully I set out. I could not regret my decision, but I took leave to upbraid my luck. The thought of Glenaicill, with the woodcock beginning to arrive and the Clanroydens imploring me to stay, saddened my journey in the morning, and the murky, coaly, midland country of the afternoon completed my depression. The drive through the woodlands of More failed to raise my spirits. I was anxious about Sibyl and Ladlaw, and this accursed country had always given me a certain eeriness on my first approaching it. You may call it silly, but I have no nerves and am little susceptible to vague sentiment. It was sheer physical dislike of the rich deep soil, the woody and antique smells, the melancholy roads and trees, and the flavor of old mystery. I am aggressively healthy and wholly Philistine. I love clear outlines and strong colors, and More with its half tints and hazy distances depressed me miserably.

Even when the road crept uphill and the trees ended, I found nothing to hearten me in the moorland which succeeded. It was genuine moorland, close on eight hundred feet above the sea, and through it ran this old grass-grown coach road. Low hills rose to the left, and to the right, after some miles of peat, flared the chimneys of pits and oil works. Straight in front the moor ran out into the horizon, and there in the centre was the last dying spark of the sun. The place was as still as the grave save for the crunch of our wheels on the grassy road, but the flaring lights to the north seemed to endow it with life. I have rarely had so keenly the feeling of movement in the inanimate world. It was an unquiet place, and I shivered nervously. Little gleams of loch came from the hollows, the burns were brown with peat, and every now and then there rose in the moor jags of sickening red stone.

I remembered that Ladlaw had talked about the place as the old Manann, the holy land of the ancient races. I had paid little attention at the time, but now it struck me that the old peoples had been wise in their choice. There was something uncanny in this soil and air. Framed in dank mysterious woods and a country of coal and ironstone, at no great distance from the capital city, it was a sullen relic of a lost barbarism. Over the low hills lay a green pastoral country with bright streams and valleys, but here, in this peaty desert, there were few sheep and little cultivation. The House of More was the only dwelling, and, save for the ragged village, the wilderness was given over to the wild things of the hills. The shooting was good, but the best shooting on earth would not persuade me to make my abode in such a place. Ladlaw was ill; well, I did not wonder. You can have uplands without air, moors that are not health-giving, and a country life which is more arduous than a townsman's. I shivered again, for I seemed to have passed in a few hours from the open noon to a kind of dank twilight.

We passed the village and entered the lodge gates. Here there were trees again – little innocent new-planted firs, which flourished ill. Some large plane trees grew near the house, and there were thickets upon thickets of the ugly elderberry. Even in the half darkness I could see that the lawns were trim and the flower beds respectable for the season; doubtless Sibyl looked after the gardeners. The oblong whitewashed house, more like a barrack than ever, opened suddenly on my sight, and I experienced my first sense of comfort since I left Glenaicill. Here I should find warmth and company; and sure enough, the hall door was wide open, and in the great flood of light which poured from it Sibyl stood to welcome me.

She ran down the steps as I dismounted, and, with a word to the groom, caught my arm and drew me into the shadow. "Oh, Henry, it was so good of you to come. You mustn't let Bob think that you know he is ill. We don't talk about it. I'll tell you afterwards. I want you to cheer him up. Now we must go in, for he is in the hall expecting you."

While I stood blinking in the light, Ladlaw came forward with outstretched hand and his usual cheery greeting. I looked at him and saw nothing unusual in his appearance; a little drawn at the lips, perhaps, and heavy below the eyes, but still fresh-colored and healthy. It was Sibyl who showed change. She was very pale, her pretty eyes were deplorably mournful, and in place of her delightful shyness there were the self-confidence and composure of pain. I was honestly shocked, and as I dressed my heart was full of hard thoughts about Ladlaw. What could his illness mean? He seemed well and cheerful, while Sibyl was pale; and yet it was Sibyl who had written the postscript. As I warmed myself by the fire, I resolved that this particular family difficulty was my proper business.

The Ladlaws were waiting for me in the drawing-room. I noticed something new and strange in Sibyl's demeanor. She looked to her husband with a motherly, protective air, while Ladlaw, who had been the extreme of masculine independence, seemed to cling to his wife with a curious appealing fidelity. In conversation he did little more than echo her words. Till dinner was announced he spoke of the weather, the shooting, and Mabel Clanroyden. Then he did a queer thing; for when I was about to offer my arm to Sibyl he forestalled me, and clutching her right arm with his left hand led the way to the dining room, leaving me to follow in some bewilderment.

I have rarely taken part in a more dismal meal. The House of More has a pretty Georgian paneling through most of the rooms, but in the dining room the walls are level and painted a dull stone color. Abraham offered up Isaac in a ghastly picture in front of me. Some photographs of the Quorn hung over the mantelpiece, and five or six drab ancestors filled up the remaining space. But one thing was new and startling. A great marble bust, a genuine antique, frowned on me from a pedestal. The head was in the late Roman style, clearly of some emperor, and in its commonplace environment the great brows, the massive neck, and the mysterious solemn lips had a surprising effect. I nodded toward the thing, and asked what it represented.

Ladlaw grunted something which I took for "Justinian," but he never raised his eyes from his plate. By accident I caught Sibyl's glance. She looked toward the bust, and laid a finger on her lips.

The meal grew more doleful as it advanced. Sibyl scarcely touched a dish, but her husband ate ravenously of everything. He was a strong, thickset man, with a square kindly face burned brown by the sun. Now he seemed to have suddenly coarsened. He gobbled with undignified haste, and his eye was extraordinarily vacant. A question made him start, and he would turn on me a face so strange and inert that I repented the interruption.

I asked him about the autumn's sport. He collected his wits with difficulty. He thought it had been good, on the whole, but he had shot badly. He had not been quite so fit as usual. No, he had had nobody staying with him. Sibyl had wanted to be alone. He was afraid the moor might have been undershot, but he would make a big day with keepers and farmers before the winter.

"Bob has done pretty well," Sibyl said. "He hasn't been out often, for the weather has been very bad here. You can have no idea, Henry, how horrible this moorland place of ours can be when it tries. It is one great sponge sometimes, with ugly red burns and mud to the ankles."

"I don't think it's healthy," said I.

Ladlaw lifted his face. "Nor do I. I think it's intolerable, but I am so busy I can't get away." Once again I caught Sibyl's warning eye as I was about to question him on his business.

Clearly the man's brain had received a shock, and he was beginning to suffer from hallucinations. This could be the only explanation, for he had always led a temperate life. The distrait, wandering manner was the only sign of his malady, for otherwise he seemed normal and mediocre as ever. My heart grieved for Sibyl, alone with him in this wilderness.

Then he broke the silence. He lifted his head and looked nervously around till his eye fell on the Roman bust.

"Do you know that this countryside is the old Manann?" he said.

It was an odd turn to the conversation, but I was glad of a sign of intelligence. I answered that I had heard so.

"It's a queer name," he said oracularly, "but the thing it stood for was queerer, Manann, Manaw," he repeated, rolling the words on his tongue. As he spoke, he glanced sharply, and, as it seemed to me, fearfully, at his left side.

The movement of his body made his napkin slip from his left knee and fall on the floor. It leaned against his leg, and he started from its touch as if he had been bitten by a snake. I have never seen a more sheer and transparent terror on a man's face. He got to his feet, his strong frame shaking like a rush. Sibyl ran round to his side, picked up the napkin and flung it on a sideboard. Then she stroked his hair as one would stroke a frightened horse. She called him by his old boy's name of Robin, and at her touch and voice he became quiet. But the particular course then in progress was removed, untasted.

In a few minutes he seemed to have forgotten his behavior, for he took up the former conversation. For a time he spoke well and briskly. "You lawyers," he said, "understand only the dry framework of the past. You cannot conceive the rapture, which only the antiquary can feel, of constructing in every detail an old culture. Take this Manann. If I could explore the secret of these moors, I would write the world's greatest book. I would write of that prehistoric life when man was knit close to nature. I would describe the people who were brothers of the red earth and the red rock and the red streams of the hills. Oh, it would be horrible, but superb, tremendous! It would be more than a piece of history; it would be a new gospel, a new theory of life. It would kill materialism once and for all. Why, man, all the poets who have deified and personified nature would not do an eighth part of my work. I would show you the unknown, the hideous, shrieking mystery at the back of this simple nature. Men would see the profundity of the old crude faiths which they affect to despise. I would make a picture of our shaggy, sombre-eyed forefather, who heard strange things in the hill silences. I would show him brutal and terror-stricken, but wise, wise, God alone knows how wise! The Romans knew it, and they learned what they could from him, though he did not tell them much. But we have some of his blood in us, and we may go deeper. Manann! A queer land nowadays! I sometimes love it and sometimes hate it, but I always fear it. It is like that statue, inscrutable."

I would have told him that he was talking mystical nonsense, but I had looked toward the bust, and my rudeness was checked on my lips. The moor might be a common piece of ugly waste land, but the statue was inscrutable, – of that there was no doubt. I hate your cruel heavy-mouthed Roman busts; to me they have none of the beauty of life, and little of the interest of art. But my eyes were fastened on this as they had never before looked on marble. The oppression of the heavy woodlands, the mystery of the silent moor, seemed to be caught and held in this face. It was the intangible mystery of culture on the verge of savagery – a cruel, lustful wisdom, and yet a kind of bitter austerity which laughed at the game of life and stood aloof. There was no weakness in the heavy-veined brow and slumbrous eyelids. It was the face of one who had conquered the world, and found it dust and ashes; one who had eaten of the tree of the knowledge of good and evil, and scorned human wisdom. And at the same time, it was the face of one who knew uncanny things, a man who was the intimate of the half-world and the dim background of life. Why on earth I should connect the Roman grandee with the moorland parish of More I cannot say, but the fact remains that there was that in the face which I knew had haunted me through the woodlands and bogs of the place – a sleepless, dismal, incoherent melancholy.

I have identified the bust, which, when seen under other circumstances, had little power to affect me. It was a copy of the head of Justinian in the Tesci Museum at Venice, and several duplicates exist, dating apparently from the seventh century, and showing traces of Byzantine decadence in the scroll work on the hair. It is engraved in M. Delacroix's Byzantium, and, I think, in Windscheid's Pandektenlehrbuch.

"I bought that at Colenzo's," Ladlaw said, "because it took my fancy. It matches well with this place?"

I thought it matched very ill with his drab walls and Quorn photographs, but I held my peace.

"Do you know who it is?" he asked. "It is the head of the greatest man the world has ever seen. You are a lawyer and know your Justinian."

The Pandects are scarcely part of the daily work of a common-law barrister. I had not looked into them since I left college.

"I know that he married an actress," I said, "and was a sort of all-round genius. He made law, and fought battles, and had rows with the Church. A curious man! And wasn't there some story about his selling his soul to the devil, and getting law in exchange? Rather a poor bargain!"

I chattered away, sillily enough, to dispel the gloom of that dinner table. The result of my words was unhappy. Ladlaw gasped and caught at his left side, as if in pain. Sibyl, with tragic eyes, had been making signs to me to hold my peace. Now she ran round to her husband's side and comforted him like a child. As she passed me, she managed to whisper in my ear to talk to her only, and let her husband alone.

For the rest of dinner I obeyed my orders to the letter. Ladlaw ate his food in gloomy silence, while I spoke to Sibyl of our relatives and friends, of London, Glenaicill, and any random subject. The poor girl was dismally forgetful, and her eye would wander to her husband with wifely anxiety. I remember being suddenly overcome by the comic aspect of it all. Here were we three fools alone in the dank upland: one of us sick and nervous, talking out-of-the-way nonsense about Manann and Justinian, gobbling his food and getting scared at his napkin; another gravely anxious; and myself at my wits' end for a solution. It was a Mad Tea-Party with a vengeance: Sibyl the melancholy little Dormouse, and Ladlaw the incomprehensible Hatter. I laughed aloud, but checked myself when I caught my cousin's eye. It was really no case for finding humor. Ladlaw was very ill, and Sibyl's face was getting deplorably thin.

I welcomed the end of that meal with unmannerly joy, for I wanted to speak seriously with my host. Sibyl told the butler to have the lamps lighted in the library. Then she leaned over toward me and spoke low and rapidly: "I want you to talk with Bob. I'm sure you can do him good. You'll have to be very patient with him, and very gentle. Oh, please try to find out what is wrong with him. He won't tell me, and I can only guess."

The butler returned with word that the library was ready to receive us, and Sibyl rose to go. Ladlaw half rose, protesting, making the most curious feeble clutches to his side. His wife quieted him. "Henry will look after you, dear," she said. "You are going into the library to smoke." Then she slipped from the room, and we were left alone.

He caught my arm fiercely with his left hand, and his grip nearly made me cry out. As we walked down the hall, I could feel his arm twitching from the elbow to the shoulder. Clearly he was in pain, and I set it down to some form of cardiac affection, which might possibly issue in paralysis.

I settled him in the biggest armchair, and took one of his cigars. The library is the pleasantest room in the house, and at night, when a peat fire burned on the old hearth and the great red curtains were drawn, it used to be the place for comfort and good talk. Now I noticed changes. Ladlaw's bookshelves had been filled with the Proceedings of antiquarian societies and many light-hearted works on sport. But now the Badminton library had been cleared out of a shelf where it stood most convenient to the hand, and its place taken by an old Leyden reprint of Justinian. There were books on Byzantine subjects of which I never dreamed he had heard the names; there were volumes of history and speculation, all of a slightly bizarre kind; and to crown everything, there were several bulky medical works with gaudily colored plates. The old atmosphere of sport and travel had gone from the room with the medley of rods, whips, and gun cases which used to cumber the tables. Now the place was moderately tidy and somewhat learned, and I did not like it.

Ladlaw refused to smoke, and sat for a little while in silence. Then of his own accord he broke the tension.

"It was devilish good of you to come, Harry. This is a lonely place for a man who is a bit seedy."

"I thought you might be alone," I said, "so I looked you up on my way down from Glenaicill. I'm sorry to find you feeling ill."

"Do you notice it?" he asked sharply.

"It's tolerably patent," I said. "Have you seen a doctor?"

He said something uncomplimentary about doctors, and kept looking at me with his curious dull eyes.

I remarked the strange posture in which he sat, his head screwed round to his right shoulder, and his whole body a protest against something at his left hand.

"It looks like a heart," I said. "You seem to have pains in your left side."

Again a spasm of fear. I went over to him and stood at the back of his chair.

"Now for goodness" sake, my dear fellow, tell me what is wrong. You're scaring Sibyl to death. It's lonely work for the poor girl, and I wish you would let me help you."

He was lying back in his chair now, with his eyes half shut, and shivering like a frightened colt. The extraordinary change in one who had been the strongest of the strong kept me from realizing his gravity. I put a hand on his shoulder, but he flung it off.

For God's sake, sit down!" he said hoarsely. "I'm going to tell you, but I'll never make you understand."

I sat down promptly opposite him.

"It's the devil," he said very solemnly.

I am afraid that I was rude enough to laugh. He took no notice, but sat, with the same tense, miserable air, staring over my head.

"Right," said I. "Then it is the devil. It's a new complaint, so it's as well I did not bring a doctor. How does it affect you?"

He made the old impotent clutch at the air with his left hand. I had the sense to become grave at once. Clearly this was some serious mental affection, some hallucination born of physical pain.

Then he began to talk in a low voice, very rapidly, with his head bent forward like a hunted animal's. I am not going to set down what he told me in his own words, for they were incoherent often, and there was much repetition. But I am going to write the gist of the odd story which took my sleep away on that autumn night, with such explanations and additions I think needful. The fire died down, the wind arose, the hour grew late, and still he went on in his mumbling recitative. I forgot to smoke, forgot my comfort – everything but the odd figure of my friend and his inconceivable romance. And the night before I had been in cheerful Glenaicill!

He had returned to the House of More, he said, in the latter part of May, and shortly after he fell ill. It was a trifling sickness, – influenza or something, – but he had never quite recovered. The rainy weather of June depressed him, and the extreme heat of July made him listless and weary. A kind of insistent sleepiness hung over him, and he suffered much from nightmare. Toward the end of July his former health returned, but he was haunted with a curious oppression. He seemed to himself to have lost the art of being alone. There was a perpetual sound in his left ear, a kind of moving and rustling at his left side, which never left him by night or day. In addition, he had become the prey of nerves and an insensate dread of the unknown.

Ladlaw, as I have explained, was a commonplace man, with fair talents, a mediocre culture, honest instincts, and the beliefs and incredulities of his class. On abstract grounds, I should have declared him an unlikely man to be the victim of an hallucination. He had a kind of dull bourgeois rationalism, which used to find reasons for all things in heaven and earth. At first he controlled his dread with proverbs. He told himself it was the sequel of his illness or the light-headedness of summer heat on the moors. But it soon outgrew his comfort. It became a living second presence, an alter ego which dogged his footsteps. He grew acutely afraid of it. He dared not be alone for a moment, and clung to Sibyl's company despairingly. She went off for a week's visit in the beginning of August, and he endured for seven days the tortures of the lost. The malady advanced upon him with swift steps. The presence became more real daily. In the early dawning, in the twilight, and in the first hour of the morning it seemed at times to take a visible bodily form. A kind of amorphous featureless shadow would run from his side into the darkness, and he would sit palsied with terror. Sometimes, in lonely places, his footsteps sounded double, and something would brush elbows with him. Human society alone exorcised it. With Sibyl at his side he was happy; but as soon as she left him, the thing came slinking back from the unknown to watch by him. Company might have saved him, but joined to his affliction was a crazy dread of his fellows. He would not leave his moorland home, but must bear his burden alone among the wild streams and mosses of that dismal place.

The 12th came, and he shot wretchedly, for his nerve had gone to pieces. He stood exhaustion badly, and became a dweller about the doors. But with this bodily inertness came an extraordinary intellectual revival. He read widely in a blundering way, and he speculated unceasingly. It was characteristic of the man that as soon as he left the paths of the prosaic he should seek his supernatural in a very concrete form. He assumed that he was haunted by the devil – the visible personal devil in whom our fathers believed. He waited hourly for the shape at his side to speak, but no words came. The Accuser of the Brethren in all but tangible form was his ever present companion. He felt, he declared, the spirit of old evil entering subtly into his blood. He sold his soul many times over, and yet there was no possibility of resistance. It was a Visitation more undeserved than Job's, and a thousandfold more awful.

For a week or more he was tortured with a kind of religious mania. When a man of a healthy secular mind finds himself adrift on the terrible ocean of religious troubles he is peculiarly helpless, for he has not the most rudimentary knowledge of the winds and tides. It was useless to call up his old carelessness; he had suddenly dropped into a new world where old proverbs did not apply. And all the while, mind you, there was the shrinking terror of it – an intellect all alive to the torture and the most unceasing physical fear. For a little he was on the far edge of idiocy.

Then by accident it took a new form. While sitting with Sibyl one day in the library, he began listlessly to turn over the leaves of an old book. He read a few pages, and found the hint to a story like his own. It was some French Life of Justinian, one of the unscholarly productions of last century, made up of stories from Procopius and tags of Roman law. Here was his own case written down in black and white; and the man had been a king of kings. This was a new comfort, and for a little – strange though it may seem – he took a sort of pride in his affliction. He worshiped the great Emperor, and read every scrap he could find on him, not excepting the Pandects and the Digest. He sent for the bust in the dining room, paying a fabulous price. Then he settled himself to study his imperial prototype, and the study became an idolatry. As I have said, Ladlaw was a man of ordinary talents, and certainly of meagre imaginative power. And yet from the lies of the Secret History and the crudities of German legalists he had constructed a marvelous portrait of a man. Sitting there in the half-lighted room, he drew the picture: the quiet cold man with his inheritance of Dacian mysticism, holding the great world in fee, giving it law and religion, fighting its wars, building its churches, and yet all the while intent upon his own private work of making his peace with his soul – the churchman and warrior whom all the world worshiped, and yet one going through life with his lip quivering. He Watched by the Threshold ever at the left side. Sometimes at night, in the great Brazen Palace, warders heard the Emperor walking in the dark corridors, alone, and yet not alone; for once, when a servant entered with a lamp, he saw his master with a face as of another world, and something beside him which had no face or shape, but which he knew to be that hoary Evil which is older than the stars.

Crazy nonsense! I had to rub my eyes to assure myself that I was not sleeping. No! There was my friend with his suffering face, and it was the library of More.

And then he spoke of Theodora, – actress, harlot, devote, empress. For him the lady was but another part of the uttermost horror, a form of the shapeless thing at his side. I felt myself falling under the fascination. I have no nerves and little imagination, but in a flash I seemed to realize something of that awful featureless face, crouching ever at a man's hand, till darkness and loneliness come, and it rises to its mastery. I shivered as I looked at the man in the chair before me. These dull eyes of his were looking upon things I could not see, and I saw their terror. I realized that it was grim earnest for him. Nonsense or no, some devilish fancy had usurped the place of his sanity, and he was being slowly broken upon the wheel. And then, when his left hand twitched, I almost cried out. I had thought it comic before; now it seemed the last proof of tragedy.

He stopped, and I got up with loose knees and went to the window. Better the black night than the intangible horror within. I flung up the sash and looked out across the moor. There was no light; nothing but an inky darkness and the uncanny rustle of elder bushes. The sound chilled me, and I closed the window.

"The land is the old Manann," Ladlaw was saying. "We are beyond the pale here. Do you hear the wind?"

I forced myself back into sanity and looked at my watch. It was nearly one o'clock.

"What ghastly idiots we are!" I said. "I am off to bed."

Ladlaw looked at me helplessly. "For God's sake, don't leave me alone!" he moaned. "Get Sibyl."

We went together back to the hall, while he kept the same feverish grasp on my arm. Some one was sleeping in a chair by the hall fire, and to my distress I recognized my hostess. The poor child must have been sadly wearied. She came forward with her anxious face.

"I'm afraid Bob has kept you very late, Henry," she said. "I hope you will sleep well. Breakfast at nine, you know." And then I left them.

Over my bed there was a little picture, a reproduction of some Italian work, of Christ and the Demoniac. Some impulse made me hold my candle up to it. The madman's face was torn with passion and suffering, and his eye had the pained furtive expression which I had come to know. And by his left side there was a dim shape crouching.

I got into bed hastily, but not to sleep. I felt that my reason must be going. I had been pitchforked from our clear and cheerful modern life into the mists of old superstition. Old tragic stories of my Calvinist upbringing returned to haunt me. The man dwelt in by a devil was no new fancy, but I believed that science had docketed and analyzed and explained the devil out of the world. I remembered my dabblings in the occult before I settled down to law – the story of Donisarius, the monk of Padua, the unholy legend of the Face of Proserpine, the tales of succubi and incubi, the Leannain Sith and the Hidden Presence. But here was something stranger still. I had stumbled upon that very possession which fifteen hundred years ago had made the monks of New Rome tremble and cross themselves. Some devilish occult force, lingering through the ages, had come to life after a long sleep. God knows what earthly connection there was between the splendid Emperor of the World and my prosaic friend, or between the glittering shores of the Bosporus and this moorland parish! But the land was the old Manann! The spirit may have lingered in the earth and air, a deadly legacy from Pict and Roman. I had felt the uncanniness of the place; I had augured ill of it from the first. And then in sheer disgust I rose and splashed my face with cold water.

I lay down again, laughing miserably at my credulity. That I, the sober and rational, should believe in this crazy fable was too palpably absurd. I would steel my mind resolutely against such harebrained theories. It was a mere bodily ailment – liver out of order, weak heart, bad circulation, or something of that sort. At the worst it might be some affection of the brain, to be treated by a specialist. I vowed to myself that next morning the best doctor in Edinburgh should be brought to More.

The worst of it was that my duty compelled me to stand my ground. I foresaw the few remaining weeks of my holiday blighted. I should be tied to this moorland prison, a sort of keeper and nurse in one, tormented by silly fancies. It was a charming prospect, and the thought of Glenaicill and the woodcock made me bitter against Ladlaw. But there was no way out of it. I might do Ladlaw good, and I could not have Sibyl worn to death by his vagaries.

My ill nature comforted me, and I forgot the horror of the thing in its vexation. After that I think I fell asleep and dozed uneasily till morning. When I woke I was in a better frame of mind. The early sun had worked wonders with the moorland. The low hills stood out fresh-colored and clear against a pale October sky; the elders sparkled with frost; the raw film of morn was rising from the little loch in tiny clouds. It was a cold, rousing day, and I dressed in good spirits and went down to breakfast.

I found Ladlaw looking ruddy and well; very different from the broken man I remembered of the night before. We were alone, for Sibyl was breakfasting in bed. I remarked on his ravenous appetite, and he smiled cheerily. He made two jokes during the meal; he laughed often, and I began to forget the events of the previous day. It seemed to me that I might still flee from More with a clear conscience. He had forgotten about his illness. When I touched distantly upon the matter he showed a blank face.

It might be that the affection had passed; on the other hand, it might return to him at the darkening. I had no means to decide. His manner was still a trifle distrait and peculiar, and I did not like the dullness in his eye. At any rate, I should spend the day in his company, and the evening would decide the question.

I proposed shooting, which he promptly vetoed. He was no good at walking, he said, and the birds were wild. This seriously limited the possible occupations. Fishing there was none, and hill-climbing was out of the question. He proposed a game at billiards, and I pointed to the glory of the morning. It would have been sacrilege to waste such sunshine in knocking balls about. Finally we agreed to drive somewhere and have lunch, and he ordered the dogcart.

In spite of all forebodings I enjoyed the day. We drove in the opposite direction from the woodland parts, right away across the moor to the coal country beyond. We lunched at the little mining town of Borrowmuir, in a small and noisy public house. The roads made bad going, the country was far from pretty, and yet the drive did not bore me. Ladlaw talked incessantly – talked as I had never heard man talk before. There was something indescribable in all he said, a different point of view, a lost groove of thought, a kind of innocence and archaic shrewdness in one. I can only give you a hint of it, by saying that it was like the mind of an early ancestor placed suddenly among modern surroundings. It was wise with a remote wisdom, and silly (now and then) with a quite antique and distant silliness.

I will give instances of both. He provided me with a theory of certain early fortifications, which must be true, which commends itself to the mind with overwhelming conviction, and yet which is so out of the way of common speculation that no man could have guessed it. I do not propose to set down the details, for I am working at it on my own account. Again, he told me the story of an old marriage custom, which till recently survived in this district – told it with full circumstantial detail and constant allusions to other customs which he could not possibly have known of. Now for the other side. He explained why well water is in winter warmer than a running stream, and this was his explanation: at the antipodes our winter is summer, consequently, the water of a well which comes through from the other side of the earth must be warm in winter and cold in summer, since in our summer it is winter there. You perceive what this is. It is no mere silliness, but a genuine effort of an early mind, which had just grasped the fact of the antipodes, to use it in explanation.

Gradually I was forced to the belief that it was not Ladlaw who was talking to me, but something speaking through him, something at once wiser and simpler. My old fear of the devil began to depart. This spirit, the exhalation, whatever it was, was ingenuous in its way, at least in its daylight aspect. For a moment I had an idea that it was a real reflex of Byzantine thought, and that by cross-examining I might make marvelous discoveries. The ardor of the scholar began to rise in me, and I asked a question about that much-debated point, the legal status of the apocrisiarii. To my vexation he gave no response. Clearly the intelligence of this familiar had its limits.

It was about three in the afternoon, and we had gone half of our homeward journey, when signs of the old terror began to appear. I was driving, and Ladlaw sat on my left. I noticed him growing nervous and silent, shivering at the flick of the whip, and turning halfway round toward me. Then he asked me to change places, and I had the unpleasant work of driving from the wrong side. After that I do not think he spoke once till we arrived at More, but sat huddled together, with the driving rug almost up to his chin – an eccentric figure of a man.

I foresaw another such night as the last, and I confess my heart sank. I had no stomach for more mysteries, and somehow with the approach of twilight the confidence of the day departed. The thing appeared in darker colors, and I found it in my mind to turn coward. Sibyl alone deterred me. I could not bear to think of her alone with this demented being. I remembered her shy timidity, her innocence. It was monstrous that the poor thing should be called on thus to fight alone with phantoms.

When we came to the House it was almost sunset. Ladlaw got out very carefully on the right side, and for a second stood by the horse. The sun was making our shadows long, and as I stood beyond him it seemed for a moment that his shadow was double. It may have been mere fancy, for I had not time to look twice. He was standing, as I have said, with his left side next the horse. Suddenly the harmless elderly cob fell into a very panic of fright, reared upright, and all but succeeded in killing its master. I was in time to pluck Ladlaw from under its feet, but the beast had become perfectly unmanageable, and we left a groom struggling to quiet it.

In the hall the butler gave me a telegram. It was from my clerk, summoning me back at once to an important consultation.

Here was a prompt removal of my scruples. There could be no question of my remaining, for the case was one of the first importance, which I had feared might break off my holiday. The consultation fell in vacation time to meet the convenience of certain people who were going abroad, and there was the most instant demand for my presence. I must go, and at once; and, as I hunted in the timetable, I found that in three hours' time a night train for the south would pass Borrowmuir which might be stopped by special wire.

But I had no pleasure in my freedom. I was in despair about Sibyl, and I hated myself for my cowardly relief. The dreary dining room, the sinister bust, and Ladlaw crouching and quivering – the recollection, now that escape was before me, came back on my mind with the terror of a nightmare. My first thought was to persuade the Ladlaws to come away with me. I found them both in the drawing-room – Sibyl very fragile and pale, and her husband sitting as usual like a frightened child in the shadow of her skirts. A sight of him was enough to dispel my hope. The man was fatally ill, mentally, bodily; and who was I to attempt to minister to a mind diseased?

But Sibyl – she might be saved from the martyrdom. The servants would take care of him, and, if need be, a doctor might be got from Edinburgh to live in the house. So while he sat with vacant eyes staring into the twilight, I tried to persuade Sibyl to think of herself. I am frankly a sun worshiper. I have no taste for arduous duty, and the quixotic is my abhorrence. I labored to bring my cousin to this frame of mind. I told her that her first duty was to herself, and that this vigil of hers was beyond human endurance. But she had no ears for my arguments.

"While Bob is ill I must stay with him," she said always in answer, and then she thanked me for my visit, till I felt a brute and a coward. I strove to quiet my conscience, but it told me always that I was fleeing from my duty; and then, when I was on the brink of a nobler resolution, a sudden overmastering terror would take hold of me, and I would listen hysterically for the sound of the dogcart on the gravel.

At last it came, and in a sort of fever I tried to say the conventional farewells. I shook hands with Ladlaw, and when I dropped his hand it fell numbly on his knee. Then I took my leave, muttering hoarse nonsense about having had a "charming visit," and "hoping soon to see them both in town." As I backed to the door, I knocked over a lamp on a small table. It crashed on the floor and went out, and at the sound Ladlaw gave a curious childish cry. I turned like a coward, and ran across the hall to the front door, and scrambled into the dogcart.

The groom would have driven me sedately through the park, but I must have speed or go mad. I took the reins from him and put the horse into a canter. We swung through the gates and out into the moor road, for I could have no peace till the ghoulish elder world was exchanged for the homely ugliness of civilization. Once only I looked back, and there against the sky line, with a solitary lit window, the House of More stood lonely in the red desert.

The Dying Art

Glen Damien Campbell

THIS IS A CONFESSION, a confession of an evil that I, William Green, committed over forty years ago and which cost the life of my friend. Or so I had always believed. Thomas Crawford was the name of that friend. I don't suppose that name means anything today, celebrities are after all so quickly forgotten and replaced, but in my day he was the greatest illusionist, mentalist, hypnotist and conjuror to ever work the stage.

Tom had always seemed to me a man born for an audience. Physically he was everything one could hope of being; athletic, tall, and swarthy, he was handsome to an almost intolerable degree. Not only was he attractive but he possessed too an astonishing intellect. The body was additionally complimented with an acute mind that was given expression by a voice of upper class eloquence, refining his speech to a fluid argot, typical of someone educated the expensive way. These gifts of nature and breeding gave him an enchanting presence on stage, and, an irresistible appeal to women. Unfortunately, arrogance typically is the corollary of such assets and although in most respects Tom was a kind and liberal man, capable of great generosity at times, above all he was unashamedly narcissistic and perversely devoted to himself and the character he had created for the stage.

His star was quick to shine brightest among the many acts working the London theatres, not least because his shows were truly terrific spectacles. Women swooned as this handsome magician walked barefoot across broken glass, some of the audience would even faint at the sight of his decapitated head during the trick dubbed '*the decollation of John Baptist*' and laughter would resound when he chose the fattest, baldest man from among the audience and hypnotized him into believing he was Cary Grant.

We, Thomas and I, became acquainted early in his career while he was still performing in east end dives run by gangsters and earning extra pocket money by counting blackjack cards and, consequently, getting himself barred from all the casinos in London. I was, at that time, an itinerant pianist tickling the ivories wherever the work was and so naturally we wound up performing in many of same clubs and bars. Our paths crossed regularly enough for a friendship to blossom, and a strong and true friendship it soon became. What made our opposite characters so compatible, I'm not sure, but we were like brothers, I the jealous younger brother, but brothers nonetheless, and only once was that bond ever threatened and I suppose inevitably a woman was the cause.

Olivia Darrow was her name, an actress Tom had hired as his stage assistant. She would stalk in a gaudy leotard and distract the audience with her long perfect legs. God, how we both adored her, she was a beauty that I'm utterly at a loss to describe. Tom and I were scandalous in our pursuit of her.

"Let the better man win," declared Tom, no doubt confident that the better man was him. And, of course, he was right. The fight for Olivia's affections was a battle I was ill equipped for. I was the anti-Tom; myopic, asthmatic and gaunt to a degree so frightening that it could have seen me cast as one of Tod Browning's *Freaks*. Well, maybe I exaggerate. But, nevertheless, it was inevitably Thomas who took the prize and got to nestle between those dancer's legs of hers That was a devastating blow for me. I'd admit that now. I was crazy for her.

* * *

Well now, let's get to the heart of this confession, which I suppose starts that night after Tom's last Palladium show, October 1936. We had gone back to Tom's home in Fulham, a large detached house close to Bishop's Park and overlooking the Thames. Olivia was away visiting family if I remember correctly; she definitely wasn't home that night. They, Tom and Olivia, had been married two years by this time, no children and, to Tom's mind, happier for it. As was our custom we sat in the study with our sherry and Houdini, Tom's black tomcat, brushing up against my ankles.

The study was Tom's shrine to his art, a veritable museum of magic. Early editions, in lavish bindings, of all the most important texts were the pride of the many bookcases, but more entertaining for the guest were the original lithograph posters of sundry magical acts, varying from the haunting to the ludicrous (my personal favourite of these was a French poster that featured a devilish character holding aloft a freshly decapitated head). There was also the odd guillotine, iron maiden and cannon knocking about; the ghoulish props for his stage act.

That night, I remember we talked idly for some time, though I was quite aware that Tom was merely biding his time, he had a purpose for me that night beyond conversation, I could tell this from his demeanour. There was an agitation about him, he wouldn't be seated and would pace the floor throughout our conversation until finally he came to it.

"Enjoy the show tonight?" he asked. It was a peculiar question I remember thinking; he hadn't asked my opinion on his show in years.

"I enjoyed it very much," I answered, perhaps a little too quickly and mechanically.

"Really!" he said, "*You* enjoyed it? You do realise my act hasn't changed much in the past eight years, which is as long as I've known you, you therefore know my act probably better than anyone other than myself, and yet you still enjoy seeing the same old routine. We ought to have your pulse checked; I however was bored out of my skull."

"Well the audience still enjoy it, the seats are still full, and that's the main thing."

"No it isn't, for me to enjoy it that's the main thing. I get up on stage to entertain myself, not those Guffins, and what entertains me is their fear. The only reason the audience still enjoy my show, and probably more now than they ever did, is because my act no longer terrifies them, it's all too comfortingly familiar. I want to see fear in their eyes again. I want all the pretty young virgins in my audience to go home afraid that I lurk in shadows of their boudoirs, afraid that one day they might encounter me and that I might mesmerize them into revealing all their vulgar little fantasies. That's why I do what I do. I want my audience to believe they're watching an emissary of Lucifer."

"Well then you must give them something new," I suggested casually, but this, I could tell, was just the advice Tom had been counting on for as soon as the words were spoken that maliciously little smile of his crept right across his lupine face.

All adults I believe have a facial characteristic that betrays the child they used to be, I believe that malicious grin of Tom's betrayed his childhood nature. It was the smile of a remorseless trickster and show-off. It was easy to imagine him as a rather wicked and mischievous child grinning like that after having performed a particularly fiendish prank.

"Give them something new?" he repeated my words. "That's exactly what *we* shall do."

Straight away, I found his use of the word *we* suspicious.

"You have a new trick?" I asked.

"Perhaps," he answered nonchalantly. "Last Tuesday I drove up to Lockwood village, why I should go so far out of my way for no particular reason I don't know, but I had just been with Bea and didn't really feel ready to return home to Olivia yet. After being with Beatrice I find I need to air myself out a bit, that cheap perfume she must positively bathe in hangs in the ether around me like noxious gas. But I really shouldn't complain, after all, I probably bought it for her."

Beatrice was his mistress, one of many. I had always wished that he'd keep his affairs hidden from me, some days I could hardly look at Olivia for guilt, and looking at Olivia was one of the few great pleasures I had in life.

"Whatever the reason, some instinct compelled me to Lockwood that day," Tom continued, "and I know now that fortune was smiling on me that day. Of course you remember that Lockwood was the town where Gombrich lived and died?"

I hadn't the foggiest, but I knew the name Gombrich well enough, some days he was all Tom would deign talk about. "A magician so good he makes my cock crow" was one particularly memorable way Tom had once described him. He had died an old man in 1911, when Tom was only three years old and so consequently Tom knew him only through newspaper clippings and word of mouth, but that was enough to make him obsessed.

"Well anyway," said Tom, "in Lockwood I stumbled upon a little bric-a-brac store, full of junk mostly, actually that's being too kind, it was full of junk *entirely*. But what I did find was a heap of old newspapers, the local town rag. The rheumatic old codger who owned the store had editions from as far back as the eighteen-nineties. I even found the editions dating from the time of Gombrich's death and funeral. They were fantastic, so much more detailed than the nationals and one particular snippet of information had me doing cartwheels. Apparently Gombrich was buried with his journal, the book of all his secrets. That's where I shall find my new routine."

"You want to steal Gombrich's tricks?" I asked.

Tom glowered at me vexed.

"I will not be *stealing* his tricks," he roared. "It shall be homage, a tribute. I'll acknowledge him in performance. I shall always be his disciple. Gombrich will always be the Master. I shall see to it that his name is placed along side Dedi, Robert-Houdin and John Nevil Maskelyne in the pantheon of the black arts. Those wonderful illusions he invented should not go with him to the grave. I need that journal William. Will you help me? The drive to Lockwood is but two hours, if we leave now we'd be there by one o'clock, the deed itself shouldn't take long. I have everything we need shovels, torches and such prepared and ready."

"Tonight," I exclaimed.

"Of course tonight," snapped Tom, "you expect me to wait! I cannot wait any longer. I have the patience of a child on such matters. Think of what a treasure trove could be waiting for me in that dead man's hands."

"But it's so damn gruesome, Tom," I protested. "Do you really mean to dig up the poor man's grave?"

Delighted at having scandalized me, Tom grinned at me diabolically.

"He's quite dead, William, I assure you," he said, "I shouldn't think he'd be the slightest bit put out by us dropping by and as for the journal, well I hardly think that it's of much use to him now. What is there left for him to enter? *'Dear Journal, today my right eye was eaten by a worm.'* Ha!" he laughed fiendishly. "Come! The sooner we leave the sooner we're done."

He didn't even wait to hear my acquiescence, he simply walked out the room expecting me to follow, which of course I did.

* * *

The estimate Tom gave for the journey to Lockwood was, as customary, accurate to the minute and we arrived at the cemetery gates a little before one. Like Burke and Hare we traipsed among the gravestones, our shovels resting on our shoulders. Tom led the way. He seemed quite familiar with the cemetery grounds; the darkness seemed to be no impediment to our progress. The night, though, was everything we wouldn't have hoped for, both bitterly cold and damp.

I'm a city lad and hate the country at the best of times. It's nothing but muddy grass and cowpats as far as I can tell. But it is the isolation that I dislike above all. I need the anonymity a city provides. With such want of activity around us, increasingly, while Tom and I trudged our wellingtons disrespectfully over the graves of strangers, I felt that Heaven's spotlight was free to focus very disapprovingly upon us.

I would guess that Tom didn't share my discomfort for he didn't display the slightest jot of consternation quite the contrary actually, such macabre acts I suppose delighted him. He had always wanted to play the part of the gothic villain. He lived that fantasy out to a degree on stage.

The stage was his lair where he chained down scantily clad beauties with heaving bosoms and gleefully impaled them with swords or cut them in half. But that was theatre, this was genuine, and I must admit I found his *sang-froid* in the cemetery discomforting. I felt the occasion called for a certain solemnity and as we stood before Gombrich's gravestone within the shadow of the church spire I couldn't help but feel judgement being cast upon us.

It was a humble grave, in the end, with the briefest of inscriptions.

In Memory of
THEODOR ANTON GOMBRICH
Magician
Born 28 January 1846 – Died 04 December 1911

I saw to it that it was Tom's shovel that first broke the ground. Stupid I know but I felt this in some way helped to consolidate me in my position as a mere footman in the deed and not the mastermind, as if this would matter at some time.

We dug for about an hour before we struck the coffin's lid.

"You don't have to see inside," Tom charitably informed me. "Climb up and hand down the crowbar."

I did as I was told and then waited at the edge of the pit smoking a cigarette and trying to keep myself warm. From the sound of it Tom had quite a job breaking into the coffin but soon enough he emerged from grave bringing with him a small chest about the size of a loaf of bread.

"Got it!" he declared triumphantly. "Let's fill this back up and go."

* * *

Our journey back to London passed almost entirely in silence. Eager to return to his study and open his treasure chest, Tom took full advantage of the empty roads and drove the whole way back to London like a race car driver. Being by no means a speedster it would have been a very nervous journey home for me had I not been agitated by a morbid curiosity. *What would twenty-five years in the grave do to a body?*

The car pulled up outside my house at about three AM. At the time I lived in a small house in Hammersmith. Out of the car, I shook hands with Tom through the driver's window. He thanked me again with real sincerity. Then, just as he was about to start the motor again to leave, I finally asked: "What . . . what did it look like?"

"What did *what* look like?" teased Tom looking at me blankly despite knowing perfectly well what I meant by *it*.

"What did the *body* look like," I clarified.

Tom sniggered. "There was no body," he answered enigmatically before driving away.

I never saw him again.

The next morning I received the news that Tom had died in his sleep. Obviously I was shocked. In an instant I had lost my best friend, but however much grief the news had caused me it was nothing compared to how Olivia suffered. Upon receiving the news I immediately went to her. The condition I found her in excited me. Should I be ashamed to admit that? She was lost and needed me, and, like a votive offering, I wanted to give myself to her.

* * *

It was on the morning of Tom's funeral when I noticed the letter. It was one of a dozen or so unopened letters strewn across my bureau. I hadn't the time or inclination to handle my correspondence in the wake of Tom's death and the letters had simply begun to pile up. I was actually on my way out when it caught my eye and stopped me dead in my tracks. It was unmistakable. The writing on one of the envelopes was written in Tom's hand. What is amazing is that I could have missed this before. I would have seen that letter everyday over the past four. It must have been posted on the day of his death. Naturally, I immediately opened it and what a revelation I discovered inside.

My conscience has indelibly engraved every word of its contents upon me so that now, even after the passing of forty years, I can relate it verbatim. It read:

> *My dear friend*
> *I must once again thank you for your assistance the other night, quite a lark wouldn't you say?*
> *The rewards it has brought are indeed fantastically great, much more than I could have ever imagined. Since my earliest days, when I was only capable of the most primitive of coin tricks I have revered Gombrich as my idol. It was thoughts of him that would spur me on, but only now, now that I have his journal in my hands, do I really know anything of his genius. The chest we recovered contained two items*

*the journal and a phial of powder. The journal, I shall discuss the powder shortly,
I have just read from cover to cover. Not since I was a child, the time a lay across a
rug in my father's library reading Reginald Scot's 'The Discoverie of Witchcraft', my
introduction to the black arts, have I been so enthralled.*

*With this discovery my whole career shall be reborn and to announce this
rebirth the world shall bare witness to a trick, one of Gombrich's last and cheekiest.
For this trick the powder which I spoke of is the key. Gombrich writes that he acquired
the substance from a coloured magician in New Orleans, it's a neurotoxin derived
from a fish, which when administered gives the patient the characteristic of death,
slowing the heart to a beat practically imperceptible. This cataleptic condition
can last up to five days, and then the sleeper shall awake and take a bow as his
audience gasp in astonishment. This delightfully simple trick seems responsible
for the superstition of the living corpse found in primitive cultures. Gombrich has
dubbed the illusion The Dying Art.*

*You must be incredulous William I'm sure, such things aren't possible, but
remember that this is magic the art of the impossible.*

*Well then, if you are still incredulous you must have proof. Tonight I shall
take a draught of the powder and let it put me to sleep and in five days I shall
return from the grave. I have told no one of my intention, not even dear Olivia.
Her grief appearing genuine I imagine is tantamount to the tricks success and,
unfortunately, we have both seen her act. People must really believe that I can cheat
death. You are my sole accomplice on this matter. Do what you can to fan the flames
of publicity, for my funeral suggest a transparent coffin perhaps, so the mourners
and reporters can watch my corpse like body be interred.Oh but William, if it does
go as far as my burial be a dear and dig me up, you have some recent grave digging
experience I believe.*

Well that is all. Destroy this letter and tell no one.

THE DEVIL'S MESSIAH

Now, at last, here is my confession. Of the two requests he asked of me in that letter I
complied with only one. I burnt the letter but after the funeral I left him in the ground to
die. Why? Maybe I resented the way he arrogantly expected that I'd always be his lackey
for whatever plot he hatched, but the truth is, I loved Olivia and in those four days leading
up to Tom's funeral I became the man at her side, consoling her, making decisions for her
and supporting her in anyway I could and I realized that at her side was where I wanted to
remain. I abandoned Tom so that I could have a second chance with Olivia and I cannot
regret mydecision for two years later we were married and went on to share our lives
together for a further forty years, years I wouldn't give up for anything.

Of course, guilt haunted me at first. Countless nights I spent lying on my back in bed,
with the cover over head, imagining what it would have been like for Tom to wake up in
that garish box of his buried six feet beneath the earth. How did he die? I often wondered.
Did he scream in terror until his throat was raw, did he scratch at the lid of his coffin until
his fingers bled, before finally resigning himself to the inevitability of his slow agonizing
demise? Did he suffocate or die of starvation?

Screaming and clawing was hardly Tom's style, but could he really have kept his dignity
in such a state? Well if anyone could, Tom could of. I could see him lying there languidly,

luxuriating among his coffin's fine silk upholstery, ensconced like a foppish vampire, trying to compose some witty last words.

For a while all my private moments were sullied by some macabre fantasy about Tom's final hours. My favourites, though, were the ones that had Tom crying out in terror and fighting hopelessly for his life.

Occasionally, I even found the thought of Tom impotently crying out in terror from within his grave amusing. I'm ashamed to say it, but it's the truth. There were times when I actually giggled while imagining the splinters lacerating his precious conjuror's hands as he tried to claw his way out of his coffin. The bloodier his hands became the more amused I would become until soon I'd be howling with laughter like a bloodthirsty ghoul. With tears of mirth rolling down my cheeks, I'd watch in my mind's eye Tom's face drop as he realized two things; his certain looming death and that his obedient dog was not so obedient after all.

It was a surprise to discover what a ghoul I could be, and yet, at other times, the same scene could move me to tears of sorrow. Such morbidity of spirit I feared would be the enduring after effect of my wrong. For years I was tortured like this, however, with time I discovered that one can make peace with any sin, as I did with mine. Crowley, that old deviant, had taught Tom to define his own morality, well now I too learned that lesson as my happiness with Olivia slowly dissolved my guilt and justified my crime.

* * *

This morning I buried her. The illness has claimed her finally. In a way, I am relieved that it's over and that she can now be at peace. That was not her at the end, the dementia had corrupted her, eaten away the dear woman that I loved and left me with the bitter pith.

Over the last few months, she had even taken to calling me Tom. That hurt me. Neither of us had spoken his name in years, but evidently he had never left her thoughts. I wonder how often she thought of him while she was with me. Was I always just an inferior replacement for him? Did she ever truly stop loving him? Perhaps it was having his name returned to my conscience that brought about what I saw this morning at the cemetery.

As Olivia's coffin was being lowered into its burial plot and the priest recited a prayer I felt eyes being cast upon me. Not sympathetic eyes being mournfully bestowed upon a widow, but eyes infused with such malice that I could practically feel their touch. I looked up to find the source. The heads of my fellow mourners lowered to observe the prayer, their exhalations wreathing and rolling in the cold winter air like dragons breath. However, there was one guest who had no regard for priest's prayer.

A young gentleman in a drape-cut suit was the exception. The brim of the black fedora he wore partly shadowed his face but I could clearly see his eyes that seem to shine out from shadows like stars of ill omen. Focused intently upon me, they were wide and ablaze with hate.

He met my gaze brazenly and then gradually his lips spread full into a grin that I instantly recognised. It was Tom's malicious grin. At that moment of recognition the prayer ended, the other heads rose and the stranger seemed to disappear among the faces.

What had I seen? Could it of actually been Tom?

Could it be that after all this time 'The Dying Art' had been played on me? Was he ever even in that grave? Did he secretly know I would have done anything to win Olivia? His whole art was based on reading people and manipulating them. Has he tested my loyalty to him? Without doubt I've failed him and so now maybe he has returned to haunt my final lonely years with his psychological tricks and sorcery, to terrorize me to insanity.

I will not let that come to pass! I must know if Thomas Crawford lies in that grave or if, like some zombie, he has crawled out from it.

I write this confession in my house on Lily Foot Lane, when I am through I shall leave for the cemetery, and there, belatedly fulfil the request put to me some forty years ago. I will dig him up! And if I find Tom's rotting corpse there in that gaudy coffin of his I shall rejoice at the sight of it, perhaps even dance a merry jig, before stomping those decaying bones into dust with the heel of my shoe and then returning home to destroy these pages. I do not believe in ghosts and therefore shall not allow myself to be haunted by one.

However, if that grave is empty, if I have again played the vassal to my whilom friend's Lord of Illusion, I shall not return. I shall *never* return. If indeed tonight I find Tom's grave empty then by sunrise *you*, whoever is reading this, can find me at Putney Bridge and there, as is my custom, I'll be staring down upon the gentle undulations of the Thames, only this time, I'll be dangling from the rafters with a noose wrapped tightly around my neck.

The Yellow Sign

Robert W. Chambers

Let the red dawn surmise
What we shall do,
When this blue starlight dies
And all is through.

I

THERE ARE so many things which are impossible to explain! Why should certain chords in music make me think of the brown and golden tints of autumn foliage? Why should the Mass of Sainte Cecile send my thoughts wandering among caverns whose walls blaze with ragged masses of virgin silver? What was it in the roar and turmoil of Broadway at six o'clock that flashed before my eyes the picture of a still Breton forest where sunlight filtered through spring foliage and Sylvia bent, half curiously, half tenderly, over a small green lizard, murmuring: "To think that this is also a little ward of God!"

When I first saw the watchman his back was toward me. I looked at him indifferently until he went into the church. I paid no more attention to him than I had to any other man who lounged through Washington Square that morning, and when I shut my window and turned back into my studio I had forgotten him. Late in the afternoon, the day being warm, I raised the window again and leaned out to get a sniff of the air. A man was standing in the courtyard of the church, and I noticed him again with as little interest as I had that morning. I looked across the square to where the fountain was playing and then, with my mind filled with vague impressions of trees, asphalt drives, and the moving groups of nursemaids and holidaymakers, I started to walk back to my easel.

As I turned, my listless glance included the man below in the churchyard. His face was toward me now, and with a perfectly involuntary movement I bent to see it. At the same moment he raised his head and looked at me. Instantly I thought of a coffin-worm. Whatever it was about the man that repelled me I did not know, but the impression of a plump white grave-worm was so intense and nauseating that I must have shown it in my expression, for he turned his puffy face away with a movement which made me think of a disturbed grub in a chestnut.

I went back to my easel and motioned the model to resume her pose. After working awhile I was satisfied that I was spoiling what I had done as rapidly as possible, and I took up a palette knife and scraped the color out again. The flesh tones were sallow and unhealthy, and I did not understand how I could have painted such sickly color into a study which before that had glowed with healthy tones.

I looked at Tessie. She had not changed, and the clear flush of health dyed her neck and cheeks as I frowned.

"Is it something I've done?" she said.

"No – I've made a mess of this arm, and for the life of me I can't see how I came to paint such mud as that into the canvas," I replied.

"Don't I pose well?" she insisted.

"Of course, perfectly."

"Then it's not my fault?"

"No. It's my own."

"I'm very sorry," she said.

I told her she could rest while I applied rag and turpentine to the plague spot on my canvas, and she went off to smoke a cigarette and look over the illustrations in the Courier Français.

I did not know whether it was something in the turpentine or a defect in the canvas, but the more I scrubbed the more that gangrene seemed to spread. I worked like a beaver to get it out, and yet the disease appeared to creep from limb to limb of the study before me. Alarmed I strove to arrest it, but now the color on the breast changed and the whole figure seemed to absorb the infection as a sponge soaks up water. Vigorously I plied palette knife, turpentine, and scraper, thinking all the time what a seance I should hold with Duval who had sold me the canvas; but soon I noticed that it was not the canvas which was defective nor yet the colors of Edward. "It must be the turpentine," I thought angrily, "or else my eyes have become so blurred and confused by the afternoon light that I can't see straight." I called Tessie, the model. She came and leaned over my chair blowing rings of smoke into the air.

"What have you been doing to it?" she exclaimed.

"Nothing," I growled, "it must be this turpentine!"

"What a horrible color it is now," she continued. "Do you think my flesh resembles green cheese?"

"No, I don't," I said angrily, "did you ever know me to paint like that before?"

"No, indeed!"

"Well, then!"

"It must be the turpentine, or something," she admitted.

She slipped on a Japanese robe and walked to the window. I scraped and rubbed until I was tired and finally picked up my brushes and hurled them through the canvas with a forcible expression, the tone alone of which reached Tessie's ears.

Nevertheless she promptly began: "That's it! Swear and act silly and ruin your brushes! You have been three weeks on that study, and now look! What's the good of ripping the canvas? What creatures artists are!"

I felt about as much ashamed as I usually did after such an outbreak, and I turned the ruined canvas to the wall. Tessie helped me clean my brushes, and then danced away to dress. From the screen she regaled me with bits of advice concerning whole or partial loss of temper, until, thinking, perhaps, I had been tormented sufficiently, she came out to implore me to button her waist where she could not reach it on the shoulder.

"Everything went wrong from the time you came back from the window and talked about that horrid-looking man you saw in the churchyard," she announced.

"Yes, he probably bewitched the picture," I said, yawning. I looked at my watch.

"It's after six, I know," said Tessie, adjusting her hat before the mirror.

"Yes," I replied, "I didn't mean to keep you so long." I leaned out the window but recoiled with disgust, for the young man with the pasty face stood below in the churchyard. Tessie saw my gesture of disapproval and leaned from the window.

"Is that the man you don't like?" she whispered.

I nodded.

"I can't see his face, but he does look fat and soft. Someway or other," she continued, looking at me, "he reminds me of a dream, – and awful dream I once had. Or," she mused looking down at her shapely shoes, "was it a dream after all?"

"How should I know?" I smiled.

Tessie smiled in reply.

"You were in it," she said, "so perhaps you might know something about it."

"Tessie! Tessie!" I protested, "don't you dare flatter by saying you dream about me!"

"But I did," she insisted; "shall I tell you about it?"

"Go ahead," I replied, lighting a cigarette.

Tessie leaned back on the open window-sill and began very seriously.

"One night last winter I was lying in bed thinking about nothing at all in particular. I had been posing for you and I was tired out, yet it seemed impossible for me to sleep. I heard the bells in the city ring ten, eleven, and midnight. I must have fallen asleep about midnight because I don't remember hearing the bells after that. It seemed to me that I had scarcely closed my eyes when I dreamed that something impelled me to go to the window. I rose, and raising the sash, leaned out. Twenty-fifth Street was deserted as far as I could see. I began to be afraid; everything outside seemed so – so black and uncomfortable. Then the sound of wheels in the distance came to my ears, and it seemed to me as though that was what I must wait for. Very slowly the wheels approached, and, finally, I could make out a vehicle moving along the street.

It came nearer and nearer, and when it passed beneath my window I saw it was a hearse. Then, as I trembled with fear, the driver turned and looked straight at me. When I awoke I was standing by the open window shivering with cold, but the black-plumed hearse and the driver were gone. I dreamed this dream again in March last, and again awoke beside the open window. Last night the dream came again. You remember how it was raining; when I awoke, standing at the open window, my nightdress was soaked."

"But where did I come into the dream?" I asked.

"You – you were in the coffin; but you were not dead."

"In the coffin?"

"Yes."

"How did you know? Could you see me?"

"No; I only knew you were there."

"Had you been eating Welsh rarebits, or lobster salad?" I began laughing, but the girl interrupted me with a frightened cry.

"Hello! What's up?" I said, as she shrank into the embrasure by the window.

"The – the man below in the churchyard; – he drove the hearse."

"Nonsense," I said, but Tessie's eyes were wide with terror. I went to the window and looked out. The man was gone. "Come, Tessie," I urged, "don't be foolish. You have posed too long; you are nervous."

"Do you think I could forget that face?" she murmured. "Three times I saw that hearse pass below my window, and every time the driver turned and looked up at me. Oh, his face was so white and – and soft? It looked dead – it looked as if it had been dead a long time."

I induced the girl to sit down and swallow a glass of Marsala. Then I sat down beside her and tried to give her some advice.

"Look here, Tessie," I said, "you go to the country for a week or two, and you'll have no more dreams about hearses. You pose all day, and when night comes your nerves are upset. You can't keep this up. Then again, instead of going to bed when your day's work is done, you run off to picnics at Sulzer's Park, or go to the Eldorado or Coney Island, and when you come down here in the morning you are fagged out. There was no real hearse. That was a soft-shell crab dream."

She smiled faintly.

"What about the man in the churchyard?"

"Oh, he's an ordinary unhealthy, everyday creature."

"As true as my name is Tessie Reardon, I swear to you, Mr. Scott, that the face of the man below in the churchyard is the face of the man who drove the hearse!"

"What of it?" I said. "It's an honest trade."

"Then you think I did see a hearse?"

"Oh," I said diplomatically, "if you really did, it might not be unlikely that the man below drove it. There is nothing in that."

Tessie rose, unrolled her scented handkerchief, and taking a bit of gum from a knot in the hem, placed it in her mouth. Then drawing on her gloves she offered me her hand, with a frank, "Good-night, Mr. Scott," and walked out.

II

THE NEXT MORNING, Thomas, the bellboy, brought me the Herald and a bit of news. The church next door had been sold. I thanked Heaven for it, not that being a Catholic I had any repugnance for the congregation next door, but because my nerves were shattered by a blatant exhorter, whose every word echoed through the aisle of the church as if it had been my own rooms, and who insisted on his r's with a nasal persistence which revolted my every instinct. Then, too, there as a fiend in human shape, an organist, who reeled off some of the grand old hymns with an interpretation of his own, and I longed for the blood of a creature who could play the doxology with an amendment of minor chords which one hears only in a quartet of very young undergraduates. I believe the minister was a good man, but when he bellowed: "And the Lorrrrd said unto Moses, the Lorrrrd is a man of war; the Lorrrrd is his name. My wrath shall wax hot and I will kill you with the sworrrrd!" I wondered how many centuries of purgatory it would take to atone for such a sin.

"Who bought the property?" I asked Thomas.

"Nobody that I knows, sir. They do say the gent wot owns this 'ere 'Amilton flats was lookin' at it. 'E might be a bildin' more studios."

I walked to the window. The young man with the unhealthy face stood by the churchyard gate, and at the mere sight of him the same overwhelming repugnance took possession of me.

"By the way, Thomas," I said, "who is that fellow down there?"

Thomas sniffed. "That there worm, sir? 'E's night-watchman of the church, sir. 'E maikes me tired a-sittin' out all night on them steps and lookin' at you insultin' like. I'd a punched 'is 'ed, sir – beg pardon sir —"

"Go on, Thomas."

"One night a comin' 'ome with 'Arry, the other English boy, I sees 'im a sittin' there on them steps. We 'ad Molly and Jen with us, sir, the two girls on the tray service, an' 'e looks so insultin' at us that I up and sez: 'Wat you looking hat, you fat slug?' – beg pardon, sir, but that's 'ow I sez, sir. Then 'e don't say nothin' and I sez; 'Come out and I'll punch that puddin' 'ed.' Then I hopens the gate an' goes in, but 'e don't say nothin', only looks insultin' like. Then I 'its 'im one, but ugh! 'is 'ed was that cold and mushy it ud sicken you to touch 'im."

"What did he do then?" I asked, curiously.

"'Im? Nawthin'."

"And you, Thomas?"

The young fellow flushed in embarrassment and smiled uneasily.

"Mr. Scott, sir, I ain't no coward an' I can't make it out at all why I run. I was with the 5th Lawncers, sir, bugler at Tel-el-Kebir, an' was shot by the wells."

"You don't mean to say you ran away?"

"Yes, sir; I run."

"Why?"

"That's just what I want to know, sir. I grabbed Molly an' run, an' the rest of us just as frightened as I."

"But what were they frightened at?"

Thomas refused to answer for a while, but now my curiosity was aroused about the repulsive young man below and I pressed him. Three years' sojourn in America had not only modified Thomas' cockney dialect but had given him the American's fear of ridicule.

"You won't believe me, Mr. Scott, sir?"

"Yes, I will."

"You will lawf at me, sir?"

"Nonsense!"

He hesitated. "Well, sir, it's God's truth that when I 'it 'im 'e grabbed me wrists, sir, and when I twisted 'is soft, mushy fist one of 'is fingers come off in me 'and."

The utter loathing and horror of Thomas' face must have been reflected in my own for he added:

"It's orful, an' now when I see 'im I just go away. 'E maikes me hill."

When Thomas had gone I went to the window. The man stood beside the church-railing with both hands on the gate, but I hastily retreated to my easel again, sickened and horrified, for I saw that the middle finger of his right hand was missing.

At nine o'clock Tessie appeared and vanished behind the screen with a merry "Good-morning, Mr. Scott." While she had reappeared and taken her pose upon the model-stand I started a new canvas much to her delight. She remained silent as long as I was on the drawing, but as soon as the scrape of the charcoal ceased and I took up my fixative she began to chatter.

"Oh, I had such a lovely time last night. We went to Tony Pastor's."

"Who are 'we'?" I demanded.

"Oh, Maggie, you know, Mr. Whyte's model, and Pinkie McCormick – we call her Pinkie because she's got that beautiful red hair you artists like so much – and Lizzie Burke."

I sent a shower of fixative over the canvas and said: "Well, go on."

"We saw Kelly and Baby Barnes the skirt-dancer and – and all the rest. I made a mash."

"Then you have gone back on me, Tessie?"

She laughed and shook her head.

"He's Lizzie Burke's brother, Ed. He's a perfect gen'l'man."

I felt constrained to give her some parental advice concerning mashing, which she took with a bright smile.

"Oh, I can take care of a strange mash," she said, examining her chewing gum, "but Ed is different. Lizzie is my best friend."

Then she related how Ed had come back from the stocking mill in Lowell, Massachusetts, to find her and Lizzie grown up, and what an accomplished young man he was, and how he thought nothing of squandering half a dollar for ice-cream and oysters to celebrate his entry as clerk into the woolen department of Macy's. Before she finished I began to paint, and she resumed the pose, smiling and chattering like a sparrow. By noon I had the study fairly well rubbed in and Tessie came to look at it.

"That's better," she said.

I thought so too, and ate my lunch with a satisfied feeling that all was going well. Tessie spread her lunch on a drawing table opposite me and we drank our claret from the same bottle and lighted our cigarettes from the same match. I was very much attached to Tessie. I had watched her shoot up into a slender but exquisitely formed woman from a frail, awkward child. She had posed for me during the last three years, and among all my models she was my favorite. It would have troubled me very much indeed had she become "tough" or "fly," as the phrase goes, but I had never noticed any deterioration of her manner, and felt at heart that she was all right. She and I never discussed morals at all, and I had no intention of doing so, partly because I had none myself, and partly because I knew she would do what she liked in spite of me.

Still I did hope she would steer clear of complications, because I wished her well, and then also I had a selfish desire to retain the best model I had. I knew that mashing, as she termed it, had no significance with girls like Tessie, and that such things in America did not resemble in the least the same things in Paris. Yet, having lived with my eyes open, I also knew that somebody would take Tessie away some day in one manner or another, and though I professed to myself that marriage was nonsense, I sincerely hoped that, in this case, there would be a priest at the end of the vista.

I am a Catholic. When I listen to high mass, when I sign myself, I feel that everything, including myself, is more cheerful, and when I confess, it does me good. A man who lives as much alone as I do, must confess to somebody. Then, again, Sylvia was Catholic, and it was reason enough for me. But I was speaking of Tessie, which is very different. Tessie also was Catholic and much more devout than I, so, taking it all in all, I had little fear for my pretty model until she should fall in love. But then I knew that fate alone would decide her future for her, and I prayed inwardly that fate would keep her away from men like me and throw into her path nothing but Ed Burkes and Jimmy McCormicks, bless her sweet face!

Tessie sat blowing smoke up to the ceiling and tinkling the ice in her tumbler.

"Do you know, Kid, that I also had a dream last night?" I observed. I sometimes called her "the Kid."

"Not about that man," she laughed.

"Exactly. A dream similar to yours, only much worse."

It was foolish and thoughtless of me to say this, but you know how little tact the average painter has.

"I must have fallen asleep about 10 o'clock," I continued, "and after a while I dreamt that I awoke. So plainly did I hear the midnight bells, the wind in the tree-branches, and the whistle of steamers from the bay, that even now I can scarcely believe that I was not awake.

I seemed to be lying in a box which had a glass cover. Dimly I saw the street lamps as I passed, for I must tell you, Tessie, the box in which I reclined appeared to lie in a cushioned wagon which jolted me over a stony pavement. After a while I became impatient and tried to move but the box was too narrow. My hands were crossed on my breast so I could not raise them to help myself. I listened and then tried to call. My voice was gone. I could hear the trample of the horses attached to the wagon and even the breathing of the driver. Then another sound broke upon my ears like the raising of a window sash. I managed to turn my head a little, and found I could look, not only through the glass cover of my box, but also through the glass panes in the side of the covered vehicle. I saw houses, empty and silent, with neither light nor life about any of them excepting one. In that house a window was open on the first floor and a figure all in white stood looking down into the street. It was you."

Tessie had turned her face away from me and leaned on the table with her elbow.

"I could see your face," I resumed, "and it seemed to me to be very sorrowful. Then we passed on and turned into a narrow black lane. Presently the horses stopped. I waited and waited, closing my eyes with fear and impatience, but all was silent as the grave. After what seemed to me hours, I began to feel uncomfortable. A sense that somebody was close to me made me unclose my eyes. Then I saw the white face of the hearse-driver looking at me through the coffin-lid –"

A sob from Tessie interrupted me. She was trembling like a leaf. I saw I had made an ass of myself and attempted to repair the damage.

"Why, Tess," I said, "I only told you this to show you what influence your story might have on another person's dreams. You don't suppose I really lay in a coffin, do you? What are you trembling for? Don't you see that your dream and my unreasonable dislike for that inoffensive watchman of the church simply set my brain working as soon as I fell asleep?"

She laid her head between her arms and sobbed as if her heart would break. What a precious triple donkey I had made of myself! But I was about to break my record. I went over and put my arm about her.

"Tessie, dear, forgive me," I said; "I had no business to frighten you with such nonsense. You are too sensible a girl, too good a Catholic to believe in dreams."

Her hand tightened on mine and her head fell back upon my shoulder, but she still trembled and I petted her and comforted her.

"Come, Tess, open your eyes and smile."

Her eyes opened with a slow languid movement and met mine, but their expression was so queer that I hastened to reassure her again.

"It's all humbug, Tessie, you surely are not afraid that any harm will come to you because of that."

"No," she said, but her scarlet lips quivered.

"Then what's the matter? Are you afraid?"

"Yes. Not for myself."

"For me, then?" I demanded gaily.

"For you," she murmured in a voice almost inaudible, "I – I care – for you."

At first I started to laugh, but when I understood her, a shock passed through me and I sat like one turned to stone. This was the crowning bit of idiocy I had committed. During the moment which elapsed between her reply and my answer I thought of a thousand responses to that innocent confession. I could pass it by with a laugh, I could misunderstand her and reassure her as to my health, I could simply point out that it was impossible she could love me. But my reply was quicker than my thoughts and I might think and think now when it was too late, for I had kissed her on the mouth.

That evening I took my usual walk in Washington Park, pondering over the occurrences of the day. I was thoroughly committed. There was no back out now, and I stared the future straight in the face. I was not good, not even scrupulous, but I had no idea of deceiving either myself or Tessie. The one passion of my life lay buried in the sunlit forests of Brittany. Was it buried forever? Hope cried "No!" For three years I had been listening to the voice of Hope, and for three years I had waited for a footstep on my threshold. Had Sylvia forgotten? "No!" cried Hope.

I said that I was not good. That is true, but still I was not exactly a comic opera villain. I had led an easy-going reckless life, taking what invited me of pleasure, deploring and sometimes bitterly regretting consequences. In one thing alone, except my painting, I was serious, and that was something which lay hidden if not lost in the Breton forests.

It was too late now for me to regret what had occurred during the day. Whatever it had been, pity, a sudden tenderness for sorrow, of the more brutal instinct of gratified vanity, it was all the same now, and unless I wished to bruise an innocent heart my path lay marked before me. The fire and strength, the depth of passion of a love which I had never even suspected, with all my imagined experience in the world, left me no alternative but to respond or send her away. Whether because I am so cowardly about giving pain to others, or whether it was that I have little of the gloomy Puritan in me, I do not know, but I shrank from disclaiming responsibility for that thoughtless kiss, and in fact had no time to do so before the gates of her heart opened and the flood poured forth. Others who habitually do their duty and find a sullen satisfaction in making themselves and everybody else unhappy, might have withstood it. I did not. I dared not.

After the storm had abated I did tell her that she might better have loved Ed Burke and worn a plain gold ring, but she would not hear of it, and I thought perhaps that as long as she had decided to love somebody she could not marry, it had better be me. I, at least, could treat her with an intelligent affection, and whenever she became tired of her infatuation she could go none the worse for it. For I was decided on that point although I knew how hard it would be. I remembered the usual termination of Platonic liaisons and thought how disgusted I had been whenever I heard of one. I knew I was undertaking a great deal for so unscrupulous a man as I was, and I dreaded the future, but never for one moment did I doubt that she was safe with me. Had it been anybody but Tessie I should not have bothered my head about scruples. For it did not occur to me to sacrifice Tessie as I would have sacrificed a woman of the world.

I looked the future squarely in the face and saw the several probable endings to the affair. She would either tire of the whole thing, or become so unhappy that I should have either to marry her or go away. If I married her we would be unhappy. I with a wife unsuited to me, and she with a husband unsuitable for any woman. For my past life could scarcely entitle me to marry. If I went away she might either fall ill, recover, and marry some Eddie Burke, or she might recklessly or deliberately go and do something foolish. On the other hand if she tired of me, then her whole life would be before her with beautiful vistas of Eddie Burkes and marriage rings and twins and Harlem flats and Heaven knows what. As I strolled along through the trees by Washington Arch, I decided that she should find a substantial friend in me anyway and the future could take care of itself. Then I went into the house and put on my evening dress for the little faintly perfumed note on my dresser said, "Have a cab at the stage door at eleven," and the note was signed 'Edith'.

I took supper that night, or rather we took supper, Miss Carmichael and I, at Solari's and the dawn was just beginning to gild the cross on the Memorial Church as I entered Washington Square after leaving Edith at the Brunswick. There was not a soul in the park as I passed among the trees and took the walk which leads from the Garibaldi statue to the Hamilton Apartment House, but as I passed the churchyard I saw a figure sitting on the stone steps. In spite of myself a chill crept over me at the sight of the white puffy face, and I hastened to pass. Then he said something which might have been addressed to me or might merely have been a mutter to himself, but a sudden furious anger flamed up within me that such a creature should address me.

For an instant I felt like wheeling about and smashing my stick over his head, but I walked on, and entering the Hamilton went to my apartment. For some time I tossed about the bed trying to get the sound of his voice out of my ears, but could not. It filled my head, that muttering sound, like thick oily smoke from a fat-rendering vat or an odor of noisome decay. And as I lay and tossed about, the voice in my ears seemed more distinct, and I began to understand the words he had muttered. They came to me slowly as if I had forgotten them, and at last I could make some sense out of the sounds. It was this:

"Have you found the Yellow Sign?"

"Have you found the Yellow Sign?"

"Have you found the Yellow Sign?"

I was furious. What did he mean by that? Then with a curse upon him and his I rolled over and went to sleep, but when I awoke later I looked pale and haggard, for I had dreamed the dream of the night before and it troubled me more than I cared to think.

I dressed and went down into my studio. Tessie sat by the window, but as I came in she rose and put both arms around my neck for an innocent kiss. She looked so sweet and dainty that I kissed her again and then sat down before the easel.

"Hello! Where's the study I began yesterday?" I asked.

Tessie looked conscious, but did not answer. I began to hunt among the piles of canvases, saying, "Hurry up, Tess, and get ready; we must take advantage of the morning light."

When at last I gave up the search among the other canvases and turned to look around the room for the missing study I noticed Tessie standing by the screen with her clothing still on.

"What's the matter," I asked, "don't you feel well?"

"Yes."

"Then hurry."

"Do you want me to pose as – as I have always posed?"

Then I understood. Here was a new complication. I had lost, of course, the best nude model I had ever seen. I looked at Tessie. Her face was scarlet. Alas! Alas! We had eaten of the tree of knowledge, and Eden and native innocence were dreams of the past – I mean – for her.

I suppose she noticed the disappointment on my face, for she said: "I will pose if you wish. The study is behind the screen here where I put it."

"No," I said, "we will begin something new"; and I went to my wardrobe and picked out a Moorish costume which fairly blazed with tinsel. It was a genuine costume, and Tessie retired to the screen with it enchanted. When she came forth again I was astonished. Her long black hair was bound above her forehead with a circlet of turquoises, and the ends curled about her glittering girdle. Her feet were encased in the embroidered pointed slippers and the skirt of her costume, curiously wrought with arabesques in silver, fell to her ankles. The deep metallic blue vest embroidered with silver and the short Mauresque jacket spangled and sewn with turquoises became her wonderfully. She came up to me and held up her face smiling. I slipped my hand into my pocket and drawing out a gold chain with a cross attached, dropped it over her head.

"It's yours, Tessie."

"Mine?" she faltered.

"Yours. Now go and pose." Then with a radiant smile she ran behind the screen and presently reappeared with a little box on which was written my name.

"I had intended to give it to you when I went home tonight," she said, "but I can't wait now."

I opened the box. On the pink cotton inside lay a clasp of black onyx, on which was inlaid a curious symbol or letter in gold. It was neither Arabic nor Chinese, nor as I found afterwards did it belong to any human script.

"It's all I had to give you for a keepsake," she said, timidly.

I was annoyed, but I told her how much I should prize it, and promised to wear it always. She fastened it on my coat beneath the lapel.

"How foolish, Tess, to go and buy me such a beautiful thing as this," I said.

"I did not buy it," she laughed.

"Where did you get it?"

Then she told me how she had found it one day while coming from the Aquarium in the Battery, how she had advertised it and watched the papers, but at last gave up all hopes of finding the owner.

"That was last winter," she said, "the very day I had the first horrid dream about the hearse."

I remembered my dream of the previous night but said nothing, and presently my charcoal was flying over a new canvas, and Tessie stood motionless on the model-stand.

III

THE DAY FOLLOWING was a disastrous one for me. While moving a framed canvas from one easel to another my foot slipped on the polished floor and I fell heavily on both wrists. They were so badly sprained that it was useless to attempt to hold a brush, and I was obliged to wander about the studio, glaring at unfinished drawings and sketches until despair seized me and I sat down to smoke and twiddle my thumbs with rage. The rain blew against the windows and rattled on the roof of the church, driving me into a nervous fit with its interminable patter.

Tessie sat sewing by the window, and every now and then raised her head and looked at me with such innocent compassion that I began to feel ashamed of my irritation and looked about for something to occupy me. I had read all the papers and all the books in the library, but for the sake of something to do I went to the bookcases and shoved them open with my elbow. I knew every volume by its color and examined them all, passing slowly around the library and whistling to keep up my spirits. I was turning to go into the dining-room when my eye fell upon a book bound in yellow, standing in a corner of the top shelf of the last bookcase. I did not remember it and from the floor could not decipher the pale lettering on the back, so I went to the smoking-room and called Tessie. She came in from the studio and climbed to reach the book.

"What is it?" I asked.

"'The King in Yellow'."

I was dumbfounded. Who had placed it there? How came it to my rooms? I had long ago decided that I should never open that book, and nothing on earth could have persuaded me to buy it. Fearful lest curiosity might tempt me to open it, I had never even looked at it in book-stores. If I ever had had any curiosity to read it, the awful tragedy of young Castaigne, whom I knew, prevented me from exploring its wicked pages. I had always refused to listen to any description of it, and indeed, nobody ever ventured to discuss the second part aloud, so I had absolutely no knowledge of what those leaves might reveal. I stared at the poisonous yellow binding as I would at a snake.

"Don't touch it, Tessie," I said, "come down."

Of course my admonition was enough to arouse her curiosity, and before I could prevent it she took the book and, laughing, danced away into the studio with it. I called to her but she slipped away with a tormenting smile at my helpless hands, and I followed her with some impatience.

"Tessie!" I cried, entering the library, "listen, I am serious. Put that book away. I do not wish you to open it!" The library was empty. I went into both drawing-rooms, then into the bedrooms, laundry, kitchen, and finally returned to the library and began a systematic search. She had hidden herself so well that it was half an hour later when I discovered her crouching white and silent by the latticed window in the store-room above. At the first glance I saw she had been punished for her foolishness. 'The King in Yellow' lay at her feet, but the book was open to the second part. I looked at Tessie and saw it was too late. She had opened 'The King in Yellow'. Then I took her by the hand and led her into the studio. She seemed dazed, and when I told her to lie down on the sofa she obeyed me without a word. After a while she closed her eyes and her breathing became regular and deep, but I could not determine whether or not she slept. For a long while I sat silently beside her, but she neither stirred nor spoke, and at last I rose and entering the unused store-room took the yellow book in my least injured hand. It seemed heavy as lead, but I carried it into the studio again, and sitting down on the rug beside the sofa, opened it and read it through from beginning to end.

When, faint with the excess of my emotions, I dropped the volume and leaned wearily back against the sofa, Tessie opened her eyes and looked at me.

We had been speaking for some time in a dull and monotonous strain before I realized that we were discussing 'The King in Yellow'. Oh the sin of writing such words, – words which are clear as crystal, limpid and musical as bubbling springs, words which sparkle and glow like the poisoned diamonds of the Medicis! Oh the wickedness, the hopeless damnation of a soul who could fascinate and paralyze human creatures with such words, – words understood by the ignorant and wise alike, words which are more precious than jewels, more soothing than Heavenly music, more awful than death itself.

We talked on, unmindful of the gathering shadows, and she was begging me to throw away the clasp of black onyx quaintly inlaid with what we now knew to be the Yellow Sign. I never shall know why I refused, though even at this hour, here in my bedroom as I write this confession, I should be glad to know what it was that prevented me from tearing the Yellow Sign from my breast and casting it into the fire. I am sure I wished to do so, but Tessie pleaded with me in vain. Night fell and the hours dragged on, but still we murmured to each other of the King and the Pallid Mask, and midnight sounded from the misty spires in the fog-wrapped city. We spoke of Hastur and of Cassilda, while outside the fog rolled against the blank window-panes as the cloud waves roll and break on the shores of Hali.

The house was very silent now and not a sound from the misty streets broke the silence. Tessie lay among the cushions, her face a gray blot in the gloom, but her hands were clasped in mine and I knew that she knew and read my thoughts as I read hers, for we had understood the mystery of the Hyades and the Phantom of Truth was laid. Then as we answered each other, swiftly, silently, thought on thought, the shadows stirred in the gloom about us, and far in the distant streets we heard a sound. Nearer and nearer it came, the dull crunching of wheels, nearer, nearer and yet nearer, and now, outside the door it ceased, and I dragged myself to the window and saw a black-plumed hearse.

The gate below opened and shut, and I crept shaking to my door and bolted it, but I knew no bolts, no locks, could keep that creature out who was coming for the Yellow Sign. And now I heard him moving very softly along the hall. Now he was at the door, and the bolts rotted at his touch. Now he had entered. With eyes starting from my head I peered into the darkness, but when he came into the room I did not see him. It was only when I felt him envelop me in his cold soft grasp that I cried out and struggled with deadly fury, but my hands were useless and he tore the onyx clasp from my coat and struck me full in the face. Then, as I fell, I heard Tessie's soft cry and her spirit fled to God, and even while falling I longed to follow her, for I knew that the King in Yellow had opened his tattered mantle and there was only Christ to cry to now.

I could tell more, but I cannot see what help it will be to the world. As for me I am past human help or hope. As I lie here, writing, careless even whether or not I die before I finish, I can see the doctor gathering up his powders and phials with a vague gesture to the good priest beside me, which I understand.

They will be very curious to know the tragedy – they of the outside world who write books and print millions of newspapers, but I will write no more, and the father confessor will seal my last words with the seal of sanctity when his holy office is done. They of the outside world may send their creatures into wrecked homes and death-smitten firesides, and their newspapers will batten on blood and tears, but with me their spies must halt before the confessional. They know that Tessie is dead and that I am dying. They know how the people in the house, aroused by an infernal scream, rushed into my room and found one living and two dead, but they do not know that the doctor said as he pointed to a horrible decomposed heap on the floor – the livid corpse of the watchman from the church: "I have no theory, no explanation. That man must have been dead for months!"

I think I am dying. I wish the priest would —

Breach

Justin Coates

There are no more happy endings.

THE FOREST across the canal loomed towards him. The worst ice storm Detroit had seen in a century had done its work well, transforming the entirety of the park into frozen sculptures. The trees seemed to grasp at the air as they swayed in the howling wind. Many of their branches had already broken under the weight, falling heavily onto the icy stream below.

He eyed the forest, standing on the other side of the worn stone bridge, hands buried in his pockets. He'd seen the bridge before in pictures and its utter mundaneness came as something of a surprise. The stones embedded in the concrete were ancient, stripped of snow by the wind. Whatever handrails had once guarded the edges of the bridge were gone, long since rusted away. Except for the thick, slushy trail of blood that ran up the center of it, there was absolutely no indication of what he knew was waiting for him on the other side.

He had an idea who the blood on the bridge belonged to. Lucille Gale had been the last of seven young adults to have disappeared in a month. The first six had been found already, their bodies discovered in various locations along the banks of the Detroit river.

The first of them had his skin completely removed, expertly flayed off. The second was so badly ripped apart that it had taken a week to identify her. The third was found lying in an alleyway with lungs full of water and seaweed, a full hundred meters away from the river.

It wasn't until a fourth teenager was found with her skeleton missing that the Department took interest. They'd swooped down onto the case overnight, so desperate to get him onto the scene that they'd sent him there via translocation. From the moment he emerged from the Detroit alleyway, shaking off the horror of what he always saw when he translocated, it had been nothing but investigation with the local police and terrified civilians.

The FBI got involved when two more children turned up dead (exsanguinated and strangled with their own intestines, respectively). Federal agents were always the most difficult to deal with. They were suspicious of his badge, despite it being completely authentic. They were suspicious of how massive he was, towering over most of them, easily broader than any. They were suspicious of how much he already knew about the case, despite having arrived only a few days before them.

What made them more suspicious than anything was how quickly their bosses told them to shut up and get out of his way. The men who ran the Bureau from their offices in D.C. had no idea who he was, and none of them were interested in finding out. They had all heard the legends from those that had led the Bureau before them. They knew what happened when men like him showed up on the scene of a crime too terrible for words.

The problem stopped, and it was better to not ask questions how. Any federal involvement was quickly terminated, and the agents reassigned to different cases.

They'd remember this case for the rest of their lives. They might one day have colleagues who had similar encounters with men like him, and endlessly discuss what organization he might have represented. Theories ranged from an obscure Homeland Security cell to the CIA Special Operations Group. They would jokingly refer to men like him as 'The Others,' 'Those We Don't Speak Of', 'The Activity', or even as 'The Men in Black' if they were feeling sarcastic.

The Department knew all of this. There wasn't much they didn't.

The man took a reading. The palm-sized device lit up, whirring as he placed it on the ground. He stepped back, fishing out a pack of cigarettes and a lighter from his pocket. The twin marbles of glass atop the reader spun faster and faster, the silver liquid inside them catching the bright blue light shining from the dozen or so diodes that covered the front and back of the device. After a few frantic seconds the marbles were spinning so fast above the device the man could no longer see them. A moment later the reader gave a frantic shriek. The globes exploded in a puff of powdered glass, the liquid flying through the air but evaporating before it touched the ground.

He sighed and lit his cigarette. "Initial readings suggest an unusually high breach in the Jovlin-Knight Barrier," he said. "The presence of the remains of Lucille Gale confirms initial assumptions that she did not survive the hosting. Extreme weather patterns indicate the presence of a Midnight-Level Event occurring within the confines of the breach."

He put his smoke to his lips again. The cherry flared brightly, a tiny speck of light burning defiantly in the darkness. The FBI and the police might not have a clue what the missing teens had in common, but he had known it the moment he had visited the morgue and seen their tortured bodies.

Each of them was psychic. Very, very psychic, and Lucille Gale most of all. He doubted that any of them were fully aware of it. Perhaps they had experienced vivid dreams that later came true, or had wondered whether or not they were at fault for the power outages that followed their every outburst. If left to themselves they would have grown exponentially more powerful, most likely to the point where they would have been targeted and killed by his organization. There were very few like them that managed to make it into adulthood, and none of them managed to die of old age.

Even at their nascent stage, however, they possessed more than enough raw ability to be of use to something on the other side. Something was trying desperately to come through, something that had no place even in a nightmare. The other six teens had proven unsuitable as doorways, but judging from the cataclysmic storm that had engulfed half the county, the man guessed that Lucille Gale would prove more than adequate.

He felt the smoke burn a trail down his lungs as he considered his next words. "I still plan on crossing," he said. "Regardless of what's fueling the breach, I'll ensure sufficient distraction or damage to prevent crossover until Aegis translocation is available. Upon loss of communication, I stand by my original recommendation of an immediate kinetic on my last known position." He paused. "Not that you ever listen to what I have to say."

His answer was the howling wind, and a voice that spoke directly into his mind. He would have smiled at the response if smiling were something he was capable of. Instead he drew Jovlin's gun from its holster on his side, the massive revolver fitting snugly into his equally massive hands. He squeezed the rubberized grip, fingers caressing the raised knotwork that adorned the barrel. The man took one last drag on his cigarette, flicking it away as he strode purposely onto the bridge, careful to keep his steps within the trail of Lucille Gale's remains.

Normally crossing over required a tremendous amount of concentration and no small amount of luck. His repelling tattoos would burn so bad they'd singe his skin, and the tiny nodes lining the center of his brain would overload with static. Wearing an Aegis made it a bit easier, but even the best protection his organization could offer didn't keep out the visions. He'd been there when Jovlin had died, and it was that memory that was returned to violent life every time he translocated.

This time there were no visions, no screaming ghosts from decades past. He simply stepped out of here and into nowhere, the symbols that were carved onto his flesh flaring briefly beneath his heavy clothing. The ease of the translocation confirmed his worst fears. It took a lot of power to rend such a huge hole in reality. Whatever caused this had been very old and very, very angry. For the first time, he wondered bemusedly if he'd been right to turn down assignment to an Aegis unit.

Regardless, he was relieved to see that the trail of human remains provided him a clear path through what was otherwise a land of absolute madness. Whatever thing had nested and birthed itself in the mind of Lucille Gale had not been kind to her. The thick, black-red smear on the ground led deep into the forest which now towered thousands of feet up into the air. He thought he caught a glimpse of something massive above him, moving in the storm clouds, its barbed coils swaying lazily from the sky. The frost-covered branches of the trees were all screaming with a woman's voice, weeping and sobbing, crying for a mother and a father and the safety of home. He assumed the voice was Lucille's.

He started off down the trail, booted feet splashing noisily in gristle that seemed to grow deeper as he walked. Around him the world shifted and rearranged itself at random. The trees exploded, sending ice shards the size of buildings crashing down around him. Something massive fell out of the sky, its leathered wings curling around its dead form, crashing to the earth behind a distant mountain range that abruptly forced itself out of the frozen earth. The wind intensified, and on it he could hear a name being whispered over and over again.

He didn't recognize the name. He wondered if it was his.

The further he went along the trail, the more twisted reality became. He wondered how deep into the forest he was actually going in the real world. On more than occasion he had traveled for days inside a breach, only to find himself a step or two away from where he had started upon crossing out. Time and distance could have very little meaning in the Veiled World. Mercifully the laws of physics (usually) held sway, but those laws were easily bent or broken depending on what was causing such an awesome disturbance.

There was a place, he knew, where physics simply didn't exist. Even as he walked he could see it, far on the horizon, a thin line of shadow that seemed to swallow up even the darkness. Calling it oblivion wasn't accurate. There were things in the Nothing, things that made the horrors he dealt with on a regular occasion seem downright pleasant. He'd been to the edge before, watching reality and un-reality disappear into the howling claws of whatever waited for men and demons on the other side of existence.

Men smarter than he surmised that whatever it was had no power to enter or affect the world he sought to protect. He supposed this was true; it was hungry, and would have long since devoured the third dimension had it been capable.

The ground beneath his feet shook, and he suddenly found himself standing in a clearing. The storm-wracked sky was gone, replaced with a peaceful canvas devoid of any light save that of a full moon. The wind stopped abruptly. Snowflakes fell slowly through the air like the inside of a tumbling snow globe. A vast clearing spread out before him, the smeared remains of an overly ambitious psychic a vivid splash of red on the virgin snow.

There was a child in the clearing at the end of the trail. The boy was sobbing, his knees drawn up to his chest. The man approached him slowly. He tentatively took a step off the pathway and into the snow. His feet sunk into reassuring solid ground. The man began circling the boy, trudging through snow that came up to his shins.

"Go away," the boy said, burying his face in his arms. "Go away! I just want to be left alone."

The man didn't say anything. He'd learned long ago not to speak to the things that crawled out of the lightless spaces between the worlds. Instead he kept circling, trying to see the child's face.

"Why did you follow me?" The boy kicked his feet into the ground. "I want to be left alone! Leave me alone!"

The world around them trembled slightly, and the man cursed under his breath. "You aren't alone," he answered. He had to buy himself more time. It needed to be tricked into revealing its true self, or it might simply push him back out into reality out of annoyance. "You're with Lucille. Lucille Gale. Remember?"

Face still buried in his arms, the boy laughed. "Lucille. I remember Lucille. The other ones all ran, but Lucille wasn't afraid. She stayed. She told me that she wanted to help me." His voice changed in an instant, becoming a tone no human vocal cord could ever hope to produce. "She's rotting inside me. I cannot be bound. I cannot be harmed. I am eternal."

"You might be eternal, but your son wasn't, was he?" The warding tattoos on his skin started to prickle. That was a good sign. It was getting angry. "That's who you're pretending to be right now. Your son."

"You don't know what you're talking about," the boy sniffed, his voice that of a child's again. "I'm just a little boy, all alone in the woods."

"No, you're not. Your name is Claude Lachay. You killed your wife and son here, before it was a park. Before there were many people here at all. You started running, and when you couldn't go anymore you killed a family that tried to help you. You ate them. Do you remember? You ate them, but even that couldn't keep you from starving. You nearly died from hunger in the wilderness a hundred miles north of here." The man decided to push the issue. "You pissed yourself when the wolves came. You screamed for your mother when they started eating you, like you screamed for her every day in Hell."

The child exploded in a shower of blood. His face landed on the snow next to the man, steam pouring from its eye sockets and laughing mouth. Where the child once stood was what his organization would call a 'Class IX Paranormal Entity,' unveiled in all its horrific glory. Its three heads sprouted from between its shoulders, each of them gnashing on a tongue that flickered like a snake. A pair of arms sprouted from between its legs, their fingers ended in leech-like mouths. The skin on its bloated stomach was stretched so far it was nearly transparent. Inside it he could see the tortured face of Lucille Gale, her hands pushing desperately to get out.

The thing that was once Claude Lachay, the first serial killer to walk American soil, thundered with laughter. Its voice echoed around the clearing where it had committed its first crimes nearly three hundred and fifty years prior. "I cannot be bound. I cannot be harmed. I am eternal. I am…God!"

The first bullet fired through Jovlin's gun put an end to such boastful nonsense. Lachay roared as the round tore a fist-sized hole through the center of one of its heads. It clapped a massive hand to its face, reeling in agony. The man fired again and again, moving towards it at a flat-out run. While the danger of being forced out of the breach was over, he now faced the equally real threat of death at the target's hands. Jovlin's revolver was a powerful weapon against the denizens of the Veil, and the fact that it had already proved ineffective told him everything he needed to know.

He'd never survive a direct fight. Lachay had dragged itself out of the pit, and the mindless hate that allowed such perseverance had twisted it something wholly inhuman. Every heaving breath it took was the scream of a dying man; every guttural curse was the wheeze of lungs filling with bloody clots. It was a lord of death now, a corpse god, the grave incarnate.

There was no time to wait for armored translocation. The only option was to deny its ascension by destroying the breach, and the only way to destroy the breach was to murder the soul that was fueling it.

Each of the bullets he fired found their mark. By the time he had reached the target the man had already reloaded. He fired at point blank range, aiming at Lachay's bloated stomach. A massive, scaled hand moved to intercept the rounds. The same hand struck him hard, tossing him through the air. He fired as he flipped head over heels, managing to keep the target at bay as he rolled on the ground. It was on him by the time he righted himself, choking as its tongues whipped towards his torso and legs.

He thought about evading, considered his options, and calmly decided against it. The barbs bit into his flesh and tensed, digging into his skin. He grunted, pain dampeners flooding his system. The venom hit him a second later. He vomited, body shuddering in the throes of a seizure as the poison reached his brain. The receptors in his skull were shrieking, fighting off both the toxins and the terrifying psychic power Lachay was unleashing through its unwilling host. He caught brief glimpses of the monster's past; the last, confused looks on the faces of the Chippewa family it had butchered, the taste of human flesh in its mouth, the awful, maddening climb out of the bottom of torment back into the world of the living.

The man felt the barbs tense, followed by a violent jerking on his left leg. He looked down in time to see it come clean off, ripped away at the knee, disappearing down Lachay's gullet.

He saw his leg floating inside Lachay's bloated stomach as he fired into it again and again. Distracted, the target had no chance to defend itself. Its immense stomach popped like a blister, spewing digestive juices over the frozen earth. It dropped him as it stumbled backwards, yelping, its hands clapped over its gut. Between its massive fingers, the half-digested form of Lucille Gale spilled out. She writhed in the snow, screaming through a mouth that had fused shut.

Lachay reached for her desperately, but it was already too late. The man fired a single shot. The high-caliber shell blew her head clean off.

The clearing was completely still for a moment. Then there was an earth shattering roar that sounded all too familiar to him. The breach shuddered and tilted. The whole world sloped at a downward angle, making Lachay stumble and fall. Both monster and man went tumbling head over heels towards the edge of the forest. The man's fevered mind screamed at him to make sure he landed on the bridge. At the last second he reached out, his hand slapping down into the trail of blood, arresting his fall as he held tight to his only line back to reality.

There was another roar, and Nothingness came howling up towards them. The world below him almost completely vanished, the trees and the mountain ranges swallowed up by a mouth made of nightmares. The power of Lucille Gale, wielded ruthlessly by Lachay, had been the only thing keeping the breach open. With her death, the thin barrier between the Veiled World and what lay beyond came crashing down.

He saw Lachay land in the trees below. The monster leapt back into the clearing, scrabbling to find purchase in the snow. The man calmly fired his remaining rounds into the target, watching as each bullet hit home. With one last howl, the monster lost its grip and fell down into darkness.

The man didn't have any time to feel satisfied. The breach was collapsing, shaking apart at the seams. Like a rising tide the Void came up to greet him, laughing and screaming. He could make up indistinct shapes as it came on; shapes that reminded him of Jovlin, the smell of her hair and the sound of her voice when she told him

I'll love you until the day I die

and the look on her face when she fell, when she let go, when *she LET GO! LET GO! LET GO! LET GO AND FALL!*

"Agent Hauser."

The man looked up into glowing blue eyes. The Aegis was only a few feet above him, standing with its steel feet planted firmly in the bridge. The dying light of the breach cast wicked shadows over its black armor and menacing weapon arrays. It reached out to him, its fingers strangely slender for such a massive construct.

"We haven't much time, sir," it said. "Please take my hand to initiate translocation."

Hauser didn't hesitate. He holstered his pistol and reached for its hand. Half a dozen ports on the Aegis' back popped open with a pneumatic hiss. The construct's translocation generator came online, emitting brilliant white light as it drank in the otherworldly energy of the breach.

"Translocation imminent," it said. **"Brace for impact."**

Hauser looked down. Nothingness looked back at him, smiling. Reaching.

"Brace for impact. Brace for impact. Brace—"

He hit the snowy ground so hard it drove the air out of his lungs. He gasped, rolling onto his side. The wind that had been howling moments before seemed to calm by the moment. Soon it disappeared entirely, leaving the world still and silent in its wake.

His eyes were drawn to the cigarette he had flicked away before entering the breach. It was inches away from him, still burning. He'd been gone only seconds in the real world. He reached for it with a trembling hand, the cherry flaring brightly as he inhaled. It was almost too damp to smoke, but he'd never tasted anything better.

The Aegis was already working on his leg. Hauser felt a brief twinge of pain as it spread anti-septic paste over his wound, spraying it from a small retractable hose attached to its hip. The paste quickly turned to a murky red gel as it stopped the bleeding. In a few seconds Hauser's entire leg went numb, and he could feel the pain dampening drugs in his system start to recede.

It looked up at him, the center eye of its forehead turning a bright green as it scanned his vital signs. **I apologize,"** it said. **"I arrived as soon as I could. I had hoped to get there in time to assist you with the entity, and prevent such damage from occurring."**

Hauser managed a weak laugh. "Killing the psychic was the only way to stop it from cross over, and this..." He waved his hand at his stump. "This was the only way to get close enough for a clean shot. I'm still glad you came. If it had finished me off, someone would have needed to finish the job." Hauser paused, squinting up at the construct's expressionless face. "Who is that in there?"

The Aegis gave a metallic laugh as its visor slid back. A female face stared back at him, pale and young and covered in scars. "You might not remember me, Agent Hauser," she said, her voice soft and lilting. "I was in training for the Aegis program when you were sent on your last assignment."

"I remember you. I was there when you were initiated and picked your name. Bellona. Agent Bellona." He took another drag on his cigarette, staring up at the stars. She'd had fewer scars then. "Damned pretentious name, if you ask me."

He heard the sound of her visor slide shut as a response. **"Recovery units are en route,"** she said in the sexless voice of a machine. **"They will be here within the minute. Since he is certain your telepathic receivers have almost certainly shut down as a result of your psychic trauma, Control has asked me to extend congratulations to you on his behalf. He says he would never have authorized the kinetic strike, even if we'd lost track of you within the breach."**

Now it was Hauser's turn to laugh. "He wouldn't say that if he had seen what was in there. One of these days, something is going to come through and we'll have to blow the breach to kingdom come. One of these days, I'll be right." He leaned his head back into the freezing snow, letting it cool his head. The static from the destroyed receptors inside his skull was giving him a pounding headache. Taking one last inhale, he tossed the smoke away from him for good.

It landed solidly on the grisly path Hauser had taken into nothingness. Drowned in blood, surrounded by darkness, the light of the cigarette quickly faded and died.

The Dead Smile

F. Marion Crawford

I

SIR HUGH OCKRAM smiled as he sat by the open window of his study, in the late August afternoon. A curiously yellow cloud obscured the low sun, and the clear summer light turned lurid, as if it had been suddenly poisoned and polluted by the foul vapours of a plague. Sir Hugh's face seemed, at best, to be made of fine parchment drawn skin-tight over a wooden mask, in which two sunken eyes peered from far within. The eyes peered from under wrinkled lids, alive and watchful like toads in their holes, side by side and exactly alike. But as the light changed, a little yellow glare flashed in each. He smiled, stretching pale lips across discoloured teeth in an expression of profound self-satisfaction, blended with the most unforgiving hatred and contempt for the human doll.

Nurse Macdonald, who was a hundred years old, said that when Sir Hugh smiled he saw the faces of two women in hell – two dead women he had betrayed. The smile widened.

The hideous disease of which Sir Hugh was dying had touched his brain. His son stood beside him, tall, white and delicate as an angel in a primitive picture. And though there was deep distress in his violet eyes as he looked at his father's face, he felt the shadow of that sickening smile stealing across his own lips, parting and drawing them against his will. It was like a bad dream, for he tried not to smile and smiled the more.

Beside him – strangely like him in her wan, angelic beauty, with the same shadowy golden hair, the same sad violet eyes, the same luminously pale face – Evelyn Warburton rested one hand upon his arm. As she looked into her uncle's eyes, she could not turn her own away and she too knew that the deathly smile was hovering on her own red lips, drawing them tightly across her little teeth, while two bright tears ran down her cheeks to her mouth, and dropped from the upper to the lower lip .The smile was like the shadow of death and the seal of damnation upon her pure, young face.

"Of course," said Sir Hugh very slowly, still looking out at the trees, "if you have made your mind up to be married, I cannot hinder you, and I don't suppose you attach the smallest importance to my consent – "

"Father!" exclaimed Gabriel reproachfully.

"No. I do not deceive myself," continued the old man, smiling terribly. "You will marry when I am dead, though there is a very good reason why you had better not – why you had better not," he repeated very emphatically, and he slowly turned his toad eyes upon the lovers.

"What reason?" asked Evelyn in a frightened voice.

"Never mind the reason, my dear. You will marry just as if it did not exist." There was a long pause. "Two gone," he said, his voice lowering strangely, "and two more will be four all together forever and ever, burning, burning, burning bright."

At the last words his head sank slowly back, and the little glare of his toad eyes disappeared under the swollen lids. Sir Hugh had fallen asleep, as he often did in his illness, even while speaking.

Gabriel Ockram drew Evelyn away, and from the study they went out into the dim hall. Softly closing the door behind them, each audibly drew a breath, as though some sudden danger had been passed. As they laid their hands each in the other's, their strangely-like eyes met in a long look in which love and perfect understanding were darkened by the secret terror of an unknown thing. Their pale faces reflected each other's fear.

"It is his secret," said Evelyn at last. "He will never tell us what it is."

"If he dies with it," answered Gabriel, "let it be on his own head!"

"On his head!" echoed the dim hall. It was a strange echo. Some were frightened by it, for they said that if it were a real echo it should repeat everything and not give back a phrase here and there – now speaking, now silent. Nurse Macdonald said that the great hall would never echo a prayer when an Ockram was to die, though it would give back curses ten for one.

"On his head!" it repeated quite softly, and Evelyn started and looked round.

"It is only the echo," said Gabriel, leading her away.

They went out into the late afternoon light, and sat upon a stone seat behind the chapel, which had been built across the end of the east wing. It was very still. Not a breath stirred, and there was no sound near them. Only far off in the park a song-bird was whistling the high prelude to the evening chorus.

"It is very lonely here," said Evelyn, taking Gabriel's hand nervously and speaking as if she dreaded to disturb the silence. "If it were dark, I should be afraid."

"Of what? Of me?" Gabriel's sad eyes turned to her.

"Oh no! Never of you! But of the old Ockrams. They say they are just under our feet here in the north vault outside the chapel, all in their shrouds, with no coffins, as they used to bury them."

"As they always will. As they will bury my father, and me. They say an Ockram will not lie in a coffin."

"But it cannot be true. These are fairy tales, ghost stories!" Evelyn nestled nearer to her companion, grasping his hand more tightly as the sun began to go down.

"Of course. But there is the story of old Sir Vernon, who was beheaded for treason under James II. The family brought his body back from the scaffold in an iron coffin with heavy locks and put it in the north vault. But ever afterwards, whenever the vault was opened to bury another of the family, they found the coffin wide open, the body standing upright against the wall, and the head rolled away in a corner smiling at it."

"As Uncle Hugh smiles?" Evelyn shivered.

"Yes, I suppose so," answered Gabriel, thoughtfully. "Of course I never saw it, and the vault has not been opened for thirty years. None of us have died since then."

"And if...if Uncle Hugh dies, shall you...?" Evelyn stopped. Her beautiful thin face was quite white.

"Yes. I shall see him laid there too, with his secret, whatever it is." Gabriel sighed and pressed the girl's little hand.

"I do not like to think of it," she said unsteadily. "O Gabriel, what can the secret be? He said we had better not marry. Not that he forbade it, but he said it so strangely, and he smiled. Ugh!" Her small white teeth chattered with fear, and she looked over her shoulder while drawing still closer to Gabriel. "And, somehow, I felt it in my own face."

"So did I," answered Gabriel in a low, nervous voice. "Nurse Macdonald..." He stopped abruptly.

"What? What did she

"Oh, nothing. She has told me things.... They would frighten you, dear. Come, it is growing chilly." He rose, but Evelyn held his hand in both of hers, still sitting and looking up into his face.

"But we shall be married just the same – Gabriel! Say that we shall!"

"Of course, darling, of course. But while my father is so very ill, it is impossible – "

"O Gabriel, Gabriel, dear! I wish we were married now!" Evelyn cried in sudden distress. "I know that something will prevent it and keep us apart."

"Nothing shall!"

"Nothing?"

"Nothing human," said Gabriel Ockram, as she drew him down to her.

And their faces, that were so strangely alike, met and touched. Gabriel knew that the kiss had a marvelous savor of evil. Evelyn's lips were like the cool breath of a sweet and mortal fear that neither of them understood, for they were innocent and young. Yet she drew him to her by her lightest touch, as a sensitive plant shivers, waves its thin leaves, and bends and closes softly upon what it wants. He let himself be drawn to her willingly – as he would even if her touch had been deadly and poisonous – for he strangely loved that half voluptuous breath of fear, and he passionately desired the nameless evil something that lurked in her maiden lips.

"It is as if we loved in a strange dream," she said.

"I fear the waking," he murmured.

"We shall not wake, dear. When the dream is over it will have already turned into death, so softly that we shall not know it. But until then..."

She paused, her eyes seeking his, as their faces slowly came nearer. It was as if each had thoughts in their lips that foresaw and foreknew the other.

"Until then," she said again, very low, her mouth near to his.

"Dream – till then," he murmured.

II

NURSE MACDONALD slept sitting all bent together in a great old leather arm chair with wings – many warm blankets wrapped about her, even in summer. She would rest her feet in a bag footstool lined with sheepskin while beside her, on a wooden table, there was a little lamp that burned at night, and an old silver cup, in which there was always something to drink.

Her face was very wrinkled, but the wrinkles were so small and fine and close together that they made shadows instead of lines. Two thin locks of hair, that were turning from white to a smoky yellow, fell over her temples from under her starched white cap. Every now and then she would wake from her slumber, her eyelids drawn up in tiny folds like little pink silk curtains, and her queer blue eyes would look straight ahead through doors and walls and worlds to a far place beyond. Then she'd sleep again with her hands one upon the other on the edge of the blanket, her thumbs grown longer than the fingers with age.

It was nearly one o'clock in the night, and the summer breeze was blowing the ivy branch against the panes of the window with a hushing caress. In the small room beyond, with the door ajar, the young maid who took care of Nurse Macdonald was fast asleep. All was very quiet. The old woman breathed regularly, and her drawn lips trembled each time the breath went out.

But outside the closed window there was a face. Violet eyes were looking steadily at the ancient sleeper. Strange, as there were eighty feet from the sill of the window to the foot of the tower. It was like the face of Evelyn Warburton, yet the cheeks were thinner than Evelyn's and as white as a gleam. The eyes stared and the lips were red with life. They were dead lips painted with new blood.

Slowly Nurse Macdonald's wrinkled eyelids folded back, and she looked straight at the face at the window.

"Is it time?" she asked in her little old, faraway voice.

While she looked the face at the window changed, the eyes opened wider and wider till the white glared all round the bright violet and the bloody lips opened over gleaming teeth. The shadowy golden hair surrounding the face rose and streamed against the window in the night breeze and in answer to Nurse Macdonald's question came a sound that froze the living flesh.

It was a low-moaning voice, one that rose suddenly, like the scream of storm. Then it went from a moan to a wail, from a wail to a howl, and from a howl to the shriek of the tortured dead. He who has heard it before knows, and he can bear witness that the cry of the banshee is an evil cry to hear alone in the deep night.

When it was over and the face was gone, Nurse Macdonald shook a little in her great chair. She looked at the black square of the window, but there was nothing more there, nothing but the night and the whispering ivy branch. She turned her head to the door that was ajar, and there stood the young maid in her white gown, her teeth chattering with fright.

"It is time, child," said Nurse Macdonald. "I must go to him, for it is the end."

She rose slowly, leaning her withered hands upon the arms of the chair as the girl brought her a woollen gown, a great mantle and her crutch-stick. But very often the girl looked at the window and was unjointed with fear, and often Nurse Macdonald shook her head and said words which the maid could not understand.

"It was like the face of Miss Evelyn," said the girl, trembling.

But the ancient woman looked up sharply and angrily. Her queer blue eyes glared. She held herself up by the arm of the great chair with her left hand, and lifted up her crutch-stick to strike the maid with all her might. But she did not.

"You are a good girl," she said, "but you are a fool. Pray for wit, child. Pray for wit – or else find service in a house other than Ockram Hall. Now bring the lamp and help me up."

Each step Nurse Macdonald took was a labour in itself, and as she moved, the maid's slippers clappered alongside. By the clacking noise the other servants knew that she was coming, very long before they saw her.

No one was sleeping now, and there were lights, and whisperings, and pale faces in the corridors near Sir Hugh's bedroom. Often someone would go in, and someone would come out, but every one made way for Nurse Macdonald, who had nursed Sir Hugh's father more than eighty years ago.

The light was soft and clear in the room. Gabriel Ockram stood by his father's bedside, and there knelt Evelyn Warburton – her hair lying like a golden shadow down her shoulder, and her hands clasped nervously together. Opposite Gabriel, a nurse was trying to make Sir Hugh drink, but he would not. His lips parted, but his teeth were set. He was very, very thin now, and as his eyes caught the light sideways, they were as yellow coals.

"Do not torment him," said Nurse Macdonald to the woman who held the cup. "Let me speak to him, for his hour is come."

"Let her speak to him," said Gabriel in a dull voice.

The ancient nurse leaned to the pillow and laid the feather-weight of her withered hand – that was like a grown moth – upon Sir Hugh's yellow fingers. Then she spoke to him earnestly, while only Gabriel and Evelyn were left in the room to hear.

"Hugh Ockram," she said, "this is the end of your life; and as I saw you born, and saw your father born before you, I come to see you die. Hugh Ockram, will you tell me the truth?"

The dying man recognized the little faraway voice he had known all his life and he very slowly turned his yellow face 4o Nurse Macdonald, but he said nothing. Then she spoke again.

"Hugh Ockram, you will never see the daylight again. Will you tell the truth?"

His toad like eyes were not yet dull. They fastened themselves on her face.

"What do you want of me?" he asked, each word sounding more hollow than the last. "I have no secrets. I have lived a good life."

Nurse Macdonald laughed – a tiny, cracked laugh that made her old head bob and tremble a little, as if her neck were on a steel spring. But Sir Hugh's eyes grew red, and his pale lips began to twist.

"Let me die in peace," he said slowly.

But Nurse Macdonald shook her head, and her brown, mothlike hand left his and fluttered to his forehead.

"By the mother that bore you and died of grief for the sins you did, tell me the truth!"

Sir Hugh's lips tightened on his discoloured teeth.

"Not on earth," he answered slowly.

"By the wife who bore your son and died heartbroken, tell me the truth!"

"Neither to you in life, nor to her in eternal death."

His lips writhed, as if the words were coals between them, and a great drop of sweat rolled across the parchment of his forehead. Gabriel Ockram bit his hand as he watched his father die. But Nurse Macdonald spoke a third time.

"By the woman whom you betrayed, and who waits for you this night, Hugh Ockram, tell me the truth!"

"It is too late. Let me die in peace."

His writhing lips began to smile across his yellow teeth, and his toadlike eyes glowed like evil jewels in his head.

"There is time," said the ancient woman. "Tell me the name of Evelyn Warburton's father. Then I will let you die in peace."

Evelyn started. She stared at Nurse Macdonald, and then at her uncle.

"The name of Evelyn's father?" he repeated slowly, while the awful smile spread upon his dying face.

The light was growing strangely dim in the great room. As Evelyn looked on, Nurse Macdonald's crooked shadow on the wall grew gigantic. Sir Hugh's breath was becoming thick, rattling in his throat, as death crept in like a snake and choked it back. Evelyn prayed aloud, high and clear.

Then something rapped at the window, and she felt her hair rise upon her head. She looked around in spite of herself. And when she saw her own white face looking in at the window, her own eyes staring at her through the glass – wide and fearful – her own hair streaming against the pane, and her own lips dashed with blood, she rose slowly from the floor and stood rigid for one moment before she screamed once and fell straight back into Gabriel's arms. But the shriek that answered hers was the fear-shriek of a tormented corpse out of which the soul cannot pass for shame of deadly sins.

Sir Hugh Ockram sat upright in his deathbed, and saw and cried aloud:

"Evelyn!" His harsh voice broke and rattled in his chest as he sank down. But still Nurse Macdonald tortured him, for there was a little life left in him still.

"You have seen the mother as she waits for you, Hugh Ockram. Who was this girl Evelyn's father? What was his name?"

For the last time the dreadful smile came upon the twisted lips, very slowly, very surely now. The toad eyes glared red and the parchment face glowed a little in the flickering light; for the last time words came.

"They know it in hell."

Then the glowing eyes went out quickly. The yellow face turned waxen pale, and a great shiver ran through the thin body as Hugh Ockram died.

But in death he still smiled, for he knew his secret and kept it still. He would take it with him to the other side, to lie with him forever in the north vault of the chapel where the Ockrams lie uncoffined in their shrouds – all but one. Though he was dead, he smiled, for he had kept his treasure of evil truth to the end. There was none left to tell the name he had spoken, but there was all the evil he had not undone left to bear fruit.

As they watched – Nurse Macdonald and Gabriel, who held the still unconscious Evelyn in his arms while he looked at the father – they felt the dead smile crawling along their own lips. Then they shivered a little as they both looked at Evelyn as she lay with her head on Gabriel's shoulder, for though she was very beautiful, the same sickening smile was twisting her young mouth too, and it was like the foreshadowing of a great evil that they could not understand.

By and by they carried Evelyn out, and when she opened her eyes the smile was gone. From far away in the great house the sound of weeping and crooning came up the stairs and echoed along the dismal corridors as the women had begun to mourn the dead master in the Irish fashion. The hall had echoes of its own all that night, like the far-off wail of the banshee among forest trees.

When the time was come they took Sir Hugh in his winding-sheet on a trestle bier and bore him to the chapel, through the iron door and down the long descent to the north vault lit with tapers, to lay him by his father. The two men went in first to prepare the place, and came back staggering like drunken men, their faces white.

But Gabriel Ockram was not afraid, for he knew. When he went in, alone, he saw the body of Sir Vernon Ockram leaning upright against the stone wall. Its head lay on the ground nearby with the face turned up. The dried leather lips smiled horribly at the dried-up corpse, while the iron coffin, lined with black velvet, stood open on the floor.

Gabriel took the body in his hands – for it was very light, being quite dried by the air of the vault – and those who peeped in the door saw him lay it in the coffin again. They heard it rustle a little, as it touched the sides and the bottom, like a bundle of reeds. He also placed the head upon the shoulders and shut down the lid, which fell to with the snap of its rusty spring.

After that they laid Sir Hugh beside his father, on the trestle bier on which they had brought him, and they went back to the chapel. But when they looked into one another's faces, master and men, they were all smiling with the dead smile of the corpse they had left in the vault. They could not bear to look at one another again until it had faded away.

III

GABRIEL OCKRAM became Sir Gabriel, inheriting the baronetcy with the half-ruined fortune left by his father, and Evelyn Warburton continued to lived at Ockram Hall, in the south room that had been hers ever. since she could remember. She could not go away, for there were no relatives to whom she could have gone, and besides, there seemed to be no reason why she should not stay. The world would never trouble itself to care what the Ockrams did on their Irish estates. It was long since the Ockrams had asked anything of the world.

So Sir Gabriel took his father's place at the dark old table in the dining room, and Evelyn sat opposite to him – until such time as their mourning should be over – and they might be married at last. Meanwhile, their lives went on as before – since Sir Hugh had been a hopeless invalid during the last year of his life, and they had seen him but once a day for a little while – spending most of their time together in a strangely perfect companionship.

Though the late summer saddened into autumn, and autumn darkened into winter, and storm followed storm, and rain poured on rain through the short days and the long nights, Ockram Hall seemed less gloomy since Sir Hugh had been laid in the north vault beside his father.

At Christmastide Evelyn decked the great hall with holly and green boughs. Huge fires blazed on every hearth. The tenants were all bid to come to a New Year's dinner at which they ate and drank well, while Sir Gabriel sat at the head of the table. Evelyn came in when the port wine was brought and the most respected of the tenants made a speech to her health.

When the speechmaker said it had been a long time since there had been a Lady Ockram, Sir Gabriel shaded his eyes with his hand and looked down at the table; a faint color came into Evelyn's transparent cheeks. And, said the gray-haired farmer, it was longer still since there had been a Lady Ockram so fair as the next was to be, and he drank to the health of Evelyn Warburton.

Then the tenants all stood up and shouted for her. Sir Gabriel stood up likewise, beside Evelyn. But when the men gave the last and loudest cheer of all, there was a voice not theirs, above them all, higher, fiercer, louder – an unearthly scream-shrieking for the bride of Ockram Hall. It was so loud that the holly and the green boughs over the great chimney shook and waved as if a cool breeze were blowing over them.

The men turned very pale. Many of them set down their glasses, but others let them fall upon the floor. Looking into one another's faces, they saw that they were all smiling strangely – a dead smile – like dead Sir Hugh's.

The fear of death was suddenly upon them all, so that they fled in a panic, falling over one another like wild beasts in the burning forest when the thick smoke runs along before the flame. Tables were overturned, drinking glasses and bottles were broken in heaps, and dark red wine crawled like blood upon the polished floor.

Sir Gabriel and Evelyn were left standing alone at the head of the table before the wreck of their feast, not daring to turn to look at one another, for each knew that the other smiled.

But Gabriel's right arm held her and his left hand clasped her tight as they stared before them. But for the shadows of her hair, one might not have told their two faces apart.

They listened long, but the cry came not again, and eventually the dead smile faded from their lips as each remembered that Sir Hugh Ockram lay in the north vault smiling in his winding sheet, in the dark, because he had died with his secret.

So ended the tenants' New Year's dinner. But from that time on, Sir Gabriel grew more and more silent and his face grew even paler and thinner than before. Often, without warning and without words, he would rise from his seat as if something moved him against his will. He would go out into the rain or the sunshine to the north side of the chapel, sit on the stone bench and stare at the ground as if he could see through it, through the vault below, and through the white winding sheet in the dark, to the dead smile that would not die.

Always when he went out in that way Evelyn would come out presently and sit beside him. Once, as in the past, their beautiful faces came suddenly near; their lids drooped, and their red lips were almost joined together. But as their eyes met, they grew wide and wild, so that the white showed in a ring all round the deep violet. Their teeth chattered and their hands were like the hands of corpses, for fear of what was under their feet, and of what they knew but could not see.

Once, Evelyn found Sir Gabriel in the chapel alone, standing before the iron door that led down to the place of death with the key to the door in his hand, but he had not put it into the lock. Evelyn drew him away, shivering, for she had also been driven – in waking dreams – to see that terrible thing again, and to find out whether it had changed since it had been laid there.

"I'm going mad," said Sir Gabriel, covering his eyes with his hand as he went with her. "I see it in my sleep. I see it when I am awake. It draws me to it, day and night and unless I see it I shall die!"

"I know," answered Evelyn, "I know. It is as if threads were spun from it like a spider's, drawing us down to it." She was silent for a moment and then she started violently and grasped his arm with a man's strength, and almost screamed the words she spoke. "But we must not go there!" she cried. "We must not go!"

Sir Gabriel's eyes were half shut, and he was not moved by the agony of her face.

"I shall die, unless I see it again," he said, in a quiet voice not like his own. And all that day and that evening he scarcely spoke, thinking of it, always thinking, while Evelyn Warburton quivered from head to foot with a terror she had never known.

One grey winter morning, she went alone to Nurse Macdonald's room in the tower, and sat down beside the great leather easy chair, laying her thin white hand upon the withered fingers.

"Nurse," she said, "what was it that Uncle Hugh should have told you, that night before he died? It must have been an awful secret – and yet, though you asked him, I feel somehow that you know it, and that you know why he used to smile so dreadfully."

The old woman's head moved slowly from side to side.

"I only guess.... I shall never know," she answered slowly in her cracked little voice.

"But what do you guess? Who am I? Why did you ask who my father was? You know I am Colonel Warburton's daughter, and my mother was Lady Ockram's sister, so that Gabriel and I are cousins. My father was killed in Afghanistan. What secret can there be?"

"I do not know. I can only guess."

"Guess what?" asked Evelyn imploringly, pressing the soft withered hands, as she leaned forward. But Nurse Macdonald's wrinkled lids dropped suddenly over her queer blue eyes, and her lips shook a little with her breath, as if she were asleep.

Evelyn waited. By the fire the Irish maid was knitting fast. Her needles clicked like three or four clocks ticking against each other. But the real clock on the wall solemnly ticked alone, checking off the seconds of the woman who was a hundred years old, and had not many days left. Outside the ivy branch beat the window in the wintry blast, as it had beaten against the glass a hundred years ago.

Then as Evelyn sat there she felt again the waking of a horrible desire – the sickening wish to go down, down to the thing in the north vault, and to open the winding-sheet, and see whether it had changed; and she held Nurse Macdonald's hands as if to keep herself in her place and fight against the appalling attraction of the evil dead.

But the old cat that kept Nurse Macdonald's feet warm, lying always on the footstool, got up and stretched itself, and looked up into Evelyn's eyes, while its back arched, and its tail thickened and bristled, and its ugly pink lips drew back in a devilish grin, showing its sharp teeth. Evelyn stared at it, half fascinated by its ugliness. Then the creature suddenly put out one paw with all its claws spread, and spat at the girl. All at once the grinning cat was like the smiling corpse far down below. Evelyn shivered down to her small feet, and covered her face with her free hand, lest Nurse Macdonald should wake and see the dead smile there, for she could feel it.

The old woman had already opened her eyes again, and she touched her cat with the end of her crutch-stick, whereupon its back went down and its tail shrunk, and it sidled back to its place on the footstool. But its yellow eyes looked up sideways at Evelyn, between the slits of its lids.

"What is it that you guess, nurse?" asked the young girl again.

"A bad thing, a wicked thing. But I dare not tell you, lest it might not be true, and the very thought should blast your life. For if I guess right, he meant that you should not know, and that you two should marry and pay for his old sin with your souls."

"He used to tell us that we ought not to marry."

"Yes – he told you that, perhaps. But it was as if a man put poisoned meat before a starving beast, and said 'do not eat,' but never raised his hand to take the meat away. And if he told you that you should not marry, it was because he hoped you would; for of all men living or dead, Hugh Ockram was the falsest man that ever told a cowardly lie, and the crudest that ever hurt a weak woman, and the worst that ever loved a sin."

"But Gabriel and I love each other," said Evelyn very sadly.

Nurse Macdonald's old eyes looked far away, at sights seen long ago, and that rose in the grey winter air amid the mists of an ancient youth.

"If you love, you can die together," she said, very slowly. "Why should you live, if it is true? I am a hundred years old. What has life given me? The beginning is fire; the end is a heap of ashes; and between the end and the beginning lies all the pain of the world. Let me sleep, since I cannot die."

Then the old woman's eyes closed again, and her head sank a little lower upon her breast.

So Evelyn went away and left her asleep, with the cat asleep on the footstool. The young girl tried to forget Nurse Macdonald's words, but she could not, for she heard them over and over again in the wind, and behind her on the stairs. And as she grew sick with fear of the frightful unknown evil to which her soul was bound, she felt a bodily something pressing her, pushing her, forcing her on from the other side. She felt threads that drew her mysteriously, and when she shut her eyes, she saw in the chapel behind the altar, the low iron door through which she must pass to go to the thing.

As she lay awake at night, she drew the sheet over her face, lest she should see shadows on the wall beckoning to her. The sound of her own warm breath made whisperings in her ears, while she held the mattress with her hands, to keep from getting up and going to the chapel. It would have been easier if there had not been a way thither through the library, by a door which was never locked. It would be fearfully easy to take her candle and go softly through the sleeping house. The key of the vault lay under the altar behind a stone that turned. She knew that little secret. She could go alone and see.

But when she thought of it, she felt her hair rise on her head. She shivered so that the bed shook, then the horror went through her in a cold thrill that was agony again, like a myriad of icy needles boring into her nerves.

IV

THE OLD CLOCK in Nurse Macdonald's tower struck midnight. From her room she could hear the creaking chains, and weights in their box in the corner of the staircase, and the jarring of the rusty lever that lifted the hammer. She had heard it all her life. It struck eleven strokes clearly, and then came the twelfth with a dull half stroke, as though the hammer were too weary to go on and had fallen asleep against the bell.

The old cat got up from the footstool and stretched itself. Nurse Macdonald opened her ancient eyes and looked slowly round the room by the dim light of the night lamp. She touched the cat with her crutch-stick, and it lay down upon her feet. She drank a few drops from her cup and went to sleep again.

But downstairs Sir Gabriel sat straight up as the clock struck, for he had dreamed a fearful dream of horror, and his heart stood still. He awoke at its stopping and it beat again furiously with his breath, like a wild thing set free. No Ockram had ever known fear waking, but sometimes it came to Sir Gabriel in his sleep.

He pressed his hands to his temples as he sat up in bed. His hands were icy cold, but his head was hot. The dream faded far and in its place there came the master thought that racked his life. With the thought also came the sick twisting of his lips in the dark that would have been a smile. Far off, Evelyn Warburton dreamed that the dead smile was on her mouth, and awoke – starting with a little moan – her face in her hands, shivering.

But Sir Gabriel struck a light and got up and began to walk up and down his great room. It was midnight and he had barely slept an hour, and in the north of Ireland the winter nights are long.

"I shall go mad," he said to himself, holding his forehead. He knew that it was true. For weeks and months the possession of the thing had grown upon him like a disease, till he could think of nothing without thinking first of that. And now all at once it outgrew his strength, and he knew that he must be its instrument or lose his mind. He knew that he must do the deed he hated and feared, if he could fear anything, or that something would snap in his brain and divide him from life while he was yet alive. He took the candlestick in his hand, the old-fashioned heavy candlestick that had always been used by the head of the house. He did not think of dressing, but went as he was – in his silk night clothes and his slippers – and opened the door.

Everything was very still in the great old house. He shut the door behind him and walked noiselessly on the carpet through the long corridor. A cool breeze blew over his shoulder and blew the flame of his candle straight out. Instinctively he stopped and looked round, but all was still, and the upright flame burned steadily. He walked on, and instantly a strong draught was behind him, almost extinguishing the light. It seemed to blow him on his way, ceasing whenever he turned, coming again when he went on – invisible, icy.

Down the great staircase to the echoing hall he went, seeing nothing but the flaring flame of the candle standing away from him over the guttering wax. The cold wind blew over his shoulder and through his hair. On he passed through the open door into the library dark with old books and carved bookcases. On he went through the door with shelves and the imitated backs of books painted on it, which shut itself after him with a soft click.

He entered the low-arched passage, and though the door was shut behind him and fitted tightly in its frame, still the cold breeze blew the flame forward as he walked. He was not afraid; but his face was very pale and his eyes were wide and bright, seeing already in the dark air the picture of the thing beyond. But in the chapel he stood still, his hand on the little turning stone tablet in the back of the stone altar. On the tablet were engraved the words:

Clavis sepulchri Clarissimorum Dominorum De Ockram

(*"the key to the vault of the most illustrious lords of Ockram"*).

Sir Gabriel paused and listened. He fancied that he heard a sound far off in the great house where all had been so still, but it did not come again. Yet he waited at the last, and looked at the low iron door. Beyond it, down the long descent, lay his father uncoffined, six months dead, corrupt, terrible in his clinging shroud. The strangely preserving air of the vault could not yet have done its work completely. But on the thing's ghastly features, with their half-dried, open eyes, there would still be the frightful smile with which the man had died – the smile that haunted.

As the thought crossed Sir Gabriel's mind, he felt his lips writhing, and he struck his own mouth in wrath with the back of his hand so fiercely that a drop of blood ran down his chin, and another, and more, falling back in the gloom upon the chapel pavement. But still his bruised lips twisted themselves. He turned the tablet by the simple secret. It needed no safer fastening, for had each Ockram been coffined in pure gold, and had the door been open wide, there was not a man in Tyrone brave enough to go down to that place, save Gabriel Ockram himself, with his angel's face, his thin, white hands, and his sad unflinching eyes.

He took the great old key and set it into the lock of the iron door. The heavy, rattling noise echoed down the descent beyond like footsteps, as if a watcher had stood behind the iron and were running away within, with heavy dead feet. And though he was standing still, the cool wind was from behind him, and blew the flame of the candle against the iron panel. He turned the key.

Sir Gabriel saw that his candle was short. There were new ones on the altar, with long candlesticks, so he lit one and left his own burning on the floor. As he set it down on the pavement his lip began to bleed again, and another drop fell upon the stones.

He drew the iron door open and pushed it back against the chapel wall, so that it should not shut of itself, while he was within; and the horrible draught of the sepulchre came up out of the depths in his face, foul and dark. He went in, but though the fetid air met him, yet the flame of the tall candle was blown straight from him against the wind while he walked down the easy incline with steady steps, his loose slippers slapping the pavement as he trod.

He shaded the candle with his hand, and his fingers seemed to be made of wax and blood as the light shone through them. And in spite of him the unearthly draught forced the flame forward, till it was blue over the black wick, and it seemed as if it must go out. But he went straight on, with shining eyes.

The downward passage was wide, and he could not always see the walls by the struggling light, but he knew when he was in the place of death by the larger, drearier echo of his steps in the greater space, and by the sensation of a distant blank wall. He stood still, almost enclosing the flame of the candle in the hollow of his hand. He could see a little, .for his eyes were growing used to the gloom. Shadowy forms were outlined in the dimness, where the biers of the Ockrams stood crowded together, side by side, each with its straight, shrouded corpse, strangely preserved by the dry air, like the empty shell that the locust sheds in summer. And a few steps before him he saw clearly the dark shape of headless Sir Vernon's iron coffin, and he knew that nearest to it lay the thing he sought.

He was as brave as any of those dead men had been. They were his fathers, and he knew that sooner or later he should lie there himself, beside Sir Hugh, slowly drying to a parchment shell. But as yet, he was still alive. He closed his eyes a moment as three great drops stood on his forehead.

Then he looked again, and by the whiteness of the winding sheet he knew his father's corpse, for all the others were brown with age; and, moreover, the flame of the candle was blown toward it. He made four steps till he reached it, and suddenly the light burned straight and high, shedding a dazzling yellow glare upon the fine linen that was all white, save over the face, and where the joined hands were laid on the breast. And at those places ugly stains had spread, darkened with outlines of the features and of the tight clasped fingers. There was a frightful stench of drying death.

As Sir Gabriel looked down, something stirred behind him, softly at first, then more noisily, and something fell to the stone floor with a dull thud and rolled up to his feet. He started back and saw a withered head lying almost face upward on the pavement, grinning at him. He felt the cold sweat standing on his face, and his heart beat painfully.

For the first time in all his life that evil thing which men call fear was getting hold of him, checking his heart-strings as a cruel driver checks a quivering horse, clawing at his backbone with icy hands, lifting his hair with freezing breath, climbing up and gathering in his midriff with leaden weight.

Yet he bit his lip and bent down, holding the candle in one hand, to lift the shroud back from the head of the corpse with the other. Slowly he lifted it. It clove to the half-dried skin of the face, and his hand shook as if someone had struck him on the elbow, but half in fear and half in anger at himself, he pulled it, so that it came away with a little ripping sound. He caught his breath as he held it, not yet throwing it back, and not yet looking. The horror was working in him and he felt that old Vernon Ockram was standing up in his iron coffin, headless, yet watching him with the stump of his severed neck.

While he held his breath he felt the dead smile twisting his lips. In sudden wrath at his own misery, he tossed the death-stained linen backward, and looked at last. He ground his teeth lest he should shriek aloud. There it was, the thing that haunted him, that haunted Evelyn Warburton, that was like a blight on all that came near him.

The dead face was blotched with dark stains, and the thin, grey hair was matted about the discoloured forehead. The sunken lids were half open, and the candlelight gleamed on something foul where the toad eyes had lived.

But yet the dead thing smiled, as it had smiled in life. The ghastly lips were parted and drawn wide and tight upon the wolfish teeth, cursing still, and still defying hell to do its worst – defying, cursing, and always and forever smiling alone in the dark.

Sir Gabriel opened the sheet where the hands were. The blackened, withered fingers were closed upon something stained and mottled. Shivering from head to foot, but fighting like a man in agony for his life, he tried to take the package from the dead man's hold. But as he pulled at it the clawlike fingers seemed to close more tightly. When he pulled harder the shrunken hands and arms rose from the corpse with a horrible look of life following his motion – then as he wrenched the sealed packet loose at last, the hands fell back into their place still folded.

He set down the candle on the edge of the bier to break the seals from the stout paper. Kneeling on one knee, to get a better light, he read what was within, written long ago in Sir Hugh's queer hand. He was no longer afraid.

He read how Sir Hugh had written it all down that it might perchance be a witness of evil and of his hatred. He had written how he had loved Evelyn Warburton, his wife's sister; and how his wife had died of a broken heart with his curse upon her. He wrote how Warburton and he had fought side by side in Afghanistan, and Warburton had fallen; but Ockram had brought his comrade's wife back a full year later, and little Evelyn, her child, had been born in Ockram Hall. And he wrote how he had wearied of the mother, and she had died like her sister with his curse on her; and how Evelyn had been brought up as his niece, and how he had trusted that his son Gabriel and his daughter, innocent and unknowing, might love and marry, and the souls of the women he had betrayed might suffer yet another anguish before eternity was out. And, last of all, he hoped that some day, when nothing could be undone, the two might find his writing and live on, as man and wife, not daring to tell the truth for their children's sake and the world's word.

This he read, kneeling beside the corpse in the north vault, by the light of the altar candle. He had read it all and then he thanked God aloud that he had found the secret in time. When he finally rose to his feet and looked down at the dead face it had changed. The smile was gone from it. The jaw had fallen a little and the tired, dead lips were relaxed. And then there was a breath behind him and close to him, not cold like that which had blown the flame of the candle as he came, but warm and human. He turned suddenly.

There she stood, all in white, with her shadowy golden hair. She had risen from her bed and had followed him noiselessly. When she found him reading, she read over his shoulder.

He started violently when he saw her, for his nerves were unstrung. Then he cried out her name in that still place of death:

"Evelyn!"

"My brother!" she answered softly and tenderly, putting out both hands to meet his.

The Screaming Skull

F. Marion Crawford

I HAVE OFTEN heard it scream. No, I am not nervous, I am not imaginative, and I never believed in ghosts, unless that thing is one. Whatever it is, it hates me almost as much as it hated Luke Pratt, and it screams at me. If I were you, I would never tell ugly stories about ingenious ways of killing people, for you never can tell but that someone at the table may be tired of his or her nearest and dearest. I have always blamed myself for Mrs. Pratt's death, and I suppose I was responsible for it in a way, though heaven knows I never wished her anything but long life and happiness. If I had not told that story she might be alive yet. That is why the thing screams at me, I fancy. She was a good little woman, with a sweet temper, all things considered, and a nice gentle voice; but I remember hearing her shriek once when she thought her little boy was killed by a pistol that went off though everyone was sure that it was not loaded. It was the same scream; exactly the same, with a sort of rising quaver at the end; do you know what I mean? Unmistakable.

The truth is, I had not realized that the doctor and his wife were not on good terms. They used to bicker a bit now and then when I was here, and I often noticed that little Mrs. Pratt got very red and bit her lip hard to keep her temper, while Luke grew pale and said the most offensive things. He was that sort when he was in the nursery, I remember, and afterwards at school. He was my cousin, you know; that is how I came by this house; after he died, and his boy Charley was killed in South Africa, there were no relations left. Yes, it's a pretty little property, just the sort of thing for an old sailor like me who has taken to gardening.

One always remembers one's mistakes much more vividly than one's cleverest things, doesn't one? I've often noticed it. I was dining with the Pratts one night, when I told them the story that afterwards made so much difference. It was a wet night in November, and the sea was moaning. Hush! – if you don't speak you will hear it now... Do you hear the tide? Gloomy sound, isn't it? Sometimes, about this time of year – hallo! – there it is! Don't be frightened, man – it won't eat you – it's only a noise, after all! But I'm glad you've heard it, because there are always people who think it's the wind, or my imagination, or something. You won't hear it again tonight, I fancy, for it doesn't often come more than once. Yes – that's right. Put another stick on the fire, and a little more stuff into that weak mixture you're so fond of. Do you remember old Blauklot the carpenter, on that German ship that picked us up when the Clontarf went to the bottom? We were hove to in a howling gale one night, as snug as you please, with no land within five hundred miles, and the ship coming up and falling off as regularly as clockwork – "Biddy te boor beebles ashore tis night, poys!" old Blauklot sang out, as he went off to his quarters with the sail-maker. I often think of that, now that I'm ashore for good and all.

Yes, it was on a night like this, when I was at home for a spell, waiting to take the Olympia out on her first trip – it was on the next voyage that she broke the record, you remember – but that dates it. Ninety-two was the year, early in November.

The weather was dirty, Pratt was out of temper, and the dinner was bad, very bad indeed, which didn't improve matters, and cold, which made it worse. The poor little lady was very unhappy about it, and insisted on making a Welsh rarebit on the table to counteract the raw turnips and the half-boiled mutton. Pratt must have had a hard day. Perhaps he had lost a patient. At all events, he was in a nasty temper.

"My wife is trying to poison me, you see!" he said. "She'll succeed some day." I saw that she was hurt, and I made believe to laugh, and said that Mrs. Pratt was much too clever to get rid of her husband in such a simple way; and then I began to tell them about Japanese tricks with spun glass and chopped horsehair and the like.

Pratt was a doctor, and knew a lot more than I did about such things, but that only put me on my mettle, and I told a story about a woman in Ireland who did for three husbands before anyone suspected foul play.

Did you never hear that tale? The fourth husband managed to keep awake and caught her, and she was hanged. How did she do it? She drugged them, and poured melted lead into their ears through a little horn funnel when they were asleep... No – that's the wind whistling. It's backing up to the southward again. I can tell by the sound. Besides, the other thing doesn't often come more than once in an evening even at this time of year – when it happened. Yes, it was in November. Poor Mrs. Pratt died suddenly in her bed not long after I dined here. I can fix the date, because I got the news in New York by the steamer that followed the Olympia when I took her out on her first trip. You had the Leofric the same year? Yes, I remember. What a pair of old buffers we are coming to be, you and I. Nearly fifty years since we were apprentices together on the Clontarf. Shall you ever forget old Blauklot? "Biddy te boor beebles ashore, poys!" Ha, ha! Take a little more, with all that water. It's the old Hulstkamp I found in the cellar when this house came to me, the same I brought Luke from Amsterdam five-and-twenty years ago. He had never touched a drop of it. Perhaps he's sorry now, poor fellow.

Where did I leave off? I told you that Mrs. Pratt died suddenly – yes. Luke must have been lonely here after she was dead, I should think; I came to see him now and then, and he looked worn and nervous, and told me that his practice was growing too heavy for him, though he wouldn't take an assistant on any account. Years went on, and his son was killed in South Africa, and after that he began to be queer. There was something about him not like other people. I believe he kept his senses in his profession to the end; there was no complaint of his having made mad mistakes in cases, or anything of that sort, but he had a look about him –

Luke was a red-headed man with a pale face when he was young, and he was never stout; in middle age he turned a sandy grey, and after his son died he grew thinner and thinner, till his head looked like a skull with parchment stretched over it very tight, and his eyes had a sort of glare in them that was very disagreeable to look at. He had an old dog that poor Mrs. Pratt had been fond of, and that used to follow her everywhere. He was a bulldog, and the sweetest tempered beast you ever saw, though he had a way of hitching his upper lip behind one of his fangs that frightened strangers a good deal. Sometimes, of an evening, Pratt and Bumble – that was the dog's name – used to sit and look at each other a long time, thinking about old times, I suppose, when Luke's wife used to sit in that chair you've got. That was always her place, and this was the doctor's, where I'm sitting. Bumble used to climb up by the footstool – he was old and fat by that time, and could not jump much, and his teeth were getting shaky. He would look steadily at Luke, and Luke looked steadily at the dog, his face growing more and more like a skull with two little coals for eyes; and after about five minutes or so, though it may have been less, old Bumble would suddenly begin to shake all over, and all on a sudden he would set up an awful howl, as if he had been shot, and tumble out of the easy-chair and trot away, and hide himself under the sideboard, and lie there making odd noises.

Considering Pratt's looks in those last months, the thing is not surprising, you know. I'm not nervous or imaginative, but I can quite believe he might have sent a sensitive woman into hysterics – his head looked so much like a skull in parchment.

At last I came down one day before Christmas, when my ship was in dock and I had three weeks off. Bumble was not about, and I said casually that I supposed the old dog was dead. "Yes," Pratt answered, and I thought there was something odd in his tone even before he went on after a little pause. "I killed him," he said presently. "I could stand it no longer." I asked what it was that Luke could not stand, though I guessed well enough.

"He had a way of sitting in her chair and glaring at me, and then howling," Luke shivered a little. "He didn't suffer at all, poor old Bumble," he went on in a hurry, as if he thought I might imagine he had been cruel. "I put dionine into his drink to make him sleep soundly, and then I chloroformed him gradually, so that he could not have felt suffocated even if he was dreaming. It's been quieter since then."

I wondered what he meant, for the words slipped out as if he could not help saying them. I've understood since. He meant that he did not hear that noise so often after the dog was out of the way. Perhaps he thought at first that it was old Bumble in the yard howling at the moon, though it's not that kind of noise, is it? Besides, I know what it is, if Luke didn't. It's only a noise after all, and a noise never hurt anybody yet. But he was much more imaginative than I am. No doubt there really is something about this place that I don't understand; but when I don't understand a thing, I call it a phenomenon, and I don't take it for granted that it's going to kill me, as he did. I don't understand everything, by long odds, nor do you, nor does any man who has been to sea. We used to talk of tidal waves, for instance, and we could not account for them; now we account for them by calling them submarine earthquakes, and we branch off into fifty theories, any one of which might make earthquakes quite comprehensible if we only knew what they were. I fell in with one of them once, and the inkstand flew straight up from the table against the ceiling of my cabin. The same thing happened to Captain Lecky – I dare say you've read about it in his "Wrinkles". Very good. If that sort of thing took place ashore, in this room for instance, a nervous person would talk about spirits and levitation and fifty things that mean nothing, instead of just quietly setting it down as a "phenomenon" that has not been explained yet. My view of that voice, you see.

Besides, what is there to prove that Luke killed his wife? I would not even suggest such a thing to anyone but you. After all, there was nothing but the coincidence that poor little Mrs. Pratt died suddenly in her bed a few days after I told that story at dinner. She was not the only woman who ever died like that. Luke got the doctor over from the next parish, and they agreed that she had died of something the matter with her heart. Why not? It's common enough. Of course, there was the ladle. I never told anybody about that, and, it made me start when I found it in the cupboard in the bedroom. It was new, too – a little tinned iron ladle that had not been in the fire more than once or twice, and there was some lead in it that had been melted, and stuck to the bottom of the bowl, all grey, with hardened dross on it. But that proves nothing. A country doctor is generally a handy man, who does everything for himself, and Luke may have had a dozen reasons for melting a little lead in a ladle. He was fond of sea-fishing, for instance, and he may have cast a sinker for a night-line; perhaps it was a weight for the hall clock, or something like that. All the same, when I found it I had a rather queer sensation, because it looked so much like the thing I had described when I told them the story. Do you understand? It affected me unpleasantly, and I threw it away; it's at the bottom of the sea a mile from the Spit, and it will be jolly well rusted beyond recognizing if it's ever washed up by the tide.

You see, Luke must have bought it in the village, years ago, for the man sells just such ladles still. I suppose they are used in cooking. In any case, there was no reason why an inquisitive housemaid should find such a thing lying about, with lead in it, and wonder what it was, and perhaps talk to the maid who heard me tell the story at dinner – for that girl married the plumber's son in the village, and may remember the whole thing.

You understand me, don't you? Now that Luke Pratt is dead and gone, and lies buried beside his wife, with an honest man's tombstone at his head, I should not care to stir up anything that could hurt his memory. They are both dead, and their son, too. There was trouble enough about Luke's death, as it was.

How? He was found dead on the beach one morning, and there was a coroner's inquest. There were marks on his throat, but he had not been robbed. The verdict was that he had come to his end "By the hands or teeth of some person or animal unknown," for half the jury thought it might have been a big dog that had thrown him down and gripped his windpipe, though the skin of his throat was not broken. No one knew at what time he had gone out, nor where he had been. He was found lying on his back above high-water mark, and an old cardboard bandbox that had belonged to his wife lay under his hand, open. The lid had fallen off. He seemed to have been carrying home a skull in the box – doctors are fond of collecting such things. It had rolled out and lay near his head, and it was a remarkably fine skull, rather small, beautifully shaped and very white, with perfect teeth. That is to say, the upper jaw was perfect, but there was no lower one at all, when I first saw it.

Yes, I found it here when I came. You see, it was very white and polished, like a thing meant to be kept under a glass case, and the people did not know where it came from, nor what to do with it; so they put it back into the bandbox and set it on the shelf of the cupboard in the best bedroom, and of course they showed it to me when I took possession. I was taken down to the beach, too, to be shown the place where Luke was found, and the old fisherman explained just how he was lying, and the skull beside him. The only point he could not explain was why the skull had rolled up the sloping sand towards Luke's head instead of rolling downhill to his feet. It did not seem odd to me at the time, but I have often thought of it since, for the place is rather steep. I'll take you there tomorrow if you like – I made a sort of cairn of stones there afterwards.

When he fell down, or was thrown down – whichever happened – the bandbox struck the sand, and the lid came off, and the thing came out and ought to have rolled down. But it didn't. It was close to his head almost touching it, and turned with the face towards it. I say it didn't strike me as odd when the man told me; but I could not help thinking about It afterwards, again and again, till I saw a picture of it all when I closed my eyes; and then

I began to ask myself why the plaguey thing had rolled up instead of down, and why it had stopped near Luke's head instead of anywhere else, a yard away, for instance.

You naturally want to know what conclusion I reached, don't you? None that at all explained the rolling, at all events. But I got something else into my head, after a time, that made me feel downright uncomfortable. Oh, I don't mean as to anything supernatural! There may be ghosts, or there may not be. If there are, I'm not inclined to believe that they can hurt living people except by frightening them, and, for my part, I would rather face any shape of ghost than a fog in the Channel when it's crowded. No. What bothered me was just a foolish idea, that's all, and I cannot tell how it began, nor what made it grow till it turned into a certainty.

I was thinking about Luke and his poor wife one evening over my pipe and a dull book, when it occurred to me that the skull might possibly be hers, and I have never got rid of the thought since. You'll tell me there's no sense in it, no doubt, that Mrs. Pratt was buried like a Christian and is lying in the churchyard where they put her, and that it's perfectly monstrous to suppose her husband kept her skull in her old bandbox in his bedroom. All the same, in the face of reason, and common sense, and probability, I'm convinced that he did. Doctors do all sorts of queer things that would make men like you and me feel creepy, and those are just the things that don't seem probable, nor logical, nor sensible to us.

Then, don't you see? – if it really was her skull, poor woman, the only way of accounting for his having it is that he really killed her, and did it in that way, as the woman killed her husbands in the story, and that he was afraid there might be an examination some day which would betray him. You see, I told that too, and I believe it had really happened some fifty or sixty years ago. They dug up the three skulls, you know, and there was a small lump of lead rattling about in each one. That was what hanged the woman. Luke remembered that, I'm sure. I don't want to know what he did when he thought of it; my taste never ran in the direction of horrors, and I don't fancy you care for them either, do you? No. If you did, you might supply what is wanting to the story.

It must have been rather grim, eh? I wish I did not see the whole thing so distinctly, just as everything must have happened. He took it the night before she was buried, I'm sure, after the coffin had been shut, and when the servant girl was asleep. I would bet anything, that when he'd got it, he put something under the sheet in its place, to fill up and look like it. What do you suppose he put there, under the sheet?

I don't wonder you take me up on what I'm saying! First I tell you that I don't want to know what happened, and that I hate to think about horrors, and then I describe the whole thing to you as if I had seen it. I'm quite sure that it was her work-bag that he put there. I remember the bag very well, for she always used it of an evening; it was made of brown plush, and when it was stuffed full it was about the size of – you understand. Yes, there I am, at it again! You may laugh at me, but you don't live here alone, where it was done, and you didn't tell Luke the story about the melted lead. I'm not nervous, I tell you, but sometimes I begin to feel that I understand why some people are. I dwell on all this when I'm alone, and I dream of it, and when that thing screams – well, frankly, I don't like the noise any more than you do, though I should be used to it by this time.

I ought not to be nervous. I've sailed in a haunted ship. There was a Man in the Top, and two-thirds of the crew died of the West Coast fever inside of ten days after we anchored; but I was all right, then and afterwards. I have seen some ugly sights, too, just as you have, and all the rest of us. But nothing ever stuck in my head in the way this does. You see, I've tried to get rid of the thing, but it doesn't like that. It wants to be there in its place, in Mrs. Pratt's bandbox in the cupboard in the best bedroom. It's not happy anywhere else. How do I know that? Because I've tried it. You don't suppose that I've not tried, do you? As long as it's there it only screams now and then, generally at this time of year, but if I put it out of the house it goes on all night, and no servant will stay here twenty-four hours. As it is, I've often been left alone and have been obliged to shift for myself for a fortnight at a time. No one from the village would ever pass a night under the roof now, and as for selling the place, or even letting it, that's out of the question. The old women say that if I stay here I shall come to a bad end myself before long.

I'm not afraid of that. You smile at the mere idea that anyone could take such nonsense seriously. Quite right. It's utterly blatant nonsense, I agree with you. Didn't I tell you that it's only a noise after all when you started and looked round as if you expected to see a ghost standing behind your chair?

I may be all wrong about the skull, and I like to think that I am when I can. It may be just a fine specimen which Luke got somewhere long ago, and what rattles about inside when you shake it may be nothing but a pebble, or a bit of hard clay, or anything. Skulls that have lain long in the ground generally have something inside them that rattles don't they? No, I've never tried to get it out, whatever it is; I'm afraid it might be lead, don't you see? And if it is, I don't want to know the fact, for I'd much rather not be sure. If it really is lead, I killed her quite as much as if I had done the deed myself. Anybody must see that, I should think. As long as I don't know for certain, I have the consolation of saying that it's all utterly ridiculous nonsense, that Mrs. Pratt died a natural death and that the beautiful skull belonged to Luke when he was a student in London. But if I were quite sure, I believe I should have to leave the house; indeed I do, most certainly. As it is, I had to give up trying to sleep in the best bedroom where the cupboard is. You ask me why I don't throw it into the pond – yes, but please don't call it a "confounded bugbear" – it doesn't like being called names.

There! Lord, what a shriek! I told you so! You're quite pale, man. Fill up your pipe and draw your chair nearer to the fire, and take some more drink. Old Hollands never hurt anybody yet. I've seen a Dutchman in Java drink half a jug of Hulstkamp in a morning without turning a hair. I don't take much rum myself, because it doesn't agree with my rheumatism, but you are not rheumatic and it won't damage you. Besides, it's a very damp night outside. The wind is howling again, and it will soon be in the south-west; do you hear how the windows rattle? The tide must have turned too, by the moaning.

We should not have heard the thing again if you had not said that. I'm pretty sure we should not. Oh yes, if you choose to describe it as a coincidence, you are quite welcome, but I would rather that you should not call the thing names again, if you don't mind. It may be that the poor little woman hears, and perhaps it hurts her, don't you know? Ghosts? No! You don't call anything a ghost that you can take in your hands and look at in broad daylight, and that rattles when you shake it. Do you, now? But it's something that hears and understands; there's no doubt about that. I tried sleeping in the best bedroom when I first came to the house just because it was the best and most comfortable, but I had to give it up. It was their room, and there's the big bed she died in, and the cupboard is in the thickness of the wall, near the head, on the left. That's where it likes to be kept, in its bandbox. I only used the room for a fortnight after I came, and then I turned out and took the little room downstairs, next to the surgery, where Luke used to sleep when he expected to be called to a patient during the night.

I was always a good sleeper ashore; eight hours is my dose, eleven to seven when I'm alone, twelve to eight when I have a friend with me. But I could not sleep after three o'clock in the morning in that room – a quarter past, to be accurate – as a matter of fact, I timed it with my old pocket chronometer, which still keeps good time, and it was always at exactly seventeen minutes past three. I wonder whether that was the hour when she died?

It was not what you have heard. If it had been that, I could not have stood it two nights. It was just a start and a moan and hard breathing for a few seconds in the cupboard, and it could never have waked me under ordinary circumstances, I'm sure. I suppose you are like me in that, and we are just like other people who have been to sea. No natural sounds disturb us at all, not all the racket of a square-rigger hove to in a heavy gale, or rolling on her beam ends before the wind. But if a lead pencil gets adrift and rattles in the drawer of your cabin table you are awake in a moment. Just so – you always understand. Very well, the noise in the cupboard was no louder than that, but it waked me instantly.

I said it was like a "start". I know what I mean, but it's hard to explain without seeming to talk nonsense. Of course you cannot exactly "hear" a person "start"; at the most, you might hear the quick drawing of the breath between the parted lips and closed teeth, and the almost imperceptible sound of clothing that moved suddenly though very slightly. It was like that.

You know how one feels what a sailing vessel is going to do, two or three seconds before she does it, when one has the wheel. Riders say the same of a horse, but that's less strange, because the horse is a live animal with feelings of its own, and only poets and landsmen talk about a ship being alive, and all that. But I have always felt somehow that besides being a steaming machine or a sailing machine for carrying weights, a vessel at sea is a sensitive instrument, and a means of communication between nature and man, and most particularly the man at the wheel, if she is steered by hand. She takes her impressions directly from wind and sea, tide and stream, and transmits them to the man's hand, just as the wireless telegraphy picks up the interrupted currents aloft and turns them out below in the form of a message.

You see what I am driving at; I felt that something started in the cupboard, and I felt it so vividly that I heard it, though there may have been nothing to hear, and the sound inside my head waked me suddenly. But I really heard the other noise. It was as if it were muffled inside a box, as far away as if it came through a long-distance telephone; and yet I knew that it was inside the cupboard near the head of my bed. My hair did not bristle and my blood did not run cold that time. I simply resented being waked up by something that had no business to make a noise, any more than a pencil should rattle in the drawer of my cabin table on board ship. For I did not understand; I just supposed that the cupboard had some communication with the outside air, and that the wind had got in and was moaning through it with a sort of very faint screech. I struck a light and looked at my watch, and it was seventeen minutes past three. Then I turned over and went to sleep on my right ear. That's my good one; I'm pretty deaf with the other, for I struck the water with it when I was a lad in diving from the fore-topsail yard. Silly thing to do, it was, but the result is very convenient when I want to go to sleep when there's a noise.

That was the first night, and the same thing happened again and several times afterwards, but not regularly, though it was always at the same time, to a second; perhaps I was sometimes sleeping on my good ear, and sometimes not. I overhauled the cupboard and there was no way by which the wind could get in, or anything else, for the door makes a good fit, having been meant to keep out moths, I suppose; Mrs. Pratt must have kept her winter things in it, for it still smells of camphor and turpentine.

After about a fortnight I had had enough of the noises. So far I had said to myself that it would be silly to yield to it and take the skull out of the room. Things always look differently by daylight, don't they? But the voice grew louder – I suppose one may call it a voice – and it got inside my deaf ear, too, one night. I realized that when I was wide awake, for my good ear was jammed down on the pillow, and I ought not to have heard a foghorn in that position. But I heard that, and it made me lose my temper, unless it scared me, for sometimes the two are not far apart. I struck a light and got up, and I opened the cupboard, grabbed the bandbox and threw it out of the window, as far as I could.

Then my hair stood on end. The thing screamed in the air, like a shell from a twelve-inch gun. It fell on the other side of the road. The night was very dark, and I could not see it fall, but I know it fell beyond the road The window is just over the front door, it's fifteen yards to the fence, more or less, and the road is ten yards wide. There's a thick-set hedge beyond, along the glebe that belongs to the vicarage.

I did not sleep much more than night. It was not more than half an hour after I had thrown the bandbox out when I heard a shriek outside – like what we've had tonight, but worse, more despairing, I should call it; and it may have been my imagination, but I could have sworn that the screams came nearer and nearer each time. I lit a pipe, and walked up and down for a bit, and then took a book and sat up reading, but I'll be hanged if I can remember what I read nor even what the book was, for every now and then a shriek came up that would have made a dead man turn in his coffin.

A little before dawn someone knocked at the front door. There was no mistaking that for anything else, and I opened my window and looked down, for I guessed that someone wanted the doctor, supposing that the new man had taken Luke's house. It was rather a relief to hear a human knock after that awful noise.

You cannot see the door from above, owing to the little porch. The knocking came again, and I called out, asking who was there, but nobody answered, though the knock was repeated. I sang out again, and said that the doctor did not live here any longer. There was no answer, but it occurred to me that it might be some old countryman who was stone deaf. So I took my candle and went down to open the door. Upon my word, I was not thinking of the thing yet, and I had almost forgotten the other noises. I went down convinced that I should find somebody outside, on the doorstep, with a message. I set the candle on the hall table, so that the wind should not blow it out when I opened. While I was drawing the old-fashioned bolt I heard the knocking again. It was not loud, and it had a queer, hollow sound, now that I was close to it, I remember, but I certainly thought it was made by some person who wanted to get in.

It wasn't. There was nobody there, but as I opened the door inward, standing a little on one side, so as to see out at once, something rolled across the threshold and stopped against my foot.

I drew back as I felt it, for I knew what it was before I looked down. I cannot tell you how I knew, and it seemed unreasonable, for I am still quite sure that I had thrown it across the road. It's a French window, that opens wide, and I got a good swing when I flung it out. Besides, when I went out early in the morning, I found the bandbox beyond the thick hedge.

You may think it opened when I threw it, and that the skull dropped out; but that's impossible, for nobody could throw an empty cardboard box so far. It's out of the question; you might as well try to fling a ball of paper twenty-five yards, or a blown bird's egg.

To go back, I shut and bolted the hall door, picked the thing up carefully, and put it on the table beside the candle. I did that mechanically, as one instinctively does the right thing in danger without thinking at all – unless one does the opposite. It may seem odd, but I believe my first thought had been that somebody might come and find me there on the threshold while it was resting against my foot, lying a little on its side, and turning one hollow eye up at my face, as if it meant to accuse me. And the light and shadow from the candle played in the hollows of the eyes as it stood on the table, so that they seemed to open and shut at me. Then the candle went out quite unexpectedly, though the door was fastened and there was not the least draught; and I used up at least half a dozen matches before it would burn again.

I sat down rather suddenly, without quite knowing why. Probably I had been badly frightened, and perhaps you will admit there was no great shame in being scared. The thing had come home, and it wanted to go upstairs, back to its cupboard. I sat still and stared at it for a bit till I began to feel very cold; then I took it and carried it up and set it in its place, and I remember that I spoke to it, and promised that it should have its bandbox again in the morning. You want to know whether I stayed in the room till daybreak? Yes but I kept a light burning, and sat up smoking and reading, most likely out of fright; plain, undeniable fear, and you need not call it cowardice either, for that's not the same thing. I could not have stayed alone with that thing in the cupboard; I should have been scared to death, though I'm not more timid than other people. Confound it all, man, it had crossed the road alone, and had got up the doorstep and had knocked to be let in.

When the dawn came, I put on my boots and went out to find the bandbox. I had to go a good way round, by the gate near the high road, and I found the box open and hanging on the other side of the hedge. It had caught on the twigs by the string, and the lid had fallen off and was lying on the ground below it. That shows that it did not open till it was well over; and if it had not opened as soon as it left my hand, what was inside it must have gone beyond the road too.

That's all. I took the box upstairs to the cupboard, and put the skull back and locked it up. When the girl brought me my breakfast she said she was sorry, but that she must go, and she did not care if she lost her month's wages. I looked at her, and her face was a sort of greenish yellowish white. I pretended to be surprised, and asked what was the matter; but that was of no use, for she just turned on me and wanted to know whether I meant to stay in a haunted house, and how long I expected to live if I did, for though she noticed I was sometimes a little hard of hearing, she did not believe that even I could sleep through those screams again – and if I could, why had I been moving about the house and opening and shutting the front door, between three and four in the morning? There was no answering that, since she had heard me, so off she went, and I was left to myself. I went down to the village during the morning and found a woman who was willing to come and do the little work there is and cook my dinner, on condition that she might go home every night. As for me, I moved downstairs that day, and I have never tried to sleep in the best bedroom since. After a little while I got a brace of middle-aged Scotch servants from London, and things were quiet enough for a long time. I began by telling them that the house was in a very exposed position, and that the wind whistled round it a good deal in the autumn and winter, which had given it a bad name in the village, the Cornish people being inclined to superstition and telling ghost stories. The two hard-faced, sandy-haired sisters almost smiled, and they answered with great contempt that they had no great opinion of any Southern bogey whatever, having been in service in two

English haunted houses, where they had never seen so much as the Boy in Grey, whom they reckoned no very particular rarity in Forfarshire.

They stayed with me several months, and while they were in the house we had peace and quiet. One of them is here again now, but she went away with her sister within the year. This one – she was the cook – married the sexton, who works in my garden. That's the way of it. It's a small village and he has not much to do, and he knows enough about flowers to help me nicely, besides doing most of the hard work; for though I'm fond of exercise, I'm getting a little stiff in the hinges. He's a sober, silent sort of fellow, who minds his own business, and he was a widower when I came here – Trehearn is his name, James Trehearn. The Scottish sisters would not admit that there was anything wrong about the house, but when November came they gave me warning that they were going, on the ground that the chapel was such a long walk from here, being in the next parish, and that they could not possibly go to our church. But the younger one came back in the spring, and as soon as the banns could be published she was married to James Trehearn by the vicar, and she seems to have had no scruples about hearing him preach since then. I'm quite satisfied, if she is! The couple live in a small cottage that looks over the churchyard.

I suppose you are wondering what all this has to do with what I was talking about. I'm alone so much that when an old friend comes to see me, I sometimes go on talking just for the sake of hearing my own voice. But in this case there is really a connection of ideas. It was James Trehearn who buried poor Mrs. Pratt, and her husband after her in the same grave, and it's not far from the back of his cottage. That's the connection in my mind, you see. It's plain enough. He knows something; I'm quite sure that he does, though he's such a reticent beggar.

Yes, I'm alone in the house at night now, for Mrs. Trehearn does everything herself, and when I have a friend the sexton's niece comes in to wait on the table. He takes his wife home every evening in winter, but in summer, when there's light, she goes by herself. She's not a nervous woman, but she's less sure than she used to be that there are no bogies in England worth a Scotch-woman's notice. Isn't it amusing, the idea that Scotland has a monopoly of the supernatural? Odd sort of national pride, I call that, don't you?

That's a good fire, isn't it? When driftwood gets started at last there's nothing like it, I think. Yes, we get lots of it, for I'm sorry to say there are still a great many wrecks about here. It's a lonely coast, and you may have all the wood you want for the trouble of bringing it in. Trehearn and I borrow a cart now and then, and load it between here and the Spit. I hate a coal fire when I can get wood of any sort A log is company, even if it's only a piece of a deck beam or timber sawn off, and the salt in it makes pretty sparks. See how they fly, like Japanese hand-fireworks! Upon my word, with an old friend and a good fire and a pipe, one forgets all about that thing upstairs, especially now that the wind has moderated. It's only a lull, though, and it will blow a gale before morning.

You think you would like to see the skull? I've no objection. There's no reason why you shouldn't have a look at it, and you never saw a more perfect one in your life, except that there are two front teeth missing in the lower jaw. Oh yes – I had not told you about the jaw yet. Trehearn found it in the garden last spring when he was digging a pit for a new asparagus bed. You know we make asparagus beds six or eight feet deep here. Yes, yes – I had forgotten to tell you that. He was digging straight down, just as he digs a grave; if you want a good asparagus bed made, I advise you to get a sexton to make it for you. Those fellows have a wonderful knack at that sort of digging. Trehearn had got down about three feet when he cut into a mass of white lime in the side of the trench. He had noticed that the earth was a little looser there, though he says it had not been disturbed for a number of years. I suppose he thought that even old lime might not be good for asparagus, so he broke it out and threw it up. It was pretty hard, he says, in biggish lumps, and out of sheer force of habit he cracked the lumps with his spade as they lay outside the pit beside him; the jaw bone of the skull dropped out of one of the pieces. He thinks he must have knocked out the two front teeth in breaking up the lime, but he did not see them anywhere. He's a very experienced man in such things, as you may imagine, and he said at once that the jaw had probably belonged to a young woman, and that the teeth had been complete when she died. He brought it to me, and asked me if I wanted to keep it; if I did not, he said he would drop it into the next grave he made in the churchyard, as he supposed it was a Christian jaw, and ought to have decent burial, wherever the rest of the body might be. I told him that doctors often put bones into quicklime to whiten them nicely, and that I supposed Dr Pratt had once had a little lime pit in the garden for that purpose, and had forgotten the jaw. Trehearn looked at me quietly.

"Maybe it fitted that skull that used to be in the cupboard upstairs, sir," he said. "Maybe Dr Pratt had put the skull into the lime to clean it, or something, and when he took it out he left the lower jaw behind. There's some human hair sticking in the lime, sir."

I saw there was, and that was what Trehearn said. If he did not suspect something, why in the world should he have suggested that the jaw might fit the skull? Besides, it did. That's proof that he knows more than he cares to tell. Do you suppose he looked before she was buried? Or perhaps – when he buried Luke in the same grave – Well, well, it's of no use to go over that, is it? I said I would keep the jaw with the skull, and I took it upstairs and fitted it into its place. There's not the slightest doubt about the two belonging together, and together they are. Trehearn knows several things. We were talking about plastering the kitchen a while ago, and he happened to remember that it had not been done since the very week when Mrs. Pratt died. He did not say that the mason must have left some lime on the place, but he thought it, and that it was the very same lime he had found in the asparagus pit. He knows a lot. Trehearn is one of your silent beggars who can put two and two together. That grave is very near the back of his cottage, too, and he's one of the quickest men with a spade I ever saw. If he wanted to know the truth, he could, and no one else would ever be the wiser unless he chose to tell. In a quiet village like ours, people don't go and spend the night in the churchyard to see whether the sexton potters about by himself between ten o'clock and daylight.

What is awful to think of, is Luke's deliberation, if he did it; his cool certainty that no one would find him out; above all, his nerve, for that must have been extraordinary. I sometimes think it's bad enough to live in the place where it was done, if it really was done. I always put in the condition, you see, for the sake of his memory, and a little bit for my own sake, too.

I'll go upstairs and fetch the box in a minute. Let me light my pipe; there's no hurry! We had supper early, and it's only half-past nine o'clock. I never let a friend go to bed before twelve, or with less than three glasses – you may have as many more as you like, but you shan't have less, for the sake of old times.

It's breezing up again, do you hear? That was only a lull just now, and we are going to have a bad night. A thing happened that made me start a little when I found that the jaw fitted exactly. I'm not very easily startled in that way myself, but I have seen people make a quick movement, drawing their breath sharply, when they had thought they were alone and suddenly turned and saw someone very near them. Nobody can call that fear. You wouldn't, would you? No. Well, just when I had set the jaw in its place under the skull, the teeth closed sharply on my finger. It felt exactly as if it were biting me hard, and I confess that I jumped before I realized that I had been pressing the jaw and the skull together with my other hand. I assure you I was not at all nervous. It was broad daylight, too, and a fine day, and the sun was streaming into the best bedroom. It would have been absurd to be nervous, and it was only a quick mistaken impression, but it really made me feel queer. Somehow it made me think of the funny verdict of the coroner's jury on Luke's death, "by the hand or teeth of some person or animal unknown". Ever since that I've wished I had seen those marks on his throat, though the lower jaw was missing then.

I have often seen a man do insane things with his hands that he does not realize at all. I once saw a man hanging on by an old awning stop with one hand, leaning backward, outboard, with all his weight on it, and he was just cutting the stop with the knife in his other hand when I got my arms round him. We were in mid-ocean, going twenty knots. He had not the smallest idea what he was doing; neither had I when I managed to pinch my finger between the teeth of that thing. I can feel it now. It was exactly as if it were alive and were trying to bite me. It would if it could, for I know it hates me, poor thing! Do you suppose that what rattles about inside is really a bit of lead? Well, I'll get the box down presently, and if whatever it is happens to drop out into your hands, that's your affair. If it's only a clod of earth or a pebble, the whole matter would be off my mind, and I don't believe I should ever think of the skull again; but somehow I cannot bring myself to shake out the bit of hard stuff myself. The mere idea that it may be lead makes me confoundedly uncomfortable, yet I've got the conviction that I shall know before long. I shall certainly know. I'm sure Trehearn knows, but he's such a silent beggar. I'll go upstairs now and get it. What? You had better go with me? Ha, ha! do you think I'm afraid of a bandbox and a noise? Nonsense!

Bother the candle, it won't light! As if the ridiculous thing understood what it's wanted for! Look at that – the third match. They light fast enough for my pipe. There, do you see? It's a fresh box, just out of the tin safe where I keep the supply on account of the dampness. Oh, you think the wick of the candle may be damp, do you? All right, I'll light the beastly thing in the fire. That won't go out, at all events. Yes, it sputters a bit, but it will keep lighted now. It burns just like any other candle, doesn't it? The fact is, candles are not very good about here. I don't know where they come from, but they have a way of burning low occasionally, with a greenish flame that spits tiny sparks, and I'm often annoyed by their going out of themselves. It cannot be helped, for it will be long before we have electricity in our village. It really is rather a poor light, isn't it?

You think I had better leave you the candle and take the lamp, do you? I don't like to carry lamps about, that's the truth. I never dropped one in my life, but I have always thought I might, and it's so confoundedly dangerous if you do. Besides, I am pretty well used to these rotten candles by this time.

You may as well finish that glass while I'm getting it, for I don't mean to let you off with less than three before you go to bed. You won't have to go upstairs, either, for I've put you in the old study next to the surgery – that's where I live myself. The fact is, I never ask a friend to sleep upstairs now. The last man who did was Crackenthorpe, and he said he was kept awake all night. You remember old Crack, don't you? He stuck to the Service, and they've just made him an admiral. Yes, I'm off now – unless the candle goes out. I couldn't help asking if you remembered Crackenthorpe. If anyone had told us that the skinny little idiot he used to be was to turn out the most successful of the lot of us, we should have laughed at the idea, shouldn't we? You and I did not do badly, it's true – but I'm really going now. I don't mean to let you think that I've been putting it off by talking! As if there were anything to be afraid of! If I were scared, I should tell you so quite frankly, and get you to go upstairs with me.

Here's the box. I brought it down very carefully, so as not to disturb it, poor thing. You see, if it were shaken, the jaw might get separated from it again, and I'm sure it wouldn't like that. Yes, the candle went out as I was coming downstairs, but that was the draught from the leaky window on the landing. Did you hear anything? Yes, there was another scream. Am I pale, do you say? That's nothing. My heart is a little queer sometimes, and I went upstairs too fast. In fact, that's one reason why I really prefer to live altogether on the ground floor.

Wherever the shriek came from, it was not from the skull, for I had the box in my hand when I heard the noise, and here it is now; so we have proved definitely that the screams are produced by something else. I've no doubt I shall find out some day what makes them. Some crevice in the wall, of course, or a crack in a chimney, or a chink in the frame of a window. That's the way all ghost stories end in real life. Do you know, I'm jolly glad I thought of going up and bringing it down for you to see, for that last shriek settles the question. To think that I should have been so weak as to fancy that the poor skull could really cry out like a living thing!

Now I'll open the box, and we'll take it out and look at it under the bright light. It's rather awful to think that the poor lady used to sit there, in your chair, evening after evening, in just the same light, isn't it? But then – I've made up my mind that it's all rubbish from beginning to end, and that it's just an old skull that Luke had when he was a student and perhaps he put it into the lime merely to whiten it, and could not find the jaw.

I made a seal on the string, you see, after I had put the jaw in its place, and I wrote on the cover. There's the old white label on it still, from the milliner's, addressed to Mrs. Pratt when the hat was sent to her, and as there was room I wrote on the edge: "A skull, once the property of the late Luke Pratt, MD." I don't quite know why I wrote that, unless it was with the idea of explaining how the thing happened to be in my possession. I cannot help wondering sometimes what sort of hat it was that came in the bandbox. What colour was it, do you think? Was it a gay spring hat with a bobbing feather and pretty ribands? Strange that the very same box should hold the head that wore the finery – perhaps. No – we made up our minds that it just came from the hospital in London where Luke did his time. It's far better to look at it in that light, isn't it? There's no more connection between that skull and poor Mrs. Pratt than there was between my story about the lead and –

Good Lord! Take the lamp – don't let it go out, if you can help it – I'll have the window fastened again in a second – I say, what a gale! There, it's out! I told you so! Never mind, there's the firelight – I've got the window shut – the bolt was only half down. Was the box blown off the table? Where the deuce is it? There! That won't open again, for I've put up the bar. Good dodge, an old-fashioned bar – there's nothing like it. Now, you find the bandbox while I light the lamp. Confound those wretched matches! Yes, a pipe spill is better – it must light in the fire – hadn't thought of it – thank you – there we are again. Now, where's the box? Yes, put it back on the table, and we'll open it.

That's the first time I have ever known the wind to burst that window open; but it was partly carelessness on my part when I last shut it. Yes, of course I heard the scream. It seemed to go all round the house before it broke in at the window. That proves that it's always been the wind and nothing else, doesn't it? When it was not the wind, it was my imagination I've always been a very imaginative man: I must have been, though I did not know it. As we grow older we understand ourselves better, don't you know?

I'll have a drop of the Hulstkamp neat, by way of an exception, since you are filling up your glass. That damp gust chilled me, and with my rheumatic tendency I'm very much afraid of a chill, for the cold sometimes seems to stick in my joints all winter when it once gets in.

By George, that's good stuff! I'll just light a fresh pipe, now that everything is snug again, and then we'll open the box. I'm so glad we heard that last scream together, with the skull here on the table between us, for a thing cannot possibly be in two places at the same time, and the noise most certainly came from outside, as any noise the wind makes must. You thought you heard it scream through the room after the window was burst open? Oh yes, so did I, but that was natural enough when everything was open. Of course we heard the wind. What could one expect? Look here, please. I want you to see that the seal is intact before we open the box together. Will you take my glasses? No, you have your own. All right. The seal is sound, you see, and you can read the words of the motto easily. "Sweet and low" – that's it – because the poem goes on "Wind of the Western Sea", and says, "blow him again to me", and all that. Here is the seal on my watch chain, where it's hung for more than forty years. My poor little wife gave it to me when I was courting, and I never had any other. It was just like her to think of those words – she was always fond of Tennyson.

It's no use to cut the string, for it's fastened to the box, so I'll just break the wax and untie the knot, and afterwards we'll seal it up again. You see, I like to feel that the thing is safe in its place, and that nobody can take it out. Not that I should suspect Trehearn of meddling with it, but I always feel that he knows a lot more than he tells. You see, I've managed it without breaking the string, though when I fastened it I never expected to open the bandbox again. The lid comes off easily enough. There! Now look!

What! Nothing in it! Empty! It's gone, man, the skull is gone!

No, there's nothing the matter with me. I'm only trying to collect my thoughts. It's so strange. I'm positively certain that it was inside when I put on the seal last spring. I can't have imagined that: it's utterly impossible. If I ever took a stiff glass with a friend now and then, I would admit that I might have made some idiotic mistake when I had taken too much. But I don't, and I never did. A pint of ale at supper and half a go of rum at bedtime was the most I ever took in my good days. I believe it's always we sober fellows who get rheumatism and gout! Yet there was my seal, and there is the empty bandbox. That's plain enough.

I say, I don't half like this. It's not right. There's something wrong about it, in my opinion. You needn't talk to me about supernatural manifestations, for I don't believe in them, not a little bit! Somebody must have tampered with the seal and stolen the skull. Sometimes, when I go out to work in the garden in summer, I leave my watch and chain on the table. Trehearn must have taken the seal then, and used it, for he would be quite sure that I should not come in for at least an hour.

If it was not Trehearn – oh, don't talk to me about the possibility that the thing has got out by itself! If it has, it must be somewhere about the house, in some out-of-the-way corner, waiting. We may come upon it anywhere, waiting for us, don't you know? – just waiting in the dark. Then it will scream at me; it will shriek at me in the dark, for it hates me, I tell you!

The bandbox is quite empty. We are not dreaming, either of us. There, I turn it upside down.

What's that? Something fell out as I turned it over. It's on the floor, it s near your feet. I know it is, and we must find it. Help me to find it, man. Have you got it? For God's sake, give it to me, quickly!

Lead! I knew it when I heard it fall. I knew it couldn't be anything else by the little thud it made on the hearthrug. So it was lead after all and Luke did it.

I feel a little bit shaken up – not exactly nervous, you know, but badly shaken up, that's the fact. Anybody would, I should think. After all, you cannot say that it's fear of the thing, for I went up and brought it down – at least, I believed I was bringing it down, and that's the same thing, and by George, rather than give in to such silly nonsense, I'll take the box upstairs again and put it back in its place. It's not that. It's the certainty that the poor little woman came to her end in that way, by my fault, because I told the story. That's what is so dreadful. Somehow, I had always hoped that I should never be quite sure of it, but there is no doubting it now. Look at that!

Look at it! That little lump of lead with no particular shape. Think of what it did, man! Doesn't it make you shiver? He gave her something to make her sleep, of course, but there must have been one moment of awful agony. Think of having boiling lead poured into your brain. Think of it. She was dead before she could scream, but only think of – oh! there it is again – it's just outside – I know it's just outside – I can't keep it out of my head! – oh! – oh!

You thought I had fainted? No, I wish I had, for it would have stopped sooner. It's all very well to say that it's only a noise, and that a noise never hurt anybody – you're as white as a shroud yourself. There's only one thing to be done, if we hope to close an eye tonight. We must find it and put it back into its bandbox and shut it up in the cupboard, where it likes to be I don't know how it got out, but it wants to get in again. That's why it screams so awfully tonight – it was never so bad as this – never since I first –

Bury it? Yes, if we can find it, we'll bury it, if it takes us all night. We'll bury it six feet deep and ram down the earth over it, so that it shall never get out again, and if it screams, we shall hardly hear it so deep down. Quick, we'll get the lantern and look for it. It cannot be far away; I'm sure it's just outside – it was coming in when I shut the window, I know it.

Yes, you're quite right. I'm losing my senses, and I must get hold of myself. Don't speak to me for a minute or two; I'll sit quite still and keep my eyes shut and repeat something I know. That's the best way.

"Add together the altitude, the latitude, and the polar distance, divide by two and subtract the altitude from the half-sum; then add the logarithm of the secant of the latitude, the cosecant of the polar distance, the cosine of the half-sum and the sine of the half-sum minus the altitude" – there! Don't say that I'm out of my senses, for my memory is all right, isn't it?

Of course, you may say that it's mechanical, and that we never forget the things we learned when we were boys and have used almost every day for a lifetime. But that's the very point. When a man is going crazy, it's the mechanical part of his mind that gets out of order and won't work right; he remembers things that never happened, or he sees things that aren't real, or he hears noises when there is perfect silence. That's not what is the matter with either of us, is it?

Come, we'll get the lantern and go round the house. It's not raining – only blowing like old boots, as we used to say. The lantern is in the cupboard under the stairs in the hall, and I always keep it trimmed in case of a wreck. No use to look for the thing? I don't see how you can say that. It was nonsense to talk of burying it, of course, for it doesn't want to be buried; it wants to go back into its bandbox and be taken upstairs, poor thing! Trehearn took it out, I know, and made the seal over again. Perhaps he took it to the churchyard, and he may have meant well. I dare say he thought that it would not scream any more if it were quietly laid in consecrated ground, near where it belongs. But it has come home. Yes, that's it. He's not half a bad fellow, Trehearn, and rather religiously inclined, I think. Does not that sound natural, and reasonable, and well meant? He supposed it screamed because it was not decently buried – with the rest. But he was wrong. How should he know that it screams at me because it hates me, and because it's my fault that there was that little lump of lead in it?

No use to look for it, anyhow? Nonsense! I tell you it wants to be found – Hark! what's that knocking? Do you hear it? Knock – knock – knock – three times, then a pause, and then again. It has a hollow sound, hasn't it? It has come home. I've heard that knock before. It wants to come in and be taken upstairs in its box. It's at the front door.

Will you come with me? We'll take it in. Yes, I own that I don't like to go alone and open the door. The thing will roll in and stop against my foot, just as it did before, and the light will go out. I'm a good deal shaken by finding that bit of lead, and, besides, my heart isn't quite right – too much strong tobacco, perhaps. Besides, I'm quite willing to own that I'm a bit nervous tonight, if I never was before in my life.

That's right, come along! I'll take the box with me, so as not to come back. Do you hear the knocking? It's not like any other knocking I ever heard. If you will hold this door open, I can find the lantern under the stairs by the light from this room without bringing the lamp into the hall – it would only go out.

The thing knows we are coming – hark! It's impatient to get in. Don't shut the door till the lantern is ready, whatever you do. There will be the usual trouble with the matches, I suppose – no, the first one, by Jove! I tell you it wants to get in, so there's no trouble. All right with that door now; shut it, please. Now come and hold the lantern, for it's blowing so hard outside that I shall have to use both hands. That's it, hold the light low. Do you hear the knocking still? Here goes – I'll open just enough with my foot against the bottom of the door – now!

Catch it! it's only the wind that blows it across the floor, that's all – there s half a hurricane outside, I tell you! Have you got it? The bandbox is on the table. One minute, and I'll have the bar up. There!

Why did you throw it into the box so roughly? It doesn't like that, you know.

What do you say? Bitten your hand? Nonsense, man! You did just what I did. You pressed the jaws together with your other hand and pinched yourself. Let me see. You don't mean to say you have drawn blood? You must have squeezed hard by Jove, for the skin is certainly torn. I'll give you some carbolic solution for it before we go to bed, for they say a scratch from a skull's tooth may go bad and give trouble.

Come inside again and let me see it by the lamp. I'll bring the bandbox – never mind the lantern, it may just as well burn in the hall for I shall need it presently when I go up the stairs. Yes, shut the door if you will; it makes it more cheerful and bright. Is your finger still bleeding? I'll get you the carbolic in an instant; just let me see the thing. Ugh! There's a drop of blood on the upper jaw. It's on the eyetooth. Ghastly, isn't it? When I saw it running along the floor of the hall, the strength almost went out of my hands, and I felt my knees bending, then I understood that it was the gale, driving it over the smooth boards. You don t blame me? No, I should think not! We were boys together, and we've seen a thing or two, and we may just as well own to each other that we were both in a beastly funk when it slid across the floor at you. No wonder you pinched your finger picking it up, after that, if I did the same thing out of sheer nervousness, in broad daylight, with the sun streaming in on me.

Strange that the jaw should stick to it so closely, isn't it? I suppose it's the dampness, for it shuts like a vice – I have wiped off the drop of blood, for it was not nice to look at. I'm not going to try to open the jaws, don't be afraid! I shall not play any tricks with the poor thing, but I'll just seal the box again, and we'll take it upstairs and put it away where it wants to be. The wax is on the writing-table by the window. Thank you. It will be long before I leave my seal lying about again, for Trehearn to use, I can tell you. Explain? I don't explain natural phenomena, but if you choose to think that Trehearn had hidden it somewhere in the bushes, and that the gale blew it to the house against the door, and made it knock, as if it wanted to be let in, you're not thinking the impossible, and I'm quite ready to agree with you.

Do you see that? You can swear that you've actually seen me seal it this time, in case anything of the kind should occur again. The wax fastens the strings to the lid, which cannot possibly be lifted, even enough to get in one finger. You're quite satisfied, aren't you? Yes. Besides, I shall lock the cupboard and keep the key in my pocket hereafter. Now we can take the lantern and go upstairs. Do you know? I'm very much inclined to agree with your theory that the wind blew it against the house. I'll go ahead, for I know the stairs; just hold the lantern near my feet as we go up. How the wind howls and whistles! Did you feel the sand on the floor under your shoes as we crossed the hall? Yes – this is the door of the best bedroom. Hold up the lantern, please. This side, by the head of the bed. I left the cupboard open when I got the box. Isn't it queer how the faint odour of women's dresses will hang about an old closet for years? This is the shelf. You've seen me set the box there, and now you see me turn the key and put it into my pocket. So that's done!

Goodnight. Are you sure you're quite comfortable? It's not much of a room, but I dare say you would as soon sleep here as upstairs tonight. If you want anything, sing out; there's only a lath and plaster partition between us. There's not so much wind on this side by half. There's the Hollands on the table, if you'll have one more nightcap. No? Well, do as you please. Goodnight again, and don't dream about that thing, if you can. The following paragraph appeared in the Penraddon News, 23rd November 1906:

MYSTERIOUS DEATH OF A RETIRED SEA CAPTAIN

The village of Tredcombe is much disturbed by the strange death of Captain Charles Braddock, and all sorts of impossible stories are circulating with regard to the circumstances, which certainly seem difficult of explanation. The retired captain, who had successfully commanded in his time the largest and fastest liners belonging to one of the principal transatlantic steamship companies, was found dead in his bed on Tuesday morning in his own cottage, a quarter of a mile from the village. An examination was made at once by the local practitioner, which revealed the horrible fact that the deceased had been bitten in the throat by a human assailant, with such amazing force as to crush the windpipe and cause death. The marks of the teeth of both jaws were so plainly visible on the skin that they could be counted, but the perpetrator of the deed had evidently lost the two lower middle incisors. It is hoped that this peculiarity may help to identify the murderer, who can only be a dangerous escaped maniac. The deceased, though over sixty-five years of age, is said to have been a hale man of considerable physical strength, and it is remarkable that no signs of any struggle were visible in the room, nor could it be ascertained how the murderer had entered the house. Warning has been sent to all the insane asylums in the United Kingdom, but as yet no information has been received regarding the escape of any dangerous patient.

The coroner's Jury returned the somewhat singular verdict that Captain Braddock came to his death "by the hands or teeth of some person unknown". The local surgeon is said to have expressed privately the opinion that the maniac is a woman, a view he deduces from the small size of the jaws, as shown by the marks of the teeth. The whole affair is shrouded in mystery. Captain Braddock was a widower, and lived alone. He leaves no children.

The Child's Story

Charles Dickens

ONCE UPON A TIME, a good many years ago, there was a traveller, and he set out upon a journey. It was a magic journey, and was to seem very long when he began it, and very short when he got half way through.

He travelled along a rather dark path for some little time, without meeting anything, until at last he came to a beautiful child. So he said to the child, "What do you do here?" And the child said, "I am always at play. Come and play with me!"

So, he played with that child, the whole day long, and they were very merry. The sky was so blue, the sun was so bright, the water was so sparkling, the leaves were so green, the flowers were so lovely, and they heard such singing-birds and saw so many butteries, that everything was beautiful. This was in fine weather. When it rained, they loved to watch the falling drops, and to smell the fresh scents. When it blew, it was delightful to listen to the wind, and fancy what it said, as it came rushing from its home – where was that, they wondered! – whistling and howling, driving the clouds before it, bending the trees, rumbling in the chimneys, shaking the house, and making the sea roar in fury. But, when it snowed, that was best of all; for, they liked nothing so well as to look up at the white flakes falling fast and thick, like down from the breasts of millions of white birds; and to see how smooth and deep the drift was; and to listen to the hush upon the paths and roads.

They had plenty of the finest toys in the world, and the most astonishing picture-books: all about scimitars and slippers and turbans, and dwarfs and giants and genii and fairies, and blue-beards and bean-stalks and riches and caverns and forests and Valentines and Orsons: and all new and all true.

But, one day, of a sudden, the traveller lost the child. He called to him over and over again, but got no answer. So, he went upon his road, and went on for a little while without meeting anything, until at last he came to a handsome boy. So, he said to the boy, "What do you do here?" And the boy said, "I am always learning. Come and learn with me."

So he learned with that boy about Jupiter and Juno, and the Greeks and the Romans, and I don't know what, and learned more than I could tell – or he either, for he soon forgot a great deal of it. But, they were not always learning; they had the merriest games that ever were played. They rowed upon the river in summer, and skated on the ice in winter; they were active afoot, and active on horseback; at cricket, and all games at ball; at prisoner's base, hare and hounds, follow my leader, and more sports than I can think of; nobody could beat them. They had holidays too, and Twelfth cakes, and parties where they danced till midnight, and real Theatres where they saw palaces of real gold and silver rise out of the real earth, and saw all the wonders of the world at once. As to friends, they had such dear friends and so many of them, that I want the time to reckon them up. They were all young, like the handsome boy, and were never to be strange to one another all their lives through.

Still, one day, in the midst of all these pleasures, the traveller lost the boy as he had lost the child, and, after calling to him in vain, went on upon his journey. So he went on for a little while without seeing anything, until at last he came to a young man. So, he said to the young man, "What do you do here?" And the young man said, "I am always in love. Come and love with me."

So, he went away with that young man, and presently they came to one of the prettiest girls that ever was seen – just like Fanny in the corner there – and she had eyes like Fanny, and hair like Fanny, and dimples like Fanny's, and she laughed and coloured just as Fanny does while I am talking about her. So, the young man fell in love directly – just as Somebody I won't mention, the first time he came here, did with Fanny. Well! he was teased sometimes – just as Somebody used to be by Fanny; and they quarrelled sometimes – just as Somebody and Fanny used to quarrel; and they made it up, and sat in the dark, and wrote letters every day, and never were happy asunder, and were always looking out for one another and pretending not to, and were engaged at Christmas-time, and sat close to one another by the fire, and were going to be married very soon – all exactly like Somebody I won't mention, and Fanny!

But, the traveller lost them one day, as he had lost the rest of his friends, and, after calling to them to come back, which they never did, went on upon his journey. So, he went on for a little while without seeing anything, until at last he came to a middle-aged gentleman. So, he said to the gentleman, "What are you doing here?" And his answer was, "I am always busy. Come and be busy with me!"

So, he began to be very busy with that gentleman, and they went on through the wood together. The whole journey was through a wood, only it had been open and green at first, like a wood in spring; and now began to be thick and dark, like a wood in summer; some of the little trees that had come out earliest, were even turning brown. The gentleman was not alone, but had a lady of about the same age with him, who was his Wife; and they had children, who were with them too. So, they all went on together through the wood, cutting down the trees, and making a path through the branches and the fallen leaves, and carrying burdens, and working hard.

Sometimes, they came to a long green avenue that opened into deeper woods. Then they would hear a very little, distant voice crying, "Father, father, I am another child! Stop for me!" And presently they would see a very little figure, growing larger as it came along, running to join them. When it came up, they all crowded round it, and kissed and welcomed it; and then they all went on together.

Sometimes, they came to several avenues at once, and then they all stood still, and one of the children said, "Father, I am going to sea," and another said, "Father, I am going to India," and another, "Father, I am going to seek my fortune where I can," and another, "Father, I am going to Heaven!" So, with many tears at parting, they went, solitary, down those avenues, each child upon its way; and the child who went to Heaven, rose into the golden air and vanished.

Whenever these partings happened, the traveller looked at the gentleman, and saw him glance up at the sky above the trees, where the day was beginning to decline, and the sunset to come on. He saw, too, that his hair was turning grey. But, they never could rest long, for they had their journey to perform, and it was necessary for them to be always busy.

At last, there had been so many partings that there were no children left, and only the traveller, the gentleman, and the lady, went upon their way in company. And now the wood was yellow; and now brown; and the leaves, even of the forest trees, began to fall.

So, they came to an avenue that was darker than the rest, and were pressing forward on their journey without looking down it when the lady stopped.

"My husband," said the lady. "I am called."

They listened, and they heard a voice a long way down the avenue, say, "Mother, mother!"

It was the voice of the first child who had said, "I am going to Heaven!" and the father said, "I pray not yet. The sunset is very near. I pray not yet!"

But, the voice cried, "Mother, mother!" without minding him, though his hair was now quite white, and tears were on his face.

Then, the mother, who was already drawn into the shade of the dark avenue and moving away with her arms still round his neck, kissed him, and said, "My dearest, I am summoned, and I go!" And she was gone. And the traveller and he were left alone together.

And they went on and on together, until they came to very near the end of the wood: so near, that they could see the sunset shining red before them through the trees.

Yet, once more, while he broke his way among the branches, the traveller lost his friend. He called and called, but there was no reply, and when he passed out of the wood, and saw the peaceful sun going down upon a wide purple prospect, he came to an old man sitting on a fallen tree. So, he said to the old man, "What do you do here?" And the old man said with a calm smile, "I am always remembering. Come and remember with me!"

So the traveller sat down by the side of that old man, face to face with the serene sunset; and all his friends came softly back and stood around him. The beautiful child, the handsome boy, the young man in love, the father, mother, and children: every one of them was there, and he had lost nothing. So, he loved them all, and was kind and forbearing with them all, and was always pleased to watch them all, and they all honoured and loved him. And I think the traveller must be yourself, dear Grandfather, because this what you do to us, and what we do to you.

The Leather Funnel

Arthur Conan Doyle

MY FRIEND, Lionel Dacre, lived in the Avenue de Wagram, Paris. His house was that small one, with the iron railings and grass plot in front of it, on the left-hand side as you pass down from the Arc de Triomphe. I fancy that it had been there long before the avenue was constructed, for the grey tiles were stained with lichens, and the walls were mildewed and discoloured with age. It looked a small house from the street, five windows in front, if I remember right, but it deepened into a single long chamber at the back. It was here that Dacre had that singular library of occult literature, and the fantastic curiosities which served as a hobby for himself, and an amusement for his friends.

A wealthy man of refined and eccentric tastes, he had spent much of his life and fortune in gathering together what was said to be a unique private collection of Talmudic, cabalistic, and magical works, many of them of great rarity and value. His tastes leaned toward the marvellous and the monstrous, and I have heard that his experiments in the direction of the unknown have passed all the bounds of civilization and of decorum. To his English friends he never alluded to such matters, and took the tone of the student and virtuoso; but a Frenchman whose tastes were of the same nature has assured me that the worst excesses of the black mass have been perpetrated in that large and lofty hall, which is lined with the shelves of his books, and the cases of his museum.

Dacre's appearance was enough to show that his deep interest in these psychic matters was intellectual rather than spiritual. There was no trace of asceticism upon his heavy face, but there was much mental force in his huge, dome-like skull, which curved upward from amongst his thinning locks, like a snowpeak above its fringe of fir trees. His knowledge was greater than his wisdom, and his powers were far superior to his character. The small bright eyes, buried deeply in his fleshy face, twinkled with intelligence and an unabated curiosity of life, but they were the eyes of a sensualist and an egotist. Enough of the man, for he is dead now, poor devil, dead at the very time that he had made sure that he had at last discovered the elixir of life. It is not with his complex character that I have to deal, but with the very strange and inexplicable incident which had its rise in my visit to him in the early spring of the year '82.

I had known Dacre in England, for my researches in the Assyrian Room of the British Museum had been conducted at the time when he was endeavouring to establish a mystic and esoteric meaning in the Babylonian tablets, and this community of interests had brought us together. Chance remarks had led to daily conversation, and that to something verging upon friendship. I had promised him that on my next visit to Paris I would call upon him. At the time when I was able to fulfil my compact I was living in a cottage at Fontainebleau, and as the evening trains were inconvenient, he asked me to spend the night in his house.

"I have only that one spare couch," said he, pointing to a broad sofa in his large salon; "I hope that you will manage to be comfortable there."

It was a singular bedroom, with its high walls of brown volumes, but there could be no more agreeable furniture to a bookworm like myself, and there is no scent so pleasant to my nostrils as that faint, subtle reek which comes from an ancient book. I assured him that I could desire no more charming chamber, and no more congenial surroundings.

"If the fittings are neither convenient nor conventional, they are at least costly," said he, looking round at his shelves. "I have expended nearly a quarter of a million of money upon these objects which surround you. Books, weapons, gems, carvings, tapestries, images – there is hardly a thing here which has not its history, and it is generally one worth telling."

He was seated as he spoke at one side of the open fireplace, and I at the other. His reading-table was on his right, and the strong lamp above it ringed it with a very vivid circle of golden light. A half-rolled palimpsest lay in the centre, and around it were many quaint articles of bric-a-brac. One of these was a large funnel, such as is used for filling wine casks. It appeared to be made of black wood, and to be rimmed with discoloured brass.

"That is a curious thing," I remarked. "What is the history of that?"

"Ah!" said he, "it is the very question which I have had occasion to ask myself. I would give a good deal to know. Take it in your hands and examine it."

I did so, and found that what I had imagined to be wood was in reality leather, though age had dried it into an extreme hardness. It was a large funnel, and might hold a quart when full. The brass rim encircled the wide end, but the narrow was also tipped with metal.

"What do you make of it?" asked Dacre.

"I should imagine that it belonged to some vintner or maltster in the Middle Ages," said I. "I have seen in England leather drinking flagons of the seventeenth century – 'black jacks' as they were called – which were of the same colour and hardness as this filler."

"I dare say the date would be about the same," said Dacre, "and, no doubt, also, it was used for filling a vessel with liquid. If my suspicions are correct, however, it was a queer vintner who used it, and a very singular cask which was filled. Do you observe nothing strange at the spout end of the funnel."

As I held it to the light I observed that at a spot some five inches above the brass tip the narrow neck of the leather funnel was all haggled and scored, as if someone had notched it round with a blunt knife. Only at that point was there any roughening of the dead black surface.

"Someone has tried to cut off the neck."

"Would you call it a cut?"

"It is torn and lacerated. It must have taken some strength to leave these marks on such tough material, whatever the instrument may have been. But what do you think of it? I can tell that you know more than you say."

Dacre smiled, and his little eyes twinkled with knowledge.

"Have you included the psychology of dreams among your learned studies?" he asked.

"I did not even know that there was such a psychology."

"My dear sir, that shelf above the gem case is filled with volumes, from Albertus Magnus onward, which deal with no other subject. It is a science in itself."

"A science of charlatans "

"The charlatan is always the pioneer. From the astrologer came the astronomer, from the alchemist the chemist, from the mesmerist the experimental psychologist. The quack of yesterday is the professor of tomorrow. Even such subtle and elusive things as dreams will in time be reduced to system and order. When that time comes the researches of our friends on the bookshelf yonder will no longer be the amusement of the mystic, but the foundations of a science."

"Supposing that is so, what has the science of dreams to do with a large, black, brass-rimmed funnel?"

"I will tell you. You know that I have an agent who is always on the look-out for rarities and curiosities for my collection. Some days ago he heard of a dealer upon one of the Quais who had acquired some old rubbish found in a cupboard in an ancient house at the back of the Rue Mathurin, in the Quartier Latin. The dining-room of this old house is decorated with a coat of arms, chevrons, and bars rouge upon a field argent, which prove, upon inquiry, to be the shield of Nicholas de la Reynie, a high official of King Louis XIV. There can be no doubt that the other articles in the cupboard date back to the early days of that king. The inference is, therefore, that they were all the property of this Nicholas de la Reynie, who was, as I understand, the gentleman specially concerned with the maintenance and execution of the Draconic laws of that epoch."

"What then?"

"I would ask you now to take the funnel into your hands once more and to examine the upper brass rim. Can you make out any lettering upon it?"

There were certainly some scratches upon it, almost obliterated by time. The general effect was of several letters, the last of which bore some resemblance to a B.

"You make it a B?"

"Yes, I do."

"So do I. In fact, I have no doubt whatever that it is a B."

"But the nobleman you mentioned would have had R for his initial."

"Exactly! That's the beauty of it. He owned this curious object, and yet he had someone else's initials upon it. Why did he do this?"

"I can't imagine; can you?"

"Well, I might, perhaps, guess. Do you observe something drawn a little farther along the rim?"

"I should say it was a crown."

"It is undoubtedly a crown; but if you examine it in a good light, you will convince yourself that it is not an ordinary crown. It is a heraldic crown – a badge of rank, and it consists of an alternation of four pearls and strawberry leaves, the proper badge of a marquis. We may infer, therefore, that the person whose initials end in B was entitled to wear that coronet."

"Then this common leather filler belonged to a marquis?"

Dacre gave a peculiar smile.

"Or to some member of the family of a marquis," said he. "So much we have clearly gathered from this engraved rim."

"But what has all this to do with dreams?" I do not know whether it was from a look upon Dacre's face, or from some subtle suggestion in his manner, but a feeling of repulsion, of unreasoning horror, came upon me as I looked at the gnarled old lump of leather.

"I have more than once received important information through my dreams," said my companion in the didactic manner which he loved to affect. "I make it a rule now when I am in doubt upon any material point to place the article in question beside me as I sleep, and to hope for some enlightenment. The process does not appear to me to be very obscure, though it has not yet received the blessing of orthodox science. According to my theory, any object which has been intimately associated with any supreme paroxysm of human emotion, whether it be joy or pain, will retain a certain atmosphere or association which it is capable of communicating to a sensitive mind. By a sensitive mind I do not mean an abnormal one, but such a trained and educated mind as you or I possess."

"You mean, for example, that if I slept beside that old sword upon the wall, I might dream of some bloody incident in which that very sword took part?"

"An excellent example, for, as a matter of fact, that sword was used in that fashion by me, and I saw in my sleep the death of its owner, who perished in a brisk skirmish, which I have been unable to identify, but which occurred at the time of the wars of the Frondists. If you think of it, some of our popular observances show that the fact has already been recognized by our ancestors, although we, in our wisdom, have classed it among superstitions."

"For example?"

"Well, the placing of the bride's cake beneath the pillow in order that the sleeper may have pleasant dreams. That is one of several instances which you will find set forth in a small brochure which I am myself writing upon the subject. But to come back to the point, I slept one night with this funnel beside me, and I had a dream which certainly throws a curious light upon its use and origin."

"What did you dream?"

"I dreamed – " He paused, and an intent look of interest came over his massive face. "By Jove, that's well thought of," said he. "This really will be an exceedingly interesting experiment. You are yourself a psychic subject – with nerves which respond readily to any impression."

"I have never tested myself in that direction."

"Then we shall test you tonight. Might I ask you as a very great favour, when you occupy that couch tonight, to sleep with this old funnel placed by the side of your pillow?"

The request seemed to me a grotesque one; but I have myself, in my complex nature, a hunger after all which is bizarre and fantastic. I had not the faintest belief in Dacre's theory, nor any hopes for success in such an experiment; yet it amused me that the experiment should be made. Dacre, with great gravity, drew a small stand to the head of my settee, and placed the funnel upon it. Then, after a short conversation, he wished me good night and left me.

I sat for some little time smoking by the smouldering fire, and turning over in my mind the curious incident which had occurred, and the strange experience which might lie before me. Sceptical as I was, there was something impressive in the assurance of Dacre's manner, and my extraordinary surroundings, the huge room with the strange and often sinister objects which were hung round it, struck solemnity into my soul. Finally I undressed, and turning out the lamp, I lay down. After long tossing I fell asleep. Let me try to describe as accurately as I can the scene which came to me in my dreams. It stands out now in my memory more clearly than anything which I have seen with my waking eyes. There was a room which bore the appearance of a vault. Four spandrels from the corners ran up to join a sharp, cup-shaped roof. The architecture was rough, but very strong. It was evidently part of a great building.

Three men in black, with curious, top-heavy, black velvet hats, sat in a line upon a red-carpeted dais. Their faces were very solemn and sad. On the left stood two long-gowned men with portfolios in their hands, which seemed to be stuffed with papers. Upon the right, looking toward me, was a small woman with blonde hair and singular, light-blue eyes – the eyes of a child. She was past her first youth, but could not yet be called middle-aged.

Her figure was inclined to stoutness and her bearing was proud and confident. Her face was pale, but serene. It was a curious face, comely and yet feline, with a subtle suggestion of cruelty about the straight, strong little mouth and chubby jaw. She was draped in some sort of loose, white gown. Beside her stood a thin, eager priest, who whispered in her ear, and continually raised a crucifix before her eyes. She turned her head and looked fixedly past the crucifix at the three men in black, who were, I felt, her judges.

As I gazed the three men stood up and said something, but I could distinguish no words, though I was aware that it was the central one who was speaking. They then swept out of the room, followed by the two men with the papers. At the same instant several rough-looking fellows in stout jerkins came bustling in and removed first the red carpet, and then the boards which formed the dais, so as to entirely clear the room. When this screen was removed I saw some singular articles of furniture behind it. One looked like a bed with wooden rollers at each end, and a winch handle to regulate its length. Another was a wooden horse. There were several other curious objects, and a number of swinging cords which played over pulleys. It was not unlike a modern gymnasium.

When the room had been cleared there appeared a new figure upon the scene. This was a tall, thin person clad in black, with a gaunt and austere face. The aspect of the man made me shudder. His clothes were all shining with grease and mottled with stains. He bore himself with a slow and impressive dignity, as if he took command of all things from the instant of his entrance. In spite of his rude appearance and sordid dress, it was now his business, his room, his to command. He carried a coil of light ropes over his left forearm. The lady looked him up and down with a searching glance, but her expression was unchanged. It was confident – even defiant. But it was very different with the priest. His face was ghastly white, and I saw the moisture glisten and run on his high, sloping forehead. He threw up his hands in prayer and he stooped continually to mutter frantic words in the lady's ear.

The man in black now advanced, and taking one of the cords from his left arm, he bound the woman's hands together. She held them meekly toward him as he did so. Then he took her arm with a rough grip and led her toward the wooden horse, which was little higher than her waist. On to this she was lifted and laid, with her back upon it, and her face to the ceiling, while the priest, quivering with horror, had rushed out of the room. The woman's lips were moving rapidly, and though I could hear nothing I knew that she was praying. Her feet hung down on either side of the horse, and I saw that the rough varlets in attendance had fastened cords to her ankles and secured the other ends to iron rings in the stone floor.

My heart sank within me as I saw these ominous preparations, and yet I was held by the fascination of horror, and I could not take my eyes from the strange spectacle. A man had entered the room with a bucket of water in either hand. Another followed with a third bucket. They were laid beside the wooden horse. The second man had a wooden dipper – a bowl with a straight handle – in his other hand. This he gave to the man in black. At the same moment one of the varlets approached with a dark object in his hand, which even in my dream filled me with a vague feeling of familiarity. It was a leather filler. With horrible energy he thrust it – but I could stand no more. My hair stood on end with horror. I writhed, I struggled, I broke through the bonds of sleep, and I burst with a shriek into my own life, and found myself lying shivering with terror in the huge library, with the moonlight flooding through the window and throwing strange silver and black traceries upon the opposite wall. Oh, what a blessed relief to feel that I was back in the nineteenth century – back out of that mediaeval vault into a world where men had human hearts within their bosoms. I sat up on my couch, trembling in every limb, my mind divided between thankfulness and horror. To think that such things were ever done – that they could be done without God striking the villains dead. Was it all a fantasy, or did it really stand for something which had happened in the black, cruel days of the world's history? I sank my throbbing head upon my shaking hands. And then, suddenly, my heart seemed to stand still in my bosom, and I could not even scream, so great was my terror. Something was advancing toward me through the darkness of the room.

It is a horror coming upon a horror which breaks a man's spirit. I could not reason, I could not pray; I could only sit like a frozen image, and glare at the dark figure which was coming down the great room. And then it moved out into the white lane of moonlight, and I breathed once more. It was Dacre, and his face showed that he was as frightened as myself.

"Was that you? For God's sake what's the matter?" he asked in a husky voice.

"Oh, Dacre, I am glad to see you! I have been down into hell. It was dreadful."

"Then it was you who screamed?"

"I dare say it was."

"It rang through the house. The servants are all terrified." He struck a match and lit the lamp. "I think we may get the fire to burn up again," he added, throwing some logs upon the embers. "Good God, my dear chap, how white you are! You look as if you had seen a ghost."

"So I have – several ghosts."

"The leather funnel has acted, then?"

"I wouldn't sleep near the infernal thing again for all the money you could offer me."

Dacre chuckled.

"I expected that you would have a lively night of it," said he. "You took it out of me in return, for that scream of yours wasn't a very pleasant sound at two in the morning. I suppose from what you say that you have seen the whole dreadful business."

"What dreadful business?"

"The torture of the water – the 'Extraordinary Question,' as it was called in the genial days of 'Le Roi Soleil.' Did you stand it out to the end?"

"No, thank God, I awoke before it really began."

"Ah! it is just as well for you. I held out till the third bucket. Well, it is an old story, and they are all in their graves now, anyhow, so what does it matter how they got there? I suppose that you have no idea what it was that you have seen?"

"The torture of some criminal. She must have been a terrible malefactor indeed if her crimes are in proportion to her penalty."

"Well, we have that small consolation," said Dacre, wrapping his dressing-gown round him and crouching closer to the fire. "They were in proportion to her penalty. That is to say, if I am correct in the lady's identity."

"How could you possibly know her identity?"

For answer Dacre took down an old vellum-covered volume from the shelf.

"Just listen to this," said he; "it is in the French of the seventeenth century, but I will give a rough translation as I go. You will judge for yourself whether I have solved the riddle or not.

"*The prisoner was brought before the Grand Chambers and Tournelles of Parliament, sitting as a court of justice, charged with the murder of Master*

Dreux d'Aubray, her father, and of her two brothers, MM. d'Aubray, one being civil lieutenant, and the other a counsellor of Parliament. In person it seemed hard to believe that she had really done such wicked deeds, for she was of a mild appearance, and of short stature, with a fair skin and blue eyes. Yet the Court, having found her guilty, condemned her to the ordinary and to the extraordinary question in order that she might be forced to name her accomplices, after which she should be carried in a cart to the Place de Greve, there to have her head cut off, her body being afterwards burned and her ashes scattered to the winds.'

"The date of this entry is July 16, 1676."

"It is interesting," said I, "but not convincing. How do you prove the two women to be the same?"

"I am coming to that. The narrative goes on to tell of the woman's behaviour when questioned. 'When the executioner approached her she recognized him by the cords which he held in his hands, and she at once held out her own hands to him, looking at him from head to foot without uttering a word.' How's that?"

"Yes, it was so."

"'She gazed without wincing upon the wooden horse and rings which had twisted so many limbs and caused so many shrieks of agony. When her eyes fell upon the three pails of water, which were all ready for her, she said with a smile, "All that water must have been brought here for the purpose of drowning me, Monsieur. You have no idea, I trust, of making a person of my small stature swallow it all."' Shall I read the details of the torture?"

"No, for Heaven's sake, don't."

"Here is a sentence which must surely show you that what is here recorded is the very scene which you have gazed upon tonight: 'The good Abbe Pirot, unable to contemplate the agonies which were suffered by his penitent, had hurried from the room.' Does that convince you?"

"It does entirely. There can be no question that it is indeed the same event. But who, then, is this lady whose appearance was so attractive and whose end was so horrible?"

For answer Dacre came across to me, and placed the small lamp upon the table which stood by my bed. Lifting up the ill-omened filler, he turned the brass rim so that the light fell full upon it. Seen in this way the engraving seemed clearer than on the night before.

"We have already agreed that this is the badge of a marquis or of a marquise," said he. "We have also settled that the last letter is B."

"It is undoubtedly so."

"I now suggest to you that the other letters from left to right are, M, M, a small d, A, a small d, and then the final B."

"Yes, I am sure that you are right. I can make out the two small d's quite plainly."

"What I have read to you tonight," said Dacre, "is the official record of the trial of Marie Madeleine d'Aubray, Marquise de Brinvilliers, one of the most famous poisoners and murderers of all time."

I sat in silence, overwhelmed at the extraordinary nature of the incident, and at the completeness of the proof with which Dacre had exposed its real meaning. In a vague way I remembered some details of the woman's career, her unbridled debauchery, the cold-blooded and protracted torture of her sick father, the murder of her brothers for motives of petty gain. I recollected also that the bravery of her end had done something to atone for the horror of her life, and that all Paris had sympathized with her last moments, and blessed her as a martyr within a few days of the time when they had cursed her as a murderess. One objection, and one only, occurred to my mind.

"How came her initials and her badge of rank upon the filler? Surely they did not carry their mediaeval homage to the nobility to the point of decorating instruments of torture with their titles?"

"I was puzzled with the same point," said Dacre, "but it admits of a simple explanation. The case excited extraordinary interest at the time, and nothing could be more natural than that La Reynie, the head of the police, should retain this filler as a grim souvenir. It was not often that a marchioness of France underwent the extraordinary question. That he should engrave her initials upon it for the information of others was surely a very ordinary proceeding upon his part."

"And this?" I asked, pointing to the marks upon the leather neck.

"She was a cruel tigress," said Dacre, as he turned away. "I think it is evident that like other tigresses her teeth were both strong and sharp."

In Search of a New Wilhelm

John H. Dromey

IMAGINE a hyperactive cricket on steroids frenetically rubbing its wings together to the polyphonous counterpoint accompaniment of a handful of fingernails scratching a chalkboard. The resulting atonal musical rendition could be likened to a soothing lullaby when compared to the dissonant sounds that were emanating from the walls of a cramped apartment and assaulting the ears of the two occupants.

One of them – an industrious young man, who had been setting up an array of sophisticated recording devices – took a brief time out from what he was doing.

He raised his voice to comment, "That is unquestionably the most irritating sound I've ever heard in my life. What do you think?"

The heavyset, middle-aged man in an overstuffed easy chair was slow to respond. "I agree, but what's your point?"

"I think you know," the young man said. He pulled a remote control device out of his pocket and pressed a button. The stridulation ceased abruptly. "That's better," he said. "Now we can have a quiet talk."

"Who are you?" the man in the chair asked.

"I'm Max. We talked on the phone earlier when I set up this appointment. Is it all right for me to call you Hank, or do you prefer Henry, or maybe Mr. Simpson?"

"Take your pick. What is it you do for a living, Max?"

"I'm a psychic detective, Hank. I investigate reports of unexplained phenomena. The truth of the matter is my fancy title doesn't really apply to most of the work I do. There's usually a simple, down-to-earth explanation for even the most bizarre situations."

"Why did you bring all those gadgets in here? I didn't ask for your services."

"You didn't need to, Hank. One of your tenants did. Actually, two of them did, but that's getting ahead of the story."

"You mean those peculiar sounds we heard earlier made them think my places are haunted. Who snitched?"

"Their names aren't relevant. You know who I'm talking about anyway, since you have a finite number of rental properties, and whether or not you have enough real estate holdings to qualify for the title slumlord, you certainly act like one. It must be a challenging profession in a town like this where the laws favor the renters. I understand it's next to impossible to get someone evicted."

"Tell me about it. All I get are deadbeats and chronic complainers."

"Sometimes you get what you deserve," Max said. "I'd have to be desperate to pay good money to live in a dump like this."

"You don't plan to rent the place? Why are we here then?" Hank asked.

"I'm here as an observer to see you get your comeuppance. Perhaps I should warn you, you're not going to like it."

"What's to stop me from leaving right now?"

"Go ahead."

Hank remained motionless. "I can't move," he said. "What did you do to me?"

Max shrugged his shoulders. "Me? Nothing."

"Am I your prisoner?"

"Not mine. I haven't done anything to you, Hank, and I won't. I'm here to watch." Max moved over to a camera mounted on a tripod and looked at the viewing screen. "Let's see now. What's wrong with this picture? Oh, I know. You're overdressed." He walked over to the chair, ripped open Hank's shirt, and then pulled up the man's T-shirt to expose his ample midriff.

"You just ruined my shirt," Hank said, "after telling me you weren't going to do anything to me. You lied."

"No, I didn't. I caused a little damage to your shirt, sure enough, but that was for your next visitor's benefit, not yours."

"What are you talking about?"

"You've already had one visitor tonight, Hank, not counting me. The reason you can't move is that you've been injected with insect venom. It's a powerful nerve agent, similar to curare but with perhaps one important distinction: its full effect doesn't rise above the brain stem. I'm guessing that's why you're still able to communicate. Apparently there's a mild, analgesic quality to the injected poison that induces a feeling of euphoria and keeps the victim calm."

"You're talking nonsense," Hank said.

"Part of what I've said was sheer speculation on my part, I admit, but in addition to that, I did my homework. I talked to a shaman."

"A what?"

"A medicine man. According to his tribe's oral tradition, about a millennium ago, certainly in pre-Columbian times, there was a highly unusual event one autumn evening. Tribal scouts located a large buffalo herd mid-afternoon, but it was nearly sundown by the time the main hunting party arrived. They decided to wait and watch until morning. Sometime during the night the hunters were disturbed by the strident bellowing of several bulls, a sound unlike anything they'd ever heard before. The next morning, the bulk of the herd had moved on, but there were several adult males left behind – their motionless bodies sprawled on the ground.

Although buffalo wallows by their very nature have exposed earth in them, the dusty soil is usually relatively smooth. Something, however, other than pawing hoofs had churned up the nearby terrain. By looking into the eyes of the fallen buffalo, the scouts discovered that the abandoned beasts were still alive. After that, the hunters kept their distance. Fearing the creatures were ill and that the meat might be contaminated, the hunting party went off in pursuit of the main herd.

Several moons later, when members of the tribe passed through those same hunting grounds again, they found hollow carcasses with the outer skin intact, except for a gaping breach in the abdomen. Despite the passage of time, there was no indication that the site had been visited by buzzards, crows, or any of the other carrion eaters common to the region. What had killed the buffalo and consumed them from the inside? The shaman didn't know. The event was an unsolved mystery that had become part of the tribe's unwritten folklore."

Hank had a question. "So, where has this primordial figment of your imagination been for the last thousand years, or so, and why did it disappear for so long?"

"Who knows? Maybe the creepy-crawly creatures were too successful in their reproductive efforts and ultimately were responsible for the disappearance of the dinosaurs. In order to avoid extinction themselves, the parasites had to downsize their prey and go into extended periods of underground hibernation, similar to the seventeen-year locust, or cicadas, or whatever you call them, but with a much longer cycle between one emergence and the next."

The landlord was still not convinced. "It seems to me you took that medicine man's tidbit of information and embellished it with outlandish details."

Max shook his head. "I simply added a bit of anecdotal knowledge to what I already knew."

"Which is not much, I'm guessing," Hank said.

"You might be surprised by what I've learned. I know, for example, precisely where you got your soundtrack."

"How could you?"

"Your tenant on Maple Street called me a few days ago and had me listen to that irritating noise over the phone. He said he'd called you first, but had got no satisfaction. Evidently, you recorded your tenant's call. That was the source of the playback you used to drive out the renter from this place, but not before he'd lodged a complaint with me. With his permission, I searched the premises, and I located the hidden amplifier and speakers you'd installed. I bought a compatible remote control device, and then I invited you over to have a chat."

Hank was still frozen in place. "You did more than that," he said. "We've talked. Now, I'd like for you to pack up your gear and leave. You don't look like a cold-blooded killer to me. I'd ask you to call an ambulance, but I feel fine. I'll just have to wait for the effects of the drug you shot me with to wear off."

"You're deluding yourself, Hank. The crucial question now is: are you as healthy as a buffalo? If you are, your visitors will likely proceed to phase two."

"You're making all of this up as you go along in an attempt to scare me, aren't you?"

"No," Max said. "That last part is based on firsthand observation. There's an extended delay between the initial injection and the follow-up."

"What makes you think that?"

"I saw what happened to your Maple Street tenant. He told me he had no intention of breaking his lease, and he refused to move out even temporarily. One day, his phone calls to me became more and more frequent, and his pleas for my help increasingly desperate. I was out of town at the time, communicating with a cell phone, but I assured him I'd talk to him in person as soon as I returned home. He kept calling anyway. At one point, I began to suspect the incessant chittering sound – which seemed to increase in volume with each call he made – somehow had affected his ability to think clearly.

Despite that, he finally convinced me to cut short my trip and go to see him as soon as possible, but I got there too late. The man told me he'd been bitten, or stung, while I was in transit. The poor fellow was already immobilized from the neck down by the venom. Even though I could plainly see for myself that – with the exception of his shallow breathing – his torso and extremities were deathly still, I doubted his story at first, simply because he sounded so calm and unconcerned about his predicament as he recounted the details. I had only a couple of minutes to talk to him before a female of the species showed up. She was large and her carapace was armor-plated like an armadillo. There was nothing I could do for the man."

"If your tale gets any taller, you'll force me to remodel this place with higher ceilings." A high-pitched chirping sound punctuated Hank's facetious comment. "Haven't you annoyed me enough, Max? Why did you turn that insect sound on again?"

"I didn't."

"Liar!"

"Listen carefully," Max said. "What you recorded was a calling signal sent out by a drone to announce the discovery of a suitable host. The sound we're hearing now has a slightly different pitch and cadence to it. I think it's a courting call. If so, that means the queen is nearby. You might have overlooked the tiny drone earlier, but her royal majesty is large enough to get your full attention."

"How large?"

"About the size of a large cat or a small dog."

"If she's that big, how will she get into the house?"

"Through the pet door you installed so you could introduce an occasional raccoon into the house in your ongoing efforts to maintain a high turnover rate among your renters. I'll bet you've never returned a security deposit in your life."

"If all you say is true, why didn't a female show up at this house earlier and attack Smitty?"

"He's not her type. Neither am I. We're both too skinny. You on the other hand...." Max left the sentence unfinished.

"I'm getting tired of this harassment," Max said. "How much are those other guys paying you? I'll double your fee to leave me alone."

"My other clients aren't paying me anything. I'm working pro bono. With your offer on the table, though, I now have a choice of double or nothing. I'll take nothing, but that doesn't mean I won't be compensated later on. That reminds me, I need to get a model release from you."

"I won't sign it. In fact, I can't. You've seen to that."

"You're wrong on both counts," Max said. "I brought an ink pad. Are you right-handed or left?"

Hank declined to answer.

"Why don't I just get your thumb print from the hand that's closer to me?"

He did.

"What next?" Hank asked.

"Now, we wait."

"For what?"

"I'm not supposed to tell you," Max said.

"Why not?"

"I was given a stern warning by a couple of suits who work for an agency, which – according to them – is so secret they don't even carry credentials."

"What made you think they were legit?"

"They weren't alone. They were accompanied by a guy from Homeland Security and representatives from a couple of intelligence agencies with acronyms you'd most likely recognize."

"What happened to the Maple Street tenant?" Hank asked.

"A hazmat team from the Center for Disease Control took him away somewhere."

"Wait a minute. If you're sworn to secrecy, there's no way you can make money from this recording. This has to be a hoax."

Max shook his head.

"You're wrong again. It's true that I'm documenting every detail I possibly can of this deadly encounter you're having with an antagonistic species. I even have a motion-activated camera in the basement to record the creature's offspring as they burrow into the earth. If it weren't for the dirt floor down there, you might have been spared, but in a perverse way I'm pleased you were too cheap to fix the place up. The visuals should be stunning, but I have no plans to show them to anyone else, let alone try to sell them."

"Where's the profit come from then?"

"I thought you'd never ask, Hank. What I'm counting on is discovering a new Wilhelm."

"A what?"

"A particularly memorable scream that's used over and over again on Hollywood movie soundtracks. A Wilhelm. There are two or three versions already in use. I'm sure you've heard at least one of them. Your contribution will surely make the others pale by comparison and should prove highly lucrative for me." .

"Aren't you forgetting the alleged injection of venom makes me feel good? According to your earlier description, I should be impervious to pain. If so, you can't make me scream and neither can your mythical monster."

"I'm disappointed in you, Hank. Have you forgotten the bellowing of the buffalo? I suspect the queen wants to know she's laying her eggs in a viable host. Maybe she injects an antidote for the painkiller just before her ovipositor penetrates your bellybutton."

"You expect me to believe that?"

Max held up his hand for Hank to be quiet and then cupped his hand behind his ear. "Listen. Can you hear that scratching sound? The queen's claws are scraping on the linoleum that covers the kitchen floor."

"I don't hear anything," Hank said.

"That's because she's stopped moving for some reason." Max stepped to one side and looked through the arched entranceway between the two rooms. "She's sniffing the air that's coming up the cellar stairs. I left the door open so her kiddies can have easy access. She's lowered her head now and is getting ready to move. Apparently, she's satisfied with the layout of the hatchery. Here she comes."

Hank's face showed that he not only heard the renewed sound of scratching claws, but he also recognized its significance. "Don't just stand there," he said with a slight quiver in his voice. "Get me away from that thing."

"As I told you before, Hank, I'm only here as an observer. I plan to let nature take its course. Obviously, I know what's going to happen next because I've seen it before, but there is one big difference."

"What's that?"

Max opened a carrying case and withdrew a headset designed to be worn while running a lawn mower or operating heavy equipment. "This time I brought ear protection."

Leonora

Elise Forier Edie

ROUNDSBY TOSSED ME A CROQUET MALLET. "You're not required to kill anyone," he said. "Just give them something to remember you by."

"I'm not exactly memorable," I said.

"Well. Now you will be."

"As an Anonymous Destroyer, Roundsby?" The irony escaped him, of course.

"As the Demon Diggs." Roundsby fairly wiggled with pleasure at his own wit. Roundsby delighted easily. It was part of his charm.

"I have planned our Bonfire Night perfectly," he said, holding aloft a finger. "We shall first avail ourselves of the expertise of the lovely Misses Haddie and Leonora of Drury Lane." A second finger joined the first. "Then we shall take to the streets with dozens of other demons, having our way, as they say, while stoking the fires of faith." A third finger popped up next to the other two. "At which point, we shall return to the Misses, who will sing 'Hail the Conquering Heroes', or something even better." He waggled his eyebrows as the fourth finger lifted and joined the others for an obscene gesture. "And then – the plat de résistance, my friend – we will be summarily divested of our disguises and allowed to partake of certain pleasures that only conquering heroes – and demons – may claim. And all this, all these riches, Diggs, will be yours simply for keeping me company, on this Guy Fawkes revelry."

I smiled in spite of myself. "Masks, violence and dabbing it up with actresses – you're a veritable cliché Roundsby."

"I'm a purveyor of pleasures, sir, and don't you forget it."

Roundsby got his name from fisticuffs at Eton, but he was Nicholas Bristow-Craig to his peers, Nickie to his whores, and a beloved but definite disappointment to his father, the viscount. Roundsby and I had met over the gaming tables some days before. He was under the impression that I lacked polish and experience and fancied he was bestowing an education in vice on my shy and retiring person. I let him believe what he liked. He was young and beautiful. He amused me. I quite regretted having to destroy him. Still, I hefted my croquet mallet, and followed him out the door.

The Misses Haddie and Leonora lived in an apartment near Covent Garden. Every surface in their rooms appeared to be dusted with powder, fringe and bottles of cheap scent. Haddie was the redhead, ticklish and plump, all lusty curves and throaty laughs. Leonora was the brunette, Romany-tinged, slight as a swan, and probably not a day over fifteen. Her clear, dark eyes glistened like polished stones. Roundsby pushed her towards me with a wink and a smile. "She's yours, Diggs. To have and … well, whatever you like."

Leonora and I regarded one another. She gestured for me to sit on her messy bed, amidst a collection of shawls. She sat carefully beside me.

"Nickie says you are to be a painted devil." Her voice, like crystallized honey, was both gritty and sweet. She reached for my face but I stopped her, plucking her small hand from the air before it touched my flesh.

"I won't be painted," I said firmly.

She glanced at the gloves I wore, fine black leather, soft as a shadow. "What will you have, then?" she asked calmly.

"By chance, do you have a mask?"

She lifted her chin and nodded shortly; she was clearly used to unusual garb and strange requests. I watched her rise, hiking up her long skirts before hopping across the room to rummage through a trunk. She had a pronounced birthmark in the shape of a ship on her smooth upper thigh. I wanted to lick it, but smothered the impulse. It wouldn't fit with the picture Roundsby had of me.

From across the room, on Haddie's bed, he said, "Diggs, you must have Leonora read your cards before the night is over. It's a lark and she's a wonder."

I lifted the corners of my mouth. "Do you mean to damn my soul for all eternity, Roundsby? And I thought you were my friend."

"I want you to live a little, that's all."

"I am,' I said, smiling at my own joke.

"Hold still," Haddie fussed at Roundsby. Having secured a suitable pantomime cape from a pile of costume pieces on her bed, she was now laying out an array of tiny paint pots and jars. "I have to start on your mouth, so just stop talking, your Lordship."

"My lady decrees." He dimpled and surrendered himself to her hands.

Leonora's small face suddenly jumped into my vision. A black mask dangled from her fingertips. "Will this do, sir?" she asked.

"Give it to me," I said.

I placed the mask on my face, but fumbled with the ribbons meant to secure it. The gloves have their uses, but bedevil attempts to be dexterous with buttons or ties.

"I can help you," she said.

"I don't think you want to," I muttered

A pause and then, very softly, "Are you meant for me, then?"

The question took me by surprise. I would have inhaled sharply, if I could. Instead, the mask fell to the bed as I stared at her. I am generally not recognized for what I am until it is much too late. Her face was perfectly blank, but her eyes betrayed her fear.

I said at last, "No. I am not for you." Then, a little dismayed, I added, "What gave it away?"

"I know a curse when I see one. My granny liked to curse people. I saw what some of them did." She shrugged tightly. "If I spread your cards, there'd just be these: the Devil, the Hanged Man, the Tower. The rest blank. I've seen it before. It don't make sense, but your kind aren't about sense-making, are you? You're about killing."

I could have snapped her neck right there. Instead, I pulled her close. Some things don't make sense, it's true.

"Listen, Leonora," I said. "Point, scream, wave a crucifix, chant in Latin, things will get very unpleasant for everyone, including you. I can't be stopped. Your grandmother surely taught you that. Play nice however, and you shall have a good story to tell about tonight. You choose. Right now."

I wondered what she'd do next. To my mind, she had infinite options, but only one path that would not end with her dead and devoured. She glanced at Haddie and Roundsby. She looked at me for a long time, like a girl who has woken to find a lion in her room. Then she suddenly jumped on the bed beside me, hiking up her skirt once more, giving me a tantalizing glimpse of that little ship on her thigh. She surprised me; so much I was startled. She surprised me even more when a second later she set about deftly tightening the mask's black ribbons. I felt it settle, molding to my face. She crawled back around to check the fit.

"Aren't you afraid of me?" I asked.

"Terrified," she said. "But it's not my place to stand in your way. And Nickie gave me coin to help you dress." She touched the mask, clearly not satisfied with its security. "And you're right, I can't stop you. You can't stop yourself, I think. I don't believe you have any will of your own. Do you?"

I didn't answer her. It's not something I like to talk about. I felt her crawl behind me again, her slight weight barely shifting the mattress. "Are you here for Nickie?" she asked.

"That's none of your business."

"I know. It's just a lot of lords are nasty. But he's nice."

"I think so too," I said. "If it helps."

She was silent, tightening the ribbons, her body warm and soft at my back. I closed my eyes, enjoying her nimble fingers on my scalp. As a rule I don't let human beings touch me. They're much more likely to get a whiff of what I am, if they brush up against my chest, or try to hold my hand. And their proximity can make me hungry. Leonora was no exception. She smelled faintly of clary sage, a slice of freshness in an otherwise fetid room. I thought of the little birthmark on her leg, her arms so slender I could crunch them with my teeth. I felt her crawl to the front of me again, and opened my eyes to meet her solemn gaze. Her irises had black and gold spots in them. They reminded me of something I couldn't quite recall.

"Were you always a devil?" she asked, her little fingers again checking the mask.

"No," I said. "I was not."

"What were you before? A man?"

"No. I was never a man."

I waited for the next inevitable question. But she didn't ask it. Instead, she cocked her head to one side, appraising me. "I think you need a hat." Then she smiled suddenly, like a shaft of sunlight through a black curtain, and brushed the hair from my forehead, where it had gotten caught up in the mask.

I felt something in my throat. At first, I didn't know what it was; it had been such a very long time. I watched, as she turned, her thin feet padding across the room, the scent of wild herbs wafting in her wake. I observed the cascade of her black hair shimmering in the lamplight. Her tiny hand pulled a slouchy hat from a peg on the wall. She whirled, holding it aloft, an eyebrow raised in silent inquiry.

I realized what had happened. And my insides shattered, like a wineglass dropped on a stone hearth.

I came to myself only moments later, Leonora adjusting the hat, trying to slouch it to one side. I batted at her hands and grabbed her wrist again, ignoring her cry of alarm. This time, I pressed her palm to my chest, where no heart had ever beat, nor ever would.

The story of her life unfurled in my mind's eye like a tattered banner. The squalid childhood, full of cold mornings and firelit nights, the tents and caravans, strung through the country, like beads of dew on a cobweb. Bouts of starvation. Scraps of sweetness. Slices of pain. A half brother who raped her. A sister who offered nurture. A rake she wasted her love on. His inevitable cruel rejection, her subsequent escape to London. And the rapture, the rapture, the rapture of her innocence, kept whole even in the midst of a life that had been one dreary episode followed by another, stained bricks in a road going to nowhere. Still her soul was a shining light glowing incongruously in filth. It cut through my darkness, as bright and clear as a star.

I released her. She shook to her bones. "Why did you do that? Why?" she asked.

I trembled in tandem. "You made me remember what I lost." I was disgusted and frightened to hear my voice thick with longing.

The connection between us still lingered, a taut string plucked, singing. "I swear didn't mean to hurt you," she whispered.

"Yes. Yes, I know."

Hell has nothing to do with fire pits or brimstone. Hell is knowing plainly that heaven is out of reach forever. Sometimes years grind by and the memory of loss retreats. Then a bolt of illumination renders every regret suddenly, achingly clear. God sends children, harlots and beggars to perform these miracles, to love suddenly and purely, without conditions. They are his true agents, not the bishops, not even the angels.

I am old. I rallied. I clenched my fists and the grief passed, leaving rage in its place.

"Are you ready, Diggs?" Roundsby asked suddenly.

I tore my gaze from Leonora to look over at my companion. His doxy had painted him in a series of lurid stripes. A pair of similarly decorated horns protruded from his head.

"You look frightful," I managed to say cheerfully.

"You look utterly boring," he crowed. "Couldn't little Leonora have fixed you up with something better than a black mask and a hat?"

I lifted my mouth in a smile. "You've said so yourself a dozen times – I'm a terribly boring person, Roundsby. Don't blame the girl. She did her best."

"Alastair Diggs, sometimes I despair of you."

"Alastor," Leonora echoed, faintly.

I flinched when she said what I was. What I am.

Roundsby shot her a puzzled glance while Haddie called from her bed. "You look pale, my dear. Are you ill?"

"He just bored the poor thing to death," Roundsby chuckled. Then to me he added. "Come, lad. Let us go be devils."

I took up my mallet. I smiled at him. "It's what I live for," I said.

At the doorway Leonora reached out her hand again to brush my hair with one tiny finger. "I'm sorry you have to suffer," she said softly.

She almost brought me to my knees.

Outside, the air was cool and wet. London's nighttime fog blanketed the streets. Fires and pyrotechnics blossomed the gloom, turning the air a lurid green. Roundsby and I headed toward the church with other revelers, some carrying torches and sparklers, others masked and bewigged in an array of startling disguises. Flaming Guys decked street corners. Explosions rocked the cobblestones. Shrieks and cries echoed through the eerily lit alleyways.

Roundsby had chosen a silver headed walking stick for his weapon. It looked decidedly at odds with his striped countenance and festive horns. He neither noticed nor cared. He was enjoying himself immensely. He caught me looking at him and smiled.

I didn't stop to wonder if the moment was right. I just lifted my cudgel and I bashed it on his skull. He died with a smile on his lips.

Things got rather gloriously messy after that, with his brains spattering my face in warm flecks, and fat drops of blood landing on my lips. I continued beating his body until he was a mass of gobbets and bone splinters, the walls around us drenched with his pieces. Then I ate his flesh, what I could of it, stuffing wads in my face. Poor Roundsby. He was so warm; everything about him was warm as Venus. I lost myself in a murderous dream.

Afterwards, I sat next to what was left of him. I wasn't tired, of course. I don't get tired. I had worked off most of my wrath, however. There was still some malingering bolts of regret, memories of everything I lost with the Fall, sensations that the English language wraps in short words that say nothing at all: love, peace, bliss, grace. So I sat with Roundsby's remains for some time while I struggled to recalibrate.

His head had been smashed almost perfectly flat, but one eye remained miraculously intact. It seemed to stare up at me, bewildered, in a nest of scarlet tissue, above a scattering of broken teeth.

I told him: "It wasn't supposed to end this way, old chum. We had farther to go down the road together. A few more fetes, a few more debts, before your utter ruination. My job is to break your father's heart, not make you a Guy Fawkes casualty. But she made me crazy, Roundsby. And your father will be broken hearted enough, with you having come to this."

Poor Roundsby had nothing to contribute to the discussion. His eye, starting to film over, just stared.

"You probably admired your father," I said. "Everyone else does. Peer of the realm. Landed aristocrat. Member of Parliament. Decorated solider. But do you know how he survived the Crimean War unscathed?"

Roundsby didn't answer. Rain began to fall in cool drops on both of us. I lifted my face.

I said, "He had a habit of fleeing the battle. Blames this phenomenon on a gun-shy steed, despite being an expert horseman. His maneuvers cost the lives of thousands of good men, Roundsby, but your father strutted home, proud as a tom turkey. One of his men, a Greek under his command, lost his legs, his son, and his manhood, all thanks to your father's incompetence on the battlefield. The man remains uncompensated for his losses. I suppose you could call me his compensation. The Greeks know how to curse a man properly, after all."

A firework exploded nearby, making the gore around me shine with silver light.

"It's too bad you went to Eton and Oxford, Roundsby. If you'd been brought up by a gypsy grandmother, you would have recognized an alastor too, and perhaps taken steps to be rid of me. But you were brought up by a self-satisfied prig of a coward, and so here you are, dead at twenty-four. Forgive me, old boy. I am a curse. I am accursed. Either way, the gypsy girl was right. I am a servant of the devil and I have no free will."

I left him where he lay in the rain.

I would have to go to Sheffield next, where the viscount wintered. There, I would ingratiate myself. Roundsby's father would be an easy mark. He would welcome a bright, comely, young man into his home, so soon after his son's death. Once there, I would ruin him even more thoroughly. Having devoured his heir, I would also destroy his lands, decimate his fortune, wreck his health. It was, as they say, my calling.

But first, I found myself stopping near Covent Garden.

She waited by the window, as if expecting me. Somehow, on the one night of the year when every Catholic Church was surrounded by ruffians and revelers, Leonora had managed to secure some holy water, and had sprinkled all the thresholds and windowsills. Wise girl. It gave off a faint, electric scent, and crackled in the rain. She looked down at me, her beautiful face lit by blue and red fireworks. I wanted to stand there and watch her until the night died.

She opened the window. "The holy water keeps you out?" she called.

"Your grandmother taught you well, Leonora."

"Why are you here, alastor? I thought you weren't for me."

I told the truth. "Yours is the first pure soul I've encountered in centuries."

"And you want to kill it?"

"No," I said. "I wanted to remember."

"What?"

She made me helpless, the devil take me. "What it was like before. Before I fell."

I could see that moved her. "Oh," she said. Then more softly she added, "oh." The fear in her eyes melted. She said, "Wait, I'll come down." Her small hands gathered a shawl around her shoulders. She started to turn from the window.

She was mine. She was mine. I don't know. I don't know. Maybe it was a memory of light. How the stars and trees and stones and grubs sing praises, all day long, if you listen. But I cried, "Stay, Leonora. Stay there, please. Stay if you value your life."

She hesitated. I waited. Then she whispered, "I'm sorry," and closed the window.

She wept while she did it. And each tear on her face was like a hot needle thrust in my bones. Eventually, like the rain, the pain went away.

Then I went on to Sheffield and ruined the viscount. Later, I was summoned by someone else and defaced yet another life. And so, ad infinitum. It is, after all, what I do.

I never saw Leonora again. I am not free to wander, or pay calls, after all. I am an infernal instrument. Still, I long for her sometimes. I worry she will die in squalor. I wonder what pains she feels. A pure soul on Earth is a boon to those it touches, but it's no guarantee of wealth, or luck or a happy life. It never has been. Not in the mortal realms.

I worry she will die without knowing the gift she gave me. For standing under her window in the damp, I was given a choice. To defile, or not. To crush or not. To kill or not. A choice, sure as tares, and I seized it. For an instant, my will spun free. I clutched her life in my palms and I chose not to take it. I did not taste or touch her flesh. Instead, for a second, I tasted freedom. And freedom was far sweeter than even the clear morning sky.

Will another chance come my way again? I do not know. But this is how divine messages are sent. By way of harlots in rented rooms, who give away their love so freely. In the corridors of hell where I wander in between summonings, I whisper her name, "Leonora". I whisper her name, like the mad poet, and sometimes it sounds like hope.

A Game of Conquest

David A. Elsensohn

"THANK YOU, GODWIN, that will be all for tonight," said Ashton. Tapping excess ink from the nib, he signed with a firm hand and stabbed the pen into the inkwell.

"If you're certain, sir," intoned the butler, pulling the great windows shut and drawing the velvet curtains. "The night is very chilly, and I needn't tell you how drafty the walls are."

"No, Godwin, you needn't. I will be fine. Stoke up the fire if it makes you feel better," chuckled Ashton. "Tell Lillian I will be upstairs shortly." The elderly manservant threatened the logs with a silver-tipped poker, gave a crisp nod and strode out.

The study was cold, but Ashton liked it whatever the weather; it was his sanctuary, his throne room. Decades of reading ledgers, writing important letters, meeting with other gentlemen to drink Armagnac and decide the fate of countries had passed in this study. Oaken shelves held yards of books. Gilded-frame paintings of past Ashtons gazed calmly from the walls. A velvet couch luxuriated near a small table with a chess board on it. The room smelled of distant smoke and history.

John Francis Ashton, Esq., formerly of Crump, Ashton and Ludlow, was in his sixties but looked younger, with a broad forehead and grand sideburns framing a strong jaw. His bearing was straight and his hair was shot with enough salt and pepper for respectability. He was a man of business. Deep set blue eyes scanned his writing for error; satisfied, he placed the letter atop the desk to dry.

He drew in a mouthful from his Philippine cigar and laid it to rest in its marble block, then leaned back and gazed at the great ship's wheel hanging over the mantel. It was a keepsake from the last clipper he owned back in 1833, before he retired. He had never helmed one of his possessions, but had always relished walking on board after it returned from China laden with silver, sails booming in the wind, deck holystoned and gleaming. He would listen to gentle creaks and snaps, would take in the scent of salt and wood and tar and thank Providence for his lot in life. It was ten years later, and he lived comfortably still on old proceeds and property.

A log groaned and snapped in the fireplace. He pulled his waistcoat tighter about him, grateful that he still wore vest and shawl collar instead of his bedclothes. It was cold. The fire writhed fitfully behind the grate without touching the room. The night air pressed against the windows, bleeding through the glass and the heavy curtains. He shook his head, picked up the pen, and dotted the ink from its tip.

"Ashton," called a cold voice.

John Francis started at the sound, head whirling first to the door, then searching the study. His eyes widened. A man stood in the darkened corner near the fireplace. A man he knew, once.

"... Ludlow?"

The figure slipped forward into the firelight, gaunt and dour.

"It is you, Ludlow! I haven't seen you in years. How did you get in..." Ashton started. He was looking at his old business partner, but William Ludlow was not wholly there. The firelight shone into him, casting sickly shadows against the inside of his skin. Hair hung in strings around his neck and sideburns, giving his thin face the appearance of jaws. His nose was crooked, his waistcoat dark.

"I have been here a while, Ashton," crooned William Ludlow. "Standing here, in the corner, watching you." He moved forward onto the carpet, silently.

Ashton's tongue cleaved to his palate. He pushed away from his desk, pen and cigar forgotten. "You... you aren't real, sir," he stammered. "I am tired, and must go to bed."

"Real enough, Ashton," said Ludlow, teeth cracking in a vile grin. The air in the room went colder with an almost audible sigh. "I am here to take you with me."

"Take me? But... you aren't dead, are you, Ludlow? Oh, God," moaned Ashton, lurching to his feet and steadying himself on the desk. The fire's glow could be seen inside Ludlow, curling vaguely around tissue and bone like sheets laid over furniture.

Ludlow had black eyes, and they glimmered. "Didn't you know? Five years back. After Crump died. You're the last of us, and the worst. When they sent for someone to bring you, I leapt at the chance, believe me."

"I have had too much brandy," tried Ashton. His stomach fluttered.

Ludlow ignored him, gliding around the room in small paces, hands clasped behind his back. "You've done very well for yourself, John," he said, head askew, looking at the book titles. They could almost be seen behind his shadowed figure. He stopped in front of a painting. "All that silver from Canton buys a lot of gilt for picture frames." He traced a pale finger down the canvas, gazing at the woman rendered within. The artist's brush had given her face touches of sadness. "Lillian."

"I am not ready to die!" gasped Ashton. "I am still hale. I am a God-fearing gentleman. There is a mistake."

Ludlow pulled his gaze away from the woman in the picture, faced Ashton with eyes glinting. "Neither God nor Devil has anything to do with it, villain."

"I will not go."

"You must," said Ludlow, relentless. "This is how it happens for everyone. Someone is sent for you when it is your time, and you are brought. Deny it all you like. I did."

"There must be something we can do," Ashton insisted, struggling to keep his English composure. He thought furiously, then brightened. "A wager. A game. For more time."

The apparition's eyes blazed, and he spun, spitting words. "Like what, Ashton, a friendly game of Whist? Or do you think to be Faust, and I am your Mephistophilis?"

Ashton gestured at the wall under the largest of the windows, where a marble-inlaid chessboard, its stone armies at attention, lay on a round table between two chairs. "Yes, Ludlow, yes. For an old friend."

"Friend, is it." Ludlow moved to the table. One of the kings lay on its side, blown over by the nightly wind before Godwin had closed the window. He touched the pitted stone piece, righted it. "How well-trodden a path, John. Playing chess against your death. Like those old cathedral paintings. But why should I?"

John Ashton straightened and regained a measure of himself. "A wager. Play a game of chess against me. If I win you will leave me be. If I lose..." his voice faltered as William Ludlow fixed him with black, abyssal eyes. "If I lose, I will go with you."

They looked at and through each other. Ashton adjusted his vest. Ludlow glowered.

"I will see about it," said Ludlow finally. He turned toward the door, head half cocked as if listening to something beyond the room. "Don't try to leave, Ashton. Don't try." His body seemed to go soft, buckling into itself, and winked out.

Ashton fell into his desk chair with chest heaving. He could not stop his hands from shaking. He must keep his reserve in the face of adversity, a stiff upper lip, but against what? A dream? Hell? Ashton took a shuddering draw from his cigar and let earthy smoke fill the air. He had not had too much brandy, nor was he sick. He looked around his room, at the wheel, at the paintings, at the aged footlocker behind his desk. The woman in the painting looked pensively downward, as if pleading. A sudden desire struck him, and he knelt suddenly before the footlocker and fumbled a key into it. He pulled a locket from its depths, clicked it open, took in breath and hope. The tiny picture was, he thought, so much more real than the great and solemn painting on the wall. Lillian was so beautiful when the locket had been made, and she still was. He wanted to go upstairs to her, wish her goodnight, perhaps kiss her. They had spoken so little for the last few years. So beautiful.

This time the voice was next to his ear. "We accept."

Ashton cried out, almost falling backward. "Damn you, Ludlow." He pushed the locket into his vest pocket. The apparition, standing over him, gazed down his long nose, and said nothing. He looked over at the stand with a decanter and several small snifters, moved to it. He lifted a dusty bottle from a shelf underneath.

"Still prefer Armagnac?" He glanced over at Ashton. "Hm. Château de Bourdieu. Pour one for me."

"You can drink?"

"I can remember."

While Ashton nervously poured the amber liquid into two snifters, Ludlow drifted to the small table by the window and sat, waiting. He took the snifter from Ashton and raised it to an eye as glassy and swirling as the brandy. He sipped and glared.

Ashton took a shallow breath, regarded the silent board and his eerie companion, and sat across from him. He hid a pawn from each side underneath the table, then brought up his two fists. Ludlow looked pointedly at the right, and Ashton opened it. White.

"I will go first, then," murmured William Ludlow. "And last."

"Don't be too sure, old man," huffed Ashton. "You could never beat me at chess."

"So cocksure until the end," said the other. "Remember, I was the one who took all those trips to Calcutta, to Burma, to Canton. What else is there to do during a month at sea than to play against the captain?" His grin bore into Ashton, who knew all too well Ludlow's resentment. The company had always sent Ludlow on the voyages; he hadn't wanted to be a ship's purser but had a better head for languages and currency conversion. Always outvoted by Ashton and Crump, it had been Ludlow who suffered sickness, counted casks or bribed Indian officials. His two older partners stayed in England, arranging transactions, hiring crews, appearing at events, and enjoying the benefits of membership in the Shipowners Society.

They began. In Ludlow's translucent fingers a knight leapt from its place and landed before his line of pale soldiers. A bold yet orthodox move from his king's right. Ashton matched him, moving pawns forward to clear the way for his bishops, and slowly their armies began their advance. Neither wasted time with defense and terrain. Both men were aggressive players, delving into ancestral memory of battles past, sacrificing too much in their push to possess and destroy. Both of Ashton's bishops fell to Ludlow's rapacious white knight; the knight was swarmed by black pawns bent on revenge. Years of business, of dislike, of distrust, made the pieces fly over the board.

Ashton paused, mopped his forehead with a sleeve. Sweat sat cold on his brow. He hauled up his mind from the game, an anchor from murky depths. "Ludlow," he said. "What happened? How did you die?"

"You act so innocent," sneered Ludlow, standing. The table rattled with his anger. "It was you, Ashton. After Crump died, you sold our last ship and the business and retired on the proceeds, you insufferable bastard. What of me?"

"I thought you were doing well. I thought you would stay in Hong Kong, William," said Ashton.

"How, John? The war was still on. Oh, yes, when Hong Kong came to be, you did quite well, didn't you? And you stayed very carefully out of it, like you stayed out of everything except the silver coffers. You and Crump both, two ravens plucking my eyeballs. Do you even know how you made your money?"

Ashton looked down at his king, hiding behind a rook who had switched places with it, ready to die to save its lord. He knew. It was something one did at the time, following the lead of the East India Company. Clipper ships were filled with machinery parts and textiles and sent to India, where they emptied their holds in return for opium. Balls of the sticky narcotic were stuffed into chests, sealed with pitch, stamped with a trademark, and sent east, to be snapped up by hungry nobles whose hands flowed with silver and silk. It was a brutally efficient triangle of corruption. Gentlemen grew rich. It was a perfectly respectable, worthy, unmentionable blasphemy. It was part of the Empire.

Ludlow sat down, regarded his former partner. "I remember a paper I signed, Ashton. Let's see... I, William Claxton Ludlow, do hereby give notice, that I intend to present a petition to the Court of Bankruptcy – sound familiar, Ashton? You floated through all those circles, shaking hands with notaries and notables – praying to be examined, et cetera, my debts, estate and effects, et cetera, full disclosure and surrender of... you know how it goes."

Ashton scowled. "I had nothing to do with that. What you did with your share after we closed is your concern."

"What share? You'd taken all the money when you sold the business. I'd sent you a letter, Ashton. I asked you for help. Nothing. I died penniless."

"That is not my doing, Ludlow!" shouted Ashton. "It is your affair, and I will not –"

A polite knock sounded at the door. Ludlow glimmered, rose up and floated toward it; he had vanished by the time it opened.

"Sir?" asked Godwin in nightgown and candle. "Are you well?"

"I am, Godwin, as I said," said Ashton, too harshly.

The elderly man looked over at the unfinished game, the two glasses – one filled, one empty – and the red face of his master, and kept his face blank as only an English butler can. The air around him swam; his candle flickered. Godwin hugged himself, and his breath could almost be seen. "As you say, sir. Mrs. Ashton wished me to check upon you. She doesn't wish you to catch your death."

"Thank you, Godwin, God damn it, that will be all."

The door closed, showing Ludlow glaring where Godwin had stood. He drifted back to the table, bringing cold with him. They resumed the game. He dragged a rook across the board like a coffin over dirt, but his eyes never left Ashton's except to flash downward at the other man's vest.

"Who is that in the locket, John? Is that Lillian?"

Ashton was grim, playing. He drove his army across the middle of the board as Ludlow retreated and parried; the black queen had come forth, and she pushed pawns ahead of her without mercy. One of Ludlow's bishops perished beneath her wrath, and a rook. Ashton was playing for his life, and extended himself dangerously far. "Check!" he snapped, and Ludlow scrambled to pull his king from peril. The move had exposed Ashton's side, however, and the white enemy crept toward his own leader. He bolstered his defenses and soon another smoky lull spread over the battlefield.

Ludlow rocked his queen back and forth on her tiny pedestal. "Is she well, John? I should like to see her."

"Don't you dare, Ludlow. Don't you dare touch her." Ashton was livid. "Maybe you will take me, and maybe you won't, but you will leave Lillian alone. She is not part of this."

William Ludlow's eyes stabbed out from under dark brows. "I would never hurt her, you know that I would not. I loved her, Ashton. I loved her before you did." Ashton shot a look at his opponent, but Ludlow stared at the locket hidden beneath the silk vest.

It had been a near thing, Lillian's love. She was a gift of honesty and serenity for which both men strove, callous men who lived in a world of economic empire, fighting to fill their own souls sucked empty by commerce and divine right. She could be a statue carved in prudence, or melt into breathless girlhood. The scent of jasmine and roses followed where she walked. Both men would kill for her; one of them had died. Ashton looked up at Ludlow in doubt. Lillian had chosen to be an Ashton, hadn't she? She had married him, had chosen to be his. Ludlow was always half a world away, and John was a comfortable, respectable presence.

The cold voice pulled him from reverie. "Any children, Ashton? Any sons?"

"No," Ashton whispered. There had been two. Neither had lived past swaddling clothes.

"There is no one to take up where you left off, then," said Ludlow. "A pity."

"There will be me," said Ashton through clenched teeth. "You are losing the game, Ludlow."

The door clicked. "John?"

Lillian was there, candle in hand, greying hair bound behind her. A tall, willowy woman, her gentle beauty had settled beneath wrinkles around her brown eyes. She did not see Ludlow, but he saw her; his gaze was drawn like a magnet. His body flickered as memories flooded into him.

"I am fine, dearest," said John. "I will be there soon. Please return to bed." He realized suddenly that he loved her, as much as a man should. She had slipped from his mind for so long, almost unnoticed, a proper wife, an elegant companion for dinner parties; more, a serene presence that never complained, never wept openly for the loss of their sons. He had devoted himself to worldly things, raced to possess everything so that it could be used to obtain more. He no longer knew if he had done right.

She looked uncertain, but closed the door, leaving behind a smile still lovely after so many echoing years. Ludlow lowered his head in bitterness.

"You even took her, Ashton. You even took her," he whispered. Ashton looked up and saw a different face on his old partner. A ghost, weeping with rage.

They played, and the fire began to die; the Philippine cigar had faded to grey. Shadows stretched and writhed along the walls. Ashton's rook kept a bloody vigil along one side of the battlefield, pushing Ludlow's leaders to the corner. Ludlow pounced forward, offering a bishop, and the rook crushed it, only to be taken a moment later by a pawn. Kings muttered and fretted and took careful steps behind their retinue. Both queens circled each other, tigers vying for the other's kill.

"I am glad that she's well," said Ludlow. "I really am. I cared for her."

"So do I," said John, gazing wistfully at the door where her presence still seemed to linger. He could smell jasmine and roses. "Perhaps I hadn't noticed."

"Oh, and Ashton?" A hint of flame sparked in Ludlow's eye. "Checkmate."

Thing in the Bucket

Eric Esser

WHENEVER THE VILLAGERS of Drumby Hole fell ill, the weak-minded among them sought the cunning woman who lived out past the Long Mynd, but good Christians went to Alexander Pritcher's barbershop across from the village green. Pritcher's medicinals did not have the power of the cunning woman's, but he was adept with a lance and could bleed most infirmities away. Villagers with colds or infections or deep sorrows of the heart came to him to drain the darkness from them.

Blood often spilled from Pritcher's bowl as he worked, or sprayed when he made fresh incisions, so every evening after closing, he cleaned the floor of his shop before the village cats got to it. One winter's evening, just as he was finishing, Sarah Penny, a young barmaid at the village tavern, knocked on the door.

She was a blossoming girl of thirteen, not yet old enough to know what power her beauty would have over men. Her hair was long and flaxen and her skin so supple it glowed even in the waning light. She had always been kind to Pritcher on those occasions when he'd supped at the tavern alone. Pritcher was awkward around women, but Sarah made him feel as if it didn't matter. She wasn't like that older maid; there was no judgment in her.

This evening Pritcher almost did not recognize her. She looked up at him with eyes wide, like a dog that had been beaten by its master for some reason it didn't understand.

"Do you need to sit down?" he asked.

She nodded. He took her hand and guided her to his big barber's chair and brought her a cup of ginger tea. She had a faint sallowness beneath the eyes from too much black bile secreted by the gallbladder. Something had frightened her.

"Are you all right?" he said.

She whispered, "I am bleeding."

Pritcher dealt in the art of the bleed, so it was unsurprising she had come to him. "Can you show me?"

"From inside." She pressed her belly, then brushed at her petticoat.

Pritcher considered Sarah's young age and air of shame, and then smiled. "You mean it is worse than usual? Or at the wrong time?"

"What do you mean?"

"The time of month you bleed."

She stared at him blankly. Was it possible she did not know? Her parents had died some years before, so she'd been raised by the barkeep, Elias Grubbs. He was well-meaning, but not the brightest man, and a widower without daughters of his own. Such subjects were not spoken of in Drumby Hole between young girls; the vicar taught them not to succumb to the corruption of flesh, to focus on God when it tempted them.

Surely someone must have taken an interest. That older barmaid, perhaps. "Has Lizzy never mentioned the curse?"

Sarah shook her head. "I'm cursed?" Her voice trembled.

Pritcher patted her hand. "You will be fine. You bleed because your womb is open and ready to receive a man's seed."

She looked at her belly. "Will it happen again?"

"Every cycle of the moon."

"It lasts a month?"

Pritcher tried to laugh casually, so as to reassure her. "No, my dear. Three or four days. A week at most." He grabbed a clean rag from his cupboard. "See, you can take a cloth and fold it up and pin it beneath your smock to catch the blood." He presented her the folded cloth with a smile.

She turned away. She seemed horrified. He was not surprised. Most people found the idea of bleeding unnatural, as if all that was in them should stay inside. Pritcher knew better because of how he changed people as he bled them. He drew away not just sickness but qualities. Happiness, sadness, good, evil, impure cravings, and saintliness. The blood contained them all, and thus they could be drained away by one who knew the secret of it – where to cut and how much to spill.

"There must be something you can do," she said.

"But it is natural."

She gripped the sleeve of his shirt and beseeched him with her eyes. "Please."

He wanted to help, if only because he could hardly believe how easily he was speaking to such a beautiful girl. He could offer her a balm of mandrake for the pain. Barbers were forbidden by law from practising the arts of the apothecary, but Pritcher did anyway. If he did not help the villagers, they would have to risk their souls on the arcane cures of the cunning woman. The nearest licensed practitioner was a day's journey away.

But before he spoke, another idea struck him. He had worked with many kinds of blood from people of many different dispositions, but never the birthing blood. The sort of blood from which whole people grow.

He might never again have such an opportunity, and Sarah would be very grateful. But he would require more than the drips and clots he could wring from her smock.

"There is one thing," he said. "A potion. It will empty your womb all at once. But...there will be some pain."

"Oh, thank you," she said without hesitation.

He pulled out a book, an old herbal with a recipe meant for unwed mothers-to-be. He lit a fire, set a kettle on, blended the ingredients together, and let them come to a boil, then simmer. Once the potion cooled, he filled a cup for her to drink.

"It tastes like wet dirt!" she said, and he laughed. He asked about her day and how her job at the tavern was going. He enjoyed the way she looked down sometimes as she spoke to him. Perhaps they could become friends.

And then quite suddenly the glow of her cheeks dulled to sickly green. Her head tipped forward. He had not expected the potion to work so fast. He caught her at the shoulders and led her to the room behind his shop. He lay a blanket and a couple of rags on his bed and propped a pillow against the wall. He centered a shallow pan on the rags.

"What is this?" She stared through him into the middle distance.

"Catch as much blood as you can," he said. "I will examine it afterward to make sure everything is all right."

She lay on the bed over the pan with her back against the pillow. He set a damp cloth on her head and let her catch her breath. The blood had drained from her face. It made him nervous. He had used the potion before, but never on a woman not pregnant or one so young. He ran back into his shop and dropped the crossbar across the front door, and then pulled closed the shutters and even the door of the back room. If there were any problems, passersby overhearing would make things worse.

He drew a stool to her side, sat down, and watched her for signs of fainting or seizure. She kept her eyes closed and breathed deeply and slowly. She bent forward. It must be the pain of her womb opening. Her blood began to flow. It was dark and clotted at first, but soon turned glistening bright red. He caught a whiff of rust and iron.

He squeezed her hand. "You are doing wonderfully." He lied, as much to himself as to her. He feared he had made a mistake and prayed there were not consequences.

"It hurts," she whispered.

"It's perfectly natural," he said.

She cried out.

"Please, it is better if you're quiet," he said, but her wail grew louder, like a gale through gaps in an old house.

She gripped his arm, and her fingernails cut him, but it was all right because it was his fault she suffered like this.

Eventually she succumbed and fell into a deep slumber, but it was hours before the flow of blood dwindled. He took away the pan, poured the blood into one of his measuring bowls, and set it on the table. There was much more blood than he would have thought. He watched the rise and fall of her chest; even with her flesh turned so ghostly, he longed to reach out and pet her. Her hair was so thick with sweat it had the consistency of seaweed.

It was late. If he could not get her back to the tavern tonight, there would be talk. He grabbed a sponge and a bucket of water, then carefully slipped the remaining rags out from beneath her legs and began to clean her.

She awoke with a start. He looked up from between her legs. She tried to push her petticoat down around her waist.

"How do you feel?" he said. .

"What's happening?" she said.

"You're all right."

She pulled herself from the bed and stumbled through the back room doorway into the shop. Patches of scarlet stained the back of her skirt like a birthmark.

"You must rest," he called. He followed her and set his hand on her shoulder to comfort her but she brushed it away. She fumbled with the crossbar, pushed the door open, and ran from the shop without looking him in the eye.

A few of the village cats dashed in the open door. They sniffed around the chair, then headed to the back room. Pritcher watched Sarah weave down the street toward the tavern. He longed to run after her, to explain he hadn't meant her to suffer, but if he left the bowl with the cats, it would be empty when he returned.

He locked the door and went back to the bowl. The cats lapped at it and what had spilled onto the bed and the floor. He wondered again if he should go after Sarah, but she would be at the tavern by now, with people watching.

Instead, he scattered the cats and ran his finger through the bowl, through warm blood and irregular clots. He raised it to his nose and inhaled its earthy fragrance. He touched a little to his tongue. It tasted of sweat and iron, underlain by an unfamiliar richness.

He was exhausted, but if he was to perform this experiment properly, he had best do it right away. So he took the bowl, found a warm, dark place, and seeded it.

He hid it on a high shelf cluttered with too many vials and bottles for cats to climb on it. He dripped in a blend of herbs he used to keep blood flowing in patients who clotted too quickly and covered the bowl with a damp cloth.

He went to the tavern the next day looking for Sarah, but she was not working. She was probably tired from her ordeal and had to rest. He wanted to ask after her, but was afraid that if something had befallen her, he might be blamed. Instead, he went back to his shop and checked on the bowl. He saw no change; he told himself he expected none but could not help feeling disappointed.

For the next few days he did not see her, though he took every meal at the tavern. He sat quietly at the long trestle table and ate his roast pigeon and listened to the conversations of others. Finally he overheard someone asking where she was; Grubbs replied that she was unwell, but the cunning woman was treating her.

Pritcher returned to his shop dejected. If only he could explain to her what had happened. He checked on the bowl and her bright red blood cheered him a little. He wiped down the edges and covered it with a fresh cloth. He inspected it often, setting it out if it was too warm and tucking it away if it was too cold. He imagined what he would have said to Sarah if their conversation had continued. He wished he had talked to her more before that night. Maybe he could have made it easier for her.

Then one morning he lifted the cloth from the bowl and noticed the blood line had fallen. The insides of his bowls were traced in concentric measuring rings; he could see it had lost almost a half ounce. The blood was drying out.

He needed to bleed Sarah again. It would help her recover and give him something to put in his bowl to stop it from drying. He went to the tavern right away.

"Sarah's been ill too long," he told Grubbs. "That cunning woman doesn't know what she's doing. A bleeding is what she needs. Free of charge."

Grubbs nodded amiably, but when Pritcher returned later for Sarah's answer, his smile was gone. "No need, barber, no need," Grubbs said coldly.

* * *

If Pritcher couldn't have Sarah's blood, he could do the next best thing. Every day he saved a little of the blood he drained from certain patients, and then fed it into the bowl. He was careful not to use the bad blood he drained from most clients, those with ailments like pox or tumors. Instead he carefully mimicked the blood of a young girl's womb by feeding the bowl only the blood of fertile women who came to him to enliven their spirits or still the restlessness in their hearts. He usually took a pint or two from each patient, and he only needed a few ounces for the bowl. He never emptied it for fear he might spill Sarah's blood with the special properties of her womb or any seed of his that had sprouted.

He found he enjoyed the process; every time he sprinkled in more blood, he recalled the particular lady from whom he had drawn it: the curve of her neck or full swell of her lip or bosom; each woman passed through his fingers as her blood spilled across them. But every night as he stared into the bowl, looking for some sign of life, it was Sarah he thought of, bleeding into it.

And then one day when Pritcher sat down at the tavern's long table, there she was, Sarah, behind the bar like some miracle. She was pale and moved more slowly than she had, but she smiled as villagers wished her well or teased her for taking a holiday.

Pritcher waved and caught her eye. She half smiled, then said something to Grubbs and disappeared into the back. Lizzy brought him his plate and ale.

"How is Sarah?" he said.

"She's busy."

He was hurt Sarah did not want to talk to him, but also relieved she was all right. She probably did have a lot of work to catch up with after having been ill so long. That night he lit a candle and set it by the bowl. He fed a few ounces of choice blood into it. He stared into the blood and whispered what he might say to Sarah if she let him.

"You are so beautiful."

A ripple fluttered across the surface of the blood. Something flickered like a tadpole through the bowl toward the new blood, though it was pale, unlike any tadpole he had seen.

Pritcher scrambled to find his magnifying glass. He dripped in more blood to bring whatever it was to the surface, but it was so fast he could not make out any detail. He watched it for an hour, uncertain it was real. But it was alive. He'd been a fool to doubt. He wondered how long it had been hiding in the blood, too small to see.

That first day he was very nervous for it; it had come alive so suddenly there seemed no reason it might not die just as fast. He checked on it in every spare moment, making sure the blood level was still high, the temperature just right. He fed it more fresh blood and it shook its tail, twirling like a bird through the sky. He laughed, and it swam a tiny circle.

In the evening, he took the bowl to his bedside and set it by his oil lamp to keep it warm. He concocted an elaborate story to explain it to the village: he would find it on his doorstep one morning with a note saying a distant cousin entrusted it to his care until her return. He might have to marry someone to help him raise it. Maybe Sarah would see herself in it and feel compelled to be a mother to it. He wondered if it would be a boy or a girl. He fell asleep dreaming of everything it might become.

It grew rapidly under his care, much faster than it would have in the womb. Initially this encouraged him. He was doing such a good job tending it. He stopped taking meals at the tavern because he was afraid to leave it alone for long, and because Sarah disappeared whenever he was there. Also the judgmental looks from Grubbs and Lizzy made him uncomfortable.

He called it "my little one," and every night, when he took it to his bedside, he told it stories: tales of faeries who lived beneath the barrows and sirens who seduced men to their doom. He heard it sometimes, tail slapping against wood when he reached a particularly satisfying moment. When he dimmed the light to turn in for the night, it sloshed about because, just like him, it must not want the evening to end. He sang a lullaby over the bowl until it stilled.

Three weeks later, he put several pints he had saved from his choice lady patients into a pot, then poured in the contents of the bowl. His little one plopped down quickly, but he caught a glimpse of sleek flesh and arms stretched out like elegant fins with dainty fingers on the ends. He laughed aloud. It was beautiful. He hoped it was a she, he decided.

But then it became too large for the pot and banged back and forth against either side of it whenever the blood grew stale. He moved it into a bucket, which required a great deal more blood to fill and keep full. He made most of his money from shaves and haircuts and dental extractions; he performed perhaps a dozen bloodlettings a week.

It was not enough.

He waited outside the tavern for Sarah on market day. He had seen her shopping among the stalls and thought she rarely failed to go. He needed to talk to her; she had what his little one needed, if only she would give it to him.

She appeared at a window on the second story, and looked on him in the street. He waved and gestured for her to come down. Lizzy appeared behind her and drew her away. Grubbs came out instead. "Best keep taking your meals in your shop for a while, eh, barber?" he said.

Pritcher understood. Sarah had not yet forgiven him. It should not have surprised him. But he had his little one.

He took his responsibilities as a healer very seriously, but when the next of his special ladies returned for a bleeding, he took four pints instead of one. Her face passed from pale to green, and looked as lost as Sarah's had that first evening. He fed her an apricot pastry from Goodrich's bakery so she wouldn't faint, but she still had to sit quietly in his barbershop for a few hours, staring listlessly into space.

"What happened to Nelly?" asked one of Pritcher's best customers as he examined her with a cocked eyebrow before sitting down for a trim. Pritcher could tell what he really wanted to know was whether the next time he fell ill it would happen to him too.

As much as it pained Pritcher, he bled more from each of his special ladies but they fared no better. In the end, he had no choice but to use men's blood. He only occasionally treated gentlemen clients without serious illness who took the bleed to improve their overall disposition and vigor, but villagers were in and out of his shop all day, mostly men come for a shave.

"You've got a certain jaundice beneath the skin," he'd say to them. "I'd recommend we take a pint, if you've time." Not many agreed. It was easier if one of his special ladies recovered in the corner so they could leer at her as they bled. Some tried to joke with him about how best to treat a woman in such a stupor.

He felt dirty as he poured their blood into the bucket with that of his special ladies. His little one at first dashed toward the blood, then shivered and sulked in the deep recesses of the bucket. He lured it toward the surface by dimming the lights and singing a lullaby, but it rose reluctantly. He felt as if this new blood made it suspicious of him.

But it was like the bucket had a hole he could not see; he did not know where all the blood went. The bloodline was always descending, his little one always growing bigger, and it cried out when the blood lowered too far. He heard it in his shop as he held a straight razor to a client's cheek, like the squeal of a goat having its throat cut.

"Probably just one of the cats gotten into something," Pritcher said as he ran back with no blood to give it. After a moment's hesitation, he opened his own artery and drained a pint. When he stumbled back to his client in a fog, he realized he would never be able to do it often enough to make any difference.

He agonized over what to do. He could not let it die. He loved it, and he thought it loved him too. He could think of nothing but feeding it all the blood he had.

He fed it blood from patients with dropsy and infection and deep melancholy. He did not want to, for he knew what darkness such blood contained. He knew in theory he could bleed away not only darkness, but light, but none of his training or sources explained the mechanics of that process; indeed, to transform a person in such a way would be an abomination.

He would have done it if he knew how. His little one cried out when he fed it the bad blood, the dirty blood, and coughed it up many times before swallowing. It shook with seizure or rammed itself into the side of the bucket hard enough that blood leaked from between staves.

Pritcher came to his bedroom and found blood splattered across the walls and a thick black sludge that smelled of bile. He sat on his stool, leaned over the bucket, and sang to it. The bucket vibrated with a deep moan he felt more than heard. Once or twice his little one flittered toward the surface. The blood was thick and opaque and his little one moved quickly, but he could have sworn its flesh was harder and rougher than it had been, rougher than a baby's should be.

He turned his gaze from the bucket. He was doing this to his little one. It transformed as it brought what he fed it to life. He lay awake that night, listening, bucket near the side of his bed. Sometimes he thought he heard it crying. He needed healthier blood, but he could not draw any more from his patients and could hardly ask for volunteers. He wished there were some way to restore his little one to Sarah's womb; perhaps if she spread her legs for him again and squatted over the bucket, his little one might crawl up to where it was meant to be.

After the sun set, before the moon rose, he slipped out to the pastures, lured an untended sheep from its flock with an apple, and cut its throat. He did not use scalpels, for fear his skill might be recognized; he chopped at its throat with a cleaver. He drained four buckets of blood and then ran away before anyone saw.

He had hoped sheep's blood might soothe his little one, but it did not. Strange twisting sounds came from the bucket, and jets of blood vomited out of it across the walls of his bedroom. He tried not to look down as he fed it. In the corner of his eye he thought he saw the irregular outline of matted fur, the sharp angles of hooves. He slept as best he could in his chair in the shop with the door to his back room barred.

Every few days he drained another animal, be it sheep, goat, or cow. The petty constable led patrols of farmers through the countryside, hunting the creature that attacked their livestock. Rumors spread of a beast that rose from the barrows when the sun set, but calmer heads knew the cut of a blade when they saw one. Some vandal among them did this, the villagers said, probably as part of forbidden rituals, and when they caught him, he would hang. The people watched each other, and too often Pritcher felt their gazes fall on him and linger. People who had always ignored him asked him how he was doing and what he'd been up to. When he saw the constable speaking in whispers with Grubbs and the vicar, he knew they would come for him.

Pritcher sat up late with his lantern and cleaver, needing to go out, knowing he dare not. He could not feed the thing in the bucket anymore, come what may. He might not even need to. It was big now, bigger than a baby when it's born; if the bloodline fell far enough, it might simply emerge into the world.

He realized he had not seen the cats recently, and had not thought to hide the bucket from them.

Though he loved his little one, he also hated it. He hated what it made him do and the dread it stuck in the pit of his stomach. He knew what was in that bucket, even if he had never seen it clearly. Most of the blood he had fed it contained only the worst in people, only those parts they would not have if they were perfect, if they were like God. He knew now how foolish he had been to think he could raise this thing, or tell the village about it.

It could not be here when they came for him.

He pulled out his old herbal with the recipe he had made for Sarah and set the kettle on. It cautioned to use only small amounts of savin and devil's flower to prevent the mother from going the way of the unborn, but Pritcher put in all he had.

When it was ready, he stood above the bucket and looked down at the blood for the first time in weeks. It was still. His own face looked back at him. A ripple passed through his jaw to his brow as the thing swam near the surface. He would have done anything for it, and yet he did everything wrong. He thought about everything it might have been, if only he could have given it what it needed. He saw the life they might have shared, and then that life destroyed. It was like he was dying too. Who would he have been if he could have known it better, if he had not corrupted it?

He poured the poison in slowly, for it was still hot, and he did not want his little one to burn. When he finished, he sat by the bucket, sobbing and trying to hold himself in the way his little one might have one day had it lived, telling himself he had no choice but knowing things had come to this only because of his choices. He was thankful his little one made no sound. When enough time passed, he pulled out a sack, so he could take it into the forest to bury. He could not bury it on hallowed ground, but at least it would rest in the warm earth.

He rolled up his sleeves, took a breath, then plunged his hands and forearms into the blood. He had to hurry or the poison might penetrate his skin and sicken him, but he found his little one almost at once. It was the first time he had touched it; his heart missed a beat. Its flesh was warm and soft and fresh.

He carefully pulled it out, then set it on a clean cloth. There were no tails nor horns nor fur. In fact it looked just like him: the same crooked nose, the same thin lips, the same little white scars on its forearm where Sarah's nails had cut him. Its face was blue and its eyes and mouth set open, as if in amazement.

Pritcher assured himself again what a wicked creature it must be on the inside, after imbibing all those vile influences. He did not put it in the sack, but only watched it awhile, feeling the weight of his sins.

A knocking on the back door of his barbershop roused him. He heard the shouts of many men. The constable called out to him, asking why his lamps always burned so late and if he knew anything about all the animals that had been killed.

He glanced toward the sack, the fire pit, the door. He picked his little one up and slipped it back into its bucket of blood, though it did not sink into it, but floated. He wiped his hands as best he could on the cloth and rose to open the door.

The Murdered Cousin

Sheridan Le Fanu

"And they lay wait for their own blood: they lurk privily for their own lives.
"So are the ways of every one that is greedy of gain; which taketh
away the life of the owner thereof."

THIS STORY of the Irish peerage is written, as nearly as possible, in the very words in which it was related by its 'heroine', the late Countess D—, and is therefore told in the first person.

My mother died when I was an infant, and of her I have no recollection, even the faintest. By her death my education was left solely to the direction of my surviving parent. He entered upon his task with a stern appreciation of the responsibility thus cast upon him. My religious instruction was prosecuted with an almost exaggerated anxiety; and I had, of course, the best masters to perfect me in all those accomplishments which my station and wealth might seem to require. My father was what is called an oddity, and his treatment of me, though uniformly kind, was governed less by affection and tenderness, than by a high and unbending sense of duty. Indeed I seldom saw or spoke to him except at meal-times, and then, though gentle, he was usually reserved and gloomy. His leisure hours, which were many, were passed either in his study or in solitary walks; in short, he seemed to take no further interest in my happiness or improvement, than a conscientious regard to the discharge of his own duty would seem to impose.

Shortly before my birth an event occurred which had contributed much to induce and to confirm my father's unsocial habits; it was the fact that a suspicion of *murder* had fallen upon his younger brother, though not sufficiently definite to lead to any public proceedings, yet strong enough to ruin him in public opinion. This disgraceful and dreadful doubt cast upon the family name, my father felt deeply and bitterly, and not the less so that he himself was thoroughly convinced of his brother's innocence. The sincerity and strength of this conviction he shortly afterwards proved in a manner which produced the catastrophe of my story.

Before, however, I enter upon my immediate adventures, I ought to relate the circumstances which had awakened that suspicion to which I have referred, inasmuch as they are in themselves somewhat curious, and in their effects most intimately connected with my own after-history.

My uncle, Sir Arthur Tyrrell, was a gay and extravagant man, and, among other vices, was ruinously addicted to gaming. This unfortunate propensity, even after his fortune had suffered so severely as to render retrenchment imperative, nevertheless continued to engross him, nearly to the exclusion of every other pursuit. He was, however, a proud, or rather a vain man, and could not bear to make the diminution of his income a matter of triumph to those with whom he had hitherto competed; and the consequence was, that he frequented no longer the expensive haunts of his dissipation, and retired from the gay world, leaving his coterie to discover his reasons as best they might. He did not, however, forego his favourite vice, for though he could not worship his great divinity in those costly temples where he was formerly wont to take his place, yet he found it very possible to bring about him a sufficient number of the votaries of chance to answer all his ends. The consequence was, that Carrickleigh, which was the name of my uncle's residence, was never without one or more of such visiters as I have described. It happened that upon one occasion he was visited by one Hugh Tisdall, a gentleman of loose, and, indeed, low habits, but of considerable wealth, and who had, in early youth, travelled with my uncle upon the Continent. The period of this visit was winter, and, consequently, the house was nearly deserted excepting by its ordinary inmates; it was, therefore, highly acceptable, particularly as my uncle was aware that his visiter's tastes accorded exactly with his own.

Both parties seemed determined to avail themselves of their mutual suitability during the brief stay which Mr. Tisdall had promised; the consequence was, that they shut themselves up in Sir Arthur's private room for nearly all the day and the greater part of the night, during the space of almost a week, at the end of which the servant having one morning, as usual, knocked at Mr. Tisdall's bed-room door repeatedly, received no answer, and, upon attempting to enter, found that it was locked. This appeared suspicious, and the inmates of the house having been alarmed, the door was forced open, and, on proceeding to the bed, they found the body of its occupant perfectly lifeless, and hanging halfway out, the head downwards, and near the floor. One deep wound had been inflicted upon the temple, apparently with some blunt instrument, which had penetrated the brain, and another blow, less effective – probably the first aimed – had grazed his head, removing some of the scalp. The door had been double locked upon the *inside*, in evidence of which the key still lay where it had been placed in the lock. The window, though not secured on the interior, was closed; a circumstance not a little puzzling, as it afforded the only other mode of escape from the room. It looked out, too, upon a kind of court-yard, round which the old buildings stood, formerly accessible by a narrow doorway and passage lying in the oldest side of the quadrangle, but which had since been built up, so as to preclude all ingress or egress; the room was also upon the second story, and the height of the window considerable; in addition to all which the stone window-sill was much too narrow to allow of any one's standing upon it when the window was closed. Near the bed were found a pair of razors belonging to the murdered man, one of them upon the ground, and both of them open. The weapon which inflicted the mortal wound was not to be found in the room, nor were any footsteps or other traces of the murderer discoverable. At the suggestion of Sir Arthur himself, the coroner was instantly summoned to attend, and an inquest was held. Nothing, however, in any degree conclusive was elicited. The walls, ceiling, and floor of the room were carefully examined, in order to ascertain whether they contained a trap-door or other concealed mode of entrance, but no such thing appeared. Such was the minuteness of investigation employed, that, although the grate had contained a large fire during the night, they proceeded to examine even the very chimney, in order to discover whether escape by it were possible. But this attempt, too, was fruitless, for the chimney, built in the old fashion, rose in a perfectly perpendicular line from the hearth, to a height of nearly fourteen feet above the roof, affording in its interior scarcely the possibility of ascent, the flue being smoothly plastered, and sloping towards the top like an inverted funnel; promising, too, even if the summit were attained, owing to its great height, but a precarious descent upon the sharp and steep-ridged roof; the ashes, too, which lay in the grate, and the soot, as far as it could be seen, were undisturbed, a circumstance almost conclusive upon the point.

Sir Arthur was of course examined. His evidence was given with clearness and unreserve, which seemed calculated to silence all suspicion. He stated that, up to the day and night immediately preceding the catastrophe, he had lost to a heavy amount, but that, at their last sitting, he had not only won back his original loss, but upwards of £4,000 in addition; in evidence of which he produced an acknowledgment of debt to that amount in the handwriting of the deceased, bearing date the night of the catastrophe. He had mentioned the circumstance to Lady Tyrrell, and in presence of some of his domestics; which statement was supported by *their* respective evidence. One of the jury shrewdly observed, that the circumstance of Mr. Tisdall's having sustained so heavy a loss might have suggested to some ill-minded persons, accidentally hearing it, the plan of robbing him, after having murdered him in such a manner as might make it appear that he had committed suicide; a supposition which was strongly supported by the razors having been found thus displaced and removed from their case. Two persons had probably been engaged in the attempt, one watching by the sleeping man, and ready to strike him in case of his awakening suddenly, while the other was procuring the razors and employed in inflicting the fatal gash, so as to make it appear to have been the act of the murdered man himself. It was said that while the juror was making this suggestion Sir Arthur changed colour. There was nothing, however, like legal evidence to implicate him, and the consequence was that the verdict was found against a person or persons unknown, and for some time the matter was suffered to rest, until, after about five months, my father received a letter from a person signing himself Andrew Collis, and representing himself to be the cousin of the deceased. This letter stated that his brother, Sir Arthur, was likely to incur not merely suspicion but personal risk, unless he could account for certain circumstances connected with the recent murder, and contained a copy of a letter written by the deceased, and dated the very day upon the night of which the murder had been perpetrated. Tisdall's letter contained, among a great deal of other matter, the passages which follow:

"I have had sharp work with Sir Arthur: he tried some of his stale tricks, but soon found that *I* was Yorkshire, too; it would not do – you understand me. We went to the work like good ones, head, heart, and soul; and in fact, since I came here, I have lost no time. I am rather fagged, but I am sure to be well paid for my hardship; I never want sleep so long as I can have the music of a dice-box, and wherewithal to pay the piper. As I told you, he tried some of his queer turns, but I foiled him like a man, and, in return, gave him more than he could relish of the genuine *dead knowledge*. In short, I have plucked the old baronet as never baronet was plucked before; I have scarce left him the stump of a quill. I have got promissory notes in his hand to the amount of —; if you like round numbers, say five-and-twenty thousand pounds, safely deposited in my portable strong box, alias, double-clasped pocket-book. I leave this ruinous old rat-hole early on tomorrow, for two reasons: first, I do not want to play with Sir Arthur deeper than I think his security would warrant; and, secondly, because I am safer a hundred miles away from Sir Arthur than in the house with him. Look you, my worthy, I tell you this between ourselves – I may be wrong – but, by —, I am sure as that I am now living, that Sir A— attempted to poison me last night. So much for old friendship on both sides. When I won the last stake, a heavy one enough, my friend leant his forehead upon his hands, and you'll laugh when I tell you that his head literally smoked like a hot dumpling. I do not know whether his agitation was produced by the plan which he had against me, or by his having lost so heavily; though it must be allowed that he had reason to be a little funked, whichever way his thoughts went; but he pulled the bell, and ordered two bottles of Champagne. While the fellow was bringing them, he wrote a promissory note to the full amount, which he signed, and, as the man came in with the bottles and glasses, he desired him to be off. He filled a glass for me, and, while he thought my eyes were off, for I was putting up his note at the time, he dropped something slyly into it, no doubt to sweeten it; but I saw it all, and, when he handed it to me, I said, with an emphasis which he might easily understand, 'There is some sediment in it, I'll not drink it.' 'Is there?' said he, and at the same time snatched it from my hand and threw it into the fire. What do you think of that? Have I not a tender bird in hand? Win or lose, I will not play beyond five thousand tonight, and tomorrow sees me safe out of the reach of Sir Arthur's Champagne."

Of the authenticity of this document, I never heard my father express a doubt; and I am satisfied that, owing to his strong conviction in favour of his brother, he would not have admitted it without sufficient inquiry, inasmuch as it tended to confirm the suspicions which already existed to his prejudice. Now, the only point in this letter which made strongly against my uncle, was the mention of the "double-clasped pocket-book," as the receptacle of the papers likely to involve him, for this pocket-book was not forthcoming, nor anywhere to be found, nor had any papers referring to his gaming transactions been discovered upon the dead man.

But whatever might have been the original intention of this man, Collis, neither my uncle nor my father ever heard more of him; he published the letter, however, in Faulkner's newspaper, which was shortly afterwards made the vehicle of a much more mysterious attack. The passage in that journal to which I allude, appeared about four years afterwards, and while the fatal occurrence was still fresh in public recollection. It commenced by a rambling preface, stating that "a *certain person* whom *certain* persons thought to be dead, was not so, but living, and in full possession of his memory, and moreover, ready and able to make *great* delinquents tremble": it then went on to describe the murder, without, however, mentioning names; and in doing so, it entered into minute and circumstantial particulars of which none but an *eye-witness* could have been possessed, and by implications almost too unequivocal to be regarded in the light of insinuation, to involve the *"titled gambler"* in the guilt of the transaction.

My father at once urged Sir Arthur to proceed against the paper in an action of libel, but he would not hear of it, nor consent to my father's taking any legal steps whatever in the matter. My father, however, wrote in a threatening tone to Faulkner, demanding a surrender of the author of the obnoxious article; the answer to this application is still in my possession, and is penned in an apologetic tone: it states that the manuscript had been handed in, paid for, and inserted as an advertisement, without sufficient inquiry, or any knowledge as to whom it referred. No step, however, was taken to clear my uncle's character in the judgment of the public; and, as he immediately sold a small property, the application of the proceeds of which were known to none, he was said to have disposed of it to enable himself to buy off the threatened information; however the truth might have been, it is certain that no charges respecting the mysterious murder were afterwards publicly made against my uncle, and, as far as external disturbances were concerned, he enjoyed henceforward perfect security and quiet.

A deep and lasting impression, however, had been made upon the public mind, and Sir Arthur Tyrrell was no longer visited or noticed by the gentry of the county, whose attentions he had hitherto received. He accordingly affected to despise those courtesies which he no longer enjoyed, and shunned even that society which he might have commanded. This is all that I need recapitulate of my uncle's history, and I now recur to my own.

Although my father had never, within my recollection, visited, or been visited by my uncle, each being of unsocial, procrastinating, and indolent habits, and their respective residences being very far apart – the one lying in the county of Galway, the other in that of Cork – he was strongly attached to his brother, and evinced his affection by an active correspondence, and by deeply and proudly resenting that neglect which had branded Sir Arthur as unfit to mix in society.

When I was about eighteen years of age, my father, whose health had been gradually declining, died, leaving me in heart wretched and desolate, and, owing to his habitual seclusion, with few acquaintances, and almost no friends. The provisions of his will were curious, and when I was sufficiently come to myself to listen to, or comprehend them, surprised me not a little: all his vast property was left to me, and to the heirs of my body, for ever; and, in default of such heirs, it was to go after my death to my uncle, Sir Arthur, without any entail. At the same time, the will appointed him my guardian, desiring that I might be received within his house, and reside with his family, and under his care, during the term of my minority; and in consideration of the increased expense consequent upon such an arrangement, a handsome allowance was allotted to him during the term of my proposed residence. The object of this last provision I at once understood; my father desired, by making it the direct apparent interest of Sir Arthur that I should die without issue, while at the same time he placed my person wholly in his power, to prove to the world how great and unshaken was his confidence in his brother's innocence and honour.

It was a strange, perhaps an idle scheme, but as I had been always brought up in the habit of considering my uncle as a deeply injured man, and had been taught, almost as a part of my religion, to regard him as the very soul of honour, I felt no further uneasiness respecting the arrangement than that likely to affect a shy and timid girl at the immediate prospect of taking up her abode for the first time in her life among strangers. Previous to leaving my home, which I felt I should do with a heavy heart, I received a most tender and affectionate letter from my uncle, calculated, if anything could do so, to remove the bitterness of parting from scenes familiar and dear from my earliest childhood, and in some degree to reconcile me to the measure.

It was upon a fine autumn day that I approached the old domain of Carrickleigh. I shall not soon forget the impression of sadness and of gloom which all that I saw produced upon my mind; the sunbeams were falling with a rich and melancholy lustre upon the fine old trees, which stood in lordly groups, casting their long sweeping shadows over rock and sward; there was an air of neglect and decay about the spot, which amounted almost to desolation, and mournfully increased as we approached the building itself, near which the ground had been originally more artificially and carefully cultivated than elsewhere, and where consequently neglect more immediately and strikingly betrayed itself.

As we proceeded, the road wound near the beds of what had been formerly two fish-ponds, which were now nothing more than stagnant swamps, overgrown with rank weeds, and here and there encroached upon by the straggling underwood; the avenue itself was much broken; and in many places the stones were almost concealed by grass and nettles; the loose stone walls which had here and there intersected the broad park, were, in many places, broken down, so as no longer to answer their original purpose as fences; piers were now and then to be seen, but the gates were gone; and to add to the general air of dilapidation, some huge trunks were lying scattered through the venerable old trees, either the work of the winter storms, or perhaps the victims of some extensive but desultory scheme of denudation, which the projector had not capital or perseverance to carry into full effect.

After the carriage had travelled a full mile of this avenue, we reached the summit of a rather abrupt eminence, one of the many which added to the picturesqueness, if not to the convenience of this rude approach; from the top of this ridge the grey walls of Carrickleigh were visible, rising at a small distance in front, and darkened by the hoary wood which crowded around them; it was a quadrangular building of considerable extent, and the front, where the great entrance was placed, lay towards us, and bore unequivocal marks of antiquity; the time-worn, solemn aspect of the old building, the ruinous and deserted appearance of the whole place, and the associations which connected it with a dark page in the history of my family, combined to depress spirits already predisposed for the reception of sombre and dejecting impressions. When the carriage drew up in the grass-grown court-yard before the hall-door, two lazy-looking men, whose appearance well accorded with that of the place which they tenanted, alarmed by the obstreperous barking of a great chained dog, ran out from some half-ruinous outhouses, and took charge of the horses; the hall-door stood open, and I entered a gloomy and imperfectly-lighted apartment, and found no one within it. However, I had not long to wait in this awkward predicament, for before my luggage had been deposited in the house, indeed before I had well removed my cloak and other muffles, so as to enable me to look around, a young girl ran lightly into the hall, and kissing me heartily and somewhat boisterously exclaimed, "My dear cousin, my dear Margaret – I am so delighted – so out of breath, we did not expect you till ten o'clock; my father is somewhere about the place, he must be close at hand. James – Corney – run out and tell your master; my brother is seldom at home, at least at any reasonable hour; you must be so tired – so fatigued – let me show you to your room; see that Lady Margaret's luggage is all brought up; you must lie down and rest yourself. Deborah, bring some coffee – up these stairs; we are so delighted to see you – you cannot think how lonely I have been; how steep these stairs are, are not they? I am so glad you are come – I could hardly bring myself to believe that you were really coming; how good of you, dear Lady Margaret." There was real good nature and delight in my cousin's greeting, and a kind of constitutional confidence of manner which placed me at once at ease, and made me feel immediately upon terms of intimacy with her. The room into which she ushered me, although partaking in the general air of decay which pervaded the mansion and all about it, had, nevertheless, been fitted up with evident attention to comfort, and even with some dingy attempt at luxury; but what pleased me most was that it opened, by a second door, upon a lobby which communicated with my fair cousin's apartment; a circumstance which divested the room, in my eyes, of the air of solitude and sadness which would otherwise have characterised it, to a degree almost painful to one so depressed and agitated as I was.

After such arrangements as I found necessary were completed, we both went down to the parlour, a large wainscotted room, hung round with grim old portraits, and, as I was not sorry to see, containing, in its ample grate, a large and cheerful fire. Here my cousin had leisure to talk more at her ease; and from her I learned something of the manners and the habits of the two remaining members of her family, whom I had not yet seen. On my arrival I had known nothing of the family among whom I was come to reside, except that it consisted of three individuals, my uncle, and his son and daughter, Lady Tyrrell having been long dead; in addition to this very scanty stock of information, I shortly learned from my communicative companion, that my uncle was, as I had suspected, completely retired in his habits, and besides that, having been, so far back as she could well recollect, always rather strict, as reformed rakes frequently become, he had latterly been growing more gloomily and sternly religious than heretofore. Her account of her brother was far less favourable, though she did not say anything directly to his disadvantage. From all that I could gather from her, I was led to suppose that he was a specimen of the idle, coarse-mannered, profligate 'squirearchy' – a result which might naturally have followed from the circumstance of his being, as it were, outlawed from society, and driven for companionship to grades below his own – enjoying, too, the dangerous prerogative of spending a good deal of money. However, you may easily suppose that I found nothing in my cousin's communication fully to bear me out in so very decided a conclusion.

I awaited the arrival of my uncle, which was every moment to be expected, with feelings half of alarm, half of curiosity – a sensation which I have often since experienced, though to a less degree, when upon the point of standing for the first time in the presence of one of whom I have long been in the habit of hearing or thinking with interest. It was, therefore, with some little perturbation that I heard, first a slight bustle at the outer door, then a slow step traverse the hall, and finally witnessed the door open, and my uncle enter the room. He was a striking looking man; from peculiarities both of person and of dress, the whole effect of his appearance amounted to extreme singularity. He was tall, and when young his figure must have been strikingly elegant; as it was, however, its effect was marred by a very decided stoop; his dress was of a sober colour, and in fashion anterior to any thing which I could remember. It was, however, handsome, and by no means carelessly put on; but what completed the singularity of his appearance was his uncut, white hair, which hung in long, but not at all neglected curls, even so far as his shoulders, and which combined with his regularly classic features, and fine dark eyes, to bestow upon him an air of venerable dignity and pride, which I have seldom seen equalled elsewhere. I rose as he entered, and met him about the middle of the room; he kissed my cheek and both my hands, saying:

"You are most welcome, dear child, as welcome as the command of this poor place and all that it contains can make you. I am rejoiced to see you – truly rejoiced. I trust that you are not much fatigued; pray be seated again." He led me to my chair, and continued, "I am glad to perceive you have made acquaintance with Emily already; I see, in your being thus brought together, the foundation of a lasting friendship. You are both innocent, and both young. God bless you – God bless you, and make you all that I could wish."

He raised his eyes, and remained for a few moments silent, as if in secret prayer. I felt that it was impossible that this man, with feelings manifestly so tender, could be the wretch that public opinion had represented him to be. I was more than ever convinced of his innocence. His manners were, or appeared to me, most fascinating. I know not how the lights of experience might have altered this estimate. But I was then very young, and I beheld in him a perfect mingling of the courtesy of polished life with the gentlest and most genial virtues of the heart. A feeling of affection and respect towards him began to spring up within me, the more earnest that I remembered how sorely he had suffered in fortune and how cruelly in fame. My uncle having given me fully to understand that I was most welcome, and might command whatever was his own, pressed me to take some supper; and on my refusing, he observed that, before bidding me good night, he had one duty further to perform, one in which he was convinced I would cheerfully acquiesce. He then proceeded to read a chapter from the Bible; after which he took his leave with the same affectionate kindness with which he had greeted me, having repeated his desire that I should consider every thing in his house as altogether at my disposal. It is needless to say how much I was pleased with my uncle – it was impossible to avoid being so; and I could not help saying to myself, if such a man as this is not safe from the assaults of slander, who is? I felt much happier than I had done since my father's death, and enjoyed that night the first refreshing sleep which had visited me since that calamity. My curiosity respecting my male cousin did not long remain unsatisfied; he appeared upon the next day at dinner. His manners, though not so coarse as I had expected, were exceedingly disagreeable; there was an assurance and a forwardness for which I was not prepared; there was less of the vulgarity of manner, and almost more of that of the mind, than I had anticipated. I felt quite uncomfortable in his presence; there was just that confidence in his look and tone, which would read encouragement even in mere toleration; and I felt more disgusted and annoyed at the coarse and extravagant compliments which he was pleased from time to time to pay me, than perhaps the extent of the atrocity might fully have warranted. It was, however, one consolation that he did not often appear, being much engrossed by pursuits about which I neither knew nor cared anything; but when he did, his attentions, either with a view to his amusement, or to some more serious object, were so obviously and perseveringly directed to me, that young and inexperienced as I was, even *I* could not be ignorant of their significance. I felt more provoked by this odious persecution than I can express, and discouraged him with so much vigour, that I did not stop even at rudeness to convince him that his assiduities were unwelcome; but all in vain.

This had gone on for nearly a twelvemonth, to my infinite annoyance, when one day, as I was sitting at some needlework with my companion, Emily, as was my habit, in the parlour, the door opened, and my cousin Edward entered the room. There was something, I thought, odd in his manner, a kind of struggle between shame and impudence, a kind of flurry and ambiguity, which made him appear, if possible, more than ordinarily disagreeable.

"Your servant, ladies," he said, seating himself at the same time; "sorry to spoil your *tête-à-tête*; but never mind, I'll only take Emily's place for a minute or two, and then we part for a while, fair cousin. Emily, my father wants you in the corner turret; no shilly, shally, he's in a hurry." She hesitated. "Be off – tramp, march, I say," he exclaimed, in a tone which the poor girl dared not disobey.

She left the room, and Edward followed her to the door. He stood there for a minute or two, as if reflecting what he should say, perhaps satisfying himself that no one was within hearing in the hall. At length he turned about, having closed the door, as if carelessly, with his foot, and advancing slowly, in deep thought, he took his seat at the side of the table opposite to mine. There was a brief interval of silence, after which he said:

"I imagine that you have a shrewd suspicion of the object of my early visit; but I suppose I must go into particulars. Must I?"

"I have no conception," I replied, "what your object may be."

"Well, well," said he becoming more at his ease as he proceeded, "it may be told in a few words. You know that it is totally impossible, quite out of the question, that an off-hand young fellow like me, and a good-looking girl like yourself, could meet continually as you and I have done, without an attachment – a liking growing up on one side or other; in short, I think I have let you know as plainly as if I spoke it, that I have been in love with you, almost from the first time I saw you." He paused, but I was too much horrified to speak. He interpreted my silence favourably. "I can tell you," he continued, "I'm reckoned rather hard to please, and very hard to *hit*. I can't say when I was taken with a girl before, so you see fortune reserved me."

Here the odious wretch actually put his arm round my waist: the action at once restored me to utterance, and with the most indignant vehemence I released myself from his hold, and at the same time said:

"I *have*, sir, of course, perceived your most disagreeable attentions; they have long been a source of great annoyance to me; and you must be aware that I have marked my disapprobation, my disgust, as unequivocally as I possibly could, without actual indelicacy."

I paused, almost out of breath from the rapidity with which I had spoken; and without giving him time to renew the conversation, I hastily quitted the room, leaving him in a paroxysm of rage and mortification. As I ascended the stairs, I heard him open the parlour-door with violence, and take two or three rapid strides in the direction in which I was moving. I was now much frightened, and ran the whole way until I reached my room, and having locked the door, I listened breathlessly, but heard no sound. This relieved me for the present; but so much had I been overcome by the agitation and annoyance attendant upon the scene which I had just passed through, that when my cousin Emily knocked at the door, I was weeping in great agitation. You will readily conceive my distress, when you reflect upon my strong dislike to my cousin Edward, combined with my youth and extreme inexperience. Any proposal of such a nature must have agitated me; but that it should come from the man whom, of all others, I instinctively most loathed and abhorred, and to whom I had, as clearly as manner could do it, expressed the state of my feelings, was almost too annoying to be borne; it was a calamity, too, in which I could not claim the sympathy of my cousin Emily, which had always been extended to me in my minor grievances. Still I hoped that it might not be unattended with good; for I thought that one inevitable and most welcome consequence would result from this painful *éclaircissement*, in the discontinuance of my cousin's odious persecution.

When I arose next morning, it was with the fervent hope that I might never again behold his face, or even hear his name; but such a consummation, though devoutedly to be wished, was hardly likely to occur. The painful impressions of yesterday were too vivid to be at once erased; and I could not help feeling some dim foreboding of coming annoyance and evil. To expect on my cousin's part anything like delicacy or consideration for me, was out of the question. I saw that he had set his heart upon my property, and that he was not likely easily to forego such a prize, possessing what might have been considered opportunities and facilities almost to compel my compliance. I now keenly felt the unreasonableness of my father's conduct in placing me to reside with a family, with all the members of which, with one exception, he was wholly unacquainted, and I bitterly felt the helplessness of my situation. I determined, however, in the event of my cousin's persevering in his addresses, to lay all the particulars before my uncle, although he had never, in kindness or intimacy, gone a step beyond our first interview, and to throw myself upon his hospitality and his sense of honour for protection against a repetition of such annoyances.

My cousin's conduct may appear to have been an inadequate cause for such serious uneasiness; but my alarm was awakened neither by his acts nor by words, but entirely by his manner, which was strange and even intimidating. At the beginning of our yesterday's interview, there was a sort of bullying swagger in his air, which, towards the end, gave place to something bordering upon the brutal vehemence of an undisguised ruffian, a transition which had tempted me into a belief that he might seek, even forcibly, to extort from me a consent to his wishes, or by means still more horrible, of which I scarcely dared to trust myself to think, to possess himself of my property.

I was early next day summoned to attend my uncle in his private room, which lay in a corner turret of the old building; and thither I accordingly went, wondering all the way what this unusual measure might prelude. When I entered the room, he did not rise in his usual courteous way to greet me, but simply pointed to a chair opposite to his own; this boded nothing agreeable. I sat down, however, silently waiting until he should open the conversation.

"Lady Margaret," at length he said, in a tone of greater sternness than I thought him capable of using, "I have hitherto spoken to you as a friend, but I have not forgotten that I am also your guardian, and that my authority as such gives me a right to controul your conduct. I shall put a question to you, and I expect and will demand a plain, direct answer. Have I rightly been informed that you have contemptuously rejected the suit and hand of my son Edward?"

I stammered forth with a good deal of trepidation:

"I believe, that is, I have, sir, rejected my cousin's proposals; and my coldness and discouragement might have convinced him that I had determined to do so."

"Madame," replied he, with suppressed, but, as it appeared to me, intense anger, "I have lived long enough to know that *coldness and discouragement,* and such terms, form the common cant of a worthless coquette. You know to the full, as well as I, that *coldness and discouragement* may be so exhibited as to convince their object that he is neither distasteful nor indifferent to the person who wears that manner. You know, too, none better, that an affected neglect, when skillfully managed, is amongst the most formidable of the allurements which artful beauty can employ. I tell you, madame, that having, without one word spoken in discouragement, permitted my son's most marked attentions for a twelvemonth or more, you have no *right* to dismiss him with no further explanation than demurely telling him that you had always looked coldly upon him, and neither your wealth nor *your ladyship* (there was an emphasis of scorn on the word which would have become Sir Giles Overreach himself) can warrant you in treating with contempt the affectionate regard of an honest heart."

I was too much shocked at this undisguised attempt to bully me into an acquiescence in the interested and unprincipled plan for their own aggrandisement, which I now perceived my uncle and his son had deliberately formed, at once to find strength or collectedness to frame an answer to what he had said. At length I replied, with a firmness that surprised myself:

"In all that you have just now said, sir, you have grossly misstated my conduct and motives. Your information must have been most incorrect, as far as it regards my conduct towards my cousin; my manner towards him could have conveyed nothing but dislike; and if anything could have added to the strong aversion which I have long felt towards him, it would be his attempting thus to frighten me into a marriage which he knows to be revolting to me, and which is sought by him only as a means for securing to himself whatever property is mine."

As I said this, I fixed my eyes upon those of my uncle, but he was too old in the world's ways to falter beneath the gaze of more searching eyes than mine; he simply said:

"Are you acquainted with the provisions of your father's will?"

I answered in the affirmative; and he continued: "Then you must be aware that if my son Edward were, which God forbid, the unprincipled, reckless man, the ruffian you pretend to think him" – (here he spoke very slowly, as if he intended that every word which escaped him should be registered in my memory, while at the same time the expression of his countenance underwent a gradual but horrible change, and the eyes which he fixed upon me became so darkly vivid, that I almost lost sight of everything else) – "if he were what you have described him, do you think, child, he would have found no shorter way than marriage to gain his ends? A single blow, an outrage not a degree worse than you insinuate, would transfer your property to us!!"

I stood staring at him for many minutes after he had ceased to speak, fascinated by the terrible, serpent-like gaze, until he continued with a welcome change of countenance:

"I will not speak again to you, upon this topic, until one month has passed. You shall have time to consider the relative advantages of the two courses which are open to you. I should be sorry to hurry you to a decision. I am satisfied with having stated my feelings upon the subject, and pointed out to you the path of duty. Remember this day month; not one word sooner."

He then rose, and I left the room, much agitated and exhausted.

This interview, all the circumstances attending it, but most particularly the formidable expression of my uncle's countenance while he talked, though hypothetically, of *murder*, combined to arouse all my worst suspicions of him. I dreaded to look upon the face that had so recently worn the appalling livery of guilt and malignity. I regarded it with the mingled fear and loathing with which one looks upon an object which has tortured them in a night-mare.

In a few days after the interview, the particulars of which I have just detailed, I found a note upon my toilet-table, and on opening it I read as follows:

> *"My Dear Lady Margaret,*
> *You will be, perhaps, surprised to see a strange face in your room today. I have dismissed your Irish maid, and secured a French one to wait upon you; a step rendered necessary by my proposing shortly to visit the Continent with all my family.*
> *Your faithful guardian,*
> *ARTHUR TYRELL."*

On inquiry, I found that my faithful attendant was actually gone, and far on her way to the town of Galway; and in her stead there appeared a tall, raw-boned, ill-looking, elderly Frenchwoman, whose sullen and presuming manners seemed to imply that her vocation had never before been that of a lady's-maid. I could not help regarding her as a creature of my uncle's, and therefore to be dreaded, even had she been in no other way suspicious.

Days and weeks passed away without any, even a momentary doubt upon my part, as to the course to be pursued by me. The allotted period had at length elapsed; the day arrived upon which I was to communicate my decision to my uncle. Although my resolution had never for a moment wavered, I could not shake off the dread of the approaching colloquy; and my heart sank within me as I heard the expected summons. I had not seen my cousin Edward since the occurrence of the grand *éclaircissement*; he must have studiously avoided me; I suppose from policy, it could not have been from delicacy. I was prepared for a terrific burst of fury from my uncle, as soon as I should make known my determination; and I not unreasonably feared that some act of violence or of intimidation would next be resorted to. Filled with these dreary forebodings, I fearfully opened the study door, and the next minute I stood in my uncle's presence. He received me with a courtesy which I dreaded, as arguing a favourable anticipation respecting the answer which I was to give; and after some slight delay he began by saying

"It will be a relief to both of us, I believe, to bring this conversation as soon as possible to an issue. You will excuse me, then, my dear niece, for speaking with a bluntness which, under other circumstances, would be unpardonable. You have, I am certain, given the subject of our last interview fair and serious consideration; and I trust that you are now prepared with candour to lay your answer before me. A few words will suffice; we perfectly understand one another."

He paused; and I, though feeling that I stood upon a mine which might in an instant explode, nevertheless answered with perfect composure: "I must now, sir, make the same reply which I did upon the last occasion, and I reiterate the declaration which I then made, that I never can nor will, while life and reason remain, consent to a union with my cousin Edward."

This announcement wrought no apparent change in Sir Arthur, except that he became deadly, almost lividly pale. He seemed lost in dark thought for a minute, and then, with a slight effort, said, "You have answered me honestly and directly; and you say your resolution is unchangeable; well, would it had been otherwise – would it had been otherwise – but be it as it is; I am satisfied."

He gave me his hand – it was cold and damp as death; under an assumed calmness, it was evident that he was fearfully agitated. He continued to hold my hand with an almost painful pressure, while, as if unconsciously, seeming to forget my presence, he muttered, "Strange, strange, strange, indeed! fatuity, helpless fatuity!" there was here a long pause. "Madness *indeed* to strain a cable that is rotten to the very heart; it must break – and then – all goes." There was again a pause of some minutes, after which, suddenly changing his voice and manner to one of wakeful alacrity, he exclaimed,

"Margaret, my son Edward shall plague you no more. He leaves this country tomorrow for France; he shall speak no more upon this subject – never, never more; whatever events depended upon your answer must now take their own course; but as for this fruitless proposal, it has been tried enough; it can be repeated no more."

At these words he coldly suffered my hand to drop, as if to express his total abandonment of all his projected schemes of alliance; and certainly the action, with the accompanying words, produced upon my mind a more solemn and depressing effect than I believed possible to have been caused by the course which I had determined to pursue; it struck upon my heart with an awe and heaviness which *will* accompany the accomplishment of an important and irrevocable act, even though no doubt or scruple remains to make it possible that the agent should wish it undone.

"Well," said my uncle, after a little time, "we now cease to speak upon this topic, never to resume it again. Remember you shall have no farther uneasiness from Edward; he leaves Ireland for France tomorrow; this will be a relief to you; may I depend upon your *honour* that no word touching the subject of this interview shall ever escape you?" I gave him the desired assurance; he said, "It is well; I am satisfied; we have nothing more, I believe, to say upon either side, and my presence must be a restraint upon you, I shall therefore bid you farewell." I then left the apartment, scarcely knowing what to think of the strange interview which had just taken place.

On the next day my uncle took occasion to tell me that Edward had actually sailed, if his intention had not been prevented by adverse winds or weather; and two days after he actually produced a letter from his son, written, as it said, *on board*, and despatched while the ship was getting under weigh. This was a great satisfaction to me, and as being likely to prove so, it was no doubt communicated to me by Sir Arthur.

During all this trying period I had found infinite consolation in the society and sympathy of my dear cousin Emily. I never, in after-life, formed a friendship so close, so fervent, and upon which, in all its progress, I could look back with feelings of such unalloyed pleasure, upon whose termination I must ever dwell with so deep, so yet unembittered a sorrow. In cheerful converse with her I soon recovered my spirits considerably, and passed my time agreeably enough, although still in the utmost seclusion. Matters went on smoothly enough, although I could not help sometimes feeling a momentary, but horrible uncertainty respecting my uncle's character; which was not altogether unwarranted by the circumstances of the two trying interviews, the particulars of which I have just detailed. The unpleasant impression which these conferences were calculated to leave upon my mind was fast wearing away, when there occurred a circumstance, slight indeed in itself, but calculated irrepressibly to awaken all my worst suspicions, and to overwhelm me again with anxiety and terror.

I had one day left the house with my cousin Emily, in order to take a ramble of considerable length, for the purpose of sketching some favourite views, and we had walked about half a mile when I perceived that we had forgotten our drawing materials, the absence of which would have defeated the object of our walk. Laughing at our own thoughtlessness, we returned to the house, and leaving Emily outside, I ran upstairs to procure the drawing-books and pencils which lay in my bed-room. As I ran up the stairs, I was met by the tall, ill-looking Frenchwoman, evidently a good deal flurried; "*Que veut Madame?*" said she, with a more decided effort to be polite, than I had ever known her make before. "No, no – no matter," said I, hastily running by her in the direction of my room. "Madame," cried she, in a high key, "*restez ici s'il vous plaît, votre chambre n'est pas faite.*"

I continued to move on without heeding her. She was some way behind me, and feeling that she could not otherwise prevent my entrance, for I was now upon the very lobby, she made a desperate attempt to seize hold of my person; she succeeded in grasping the end of my shawl, which she drew from my shoulders, but slipping at the same time upon the polished oak floor, she fell at full length upon the boards.

A little frightened as well as angry at the rudeness of this strange woman, I hastily pushed open the door of my room, at which I now stood, in order to escape from her; but great was my amazement on entering to find the apartment preoccupied. The window was open, and beside it stood two male figures; they appeared to be examining the fastenings of the casement, and their backs were turned towards the door. One of them was my uncle; they both had turned on my entrance, as if startled; the stranger was booted and cloaked, and wore a heavy, broad-leafed hat over his brows; he turned but for a moment, and averted his face; but I had seen enough to convince me that he was no other than my cousin Edward.

My uncle had some iron instrument in his hand, which he hastily concealed behind his back; and coming towards me, said something as if in an explanatory tone; but I was too much shocked and confounded to understand what it might be. He said something about "*repairs* – window-frames – cold, and safety." I did not wait, however, to ask or to receive explanations, but hastily left the room. As I went down stairs I thought I heard the voice of the Frenchwoman in all the shrill volubility of excuse, and others uttering suppressed but vehement imprecations, or what seemed to me to be such.

I joined my cousin Emily quite out of breath. I need not say that my head was too full of other things to think much of drawing for that day. I imparted to her frankly the cause of my alarms, but, at the same time, as gently as I could; and with tears she promised vigilance, devotion, and love. I never had reason for a moment to repent the unreserved confidence which I then reposed in her. She was no less surprised than I at the unexpected appearance of Edward, whose departure for France neither of us had for a moment doubted, but which was now proved by his actual presence to be nothing more than an imposture practised, I feared, for no good end. The situation in which I had found my uncle had very nearly removed all my doubts as to his designs; I magnified suspicions into certainties, and dreaded night after night that I should be murdered in my bed. The nervousness produced by sleepless nights and days of anxious fears increased the horrors of my situation to such a degree, that I at length wrote a letter to a Mr. Jefferies, an old and faithful friend of my father's, and perfectly acquainted with all his affairs, praying him, for God's sake, to relieve me from my present terrible situation, and communicating without reserve the nature and grounds of my suspicions. This letter I kept sealed and directed for two or three days always about my person, for discovery would have been ruinous, in expectation of an opportunity, which might be safely trusted, of having it placed in the post-office; as neither Emily nor I were permitted to pass beyond the precincts of the demesne itself, which was surrounded by high walls formed of dry stone, the difficulty of procuring such an opportunity was greatly enhanced.

At this time Emily had a short conversation with her father, which she reported to me instantly. After some indifferent matter, he had asked her whether she and I were upon good terms, and whether I was unreserved in my disposition. She answered in the affirmative; and he then inquired whether I had been much surprised to find him in my chamber on the other day. She answered that I had been both surprised and amused. "And what did she think of George Wilson's appearance?" "Who?" inquired she. "Oh! the architect," he answered, "who is to contract for the repairs of the house; he is accounted a handsome fellow." "She could not see his face," said Emily, "and she was in such a hurry to escape that she scarcely observed him." Sir Arthur appeared satisfied, and the conversation ended.

This slight conversation, repeated accurately to me by Emily, had the effect of confirming, if indeed any thing was required to do so, all that I had before believed as to Edward's actual presence; and I naturally became, if possible, more anxious than ever to despatch the letter to Mr. Jefferies. An opportunity at length occurred. As Emily and I were walking one day near the gate of the demesne, a lad from the village happened to be passing down the avenue from the house; the spot was secluded, and as this person was not connected by service with those whose observation I dreaded, I committed the letter to his keeping, with strict injunctions that he should put it, without delay, into the receiver of the town post-office; at the same time I added a suitable gratuity, and the man having made many protestations of punctuality, was soon out of sight. He was hardly gone when I began to doubt my discretion in having trusted him; but I had no better or safer means of despatching the letter, and I was not warranted in suspecting him of such wanton dishonesty as a disposition to tamper with it; but I could not be quite satisfied of its safety until I had received an answer, which could not arrive for a few days. Before I did, however, an event occurred which a little surprised me. I was sitting in my bed-room early in the day, reading by myself, when I heard a knock at the door. "Come in," said I, and my uncle entered the room. "Will you excuse me," said he, "I sought you in the parlour, and thence I have come here. I desired to say a word to you. I trust that you have hitherto found my conduct to you such as that of a guardian towards his ward should be." I dared not withhold my assent. "And," he continued, "I trust that you have not found me harsh or unjust, and that you have perceived, my dear niece, that I have sought to make this poor place as agreeable to you as may be?" I assented again; and he put his hand in his pocket, whence he drew a folded paper, and dashing it upon the table with startling emphasis he said, "Did you write that letter?" The sudden and fearful alteration of his voice, manner, and face, but more than all, the unexpected production of my letter to Mr. Jefferies, which I at once recognised, so confounded and terrified me, that I felt almost choking. I could not utter a word. "Did you write that letter?" he repeated, with slow and intense emphasis. "You did, liar and hypocrite. You dared to write that foul and infamous libel; but it shall be your last. Men will universally believe you mad, if I choose to call for an inquiry. I can make you appear so. The suspicions expressed in this letter are the hallucinations and alarms of a moping lunatic. I have defeated your first attempt, madam; and by the holy God, if ever you make another, chains, darkness, and the keeper's whip shall be your portion." With these astounding words he left the room, leaving me almost fainting.

I was now almost reduced to despair; my last cast had failed; I had no course left but that of escaping secretly from the castle, and placing myself under the protection of the nearest magistrate. I felt if this were not done, and speedily, that I should be *murdered*. No one, from mere description, can have an idea of the unmitigated horror of my situation; a helpless, weak, inexperienced girl, placed under the power, and wholly at the mercy of evil men, and feeling that I had it not in my power to escape for one moment from the malignant influences under which I was probably doomed to fall; with a consciousness, too, that if violence, if murder were designed, no human being would be near to aid me; my dying shriek would be lost in void space.

I had seen Edward but once during his visit, and as I did not meet him again, I began to think that he must have taken his departure; a conviction which was to a certain degree satisfactory, as I regarded his absence as indicating the removal of immediate danger. Emily also arrived circuitously at the same conclusion, and not without good grounds, for she managed indirectly to learn that Edward's black horse had actually been for a day and part of a night in the castle stables, just at the time of her brother's supposed visit. The horse had gone, and as she argued, the rider must have departed with it.

This point being so far settled, I felt a little less uncomfortable; when being one day alone in my bed-room, I happened to look out from the window, and to my unutterable horror, I beheld peering through an opposite casement, my cousin Edward's face. Had I seen the evil one himself in bodily shape, I could not have experienced a more sickening revulsion. I was too much appalled to move at once from the window, but I did so soon enough to avoid his eye. He was looking fixedly down into the narrow quadrangle upon which the window opened. I shrunk back unperceived, to pass the rest of the day in terror and despair. I went to my room early that night, but I was too miserable to sleep. .

At about twelve o'clock, feeling very nervous, I determined to call my cousin Emily, who slept, you will remember, in the next room, which communicated with mine by a second door. By this private entrance I found my way into her chamber, and without difficulty persuaded her to return to my room and sleep with me. We accordingly lay down together, she undressed, and I with my clothes on, for I was every moment walking up and down the room, and felt too nervous and miserable to think of rest or comfort. Emily was soon fast asleep, and I lay awake, fervently longing for the first pale gleam of morning, and reckoning every stroke of the old clock with an impatience which made every hour appear like six.

It must have been about one o'clock when I thought I heard a slight noise at the partition door between Emily's room and mine, as if caused by somebody's turning the key in the lock. I held my breath, and the same sound was repeated at the second door of my room, that which opened upon the lobby; the sound was here distinctly caused by the revolution of the bolt in the lock, and it was followed by a slight pressure upon the door itself, as if to ascertain the security of the lock. The person, whoever it might be, was probably satisfied, for I heard the old boards of the lobby creak and strain, as if under the weight of somebody moving cautiously over them. My sense of hearing became unnaturally, almost painfully acute. I suppose the imagination added distinctness to sounds vague in themselves. I thought that I could actually hear the breathing of the person who was slowly returning along the lobby.

At the head of the staircase there appeared to occur a pause; and I could distinctly hear two or three sentences hastily whispered; the steps then descended the stairs with apparently less caution. I ventured to walk quickly and lightly to the lobby door, and attempted to open it; it was indeed fast locked upon the outside, as was also the other. I now felt that the dreadful hour was come; but one desperate expedient remained – it was to awaken Emily, and by our united strength, to attempt to force the partition door, which was slighter than the other, and through this to pass to the lower part of the house, whence it might be possible to escape to the grounds, and so to the village. I returned to the bedside, and shook Emily, but in vain; nothing that I could do availed to produce from her more than a few incoherent words; it was a death-like sleep. She had certainly drunk of some narcotic, as, probably, had I also, in spite of all the caution with which I had examined every thing presented to us to eat or drink. I now attempted, with as little noise as possible, to force first one door, then the other; but all in vain. I believe no strength could have affected my object, for both doors opened inwards. I therefore collected whatever moveables I could carry thither, and piled them against the doors, so as to assist me in whatever attempts I should make to resist the entrance of those without. I then returned to the bed and endeavoured again, but fruitlessly, to awaken my cousin. It was not sleep, it was torpor, lethargy, death. I knelt down and prayed with an agony of earnestness; and then seating myself upon the bed, I awaited my fate with a kind of terrible tranquillity.

I heard a faint clanking sound from the narrow court which I have already mentioned, as if caused by the scraping of some iron instrument against stones or rubbish. I at first determined not to disturb the calmness which I now experienced, by uselessly watching the proceedings of those who sought my life; but as the sounds continued, the horrible curiosity which I felt overcame every other emotion, and I determined, at all hazards, to gratify it. I, therefore, crawled upon my knees to the window, so as to let the smallest possible portion of my head appear above the sill.

The moon was shining with an uncertain radiance upon the antique grey buildings, and obliquely upon the narrow court beneath; one side of it was therefore clearly illuminated, while the other was lost in obscurity, the sharp outlines of the old gables, with their nodding clusters of ivy, being at first alone visible. Whoever or whatever occasioned the noise which had excited my curiosity, was concealed under the shadow of the dark side of the quadrangle. I placed my hand over my eyes to shade them from the moonlight, which was so bright as to be almost dazzling, and, peering into the darkness, I first dimly, but afterwards gradually, almost with full distinctness, beheld the form of a man engaged in digging what appeared to be a rude hole close under the wall. Some implements, probably a shovel and pickaxe, lay beside him, and to these he every now and then applied himself as the nature of the ground required. He pursued his task rapidly, and with as little noise as possible. "So," thought I, as shovelful after shovelful, the dislodged rubbish mounted into a heap, "they are digging the grave in which, before two hours pass, I must lie, a cold, mangled corpse. I am *theirs* – I cannot escape." I felt as if my reason was leaving me. I started to my feet, and in mere despair I applied myself again to each of the two doors alternately. I strained every nerve and sinew, but I might as well have attempted, with my single strength, to force the building itself from its foundations. I threw myself madly upon the ground, and clasped my hands over my eyes as if to shut out the horrible images which crowded upon me.

The paroxysm passed away. I prayed once more with the bitter, agonised fervour of one who feels that the hour of death is present and inevitable. When I arose, I went once more to the window and looked out, just in time to see a shadowy figure glide stealthily along the wall. The task was finished. The catastrophe of the tragedy must soon be accomplished. I determined now to defend my life to the last; and that I might be able to do so with some effect, I searched the room for something which might serve as a weapon; but either through accident, or else in anticipation of such a possibility, every thing which might have been made available for such a purpose had been removed.

I must then die tamely and without an effort to defend myself. A thought suddenly struck me; might it not be possible to escape through the door, which the assassin must open in order to enter the room? I resolved to make the attempt. I felt assured that the door through which ingress to the room would be effected was that which opened upon the lobby. It was the more direct way, besides being, for obvious reasons, less liable to interruption than the other. I resolved, then, to place myself behind a projection of the wall, the shadow would serve fully to conceal me, and when the door should be opened, and before they should have discovered the identity of the occupant of the bed, to creep noiselessly from the room, and then to trust to Providence for escape. In order to facilitate this scheme, I removed all the lumber which I had heaped against the door; and I had nearly completed my arrangements, when I perceived the room suddenly darkened, by the close approach of some shadowy object to the window. On turning my eyes in that direction, I observed at the top of the casement, as if suspended from above, first the feet, then the legs, then the body, and at length the whole figure of a man present itself. It was Edward Tyrrell. He appeared to be guiding his descent so as to bring his feet upon the centre of the stone block which occupied the lower part of the window; and having secured his footing upon this, he kneeled down and began to gaze into the room. As the moon was gleaming into the chamber, and the bed-curtains were drawn, he was able to distinguish the bed itself and its contents. He appeared satisfied with his scrutiny, for he looked up and made a sign with his hand. He then applied his hands to the window-frame, which must have been ingeniously contrived for the purpose, for with apparently no resistance the whole frame, containing casement and all, slipped from its position in the wall, and was by him lowered into the room. The cold night wind waved the bed-curtains, and he paused for a moment; all was still again, and he stepped in upon the floor of the room. He held in his hand what appeared to be a steel instrument, shaped something like a long hammer. This he held rather behind him, while, with three long, *tip-toe* strides, he brought himself to the bedside. I felt that the discovery must now be made, and held my breath in momentary expectation of the execration in which he would vent his surprise and disappointment. I closed my eyes; there was a pause, but it was a short one. I heard two dull blows, given in rapid succession; a quivering sigh, and the long-drawn, heavy breathing of the sleeper was for ever suspended. I unclosed my eyes, and saw the murderer fling the quilt across the head of his victim; he then, with the instrument of death still in his hand, proceeded to the lobby-door, upon which he tapped sharply twice or thrice. A quick step was then heard approaching, and a voice whispered something from without. Edward answered, with a kind of shuddering chuckle, "Her ladyship is past complaining; unlock the door, in the devil's name, unless you're afraid to come in, and help me to lift her out of the window." The key was turned in the lock, the door opened, and my uncle entered the room. I have told you already that I had placed myself under the shade of a projection of the wall, close to the door. I had instinctively shrunk down cowering towards the ground on the entrance of Edward through the window. When my uncle entered the room, he and his son both stood so very close to me that his hand was every moment upon the point of touching my face. I held my breath, and remained motionless as death.

"You had no interruption from the next room?" said my uncle.

"No," was the brief reply.

"Secure the jewels, Ned; the French harpy must not lay her claws upon them. You're a steady hand, by G—d; not much blood – eh?"

"Not twenty drops," replied his son, "and those on the quilt."

"I'm glad it's over," whispered my uncle again; "we must lift the – the *thing* through the window, and lay the rubbish over it."

They then turned to the bedside, and, winding the bed-clothes round the body, carried it between them slowly to the window, and exchanging a few brief words with some one below, they shoved it over the window-sill, and I heard it fall heavily on the ground underneath.

"I'll take the jewels," said my uncle; "there are two caskets in the lower drawer."

He proceeded, with an accuracy which, had I been more at ease, would have furnished me with matter of astonishment, to lay his hand upon the very spot where my jewels lay; and having possessed himself of them, he called to his son:

"Is the rope made fast above?"

"I'm no fool; to be sure it is," replied he.

They then lowered themselves from the window; and I rose lightly and cautiously, scarcely daring to breathe, from my place of concealment, and was creeping towards the door, when I heard my uncle's voice, in a sharp whisper, exclaim, "Get up again; G—d d—n you, you've forgot to lock the room door"; and I perceived, by the straining of the rope which hung from above, that the mandate was instantly obeyed. Not a second was to be lost. I passed through the door, which was only closed, and moved as rapidly as I could, consistently with stillness, along the lobby. Before I had gone many yards, I heard the door through which I had just passed roughly locked on the inside. I glided down the stairs in terror, lest, at every corner, I should meet the murderer or one of his accomplices. I reached the hall, and listened, for a moment, to ascertain whether all was silent around. No sound was audible; the parlour windows opened on the park, and through one of them I might, I thought, easily effect my escape. Accordingly, I hastily entered; but, to my consternation, a candle was burning in the room, and by its light I saw a figure seated at the dinner-table, upon which lay glasses, bottles, and the other accompaniments of a drinking party. Two or three chairs were placed about the table, irregularly, as if hastily abandoned by their occupants. A single glance satisfied me that the figure was that of my French attendant. She was fast asleep, having, probably, drank deeply. There was something malignant and ghastly in the calmness of this bad woman's features, dimly illuminated as they were by the flickering blaze of the candle. A knife lay upon the table, and the terrible thought struck me—"Should I kill this sleeping accomplice in the guilt of the murderer, and thus secure my retreat?" Nothing could be easier; it was but to draw the blade across her throat, the work of a second.

An instant's pause, however, corrected me. "No," thought I, "the God who has conducted me thus far through the valley of the shadow of death, will not abandon me now. I will fall into their hands, or I will escape hence, but it shall be free from the stain of blood; His will be done." I felt a confidence arising from this reflection, an assurance of protection which I cannot describe. There were no other means of escape, so I advanced, with a firm step and collected mind, to the window. I noiselessly withdrew the bars, and unclosed the shutters; I pushed open the casement, and without waiting to look behind me, I ran with my utmost speed, scarcely feeling the ground beneath me, down the avenue, taking care to keep upon the grass which bordered it. I did not for a moment slacken my speed, and I had now gained the central point between the park-gate and the mansion-house.

Here the avenue made a wider circuit, and in order to avoid delay, I directed my way across the smooth sward round which the carriageway wound, intending, at the opposite side of the level, at a point which I distinguished by a group of old birch trees, to enter again upon the beaten track, which was from thence tolerably direct to the gate. I had, with my utmost speed, got about half way across this broad flat, when the rapid tramp of a horse's hoofs struck upon my ear. My heart swelled in my bosom, as though I would smother. The clattering of galloping hoofs approached; I was pursued; they were now upon the sward on which I was running; there was not a bush or a bramble to shelter me; and, as if to render escape altogether desperate, the moon, which had hitherto been obscured, at this moment shone forth with a broad, clear light, which made every object distinctly visible.

The sounds were now close behind me. I felt my knees bending under me, with the sensation which unnerves one in a dream. I reeled, I stumbled, I fell; and at the same instant the cause of my alarm wheeled past me at full gallop. It was one of the young fillies which pastured loose about the park, whose frolics had thus all but maddened me with terror. I scrambled to my feet, and rushed on with weak but rapid steps, my sportive companion still galloping round and round me with many a frisk and fling, until, at length, more dead than alive, I reached the avenue-gate, and crossed the stile, I scarce knew how. I ran through the village, in which all was silent as the grave, until my progress was arrested by the hoarse voice of a sentinel, who cried "Who goes there?" I felt that I was now safe. I turned in the direction of the voice, and fell fainting at the soldier's feet. When I came to myself, I was sitting in a miserable hovel, surrounded by strange faces, all bespeaking curiosity and compassion. Many soldiers were in it also; indeed, as I afterwards found, it was employed as a guard-room by a detachment of troops quartered for that night in the town. In a few words I informed their officer of the circumstances which had occurred, describing also the appearance of the persons engaged in the murder; and he, without further loss of time than was necessary to procure the attendance of a magistrate, proceeded to the mansion-house of Carrickleigh, taking with him a party of his men. But the villains had discovered their mistake, and had effected their escape before the arrival of the military.

The Frenchwoman was, however, arrested in the neighbourhood upon the next day. She was tried and condemned at the ensuing assizes; and previous to her execution confessed that "*she had a hand in making* Hugh Tisdall's bed." *She had been a housekeeper in the castle at the* time, and a *chère amie* of my uncle's. She was, in reality, able to speak English like a native, but had exclusively used the French language, I suppose to facilitate her designs. She died the same hardened wretch she had lived, confessing her crimes only, as she alleged, that her doing so might involve Sir Arthur Tyrrell, the great author of her guilt and misery, and whom she now regarded with unmitigated detestation.

With the particulars of Sir Arthur's and his son's escape, as far as they are known, you are acquainted. You are also in possession of their after fate; the terrible, the tremendous retribution which, after long delays of many years, finally overtook and crushed them. Wonderful and inscrutable are the dealings of God with his creatures!

Deep and fervent as must always be my gratitude to heaven for my deliverance, effected by a chain of providential occurrences, the failing of a single link of which must have ensured my destruction, it was long before I could look back upon it with other feelings than those of bitterness, almost of agony. The only being that had ever really loved me, my nearest and dearest friend, ever ready to sympathise, to counsel, and to assist; the gayest, the gentlest, the warmest heart; the only creature on earth that cared for me; her life had been the price of my deliverance; and I then uttered the wish, which no event of my long and sorrowful life has taught me to recall, that she had been spared, and that, in her stead, I were mouldering in the grave, forgotten, and at rest.

The Grey Woman

Elizabeth Gaskell

Portion I

THERE IS A MILL by the Neckar-side, to which many people resort for coffee, according to the fashion which is almost national in Germany. There is nothing particularly attractive in the situation of this mill; it is on the Mannheim (the flat and unromantic) side of Heidelberg. The river turns the mill-wheel with a plenteous gushing sound; the out-buildings and the dwelling-house of the miller form a well-kept dusty quadrangle. Again, further from the river, there is a garden full of willows, and arbours, and flower-beds not well kept, but very profuse in flowers and luxuriant creepers, knotting and looping the arbours together. In each of these arbours is a stationary table of white painted wood, and light moveable chairs of the same colour and material.

I went to drink coffee there with some friends in 184—. The stately old miller came out to greet us, as some of the party were known to him of old. He was of a grand build of a man, and his loud musical voice, with its tone friendly and familiar, his rolling laugh of welcome, went well with the keen bright eye, the fine cloth of his coat, and the general look of substance about the place. Poultry of all kinds abounded in the mill-yard, where there were ample means of livelihood for them strewed on the ground; but not content with this, the miller took out handfuls of corn from the sacks, and threw liberally to the cocks and hens that ran almost under his feet in their eagerness. And all the time he was doing this, as it were habitually, he was talking to us, and ever and anon calling to his daughter and the serving-maids, to bid them hasten the coffee we had ordered. He followed us to an arbour, and saw us served to his satisfaction with the best of everything we could ask for; and then left us to go round to the different arbours and see that each party was properly attended to; and, as he went, this great, prosperous, happy-looking man whistled softly one of the most plaintive airs I ever heard.

'His family have held this mill ever since the old Palatinate days; or rather, I should say, have possessed the ground ever since then, for two successive mills of theirs have been burnt down by the French. If you want to see Scherer in a passion, just talk to him of the possibility of a French invasion.'

But at this moment, still whistling that mournful air, we saw the miller going down the steps that led from the somewhat raised garden into the mill-yard; and so I seemed to have lost my chance of putting him in a passion.

We had nearly finished our coffee, and our 'kucken,' and our cinnamon cake, when heavy splashes fell on our thick leafy covering; quicker and quicker they came, coming through the tender leaves as if they were tearing them asunder; all the people in the garden were hurrying under shelter, or seeking for their carriages standing outside. Up the steps the miller came hastening, with a crimson umbrella, fit to cover every one left in the garden, and followed by his daughter, and one or two maidens, each bearing an umbrella.

'Come into the house – come in, I say. It is a summer-storm, and will flood the place for an hour or two, till the river carries it away. Here, here.'

And we followed him back into his own house. We went into the kitchen first. Such an array of bright copper and tin vessels I never saw; and all the wooden things were as thoroughly scoured. The red tile floor was spotless when we went in, but in two minutes it was all over slop and dirt with the tread of many feet; for the kitchen was filled, and still the worthy miller kept bringing in more people under his great crimson umbrella. He even called the dogs in, and made them lie down under the tables.

His daughter said something to him in German, and he shook his head merrily at her. Everybody laughed.

'What did she say?' I asked.

'She told him to bring the ducks in next; but indeed if more people come we shall be suffocated. What with the thundery weather, and the stove, and all these steaming clothes, I really think we must ask leave to pass on. Perhaps we might go in and see Frau Scherer.'

My friend asked the daughter of the house for permission to go into an inner chamber and see her mother. It was granted, and we went into a sort of saloon, over-looking the Neckar; very small, very bright, and very close. The floor was slippery with polish; long narrow pieces of looking-glass against the walls reflected the perpetual motion of the river opposite; a white porcelain stove, with some old-fashioned ornaments of brass about it; a sofa, covered with Utrecht velvet, a table before it, and a piece of worsted-worked carpet under it; a vase of artificial flowers; and, lastly, an alcove with a bed in it, on which lay the paralysed wife of the good miller, knitting busily, formed the furniture. I spoke as if this was all that was to be seen in the room; but, sitting quietly, while my friend kept up a brisk conversation in a language which I but half understood, my eye was caught by a picture in a dark corner of the room, and I got up to examine it more nearly.

It was that of a young girl of extreme beauty; evidently of middle rank. There was a sensitive refinement in her face, as if she almost shrank from the gaze which, of necessity, the painter must have fixed upon her. It was not over-well painted, but I felt that it must have been a good likeness, from this strong impress of peculiar character which I have tried to describe. From the dress, I should guess it to have been painted in the latter half of the last century. And I afterwards heard that I was right.

There was a little pause in the conversation.

'Will you ask Frau Scherer who this is?'

My friend repeated my question, and received a long reply in German. Then she turned round and translated it to me.

'It is the likeness of a great-aunt of her husband's.' (My friend was standing by me, and looking at the picture with sympathetic curiosity.) 'See! here is the name on the open page of this Bible, "Anna Scherer, 1778." Frau Scherer says there is a tradition in the family that this pretty girl, with her complexion of lilies and roses, lost her colour so entirely through fright, that she was known by the name of the Grey Woman. She speaks as if this Anna Scherer lived in some state of life-long terror. But she does not know details; refers me to her husband for them. She thinks he has some papers which were written by the original of that picture for her daughter, who died in this very house not long after our friend there was married. We can ask Herr Scherer for the whole story if you like.'

'Oh yes, pray do!' said I. And, as our host came in at this moment to ask how we were faring, and to tell us that he had sent to Heidelberg for carriages to convey us home, seeing no chance of the heavy rain abating, my friend, after thanking him, passed on to my request.

'Ah!' said he, his face changing, 'the aunt Anna had a sad history. It was all owing to one of those hellish Frenchmen; and her daughter suffered for it – the cousin Ursula, as we all called her when I was a child. To be sure, the good cousin Ursula was his child as well. The sins of the fathers are visited on their children. The lady would like to know all about it, would she? Well, there are papers – a kind of apology the aunt Anna wrote for putting an end to her daughter's engagement – or rather facts which she revealed, that prevented cousin Ursula from marrying the man she loved; and so she would never have any other good fellow, else I have heard say my father would have been thankful to have made her his wife.' All this time he was rummaging in the drawer of an old-fashioned bureau, and now he turned round, with a bundle of yellow MSS. in his hand, which he gave to my friend, saying, 'Take it home, take it home, and if you care to make out our crabbed German writing, you may keep it as long as you like, and read it at your leisure. Only I must have it back again when you have done with it, that's all.'

And so we became possessed of the manuscript of the following letter, which it was our employment, during many a long evening that ensuing winter, to translate, and in some parts to abbreviate. The letter began with some reference to the pain which she had already inflicted upon her daughter by some unexplained opposition to a project of marriage; but I doubt if, without the clue with which the good miller had furnished us, we could have made out even this much from the passionate, broken sentences that made us fancy that some scene between the mother and daughter – and possibly a third person – had occurred just before the mother had begun to write.

'Thou dost not love thy child, mother! Thou dost not care if her heart is broken!' Ah, God! and these words of my heart-beloved Ursula ring in my ears as if the sound of them would fill them when I lie a-dying. And her poor tear-stained face comes between me and everything else. Child! hearts do not break; life is very tough as well as very terrible. But I will not decide for thee. I will tell thee all; and thou shalt bear the burden of choice. I may be wrong; I have little wit left, and never had much, I think; but an instinct serves me in place of judgement, and that instinct tells me that thou and thy Henri must never be married. Yet I may be in error. I would fain make my child happy. Lay this paper before the good priest Schriesheim; if, after reading it, thou hast doubts which make thee uncertain. Only I will tell thee all now, on condition that no spoken word ever passes between us on the subject. It would kill me to be questioned. I should have to see all present again.

My father held, as thou knowest, the mill on the Neckar, where thy new-found uncle, Scherer, now lives. Thou rememberest the surprise with which we were received there last vintage twelvemonth. How thy uncle disbelieved me when I said that I was his sister Anna, whom he had long believed to be dead, and how I had to lead thee underneath the picture, painted of me long ago, and point out, feature by feature, the likeness between it and thee; and how, as I spoke, I recalled first to my own mind, and then by speech to his, the details of the time when it was painted; the merry words that passed between us then, a happy boy and girl; the position of the articles of furniture in the room; our father's habits; the cherry-tree, now cut down, that shaded the window of my bedroom, through which my brother was wont to squeeze himself, in order to spring on to the topmost bough that would bear his weight; and thence would pass me back his cap laden with fruit to where I sat on the window-sill, too sick with fright for him to care much for eating the cherries.

And at length Fritz gave way, and believed me to be his sister Anna, even as though I were risen from the dead. And thou rememberest how he fetched in his wife, and told her that I was not dead, but was come back to the old home once more, changed as I was. And she would scarce believe him, and scanned me with a cold, distrustful eye, till at length – for I knew her of old as Babette Müller – I said that I was well-todo, and needed not to seek out friends for what they had to give. And then she asked – not me, but her husband – why I had kept silent so long, leading all – father, brother, every one that loved me in my own dear home – to esteem me dead. And then thine uncle (thou rememberest?) said he cared not to know more than I cared to tell; that I was his Anna, found again, to be a blessing to him in his old age, as I had been in his boyhood. I thanked him in my heart for his trust; for were the need for telling all less than it seems to me now I could not speak of my past life. But she, who was my sister-in-law still, held back her welcome, and, for want of that, I did not go to live in Heidelberg as I had planned beforehand, in order to be near my brother Fritz, but contented myself with his promise to be a father to my Ursula when I should die and leave this weary world.

That Babette Müller was, as I may say, the cause of all my life's suffering. She was a baker's daughter in Heidelberg – a great beauty, as people said, and, indeed, as I could see for myself I, too – thou sawest my picture – was reckoned a beauty, and I believe I was so. Babette Müller looked upon me as a rival. She liked to be admired, and had no one much to love her. I had several people to love me – thy grandfather, Fritz, the old servant Kätchen, Karl, the head apprentice at the mill – and I feared admiration and notice, and the being stared at as the 'Schöne Müllerin,' whenever I went to make my purchases in Heidelberg.

Those were happy, peaceful days. I had Kätchen to help me in the housework, and whatever we did pleased my brave old father, who was always gentle and indulgent towards us women, though he was stern enough with the apprentices in the mill. Karl, the oldest of these, was his favourite; and I can see now that my father wished him to marry me, and that Karl himself was desirous to do so. But Karl was rough-spoken, and passionate – not with me, but with the others – and I shrank from him in a way which, I fear, gave him pain. And then came thy uncle Fritz's marriage; and Babette was brought to the mill to be its mistress. Not that I cared much for giving up my post, for, in spite of my father's great kindness, I always feared that I did not manage well for so large a family (with the men, and a girl under Kätchen, we sat down eleven each night to supper). But when Babette began to find fault with Kätchen, I was unhappy at the blame that fell on faithful servants; and by-and-by I began to see that Babette was egging on Karl to make more open love to me, and, as she once said, to get done with it, and take me off to a home of my own. My father was growing old, and did not perceive all my daily discomfort. The more Karl advanced, the more I disliked him. He was good in the main, but I had no notion of being married, and could not bear any one who talked to me about it.

Things were in this way when I had an invitation to go to Carlsruhe to visit a schoolfellow, of whom I had been very fond. Babette was all for my going; I don't think I wanted to leave home, and yet I had been very fond of Sophie Rupprecht. But I was always shy among strangers. Somehow the affair was settled for me, but not until both Fritz and my father had made inquiries as to the character and position of the Rupprechts. They learned that the father had held some kind of inferior position about the Grand-duke's court, and was now dead, leaving a widow, a noble lady, and two daughters, the elder of whom was Sophie, my friend. Madame Rupprecht was not rich, but more than respectable – genteel. When this was ascertained, my father made no opposition to my going; Babette forwarded it by all the means in her power, and even my dear Fritz had his word to say in its favour. Only Kätchen was against it – Kätchen and Karl. The opposition of Karl did more to send me to Carlsruhe than anything. For I could have objected to go; but when he took upon himself to ask what was the good of going a-gadding, visiting strangers of whom no one knew anything, I yielded to circumstances – to the pulling of Sophie and the pushing of Babette. I was silently vexed, I remember, at Babette's inspection of my clothes; at the way in which she settled that this gown was too old-fashioned, or that too common, to go with me on my visit to a noble lady; and at the way in which she took upon herself to spend the money my father had given me to buy what was requisite for the occasion. And yet I blamed myself, for every one else thought her so kind for doing all this; and she herself meant kindly, too.

At last I quitted the mill by the Neckar-side. It was a long day's journey, and Fritz went with me to Carlsruhe. The Rupprechts lived on the third floor of a house a little behind one of the principal streets, in a cramped-up court, to which we gained admittance through a doorway in the street. I remember how pinched their rooms looked after the large space we had at the mill, and yet they had an air of grandeur about them which was new to me, and which gave me pleasure, faded as some of it was. Madame Rupprecht was too formal a lady for me; I was never at my ease with her; but Sophie was all that I had recollected her at school: kind, affectionate, and only rather too ready with her expressions of admiration and regard. The little sister kept out of our way; and that was all we needed, in the first enthusiastic renewal of our early friendship. The one great object of Madame Rupprecht's life was to retain her position in society; and as her means were much diminished since her husband's death, there was not much comfort, though there was a great deal of show, in their way of living; just the opposite of what it was at my father's house. I believe that my coming was not too much desired by Madame Rupprecht, as I brought with me another mouth to be fed; but Sophie had spent a year or more in entreating for permission to invite me, and her mother, having once consented, was too well bred not to give me a stately welcome.

The life in Carlsruhe was very different from what it was at home. The hours were later, the coffee was weaker in the morning, the pottage was weaker, the boiled beef less relieved by other diet, the dresses finer, the evening engagements constant. I did not find these visits pleasant. We might not knit, which would have relieved the tedium a little; but we sat in a circle, talking together, only interrupted occasionally by a gentleman, who, breaking out of the knot of men who stood near the door, talking eagerly together, stole across the room on tiptoe, his hat under his arm, and, bringing his feet together in the position we called the first at the dancing-school, made a low bow to the lady he was going to address. The first time I saw these manners I could not help smiling; but Madame Rupprecht saw me, and spoke to me next morning rather severely, telling me that, of course, in my country breeding I could have seen nothing of court manners, or French fashions, but that that was no reason for my laughing at them. Of course I tried never to smile again in company. This visit to Carlsruhe took place in '89, just when every one was full of the events taking place at Paris; and yet at Carlsruhe French fashions were more talked of than French politics. Madame Rupprecht, especially, thought a great deal of all French people. And this again was quite different to us at home. Fritz could hardly bear the name of a Frenchman; and it had nearly been an obstacle to my visit to Sophie that her mother preferred being called Madame to her proper title of Frau.

One night I was sitting next to Sophie, and longing for the time when we might have supper and go home, so as to be able to speak together, a thing forbidden by Madame Rupprecht's rules of etiquette, which strictly prohibited any but the most necessary conversation passing between members of the same family when in society. I was sitting, I say, scarcely keeping back my inclination to yawn, when two gentlemen came in, one of whom was evidently a stranger to the whole party, from the formal manner in which the host led him up, and presented him to the hostess. I thought I had never seen any one so handsome or so elegant. His hair was powdered, of course, but one could see from his complexion that it was fair in its natural state. His features were as delicate as a girl's, and set off by two little 'mouches,' as we called patches in those days, one at the left corner of his mouth, the other prolonging, as it were, the right eye. His dress was blue and silver. I was so lost in admiration of this beautiful young man, that I was as much surprised as if the angel Gabriel had spoken to me, when the lady of the house brought him forward to present him to me. She called him Monsieur de la Tourelle, and he began to speak to me in French; but though I understood him perfectly, I dared not trust myself to reply to him in that language. Then he tried German, speaking it with a kind of soft lisp that I thought charming. But, before the end of the evening, I became a little tired of the affected softness and effeminacy of his manners, and the exaggerated compliments he paid me, which had the effect of making all the company turn round and look at me. Madame Rupprecht was, however, pleased with the precise thing that displeased me. She liked either Sophie or me to create a sensation; of course she would have preferred that it should have been her daughter, but her daughter's friend was next best. As we went away, I heard Madame Rupprecht and Monsieur de la Tourelle reciprocating civil speeches with might and main, from which I found out that the French gentleman was coming to call on us the next day. I do not know whether I was more glad or frightened, for I had been kept upon stilts of good manners all the evening. But still I was flattered when Madame Rupprecht spoke as if she had invited him, because he had shown pleasure in my society, and even more gratified by Sophie's ungrudging delight at the evident interest I had excited in so fine and agreeable a gentleman. Yet, with all this, they had hard work to keep me from running out of the salon the next day, when we heard his voice inquiring at the gate on the stairs for Madame Rupprecht. They had made me put on my Sunday gown, and they themselves were dressed as for a reception.

When he was gone away, Madame Rupprecht congratulated me on the conquest I had made; for, indeed, he had scarcely spoken to anyone else, beyond what mere civility required, and had almost invited himself to come in the evening to bring some new song, which was all the fashion in Paris, he said. Madame Rupprecht had been out all morning, as she told me, to glean information about Monsieur de la Tourelle. He was a propriétaire, had a small château on the Vosges mountains; he owned land there, but had a large income from some sources quite independent of this property. Altogether, he was a good match, as she emphatically observed. She never seemed to think that I could refuse him after this account of his wealth, nor do I believe she would have allowed Sophie a choice, even had he been as old and ugly as he was young and handsome. I do not quite know – so many events have come to pass since then, and blurred the clearness of my recollections – if I loved him or not. He was very much devoted to me; he almost frightened me by the excess of his demonstrations of love. And he was very charming to everybody around me, who all spoke of him as the most fascinating of men, and of me as the most fortunate of girls. And yet I never felt quite at my ease with him. I was always relieved when his visits were over, although I missed his presence when he did not come. He prolonged his visit to the friend with whom he was staying at Carlsruhe, on purpose to woo me. He loaded me with presents, which I was unwilling to take, only Madame Rupprecht seemed to consider me an affected prude if I refused them. Many of these presents consisted of articles of valuable old jewellery, evidently belonging to his family;

by accepting these I doubled the ties which were formed around me by circumstances even more than by my own consent. In those days we did not write letters to absent friends as frequently as is done now, and I had been unwilling to name him in the few letters that I wrote home. At length, however, I learned from Madame Rupprecht that she had written to my father to announce the splendid conquest I had made, and to request his presence at my betrothal. I started with astonishment. I had not realized that affairs had gone so far as this. But when she asked me, in a stern, offended manner, what I had meant by my conduct if I did not intend to marry Monsieur de la Tourelle – I had received his visits, his presents, all his various advances without showing any unwillingness or repugnance – (and it was all true; I had shown no repugnance, though I did not wish to be married to him, – at least, not so soon) – what could I do but hang my head, and silently consent to the rapid enunciation of the only course which now remained for me if I would not be esteemed a heartless coquette all the rest of my days?

There was some difficulty, which I afterwards learnt that my sister-in-law had obviated, about my betrothal taking place from home. My father, and Fritz especially, were for having me return to the mill, and there be betrothed, and from thence be married. But the Rupprechts and Monsieur de la Tourelle were equally urgent on the other side; and Babette was unwilling to have the trouble of the commotion at the mill; and also, I think, a little disliked the idea of the contrast of my grander marriage with her own.

So my father and Fritz came over to the betrothal. They were to stay at an inn in Carlsruhe for a fortnight, at the end of which time the marriage was to take place. Monsieur de la Tourelle told me he had business at home, which would oblige him to be absent during the interval between the two events; and I was very glad of it, for I did not think that he valued my father and my brother as I could have wished him to do. He was very polite to them; put on all the soft, grand manner, which he had rather dropped with me; and complimented us all round, beginning with my father and Madame Rupprecht, and ending with little Alwina. But he a little scoffed at the old-fashioned church ceremonies which my father insisted on; and I fancy Fritz must have taken some of his compliments as satire, for I saw certain signs of manner by which I knew that my future husband, for all his civil words, had irritated and annoyed my brother. But all the money arrangements were liberal in the extreme, and more than satisfied, almost surprised, my father. Even Fritz lifted up his eyebrows and whistled. I alone did not care about anything. I was bewitched, – in a dream, – a kind of despair. I had got into a net through my own timidity and weakness, and I did not see how to get out of it. I clung to my own home-people that fortnight as I had never done before. Their voices, their ways were all so pleasant and familiar to me, after the constraint in which I had been living. I might speak and do as I liked without being corrected by Madame Rupprecht, or reproved in a delicate, complimentary way by Monsieur de la Tourelle. One day I said to my father that I did not want to be married, that I would rather go back to the dear old mill; but he seemed to feel this speech of mine as a dereliction of duty as great as if I had committed perjury; as if, after the ceremony of betrothal, no one had any right over me but my future husband. And yet he asked me some solemn questions; but my answers were not such as to do me any good.

'Dost thou know any fault or crime in this man that should prevent God's blessing from resting on thy marriage with him? Dost thou feel aversion or repugnance to him in any way?'

And to all this what could I say? I could only stammer out that I did not think I loved him enough; and my poor old father saw in this reluctance only the fancy of a silly girl who did not know her own mind, but who had now gone too far to recede.

So we were married, in the Court chapel, a privilege which Madame Rupprecht had used no end of efforts to obtain for us, and which she must have thought was to secure us all possible happiness, both at the time and in recollection afterwards.

We were married; and after two days spent in festivity at Carlsruhe, among all our new fashionable friends there, I bade good-by for ever to my dear old father. I had begged my husband to take me by way of Heidelberg to his old castle in the Vosges; but I found an amount of determination, under that effeminate appearance and manner, for which I was not prepared, and he refused my first request so decidedly that I dared not urge it. 'Henceforth, Anna,' said he, 'you will move in a different sphere of life; and though it is possible that you may have the power of showing favour to your relations from time to time, yet much or familiar intercourse will be undesirable, and is what I cannot allow.' I felt almost afraid, after this formal speech, of asking my father and Fritz to come and see me; but, when the agony of bidding them farewell overcame all my prudence, I did beg them to pay me a visit ere long. But they shook their heads, and spoke of business at home, of different kinds of life, of my being a Frenchwoman now. Only my father broke out at last with a blessing, and said, 'If my child is unhappy – which God forbid – let her remember that her father's house is ever open to her.' I was on the point of crying out, 'Oh! take me back then now, my father! oh, my father!' when I felt, rather than saw, my husband present near me. He looked on with a slightly contemptuous air; and, taking my hand in his, he led me weeping away, saying that short farewells were always the best when they were inevitable.

It took us two days to reach his château in the Vosges, for the roads were bad and the way difficult to ascertain. Nothing could be more devoted than he was all the time of the journey. It seemed as if he were trying in every way to make up for the separation which every hour made me feel the more complete between my present and my former life. I seemed as if I were only now wakening up to a full sense of what marriage was, and I dare say I was not a cheerful companion on the tedious journey. At length, jealousy of my regret for my father and brother got the better of M. de la Tourelle, and he became so much displeased with me that I thought my heart would break with the sense of desolation. So it was in no cheerful frame of mind that we approached Les Rochers, and I thought that perhaps it was because I was so unhappy that the place looked so dreary. On one side, the château looked like a raw new building, hastily run up for some immediate purpose, without any growth of trees or underwood near it, only the remains of the stone used for building, not yet cleared away from the immediate neighbourhood, although weeds and lichens had been suffered to grow near and over the heaps of rubbish; on the other, were the great rocks from which the place took its name, and rising close against them, as if almost a natural formation, was the old castle, whose building dated many centuries back.

It was not large nor grand, but it was strong and picturesque, and I used to wish that we lived in it rather than in the smart, half-furnished apartment in the new edifice, which had been hastily got ready for my reception. Incongruous as the two parts were, they were joined into a whole by means of intricate passages and unexpected doors, the exact positions of which I never fully understood. M. de la Tourelle led me to a suite of rooms set apart for me, and formally installed me in them, as in a domain of which I was sovereign. He apologised for the hasty preparation which was all he had been able to make for me, but promised, before I asked, or even thought of complaining, that they should be made as luxurious as heart could wish before many weeks had elapsed. But when, in the gloom of an autumnal evening, I caught my own face and figure reflected in all the mirrors, which showed only a mysterious background in the dim light of the many candles which failed to illuminate the great proportions of the half-furnished salon, I clung to M. de la Tourelle, and begged to be taken to the rooms he had occupied before his marriage, he seemed angry with me, although he affected to laugh, and so decidedly put aside the notion of my having any other rooms but these, that I trembled in silence at the fantastic figures and shapes which my imagination called up as peopling the background of those gloomy mirrors. There was my boudoir, a little less dreary – my bedroom, with its grand and tarnished furniture, which I commonly made into my sitting-room, locking up the various doors which led into the boudoir, the salon, the passages – all but one, through which M. de la Tourelle always entered from his own apartments in the older part of the castle. But this preference of mine for occupying my bedroom annoyed M. de la Tourelle, I am sure, though he did not care to express his displeasure. He would always allure me back into the salon, which I disliked more and more from its complete separation from the rest of the building by the long passage into which all the doors of my apartment opened. This passage was closed by heavy doors and portières, through which I could not hear a sound from the other parts of the house, and, of course, the servants could not hear any movement or cry of mine unless expressly summoned. To a girl brought up as I had been in a household where every individual lived all day in the sight of every other member of the family, never wanted either cheerful words or the sense of silent companionship, this grand isolation of mine was very formidable; and the more so, because M. de la Tourelle, as landed proprietor, sportsman, and what not, was generally out of doors the greater part of every day, and sometimes for two or three days at a time. I had no pride to keep me from associating with the domestics; it would have been natural to me in many ways to have sought them out for a word of sympathy in those dreary days when I was left so entirely to myself, had they been like our kindly German servants. But I disliked them, one and all; I could not tell why. Some were civil, but there was a familiarity in their civility which repelled me; others were rude, and treated me more as if I were an intruder than their master's chosen wife; and yet of the two sets I liked these last the best.

The principal male servant belonged to this latter class. I was very much afraid of him, he had such an air of suspicious surliness about him in all he did for me; and yet M. de la Tourelle spoke of him as most valuable and faithful. Indeed, it sometimes struck me that Lefebvre ruled his master in some things; and this I could not make out. For, while M. de la Tourelle behaved towards me as if I were some precious toy or idol, to be cherished, and fostered, and petted, and indulged, I soon found out how little I, or, apparently, any one else, could bend the terrible will of the man who had on first acquaintance appeared to me too effeminate and languid to exert his will in the slightest particular. I had learnt to know his face better now; and to see that some vehement depth of feeling, the cause of which I could not fathom, made his grey eye glitter with pale light, and his lips contract, and his delicate cheek whiten on certain occasions. But all had been so open and above board at home, that I had no experience to help me to unravel any mysteries among those who lived under the same roof. I understood that I had made what Madame Rupprecht and her set would have called a great marriage, because I lived in château with many servants, bound ostensibly to obey me as a mistress. I understood that M. de la Tourelle was fond enough of me in his way – proud of my beauty, I dare say (for he often enough spoke about it to me) – but he was also jealous, and suspicious, and uninfluenced by my wishes, unless they tallied with his own. I felt at this time as if I could have been fond of him too, if he would have let me; but I was timid from my childhood, and before long my dread of his displeasure (coming down like thunder into the midst of his love, for such slight causes as a hesitation in reply, a wrong word, or a sigh for my father), conquered my humorous inclination to love one who was so handsome, so accomplished, so indulgent and devoted. But if I could not please him when indeed I loved him, you may imagine how often I did wrong when I was so much afraid of him as to quietly avoid his company for fear of his outbursts of passion. One thing I remember noticing, that the more M. de la Tourelle was displeased with me, the more Lefebvre seemed to chuckle; and when I was restored to favour, sometimes on as sudden an impulse as that which occasioned my disgrace, Lefebvre would look askance at me with his cold, malicious eyes, and once or twice at such times he spoke most disrespectfully to M. de la Tourelle.

I have almost forgotten to say that, in the early days of my life at Les Rochers, M. de la Tourelle, in contemptuous indulgent pity at my weakness in disliking the dreary grandeur of the salon, wrote up to the milliner in Paris from whom my corbeille de mariage had come, to desire her to look out for me a maid of middle age, experienced in the toilette, and with so much refinement that she might on occasion serve as companion to me.

Portion II

A NORMAN WOMAN, Amante by name, was sent to Les Rochers by the Paris milliner, to become my maid. She was tall and handsome, though upwards of forty, and somewhat gaunt. But, on first seeing her, I liked her; she was neither rude nor familiar in her manners, and had a pleasant look of straightforwardness about her that I had missed in all the inhabitants of the château, and had foolishly set down in my own mind as a national want. Amante was directed by M. de la Tourelle to sit in my boudoir, and to be always within call. He also gave her many instructions as to her duties in matters which, perhaps, strictly belonged to my department of management. But I was young and inexperienced, and thankful to be spared any responsibility.

I daresay it was true what M. de la Tourelle said – before many weeks had elapsed – that, for a great lady, a lady of a castle, I became sadly too familiar with my Norman waiting-maid. But you know that by birth we were not very far apart in rank: Amante was the daughter of a Norman farmer, I of a German miller; and besides that, my life was so lonely! It almost seemed as if I could not please my husband. He had written for some one capable of being my companion at times, and now he was jealous of my free regard for her – angry because I could sometimes laugh at her original tunes and amusing proverbs, while when with him I was too much frightened to smile.

From time to time families from a distance of some leagues drove through the bad roads in their heavy carriages to pay us a visit, and there was an occasional talk of our going to Paris when public affairs should be a little more settled. These little events and plans were the only variations in my life for the first twelve months, if I except the alternations in M. de la Tourelle's temper, his unreasonable anger, and his passionate fondness.

Perhaps one of the reasons that made me take pleasure and comfort in Amante's society was, that whereas I was afraid of everybody (I do not think I was half as much afraid of things as of persons), Amante feared no one. She would quietly beard Lefebvre, and he respected her all the more for it; she had a knack of putting questions to M. de la Tourelle, which respectfully informed him that she had detected the weak point, but forebore to press him too closely upon it out of deference to his position as her master. And with all her shrewdness to others, she had quite tender ways with me; all the more so at this time because she knew, what I had not yet ventured to tell M. de la Tourelle, that by-and-by I might become a mother – that wonderful object of mysterious interest to single women, who no longer hope to enjoy such blessedness themselves.

It was once more autumn; late in October. But I was reconciled to my habitation; the walls of the new part of the building no longer looked bare and desolate; the débris had been so far cleared away by M. de la Tourelle's desire as to make me a little flower-garden, in which I tried to cultivate those plants that I remembered as growing at home. Amante and I had moved the furniture in the rooms, and adjusted it to our liking; my husband had ordered many an article from time to time that he thought would give me pleasure, and I was becoming tame to my apparent imprisonment in a certain part of the great building, the whole of which I had never yet explored. It was October, as I say, once more. The days were lovely, though short in duration, and M. de la Tourelle had occasion, so he said, to go to that distant estate the superintendence of which so frequently took him away from home. He took Lefebvre with him, and possibly some more of the lacqueys; he often did. And my spirits rose a little at the thought of his absence; and then the new sensation that he was the father of my unborn babe came over me, and I tried to invest him with this fresh character. I tried to believe that it was his passionate love for me that made him so jealous and tyrannical, imposing, as he did, restrictions on my very intercourse with my dear father, from whom I was so entirely separated, as far as personal intercourse was concerned.

I had, it is true, let myself go into a sorrowful review of all the troubles which lay hidden beneath the seeming luxury of my life. I knew that no one cared for me except my husband and Amante; for it was clear enough to see that I, as his wife, and also as a parvenue, was not popular among the few neighbours who surrounded us; and as for the servants; the women were all hard and impudent-looking, treating me with a semblance of respect that had more of mockery than reality in it; while the men had a lurking kind of fierceness about them, sometimes displayed even to M. de la Tourelle, who on his part, it must be confessed, was often severe even to cruelty in his management of them. My husband loved me, I said to my-self, but I said it almost in the form of a question. His love was shown fitfully, and more in ways calculated to please himself than to please me. I felt that for no wish of mine would he deviate one tittle from any predetermined course of action. I had learnt the inflexibility of those thin delicate lips; I knew how anger would turn his fair complexion to deadly white, and bring the cruel light into his pale blue eyes. The love I bore to any one seemed to be a reason for his hating them, and so I went on pitying myself one long dreary afternoon during that absence of his of which I have spoken, only sometimes remembering to check myself in my murmurings by thinking of the new unseen link between us, and then crying afresh to think how wicked I was. Oh, how well I remember that long October evening! Amante came in from time to time, talking away to cheer me – talking about dress and Paris, and I hardly know what, but from time to time looking at me keenly with her friendly dark eyes, and with serious interest, too, though all her words were about frivolity. At length she heaped the fire with wood, drew the heavy silken curtains close; for I had been anxious hitherto to keep them open, so that I might see the pale moon mounting the skies, as I used to see her – the same moon – rise from behind the Kaiser Stuhl at Heidelberg; but the sight made me cry, so Amante shut it out. She dictated to me as a nurse does to a child.

'Now, madame must have the little kitten to keep her company,' she said, 'while I go and ask Marthon for a cup of coffee.' I remember that speech, and the way it roused me, for I did not like Amante to think I wanted amusing by a kitten. It might be my petulance, but this speech – such as she might have made to a child – annoyed me, and I said that I had reason for my lowness of spirits – meaning that they were not of so imaginary a nature that I could be diverted from them by the gambols of a kitten. So, though I did not choose to tell her all, I told her a part; and as I spoke, I began to suspect that the good creature knew much of what I withheld, and that the little speech about the kitten was more thoughtfully kind than it had seemed at first. I said that it was so long since I had heard from my father; that he was an old man, and so many things might happen – I might never see him again – and I so seldom heard from him or my brother. It was a more complete and total separation than I had ever anticipated when I married, and something of my home and of my life previous to my marriage I told the good Amante; for I had not been brought up as a great lady, and the sympathy of any human being was precious to me.

Amante listened with interest, and in return told me some of the events and sorrows of her own life. Then, remembering her purpose, she set out in search of the coffee, which ought to have been brought to me an hour before; but, in my husband's absence, my wishes were but seldom attended to, and I never dared to give orders.

Presently she returned, bringing the coffee and a great large cake.

'See!' said she, setting it down. 'Look at my plunder. Madame must eat. Those who eat always laugh. And, besides, I have a little news that will please madame.' Then she told me that, lying on a table in the great kitchen, was a bundle of letters, come by the courier from Strasburg that very afternoon: then, fresh from her conversation with me, she had hastily untied the string that bound them, but had only just traced out one that she thought was from Germany, when a servant-man came in, and, with the start he gave her, she dropped the letters, which he picked up, swearing at her for having untied and disarranged them. She told him that she believed there was a letter there for her mistress; but he only swore the more, saying, that if there was it was no business of hers, or of his either, for that he had the strictest orders always to take all letters that arrived during his master's absence into the private sitting-room of the latter – a room into which I had never entered, although it opened out of my husband's dressing-room.

I asked Amante if she had not conquered and brought me this letter. No, indeed, she replied, it was almost as much as her life was worth to live among such a set of servants: it was only a month ago that Jacques had stabbed Valentin for some jesting talk. Had I never missed Valentin – that handsome young lad who carried up the wood into my salon? Poor fellow! he lies dead and cold now, and they said in the village he had put an end to himself, but those of the household knew better. Oh! I need not be afraid; Jacques was gone, no one knew where; but with such people it was not safe to upbraid or insist. Monsieur would be at home the next day, and it would not be long to wait.

But I felt as if I could not exist till the next day, without the letter. It might be to say that my father was ill, dying – he might cry for his daughter from his death-bed! In short, there was no end to the thoughts and fancies that haunted me. It was of no use for Amante to say that, after all, she might be mistaken – that she did not read writing well – that she had but a glimpse of the address; I let my coffee cool, my food all became distasteful, and I wrung my hands with impatience to get at the letter, and have some news of my dear ones at home. All the time, Amante kept her imperturbable good temper, first reasoning, then scolding. At last she said, as if wearied out, that if I would consent to make a good supper, she would see what could be done as to our going to monsieur's room in search of the letter, after the servants were all gone to bed. We agreed to go together when all was still, and look over the letters; there could be no harm in that; and yet, somehow, we were such cowards we dared not do it openly and in the face of the household.

Presently my supper came up – partridges, bread, fruits, and cream. How well I remember that supper! We put the untouched cake away in a sort of buffet, and poured the cold coffee out of the window, in order that the servants might not take offence at the apparent fancifulness of sending down for food I could not eat. I was so anxious for all to be in bed, that I told the footman who served that he need not wait to take away the plates and dishes, but might go to bed. Long after I thought the house was quiet, Amante, in her caution, made me wait. It was past eleven before we set out, with cat-like steps and veiled light, along the passages, to go to my husband's room and steal my own letter, if it was indeed there; a fact about which Amante had become very uncertain in the progress of our discussion.

To make you understand my story, I must now try to explain to you the plan of the château. It had been at one time a fortified place of some strength, perched on the summit of a rock, which projected from the side of the mountain. But additions had been made to the old building (which must have borne a strong resemblance to the castles overhanging the Rhine), and these new buildings were placed so as to command a magnifi-cent view, being on the steepest side of the rock, from which the mountain fell away, as it were, leaving the great plain of France in full survey. The ground-plan was something of the shape of three sides of an oblong; my apartments in the modern edifice occupied the narrow end, and had this grand prospect. The front of the castle was old, and ran parallel to the road far below. In this were contained the offices and public rooms of various descriptions, into which I never penetrated. The back wing (considering the new building, in which my apartments were, as the centre) consisted of many rooms, of a dark and gloomy character, as the mountain-side shut out much of the sun, and heavy pine woods came down within a few yards of the windows. Yet on this side – on a projecting plateau of the rock – my husband had formed the flower-garden of which I have spoken; for he was a great cultivator of flowers in his leisure moments.

Now my bedroom was the corner room of the new buildings on the part next to the mountains. Hence I could have let myself down into the flower-garden by my hands on the windowsill on one side, without danger of hurting myself; while the windows at right angles with these looked sheer down a descent of a hundred feet at least. Going still farther along this wing, you came to the old building; in fact, these two fragments of the ancient castle had formerly been attached by some such connecting apartments as my husband had rebuilt. These rooms belonged to M. de la Tourelle. His bedroom opened into mine, his dressing-room lay beyond; and that was pretty nearly all I knew, for the servants, as well as he himself, had a knack of turning me back, under some pretence, if ever they found me walking about alone, as I was inclined to do, when first I came, from a sort of curiosity to see the whole of the place of which I found myself mistress. M. de la Tourelle never encouraged me to go out alone, either in a carriage or for a walk, saying always that the roads were unsafe in those disturbed times; indeed, I have sometimes fancied since that the flower-garden, to which the only access from the castle was through his rooms, was designed in order to give me exercise and employment under his own eye.

But to return to that night. I knew, as I have said, that M. de la Tourelle's private room opened out of his dressing-room, and this out of his bedroom, which again opened into mine, the corner-room. But there were other doors into all these rooms, and these doors led into a long gallery, lighted by windows, looking into the inner court. I do not remember our consulting much about it; we went through my room into my husband's apartment through the dressing-room, but the door of communication into his study was locked, so there was nothing for it but to turn back and go by the gallery to the other door. I recollect noticing one or two things in these rooms, then seen by me for the first time. I remember the sweet perfume that hung in the air, the scent bottles of silver that decked his toilet-table, and the whole apparatus for bathing and dressing, more luxurious even than those which he had provided for me. But the room itself was less splendid in its proportions than mine. In truth, the new buildings ended at the entrance to my husband's dressing-room. There were deep window recesses in walls eight or nine feet thick, and even the partitions between the chambers were three feet deep; but over all these doors or windows there fell thick, heavy draperies, so that I should think no one could have heard in one room what passed in another. We went back into my room, and out into the gallery. We had to shade our candle, from a fear that possessed us, I don't know why, lest some of the servants in the opposite wing might trace our progress towards the part of the castle unused by any one except my husband. Somehow, I had always the feeling that all the domestics, except Amante, were spies upon me, and that I was trammelled in a web of observation and unspoken limitation extending over all my actions.

There was a light in the upper room; we paused, and Amante would have again retreated, but I was chafing under the delays. What was the harm of my seeking my father's unopened letter to me in my husband's study? I, generally the coward, now blamed Amante for her unusual timidity. But the truth was, she had far more reason for suspicion as to the proceedings of that terrible household than I had ever known of. I urged her on, I pressed on myself; we came to the door, locked, but with the key in it; we turned it, we entered; the letters lay on the table, their white oblongs catching the light in an instant, and revealing themselves to my eager eyes, hungering after the words of love from my peaceful, distant home.

But just as I pressed forward to examine the letters, the candle which Amante held, caught in some draught, went out, and we were in darkness. Amante proposed that we should carry the letters back to my salon, collecting them as well as we could in the dark, and returning all but the expected one for me; but I begged her to return to my room, where I kept tinder and flint, and to strike a fresh light; and I remained alone in the room, of which I could only just distinguish the size, and the principal articles of furniture: a large table, with a deep, overhanging cloth, in the middle, escritoires and other heavy articles against the walls; all this I could see as I stood there, my hand on the table close by the letters, my face towards the window, which, both from the darkness of the wood growing high up the mountain-side and the faint light of the declining moon, seemed only like an oblong of paler purpler black than the shadowy room. How much I remembered from my one instantaneous glance before the candle went out, how much I saw as my eyes became accustomed to the darkness, I do not know, but even now, in my dreams, comes up that room of horror, distinct in its profound shadow. Amante could hardly have been gone a minute before I felt an additional gloom before the window, and heard soft movements outside – soft, but resolute, and continued until the end was accomplished, and the window raised.

In mortal terror of people forcing an entrance at such an hour, and in such a manner as to leave no doubt of their purpose, I would have turned to fly when first I heard the noise, only that I feared by any quick motion to catch their attention, as I also ran the danger of doing by opening the door, which was all but closed and to whose handlings I was unaccustomed. Again, quick as lightning, I bethought me of the hiding-place between the locked door to my husband's dressing-room and the portière which covered it; but I gave that up, I felt as if I could not reach it without screaming or fainting. So I sank down softly, and crept under the table, hidden as I hoped, by the great, deep table-cover, with its heavy fringe. I had not recovered my swooning senses fully, and was trying to reassure myself as to my being in a place of comparative safety, for, above all things, I dreaded the betrayal of fainting, and struggled hard for such courage as I might attain by deadening myself to the danger I was in by inflicting intense pain on myself. You have often asked me the reason of that mark on my hand; it was there, in my agony, I bit out a piece of flesh with my relentless teeth, thankful for the pain, which helped to numb my terror. I say, I was but just concealed within I heard the window lifted, and one after another stepped over the sill, and stood by me so close that I could have touched their feet. Then they laughed and whispered; my brain swam so that I could not tell the meaning of their words, but I heard my husband's laughter among the rest – low, hissing, scornful – as he kicked something heavy that they had dragged in over the floor, and which layed near me; so near, that my husband's kick, in touching it, touched me too. I don't know why – I can't tell how – but some feeling, and not curiosity, prompted me to put out my hand, ever so softly, ever so little, and feel in the darkness for what lay spurned beside me. I stole my groping palm upon the clenched and chilly hand of a corpse!

Strange to say, this roused me to instant vividness of thought. Till this moment I had almost forgotten Amante; now I planned with feverish rapidity how I could give her a warning not to return; or rather, I should say, I tried to plan, for all my projects were utterly futile, as I might have seen from the first. I could only hope she would hear the voices of those who were now busy in trying to kindle a light, swearing awful oaths at the mislaid articles which would have enabled them to strike fire. I heard her step outside coming nearer and nearer; I saw from my hiding-place the line of light beneath the door more and more distinctly; close to it her footstep paused; the men inside – at the time I thought they had been only two, but I found out afterwards there were three – paused in their endeavours, and were quite still, as breathless as myself, I suppose. Then she slowly pushed the door open with gentle motion, to save her flickering candle from being again extinguished. For a moment all was still. Then I heard my husband say, as he advanced towards her (he wore riding-boots, the shape of which I knew well, as I could see them in the light):

'Amante, may I ask what brings you here into my private room?'

He stood between her and the dead body of a man, from which ghastly heap I shrank away as it almost touched me, so close were we all together. I could not tell whether she saw it or not; I could give her no warning, nor make any dumb utterance of signs to bid her what to say – if, indeed, I knew myself what would be best for her to say.

Her voice was quite changed when she spoke; quite hoarse, and very low; yet it was steady enough as she said, what was the truth, that she had come to look for a letter which she believed had arrived for me from Germany. Good, brave Amante! Not a word about me. M. de la Tourelle answered with a grim blasphemy and a fearful threat. He would have no one prying into his premises; madame should have her letters, if there were any, when he chose to give them to her, if, indeed, he thought it well to give them to her at all. As for Amante, this was her first warning, but it was also her last; and, taking the candle out of her hand, he turned her out of the room, his companions discreetly making a screen, so as to throw the corpse into deep shadow. I heard the key turn in the door after her – if I had ever had any thought of escape it was gone now. I only hoped that whatever was to befall me might soon be over, for the tension of nerve was growing more than I could bear. The instant she could be supposed to be out of hearing, two voices began speaking in the most angry terms to my husband, upbraiding him for not having detained her, gagged her – nay, one was for killing her, saying he had seen her eye fall on the face of the dead man, whom he now kicked in his passion. Though the form of their speech was as if they were speaking to equals, yet in their tone there was something of fear. I am sure my husband was their superior, or captain, or somewhat. He replied to them almost as if he were scoffing at them, saying it was such an expenditure of labour having to do with fools; that, ten to one, the woman was only telling the simple truth, and that she was frightened enough by discovering her master in his room to be thankful to escape and return to her mistress, to whom he could easily explain on the morrow how he happened to return in the dead of night. But his companions fell to cursing me, and saying that since M. de la Tourelle had been married he was fit for nothing but to dress himself fine and scent himself with perfume; that, as for me, they could have got him twenty girls prettier, and with far more spirit in them. He quietly answered that I suited him, and that was enough. All this time they were doing something – I could not see what – to the corpse; sometimes they were too busy rifling the dead body, I believe, to talk; again they let it fall with a heavy, resistless thud, and took to quarrelling. They taunted my husband with angry vehemence, enraged at his scoffing and scornful replies, his mocking laughter. Yes, holding up his poor dead victim, the better to strip him of whatever he wore that was valuable, I heard my husband laugh just as he had done when exchanging repartees in the little salon of the Rupprechts at Carlsruhe. I hated and dreaded him from that moment. At length, as if to make an end of the subject, he said, with cool determination in his voice:

'Now, my good friends, what is the use of all this talking, when you know in your hearts that, if I suspected my wife of knowing more than I chose of my affairs, she would not outlive the day? Remember Victorine. Because she merely joked about my affairs in an imprudent manner, and rejected my advice to keep a prudent tongue – to see what she liked, but ask nothing and say nothing – she has gone a long journey – longer than to Paris.'

'But this one is different to her; we knew all that Madame Victorine knew, she was such a chatterbox; but this one may find out a vast deal, and never breathe a word about it, she is so sly. Some fine day we may have the country raised, and the gendarmes down upon us from Strasburg, and all owing to your pretty doll, with her cunning ways of coming over you.'

I think this roused M. de la Tourelle a little from his contemptuous indifference, for he ground an oath through his teeth, and said, 'Feel! this dagger is sharp, Henri. If my wife breathes a word, and I am such a fool as not to have stopped her mouth effectually before she can bring down gendarmes upon us, just let that good steel find its way to my heart. Let her guess but one tittle, let her have but one slight suspicion that I am not a "grand propriétaire," much less imagine that I am a chief of chauffeurs, and she follows Victorine on the long journey beyond Paris that very day.'

'She'll outwit you yet; or I never judged women well. Those still silent ones are the devil. She'll be off during some of your absences, having picked out some secret that will break us all on the wheel.'

'Bah!' said his voice; and then in a minute he added, 'Let her go if she will. But, where she goes, I will follow; so don't cry before you're hurt.'

By this time, they had nearly stripped the body; and the conversation turned on what they should do with it. I learnt that the dead man was the Sieur de Poissy, a neighbouring gentleman, whom I had often heard of as hunting with my husband. I had never seen him, but they spoke as if he had come upon them while they were robbing some Cologne merchant, torturing him after the cruel practice of the chauffeurs, by roasting the feet of their victims in order to compel them to reveal any hidden circumstances connected with their wealth, of which the chauffeurs afterwards made use; and this Sieur de Poissy coming down upon them, and recognising M. de la Tourelle, they had killed him, and brought him thither after nightfall. I heard him whom I called my husband, laugh his little light laugh as he spoke of the way in which the dead body had been strapped before one of the riders, in such a way that it appeared to any passer-by as if, in truth, the murderer were tenderly supporting some sick person. He repeated some mocking reply of double meaning, which he himself had given to some one who made inquiry. He enjoyed the play upon words, softly applauding his own wit. And all the time the poor helpless outstretched arms of the dead lay close to his dainty boot! Then another stooped (my heart stopped beating), and picked up a letter lying on the ground – a letter that had dropped out of

M. de Poissy's pocket – a letter from his wife, full of tender words of endearment and pretty babblings of love. This was read aloud, with coarse ribald comments on every sentence, each trying to outdo the previous speaker. When they came to some pretty words about a sweet Maurice, their little child away with its mother on some visit, they laughed at M. de la Tourelle, and told him that he would be hearing such woman's drivelling some day. Up to that moment, I think, I had only feared him, but his unnatural, half-ferocious reply made me hate even more than I dreaded him. But now they grew weary of their savage merriment; the jewels and watch had been apprised, the money and papers examined; and apparently there was some necessity for the body being interred quietly and before daybreak. They had not dared to leave him where he was slain for fear lest people should come and recognise him, and raise the hue and cry upon them. For they all along spoke as if it was their constant endeavour to keep the immediate neighbourhood of Les Rochers in the most orderly and tranquil condition, so as never to give cause for visits from the gendarmes. They disputed a little as to whether they should make their way into the castle larder through the gallery, and satisfy their hunger before the hasty interment, or afterwards. I listened with eager feverish interest as soon as this meaning of their speeches reached my hot and troubled brain, for at the time the words they uttered seemed only to stamp themselves with terrible force on my memory, so that I could hardly keep from repeating them aloud like a dull, miserable, unconscious echo; but my brain was numb to the sense of what they said, unless I myself were named, and then, I suppose, some instinct of self-preservation stirred within me, and quickened my sense. And how I strained my ears, and nerved my hands and limbs, beginning to twitch with convulsive movements, which I feared might betray me! I gathered every word they spoke, not knowing which proposal to wish for, but feeling that whatever was finally decided upon, my only chance of escape was drawing near. I once feared lest my husband should go to his bedroom before I had had that one chance, in which case he would most likely have perceived my absence. He said that his hands were soiled (I shuddered, for it might be with life-blood), and he would go and cleanse them; but some bitter jest turned his purpose, and he left the room with the other two – left it by the gallery door. Left me alone in the dark with the stiffening corpse!

Now, now was my time, if ever; and yet I could not move. It was not my cramped and stiffened joints that crippled me, it was the sensation of that dead man's close presence. I almost fancied – I almost fancy still – I heard the arm nearest to me move; lift itself up, as if once more imploring, and fall in dead despair. At that fancy – if fancy it were – I screamed aloud in mad terror, and the sound of my own strange voice broke the spell. I drew myself to the side of the table farthest from the corpse, with as much slow caution as if I really could have feared the clutch of that poor dead arm, powerless for evermore. I softly raised myself up, and stood sick and trembling, holding by the table, too dizzy to know what to do next. I nearly fainted, when a low voice spoke – when Amante, from the outside of the door, whispered, 'Madame!' The faithful creature had been on the watch, had heard my scream, and having seen the three ruffians troop along the gallery down the stairs, and across the court to the offices in the other wing of the castle, she had stolen to the door of the room in which I was. The sound of her voice gave me strength; I walked straight towards it, as one benighted on a dreary moor, suddenly perceiving the small steady light which tells of human dwellings, takes heart, and steers straight onward. Where I was, where that voice was, I knew not; but go to it I must, or die. The door once opened – I know not by which of us – I fell upon her neck, grasping her tight, till my hands ached with the tension of their hold. Yet she never uttered a word. Only she took me up in her vigorous arms, and bore me to my room, and laid me on my bed. I do not know more; as soon as I was placed there I lost sense; I came to myself with a horrible dread lest my husband was by me, with a belief that he was in the room, in hiding, waiting to hear my first words, watching for the least sign of the terrible knowledge I possessed to murder me. I dared not breathe quicker, I measured and timed each heavy inspiration; I did not speak, nor move, nor even open my eyes, for long after I was in my full, my miserable senses. I heard some one treading softly about the room, as if with a purpose, not as if for curiosity, or merely to beguile the time; some one passed in and out of the salon; and I still lay quiet, feeling as if death were inevitable, but wishing that the agony of death were past. Again faintness stole over me; but just as I was sinking into the horrible feeling of nothingness, I heard Amante's voice close to me, saying:

'Drink this, madame, and let us begone. All is ready.'

I let her put her arm under my head and raise me, and pour something down my throat. All the time she kept talking in a quiet, measured voice, unlike her own, so dry and authoritative; she told me that a suit of her clothes lay ready for me, that she herself was as much disguised as the circumstances permitted her to be, that what provisions I had left from my supper were stowed away in her pockets, and so she went on, dwelling on little details of the most commonplace description, but never alluding for an instant to the fearful cause why flight was necessary. I made no inquiry as to how she knew, or what she knew. I never asked her either then or afterwards, I could not bear it – we kept our dreadful secret close. But I suppose she must have been in the dressing-room adjoining, and heard all.

In fact, I dared not speak even to her, as if there were anything beyond the most common event in life in our preparing thus to leave the house of blood by stealth in the dead of night. She gave me directions – short condensed directions, without reasons – just as you do to a child; and like a child I obeyed her. She went often to the door and listened; and often, too, she went to the window, and looked anxiously out. For me, I saw nothing but her, and I dared not let my eyes wander from her for a minute; and I heard nothing in the deep midnight silence but her soft movements, and the heavy beating of my own heart. At last she took my hand, and led me in the dark, through the salon, once more into the terrible gallery, where across the black darkness the windows admitted pale sheeted ghosts of light upon the floor. Clinging to her I went; unquestioning – for she was human sympathy to me after the isolation of my unspeakable terror. On we went, turning to the left instead of to the right, past my suite of sitting-rooms where the gilding was red with blood, into that unknown wing of the castle that fronted the main road lying parallel far below. She guided me along the basement passages to which we had now descended, until we came to a little open door, through which the air blew chill and cold, bringing for the first time a sensation of life to me. The door led into a kind of cellar, through which we groped our way to an opening like window, but which, instead of being glazed, was only fenced with iron bars, two of which were loose, as Amante evidently knew, for she took them out with the ease of one who had performed the action often before, and then helped me to follow her out into the free, open air.

We stole round the end of the building, and on turning the corner – she first – I felt her hold on me tighten for an instant, and the next step I, too, heard distant voices, and the blows of a spade upon the heavy soil, for the night was very warm and still.

We had not spoken a word; we did not speak now. Touch was safer and as expressive. She turned down towards the high road; I followed. I did not know the path; we stumbled again and again, and I was much bruised; so doubtless was she; but bodily pain did me good. At last, we were on the plainer path of the high road.

I had such faith in her that I did not venture to speak, even when she paused, as wondering to which hand she should turn. But now, for the first time, she spoke:

'Which way did you come when he brought you here first?'

I pointed, I could not speak.

We turned in the opposite direction; still going along the high road. In about an hour, we struck up to the mountainside, scrambling far up before we even dared to rest; far up and away again before day had fully dawned. Then we looked about for some place of rest and concealment: and now we dared to speak in whispers. Amante told me that she had locked the door of communication between his bedroom and mine, and, as in a dream, I was aware that she had also locked and brought away the key of the door between the latter and the salon.

'He will have been too busy this night to think much about you – he will suppose you are asleep – I shall be the first to be missed; but they will only just now be discovering our loss.'

I remember those last words of hers made me pray to go on; I felt as if we were losing precious time in thinking either of rest or concealment; but she hardly replied to me, so busy was she in seeking out some hiding-place. At length, giving it up in despair, we proceeded onwards a little way; the mountain-side sloped downwards rapidly, and in the full morning light we saw ourselves in a narrow valley, made by a stream which forced its way along it. About a mile lower down there rose the pale blue smoke of a village, a mill-wheel was lashing up the water close at hand, though out of sight. Keeping under the cover of every sheltering tree or bush, we worked our way down past the mill, down to a one-arched bridge, which doubtless formed part of the road between the village and the mill.

'This will do,' said she; and we crept under the space, and climbing a little way up the rough stonework, we seated ourselves on a projecting ledge, and crouched in the deep damp shadow. Amante sat a little above me, and made me lay my head on her lap. Then she fed me, and took some food herself; and opening out her great dark cloak, she covered up every light-coloured speck about us; and thus we sat, shivering and shuddering, yet feeling a kind of rest through it all, simply from the fact that motion was no longer imperative, and that during the daylight our only chance of safety was to be still. But the damp shadow in which we were sitting was blighting, from the circumstance of the sunlight never penetrating there; and I dreaded lest, before night and the time for exertion again came on, I should feel illness creeping all over me. To add to our discomfort, it had rained the whole day long, and the stream, fed by a thousand little mountain brooklets, began to swell into a torrent, rushing over the stones with a perpetual and dizzying noise.

Every now and then I was wakened from the painful doze into which I continually fell, by a sound of horses' feet over our head: sometimes lumbering heavily as if dragging a burden, sometimes rattling and galloping; and with the sharper cry of men's voices coming cutting through the roar of the waters. At length, day fell. We had to drop into the stream, which came above our knees as we waded to the bank. There we stood, stiff and shivering. Even Amante's courage seemed to fail.

'We must pass this night in shelter, somehow,' said she. For indeed the rain was coming down pitilessly. I said nothing. I thought that surely the end must be death in some shape; and I only hoped that to death might not be added the terror of the cruelty of men. In a minute or so she had resolved on her course of action. We went up the stream to the mill. The familiar sounds, the scent of the wheat, the flour whitening the walls – all reminded me of home, and it seemed to me as if I must struggle out of this nightmare and waken, and find myself once more a happy girl by the Neckar side. They were long in unbarring the door at which Amante had knocked: at length, an old feeble voice inquired who was there, and what was sought? Amante answered shelter from the storm for two women; but the old woman replied, with suspicious hesitation, that she was sure it was a man who was asking for shelter, and that she could not let us in. But at length she satisfied herself, and unbarred the heavy door, and admitted us. She was not an unkindly woman; but her thoughts all travelled in one circle, and that was, that her master, the miller, had told her on no account to let any man into the place during his absence, and that she did not know if he would not think two women as bad; and yet that as we were not men, no one could say she had disobeyed him, for it was a shame to let a dog be out such a night as this. Amante, with ready wit, told her to let no one know that we had taken shelter there that night, and that then her master could not blame her; and while she was thus enjoining secrecy as the wisest course, with a view to far other people than the miller, she was hastily helping me to take off my wet clothes, and spreading them, as well as the brown mantle that had covered us both, before the great stove which warmed the room with the effectual heat that the old woman's failing vitality required. All this time the poor creature was discussing with herself as to whether she had disobeyed orders, in a kind of garrulous way that made me fear much for her capability of retaining anything secret if she was questioned. By-and-by, she wandered away to an unnecessary revelation of her master's whereabouts: gone to help in the search for his landlord, the Sieur de Poissy, who lived at the chateau just above, and who had not returned from his chase the day before; so the intendant imagined he might have met with some accident, and had summoned the neighbours to beat the forest and the hill-side. She told us much besides, giving us to understand that she would fain meet with a place as housekeeper where there were more servants and less to do, as her life here was very lonely and dull, especially since her master's son had gone away – gone to the wars. She then took her supper, which was evidently apportioned out to her with a sparing hand, as, even if the idea had come into her head, she had not enough to offer us any. Fortunately, warmth was all that we required, and that, thanks to Amante's cares, was returning to our chilled bodies.

After supper, the old woman grew drowsy; but she seemed uncomfortable at the idea of going to sleep and leaving us still in the house. Indeed, she gave us pretty broad hints as to the propriety of our going once more out into the bleak and stormy night; but we begged to be allowed to stay under shelter of some kind; and, at last, a bright idea came over her, and she bade us mount by a ladder to a kind of loft, which went half over the lofty mill-kitchen in which we were sitting. We obeyed her – what else could we do? – and found ourselves in a spacious floor, without any safeguard or wall, boarding, or railing, to keep us from falling over into the kitchen in case we went too near the edge. It was, in fact, the store-room or garret for the household. There was bedding piled up, boxes and chests, mill sacks, the winter store of apples and nuts, bundles of old clothes, broken furniture, and many other things. No sooner were we up there, than the old woman dragged the ladder, by which we had ascended, away with a chuckle, as if she was now secure that we could do no mischief, and sat herself down again once more, to doze and await her master's return. We pulled out some bedding, and gladly laid ourselves down in our dried clothes and in some warmth, hoping to have the sleep we so much needed to refresh us and prepare us for the next day. But I could not sleep, and I was aware, from her breathing, that Amante was equally wakeful. We could both see through the crevices between the boards that formed the flooring into the kitchen below, very partially lighted by the common lamp that hung against the wall near the stove on the opposite side to that on which we were.

Portion III

FAR ON in the night there were voices outside reached us in our hiding-place; an angry knocking at the door, and we saw through the chinks the old woman rouse herself up to go and open it for her master, who came in, evidently half drunk. To my sick horror, he was followed by Lefebvre, apparently as sober and wily as ever. They were talking together as they came in, disputing about something; but the miller stopped the conversation to swear at the old woman for having fallen asleep, and, with tipsy anger, and even with blows, drove the poor old creature out of the kitchen to bed. Then he and Lefebvre went on talking – about the Sieur de Poissy's disappearance. It seemed that Lefebvre had been out all day, along with other of my husband's men, ostensibly assisting in the search; in all probability trying to blind the Sieur de Poissy's followers by putting them on a wrong scent, and also, I fancied, from one or two of Lefebvre's sly questions, combining the hidden purpose of discovering us.

Although the miller was tenant and vassal to the Sieur de Poissy, he seemed to me to be much more in league with the people of M. de la Tourelle. He was evidently aware, in part, of the life which Lefebvre and the others led; although, again, I do not suppose he knew or imagined one-half of their crimes; and also, I think, he was seriously interested in discovering the fate of his master, little suspecting Lefebvre of murder or violence. He kept talking himself, and letting out all sorts of thoughts and opinions; watched by the keen eyes of Lefebvre gleaming out below his shaggy eyebrows. It was evidently not the cue of the latter to let out that his master's wife had escaped from that vile and terrible den; but though he never breathed a word relating to us, not the less was I certain he was thirsting for our blood, and lying in wait for us at every turn of events. Presently he got up and took his leave; and the miller bolted him out, and stumbled off to bed. Then we fell asleep, and slept sound and long.

The next morning, when I awoke, I saw Amante, half raised, resting on one hand, and eagerly gazing, with straining eyes, into the kitchen below. I looked too, and both heard and saw the miller and two of his men eagerly and loudly talking about the old woman, who had not appeared as usual to make the fire in the stove, and prepare her master's breakfast, and who now, late on in the morning, had been found dead in her bed; whether from the effect of her master's blows the night before, or from natural causes, who can tell? The miller's conscience upbraided him a little, I should say, for he was eagerly declaring his value for his housekeeper, and repeating how often she had spoken of the happy life she led with him. The men might have their doubts, but they did not wish to offend the miller, and all agreed that the necessary steps should be taken for a speedy funeral. And so they went out, leaving us in our loft, but so much alone, that, for the first time almost, we ventured to speak freely, though still in hushed voice, pausing to listen continually. Amante took a more cheerful view of the whole occurrence than I did. She said that, had the old woman lived, we should have had to depart that morning, and that this quiet departure would have been the best thing we could have had to hope for, as, in all probability, the housekeeper would have told her master of us and of our resting-place, and this fact would, sooner or later, have been brought to the knowledge of those from whom we most desired to keep it concealed; but that now we had time to rest, and a shelter to rest in, during the first hot pursuit, which we knew to a fatal certainty was being carried on. The remnants of our food, and the stored-up fruit, would supply us with provision; the only thing to be feared was, that something might be required from the loft, and the miller or someone else mount up in search of it. But even then, with a little arrangement of boxes and chests, one part might be so kept in shadow that we might yet escape observation. All this comforted me a little; but, I asked, how were we ever to escape? The ladder was taken away, which was our only means of descent. But Amante replied that she could make a sufficient ladder of the rope lying coiled among other things, to drop us down the ten feet or so – with the advantage of its being portable, so that we might carry it away, and thus avoid all betrayal of the fact that any one had ever been hidden in the loft.

During the two days that intervened before we did escape, Amante made good use of her time. She looked into every box and chest during the man's absence at his mill; and finding in one box an old suit of man's clothes, which had probably belonged to the miller's absent son, she put them on to see if they would fit her; and, when she found that they did, she cut her own hair to the shortness of a man's, made me clip her black eyebrows as close as though they had been shaved, and by cutting up old corks into pieces such as would go into her cheeks, she altered both the shape of her face and her voice to a degree which I should not have believed possible.

All this time I lay like one stunned; my body resting, and renewing its strength, but I myself in an almost idiotic state – else surely I could not have taken the stupid interest which I remember I did in all Amante's energetic preparations for disguise. I absolutely recollect once the feeling of a smile coming over my stiff face as some new exercise of her cleverness proved a success.

But towards the second day, she required me, too, to exert myself; and then all my heavy despair returned. I let her dye my fair hair and complexion with the decaying shells of the stored-up walnuts, I let her blacken my teeth, and even voluntarily broke a front tooth the better to effect my disguise. But through it all I had no hope of evading my terrible husband. The third night the funeral was over, the drinking ended, the guests gone; the miller put to bed by his men, being too drunk to help himself. They stopped a little while in the kitchen, talking and laughing about the new housekeeper likely to come; and they, too, went off, shutting, but not locking the door. Everything favoured us. Amante had tried her ladder on one of the two previous nights, and could, by a dexterous throw from beneath, unfasten it from the hook to which it was fixed, when it had served its office; she made up a bundle of worthless old clothes in order that we might the better preserve our characters of a travelling pedlar and his wife; she stuffed a hump on her back, she thickened my figure, she left her own clothes deep down beneath a heap of others in the chest from which she had taken the man's dress which she wore; and with a few francs in her pocket – the sole money we had either of us had about us when we escaped – we let ourselves down the ladder, unhooked it, and passed into the cold darkness of night again.

We had discussed the route which it would be well for us to take while we lay perdues in our loft. Amante had told me then that her reason for inquiring, when we first left Les Rochers, by which way I had first been brought to it, was to avoid the pursuit which she was sure would first be made in the direction of Germany; but that now she thought we might return to that district of country where my German fashion of speaking French would excite least observation. I thought that Amante herself had something peculiar in her accent, which I had heard M. de la Tourelle sneer at as Norman patois; but I said not a word beyond agreeing to her proposal that we should bend our steps towards Germany. Once there, we should, I thought, be safe. Alas! I forgot the unruly time that was overspreading all Europe, overturning all law, and all the protection which law gives.

How we wandered – not daring to ask our way – how we lived, how we struggled through many a danger and still more terrors of danger, I shall not tell you now. I will only relate two of our adventures before we reached Frankfort. The first, although fatal to an innocent lady, was yet, I believe, the cause of my safety; the second I shall tell you, that you may understand why I did not return to my former home, as I had hoped to do when we lay in the miller's loft, and I first became capable of groping after an idea of what my future life might be. I cannot tell you how much in these doubtings and wanderings I became attached to Amante. I have sometimes feared since, lest I cared for her only because she was so necessary to my own safety; but, no! it was not so; or not so only, or principally. She said once that she was flying for her own life as well as for mine; but we dared not speak much on our danger, or on the horrors that had gone before. We planned a little what was to be our future course; but even for that we did not look forward long; how could we, when every day we scarcely knew if we should see the sun go down? For Amante knew or conjectured far more than I did of the atrocity of the gang to which M. de la Tourelle belonged; and every now and then, just as we seemed to be sinking into the calm of security, we fell upon traces of a pursuit after us in all directions. Once I remember – we must have been nearly three weeks wearily walking through unfrequented ways, day after day, not daring to make inquiry as to our whereabouts, nor yet to seem purposeless in our wanderings – we came to a kind of lonely roadside farrier's and blacksmith's. I was so tired, that Amante declared that, come what might, we would stay there all night; and accordingly she entered the house, and boldly announced herself as a travelling tailor, ready to do any odd jobs of work that might be required, for a night's lodging and food for herself and wife. She had adopted this plan once or twice before, and with good success; for her father had been a tailor in Rouen, and as a girl she had often helped him with his work, and knew the tailors' slang and habits, down to the particular whistle and cry which in France tells so much to those of a trade. At this blacksmith's, as at most other solitary houses far away from a town, there was not only a store of men's clothes laid by as wanting mending when the housewife could afford time, but there was a natural craving after news from a distance, such news as a wandering tailor is bound to furnish. The early November afternoon was closing into evening, as we sat down, she cross-legged on the great table in the blacksmith's kitchen, drawn close to the window, I close behind her, sewing at another part of the same garment, and from time to time well scolded by my seeming husband. All at once she turned round to speak to me. It was only one word, 'Courage!' I had seen nothing; I sat out of the light; but I turned sick for an instant, and then I braced myself up into a strange strength of endurance to go through I knew not what.

The blacksmith's forge was in a shed beside the house, and fronting the road. I heard the hammers stop plying their continual rhythmical beat. She had seen why they ceased. A rider had come up to the forge and dismounted, leading his horse in to be re-shod. The broad red light of the forge-fire had revealed the face of the rider to Amante, and she apprehended the consequence that really ensued.

The rider, after some words with the blacksmith, was ushered in by him into the house-place where we sat.

'Here, good wife, a cup of wine and some galette for this gentleman.'

'Anything, anything, madame, that I can eat and drink in my hand while my horse is being shod. I am in haste, and must get on to Forbach tonight.'

The blacksmith's wife lighted her lamp; Amante had asked her for it five minutes before. How thankful we were that she had not more speedily complied with our request! As it was, we sat in dusk shadow, pretending to stitch away, but scarcely able to see. The lamp was placed on the stove, near which my husband, for it was he, stood and armed himself. By-and-by he turned round, and looked all over the room, taking us in with about the same degree of interest as the inanimate furniture. Amante, cross-legged, fronting him, stooped over her work, whistling softly all the while. He turned again to the stove, impatiently rubbing his hands. He had finished his wine and galette, and wanted to be off.

'I am in haste, my good woman. Ask thy husband to get on more quickly. I will pay him double if he makes haste.'

The woman went out to do his bidding; and he once more turned round to face us. Amante went on to the second part of the tune. He took it up, whistled a second for an instant or so, and then the blacksmith's wife re-entering, he moved towards her, as if to receive her answer the more speedily.

'One moment, monsieur – only one moment. There was a nail out of the off-foreshoe which my husband is replacing; it would delay monsieur again if that shoe also came off.'

'Madame is right,' said he, 'but my haste is urgent. If madame knew my reasons, she would pardon my impatience. Once a happy husband, now a deserted and betrayed man, I pursue a wife on whom I lavished all my love, but who has abused my confidence, and fled from my house, doubtless to some paramour; carrying off with her all the jewels and money on which she could lay her hands. It is possible madame may have heard or seen something of her; she was accompanied in her flight by a base, profligate woman from Paris, whom I, unhappy man, had myself engaged for my wife's waiting-maid, little dreaming what corruption I was bringing into my house!'

'Is it possible?' said the good woman, throwing up her hands.

Amante went on whistling a little lower, out of respect to the conversation.

'However, I am tracing the wicked fugitives; I am on their track' (and the handsome, effeminate face looked as ferocious as any demon's). 'They will not escape me; but every minute is a minute of misery to me, till I meet my wife. Madame has sympathy, has she not?'

He drew his face into a hard, unnatural smile, and then both went out to the forge, as if once more to hasten the blacksmith over his work.

Amante stopped her whistling for one instant.

'Go on as you are, without change of an eyelid even; in a few minutes he will be gone, and it will be over!'

It was a necessary caution, for I was on the point of giving way, and throwing myself weakly upon her neck. We went on; she whistling and stitching, I making semblance to sew. And it was well we did so; for almost directly he came back for his whip, which he had laid down and forgotten; and again I felt one of those sharp, quick-scanning glances, sent all round the room, and taking in all.

Then we heard him ride away; and then, it had been long too dark to see well, I dropped my work, and gave way to my trembling and shuddering. The blacksmith's wife returned. She was a good creature. Amante told her I was cold and weary, and she insisted on my stopping my work, and going to sit near the stove; hastening, at the same time, her preparations for supper, which, in honour of us, and of monsieur's liberal payment, was to be a little less frugal than ordinary. It was well for me that she made me taste a little of the cider-soup she was preparing, or I could not have held up, in spite of Amante's warning look, and the remembrance of her frequent exhortations to act resolutely up to the characters we had assumed, whatever befell. To cover my agitation, Amante stopped her whistling, and began to talk; and, by the time the blacksmith came in, she and the good woman of the house were in full flow. He began at once upon the handsome gentleman, who had paid him so well; all his sympathy was with him, and both he and his wife only wished he might overtake his wicked wife, and punish her as she deserved. And then the conversation took a turn, not uncommon to those whose lives are quiet and monotonous; every one seemed to vie with each other in telling about some horror; and the savage and mysterious band of robbers called the Chauffeurs, who infested all the roads leading to the Rhine, with Schinderhannes at their head, furnished many a tale which made the very marrow of my bones run cold, and quenched even Amante's power of talking. Her eyes grew large and wild, her cheeks blanched, and for once she sought by her looks help from me. The new call upon me roused me. I rose and said, with their permission my husband and I would seek our bed, for that we had travelled far and were early risers. I added that we would get up betimes, and finish our piece of work. The blacksmith said we should be early birds if we rose before him; and the good wife seconded my proposal with kindly bustle. One other such story as those they had been relating, and I do believe Amante would have fainted.

As it was, a night's rest set her up; we arose and finished our work betimes, and shared the plentiful breakfast of the family. Then we had to set forth again; only knowing that to Forbach we must not go, yet believing, as was indeed the case, that Forbach lay between us and that Germany to which we were directing our course. Two days more we wandered on, making a round, I suspect, and returning upon the road to Forbach, a league or two nearer to that town than the blacksmith's house. But as we never made inquiries I hardly knew where we were, when we came one night to a small town, with a good large rambling inn in the very centre of the principal street. We had begun to feel as if there were more safety in towns than in the loneliness of the country. As we had parted with a ring of mine not many days before to a travelling jeweller, who was too glad to purchase it far below its real value to make many inquiries as to how it came into the possession of a poor working tailor, such as Amante seemed to be, we resolved to stay at this inn all night, and gather such particulars and information as we could by which to direct our onward course.

We took our supper in the darkest corner of the salle-àmanger, having previously bargained for a small bedroom across the court, and over the stables. We needed food sorely; but we hurried on our meal from dread of any one entering that public room who might recognize us. Just in the middle of our meal, the public diligence drove lumbering up under the porte-cochère, and disgorged its passengers. Most of them turned into the room where we sat, cowering and fearful, for the door was opposite to the porter's lodge, and both opened on to the wide-covered entrance from the street. Among the passengers came in a young, fair-haired lady, attended by an elderly French maid. The poor young creature tossed her head, and shrank away from the common room, full of evil smells and promiscuous company, and demanded, in German French, to be taken to some private apartment. We heard that she and her maid had come in the coupé, and, probably from pride, poor young lady! she had avoided all association with her fellow-passengers, thereby exciting their dislike and ridicule. All these little pieces of hearsay had a significance to us afterwards, though, at the time, the only remark made that bore upon the future was Amante's whisper to me that the young lady's hair was exactly the colour of mine, which she had cut off and burnt in the stove in the miller's kitchen in one of her descents from our hiding-place in the loft.

As soon as we could, we struck round in the shadow, leaving the boisterous and merry fellow-passengers to their supper. We crossed the court, borrowed a lantern from the ostler, and scrambled up the rude step to our chamber above the stable. There was no door into it; the entrance was the hole into which the ladder fitted. The window looked into the court. We were tired and soon fell asleep. I was wakened by a noise in the stable below. One instant of listening, and I wakened Amante, placing my hand on her mouth, to prevent any exclamation in her half-roused state. We heard my husband speaking about his horse to the ostler. It was his voice. I am sure of it. Amante said so too. We durst not move to rise and satisfy ourselves. For five minutes or so he went on giving directions. Then he left the stable, and, softly stealing to our window, we saw him cross the court and re-enter the inn. We consulted as to what we should do. We feared to excite remark or suspicion by descending and leaving our chamber, or else immediate escape was our strongest idea. Then the ostler left the stable, locking the door on the outside.

'We must try and drop through the window – if, indeed, it is well to go at all,' said Amante.

With reflection came wisdom. We should excite suspicion by leaving without paying our bill. We were on foot, and might easily be pursued. So we sat on our bed's edge, talking and shivering, while from across the court the laughter rang merrily, and the company slowly dispersed one by one, their lights flitting past the windows as they went upstairs and settled each one to his rest.

We crept into our bed, holding each other tight, and listening to every sound, as if we thought we were tracked, and might meet our death at any moment. In the dead of night, just at the profound stillness preceding the turn into another day, we heard a soft, cautious step crossing the yard. The key into the stable was turned – some one came into the stable – we felt rather than heard him there. A horse started a little, and made a restless movement with his feet, then whinnied recognition. He who had entered made two or three low sounds to the animal, and then led him into the court. Amante sprang to the window with the noiseless activity of a cat. She looked out, but dared not speak a word. We heard the great door into the street open – a pause for mounting, and the horse's footsteps were lost in distance.

Then Amante came back to me. 'It was he! he is gone!' said she, and once more we lay down, trembling and shaking.

This time we fell sound asleep. We slept long and late. We were wakened by many hurrying feet, and many confused voices; all the world seemed awake and astir. We rose and dressed ourselves, and coming down we looked around among the crowd collected in the court-yard, in order to assure ourselves he was not there before we left the shelter of the stable.

The instant we were seen, two or three people rushed to us.

'Have you heard? – Do you know? – That poor young lady – oh, come and see!' and so we were hurried, almost in spite of ourselves, across the court, and up the great open stairs of the main building of the inn, into a bed-chamber, where lay the beautiful young German lady, so full of graceful pride the night before, now white and still in death. By her stood the French maid, crying and gesticulating.

'Oh, madame! if you had but suffered me to stay with you! Oh! the baron, what will he say?' and so she went on. Her state had but just been discovered; it had been supposed that she was fatigued, and was sleeping late, until a few minutes before. The surgeon of the town had been sent for, and the landlord of the inn was trying vainly to enforce order until he came, and, from time to time, drinking little cups of brandy, and offering them to the guests, who were all assembled there, pretty much as the servants were doing in the courtyard.

At last the surgeon came. All fell back, and hung on the words that were to fall from his lips.

'See!' said the landlord. 'This lady came last night by the diligence with her maid. Doubtless, a great lady, for she must have a private sitting-room.'

'She was Madame the Baroness de Rœder,' said the French maid.

'And was difficult to please in the matter of supper, and a sleeping-room. She went to bed well, though fatigued. Her maid left her – ' 'I begged to be allowed to sleep in her room, as we were in a strange inn, of the character of which we knew nothing; but she would not let me, my mistress was such a great lady.'

'And slept with my servants,' continued the landlord. 'This morning we thought madame was still slumbering; but when eight, nine, ten, and near eleven o'clock came, I bade her maid use my pass-key, and enter her room —"

'The door was not locked, only closed. And here she was found – dead is she not, monsieur? – with her face down on her pillow, and her beautiful hair all scattered wild; she never would let me tie it up, saying it made her head ache. Such hair!' said the waiting-maid, lifting up a long golden tress, and letting it fall again.

I remembered Amante's words the night before, and crept close up to her.

Meanwhile, the doctor was examining the body underneath the bed-clothes, which the landlord, until now, had not allowed to be disarranged. The surgeon drew out his hand, all bathed and stained with blood; and holding up a short, sharp knife, with a piece of paper fastened round it.

'Here has been foul play,' he said. 'The deceased lady has been murdered. This dagger was aimed straight at her heart.' Then putting on his spectacles, he read the writing on the bloody paper, dimmed and horribly obscured as it was:

Numéro Un.

Ainsi les Chauffeurs se vengent.

'Let us go!' said I to Amante. 'Oh, let us leave this horrible place!'

'Wait a little,' said she. 'Only a few minutes more. It will be better.'

Immediately the voices of all proclaimed their suspicions of the cavalier who had arrived last the night before. He had, they said, made so many inquiries about the young lady, whose supercilious conduct all in the salle-à-manger had been discussing on his entrance. They were talking about her as we left the room; he must have come in directly afterwards, and not until he had learnt all about her, had he spoken of the business which necessitated his departure at dawn of day, and made his arrangements with both landlord and ostler for the possession of the keys of the stable and porte-cochère. In short, there was no doubt as to the murderer, even before the arrival of the legal functionary who had been sent for by the surgeon; but the word on the paper chilled every one with terror. Les Chauffeurs, who were they? No one knew, some of the gang might even then be in the room overhearing, and noting down fresh objects for vengeance. In Germany, I had heard little of this terrible gang, and I had paid no greater heed to the stories related once or twice about them in Carlsruhe than one does to tales about ogres. But here in their very haunts, I learnt the full amount of the terror they inspired. No one would be legally responsible for any evidence criminating the murderer. The public prosecutor shrank from the duties of his office. What do I say? Neither Amante nor I, knowing far more of the actual guilt of the man who had killed that poor sleeping young lady, durst breathe a word. We appeared to be wholly ignorant of everything: we, who might have told so much. But how could we? we were broken down with terrific anxiety and fatigue, with the knowledge that we, above all, were doomed victims; and that the blood, heavily dripping from the bed-clothes on to the floor, was dripping thus out of the poor dead body, because, when living, she had been mistaken for me.

At length Amante went up to the landlord, and asked permission to leave his inn, doing all openly and humbly, so as to excite neither ill-will nor suspicion. Indeed, suspicion was otherwise directed, and he willingly gave us leave to depart. A few days afterwards we were across the Rhine, in Germany, making our way towards Frankfort, but still keeping our disguises, and Amante still working at her trade.

On the way, we met a young man, a wandering journeyman from Heidelberg. I knew him, although I did not choose that he should know me. I asked him, as carelessly as I could, how the old miller was now? He told me he was dead. This realization of the worst apprehensions caused by his long silence shocked me inexpressibly. It seemed as though every prop gave way from under me. I had been talking to Amante only that very day of the safety and comfort of the home that awaited her in my father's house; of the gratitude which the old man would feel towards her; and how there, in that peaceful dwelling, far away from the terrible land of France, she should find ease and security for all the rest of her life. All this I thought I had to promise, and even yet more had I looked for, for myself. I looked to the unburdening of my heart and conscience by telling all I knew to my best and wisest friend. I looked to his love as a sure guidance as well as a comforting stay, and, behold, he was gone away from me for ever!

I had left the room hastily on hearing of this sad news from the Heidelberger. Presently, Amante followed.

'Poor madame,' said she, consoling me to the best of her ability. And then she told me by degrees what more she had learned respecting my home, about which she knew almost as much as I did, from my frequent talks on the subject both at Les Rochers and on the dreary, doleful road we had come along. She had continued the conversation after I left, by asking about my brother and his wife. Of course, they lived on at the mill, but the man said (with what truth I know not, but I believed it firmly at the time) that Babette had completely got the upper hand of my brother, who only saw through her eyes and heard with her ears. That there had been much Heidelberg gossip of late days about her sudden intimacy with a grand French gentleman who had appeared at the mill – a relation, by marriage – married, in fact, to the miller's sister, who, by all accounts, had behaved abominably and ungratefully. But that was no reason for Babette's extreme and sudden intimacy with him, going about everywhere with the French gentleman; and since he left (as the Heidelberger said he knew for a fact) corresponding with him constantly. Yet her husband saw no harm in it all, seemingly; though, to be sure, he was so out of spirits, what with his father's death and the news of his sister's infamy, that he hardly knew how to hold up his head.

'Now,' said Amante, 'all this proves that M. de la Tourelle has suspected that you would go back to the nest in which you were reared, and that he has been there, and found that you have not yet returned; but probably he still imagines that you will do so, and has accordingly engaged your sister-in-law as a kind of informant. Madame has said that her sister-in-law bore her no extreme good-will; and the defamatory story he has got the start of us in spreading, will not tend to increase the favour in which your sister-in-law holds you. No doubt the assassin was retracing his steps when we met him near Forbach, and having heard of the poor German lady, with her French maid, and her pretty blonde complexion, he followed her. If madame will still be guided by me – and, my child, I beg of you still to trust me,' said Amante, breaking out of her respectful formality into the way of talking more natural to those who had shared and escaped from common dangers – more natural, too, where the speaker was conscious of a power of protection which the other did not possess – 'we will go on to Frankfort, and lose ourselves, for a time, at least, in the numbers of people who throng a great town; and you have told me that Frankfort is a great town. We will still be husband and wife; we will take a small lodging, and you shall house-keep and live in-doors. I, as the rougher and the more alert, will continue my father's trade, and seek work at the tailors' shops.'

I could think of no better plan, so we followed this out. In a back street at Frankfort we found two furnished rooms to let on a sixth story. The one we entered had no light from day; a dingy lamp swung perpetually from the ceiling, and from that, or from the open door leading into the bedroom beyond, came our only light. The bedroom was more cheerful, but very small. Such as it was, it almost exceeded our possible means. The money from the sale of my ring was almost exhausted, and Amante was a stranger in the place, speaking only French, moreover, and the good Germans were hating the French people right heartily. However, we succeeded better than our hopes, and even laid by a little against the time of my confinement. I never stirred abroad, and saw no one, and Amante's want of knowledge of German kept her in a state of comparative isolation.

At length my child was born – my poor worse than fatherless child. It was a girl, as I had prayed for. I had feared lest a boy might have something of the tiger nature of its father, but a girl seemed all my own. And yet not all my own, for the faithful Amante's delight and glory in the babe almost exceeded mine; in outward show it certainly did.

We had not been able to afford any attendance beyond what a neighbouring sage-femme could give, and she came frequently, bringing in with her a little store of gossip, and wonderful tales culled out of her own experience, every time. One day she began to tell me about a great lady in whose service her daughter had lived as scullion, or some such thing. Such a beautiful lady! with such a handsome husband. But grief comes to the palace as well as to the garret, and why or wherefore no one knew, but somehow the Baron de Rœder must have incurred the vengeance of the terrible Chauffeurs; for not many months ago, as madame was going to see her relations in Alsace, she was stabbed dead as she lay in bed at some hotel on the road. Had I not seen it in the Gazette? Had I not heard? Why, she had been told that as far off as Lyons there were placards offering a heavy reward on the part of the Baron de Rœder for information respecting the murderer of his wife. But no one could help him, for all who could bear evidence were in such terror of the Chauffeurs; there were hundreds of them she had been told, rich and poor, great gentlemen and peasants, all leagued together by most frightful oaths to hunt to the death any one who bore witness against them; so that even they who survived the tortures to which the Chauffeurs subjected many of the people whom they plundered, dared not to recognise them again, would not dare, even did they see them at the bar of a court of justice; for, if one were condemned, were there not hundreds sworn to avenge his death?

I told all this to Amante, and we began to fear that if M. de la Tourelle, or Lefebvre, or any of the gang at Les Rochers, had seen these placards, they would know that the poor lady stabbed by the former was the Baroness de Rœder, and that they would set forth again in search of me.

This fresh apprehension told on my health and impeded my recovery. We had so little money we could not call in a physician, at least, not one in established practice. But Amante found out a young doctor for whom, indeed, she had sometimes worked; and offering to pay him in kind, she brought him to see me, her sick wife. He was very gentle and thoughtful, though, like ourselves, very poor. But he gave much time and consideration to the case, saying once to Amante that he saw my constitution had experienced some severe shock from which it was probable that my nerves would never entirely recover. By-and-by I shall name this doctor, and then you will know, better than I can describe, his character.

I grew strong in time – stronger, at least. I was able to work a little at home, and to sun myself and my baby at the garret-window in the roof. It was all the air I dared to take. I constantly wore the disguise I had first set out with; as constantly had I renewed the disfiguring dye which changed my hair and complexion. But the perpetual state of terror in which I had been during the whole months succeeding my escape from Les Rochers made me loathe the idea of ever again walking in the open daylight, exposed to the sight and recognition of every passer-by. In vain Amante reasoned – in vain the doctor urged. Docile in every other thing, in this I was obstinate. I would not stir out. One day Amante returned from her work, full of news – some of it good, some such as to cause us apprehension. The good news was this; the master for whom she worked as journeyman was going to send her with some others to a great house at the other side of Frankfort, where there were to be private theatricals, and where many new dresses and much alteration of old ones would be required. The tailors employed were all to stay at this house until the day of representation was over, as it was at some distance from the town, and no one could tell when their work would be ended. But the pay was to be proportionately good.

The other thing she had to say was this: she had that day met the travelling jeweller to whom she and I had sold my ring. It was rather a peculiar one, given to me by my husband; we had felt at the time that it might be the means of tracing us, but we were penniless and starving, and what else could we do? She had seen that this Frenchman had recognised her at the same instant that she did him, and she thought at the same time that there was a gleam of more than common intelligence on his face as he did so. This idea had been confirmed by his following her for some way on the other side of the street; but she had evaded him with her better knowledge of the town, and the increasing darkness of the night. Still it was well that she was going to such a distance from our dwelling on the next day; and she had brought me in a stock of provisions, begging me to keep within doors, with a strange kind of fearful oblivion of the fact that I had never set foot beyond the threshold of the house since I had first entered it – scarce ever ventured down the stairs. But, although my poor, my dear, very faithful Amante was like one possessed that last night, she spoke continually of the dead, which is a bad sign for the living. She kissed you – yes! it was you, my daughter, my darling, whom I bore beneath my bosom away from the fearful castle of your father – I call him so for the first time, I must call him so once again before I have done – Amante kissed you, sweet baby, blessed little comforter, as if she never could leave off. And then she went away, alive.

Two days, three days passed away. That third evening I was sitting within my bolted doors – you asleep on your pillow by my side – when a step came up the stair, and I knew it must be for me; for ours were the top-most rooms. Some one knocked; I held my very breath. But some one spoke, and I knew it was the good Doctor Voss. Then I crept to the door, and answered.

'Are you alone?' asked I.

'Yes,' said he, in a still lower voice. 'Let me in.' I let him in, and he was as alert as I in bolting and barring the door. Then he came and whispered to me his doleful tale. He had come from the hospital in the opposite quarter of the town, the hospital which he visited; he should have been with me sooner, but he had feared lest he should be watched. He had come from Amante's death-bed. Her fears of the jeweller were too well founded. She had left the house where she was employed that morning, to transact some errand connected with her work in the town; she must have been followed, and dogged on her way back through solitary wood-paths, for some of the wood-rangers belonging to the great house had found her lying there, stabbed to death, but not dead; with the poniard again plunged through the fatal writing, once more; but this time with the word 'un' underlined, so as to show that the assassin was aware of his precious mistake.

Numéro Un.

Ainsi les Chauffeurs se vengent.

They had carried her to the house, and given her restoratives till she had recovered the feeble use of her speech. But, oh, faithful, dear friend and sister! even then she remembered me, and refused to tell (what no one else among her fellow workmen knew), where she lived or with whom. Life was ebbing away fast, and they had no resource but to carry her to the nearest hospital, where, of course, the fact of her sex was made known. Fortunately both for her and for me, the doctor in attendance was the very Doctor Voss whom we already knew. To him, while awaiting her confessor, she told enough to enable him to understand the position in which I was left; before the priest had heard half her tale Amante was dead.

Doctor Voss told me he had made all sorts of détours, and waited thus, late at night, for fear of being watched and followed. But I do not think he was. At any rate, as I afterwards learnt from him, the Baron Rœder, on hearing of the similitude of this murder with that of his wife in every particular, made such a search after the assassins, that, although they were not discovered, they were compelled to take to flight for the time.

I can hardly tell you now by what arguments Dr. Voss, at first merely my benefactor, sparing me a portion of his small modicum, at length persuaded me to become his wife. His wife he called it, I called it; for we went through the religious ceremony too much slighted at the time, and as we were both Lutherans, and M. de la Tourelle had pretended to be of the reformed religion, a divorce from the latter would have been easily procurable by German law both ecclesiastical and legal, could we have summoned so fearful a man into any court.

The good doctor took me and my child by stealth to his modest dwelling; and there I lived in the same deep refinement, never seeing the full light of day, although when the dye had once passed away from my face my husband did not wish me to renew it. There was no need; my yellow hair was grey, my complexion was ashen-coloured, no creature could have recognized the fresh-coloured, bright-haired young woman of eighteen months before. The few people whom I saw knew me only as Madame Voss; a widow much older than himself, whom Dr. Voss had secretly married. They called me the Grey Woman.

He made me give you his surname. Till now you have known no other father – while he lived you needed no father's love. Once only, only once more, did the old terror come upon me. For some reason which I forget, I broke through my usual custom, and went to the window of my room for some purpose, either to shut or to open it. Looking out into the street for an instant, I was fascinated by the sight of M. de la Tourelle, gay, young, elegant as ever, walking along on the opposite side of the street. The noise I had made with the window caused him to look up; he saw me, an old grey woman, and he did not recognize me! Yet it was not three years since we had parted, and his eyes were keen and dreadful like those of the lynx.

I told M. Voss, on his return home, and he tried to cheer me, but the shock of seeing M. de la Tourelle had been too terrible for me. I was ill for long months afterwards.

Once again I saw him. Dead. He and Lefebvre were at last caught; hunted down by the Baron de Rœder in some of their crimes. Dr. Voss had heard of their arrest; their condemnation, their death; but he never said a word to me, until one day he bade me show him that I loved him by my obedience and my trust. He took me a long carriage journey, where to I know not, for we never spoke of that day again; I was led through a prison, into a closed court-yard, where, decently draped in the last robes of death, concealing the marks of decapitation, lay M. de la Tourelle, and two or three others, whom I had known at Les Rochers.

After that conviction Dr. Voss tried to persuade me to return to a more natural mode of life, and to go out more. But although I sometimes complied with his wish, yet the old terror was ever strong upon me, and he, seeing what an effort it was, gave up urging me at last.

You know all the rest. How we both mourned bitterly the loss of that dear husband and father – for such I will call him ever

– and as such you must consider him, my child, after this one revelation is over.

Why has it been made, you ask. For this reason, my child. The lover, whom you have only known as M. Lebrun, a French artist, told me but yesterday his real name, dropped because the blood-thirsty republicans might consider it as too aristocratic. It is Maurice de Poissy.

Worth the Having

Michael Paul Gonzalez

How does it feel?

It asks this as it cuts deep into the inner thigh, flesh and fat zippering apart, its tongue probing into the fresh wound.

How are you doing?

The thing wouldn't want an answer even if there was one. It only wants screams.

This is going to be worth it. You're going to love next year. This will make it worth the having.

I used to wonder what could be worth this. The heat of its palms pushing legs apart. The cold, slow rivulets of saliva dripping down like icy syrup, washed away with slowing pulses of hot blood. That single tooth in its lower jaw, barbed and curved. That awful, knowing smile from the puckered sphincter of its mouth. This year, I finally understand that phrase, worth the having. This year, the final year of our horrible agreement – the thing still uses that word, agreement, as if I wanted any of this – I understand it all.

Twenty-two years ago, I cut across the backyard of Mikey Slater's dad's house. This was the night before Halloween; the night, I'd later learn, that the thing would stretch its legs and go for a walk. The thing was the reason for the season, the whole tradition of Halloween had started because of it. Masks, costumes, disguises, none of it for fun. All of it primal camouflage to help the prey hide from the predator.

Nobody remembers that part of the tradition anymore. Not even the thing itself. It just knows to walk the night before Halloween. And it walks to me. I don't ask where it goes when it leaves me or what it does on Halloween night. I'm just glad it's gone.

Anyway, Mikey Slater. His parents had been divorced a few years, and I treated our hangout like a second home. The other bonus was that it was a quick end-around the neighborhood when I needed to get home fast. I was on my way home from checking out Mikey's Halloween costume at his mom's house and had about two minutes to get home before dinner was cold and my ass would get spanked.

We'd made a pact to dress as characters from this cartoon about interstellar knights. We had some great things rigged to our costumes, lights and fake swords, the whole works. We expected that tomorrow night, we'd barely be able to do any trick or treating since we'd be mobbed by admirers wondering how we obtained these amazing costumes.

I vaulted the six foot wooden, slatted fence, landed soft in the garden, not caring if my presence was announced or not, since Mikey's dad never cared if I cut through.

And then I saw Mr Slater lying in the grass near the backdoor, naked. Another person straddled him, pinning his arms down. Pale skin, soft curves, it looked like a woman. The back did, anyway. The head was too small, and bald with a Mohawk of downy feathers. This thing, this silhouette dipped down, the head bobbing just above Mr.

Slater's crotch. I was young, but not so young that I didn't have a small clue about what I might be seeing.

I heard a whisper: *Almost done, almost done. Next year is going to be fantastic. This will all be worth it.*

And Mr. Slater replied, "No, no, no. No more. There's nothing I want. Everything I want is gone…" Occasionally he hissed, his breath, stifling a scream.

Pleasure wasn't part of this.

"No more! No more, please!"

You must want something. It's you and I forever. If you don't want anything…

And here the thing yanked a hand back from Mr. Slater's thigh, and that's when I noticed the blood, and the flap of flayed skin that I'd initially mistaken for underwear pulled down.

I tried to turn around, grabbed the fence to bail out. I wanted to get out of there, wanted to be home.

You…want?

It whipped its head around at me, and I felt its voice in my head more than I heard it.

"Take him! Take him!" Mr. Slater cried out, pointing at me.

I can't explain any of what happened next. Can't explain the face I saw when I locked eyes with the thing. Can't explain the speed with which it moved. It crossed the yard in three hitching strides, seizing my ankle as I tried to get out of the yard. I flopped my upper body over the fence and struggled for anything to grab, to pull, to get free.

I heard a whisper…no, felt it.

Mine.

One quick bite on my ankle. A burning pain, searing, electric.

Make a wish before you go to bed. Think about what you want next year more than anything. We have an agreement now.

It wasn't a question or an offer.

It released me and I dropped to the ground in the alley behind the fence.

I reached to my ankle. There was a fading flash of pain and burning, but no blood. No cut.

Mikey's dad came stumbling around the corner, wearing nothing but a pair of shorts, holding a handgun. "Is it still here? Is it?"

I said nothing. What could I say? What the hell was happening?

"My God, if you hadn't shown up… I'd…I'm free." He smiled at me and turned away. There was a flash in his eyes, a moment where he was teetering between life and death, that gun the fulcrum between finishing something very bad or starting something new. His hand rose slowly.

"But, don't, Mikey…" Those were the only three words in the mess behind my lips that could break through. It was enough. His hand swung free and heavy.

"I'm sorry. I'm so sorry. Try to… just… try to think of good things for yourself." He looked at the gun again. "Heh. What the hell was I gonna do with this thing? Don't ever think about trying to kill it, whatever you do. Just take what you have coming and then think of good things for yourself."

I barely remembered getting home. By the time I was through my front door, the details were hazy. My ankle was fine. No cut, no scab, not even a scratch. I slid into bed, trying to remember the thing, the face, the hands, anything, but it was all gone. A haze. My gaze drifted over the shelves around my room, the random toys scattered around, the baseball bat leaning against the corner. I hopped out of bed and brought it close by, feeling like it would keep me safe, not knowing from what. As I drifted off that night, my last thought was about Little League and my wish that I wasn't too damn fat to play shortstop.

That's good enough. A whisper, shot through the center of my brain.

Cold sweat broke over my upper lip, then calmness, then sleep.

When I woke up the next morning, I'd forgotten the previous night completely. I was full of energy, light on my feet. I felt ready to take on the world. Things felt a little darker in the afternoon as I walked by Mr. Slater's house on my way to Mikey's, but I couldn't quite peg why. I saw him sitting on his porch, a strange smile on his face. I kept moving, and that night was a Halloween much like any other.

The following year I dropped a lot of weight. Got faster. Made the team. Didn't think of how or why, just attributed it to hard work and eating right.

Then early October came and I found the postcard on my pillow when I got home from school. I'd like to say I got cold chills when I picked it up, or that it felt like flesh or leathery hide, but no, just plain, cheap cardboard. Typed in a neat white font on one side, it read:

Halloween is almost here. Did you have a good year? What do you want next year? Think hard! Make it worth the having.

I wanted to show the card to my mom, but by the time she got home from work, it was gone. Every time anyone brought up Halloween, this icicle of dread would rocket down my spine, and then disappear in a haze of thoughts about candy and costumes, an itch at the back of my mind that I couldn't quite scratch.

The night before Halloween, laying my costume out before going to bed, my only thoughts were on candy and sneaking around in the dark. It was two in the morning when I woke to a great weight on top of me, pushing the blankets down tight and cocooning me inside. I opened my eyes to see a silhouette, slight shoulders that were a bit too sharp, full breasts that seemed too round, slender arms that pinned me down. It was too dark to see details. I tried to cry out for my parents, but the thing lifted a hand to my mouth, cold boneless fingers clamping down. The palm spread like cold jelly as the thing drew its hand back, forcing one, then two fingers into my mouth. There was a texture to the bottom of them, something between a snake's belly and octopus suction pads.

Shhhhh…

The whisper in my brain.

Have you thought on it?

Thought on what?

The postcard I sent. What you want for next year.

Who are you?

It doesn't matter who I am. It matters who you are. You are mine.

How did you—

Just as you hear me in your mind, I hear you in mine. You are mine.

What does that mean?

It means you are mine.

I felt the thing rock down with its pelvis, grind into my stomach.

The agreement is not without benefit to you.

I didn't agree to anything.

Does a fish agree to feed a shark? Does a tree agree to be struck by lightning? You are mine.

The thing drew closer to me, and I squeezed my eyes shut. Everything grew bright, until I could make out shapes, then colors. Then I could see it in front of me.

You don't need your ears to hear me, nor your eyes to see. You are mine.

It was mottled and grey. The torso was curved and sensuous, but the head, that too-small head. The puckered sphincter of a mouth that prolapsed in and out, exposing that single jagged tooth. The two giant eyes, bulbous and red, shot with veins but no pupils, the two smaller green eyes in between. No ears. No nose. The tuft of white feathers in a stripe over the shining bald skull. Squeezing my eyes shut tighter only seemed to draw out more clarity.

You need to understand how this works. I will show you. Think of a woman you desire.

I couldn't. I was twelve. There wasn't desire yet, only a strange fascination. An occasional stirring if I saw a woman on TV in a swimsuit or that time I sneaked a peek at my dad's private magazine collection—

The thing on top of me changed. Hair grew. The head filled in. The face melted and morphed into the perfectly sculpted features of that lady from Beach Patrol who had just done the cover shoot for Playboy. Bronze skin. Swaying breasts. A sculpted collarbone. Skin coated in a sheen of sweat, just as I'd seen her in the centerfold.

Better?

It hadn't changed the feeling of the fingers in my mouth, cold like snails, twitching and probing around my tongue.

Every year on this night, I'm going to find you. I must feed. In exchange, you will tell me something you want, and over the course of the next year, you shall have it.

But I don't want—

You are – and the fingers extended slowly, pushing against the back of my throat, gagging me – *mine. Understand it. Tell me your desire. Make it worth the having.*

I want you to leave.

Not part of the bargain. Not your place to ask. You are mine.

The fingers pushed deeper still until I could feel them sliding down into my throat. I couldn't breathe. Instinct kicked in and I began to thrash. I needed to escape. I bit down hard on the fingers, breaking the skin, cold peppery ichor oozing into my mouth.

The thing didn't draw back. It moaned. Reached up its other hand and caressed itself.

More.

It pushed hard on my mouth, wanting me to bite. I let my jaw go slack. It sighed, the kind of sigh I was too young to understand as sexually frustrated, and its fingers pulled back.

I felt my lungs suck in air. I thought I was going to die. Thoughts of school crossed my mind. Thoughts of family trips I'd never get to take. I'd never get to see Disney World—

Is that something you desire?

I nodded in spite of myself. The thing on top of me slowly morphed back to its original form, spinning around on my body so I could only see its back. I felt it pulling at the sheets covering my feet.

I want you to think harder next year. Make it good. Make it worth the having. This is scarcely worth a toe, let alone two.

"What, what—"

And I felt the cold fingers of one hand clamp down on my ankle while the other fingers slithered between my toes, constricting them, spreading them apart.

"No," I said. "Nononono please don't—"

Next year you will remember this and understand what it means when I say make it worth the having.

Its head lowered and its lips wrapped around my big toe. It sucked once, twice, then clamped down with a force I can't describe. That single tooth razored into the meat of my toe and flicked, cutting, tearing. I screamed. I had to have screamed, but there was no sound. I could feel the blood pumping out of my toe, feel the vibration of serrated tooth on bone; clamping, twisting, pulling, until it was all electricity and cold air. The thing turned to me and pursed its lips. It showed me my toe, sucking it so it bobbed in and out of its mouth before tipping its head back and swallowing. The opening between its legs pulsed and shuddered, cold slime pooling onto my sheets. It sighed.

One more.

This time I did get a scream out, a small yelp as it latched onto my second toe and began chewing again. Its leg cracked and bent around at an impossible angle until its foot was over my mouth, spreading like taffy, covering my nose and lips so that no sound could escape, no breath could enter. There was no smell, just electric pain, vibrant agony.

A crack, a tear, and more cold air. The second toe went much easier than the first. The creature arched its back and swallowed, ripples shivering down its flanks as it came again. It spun, bringing its face close to mine. I squeezed my eyes shut to no effect.

Enjoy your trip. Next year, think harder.

Without moving its torso, it raised one leg, stretched it toward my window sill. Gripping hard, it pulled itself up and out into the night.

I stared down over my soaked sheets at my foot. The silhouette in the dark room danced through the purple lightning of pain. It didn't seem to be bleeding. It didn't hurt. I didn't pass out from the pain. I passed out when I tried to count my toes and had to stop at three.

I awoke screaming as I felt someone shaking my shoulder. Unbidden, I saw that face, round and leathery and purple, hovering inches from mine.

"Honey, it's okay!"

When I opened my eyes I saw my mother's face.

"Are you feeling okay? Your bed is soaked. Did you wet the bed?"

I burst into tears, kicking at the sheets until they came free. I could feel the burning sensation in my toes still, the raw wound scraping at the fabric.

"No!" I shouted. "Look what it did! Look what it did!"

I held my foot up. Five toes. Had I not already been crying, I might have started then. Or possibly even wet the bed out of sheer joy. I wiggled my toes. Jumped out of bed.

"What's gotten into you?"

My big toe was a bit red. My second toe had a definite hard ridge beneath the skin like a scar, but they were there. They were back. I was whole. My toes were—

Mine

Mine.

"Did you stub your toe last night?" My mom grabbed my foot, poking at my toes.

No pain.

"No, I'm…Ow!"

There was a scab on the underside of my big toe. Damp sheets. No blood. Five toes.

"You need to get up! And be more careful. You get a cut like that, you show me, okay? Otherwise it could get infected and you might lose your toes. You wouldn't want that, would you?"

I blanched.

"You need to get up. It's Halloween! Big breakfast to fuel up for a big night, right?"

Her hand sank into the dampness on my sheet, the essence that the creature had left behind in its ecstasy. Her eyes became vacant, distant, as she pulled the sheet off and bunched them on the floor.

"Well. I'll wash these later. You go run along." She absently licked at her fingers as she left.

By the time I made it downstairs for breakfast, I'd forgotten about my aching toes. By the time I was out the door, my sheets were in the wash and my mind was on Halloween.

The events of the evening never returned to traumatize me. I don't remember much of the school year that followed, but I remember our vacation. The best time we'd ever had as a family. I remember years later, my parents telling me that trip had been a new beginning for them, bringing them out of a rough patch that I had been blissfully unaware of.

The next year when Halloween drew close, I got another card, this time in my lunchbox at school.

Matte black, bearing only the reminder: MAKE IT WORTH THE HAVING.

Reading those words instantly sent a spasm of pain through my foot and up my spine. I couldn't see the creature in mind, but it was omnipresent, that assault, that pain, and the reward it brought.

The night before Halloween that year, I asked if I could sleep in my parent's room. And as soon as the question left my mouth, a whisper buzzed through my brain —

Oh no, don't make them watch. Why would you do that to them?

So I didn't. I slept in my closet that year, thinking it might not find me, but I was wrong.

I could explain this. Break it down year by year and tell what happened, but that's not why I'm going to do. It's about that phrase, Make It Worth the Having.

That second time, it stood at the door of my closet, towering over me, taking on features it must have thought looked friendly, the face shifting from Santa Claus to Jesus to cartoon mice and rabbits.

I don't want you to go through this for nothing. Think big.

Please stop.

I'll stop when I'm full and finished and I'll still come back next year. Don't wish for toys. Don't wish for things for other people. Think of yourself. Remember our meeting last year, and know what's about to happen will be far worse than a few toes. Don't let this happen for nothing. Make it worth the —

I screamed hard, muffled by the gelatinous glob of fingers it had forced into my mouth again. I just wanted it to shut up. I never wanted to hear that phrase again, but I knew I would. I knew this, all of this, would be happening again, and again.

That's a big burden to put on the shoulders of a child, right? Have almost anything you want, in exchange for giving the thing what it wants. That's not accurate. In exchange for the thing *taking* what it wants. I mean, what can a child think of that would be worth that? The second year, all I could think of was sports cars. It made me try again – why ask for something I couldn't legally use? Millions of dollars? Same thing. It had to be personal. So the second year, I wished to be the fastest, strongest kid in my school.

Done.

And in exchange for that, for the next sixty minutes, the creature flayed my arms and legs with that horrible tooth, peeled back my skin and chose three strands of exposed muscle from each limb, snapping them near one tendon and pulling them out like spaghetti, lifting it as high as it would go before placing the strand in its mouth and sucking it down greedily, biting off the other end at the tendon. It held its gelatinous foot over my mouth the whole time, tiny suctioned footpads inhaling the screams that never made it into the night. Blood everywhere. Pain like I'd never felt, to that point anyway.

When it was done, it left me wide open like a biology class project pinned to a tray, trying to sleep and failing miserably. I passed out at some point and woke up in the morning, mildly sore but fully intact, testing out my newfound strength on my dad's weight bench by the end of the day. By the end of the week, I was running home from school without breaking a sweat. By the end of the school year, I was medaling in every sport I chose.

When October rolled around, and the black postcard fell out a library book I pulled from the shelf, the sinking dread in my stomach was almost matched by the excitement of the next thing I planned to ask for.

That night, it ate half of one my kidneys. Once it managed to pull the organ free it wasn't so bad, but getting there was sheer hell. Fourteen years old, I made the wish any hormonally rampaging boy would, and that year I got every girl I was interested in. Was it worth it? Hard to say. But that year I came to understand that I was addicted. That I understood what *worth the having* meant, and that my life was going to improve.

I thought I had it all figured out. I had to try something new, and something new, despite seeing the thing lick its lips, despite seeing the horrible tongue dance over that single stupid tooth in the puckered maw it called a mouth, something new was too enticing to resist. Year by year, piece by piece, I was going to become a better man.

Everything that's happened in my life is a bit of a blur, but not those nights. Those, I have perfect clarity on.

I got better-than-perfect eyesight the year it spent hours working my eyeballs free from the sockets after using one jagged nail to cut my eyelids off. More length and girth downstairs (it was my first year in college, after all), that year was sheer torture. It changed its shape to a calendar girl, arousing me, bringing me to climax orally in spite of myself, the soft supple features of the woman's body betrayed by the cold, slimy oatmeal feeling of the thing's mouth and throat. And then came the pain, my member first peeled like a raw potato with that single hooked tooth, then the soft tissue torn free, then the tongue probing into the open wound at my crotch until my testes were pulled free from my body and eaten – no, nibbled, held daintily between thumb and forefinger with pinky extended – until they were gone. That night I was on a camping trip, so the thing didn't even need to muffle my screams, and I obliged it until I was choking on my own vomit and my throat was raw. Physically, I was fine the next day, but it took me a few weeks to get the feeling of it all out of my mind. Once I did, I quickly developed a reputation as Big Man on Campus in every way imaginable. By the end of the year, every man and woman worth having knew my number.

After college, my life became career-oriented. Real Estate. Stock Market. Passive income. I wanted to be rich while having as much free time as possible to research, because I needed to know how to finish this thing. Mikey's Dad, all those years ago, had simply begged the creature to stop, and when it saw me, it did. I asked it one year if I could do the same thing. It only replied, *You are mine.*

I researched it through college and beyond, and when I had enough money to hire people, they researched it too. I couldn't be very specific with them about my reasons, of course, but I could offer grants to religious studies students, hire paranormal investigators, demonologists. Six solid years of research yielded nothing. Not a damn thing. Every ancient society, every dead culture I could study I did, end to end, to the extent that there was some buzz that I'd be nominated for a Nobel for advancing the studies so far. Nobody had heard of the thing. In college, I'd had the idea to go back and ask Mr. Slater about it, but he looked at me like I was crazy.

I wondered how much time it had spent with him, since his life wasn't so great. What if that was the first night he'd encountered it? What if the thing had been with him for years and was on a downswing, taking things away instead of granting them? I'd never know.

I was thirty five, with another Halloween approaching, a wife I loved and my first child on the way. And that was the final straw. I couldn't have this thing in my life with a child in the house. This year I was going to ask it for an exit.

This year, I received something worse than a black postcard in the mail. This year, the afternoon of what I'd come to think of as Visitation Night, we had to rush to the hospital. Complications. Our baby was lost. It made no sense. My wife was perfectly healthy, and everything had been going fine. But there was no heartbeat, no sign of life. My wife was inconsolable. She had to be sedated, and even as they were putting the IV into her, she was crying out, asking: "Will this hurt the baby? You can't give me these drugs. It'll cause complications…"

My wife refused treatment, insisted that they were mistaken. We went home, the doctor pulling me aside to suggest that we let her rest a few days, then discuss inducing labor to finish the procedure.

Finish the procedure. Just like that, our baby had somehow progressed from human being to benign growth. A mole to be scraped off. A boil to be lanced. All of those cardboard pumpkins hanging on the wall, smiling, calm. That stupid friendly skeleton on the door. They were the only witnesses.

That night, it came. Slow, silent, and sad-eyed. It sat at the foot of the couch, where I was sleeping. My wife wanted to be alone, and I didn't know what to do. I didn't notice that I'd drifted off to sleep, but one minute it wasn't there and then it was, laying a hand on my calf. I didn't feel fear. I only felt empty.

I am ready—

Just take something and go, I said.

I am ready to end our bargain.

I was speechless. It felt strange, another gut-punch, another loss, another branch pruned form the tree of my life. I wanted to dictate terms. I wanted a safe exit, but once the baby was gone… I wanted it back. I wanted it to continue. I needed it, this thing, this surety.

I will give you your child.

What?

I will give you your child. I will take it. I will be the surrogate. Tomorrow, you will be a father.

It wasn't a question or an offer.

"But my wife can't—"

She will remember nothing.

"I don't want this. You can't have it – my child. You can't. It's done."

Have I ever asked your permission for anything? The bargain ends because I say so. You are mine. Tomorrow you will be a father.

It led me to the bedroom. Made me open the door. Made sure my wife… I can't describe the look I saw on her face, how she instinctively curled her arms over her stomach, how her feral glare burned through me until *it* came into the room. Then she froze, and softened, and looked at me, her lower jaw working, trying to get out a question, to ask me what was happening.

It mounted her, stretched its arms out and wrapped those rubbery, cold fingers around her wrists, pinned her legs down, didn't bother to cover her mouth, because there was nobody to disturb with her screams. All I could do was watch. I knew what it felt like. I knew *exactly* what she was going through. I chuckled in spite of myself that she'd never be able to hold the pain of this childbirth over my head.

That single tooth tore her nightshirt open. That sphincter mouth traced kisses down her collarbone, between her breasts, suckling at her nipples until milk started to flow. Then it moved lower, elbows and shoulders dislocating so that it could keep her pinned down. Not that she was fighting at this point, only staring at me with wide eyes, panting for air until the thing's mouth reached her thighs.

How does it feel?

It asks this as it cuts deep into the inner thigh, flesh and fat zippering apart, its tongue probing into the fresh wound.

How are you doing?

The thing wouldn't want an answer even if there was one. It only wants screams.

This is going to be worth it. You're going to love next year. This will make it worth the having.

Its head stretched thin, narrowing impossibly at the mouth, the entire face a tubular beak, a hard proboscis that poked at her vulva until it found its way inside. She screamed then, my wife.

I could do nothing but watch it root, the heat of its palms pushing her legs apart. The cold, slow rivulets of saliva dripping down her sides like icy syrup, washed away with the regular and slowing pulses of her hot blood.

That single tooth in its lower jaw, barbed and curved, that awful knowing smile from the pucker of its mouth as it comes up for air, slowly retracting its head to stare at me, neck bent round the wrong way, slime coating its face, it made that hideous ring-mouth into an imitation of a smile.

It's a boy.

It plunged its beak into her stomach, slicing through skin, and fat, and muscle, splaying her open. Cold, grey slime oozed down her, mixing and pooling with her blood. That ringing, that ringing in my ears isn't ringing. It's her screaming. Screaming for the baby, screaming no, screaming my name, cursing me, damning me. Cursing the thing, even as it lowered its face to her flayed abdomen and forced its head inside.

Its back lurched up once, twice, as if taking great gulping swallows, and then it came, orgasmic shudders rippling through its spine as it straightened and stood up from the bed, staring at me, one hand cupping its swollen belly. It caressed my cheek, pushed a finger inside my mouth, pressed until my knees buckled. It lowered me onto the bed beside my wife. Tears streamed from her eyes, her organs warm and wet against my stomach. I reached out to her, stupidly, tried to cradle her in my arms.

The thing stood above us and arched its back, convulsing, straining, eyes swelling until the veins that laced them burst and bloody tears flowed. It straddled her, crouching lower and lower until it positioned its vagina above my wife's open torso. It pushed, pushed until it came…until…a child came. A membranous sac, slid out of its dilated opening and landed inside my wife. I saw through the pale pink membrane his face, calm and serene, sleeping.

Sleeping.

I woke to her screams, my wife clutching my arm, saying, "It's time! Holy shit it's time. They were wrong! My water broke! Do you feel it?"

I climbed from the bed, soaked, but not in her blood, but amniotic fluid. Aside from that, the sheets were clean in a way my memory could never be.

And we drove to the hospital, and I strode through the doors like a champion, pushing her wheelchair through the throng gathered there. I stared at the confused faces of the nurses and doctors and told them it was time.

They checked signs. They double checked charts. They made me sign waivers promising not to sue over all of this stillbirth confusion. "These things happen sometimes. We will of course be paying you for your pain and suffering in exchange for—"

I told them to shut the fuck up and do their job. We could discuss it later. There would be a later. There would be a rest of our lives. That's all that mattered.

You are all that mattered. Our son. My son. Mine.

I'm telling you all of this now before you understand it, because I never want you to hear it again. I never want you to know about any of this. It's gone. It's gone and it won't come back. It always keeps its promises. You're in my arms, with your perfect eyes, your ruddy cheeks, and I love you. More than anything. More than everything. I'm laughing at your gurgles, your tiny nose twitching, your perfect little ruby lips when they stretch into that smile, that same kind of goofy smile your mother gets. Your happy little gummy mouth that looks perfect. Perfect and normal except for that one thing that confused the doctors.

That single, smooth tiny tooth breaking through your lower gums. Doctors say this isn't unusual, they call them natal teeth. I know better. You yawn wide, showing me that tiny ivory blade, and you stare at me placidly, and I can only think.

Worth the having.

Extraneus Invokat

Ed Grabianowski

NONE OF THESE little incidents meant anything to me at first. I drew no connections. It started in the middle of a fall afternoon, sunny and crisp.

We were packing up the apartment to move. After two years in the same tiny space, we were making a little more money and moving to a slightly nicer neighborhood. The living room was a maze of cardboard boxes, stacked and taped and labeled, or hanging open, half filled with the bits and pieces of life we'd collected over our few years together.

I walked in from one of the two bedrooms with an armload of winter scarves and hats. "Should we keep these out, or do you think we'll manage to find them before it gets too cold out?" I looked at Laura, who was bent over a box with her back to me. Sun shone through the wide front windows onto her long, dark hair.

She shuddered then. Not a physical shudder, not like a seizure. More like the twitch you see when the film is about to break at a movie theater. She flickered.

I blinked, thinking something was in my eye. But she was silent and oddly still, crouching low over the box. Then I noticed her hair. Just a second ago, it had been swept sleekly across her neck and shoulders, soft and curled, but now it hung in thick, wet strings, hiding her face from my view entirely. It was all so strange, and happened so quickly, I don't really remember what I was thinking. Mostly, I was mildly irritated that she hadn't answered my question, but a numbness crept up my spine as I realized something was not right.

"Laura?" Louder, this time. Perhaps she moved slightly, I wasn't sure, but she remained silent, and my vague feelings of strangeness escalated quickly. A note of panic crept into my voice. "Is something wrong?"

She let out a sound then that I hesitate even to think about. The closest I can come to describing it is a sort of clicking sigh. At that moment she shuddered or twitched again, and it seemed as though the room brightened. Without realizing there had been a change, I saw that her hair looked as it had before, and she was busily wrapping glasses in tissue paper and lining them up in a cardboard carton.

My rising wave of dread crested then, and when I called her name again, she mistook the note of urgency for anger. She turned, frowning, and snapped. "What?"

I think I just stood there blinking stupidly at her for a moment, and already my mind had rejected the entire experience. "I, uh – I just zoned out there for a minute, sorry," I said. "Should we pack these?"

* * *

A few days later, I called her at work. One of the other women in the office answered. No, Laura wasn't in. Yes, she was a little late coming back from lunch. No, they didn't know where she'd gone.

She didn't usually leave the office for lunch, and she was hardly ever late for anything, but I didn't think twice about it at the time.

Later that week, I happened to thumb through a local newspaper, and a small article in the City News section caught my eye.

Witness claims 'stranger' walks downtown streets.

A homeless man was attacked on the city's West Side yesterday afternoon, although police are having trouble getting a description of the attacker.

Hale Thomas Donovan, 52, of no permanent address, reported the attack at 1:30 p.m., after passersby found him huddled on Dearborn St., near the Cray Island railroad bridge. He was yelling incoherently, and was 'visibly terrified', according to the police report. He was treated for trauma and released from Sisters of Mercy Medical Center, although witnesses believed the man was not physically injured.

In his statement to police, Donovan only said that he 'met a stranger' under the bridge. Police confirmed that they received two other reports that day of a 'strange person' on the city's West Side.

* * *

The apartment was mostly packed up at that point. We were living on frozen pizza eaten off of paper plates for the next few days. Every night we went to bed exhausted from packing and lugging boxes around. That night, I read in bed for a short while as Laura fell asleep beside me. She lay on her side, her back to me. When I set down my book and turned out the light, I leaned forward to kiss her goodnight. She made a soft, happy sound and snuggled back into me briefly. I was soon as sound asleep as she was.

When I awoke, I had no idea what time it was. Our alarm clock had long since been packed, and Laura was using her watch alarm to wake up for work in the morning. It was still extremely dark, the only light a feeble blue glow from the streetlight outside filtered through shade and curtains. Guessing it was about 3 a.m., I stretched sleep-stiff muscles and turned over to face Laura. She still had her back to me, sound asleep on her side. In the dim light I could see the slow, shallow rising and falling of her breath. I reached out to gently stroke her hair until I fell back to sleep.

It was ice cold and soaking wet.

I froze in place, my body instantly rigid as the memory of the afternoon packing incident flooded me with terror. My throat was tight and dry, adrenaline surging through me as I tried to keep my hand still, plotting how to withdraw without letting her know I was awake. I pulled my hand from that clammy mass as slowly as I could, fighting the urge to recoil in a panic. My fingers were tingling from fear and another, stronger numbness that spread down my arm as I tried to pull it back beneath the covers silently. Just then, she made that chittering sound again. This time, I realized what it was.

She was laughing.

I pressed myself hard against the wall on my side of the bed, heart slamming and skittering, arms pressed tight to my sides. My eyes were wide open, glaring into the darkness, watching the shape in the bed beside me for any kind of movement. I didn't know what was lying less than two feet from me. I remained that way, rigid with terror, for quite some time. I didn't sleep. I don't think I even blinked.

I never noticed a change, but at some point, I heard a soft snoring – a familiar Laura sound. I relaxed somewhat, but a few minutes later, when she stirred and rolled over, my every muscle pulled taut with apprehension. But it was just Laura, peaceful in sleep.

My fear ebbed away, and in the absence of adrenaline, my eyes refused to stay open. Although I slept soundly, I woke with stiff, sore muscles. My shoulders ached, and I remember vaguely that I'd dreamt of being chased through my childhood neighborhood, desperately hopping fences and cutting through yards to escape some unseen pursuer.

Laura came back into the bedroom just before she left for work. She looked down at me with a look of concern.

"Did you sleep ok?" she asked. "You look pale."

She reached out a hand to touch my cheek, and I flinched. Looking confused and hurt, Laura stepped back. "What?" She smelled the sleeve of her shirt. "Do I smell bad? What's wrong?"

The unconscious jolt of fear brought the previous night's encounter back to the forefront of my mind, but already the defensive mechanisms of the human psyche were at work, defusing the memory as I convinced myself it was part of my dream.

"No, it's not you. I think I was having a nightmare when I woke up, and I'm still a little foggy."

She gave a half smile and leaned down to kiss me goodbye. I reached up to give her a quick hug, feeling the warmth of her body and her soft skin against my face. Then she was gone.

* * *

That night, Laura left for a two-day conference in Memphis. I dropped her off at the airport and got back to the apartment around nine at night. There wasn't much to do, since most of the packing was finished and we were just waiting for the occupants of our new apartment to move out. I had a TV and a couch. Everything else was sealed in boxes. I ordered a pizza and settled in to watch a baseball game.

At about 1 a.m., I woke up with a stiff neck. I'd fallen asleep at an odd angle on the couch. The game was long over. An infomercial bathed the room in flickering bluish light, but I'd turned the volume very low, so I couldn't hear what they were selling. Some kind of exercise equipment.

It wasn't the infomercial or sore neck that awakened me, however. It was the early autumn chill that pervaded the apartment. Puzzled and still groggy, I sat up and realized that the door to the apartment was open. At that moment I also noticed a foul odor, like rotted meat. I walked to the door, seeing that the outer door was also hanging ajar. It was gusty out, and the night air was blowing straight down the hall. I closed both doors, certain that I hadn't forgotten to latch them shut earlier, but I could come up with no other explanation. Neither could I find any source for the smell, which was fading quickly. There was literally no other food in the house, and the garbage was outside in the dumpster. My 2 a.m. sleuthing skills exhausted, I gave up and went to bed. The night's sleep was uneventful.

* * *

On Saturday morning, I picked Laura up at the airport. That night was to be our last at the apartment, but we were still in limbo – everything packed, nothing to do but wait. Even the cable had been shut off. We spent the afternoon and evening seeing a movie and having dinner at a nearby restaurant. The televisions over the bar, usually tuned to a ball game, were buzzing with news about a recent murder. An old woman had been found mutilated in her home. They kept showing footage of a man in a suit, a detective I guess, walking out of the house with his hand over his mouth, his eyes wide with shock. Our spirits were subdued when we got home, and before long we went to bed.

That night – that unbearable, unthinkable night started out much like before. Something awoke me in the deepest hours. I had no sense of time, but it was very dark. I immediately knew something was wrong. I'd been having tense and disturbing dreams, partly from the news stories about the murder. Faceless men in suits knocking at my door, walking around the house, peering into the windows. But something other than a nightmare was contributing to my malaise.

She made the sound. That laughter. That hideous, mind-wrenching sound no human could make. My body went numb with terror and I gasped out loud. Again I shrunk to the far wall, pressed against it, my eyes frantically scanning the blackness for movement. I couldn't imagine passing another night like that, straining to hear, praying that nothing happened. But I felt the bed shift. A gout of cold air, reeking of rot, bathed my face. The shape in the bed beside me rolled over.

If I live for a thousand years, I will never forget that face. It was my wife's face, but corrupted, as though my wife was being worn by something that was not the same shape as her. The mouth was stretched in a wide rictus, literally from ear to ear. An inner set of black, oily lips curled back in a manic smile, uncovering a row of impossibly large teeth. I could see things caught in those teeth. The eyes were huge, glistening black – no iris or pupil. The nose was distorted into a thin ridge of bone with narrow slits. The scalp and hair seemed to hang loosely, as if partially detached from the skull beneath. And yet the mottled grey skin of the thin neck disappeared into my wife's pale blue night shirt.

It was an obscenity. It crawled across the bed toward me, unnaturally agile. Those eyes widened, the grin somehow stretching, the jaw working at a bizarre speed. Still that sound issued from its throat. I tried to scream, but my throat was clenched in terror. A hand gripped my shoulder, terrifyingly strong and cold as ice. Its face was inches from mine now, the mouth opening wide.

It screamed at me. It was a shrill, screeching roar of deafening volume, so loud it made my eyes hurt. As it screamed, it shook violently. The cold, wet hair flailed and fell in thick ropes across the face. But the cold black eyes stayed focused on mine.

* * *

When I awoke, the room was flooded with sun. I have no idea what happened. I can only assume that I passed out from sheer terror. Laura was already up, showering. I went to the other bathroom to wash a strange chemical taste out of my mouth. In the mirror, I noticed that thin trails of blood had seeped from the corners of my eyes, then dried.

Somehow, I got through that day. I stayed busy with loading the moving van, unloading at the new apartment, unpacking. I avoided Laura. I didn't know what to think or what to do. I finally convinced myself that whatever had happened was probably related to the apartment itself. Since we were moving, I was escaping whatever it was.

But I woke up in the middle of the night again. We were sleeping on a mattress on the floor, surrounded by boxes. My heart was slamming in my chest as I looked at Laura. She seemed to be sleeping peacefully, lying on her side facing away from me. That made it even more of a shock when I heard the sound. The laughter again.

It seemed so loud, though. I tried to get up, get out of the bed and away, but I could not move my limbs. The clicking laugh sound came again, but this time I felt it.

I felt it come from my own throat.

My limbs began moving then, but I was not in control. I was a passenger. I put my hand on Laura's shoulder, squeezing hard. It was my hand, but not my hand – grey-skinned and clawed. It woke her up.

"Hey, ow," as she rolled over and I began to pull at her shoulder. She opened her eyes and screamed just as her arm tore free. I could see clearly. Her eyes had gone glassy with terror and pain, and her scream was soon cut short. I can only hope she went into shock before most of what came next. I was not in control, but I watched it all happen.

The Three Strangers

Thomas Hardy

AMONG the few features of agricultural England which retain an appearance but little modified by the lapse of centuries, may be reckoned the high, grassy and furzy downs, coombs, or ewe-leases, as they are indifferently called, that fill a large area of certain counties in the south and south-west. If any mark of human occupation is met with hereon, it usually takes the form of the solitary cottage of some shepherd.

Fifty years ago such a lonely cottage stood on such a down, and may possibly be standing there now. In spite of its loneliness, however, the spot, by actual measurement, was not more than five miles from a county-town. Yet that affected it little. Five miles of irregular upland, during the long inimical seasons, with their sleets, snows, rains, and mists, afford withdrawing space enough to isolate a Timon or a Nebuchadnezzar; much less, in fair weather, to please that less repellent tribe, the poets, philosophers, artists, and others who "conceive and meditate of pleasant things."

Some old earthen camp or barrow, some clump of trees, at least some starved fragment of ancient hedge is usually taken advantage of in the erection of these forlorn dwellings. But, in the present case, such a kind of shelter had been disregarded. Higher Crowstairs, as the house was called, stood quite detached and undefended. The only reason for its precise situation seemed to be the crossing of two footpaths at right angles hard by, which may have crossed there and thus for a good five hundred years. Hence the house was exposed to the elements on all sides. But, though the wind up here blew unmistakably when it did blow, and the rain hit hard whenever it fell, the various weathers of the winter season were not quite so formidable on the coomb as they were imagined to be by dwellers on low ground. The raw rimes were not so pernicious as in the hollows, and the frosts were scarcely so severe. When the shepherd and his family who tenanted the house were pitied for their sufferings from the exposure, they said that upon the whole they were less inconvenienced by 'wuzzes and flames' (hoarses and phlegms) than when they had lived by the stream of a snug neighbouring valley.

The night of March 28, 182—, was precisely one of the nights that were wont to call forth these expressions of commiseration. The level rainstorm smote walls, slopes, and hedges like the clothyard shafts of Senlac and Crecy. Such sheep and outdoor animals as had no shelter stood with their buttocks to the winds; while the tails of little birds trying to roost on some scraggy thorn were blown inside-out like umbrellas. The gable-end of the cottage was stained with wet, and the eavesdroppings flapped against the wall. Yet never was commiseration for the shepherd more misplaced. For that cheerful rustic was entertaining a large party in glorification of the christening of his second girl.

The guests had arrived before the rain began to fall, and they were all now assembled in the chief or living room of the dwelling. A glance into the apartment at eight o'clock on this eventful evening would have resulted in the opinion that it was as cosy and comfortable a nook as could be wished for in boisterous weather. The calling of its inhabitant was proclaimed by a number of highly-polished sheep-crooks without stems that were hung ornamentally over the fireplace, the curl of each shining crook varying from the antiquated type engraved in the patriarchal pictures of old family Bibles to the most approved fashion of the last local sheep-fair. The room was lighted by half-a-dozen candles, having wicks only a trifle smaller than the grease which enveloped them, in candlesticks that were never used but at high-days, holy-days, and family feasts. The lights were scattered about the room, two of them standing on the chimney-piece. This position of candles was in itself significant. Candles on the chimney-piece always meant a party.

On the hearth, in front of a back-brand to give substance, blazed a fire of thorns, that crackled "like the laughter of the fool."

Nineteen persons were gathered here. Of these, five women, wearing gowns of various bright hues, sat in chairs along the wall; girls shy and not shy filled the window-bench; four men, including Charley Jake the hedge-carpenter, Elijah New the parish-clerk, and John Pitcher, a neighbouring dairyman, the shepherd's father-in-law, lolled in the settle; a young man and maid, who were blushing over tentative pourparlers on a life-companionship, sat beneath the corner-cupboard; and an elderly engaged man of fifty or upward moved restlessly about from spots where his betrothed was not to the spot where she was. Enjoyment was pretty general, and so much the more prevailed in being unhampered by conventional restrictions. Absolute confidence in each other's good opinion begat perfect ease, while the finishing stroke of manner, amounting to a truly princely serenity, was lent to the majority by the absence of any expression or trait denoting that they wished to get on in the world, enlarge their minds, or do any eclipsing thing whatever – which nowadays so generally nips the bloom and bonhomie of all except the two extremes of the social scale.

Shepherd Fennel had married well, his wife being a dairyman's daughter from a vale at a distance, who brought fifty guineas in her pocket – and kept them there, till they should be required for ministering to the needs of a coming family. This frugal woman had been somewhat exercised as to the character that should be given to the gathering. A sit-still party had its advantages; but an undisturbed position of ease in chairs and settles was apt to lead on the men to such an unconscionable deal of toping that they would sometimes fairly drink the house dry.

A dancing-party was the alternative; but this, while avoiding the foregoing objection on the score of good drink, had a counterbalancing disadvantage in the matter of good victuals, the ravenous appetites engendered by the exercise causing immense havoc in the buttery. Shepherdess Fennel fell back upon the intermediate plan of mingling short dances with short periods of talk and singing, so as to hinder any ungovernable rage in either. But this scheme was entirely confined to her own gentle mind: the shepherd himself was in the mood to exhibit the most reckless phases of hospitality.

The fiddler was a boy of those parts, about twelve years of age, who had a wonderful dexterity in jigs and reels, though his fingers were so small and short as to necessitate a constant shifting for the high notes, from which he scrambled back to the first position with sounds not of unmixed purity of tone. At seven the shrill tweedle-dee of this youngster had begun, accompanied by a booming ground-bass from Elijah New, the parish-clerk, who had thoughtfully brought with him his favourite musical instrument, the serpent. Dancing was instantaneous, Mrs. Fennel privately enjoining the players on no account to let the dance exceed the length of a quarter of an hour.

But Elijah and the boy, in the excitement of their position, quite forgot the injunction. Moreover, Oliver Giles, a man of seventeen, one of the dancers, who was enamoured of his partner, a fair girl of thirty-three rolling years, had recklessly handed a new crown-piece to the musicians, as a bribe to keep going as long as they had muscle and wind. Mrs. Fennel, seeing the steam begin to generate on the countenances of her guests, crossed over and touched the fiddler's elbow and put her hand on the serpent's mouth. But they took no notice, and fearing she might lose her character of genial hostess if she were to interfere too markedly, she retired and sat down helpless. And so the dance whizzed on with cumulative fury, the performers moving in their planet-like courses, direct and retrograde, from apogee to perigee, till the hand of the well-kicked clock at the bottom of the room had travelled over the circumference of an hour.

While these cheerful events were in course of enactment within Fennel's pastoral dwelling, an incident having considerable bearing on the party had occurred in the gloomy night without. Mrs. Fennel's concern about the growing fierceness of the dance corresponded in point of time with the ascent of a human figure to the solitary hill of Higher Crowstairs from the direction of the distant town. This personage strode on through the rain without a pause, following the little-worn path which, further on in its course, skirted the shepherd's cottage.

It was nearly the time of full moon, and on this account, though the sky was lined with a uniform sheet of dripping cloud, ordinary objects out of doors were readily visible. The sad wan light revealed the lonely pedestrian to be a man of supple frame; his gait suggested that he had somewhat passed the period of perfect and instinctive agility, though not so far as to be otherwise than rapid of motion when occasion required. At a rough guess, he might have been about forty years of age. He appeared tall, but a recruiting sergeant, or other person accustomed to the judging of men's heights by the eye, would have discerned that this was chiefly owing to his gauntness, and that he was not more than five-feet-eight or nine.

Notwithstanding the regularity of his tread, there was caution in it, as in that of one who mentally feels his way; and despite the fact that it was not a black coat nor a dark garment of any sort that he wore, there was something about him which suggested that he naturally belonged to the black-coated tribes of men. His clothes were of fustian, and his boots hobnailed, yet in his progress he showed not the mud-accustomed bearing of hobnailed and fustianed peasantry.

By the time that he had arrived abreast of the shepherd's premises the rain came down, or rather came along, with yet more determined violence. The outskirts of the little settlement partially broke the force of wind and rain, and this induced him to stand still. The most salient of the shepherd's domestic erections was an empty sty at the forward corner of his hedgeless garden, for in these latitudes the principle of masking the homelier features of your establishment by a conventional frontage was unknown. The traveller's eye was attracted to this small building by the pallid shine of the wet slates that covered it. He turned aside, and, finding it empty, stood under the pent-roof for shelter.

While he stood, the boom of the serpent within the adjacent house, and the lesser strains of the fiddler, reached the spot as an accompaniment to the surging hiss of the flying rain on the sod, its louder beating on the cabbage-leaves of the garden, on the eight or ten beehives just discernible by the path, and its dripping from the eaves into a row of buckets and pans that had been placed under the walls of the cottage. For at Higher Crowstairs, as at all such elevated domiciles, the grand difficulty of housekeeping was an insufficiency of water; and a casual rainfall was utilized by turning out, as catchers, every utensil that the house contained. Some queer stories might be told of the contrivances for economy in suds and dishwaters that are absolutely necessitated in upland habitations during the droughts of summer. But at this season there were no such exigencies; a mere acceptance of what the skies bestowed was sufficient for an abundant store.

At last the notes of the serpent ceased and the house was silent. This cessation of activity aroused the solitary pedestrian from the reverie into which he had lapsed, and, emerging from the shed, with an apparently new intention, he walked up the path to the house-door. Arrived here, his first act was to kneel down on a large stone beside the row of vessels, and to drink a copious draught from one of them. Having quenched his thirst he rose and lifted his hand to knock, but paused with his eye upon the panel. Since the dark surface of the wood revealed absolutely nothing, it was evident that he must be mentally looking through the door, as if he wished to measure thereby all the possibilities that a house of this sort might include, and how they might bear upon the question of his entry.

In his indecision he turned and surveyed the scene around. Not a soul was anywhere visible. The garden-path stretched downward from his feet, gleaming like the track of a snail the roof of the little well (mostly dry), the well-cover, the top rail of the garden-gate, were varnished with the same dull liquid glaze; while, far away in the vale, a faint whiteness of more than usual extent showed that the rivers were high in the meads. Beyond all this winked a few bleared lamplights through the beating drops – lights that denoted the situation of the county-town from which he had appeared to come. The absence of all notes of life in that direction seemed to clinch his intentions, and he knocked at the door.

Within, a desultory chat had taken the place of movement and musical sound. The hedge-carpenter was suggesting a song to the company, which nobody just then was inclined to undertake, so that the knock afforded a not unwelcome diversion.

"Walk in!" said the shepherd promptly.

The latch clicked upward, and out of the night our pedestrian appeared upon the door-mat. The shepherd arose, snuffed two of the nearest candles, and turned to look at him.

Their light disclosed that the stranger was dark in complexion and not unprepossessing as to feature. His hat, which for a moment he did not remove, hung low over his eyes, without concealing that they were large, open, and determined, moving with a flash rather than a glance round the room. He seemed pleased with his survey, and, baring his shaggy head, said, in a rich deep voice, "The rain is so heavy, friends, that I ask leave to come in and rest awhile."

"To be sure, stranger," said the shepherd. "And faith, you've been lucky in choosing your time, for we are having a bit of a fling for a glad cause – though, to be sure, a man could hardly wish that glad cause to happen more than once a year."

"Nor less," spoke up a woman. "For 'tis best to get your family over and done with, as soon as you can, so as to be all the earlier out of the fag o't."

"And what may be this glad cause?" asked the stranger.

"A birth and christening," said the shepherd.

The stranger hoped his host might not be made unhappy either by too many or too few of such episodes, and being invited by a gesture to a pull at the mug, he readily acquiesced. His manner, which, before entering, had been so dubious, was now altogether that of a careless and candid man.

"Late to be traipsing athwart this coomb – hey?" said the engaged man of fifty.

"Late it is, master, as you say. – I'll take a seat in the chimney-corner, if you have nothing to urge against it, ma'am; for I am a little moist on the side that was next the rain."

Mrs. Shepherd Fennel assented, and made room for the self-invited comer, who, having got completely inside the chimney-corner, stretched out his legs and his arms with the expansiveness of a person quite at home.

"Yes, I am rather cracked in the vamp," he said freely, seeing that the eyes of the shepherd's wife fell upon his boots, "and I am not well fitted either. I have had some rough times lately, and have been forced to pick up what I can get in the way of wearing, but I must find a suit better fit for working-days when I reach home."

"One of hereabouts?" she inquired.

"Not quite that – further up the country."

"I thought so. And so be I; and by your tongue you come from my neighbourhood."

"But you would hardly have heard of me," he said quickly. "My time would be long before yours, ma'am, you see."

This testimony to the youthfulness of his hostess had the effect of stopping her cross-examination.

"There is only one thing more wanted to make me happy," continued the newcomer. "And that is a little baccy, which I am sorry to say I am out of."

"I'll fill your pipe," said the shepherd.

"I must ask you to lend me a pipe likewise."

"A smoker, and no pipe about 'ee?"

"I have dropped it somewhere on the road."

The shepherd filled and handed him a new clay pipe, saying, as he did so, "Hand me your baccy-box – I'll fill that too, now I am about it."

The man went through the movement of searching his pockets.

"Lost that too?" said his entertainer, with some surprise.

"I am afraid so," said the man with some confusion. "Give it to me in a screw of paper." Lighting his pipe at the candle with a suction that drew the whole flame into the bowl, he resettled himself in the corner and bent his looks upon the faint steam from his damp legs, as if he wished to say no more.

Meanwhile the general body of guests had been taking little notice of this visitor by reason of an absorbing discussion in which they were engaged with the band about a tune for the next dance. The matter being settled, they were about to stand up when an interruption came in the shape of another knock at the door.

At sound of the same the man in the chimney-corner took up the poker and began stirring the brands as if doing it thoroughly were the one aim of his existence; and a second time the shepherd said, "Walk in!" In a moment another man stood upon the straw-woven door-mat. He too was a stranger.

This individual was one of a type radically different from the first. There was more of the common-place in his manner, and a certain jovial cosmopolitanism sat upon his features. He was several years older than the first arrival, his hair being slightly frosted, his eyebrows bristly, and his whiskers cut back from his cheeks. His face was rather full and flabby, and yet it was not altogether a face without power. A few grog-blossoms marked the neighbourhood of his nose. He flung back his long drab greatcoat, revealing that beneath it he wore a suit of cinder-gray shade throughout, large heavy seals, of some metal or other that would take a polish, dangling from his fob as his only personal ornament. Shaking the water-drops from his low-crowned glazed hat, he said, "I must ask for a few minutes' shelter, comrades, or I shall be wetted to my skin before I get to Casterbridge."

"Make yourself at home, master," said the shepherd, perhaps a trifle less heartily than on the first occasion. Not that Fennel had the least tinge of niggardliness in his composition; but the room was far from large, spare chairs were not numerous, and damp companions were not altogether desirable at close quarters for the women and girls in their bright-coloured gowns.

However, the second comer, after taking off his greatcoat, and hanging his hat on a nail in one of the ceiling-beams as if he had been specially invited to put it there, advanced and sat down at the table. This had been pushed so closely into the chimney-corner, to give all available room to the dancers, that its inner edge grazed the elbow of the man who had ensconced himself by the fire; and thus the two strangers were brought into close companionship. They nodded to each other by way of breaking the ice of unacquaintance, and the first stranger handed his neighbour the family mug – a huge vessel of brown ware, having its upper edge worn away like a threshold by the rub of whole generations of thirsty lips that had gone the way of all flesh, and bearing the following inscription burnt upon its rotund side in yellow letters:

THERE IS NO FUN UNTILL I CUM.

The other man, nothing loth, raised the mug to his lips, and drank on, and on, and on – till a curious blueness overspread the countenance of the shepherd's wife, who had regarded with no little surprise the first stranger's free offer to the second of what did not belong to him to dispense.

"I knew it!" said the toper to the shepherd with much satisfaction. "When I walked up your garden before coming in, and saw the hives all of a row, I said to myself, 'Where there's bees there's honey, and where there's honey there's mead.' But mead of such a truly comfortable sort as this I really didn't expect to meet in my older days." He took yet another pull at the mug, till it assumed an ominous elevation.

"Glad you enjoy it!" I said the shepherd warmly.

"It is goodish mead," assented Mrs. Fennel, with an absence of enthusiasm which seemed to say that it was possible to buy praise for one's cellar at too heavy a price. "It is trouble enough to make – and really I hardly think we shall make any more. For honey sells well, and we ourselves can make shift with a drop o' small mead and metheglin for common use from the comb-washings."

"O, but you'll never have the heart!" reproachfully cried the stranger in cinder-gray, after taking up the mug a third time and setting it down empty. "I love mead, when 'tis old like this, as I love to go to church o' Sundays, or to relieve the needy any day of the week."

"Ha, ha, ha!" said the man in the chimney-corner, who, in spite of the taciturnity induced by the pipe of tobacco, could not or would not refrain from this slight testimony to his comrade's humour.

Now the old mead of those days, brewed of the purest first-year or maiden honey, four pounds to the gallon – with its due complement of white of eggs, cinnamon, ginger, cloves, mace, rosemary, yeast, and processes of working, bottling, and cellaring – tasted remarkably strong; but it did not taste so strong as it actually was. Hence, presently, the stranger in cinder-gray at the table, moved by its creeping influence, unbuttoned his waistcoat, threw himself back in his chair, spread his legs, and made his presence felt in various ways.

"Well, well, as I say," he resumed, "I am going to Casterbridge, and to Casterbridge I must go. I should have been almost there by this time; but the rain drove me into your dwelling, and I'm not sorry for it."

"You don't live in Casterbridge?" said the shepherd.

"Not as yet; though I shortly mean to move there."

"Going to set up in trade, perhaps?"

"No, no," said the shepherd's wife. "It is easy to see that the gentleman is rich, and don't want to work at anything."

The cinder-gray stranger paused, as if to consider whether he would accept that definition of himself. He presently rejected it by answering, "Rich is not quite the word for me, dame. I do work, and I must work. And even if I only get to Casterbridge by midnight I must begin work there at eight tomorrow morning. Yes, het or wet, blow or snow, famine or sword, my day's work tomorrow must be done."

"Poor man! Then, in spite o' seeming, you be worse off than we?" replied the shepherd's wife.

Tis the nature of my trade, men and maidens. "Tis the nature of my trade more than my poverty... . But really and truly I must up and off, or I shan't get a lodging in the town." However, the speaker did not move, and directly added, "There's time for one more draught of friendship before I go; and I'd perform it at once if the mug were not dry."

"Here's a mug o' small," said Mrs. Fennel. "Small, we call it, though to be sure "tis only the first wash o' the combs."

"No," said the stranger disdainfully. "I won't spoil your first kindness by partaking o' your second."

"Certainly not," broke in Fennel. "We don't increase and multiply every day, and I'll fill the mug again." He went away to the dark place under the stairs where the barrel stood. The shepherdess followed him.

"Why should you do this?" she said reproachfully, as soon as they were alone. "He's emptied it once, though it held enough for ten people; and now he's not contented wi' the small, but must needs call for more o' the strong! And a stranger unbeknown to any of us. For my part, I don't like the look o' the man at all."

"But he's in the house, my honey; and 'tis a wet night, and a christening. Daze it, what's a cup of mead more or less? There'll be plenty more next bee-burning."

"Very well – this time, then," she answered, looking wistfully at the barrel. "But what is the man's calling, and where is he one of, that he should come in and join us like this?"

"I don't know. I'll ask him again."

The catastrophe of having the mug drained dry at one pull by the stranger in cinder-gray was effectually guarded against this time by Mrs. Fennel. She poured out his allowance in a small cup, keeping the large one at a discreet distance from him. When he had tossed off his portion the shepherd renewed his inquiry about the stranger's occupation.

The latter did not immediately reply, and the man in the chimney-corner, with sudden demonstrativeness, said, "Anybody may know my trade – I'm a wheel-wright."

"A very good trade for these parts," said the shepherd.

"And anybody may know mine – if they've the sense to find it out," said the stranger in cinder-gray.

"You may generally tell what a man is by his claws," observed the hedge-carpenter, looking at his own hands. "My fingers be as full of thorns as an old pin-cushion is of pins."

The hands of the man in the chimney-corner instinctively sought the shade, and he gazed into the fire as he resumed his pipe. The man at the table took up the hedge-carpenter's remark, and added smartly, "True; but the oddity of my trade is that, instead of setting a mark upon me, it sets a mark upon my customers."

No observation being offered by anybody in elucidation of this enigma, the shepherd's wife once more called for a song. The same obstacles presented themselves as at the former time – one had no voice, another had forgotten the first verse. The stranger at the table, whose soul had now risen to a good working temperature, relieved the difficulty by exclaiming that, to start the company, he would sing himself. Thrusting one thumb into the armhole of his waistcoat, he waved the other hand in the air, and, with an extemporizing gaze at the shining sheep-crooks above the mantelpiece, began:

"O my trade it is the rarest one, Simple shepherds all –My trade is a sight to see; For my customers I tie, and take them up on high, And waft 'em to a far countree!"

The room was silent when he had finished the verse – with one exception, that of the man in the chimney-corner, who, at the singer's word, "Chorus!" joined him in a deep bass voice of musical relish—

"And waft 'em to a far countree!"

Oliver Giles, John Pitcher the dairyman, the parish-clerk, the engaged man of fifty, the row of young women against the wall, seemed lost in thought not of the gayest kind. The shepherd looked meditatively on the ground, the shepherdess gazed keenly at the singer, and with some suspicion; she was doubting whether this stranger were merely singing an old song from recollection, or was composing one there and then for the occasion. All were as perplexed at the obscure revelation as the guests at Belshazzar's Feast, except the man in the chimney-corner, who quietly said, "Second verse, stranger," and smoked on.

The singer thoroughly moistened himself from his lips inwards, and went on with the next stanza as requested:

"My tools are but common ones, Simple shepherds all –My tools are no sight to see: A little hempen string, and a post whereon to swing Are implements enough for me!"

Shepherd Fennel glanced round. There was no longer any doubt that the stranger was answering his question rhythmically. The guests one and all started back with suppressed exclamations. The young woman engaged to the man of fifty fainted halfway, and would have proceeded, but finding him wanting in alacrity for catching her she sat down trembling.

"O, he's the —!" whispered the people in the background, mentioning the name of an ominous public officer. "He's come to do it! 'Tis to be at Casterbridge jail tomorrow – the man for sheep-stealing – the poor clockmaker we heard of, who used to live away at Shottsford and had no work to do – Timothy Summers, whose family were a-starving, and so he went out of Shottsford by the high-road, and took a sheep in open daylight, defying the farmer and the farmer's wife and the farmer's lad, and every man jack among 'em. He" (and they nodded towards the stranger of the deadly trade) "is come from up the country to do it because there's not enough to do in his own county-town, and he's got the place here now our own county man's dead; he's going to live in the same cottage under the prison wall."

The stranger in cinder-gray took no notice of this whispered string of observations, but again wetted his lips. Seeing that his friend in the chimney-corner was the only one who reciprocated his joviality in any way, he held out his cup towards that appreciative comrade, who also held out his own. They clinked together, the eyes of the rest of the room hanging upon the singer's actions. He parted his lips for the third verse; but at that moment another knock was audible upon the door. This time the knock was faint and hesitating.

The company seemed scared; the shepherd looked with consternation towards the entrance, and it was with some effort that he resisted his alarmed wife's deprecatory glance, and uttered for the third time the welcoming words, "Walk in!"

The door was gently opened, and another man stood upon the mat. He, like those who had preceded him, was a stranger. This time it was a short, small personage, of fair complexion, and dressed in a decent suit of dark clothes.

"Can you tell me the way to—?" he began: when, gazing round the room to observe the nature of the company amongst whom he had fallen, his eyes lighted on the stranger in cinder-gray. It was just at the instant when the latter, who had thrown his mind into his song with such a will that he scarcely heeded the interruption, silenced all whispers and inquiries by bursting into his third verse:

"Tomorrow is my working day, Simple shepherds all— Tomorrow is a working day for me: For the farmer's sheep is slain, and the lad who did it ta'en, And on his soul may God ha' mercy!"

The stranger in the chimney-corner, waving cups with the singer so heartily that his mead splashed over on the hearth, repeated in his bass voice as before:

"And on his soul may God ha' mercy!"

All this time the third stranger had been standing in the doorway. Finding now that he did not come forward or go on speaking, the guests particularly regarded him. They noticed to their surprise that he stood before them the picture of abject terror – his knees trembling, his hand shaking so violently that the door-latch by which he supported himself rattled audibly: his white lips were parted, and his eyes fixed on the merry officer of justice in the middle of the room. A moment more and he had turned, closed the door, and fled.

"What a man can it be?" said the shepherd.

The rest, between the awfulness of their late discovery and the odd conduct of this third visitor, looked as if they knew not what to think, and said nothing. Instinctively they withdrew further and further from the grim gentleman in their midst, whom some of them seemed to take for the Prince of Darkness himself, till they formed a remote circle, an empty space of floor being left between them and him—

"… *circulus, cujus centrum diabolus*."

The room was so silent – though there were more than twenty people in it – that nothing could be heard but the patter of the rain against the window-shutters, accompanied by the occasional hiss of a stray drop that fell down the chimney into the fire, and the steady puffing of the man in the corner, who had now resumed his pipe of long clay.

The stillness was unexpectedly broken. The distant sound of a gun reverberated through the air – apparently from the direction of the county-town.

"Be jiggered!" cried the stranger who had sung the song, jumping up.

"What does that mean?" asked several.

"A prisoner has escaped from the jail – that's what it means."

All listened. The sound was repeated, and none of them spoke but the man in the chimney-corner, who said quietly, "I've often been told that in this county they fire a gun at such times; but I never heard it till now."

"I wonder if it is my man?" murmured the personage in cinder-gray.

"Surely it is!" said the shepherd involuntarily. "And surely we've zeed him! That little man who looked in at the door by now, and quivered like a leaf when he zeed ye and heard your song!"

"His teeth chattered, and the breath went out of his body," said the dairyman.

"And his heart seemed to sink within him like a stone," said Oliver Giles.

"And he bolted as if he'd been shot at," said the hedge-carpenter.

"True – his teeth chattered, and his heart seemed to sink; and he bolted as if he'd been shot at," slowly summed up the man in the chimney-corner.

"I didn't notice it," remarked the hangman.

"We were all a-wondering what made him run off in such a fright," faltered one of the women against the wall, "and now 'tis explained!"

The firing of the alarm-gun went on at intervals, low and sullenly, and their suspicions became a certainty. The sinister gentleman in cinder-gray roused himself. "Is there a constable here?" he asked, in thick tones. "If so, let him step forward."

The engaged man of fifty stepped quavering out from the wall, his betrothed beginning to sob on the back of the chair.

"You are a sworn constable?"

"I be, sir."

"Then, pursue the criminal at once, with assistance, and bring him back here. He can't have gone far."

"I will sir, I will – when I've got my staff. I'll go home and get it, and come sharp here, and start in a body."

"Staff! – never mind your staff; the man'll be gone!"

"But I can't do nothing without my staff – can I, William, and John, and Charles Jake? No; for there's the king's royal crown a painted on en in yaller and gold, and the lion and the unicorn, so as when I raise en up and hit my prisoner, 'tis made a lawful blow thereby. I wouldn't 'tempt to take up a man without my staff – no, not I. If I hadn't the law to gie me courage, why, instead o' my taking up him he might take up me!"

"Now, I'm a king's man myself, and can give you authority enough for this," said the formidable officer in gray. "Now then, all of ye, be ready. Have ye any lanterns?"

"Yes – have ye any lanterns? – I demand it!" said the constable.

"And the rest of you able-bodied —"

"Able-bodied men – yes – the rest of ye!" said the constable.

"Have you some good stout staves and pitch-forks—"

"Staves and pitchforks – in the name o' the law! And take 'em in yer hands and go in quest, and do as we in authority tell ye!"

Thus aroused, the men prepared to give chase. The evidence was, indeed, though circumstantial, so convincing, that but little argument was needed to show the shepherd's guests that after what they had seen it would look very much like connivance if they did not instantly pursue the unhappy third stranger, who could not as yet have gone more than a few hundred yards over such uneven country.

A shepherd is always well provided with lanterns; and, lighting these hastily, and with hurdle-staves in their hands, they poured out of the door, taking a direction along the crest of the hill, away from the town, the rain having fortunately a little abated.

Disturbed by the noise, or possibly by unpleasant dreams of her baptism, the child who had been christened began to cry heartbrokenly in the room overhead. These notes of grief came down through the chinks of the floor to the ears of the women below, who jumped up one by one, and seemed glad of the excuse to ascend and comfort the baby, for the incidents of the last half-hour greatly oppressed them. Thus in the space of two or three minutes the room on the ground-floor was deserted quite.

But it was not for long. Hardly had the sound of footsteps died away when a man returned round the corner of the house from the direction the pursuers had taken. Peeping in at the door, and seeing nobody there, he entered leisurely. It was the stranger of the chimney-corner, who had gone out with the rest. The motive of his return was shown by his helping himself to a cut piece of skimmercake that lay on a ledge beside where he had sat, and which he had apparently forgotten to take with him. He also poured out half a cup more mead from the quantity that remained, ravenously eating and drinking these as he stood. He had not finished when another figure came in just as quietly – his friend in cinder-gray.

"O – you here?" said the latter, smiling. "I thought you had gone to help in the capture." And this speaker also revealed the object of his return by looking solicitously round for the fascinating mug of old mead.

"And I thought you had gone," said the other, continuing his skimmer-cake with some effort.

"Well, on second thoughts, I felt there were enough without me," said the first confidentially, "and such a night as it is, too. Besides, 'tis the business o' the Government to take care of its criminals – not mine."

"True; so it is. And I felt as you did, that there were enough without me."

"I don't want to break my limbs running over the humps and hollows of this wild country."

"Nor I neither, between you and me."

"These shepherd-people are used to it – simple-minded souls, you know, stirred up to anything in a moment. They'll have him ready for me before the morning, and no trouble to me at all."

"They'll have him, and we shall have saved ourselves all labour in the matter."

"True, true. Well, my way is to Casterbridge; and 'tis as much as my legs will do to take me that far. Going the same way?"

"No, I am sorry to say! I have to get home over there" (he nodded indefinitely to the right), "and I feel as you do, that it is quite enough for my legs to do before bedtime."

The other had by this time finished the mead in the mug, after which, shaking hands heartily at the door, and wishing each other well, they went their several ways.

In the meantime the company of pursuers had reached the end of the hog's-back elevation which dominated this part of the down. They had decided on no particular plan of action; and, finding that the man of the baleful trade was no longer in their company, they seemed quite unable to form any such plan now. They descended in all directions down the hill, and straightway several of the party fell into the snare set by Nature for all misguided midnight ramblers over this part of the cretaceous formation. The 'lanchets," or flint slopes, which belted the escarpment at intervals of a dozen yards, took the less cautious ones unawares, and losing their footing on the rubbly steep they slid sharply downwards, the lanterns rolling from their hands to the bottom, and there lying on their sides till the horn was scorched through.

When they had again gathered themselves together, the shepherd, as the man who knew the country best, took the lead, and guided them round these treacherous inclines. The lanterns, which seemed rather to dazzle their eyes and warn the fugitive than to assist them in the exploration, were extinguished, due silence was observed; and in this more rational order they plunged into the vale. It was a grassy, briery, moist defile, affording some shelter to any person who had sought it; but the party perambulated it in vain, and ascended on the other side.

Here they wandered apart, and after an interval closed together again to report progress. At the second time of closing in they found themselves near a lonely ash, the single tree on this part of the coomb, probably sown there by a passing bird some fifty years before. And here, standing a little to one side of the trunk, as motionless as the trunk itself, appeared the man they were in quest of, his outline being well defined against the sky beyond. The band noiselessly drew up and faced him.

"Your money or your life!" said the constable sternly to the still figure.

"No, no," whispered John Pitcher. 'Tisn't our side ought to say that. That's the doctrine of vagabonds like him, and we be on the side of the law."

"Well, well," replied the constable impatiently; "I must say something, mustn't I? and if you had all the weight o' this undertaking upon your mind, perhaps you'd say the wrong thing too! – Prisoner at the bar, surrender, in the name of the Father – the Crown, I mane!"

The man under the tree seemed now to notice them for the first time, and, giving them no opportunity whatever for exhibiting their courage, he strolled slowly towards them. He was, indeed, the little man, the third stranger; but his trepidation had in a great measure gone.

"Well, travellers," he said, "did I hear ye speak to me?"

"You did: you've got to come and be our prisoner at once!" said the constable. "We arrest 'ee on the charge of not biding in Casterbridge jail in a decent proper manner to be hung tomorrow morning. Neighbours, do your duty, and seize the culpet!"

On hearing the charge, the man seemed enlightened, and, saying not another word, resigned himself with preternatural civility to the search-party, who, with their staves in their hands, surrounded him on all sides, and marched him back towards the shepherd's cottage.

It was eleven o'clock by the time they arrived. The light shining from the open door, a sound of men's voices within, proclaimed to them as they approached the house that some new events had arisen in their absence. On entering they discovered the shepherd's living room to be invaded by two officers from Casterbridge jail, and a well-known magistrate who lived at the nearest country-seat, intelligence of the escape having become generally circulated.

"Gentlemen," said the constable, "I have brought back your man – not without risk and danger; but every one must do his duty! He is inside this circle of able-bodied persons, who have lent me useful aid, considering their ignorance of Crown work. Men, bring forward your prisoner!" And the third stranger was led to the light.

"Who is this?" said one of the officials.

"The man," said the constable.

"Certainly not," said the turnkey; and the first corroborated his statement.

"But how can it be otherwise?" asked the constable. "or why was he so terrified at sight o' the singing instrument of the law who sat there?" Here he related the strange behaviour of the third stranger on entering the house during the hangman's song.

"Can't understand it," said the officer coolly. "All I know is that it is not the condemned man. He's quite a different character from this one; a gauntish fellow, with dark hair and eyes, rather good-looking, and with a musical bass voice that if you heard it once you'd never mistake as long as you lived."

"Why, souls – 'twas the man in the chimney-corner!"

"Hey – what?" said the magistrate, coming forward after inquiring particulars from the shepherd in the background. "Haven't you got the man after all?"

"Well, sir," said the constable, "he's the man we were in search of, that's true; and yet he's not the man we were in search of. For the man we were in search of was not the man we wanted, sir, if you understand my everyday way; for 'twas the man in the chimney-corner!"

"A pretty kettle of fish altogether!" said the magistrate. "You had better start for the other man at once."

The prisoner now spoke for the first time. The mention of the man in the chimney-corner seemed to have moved him as nothing else could do. "Sir," he said, stepping forward to the magistrate, "take no more trouble about me. The time is come when I may as well speak. I have done nothing; my crime is that the condemned man is my brother. Early this afternoon I left home at Shottsford to tramp it all the way to Casterbridge jail to bid him farewell. I was benighted, and called here to rest and ask the way. When I opened the door I saw before me the very man, my brother, that I thought to see in the condemned cell at Casterbridge. He was in this chimney-corner; and jammed close to him, so that he could not have got out if he had tried, was the executioner who'd come to take his life, singing a song about it and not knowing that it was his victim who was close by, joining in to save appearances. My brother looked a glance of agony at me, and I knew he meant, "Don't reveal what you see; my life depends on it." I was so terror-struck that I could hardly stand, and, not knowing what I did, I turned and hurried away."

The narrator's manner and tone had the stamp of truth, and his story made a great impression on all around. "And do you know where your brother is at the present time?" asked the magistrate.

"I do not. I have never seen him since I closed this door."

"I can testify to that, for we've been between ye ever since," said the constable.

"Where does he think to fly to? – what is his occupation?"

"He's a watch-and-clock-maker, sir."

A said "a was a wheelwright – a wicked rogue," said the constable.

"The wheels of clocks and watches he meant, no doubt," said Shepherd Fennel. "I thought his hands were palish for's trade."

"Well, it appears to me that nothing can be gained by retaining this poor man in custody," said the magistrate; "your business lies with the other, unquestionably."

And so the little man was released offhand; but he looked nothing the less sad on that account, it being beyond the power of magistrate or constable to raze out the written troubles in his brain, for they concerned another whom he regarded with more solicitude than himself. When this was done, and the man had gone his way, the night was found to be so far advanced that it was deemed useless to renew the search before the next morning.

Next day, accordingly, the quest for the clever sheep-stealer became general and keen, to all appearance at least. But the intended punishment was cruelly disproportioned to the transgression, and the sympathy of a great many country-folk in that district was strongly on the side of the fugitive.

Moreover, his marvellous coolness and daring in hob-and-nobbing with the hangman, under the unprecedented circumstances of the shepherd's party, won their admiration. So that it may be questioned if all those who ostensibly made themselves so busy in exploring woods and fields and lanes were quite so thorough when it came to the private examination of their own lofts and outhouses. Stories were afloat of a mysterious figure being occasionally seen in some old overgrown trackway or other, remote from turn-pike roads; but when a search was instituted in any of these suspected quarters nobody was found. Thus the days and weeks passed without tidings.

In brief, the bass-voiced man of the chimney-corner was never recaptured. Some said that he went across the sea, others that he did not, but buried himself in the depths of a populous city. At any rate, the gentleman in cinder-gray never did his morning's work at Casterbridge, nor met anywhere at all, for business purposes, the genial comrade with whom he had passed an hour of relaxation in the lonely house on the coomb.

The grass has long been green on the graves of Shepherd Fennel and his frugal wife; the guests who made up the christening party have mainly followed their entertainers to the tomb; the baby in whose honour they all had met is a matron in the sere and yellow leaf. But the arrival of the three strangers at the shepherd's that night, and the details connected therewith, is a story as well known as ever in the country about Higher Crowstairs.

Young Goodman Brown

Nathaniel Hawthorne

YOUNG GOODMAN BROWN came forth at sunset, into the street of Salem village, but put his head back, after crossing the threshold, to exchange a parting kiss with his young wife. And Faith, as the wife was aptly named, thrust her own pretty head into the street, letting the wind play with the pink ribbons of her cap, while she called to Goodman Brown.

"Dearest heart," whispered she, softly and rather sadly, when her lips were close to his ear, "pr'y thee, put off your journey until sunrise, and sleep in your own bed tonight. A lone woman is troubled with such dreams and such thoughts, that she's afeard of herself, sometimes. Pray, tarry with me this night, dear husband, of all nights in the year!"

"My love and my Faith," replied young Goodman Brown, "of all nights in the year, this one night must I tarry away from thee. My journey, as thou callest it, forth and back again, must needs be done 'twixt now and sunrise. What, my sweet, pretty wife, dost thou doubt me already, and we but three months married!"

"Then God bless you!" said Faith, with the pink ribbons, "and may you find all well, when you come back."

"Amen!" cried Goodman Brown. "Say thy prayers, dear Faith, and go to bed at dusk, and no harm will come to thee."

So they parted; and the young man pursued his way, until, being about to turn the corner by the meeting-house, he looked back and saw the head of Faith still peeping after him, with a melancholy air, in spite of her pink ribbons.

"Poor little Faith!" thought he, for his heart smote him. "What a wretch am I, to leave her on such an errand! She talks of dreams, too. Methought, as she spoke, there was trouble in her face, as if a dream had warned her what work is to be done tonight. But, no, no! 'twould kill her to think it. Well; she's a blessed angel on earth; and after this one night, I'll cling to her skirts and follow her to Heaven."

With this excellent resolve for the future, Goodman Brown felt himself justified in making more haste on his present evil purpose. He had taken a dreary road, darkened by all the gloomiest trees of the forest, which barely stood aside to let the narrow path creep through, and closed immediately behind. It was all as lonely as could be; and there is this peculiarity in such a solitude, that the traveller knows not who may be concealed by the innumerable trunks and the thick boughs overhead; so that, with lonely footsteps, he may yet be passing through an unseen multitude.

"There may be a devilish Indian behind every tree," said Goodman Brown to himself; and he glanced fearfully behind him, as he added, "What if the devil himself should be at my very elbow!"

His head being turned back, he passed a crook of the road, and looking forward again, beheld the figure of a man, in grave and decent attire, seated at the foot of an old tree. He arose, at Goodman Brown's approach, and walked onward, side by side with him.

"You are late, Goodman Brown," said he. "The clock of the Old South was striking, as I came through Boston; and that is full fifteen minutes agone."

"Faith kept me back awhile," replied the young man, with a tremor in his voice, caused by the sudden appearance of his companion, though not wholly unexpected.

It was now deep dusk in the forest, and deepest in that part of it where these two were journeying. As nearly as could be discerned, the second traveller was about fifty years old, apparently in the same rank of life as Goodman Brown, and bearing a considerable resemblance to him, though perhaps more in expression than features. Still, they might have been taken for father and son. And yet, though the elder person was as simply clad as the younger, and as simple in manner too, he had an indescribable air of one who knew the world, and would not have felt abashed at the governor's dinner-table, or in King William's court, were it possible that his affairs should call him thither. But the only thing about him, that could be fixed upon as remarkable, was his staff, which bore the likeness of a great black snake, so curiously wrought, that it might almost be seen to twist and wriggle itself like a living serpent. This, of course, must have been an ocular deception, assisted by the uncertain light.

"Come, Goodman Brown!" cried his fellow-traveller, "this is a dull pace for the beginning of a journey. Take my staff, if you are so soon weary."

"Friend," said the other, exchanging his slow pace for a full stop, "having kept covenant by meeting thee here, it is my purpose now to return whence I came. I have scruples, touching the matter thou wot'st of."

"Sayest thou so?" replied he of the serpent, smiling apart. "Let us walk on, nevertheless, reasoning as we go, and if I convince thee not, thou shalt turn back. We are but a little way in the forest, yet."

"Too far, too far!" exclaimed the goodman, unconsciously resuming his walk. "My father never went into the woods on such an errand, nor his father before him. We have been a race of honest men and good Christians, since the days of the martyrs. And shall I be the first of the name of Brown, that ever took this path and kept –"

"Such company, thou wouldst say," observed the elder person, interrupting his pause. "Well said, Goodman Brown! I have been as well acquainted with your family as with ever a one among the Puritans; and that's no trifle to say. I helped your grandfather, the constable, when he lashed the Quaker woman so smartly through the streets of Salem. And it was I that brought your father a pitch-pine knot, kindled at my own hearth, to set fire to an Indian village, in King Philip's War. They were my good friends, both; and many a pleasant walk have we had along this path, and returned merrily after midnight. I would fain be friends with you, for their sake."

"If it be as thou sayest," replied Goodman Brown, "I marvel they never spoke of these matters. Or, verily, I marvel not, seeing that the least rumor of the sort would have driven them from New England. We are a people of prayer, and good works to boot, and abide no such wickedness."

"Wickedness or not," said the traveller with the twisted staff, "I have a very general acquaintance here in New England. The deacons of many a church have drunk the communion wine with me; the selectmen, of divers towns, make me their chairman; and a majority of the Great and General Court are firm supporters of my interest. The governor and I, too – but these are state-secrets."

"Can this be so!" cried Goodman Brown, with a stare of amazement at his undisturbed companion. "Howbeit, I have nothing to do with the governor and council; they have their own ways, and are no rule for a simple husbandman like me. But, were I to go on with thee, how should I meet the eye of that good old man, our minister, at Salem village? Oh, his voice would make me tremble, both Sabbath-day and lecture-day!"

Thus far, the elder traveller had listened with due gravity, but now burst into a fit of irrepressible mirth, shaking himself so violently that his snake-like staff actually seemed to wriggle in sympathy.

"Ha! ha! ha!" shouted he, again and again; then composing himself, "Well, go on, Goodman Brown, go on; but, pr'y thee, don't kill me with laughing!"

"Well, then, to end the matter at once," said Goodman Brown, considerably nettled, "there is my wife, Faith. It would break her dear little heart; and I'd rather break my own!"

"Nay, if that be the case," answered the other, "e'en go thy ways, Goodman Brown. I would not, for twenty old women like the one hobbling before us, that Faith should come to any harm."

As he spoke, he pointed his staff at a female figure on the path, in whom Goodman Brown recognized a very pious and exemplary dame, who had taught him his catechism in youth, and was still his moral and spiritual adviser, jointly with the minister and Deacon Gookin.

"A marvel, truly, that Goody Cloyse should be so far in the wilderness, at night-fall!" said he. "But, with your leave, friend, I shall take a cut through the woods, until we have left this Christian woman behind. Being a stranger to you, she might ask whom I was consorting with, and whither I was going."

"Be it so," said his fellow-traveller. "Betake you to the woods, and let me keep the path."

Accordingly, the young man turned aside, but took care to watch his companion, who advanced softly along the road, until he had come within a staff's length of the old dame. She, meanwhile, was making the best of her way, with singular speed for so aged a woman, and mumbling some indistinct words, a prayer, doubtless, as she went. The traveller put forth his staff, and touched her withered neck with what seemed the serpent's tail.

"The devil!" screamed the pious old lady.

"Then Goody Cloyse knows her old friend?" observed the traveller, confronting her, and leaning on his writhing stick.

"Ah, forsooth, and is it your worship, indeed?" cried the good dame. "Yea, truly is it, and in the very image of my old gossip, Goodman Brown, the grandfather of the silly fellow that now is. But – would your worship believe it? – my broomstick hath strangely disappeared, stolen, as I suspect, by that unhanged witch, Goody Cory, and that, too, when I was all anointed with the juice of smallage and cinque-foil and wolf's-bane —"

"Mingled with fine wheat and the fat of a new-born babe," said the shape of old Goodman Brown.

"Ah, your worship knows the recipe," cried the old lady, cackling aloud. "So, as I was saying, being all ready for the meeting, and no horse to ride on, I made up my mind to foot it; for they tell me, there is a nice young man to be taken into communion tonight. But now your good worship will lend me your arm, and we shall be there in a twinkling."

"That can hardly be," answered her friend. "I may not spare you my arm, Goody Cloyse, but here is my staff, if you will."

So saying, he threw it down at her feet, where, perhaps, it assumed life, being one of the rods which its owner had formerly lent to Egyptian Magi. Of this fact, however, Goodman Brown could not take cognizance. He had cast up his eyes in astonishment, and looking down again, beheld neither Goody Cloyse nor the serpentine staff, but his fellow-traveller alone, who waited for him as calmly as if nothing had happened.

"That old woman taught me my catechism!" said the young man; and there was a world of meaning in this simple comment.

They continued to walk onward, while the elder traveller exhorted his companion to make good speed and persevere in the path, discoursing so aptly, that his arguments seemed rather to spring up in the bosom of his auditor, than to be suggested by himself. As they went, he plucked a branch of maple, to serve for a walking-stick, and began to strip it of the twigs and little boughs, which were wet with evening dew. The moment his fingers touched them, they became strangely withered and dried up, as with a week's sunshine. Thus the pair proceeded, at a good free pace, until suddenly, in a gloomy hollow of the road, Goodman Brown sat himself down on the stump of a tree, and refused to go any farther.

"Friend," said he, stubbornly, "my mind is made up. Not another step will I budge on this errand. What if a wretched old woman do choose to go to the devil, when I thought she was going to Heaven! Is that any reason why I should quit my dear Faith, and go after her?"

"You will think better of this by-and-by," said his acquaintance, composedly. "Sit here and rest yourself awhile; and when you feel like moving again, there is my staff to help you along."

Without more words, he threw his companion the maple stick, and was as speedily out of sight, as if he had vanished into the deepening gloom. The young man sat a few moments by the road-side, applauding himself greatly, and thinking with how clear a conscience he should meet the minister, in his morning-walk, nor shrink from the eye of good old Deacon Gookin. And what calm sleep would be his, that very night, which was to have been spent so wickedly, but purely and sweetly now, in the arms of Faith! Amidst these pleasant and praiseworthy meditations, Goodman Brown heard the tramp of horses along the road, and deemed it advisable to conceal himself within the verge of the forest, conscious of the guilty purpose that had brought him thither, though now so happily turned from it.

On came the hoof-tramps and the voices of the riders, two grave old voices, conversing soberly as they drew near. These mingled sounds appeared to pass along the road, within a few yards of the young man's hiding-place; but owing, doubtless, to the depth of the gloom, at that particular spot, neither the travellers nor their steeds were visible. Though their figures brushed the small boughs by the way-side, it could not be seen that they intercepted, even for a moment, the faint gleam from the strip of bright sky, athwart which they must have passed. Goodman Brown alternately crouched and stood on tip-toe, pulling aside the branches, and thrusting forth his head as far as he durst, without discerning so much as a shadow. It vexed him the more, because he could have sworn, were such a thing possible, that he recognized the voices of the minister and Deacon Gookin, jogging along quietly, as they were wont to do, when bound to some ordination or ecclesiastical council. While yet within hearing, one of the riders stopped to pluck a switch.

"Of the two, reverend Sir," said the voice like the deacon's, I had rather miss an ordination-dinner than tonight's meeting. They tell me that some of our community are to be here from Falmouth and beyond, and others from Connecticut and Rhode-Island; besides several of the Indian powows, who, after their fashion, know almost as much deviltry as the best of us. Moreover, there is a goodly young woman to be taken into communion."

"Mighty well, Deacon Gookin!" replied the solemn old tones of the minister. "Spur up, or we shall be late. Nothing can be done, you know, until I get on the ground."

The hoofs clattered again, and the voices, talking so strangely in the empty air, passed on through the forest, where no church had ever been gathered, nor solitary Christian prayed.

Whither, then, could these holy men be journeying, so deep into the heathen wilderness? Young Goodman Brown caught hold of a tree, for support, being ready to sink down on the ground, faint and overburthened with the heavy sickness of his heart. He looked up to the sky, doubting whether there really was a Heaven above him. Yet, there was the blue arch, and the stars brightening in it.

"With Heaven above, and Faith below, I will yet stand firm against the devil!" cried Goodman Brown.

While he still gazed upward, into the deep arch of the firmament, and had lifted his hands to pray, a cloud, though no wind was stirring, hurried across the zenith, and hid the brightening stars. The blue sky was still visible, except directly overhead, where this black mass of cloud was sweeping swiftly northward. Aloft in the air, as if from the depths of the cloud, came a confused and doubtful sound of voices.

Once, the listener fancied that he could distinguish the accent of town's-people of his own, men and women, both pious and ungodly, many of whom he had met at the communion-table, and had seen others rioting at the tavern. The next moment, so indistinct were the sounds, he doubted whether he had heard aught but the murmur of the old forest, whispering without a wind. Then came a stronger swell of those familiar tones, heard daily in the sunshine, at Salem village, but never, until now, from a cloud of night. There was one voice, of a young woman, uttering lamentations, yet with an uncertain sorrow, and entreating for some favor, which, perhaps, it would grieve her to obtain. And all the unseen multitude, both saints and sinners, seemed to encourage her onward.

"Faith!" shouted Goodman Brown, in a voice of agony and desperation; and the echoes of the forest mocked him, crying – "Faith! Faith!" as if bewildered wretches were seeking her, all through the wilderness.

The cry of grief, rage, and terror, was yet piercing the night, when the unhappy husband held his breath for a response. There was a scream, drowned immediately in a louder murmur of voices, fading into far-off laughter, as the dark cloud swept away, leaving the clear and silent sky above Goodman Brown. But something fluttered lightly down through the air, and caught on the branch of a tree. The young man seized it, and beheld a pink ribbon.

"My Faith is gone!" cried he, after one stupefied moment. "There is no good on earth; and sin is but a name. Come, devil! for to thee is this world given."

And maddened with despair, so that he laughed loud and long, did Goodman Brown grasp his staff and set forth again, at such a rate, that he seemed to fly along the forest-path, rather than to walk or run. The road grew wilder and drearier, and more faintly traced, and vanished at length, leaving him in the heart of the dark wilderness, still rushing onward, with the instinct that guides mortal man to evil. The whole forest was peopled with frightful sounds; the creaking of the trees, the howling of wild beasts, and the yell of Indians; while, sometimes the wind tolled like a distant church-bell, and sometimes gave a broad roar around the traveller, as if all Nature were laughing him to scorn. But he was himself the chief horror of the scene, and shrank not from its other horrors.

"Ha! ha! ha!" roared Goodman Brown, when the wind laughed at him. "Let us hear which will laugh loudest! Think not to frighten me with your deviltry! Come witch, come wizard, come Indian powow, come devil himself! and here comes Goodman Brown. You may as well fear him as he fear you!"

In truth, all through the haunted forest, there could be nothing more frightful than the figure of Goodman Brown. On he flew, among the black pines, brandishing his staff with frenzied gestures, now giving vent to an inspiration of horrid blasphemy, and now shouting forth such laughter, as set all the echoes of the forest laughing like demons around him. The fiend in his own shape is less hideous, than when he rages in the breast of man. Thus sped the demoniac on his course, until, quivering among the trees, he saw a red light before him, as when the felled trunks and branches of a clearing have been set on fire, and throw up their lurid blaze against the sky, at the hour of midnight.

He paused, in a lull of the tempest that had driven him onward, and heard the swell of what seemed a hymn, rolling solemnly from a distance, with the weight of many voices. He knew the tune; it was a familiar one in the choir of the village meeting-house. The verse died heavily away, and was lengthened by a chorus, not of human voices, but of all the sounds of the benighted wilderness, pealing in awful harmony together. Goodman Brown cried out; and his cry was lost to his own ear, by its unison with the cry of the desert.

In the interval of silence, he stole forward, until the light glared full upon his eyes. At one extremity of an open space, hemmed in by the dark wall of the forest, arose a rock, bearing some rude, natural resemblance either to an altar or a pulpit, and surrounded by four blazing pines, their tops aflame, their stems untouched, like candles at an evening meeting. The mass of foliage, that had overgrown the summit of the rock, was all on fire, blazing high into the night, and fitfully illuminating the whole field. Each pendent twig and leafy festoon was in a blaze. As the red light arose and fell, a numerous congregation alternately shone forth, then disappeared in shadow, and again grew, as it were, out of the darkness, peopling the heart of the solitary woods at once.

"A grave and dark-clad company!" quoth Goodman Brown.

In truth, they were such. Among them, quivering to-and-fro, between gloom and splendor, appeared faces that would be seen, next day, at the council-board of the province, and others which, Sabbath after Sabbath, looked devoutly heavenward, and benignantly over the crowded pews, from the holiest pulpits in the land. Some affirm, that the lady of the governor was there. At least, there were high dames well known to her, and wives of honored husbands, and widows, a great multitude, and ancient maidens, all of excellent repute, and fair young girls, who trembled lest their mothers should espy them. Either the sudden gleams of light, flashing over the obscure field, bedazzled Goodman Brown, or he recognized a score of the church-members of Salem village, famous for their especial sanctity.

Good old Deacon Gookin had arrived, and waited at the skirts of that venerable saint, his reverend pastor. But, irreverently consorting with these grave, reputable, and pious people, these elders of the church, these chaste dames and dewy virgins, there were men of dissolute lives and women of spotted fame, wretches given over to all mean and filthy vice, and suspected even of horrid crimes. It was strange to see, that the good shrank not from the wicked, nor were the sinners abashed by the saints. Scattered, also, among their palefaced enemies, were the Indian priests, or powows, who had often scared their native forest with more hideous incantations than any known to English witchcraft.

"But, where is Faith?" thought Goodman Brown; and, as hope came into his heart, he trembled.

Another verse of the hymn arose, a slow and mournful strain, such as the pious love, but joined to words which expressed all that our nature can conceive of sin, and darkly hinted at far more. Unfathomable to mere mortals is the lore of fiends. Verse after verse was sung, and still the chorus of the desert swelled between, like the deepest tone of a mighty organ. And, with the final peal of that dreadful anthem, there came a sound, as if the roaring wind, the rushing streams, the howling beasts, and every other voice of the unconverted wilderness, were mingling and according with the voice of guilty man, in homage to the prince of all. The four blazing pines threw up a loftier flame, and obscurely discovered shapes and visages of horror on the smoke-wreaths, above the impious assembly. At the same moment, the fire on the rock shot redly forth, and formed a glowing arch above its base, where now appeared a figure. With reverence be it spoken, the figure bore no slight similitude, both in garb and manner, to some grave divine of the New-England churches.

"Bring forth the converts!" cried a voice, that echoed through the field and rolled into the forest.

At the word, Goodman Brown stepped forth from the shadow of the trees, and approached the congregation, with whom he felt a loathful brotherhood, by the sympathy of all that was wicked in his heart. He could have well nigh sworn, that the shape of his own dead father beckoned him to advance, looking downward from a smoke-wreath, while a woman, with dim features of despair, threw out her hand to warn him back. Was it his mother? But he had no power to retreat one step, nor to resist, even in thought, when the minister and good old Deacon Gookin seized his arms, and led him to the blazing rock. Thither came also the slender form of a veiled female, led between Goody Cloyse, that pious teacher of the catechism, and Martha Carrier, who had received the devil's promise to be queen of hell. A rampant hag was she! And there stood the proselytes, beneath the canopy of fire.

"Welcome, my children," said the dark figure, "to the communion of your race! Ye have found, thus young, your nature and your destiny. My children, look behind you!"

They turned; and flashing forth, as it were, in a sheet of flame, the fiend-worshippers were seen; the smile of welcome gleamed darkly on every visage.

"There," resumed the sable form, "are all whom ye have reverenced from youth. Ye deemed them holier than yourselves, and shrank from your own sin, contrasting it with their lives of righteousness, and prayerful aspirations heavenward. Yet, here are they all, in my worshipping assembly! This night it shall be granted you to know their secret deeds; how hoary-bearded elders of the church have whispered wanton words to the young maids of their households; how many a woman, eager for widow's weeds, has given her husband a drink at bed-time, and let him sleep his last sleep in her bosom; how beardless youth have made haste to inherit their father's wealth; and how fair damsels – blush not, sweet ones – have dug little graves in the garden, and bidden me, the sole guest, to an infant's funeral.

By the sympathy of your human hearts for sin, ye shall scent out all the places – whether in church, bed-chamber, street, field, or forest – where crime has been committed, and shall exult to behold the whole earth one stain of guilt, one mighty blood-spot. Far more than this! It shall be yours to penetrate, in every bosom, the deep mystery of sin, the fountain of all wicked arts, and which inexhaustibly supplies more evil impulses than human power – than my power at its utmost! – can make manifest in deeds. And now, my children, look upon each other."

They did so; and, by the blaze of the hell-kindled torches, the wretched man beheld his Faith, and the wife her husband, trembling before that unhallowed altar.

"Lo! there ye stand, my children," said the figure, in a deep and solemn tone, almost sad, with its despairing awfulness, as if his once angelic nature could yet mourn for our miserable race. "Depending upon one another's hearts, ye had still hoped that virtue were not all a dream! Now are ye undeceived! Evil is the nature of mankind. Evil must be your only happiness. Welcome, again, my children, to the communion of your race!"

"Welcome!" repeated the fiend-worshippers, in one cry of despair and triumph.

And there they stood, the only pair, as it seemed, who were yet hesitating on the verge of wickedness, in this dark world. A basin was hollowed, naturally, in the rock. Did it contain water, reddened by the lurid light? or was it blood? or, perchance, a liquid flame? Herein did the Shape of Evil dip his hand, and prepare to lay the mark of baptism upon their foreheads, that they might be partakers of the mystery of sin, more conscious of the secret guilt of others, both in deed and thought, than they could now be of their own. The husband cast one look at his pale wife, and Faith at him. What polluted wretches would the next glance show them to each other, shuddering alike at what they disclosed and what they saw!

"Faith! Faith!" cried the husband. "Look up to Heaven, and resist the Wicked One!"

Whether Faith obeyed, he knew not. Hardly had he spoken, when he found himself amid calm night and solitude, listening to a roar of the wind, which died heavily away through the forest. He staggered against the rock, and felt it chill and damp, while a hanging twig, that had been all on fire, besprinkled his cheek with the coldest dew.

The next morning, young Goodman Brown came slowly into the street of Salem village, staring around him like a bewildered man. The good old minister was taking a walk along the graveyard, to get an appetite for breakfast and meditate his sermon, and bestowed a blessing, as he passed, on Goodman Brown. He shrank from the venerable saint, as if to avoid an anathema. Old Deacon Gookin was at domestic worship, and the holy words of his prayer were heard through the open window.

"What God doth the wizard pray to?" quoth Goodman Brown.

Goody Cloyse, that excellent old Christian, stood in the early sunshine, at her own lattice, catechising a little girl, who had brought her a pint of morning's milk. Goodman Brown snatched away the child, as from the grasp of the fiend himself. Turning the corner by the meeting-house, he spied the head of Faith, with the pink ribbons, gazing anxiously forth, and bursting into such joy at sight of him, that she skipt along the street, and almost kissed her husband before the whole village. But Goodman Brown looked sternly and sadly into her face, and passed on without a greeting.

Had Goodman Brown fallen asleep in the forest, and only dreamed a wild dream of a witch-meeting?

Be it so, if you will. But, alas! It was a dream of evil omen for young Goodman Brown. A stern, a sad, a darkly meditative, a distrustful, if not a desperate man, did he become, from the night of that fearful dream. On the Sabbath-day, when the congregation were singing a holy psalm, he could not listen, because an anthem of sin rushed loudly upon his ear, and drowned all the blessed strain. When the minister spoke from the pulpit, with power and fervid eloquence, and with his hand on the open Bible, of the sacred truths of our religion, and of saint-like lives and triumphant deaths, and of future bliss or misery unutterable, then did Goodman Brown turn pale, dreading lest the roof should thunder down upon the gray blasphemer and his hearers.

Often, awaking suddenly at midnight, he shrank from the bosom of Faith, and at morning or eventide, when the family knelt down at prayer, he scowled, and muttered to himself, and gazed sternly at his wife, and turned away. And when he had lived long, and was borne to his grave, a hoary corpse, followed by Faith, an aged woman, and children and grand-children, a goodly procession, besides neighbors, not a few, they carved no hopeful verse upon his tombstone; for his dying hour was gloom.

The Gateway of the Monster:
A Carnacki Mystery

William Hope Hodgson

IN RESPONSE to Carnacki's usual card of invitation to have dinner and listen to a story, I arrived promptly at 427, Cheyne Walk, to find the three others who were always invited to these happy little times, there before me. Five minutes later, Carnacki, Arkright, Jessop, Taylor and I were all engaged in the "pleasant occupation" of dining.

"You've not been long away, this time," I remarked as I finished my soup; forgetting momentarily, Carnacki's dislike of being asked even to skirt the borders of his story until such time as he was ready. Then he would not stint words.

"That's all," he replied with brevity; and I changed the subject, remarking that I had been buying a new gun, to which piece of news he gave an intelligent nod, and a smile which I think showed a genuinely good-humoured appreciation of my intentional changing of the conversation.

"As Dodgson was remarking just now, I've only been away a short time, and for a very good reason too – I've only been away a short distance. The exact locality I am afraid I must not tell you; but it is less than twenty miles from here; though, except for changing a name, that won't spoil the story. And it is a story too! One of the most extraordinary things I have ever run against.

"I received a letter a fortnight ago from a man I must call Anderson, asking for an appointment. I arranged a time, and when he came, I found that he wished me to investigate, and see whether I could not clear up a long standing and well – too well – authenticated case of what he termed 'haunting.' He gave me very full particulars, and finally, as the thing seemed to present something unique, I decided to take it up.

"Two days later, I drove to the house, late in the afternoon. I found it a very old place, standing quite alone in its own grounds. Anderson had left a letter with the butler, I found, pleading excuses for his absence, and leaving the whole house at my disposal for my investigations. The butler evidently knew the object of my visit, and I questioned him pretty thoroughly during dinner, which I had in rather lonely state. He is an old and privileged servant, and had the history of the Grey Room exact in detail. From him I learned more particulars regarding two things that Anderson had mentioned in but a casual manner. The first was that the door of the Grey Room would be heard in the dead of night to open, and slam heavily, and this even though the butler knew it was locked, and the key on the bunch in his pantry. The second was that the bedclothes would always be found torn off the bed, and hurled in a heap into a corner.

"But it was the door slamming that chiefly bothered the old butler. Many and many a time, he told me, had he lain awake and just got shivering with fright, listening; for sometimes the door would be slammed time after time – thud! thud! thud! – so that sleep was impossible.

"From Anderson, I knew already that the room had a history extending back over a hundred and fifty years. Three people had been strangled in it – an ancestor of his and his wife and child. This is authentic, as I had taken very great pains to discover, so that you can imagine it was with a feeling that I had a striking case to investigate, that I went upstairs after dinner to have a look at the Grey Room.

"Peter, the old butler, was in rather a state about my going, and assured me with much solemnity that in all the twenty years of his service, no one had ever entered that room after nightfall. He begged me, in quite a fatherly way, to wait till the morning, when there would be no danger, and then he could accompany me himself.

"Of course, I smiled a little at him, and told him not to bother. I explained that I should do no more than look around a bit, and perhaps affix a few seals. He need not fear; I was used to that sort of thing. But he shook his head, when I said that.

"'There isn't many ghosts like ours, sir,' he assured me, with mournful pride. And, by Jove! he was right, as you will see.

"I took a couple of candles, and Peter followed, with his bunch of keys. He unlocked the door; but would not come inside with me. He was evidently in a fright, and renewed his request, that I would put off my examination, until daylight. Of course, I laughed at him again, and told him he could stand sentry at the door, and catch anything that came out.

"'It never comes outside, sir,' he said, in his funny, old, solemn manner. Somehow he managed to make me feel as if I were going to have the 'creeps' right away. Anyway, it was one to him, you know.

"I left him there, and examined the room. It is a big apartment, and well furnished in the grand style, with a huge four-poster, which stands with its head to the end wall. There were two candles on the mantelpiece and two on each of the three tables that were in the room. I lit the lot, and after that the room felt a little less inhumanly dreary; though, mind you, it was quite fresh, and well kept in every way.

"After I had taken a good look round I sealed lengths of baby ribbon across the windows, along the walls, over the pictures, and over the fireplace and the wall-closets. All the time, as I worked, the butler stood just without the door, and I could not persuade him to enter; though I jested with him a little, as I stretched the ribbons, and went here and there about my work. Every now and again, he would say: 'You'll excuse me, I'm sure, sir; but I do wish you would come out, sir. I'm fair in a quake for you.'

"I told him he need not wait; but he was loyal enough in his way to what he considered his duty. He said he could not go away and leave me all alone there. He apologised; but made it very clear that I did not realise the danger of the room; and I could see, generally, that he was in a pretty frightened state. All the same, I had to make the room so that I should know if anything material entered it; so I asked him not to bother me, unless he really heard something. He was beginning to get on my nerves, and the 'feel' of the room was bad enough, without making it any nastier.

"For a time further, I worked, stretching ribbons across the floor, and sealing them, so that the merest touch would have broken them, were anyone to venture into the room in the dark with the intention of playing the fool. All this had taken me far longer than I had anticipated; and, suddenly, I heard a clock strike eleven. I had taken off my coat soon after commencing work; now, however, as I had practically made an end of all that I intended to do, I walked across to the settee, and picked it up. I was in the act of getting into it when the old butler's voice (he had not said a word for the last hour) came sharp and frightened: 'Come out, sir, quick! There's something going to happen!' Jove! but I jumped, and then, in the same moment,

one of the candles on the table to the left of the bed went out. Now whether it was the wind, or what, I do not know; but just for a moment, I was enough startled to make a run for the door; though I am glad to say that I pulled, up before I reached it. I simply could not bunk out, with the butler standing there, after having, as it were, read him a sort of lesson on 'bein' brave, y'know.' So I just turned right round, picked up the two candles off the mantelpiece, and walked across to the table near the bed. Well, I saw nothing. I blew out the candle that was still alight; then I went to those on the two other tables, and blew them out. Then, outside of the door, the old man called again: 'Oh! sir, do be told! Do be told!'

"'All right, Peter,' I said, and, by Jove, my voice was not as steady as I should have liked! I made for the door, and had a bit of work, not to start running. I took some thundering long strides, as you can imagine. Near the door, I had a sudden feeling that there was a cold wind in the room. It was almost as if the window had been suddenly opened a little. I got to the door and the old butler gave back a step, in a sort of instinctive way. 'Collar the candles, Peter!' I said, pretty sharply, and shoved them into his hands. I turned, and caught the handle, and slammed the door shut, with a crash. Somehow, do you know, as I did so, I thought I felt something pull back on it; but it must have been only fancy. I turned the key in the lock, and then again, double-locking the door. I felt easier then, and set-to and sealed the door. In addition, I put my card over the keyhole, and sealed it there; after which I pocketed the key, and went downstairs – with Peter; who was nervous and silent, leading the way. Poor old beggar! It had not struck me until that moment that he had been enduring a considerable strain during the last two or three hours.

"About midnight, I went to bed. My room lay at the end of the corridor upon which opens the door of the Grey Room. I counted the doors between it and mine, and found that five rooms lay between. And I am sure you can understand that I was not sorry. Then, just as I was beginning to undress, an idea came to me, and I took my candle and sealing-wax, and sealed the doors of all the five rooms. If any door slammed in the night, I should know just which one.

"I returned to my room, locked the door, and went to bed. I was waked suddenly from a deep sleep by a loud crash somewhere out in the passage. I sat up in bed and listened, but heard nothing. Then I lit my candle. I was in the very act of lighting it when there came the bang of a door being violently slammed, along the corridor. I jumped out of bed, and got my revolver. I unlocked my door, and went out into the passage, holding my candle high, and keeping the pistol ready. Then a queer thing happened. I could not go a step towards the Grey Room. You all know I am not really a cowardly chap. I've gone into too many cases connected with ghostly things, to be accused of that; but I tell you I funked it; simply funked it, just like any blessed kid. There was something precious unholy in the air that night. I backed into my bedroom, and shut and locked the door. Then I sat on the bed all night, and listened to the dismal thudding of a door up the corridor. The sound seemed to echo through all the house.

"Daylight came at last, and I washed and dressed. The door had not slammed for about an hour, and I was getting back my nerve again. I felt ashamed of myself; though in some ways it was silly, for when you're meddling with that sort of thing, your nerve is bound to go, sometimes. And you just have to sit quiet and call yourself a coward until daylight. Sometimes it is more than just cowardice, I fancy. I believe at times it is something warning you, and fighting *for* you. But, all the same, I always feel mean and miserable, after a time like that.

"When the day came properly, I opened my door, and, keeping my revolver handy, went quietly along the passage. I had to pass the head of the stairs, on the way, and who should I see coming up, but the old butler, carrying a cup of coffee. He had merely tucked his nightshirt into his trousers, and he had an old pair of carpet slippers on.

"'Hello, Peter!' I said, feeling suddenly cheerful; for I was as glad as any lost child to have a live human being close to me. 'Where are you off to with the refreshments?'

"The old man gave a start, and slopped some of the coffee. He stared up at me and I could see that he looked white and done-up. He came on up the stairs and held out the little tray to me. 'I'm very thankful indeed, Sir, to see you safe and well,' he said. 'I feared, one time, you might risk going into the Grey Room, Sir. I've lain awake all night, with the sound of the Door. And when it came light, I thought I'd make you a cup of coffee. I knew you would want to look at the seals, and somehow it seems safer if there's two, Sir.'

"'Peter,' I said, 'you're a brick. This is very thoughtful of you.' And I drank the coffee. 'Come along,' I told him, and handed him back the tray. 'I'm going to have a look at what the Brutes have been up to. I simply hadn't the pluck to in the night.'

"'I'm very thankful, Sir,' he replied. 'Flesh and blood can do nothing, Sir, against devils; and that's what's in the Grey Room after dark.'

"I examined the seals on all the doors, as I went along, and found them right; but when I got to the Grey Room, the seal was broken; though the card, over the keyhole, was untouched. I ripped it off, and unlocked the door, and went in, rather cautiously, as you can imagine; but the whole room was empty of anything to frighten one, and there was heaps of light. I examined all my seals, and not a single one was disturbed. The old butler had followed me in, and, suddenly, he called out:'The bedclothes, Sir!'

"I ran up to the bed, and looked over; and, surely, they were lying in the corner to the left of the bed. Jove! you can imagine how queer I felt. Something *had* been in the room. I stared for a while, from the bed, to the clothes on the floor. I had a feeling that I did not want to touch either. Old Peter, though, did not seem to be affected that way. He went over to the bed-coverings, and was going to pick them up, as, doubtless, he had done every day these twenty years back; but I stopped him. I wanted nothing touched, until I had finished my examination. This, I must have spent a full hour over, and then I let Peter straighten up the bed; after which we went out and I locked the door; for the room was getting on my nerves.

"I had a short walk, and then breakfast; after which I felt more my own man, and so returned to the Grey Room, and, with Peter's help, and one of the maids, I had everything taken out except the bed, even the very pictures. I examined the walls, floor and ceiling then, with probe, hammer and magnifying glass; but found nothing suspicious. And I can assure you, I began to realise, in very truth, that some incredible thing had been loose in the room during the past night. I sealed up everything again, and went out, locking and sealing the door, as before.

"After dinner that night, Peter and I unpacked some of my stuff, and I fixed up my camera and flashlight opposite to the door of the Grey Room, with a string from the trigger of the flashlight to the door. Then, you see, if the door were really opened, the flashlight would blare out, and there would be, possibly, a very queer picture to examine in the morning. The last thing I did, before leaving, was to uncap the lens; and after that I went off to my bedroom, and to bed; for I intended to be up at midnight; and to ensure this, I set my little alarm to call me; also I left my candle burning.

"The clock woke me at twelve, and I got up and into my dressing-gown and slippers. I shoved my revolver into my right side-pocket, and opened my door. Then, I lit my dark-room lamp, and withdrew the slide, so that it would give a clear light. I carried it up the corridor, about thirty feet, and put it down on the floor, with the open side away from me, so that it would show me anything that might approach along the dark passage. Then I went back, and sat in the doorway of my room, with my revolver handy, staring up the passage towards the place where I knew my camera stood outside the door of the Grey Room.

"I should think I had watched for about an hour and a half, when, suddenly, I heard a faint noise, away up the corridor. I was immediately conscious of a queer prickling sensation about the back of my head, and my hands began to sweat a little. The following instant, the whole end of the passage flicked into sight in the abrupt glare of the flashlight. Then came the succeeding darkness, and I peered nervously up the corridor, listening tensely, and trying to find what lay beyond the faint glow of my dark-lamp, which now seemed ridiculously dim by contrast with the tremendous blaze of the flash-powder.... And then, as I stooped forward, staring and listening, there came the crashing thud of the door of the Grey Room. The sound seemed to fill the whole of the large corridor, and go echoing hollowly through the house. I tell you, I felt horrible – as if my bones were water. Simply beastly. Jove! how I did stare, and how I listened. And then it came again – thud, thud, thud, and then a silence that was almost worse than the noise of the door; for I kept fancying that some brutal thing was stealing upon me along the corridor. And then, suddenly, my lamp was put out, and I could not see a yard before me. I realised all at once that I was doing a very silly thing, sitting there, and I jumped up. Even as I did so, I *thought* I heard a sound in the passage, and quite *near* me. I made one backward spring into my room, and slammed and locked the door. I sat on my bed, and stared at the door. I had my revolver in my hand; but it seemed an abominably useless thing. I felt that there was something the other side of that door. For some unknown reason I *knew* it was pressed up against the door, and it was soft. That was just what I thought. Most extraordinary thing to think.

"Presently I got hold of myself a bit, and marked out a pentacle hurriedly with chalk on the polished floor; and there I sat in it almost until dawn. And all the time, away up the corridor, the door of the Grey Room thudded at solemn and horrid intervals. It was a miserable, brutal night.

"When the day began to break, the thudding of the door came gradually to an end, and, at last, I got hold of my courage, and went along the corridor, in the half light, to cap the lens of my camera. I can tell you, it took some doing; but if I had not done so my photograph would have been spoilt, and I was tremendously keen to save it. I got back to my room, and then set-to and rubbed out the five-pointed star in which I had been sitting.

"Half an hour later there was a tap at my door. It was Peter with my coffee. When I had drunk it, we both went along to the Grey Room. As we went, I had a look at the seals on the other doors, but they were untouched. The seal on the door of the Grey Room was broken, as also was the string from the trigger of the flashlight; but the card over the keyhole was still there. I ripped it off and opened the door. Nothing unusual was to be seen until we came to the bed; then I saw that, as on the previous day, the bedclothes had been torn off, and hurled into the left-hand corner, exactly where I had seen them before. I felt very queer; but I did not forget to look at all the seals, only to find that not one had been broken.

"Then I turned and looked at old Peter, and he looked at me, nodding his head.

"'Let's get out of here!' I said. 'It's no place for any living human to enter, without proper protection.'

"We went out then, and I locked and sealed the door, again.

"After breakfast, I developed the negative; but it showed only the door of the Grey Room, half opened. Then I left the house, as I wanted to get certain matters and implements that might be necessary to life; perhaps to the spirit; for I intended to spend the coming night in the Grey Room.

"I got back in a cab, about half-past-five, with my apparatus, and this, Peter and I carried up to the Grey Room, where I piled it carefully in the centre of the floor. When everything was in the room, including a cat which I had brought, I locked and sealed the door, and went towards my bedroom, telling Peter I should not be down to dinner. He said, 'Yes, sir,' and went downstairs, thinking that I was going to turn in, which was what I wanted him to believe, as I knew he would have worried both me and himself, if he had known what I intended.

"But I merely got my camera and flashlight from my bedroom, and hurried back to the Grey Room. I locked and sealed myself in, and set to work, for I had a lot to do before it got dark.

"First I cleared away all the ribbons across the floor; then I carried the cat – still fastened in its basket – over towards the far wall, and left it. I returned then to the centre of the room, and measured out a space twenty-one feet in diameter, which I swept with a 'broom of hyssop.' About this I drew a circle of chalk, taking care never to step over the circle. Beyond this I smudged, with a bunch of garlic, a broad belt right around the chalked circle, and when this was complete, I took from among my stores in the centre a small jar of a certain water. I broke away the parchment and withdrew the stopper. Then, dipping my left forefinger in the little jar, I went round the circle again, making upon the floor, just within the line of chalk, the Second Sign of the Saaamaaa Ritual, and joining each Sign most carefully with the left-handed crescent. I can tell you, I felt easier when this was done and the 'water-circle' complete. Then, I unpacked some more of the stuff that I had brought, and placed a lighted candle in the "valley" of each Crescent. After that, I drew a Pentacle, so that each of the five points of the defensive star touched the chalk circle. In the five points of the star I placed five portions of bread, each wrapped in linen, and in the five "vales," five opened jars of the water I had used to make the "water circle." And now I had my first protective barrier complete.

"Now, anyone, except you who know something of my methods of investigation, might consider all this a piece of useless and foolish superstition; but you all remember the Black Veil case, in which I believe my life was saved by a very similar form of protection, whilst Aster, who sneered at it, and would not come inside, died. I got the idea from the Sigsand MS., written, so far as I can make out, in the 14th century. At first, naturally, I imagined it was just an expression of the superstition of his time; and it was not until a year later that it occurred to me to test his 'Defense,' which I did, as I've just said, in that horrible Black Veil business. You know how *that* turned out. Later, I used it several times, and always I came through safe, until that Moving Fur case. It was only a partial "Defense" there and I nearly died in the pentacle. After that I came across Professor Garder's 'Experiments with a Medium.' When they surrounded the Medium with a current, in vacuum, he lost his power – almost as if it cut him off from the Immaterial. That made me think a lot; and that is how I came to make the Electric Pentacle, which is a most marvellous 'Defense' against certain manifestations. I used the shape of the defensive star for this protection, because I have, personally, no doubt at all but that there is some extraordinary virtue in the old magic figure. Curious thing for a Twentieth Century man to admit, is it not? But then, as you all know, I never did, and never will, allow myself to be blinded by a little cheap laughter. I ask questions, and keep my eyes open!

"In this last case I had little doubt that I had run up against a supernatural monster, and I meant to take every possible care; for the danger is abominable.

"I turned to now to fit the Electric Pentacle, setting it so that each of its 'points' and 'vales' coincided exactly with the 'points' and 'vales' of the drawn pentagram upon the floor. Then I connected up the battery, and the next instant the pale blue glare from the intertwining vacuum tubes shone out.

"I glanced about me then, with something of a sigh of relief, and realised suddenly that the dusk was upon me, for the

window was grey and unfriendly. Then round at the big, empty room, over the double barrier of electric and candle light. I had an abrupt, extraordinary sense of weirdness thrust upon me in the air, you know; as it were, a sense of something inhuman impending. The room was full of the stench of bruised garlic, a smell I hate.

"I turned now to my camera, and saw that it and the flashlight were in order. Then I tested my revolver, carefully; though I had little thought that it would be needed. Yet, to what extent materialisation of an abnatural creature is possible, given favourable conditions, no one can say, and I had no idea what horrible thing I was going to see, or feel the presence of. I might, in the end, have to fight with a materialised monster. I did not know, and could only be prepared. You see, I never forgot that three people had been strangled in the bed close to me, and the fierce slamming of the door I had heard myself. I had no doubt that I was investigating a dangerous and ugly case.

"By this time the night had come; though the room was very light with the burning candles; and I found myself glancing behind me, constantly, and then all round the room. It was nervy work waiting for that thing to come. Then, suddenly, I was aware of a little, cold wind sweeping over me, coming from behind. I gave one great nerve-thrill, and a prickly feeling went all over the back of my head. Then I hove myself round with a sort of stiff jerk, and stared straight against that queer wind. It seemed to come from the corner of the room to the left of the bed – the place where both times I had found the heap of tossed bedclothes. Yet, I could see nothing unusual; no opening

– nothing!...

"Abruptly I was aware that the candles were all a-flicker in that unnatural wind... . I believe I just squatted there and stared in a horribly frightened, wooden way for some minutes. I shall never be able to let you know how disgustingly horrible it was sitting in that vile, cold wind! And then, flick! flick! all the candles round the outer barrier went out; and there was I, locked and sealed in that room, and with no light beyond the weakish blue glare of the Electric Pentacle.

"A time of abominable tenseness passed, and still that wind blew upon me; and then, suddenly, I knew that something stirred in the corner to the left of the bed. I was made conscious of it, rather by some inward, unused sense, than by either sight or sound; for the pale, short-radius glare of the Pentacle gave but a very poor light for seeing by. Yet, as I stared, something began slowly to grow upon my sight – a moving shadow, a little darker than the surrounding shadows. I lost the thing amid the vagueness, and for a moment or two I glanced swiftly from side to side, with a fresh, new sense of impending danger. Then my attention was directed to the bed. All the coverings were being drawn steadily off, with a hateful, stealthy sort of motion. I heard the slow, dragging slither of the clothes; but I could see nothing of the thing that pulled. I was aware in a funny, subconscious, introspective fashion that the 'creep' had come upon me; yet I was cooler mentally than I had been for some minutes; sufficiently so to feel that my hands were sweating coldly, and to shift my revolver, half-consciously, whilst I rubbed my right hand dry upon my knee; though never, for an instant, taking my gaze or my attention from those moving clothes.

"The faint noises from the bed ceased once, and there was a most intense silence, with only the sound of the blood beating in my head. Yet, immediately afterwards, I heard again the slurring of the bedclothes being dragged off the bed. In the midst of my nervous tension I remembered the camera, and reached round for it; but without looking away from the bed. And then, you know, all in a moment, the whole of the bed-coverings were torn off with extraordinary violence, and I heard the flump they made as they were hurled into the corner.

"There was a time of absolute quietness then for perhaps a couple of minutes; and you can imagine how horrible I felt. The bedclothes had been thrown with such savageness! And then again, the brutal unnaturalness of the thing that had just been done before me!

"Abruptly, over by the door, I heard a faint noise – a sort of crickling sound and then a pitter or two upon the floor. A great nervous thrill swept over me, seeming to run up my spine and over the back of my head; for the seal that secured the door had just been broken. Something was there. I could not see the door; at least, I mean to say that it was impossible to say how much I actually saw, and how much my imagination supplied. I made it out only as a continuation of the grey walls…. And then it seemed to me that something dark and indistinct moved and wavered there among the shadows.

"Abruptly, I was aware that the door was opening, and with an effort I reached again for my camera; but before I could aim it the door was slammed with a terrific crash that filled the whole room with a sort of hollow thunder. I jumped, like a frightened child. There seemed such a power behind the noise; as though a vast, wanton Force were 'out.' Can you understand?

"The door was not touched again; but, directly afterwards, I heard the basket, in which the cat lay, creak. I tell you, I fairly pringled all along my back. I knew that I was going to learn definitely whether what was abroad was dangerous to Life. From the cat there rose suddenly a hideous caterwaul, that ceased abruptly, and then – too late – I snapped on the flashlight. In the great glare, I saw that the basket had been overturned, and the lid was wrenched open, with the cat lying half in, and half out upon the floor. I saw nothing else, but I was full of the knowledge that I was in the presence of some Being or Thing that had power to destroy.

"During the next two or three minutes, there was an odd, noticeable quietness in the room, and you must remember I was half-blinded, for the time, because of the flashlight; so that the whole place seemed to be pitchy dark just beyond the shine of the Pentacle. I tell you it was most horrible. I just knelt there in the star, and whirled round, trying to see whether anything was coming at me.

"My power of sight came gradually, and I got a little hold of myself; and abruptly I saw the thing I was looking for, close to the 'water-circle.' It was big and indistinct, and wavered curiously, as though the shadow of a vast spider hung suspended in the air, just beyond the barrier. It passed swiftly round the circle, and seemed to probe ever towards me; but only to draw back with extraordinary jerky movements, as might a living person if they touched the hot bar of a grate.

"Round and round it moved, and round and round I turned. Then, just opposite to one of the 'vales' in the pentacles, it seemed to pause, as though preliminary to a tremendous effort. It retired almost beyond the glow of the vacuum light, and then came straight towards me, appearing to gather form and solidity as it came. There seemed a vast, malign determination behind the movement, that must succeed. I was on my knees, and I jerked back, falling on to my left hand and hip, in a wild endeavour to get back from the advancing thing. With my right hand I was grabbing madly for my revolver, which I had let slip. The brutal thing came with one great sweep straight over the garlic and the 'water-circle,' almost to the vale of the pentacle. I believe I yelled. Then, just as suddenly as it had swept over, it seemed to be hurled back by some mighty, invisible force.

"It must have been some moments before I realised that I was safe; and then I got myself together in the middle of the pentacles, feeling horribly gone and shaken, and glancing round and round the barrier; but the thing had vanished. Yet I had learnt something, for I knew now that the Grey Room was haunted by a monstrous hand.

"Suddenly, as I crouched there, I saw what had so nearly given the monster an opening through the barrier. In my movements within the pentacle I must have touched one of the jars of water; for just where the thing had made its attack the jar that guarded the 'deep' of the 'vale' had been moved to one side, and this had left one of the 'five doorways' unguarded. I put it back, quickly, and felt almost safe again, for I had found the cause and the 'defense' was still good. And I began to hope again that I should see the morning come in. When I saw that thing so nearly succeed, I'd had an awful, weak, overwhelming feeling that the 'barriers' could never bring me safe through the night against such a Force. You can understand?

"For a long time I could not see the hand; but, presently, I thought I saw, once or twice, an odd wavering, over among the shadows near the door. A little later, as though in a sudden fit of malignant rage, the dead body of the cat was picked up, and beaten with dull, sickening blows against the solid floor. That made me feel rather queer.

"A minute afterwards, the door was opened and slammed twice with tremendous force. The next instant the thing made one swift, vicious dart at me, from out of the shadows. Instinctively I started sideways from it, and so plucked my hand from upon the Electric Pentacle, where – for a wickedly careless moment – I had placed it. The monster was hurled off from the neighbourhood of the pentacles; though – owing to my inconceivable foolishness – it had been enabled for a second time to pass the outer barriers. I can tell you, I shook for a time, with sheer funk. I moved right to the centre of the pentacles again, and knelt there, making myself as small and compact as possible.

"As I knelt, there came to me presently, a vague wonder at the two 'accidents' which had so nearly allowed the brute to get at me. Was I being *influenced* to unconscious voluntary actions that endangered me? The thought took hold of me, and I watched my every movement. Abruptly, I stretched a tired leg, and knocked over one of the jars of water. Some was spilled; but because of my suspicious watchfulness, I had it upright and back within the vale while yet some of the water remained. Even as I did so, the vast, black, half-materialised hand beat up at me out of the shadows, and seemed to leap almost into my face; so nearly did it approach; but for the third time it was thrown back by some altogether enormous, over-mastering force. Yet, apart from the dazed fright in which it left me, I had for a moment that feeling of spiritual sickness, as if some delicate, beautiful, inward grace had suffered, which is felt only upon the too near approach of the abhuman, and is more dreadful, in a strange way, than any physical pain that can be suffered. I knew by this, more of the extent and closeness of the danger; and for a long time I was simply cowed by the butt-headed brutality of that Force upon my spirit. I can put it no other way.

"I knelt again in the centre of the pentacles, watching myself with more fear, almost, than the monster; for I knew now that, unless I guarded myself from every sudden impulse that came to me, I might simply work my own destruction. Do you see how horrible it all was?

"I spent the rest of the night in a haze of sick fright, and so tense that I could not make a single movement naturally. I was in such fear that any desire for action that came to me might be prompted by the Influence that I knew was at work on me. And outside of the barrier that ghastly thing went round and round, grabbing and grabbing in the air at me. Twice more was the body of the dead cat molested. The second time, I heard every bone in its body scrunch and crack. And all the time the horrible wind was blowing upon me from the corner of the room to the left of the bed.

"Then, just as the first touch of dawn came into the sky, that unnatural wind ceased, in a single moment; and I could see no sign of the hand. The dawn came slowly, and presently the wan light filled all the room, and made the pale glare of the Electric Pentacle look more unearthly. Yet, it was not until the day had fully come, that I made any attempt to leave the barrier, for I did not know but that there was some method abroad, in the sudden stopping of that wind, to entice me from the pentacles.

"At last, when the dawn was strong and bright, I took one last look round, and ran for the door. I got it unlocked, in a nervous, clumsy fashion; then locked it hurriedly, and went to my bedroom, where I lay on the bed, and tried to steady my nerves. Peter came, presently, with the coffee, and when I had drunk it, I told him I meant to have a sleep, as I had been up all night. He took the tray, and went out quietly; and after I had locked my door I turned in properly, and at last got to sleep.

"I woke about midday, and after some lunch, went up to the Grey Room. I switched off the current from the Pentacle, which I had left on in my hurry; also, I removed the body of the cat. You can understand I did not want anyone to see the poor brute. After that, I made a very careful search of the corner where the bedclothes had been thrown. I made several holes, and probed, but found nothing. Then it occurred to me to try with my instrument under the skirting. I did so, and heard my wire ring on metal. I turned the hook-end that way, and fished for the thing. At the second go, I got it. It was a small object, and I took it to the window. I found it to be a curious ring, made of some greyish metal. The curious thing about it was that it was made in the form of a pentagon; that is, the same shape as the inside of the magic pentacle, but without the "mounts" which form the points of the defensive star. It was free from all chasing or engraving.

"You will understand that I was excited, when I tell you that I felt sure I held in my hand the famous Luck Ring of the Anderson family; which, indeed, was of all things the one most intimately connected with the history of the haunting. This ring was handed on from father to son through generations, and always – in obedience to some ancient family tradition – each son had to promise never to wear the ring. The ring, I may say, was brought home by one of the Crusaders, under very peculiar circumstances; but the story is too long to go into here.

"It appears that young Sir Hulbert, an ancestor of Anderson's, made a bet, in drink, you know, that he would wear the ring that night. He did so, and in the morning his wife and child were found strangled in the bed, in the very room in which I stood. Many people, it would seem, thought young Sir Hulbert was guilty of having done the thing in drunken anger; and he, in an attempt to prove his innocence, slept a second night in the room. He also was strangled. Since, as you may imagine, no one has spent a night in the Grey Room, until I did so. The ring had been lost so long, that it had become almost a myth; and it was most extraordinary to stand there, with the actual thing in my hand, as you can understand.

"It was whilst I stood there, looking at the ring, that I got an idea. Supposing that it were, in a way, a doorway – You see what I mean? A sort of gap in the world-hedge. It was a queer idea, I know, and probably was not my own, but came to me from the Outside. You see, the wind had come from that part of the room where the ring lay. I thought a lot about it. Then the shape – the inside of a pentacle. It had no 'mounts', and without mounts, as the Sigsand MS. has it: 'Thee mownts wych are thee Five Hills of safetie. To lack is to gyve pow'r to thee daemon; and surlie to fayvor thee Evill Thynge.' You see, the very shape of the ring was significant; and I determined to test it.

"I unmade my pentacle, for it must be made afresh *and around* the one to be protected. Then I went out and locked the door; after which I left the house, to get certain matters, for neither 'yarbs nor fyre nor water' must be used a second time. I returned about seven-thirty, and as soon as the things I had brought had been carried up to the Grey Room, I dismissed Peter for the night, just as I had done the evening before. When he had gone downstairs, I let myself into the room and locked and sealed the door. I went to the place in the centre of the room where all the stuff had been packed, and set to work with all my speed to construct a barrier about me and the ring.

"I do not remember whether I explained to you. But I had reasoned that if the ring were in any way a 'medium of admission,' and it were enclosed with me in the Electric Pentacle' it would be, to express it loosely, insulated. Do you see? The Force, which had visible expression as a Hand, would have to stay beyond the Barrier which separates the Ab from the Normal; for the 'gateway' would be removed from accessibility.

"As I was saying, I worked with all my speed to get the barrier completed about me and the ring, for it was already later than I cared to be in that room 'unprotected.' Also, I had a feeling that there would be a vast effort made that night to regain the use of the ring. For I had the strongest conviction that the ring was a necessity to materialisation. You will see whether I was right.

"I completed the barriers in about an hour, and you can imagine something of the relief I felt when I saw the pale glare of the Electric Pentacle once more all about me. From then, onwards, for about two hours, I sat quietly, facing the corner from which the wind came. About eleven o'clock a queer knowledge came that something was near to me; yet nothing happened for a whole hour after that. Then, suddenly, I felt the cold, queer wind begin to blow upon me. To my astonishment, it seemed now to come from behind me, and I whipped round, with a hideous quake of fear. The wind met me in the face. It was blowing up from the floor close to me. I stared down, in a sickening maze of new frights. What on earth had I done now! The ring was there, close beside me, where I had put it. Suddenly, as I stared, bewildered, I was aware that there was something queer about the ring – funny shadowy movements and convolutions. I looked at them, stupidly. And then, abruptly, I knew that the wind was blowing up at me from the ring. A queer indistinct smoke became visible to me, seeming to pour upwards through the ring, and mix with the moving shadows. Suddenly, I realised that I was in more than any mortal danger; for the convoluting shadows about the ring were taking shape, and the death-hand was forming *within* the Pentacle. My goodness! do you realise it! I had brought the 'gateway' into the pentacles, and the brute was coming through – pouring into the material world, as gas might pour out from the mouth of a pipe.

"I should think that I knelt for a moment in a sort of stunned fright. Then, with a mad, awkward movement, I snatched at the ring, intending to hurl it out of the Pentacle. Yet it eluded me, as though some invisible, living thing jerked it hither and thither. At last, I gripped it; yet, in the same instant, it was torn from my grasp with incredible and brutal force. A great, black shadow covered it, and rose into the air, and came at me. I saw that it was the Hand, vast and nearly perfect in form. I gave one crazy yell, and jumped over the Pentacle and the ring of burning candles, and ran despairingly for the door. I fumbled idiotically and ineffectually with the key, and all the time I stared, with a fear that was like insanity, toward the Barriers. The hand was plunging towards me; yet, even as it had been unable to pass into the pentacle when the ring was without, so, now that the ring was within, it had no power to pass out. The monster was chained, as surely as any beast would be, were chains rivetted upon it.

"Even then, I got a flash of this knowledge; but I was too utterly shaken with fright, to reason; and the instant I managed to get the key turned, I sprang into the passage, and slammed the door with a crash. I locked it, and got to my room, somehow; for I was trembling so that I could hardly stand, as you can imagine. I locked myself in, and managed to get the candle lit; then I lay down on the bed, and kept quiet for an hour or two, and so I got steadied.

"I got a little sleep, later; but woke when Peter brought my coffee. When I had drunk it I felt altogether better, and took the old man along with me whilst I had a look into the Grey Room. I opened the door, and peeped in. The candles were still burning, wan against the daylight; and behind them was the pale, glowing star of the Electric Pentacle. And there in the middle was the ring… the gateway of the monster, lying demure and ordinary.

"Nothing in the room was touched, and I knew that the brute had never managed to cross the Pentacles. Then I went out, and locked the door.

"After a sleep of some hours, I left the house. I returned in the afternoon in a cab. I had with me an oxy-hydrogen jet, and two cylinders, containing the gases. I carried the things to the Grey Room, and there, in the centre of the Electric Pentacle, I erected the little furnace. Five minutes later the Luck Ring, once the 'luck,' but now the 'bane,' of the Anderson family, was no more than a little solid splash of hot metal."

Carnacki felt in his pocket, and pulled out something wrapped in tissue paper. He passed it to me. I opened it and found a small circle of greyish metal, something like lead, only harder and rather brighter.

"Well?" I asked, at length, after examining it and handing it round to the others. "Did that stop the haunting?"

Carnacki nodded. "Yes," he said. "I slept three nights in the Grey Room, before I left. Old Peter nearly fainted when he knew that I meant to; but by the third night he seemed to realise that the house was just safe and ordinary. And, you know, I believe, in his heart, he hardly approved."

Carnacki stood up and began to shake hands. "Out you go!" he said, genially. And, presently, we went, pondering to our various homes.

The Challenge from Beyond

Robert E. Howard, Frank Belknap Long, H.P. Lovecraft,

A. Merritt and C.L. Moore

GEORGE CAMPBELL opened sleep-fogged eyes upon darkness and lay gazing out of the tent flap upon the pale August night for some minutes before he roused enough even to wonder what had wakened him. There was in the keen, clear air of these Canadian woods a soporific as potent as any drug. Campbell lay quiet for a moment, sinking slowly back into the delicious borderlands of sleep, conscious of an exquisite weariness, an unaccustomed sense of muscles well used, and relaxed now into perfect ease. These were vacation's most delightful moments, after all – rest, after toil, in the clear, sweet forest night.

Luxuriously, as his mind sank backward into oblivion, he assured himself once more that three long months of freedom lay before him – freedom from cities and monotony, freedom from pedagogy and the University and students with no rudiments of interest in the geology he earned his daily bread by dinning into their obdurate ears. Freedom from –

Abruptly the delightful somnolence crashed about him. Somewhere outside the sound of tin shrieking across tin slashed into his peace. George Campbell sat up jerkily and reached for his flashlight. Then he laughed and put it down again, straining his eyes through the midnight gloom outside where among the tumbling cans of his supplies a dark anonymous little night beast was prowling. He stretched out a long arm and groped about among the rocks at the tent door for a missile. His fingers closed on a large stone, and he drew back his hand to throw.

But he never threw it. It was such a queer thing he had come upon in the dark. Square, crystal smooth, obviously artificial, with dull rounded corners. The strangeness of its rock surfaces to his fingers was so remarkable that he reached again for his flashlight and turned its rays upon the thing he held.

All sleepiness left him as he saw what it was he had picked up in his idle groping. It was clear as rock crystal, this queer, smooth cube. Quartz, unquestionably, but not in its usual hexagonal crystallized form. Somehow – he could not guess the method – it had been wrought into a perfect cube, about four inches in measurement over each worn face. For it was incredibly worn. The hard, hard crystal was rounded now until its corners were almost gone and the thing was beginning to assume the outlines of a sphere. Ages and ages of wearing, years almost beyond counting, must have passed over this strange clear thing.

But the most curious thing of all was that shape he could make out dimly in the heart of the crystal. For imbedded in its center lay a little disc of a pale and nameless substance with characters incised deep upon its quartz-enclosed surface. Wedge-shaped characters, faintly reminiscent of cuneiform writing.

George Campbell wrinkled his brows and bent closer above the little enigma in his hands, puzzling helplessly. How could such a thing as this have imbedded in pure rock crystal? Remotely a memory floated through his mind of ancient legends that called quartz crystals ice which had frozen too hard to melt again. Ice – and wedge-shaped cuneiforms – yes, didn't that sort of writing originate among the Sumerians who came down from the north in history's remotest beginnings to settle in the primitive Mesopotamian valley? Then hard sense regained control and he laughed. Quartz, of course, was formed in the earliest of earth's geological periods, when there was nothing anywhere but beat and heaving rock. Ice had not come for tens of millions of years after this thing must have been formed.

And yet – that writing. Man-made, surely, although its characters were unfamiliar save in their faint hinting at cuneiform shapes. Or could there, in a Paleozoic world, have been things with a written language who might have graven these cryptic wedges upon the quartz-enveloped disc he held? Or – might a thing like this have fallen meteor-like out of space into the unformed rock of a still molten world? Could it –

Then he caught himself up sharply and felt his ears going hot at the luridness of his own imagination. The silence and the solitude and the queer thing in his hands were conspiring to play tricks with his common sense. He shrugged and laid the crystal down at the edge of his pallet, switching off the light. Perhaps morning and a clear head would bring him an answer to the questions that seemed so insoluble now.

But sleep did not come easily. For one thing, it seemed to him as he flashed off the light, that the little cube had shone for a moment as if with sustained light before it faded into the surrounding dark. Or perhaps he was wrong. Perhaps it had been only his dazzled eyes that seemed to see the light forsake it reluctantly, glowing in the enigmatic deeps of the thing with queer persistence.

He lay there unquietly for a long while, turning the unanswered questions over and over in his mind. There was something about this crystal cube out of the unmeasured past, perhaps from the dawn of all history, that constituted a challenge that would not let him sleep.

He lay there, it seemed to him, for hours. It had been the lingering light, the luminescence that seemed so reluctant to die, which held his mind. It was as though something in the heart of the cube had awakened, stirred drowsily, become suddenly alert ... and intent upon him.

Sheer fantasy, this. He stirred impatiently and flashed his light upon his watch. Close to one o'clock; three hours more before the dawn. The beam fell and was focused upon the warm crystal cube. He held it there closely, for minutes. He snapped it out, then watched.

There was no doubt about it now. As his eyes accustomed themselves to the darkness, he saw that the strange crystal was glimmering with tiny fugitive lights deep within it like threads of sapphire lightnings. They were at its center and they seemed to him to come from the pale disk with its disturbing markings. And the disc itself was becoming larger ... the markings shifting shapes ... the cube was growing ... was it illusion brought about by the tiny lightnings....

He heard a sound. It was the very ghost of a sound, like the ghosts of harp strings being plucked with ghostly fingers. He bent closer. It came from the cube....

There was squeaking in the underbrush, a flurry of bodies and an agonized wailing like a child in death throes and swiftly stilled. Some small tragedy of the wilderness, killer and prey. He stepped over to where it had been enacted, but could see nothing. He again snapped off the flash and looked toward his tent. Upon the ground was a pale blue glimmering. It was the cube. He stooped to pick it up; then obeying some obscure warning, drew back his hand.

And again, he saw, its glow was dying. The tiny sapphire lightnings flashing fitfully, withdrawing to the disc from which they had come. There was no sound from it.

He sat, watching the luminescence glow and fade, glow and fade, but steadily becoming dimmer. It came to him that two elements were necessary to produce the phenomenon. The electric ray itself, and his own fixed attention. His mind must travel along the ray, fix itself upon the cube's heart, if its beat were to wax, until ... what?

He felt a chill of spirit, as though from contact with some alien thing. It was alien, he knew it; not of this earth. Not of earth's life. He conquered his shrinking, picked up the cube and took it into the tent. It was neither warm nor cold; except for its weight he would not have known he held it. He put it upon the table, keeping the torch turned from it; then stepped to the flap of the tent and closed it.

He went back to the table, drew up the camp chair, and turned the flash directly upon the cube, focusing it so far as he could upon its heart. He sent all his will, all his concentration, along it; focusing will and sight upon the disc as he had the light.

As though at command, the sapphire lightnings burned forth. They burst from the disc into the body of the crystal cube, then beat back, bathing the disc and the markings. Again these began to change, shifting, moving, advancing, and retreating in the blue gleaming. They were no longer cuneiform. They were things ... objects.

He heard the murmuring music, the plucked harp strings. Louder grew the sound and louder, and now all the body of the cube vibrated to their rhythm. The crystal walls were melting, growing misty as though formed of the mist of diamonds. And the disc itself was growing ... the shapes shifting, dividing and multiplying as though some door had been opened and into it companies of phantasms were pouring. While brighter, more bright grew the pulsing light.

He felt swift panic, tried to withdraw sight and will, dropped the flash. The cube had no need now of the ray ... and he could not withdraw ... could not withdraw? Why, he himself was being sucked into that disc which was now a globe within which unnameable shapes danced to a music that bathed the globe with steady radiance.

There was no tent. There was only a vast curtain of sparkling mist behind which shone the globe.... He felt himself drawn through that mist, sucked through it as if by a mighty wind, straight for the globe.

As the mist-blurred light of the sapphire suns grew more and more intense, the outlines of the globe ahead wavered and dissolved to a churning chaos. Its pallor and its motion and its music all blended themselves with the engulfing mist- bleaching it to a pale steel-colour and setting it undulantly in motion. And the sapphire suns, too, melted imperceptibly into the greying infinity of shapeless pulsation.

Meanwhile the sense of forward, outward motion grew intolerably, incredibly, cosmically swift. Every standard of speed known to earth seemed dwarfed, and Campbell knew that any such flight in physical reality would mean instant death to a human being. Even as it was – in this strange, hellish hypnosis or nightmare – the quasi-visual impression of meteor-like hurtling almost paralyzed his mind. Though there were no real points of reference in the grey, pulsing void, he felt that he was approaching and passing the speed of light itself. Finally his consciousness did go under – and merciful blackness swallowed everything.

It was very suddenly, and amidst the most impenetrable darkness, that thoughts and ideas again came to George Campbell. Of how many moments – or years – or eternities

– had elapsed since his flight through the grey void, he could form no estimate. He knew only that he seemed to be at rest and without pain. Indeed, the absence of all physical sensation was the salient quality of his condition. It made even the blackness seem less solidly black – suggesting as it did that he was rather a disembodied intelligence in a state beyond physical senses, than a corporeal being with senses deprived of their accustomed objects of perception. He could think sharply and quickly – almost preternaturally so – yet could form no idea whatsoever of his situation.

Half by instinct, he realised that he was not in his own tent. True, he might have awaked there from a nightmare to a world equally black; yet he knew this was not so. There was no camp cot beneath him – he had no hands to feel the blankets and canvas surface and flashlight that ought to be around him – there was no sensation of cold in the air – no flap through which he could glimpse the pale night outside … something was wrong, dreadfully wrong.

He cast his mind backward and thought of the fluorescent cube which had hypnotised him – of that, and all which had followed. He had known that his mind was going, yet had been unable to draw back. At the last moment there had been a shocking, panic fear – a subconscious fear beyond even that caused by the sensation of daemonic flight. It had come from some vague flash or remote recollection – just what, he could not at once tell. Some cell-group in the back of his head had seemed to find a cloudily familiar quality in the cube – and that familiarity was fraught with dim terror. Now he tried to remember what the familiarity and the terror were.

Little by little it came to him. Once – long ago, in connection with his geological life-work – he had read of something like that cube. It had to do with those debatable and disquieting clay fragments called the Eltdown Shards, dug up from pre-carboniferous strata in southern England thirty years before. Their shape and markings were so queer that a few scholars hinted at artificiality, and made wild conjectures about them and their origin. They came, clearly, from a time when no human beings could exist on the globe – but their contours and figurings were damnably puzzling. That was how they got their name.

It was not, however, in the writings of any sober scientist that Campbell had seen that reference to a crystal, disc-holding globe. The source was far less reputable, and infinitely more vivid. About 1912 a deeply learned Sussex clergyman of occultist leanings – the Reverend Arthur Brooke Winters-Hall – had professed to identify the markings on the Eltdown Shards with some of the so-called 'pre-human hieroglyphs' persistently cherished and esoterically handed down in certain mystical circles, and had published at his own expense what purported to be a 'translation' of the primal and baffling 'inscriptions' – a 'translation' still quoted frequently and seriously by occult writers. In this "translation" – a surprisingly long brochure in view of the limited number of "shards" existing – had occurred the narrative, supposedly of pre-human authorship, containing the now frightening reference.

As the story went, there dwelt on a world – and eventually on countless other worlds – of outer space a mighty order of worm-like beings whose attainments and whose control of nature surpassed anything within the range of terrestrial imagination. They had mastered the art of interstellar travel early in their career, and had peopled every habitable planet in their own galaxy - killing off the races they found.

Beyond the limits of their own galaxy – which was not ours – they could not navigate in person; but in their quest for knowledge of all space and time they discovered a means of spanning certain transgalactic gulfs with their minds. They devised peculiar objects

– strangely energized cubes of a curious crystal containing hypnotic talismen and enclosed in space-resisting spherical envelopes of an unknown substance – which could be forcibly expelled beyond the limits of their universe, and which would respond to the attraction of cool solid matter only.

These, of which a few would necessarily land on various inhabited worlds in outside universes, formed the ether-bridges needed for mental communication. Atmospheric friction burned away the protecting envelope, leaving the cube exposed and subject to discovery by the intelligent minds of the world where it fell. By its very nature, the cube would attract and rivet attention. This, when coupled with the action of light, was sufficient to set its special properties working.

The mind that noticed the cube would be drawn into it by the power of the disc, and would be sent on a thread of obscure energy to the place whence the disc had come – the remote world of the worm-like space explorers across stupendous galactic abysses. Received in one of the machines to which each cube was attuned, the captured mind would remain suspended without body or senses until examined by one of the dominant race. Then it would, by an obscure process of interchange, be pumped of all its contents. The investigator's mind would now occupy the strange machine while the captive mind occupied the interrogator's worm-like body. Then, in another interchange, the interrogator's mind would leap across boundless space to the captive's vacant and unconscious body on the trans-galactic world – animating the alien tenement as best it might, and exploring the alien world in the guise of one of its denizens.

When done with exploration, the adventurer would use the cube and its disc in accomplishing his return – and sometimes the captured mind would be restored safely to its own remote world. Not always, however, was the dominant race so kind. Sometimes, when a potentially important race capable of space travel was found, the worm-like folk would employ the cube to capture and annihilate minds by the thousands, and would extirpate the race for diplomatic reasons – using the exploring minds as agents of destruction.

In other cases sections of the worm-folk would permanently occupy a trans-galactic planet - destroying the captured minds and wiping out the remaining inhabitants preparatory to settling down in unfamiliar bodies. Never, however, could the parent civilization be quite duplicated in such a case; since the new planet would not contain all the materials necessary for the worm-race's arts. The cubes, for example, could be made only on the home planet.

Only a few of the numberless cubes sent forth ever found a landing and response on an inhabited world - since there was no such thing as aiming them at goals beyond sight or knowledge. Only three, ran the story, had ever landed on peopled worlds in our own particular universe. One of these had struck a planet near the galactic rim two thousand billion years ago, while another had lodged three billion years ago on a world near the centre of the galaxy. The third – and the only one ever known to have invaded the solar system – had reached our own earth 150,000,000 years ago.

It was with this latter that Dr. Winters-Hall's 'translation' chiefly dealt. When the cube struck the earth, he wrote, the ruling terrestrial species was a huge, cone-shaped race surpassing all others before or since in mentality and achievements. This race was so advanced that it had actually sent minds abroad in both space and time to explore the cosmos, hence recognised something of what had happened when the cube fell from the sky and certain individuals had suffered mental change after gazing at it.

Realising that the changed individuals represented invading minds, the race's leaders had them destroyed – even at the cost of leaving the displaced minds exiled in alien space. They had had experience with even stranger transitions. When, through a mental exploration of space and time, they formed a rough idea of what the cube was, they carefully hid the thing from light and sight, and guarded it as a menace. They did not wish to destroy a thing so rich in later experimental possibilities. Now and then some rash, unscrupulous adventurer would furtively gain access to it and sample its perilous powers despite the consequences – but all such cases were discovered, and safely and drastically dealt with.

Of this evil meddling the only bad result was that the worm-like outside race learned from the new exiles what had happened to their explorers on earth, and conceived a violent hatred of the planet and all its life-forms. They would have depopulated it if they could, and indeed sent additional cubes into space in the wild hope of striking it by accident in unguarded places – but that accident never came to pass.

The cone-shaped terrestrial beings kept the one existing cube in a special shrine as a relique and basis for experiments, till after aeons it was lost amidst the chaos of war and the destruction of the great polar city where it was guarded. When, fifty million years ago, the beings sent their minds ahead into the infinite future to avoid a nameless peril of inner earth, the whereabouts of the sinister cube from space were unknown.

This much, according to the learned occultist, the Eltdown Shards had said. What now made the account so obscurely frightful to Campbell was the minute accuracy with which the alien cube had been described. Every detail tallied – dimensions, consistency, heiroglyphed central disc, hypnotic effects. As he thought the matter over and over amidst the darkness of his strange situation, he began to wonder whether his whole experience with the crystal cube – indeed, its very existence – were not a nightmare brought on by some freakish subconscious memory of this old bit of extravagant, charlatanic reading. If so, though, the nightmare must still be in force; since his present apparently bodiless state had nothing of normality in it.

Of the time consumed by this puzzled memory and reflection, Campbell could form no estimate. Everything about his state was so unreal that ordinary dimensions and measurements became meaningless. It seemed an eternity, but perhaps it was not really long before the sudden interruption came. What happened was as strange and inexplicable as the blackness it succeeded. There was a sensation - of the mind rather than of the body – and all at once Campbell felt his thoughts swept or sucked beyond his control in tumultuous and chaotic fashion.

Memories arose irresponsibly and irrelevantly. All that he knew – all his personal background, traditions, experiences, scholarship, dreams, ideas, and inspirations-welled up abruptly and simultaneously, with a dizzying speed and abundance which soon made him unable to keep track of any separate concept. The parade of all his mental contents became an avalanche, a cascade, a vortex. It was as horrible and vertiginous as his hypnotic flight through space when the crystal cube pulled him. Finally it sapped his consciousness and brought on fresh oblivion.

Another measureless blank – and then a slow trickle of sensation. This time it was physical, not mental. Sapphire light, and a low rumble of distant sound. There were tactile impressions – he could realise that he was lying at full length on something, though there was a baffling strangeness about the feel of his posture. He could not reconcile the pressure of the supporting surface with his own outlines – or with the outlines of the human form at all. He tried to move his arms, but found no definite response to the attempt. Instead, there were little, ineffectual nervous twitches all over the area which seemed to mark his body.

He tried to open his eyes more widely, but found himself unable to control their mechanism. The sapphire light came in a diffused, nebulous manner, and could nowhere be voluntarily focussed into definiteness. Gradually, though, visual images began to trickle in curiously and indecisively. The limits and qualities of vision were not those which he was used to, but he could roughly correlate the sensation with what he had known as sight. As this sensation gained some degree of stability, Campbell realised that he must still be in the throes of nightmare.

He seemed to be in a room of considerable extent – of medium height, but with a large proportionate area. On every side – and he could apparently see all four sides at once – were high, narrowish slits which seemed to serve as combined doors and windows. There were singular low tables or pedestals, but no furniture of normal nature and proportions. Through the slits streamed floods of sapphire light, and beyond them could be mistily seen the sides and roofs of fantastic buildings like clustered cubes. On the walls - in the vertical panels between the slits - were strange markings of an oddly disquieting character. It was some time before Campbell understood why they disturbed him so – then he saw that they were, in repeated instances, precisely like some of the hieroglyphs on the crystal cube's disc.

The actual nightmare element, though, was something more than this. It began with the living thing which presently entered through one of the slits, advancing deliberately toward him and bearing a metal box of bizarre proportions and glassy, mirror-like surfaces. For this thing was nothing human – nothing of earth – nothing even of man's myths and dreams. It was a gigantic, pale-grey worm or centipede, as large around as a man and twice as long, with a disc-like, apparently eyeless, cilia-fringed head bearing a purple central orifice. It glided on its rear pairs of legs, with its fore part raised vertically – the legs, or at least two pairs of them, serving as arms. Along its spinal ridge was a curious purple comb, and a fan-shaped tail of some grey membrane ended its grotesque bulk. There was a ring of flexible red spikes around its neck, and from the twistings of these came clicking, twanging sounds in measured, deliberate rhythms.

Here, indeed, was outré nightmare at its height – capricious fantasy at its apex. But even this vision of delirium was not what caused George Campbell to lapse a third time into unconsciousness. It took one more thing – one final, unbearable touch – to do that. As the nameless worm advanced with its glistening box, the reclining man caught in the mirror-like surface a glimpse of what should have been his own body. Yet – horribly verifying his disordered and unfamiliar sensations – it was not his own body at all that he saw reflected in the burnished metal. It was, instead, the loathsome, pale-grey bulk of one of the great centipedes.

From that final lap of senselessness, he emerged with a full understanding of his situation. His mind was imprisoned in the body of a frightful native of an alien planet, while, somewhere on the other side of the universe, his own body was housing the monster's personality.

He fought down an unreasoning horror. Judged from a cosmic standpoint, why should his metamorphosis horrify him? Life and consciousness were the only realities in the universe. Form was unimportant. His present body was hideous only according to terrestrial standards. Fear and revulsion were drowned in the excitement of titanic adventure.

What was his former body but a cloak, eventually to be cast off at death anyway? He had no sentimental illusions about the life from which he had been exiled. What had it ever given him save toil, poverty, continual frustration and repression? If this life before him offered no more, at least it offered no less. Intuition told him it offered more – much more.

With the honesty possible only when life is stripped to its naked fundamentals, he realized that he remembered with pleasure only the physical delights of his former life. But he had long ago exhausted all the physical possibilities contained in that earthly body. Earth held no new thrills. But in the possession of this new, alien body he felt promises of strange, exotic joys.

A lawless exultation rose in him. He was a man without a world, free of all conventions or inhibitions of Earth, or of this strange planet, free of every artificial restraint in the universe. He was a god! With grim amusement he thought of his body moving in earth's business and society, with all the while an alien monster staring out of the windows that were George Campbell's eyes on people who would flee if they knew.

Let him walk the earth slaying and destroying as he would. Earth and its races no longer had any meaning to George Campbell. There he had been one of a billion nonentities, fixed in place by a mountainous accumulation of conventions, laws and manners, doomed to live and die in his sordid niche. But in one blind bound he had soared above the commonplace. This was not death, but re-birth – the birth of a full-grown mentality, with a new-found freedom that made little of physical captivity on Yekub.

He started. Yekub! It was the name of this planet, but how had he known? Then he knew, as he knew the name of him whose body he occupied- Tothe. Memory, deep grooved in Tothe's brain, was stirring in him - shadows of the knowledge Tothe had. Carved deep in the physical tissues of the brain, they spoke dimly as implanted instincts to George Campbell; and his human consciousness seized them and translated them to show him the way not only to safety and freedom, but to the power his soul, stripped to its primitive impulses, craved. Not as a slave would he dwell on Yekub, but as a king! Just as of old barbarians had sat on the throne of lordly empires.

For the first time he turned his attention to his surroundings. He still lay on the couch-like thing in the midst of that fantastic room, and the centipede man stood before him, holding the polished metal object, and clashing its neck-spikes. Thus it spoke to him, Campbell knew, and what it said he dimly understood, through the implanted thought processes of Tothe, just as he knew the creature was Yukth, supreme lord of science.

But Campbell gave no heed, for he had made his desperate plan, a plan so alien to the ways of Yekub that it was beyond Yukth's comprehension and caught him wholly unprepared. Yukth, like Campbell, saw the sharp-pointed metal shard on a nearby table, but to Yukth it was only a scientific implement. He did not even know it could be used as a weapon. Campbell's earthly mind supplied the knowledge and the action that followed, driving Tothe's body into movements no man of Yekub had ever made before.

Campbell snatched the pointed shard and struck, ripping savagely upward. Yukth reared and toppled, his entrails spilling on the floor. In an instant Campbell was streaking for a door. His speed was amazing, exhilarating, first fulfillment of the promise of novel physical sensations.

As he ran, guided wholly by the instinctive knowledge implanted in Tothe's physical reflexes, it was as if he were borne by a separate consciousness in his legs. Tothe's body was bearing him along a route it had traversed ten thousand times when animated by Tothe's mind.

Down a winding corridor he raced, up a twisted stair, through a carved door, and the same instincts that had brought him there told him he had found what he sought. He was in a circular room with a domed roof from which shone a livid blue light. A strange structure rose in the middle of the rainbow-hued floor, tier on tier, each of a separate, vivid color. The ultimate tier was a purple cone, from the apex of which a blue smoky mist drifted upward to a sphere that poised in mid-air – a sphere that shone like translucent ivory.

This, the deep-grooved memories of Tothe told Campbell, was the god of Yekub, though why the people of Yekub feared and worshipped it had been forgotten a million years. A worm-priest stood between him and the altar which no hand of flesh had ever touched. That it could be touched was a blasphemy that had never occurred to a man of Yekub. The worm-priest stood in frozen horror until Campbell's shard ripped the life out of him.

On his centipede-legs Campbell clambered the tiered altar, heedless of its sudden quiverings, heedless of the change that was taking place in the floating sphere, heedless of the smoke that now billowed out in blue clouds. He was drunk with the feel of power. He feared the superstitions of Yekub no more than he feared those of earth. With that globe in his hands he would be king of Yekub. The worm men would dare deny him nothing, when he held their god as hostage. He reached a hand for the ball – no longer ivory-hued, but red as blood....

Out of the tent into the pale August night walked the body of George Campbell. It moved with a slow, wavering gait between the bodies of enormous trees, over a forest path strewed with sweet scented pine needles. The air was crisp and cold. The sky was an inverted bowl of frosted silver flecked with stardust, and far to the north the Aurora Borealis splashed streamers of fire.

The head of the walking man lolled hideously from side to side. From the corners of his lax mouth drooled thick threads of amber froth, which fluttered in the night breeze. He walked upright at first, as a man would walk, but gradually as the tent receded, his posture altered. His torso began almost imperceptibly to slant, and his limbs to shorten.

In a far-off world of outer space the centipede creature that was George Campbell clasped to its bosom a god whose lineaments were red as blood, and ran with insect-like quiverings across a rainbow-hued hall and out through massive portals into the bright glow of alien suns.

Weaving between the trees of earth in an attitude that suggested the awkward loping of a werebeast, the body of George Campbell was fulfilling a mindless destiny. Long, claw-tipped fingers dragged leaves from a carpet of odorous pine needles as it moved toward a wide expanse of gleaming water.

In the far-off, extra-galactic world of the worm people, George Campbell moved between cyclopean blocks of black masonry down long, fern-planted avenues holding aloft the round red god.

There was a harsh animal cry in the underbrush near the gleaming lake on earth where the mind of a worm creature dwelt in a body swayed by instinct. Human teeth sank into soft animal fur, tore at black animal flesh. A little silver fox sank its fangs in frantic retaliation into a furry human wrist, and thrashed about in terror as its blood spurted. Slowly the body of George Campbell arose, its mouth splashed with fresh blood. With upper limbs swaying oddly it moved towards the waters of the lake.

As the variform creature that was George Campbell crawled between the black blocks of stone thousands of worm-shapes prostrated themselves in the scintillating dust before it. A godlike power seemed to emanate from its weaving body as it moved with a slow, undulant motion toward a throne of spiritual empire transcending all the sovereignties of earth.

A trapper stumbling wearily through the dense woods of earth near the tent where the worm-creature dwelt in the body of George Campbell came to the gleaming waters of the lake and discerned something dark floating there. He had been lost in the woods all night, and weariness enveloped him like a leaden cloak in the pale morning light.

But the shape was a challenge that he could not ignore. Moving to the edge of the water he knelt in the soft mud and reached out toward the floating bulk. Slowly he pulled it to the shore.

Far off in outer space the worm-creature holding the glowing red god ascended a throne that gleamed like the constellation Cassiopeia under an alien vault of hyper-suns. The great deity that he held aloft energized his worm tenement, burning away in the white fire of a supermundane spirituality all animal dross.

On earth the trapper gazed with unutterable horror into the blackened and hairy face of the drowned man. It was a bestial face, repulsively anthropoid in contour, and from its twisted, distorted mouth black ichor poured.

"He who sought your body in the abysses of Time will occupy an unresponsive tenement," said the red god. "No spawn of Yekub can control the body of a human.

"On all earth, living creatures rend one another, and feast with unutterable cruelty on their kith and kin. No worm-mind can control a bestial man-body when it yearns to raven. Only man-minds instinctively conditioned through the course of ten thousand generations can keep the human instincts in thrall. Your body will destroy itself on earth, seeking the blood of its animal kin, seeking the cool water where it can wallow at its ease. Seeking eventually destruction, for the death-instinct is more powerful in it than the instincts of life and it will destroy itself in seeking to return to the slime from which it sprang."

Thus spoke the round red god of Yekub in a far-off segment of the space-time continuum to George Campbell as the latter, with all human desire purged away, sat on a throne and ruled an empire of worms more wisely, kindly, and benevolently than any man of earth had ever ruled an empire of men.

The opening words of each new author's text is indicated below:
From "George Campbell opened sleep-fogged eyes..." – C.L. Moore
From "He lay there, it seemed to him..." – A. Merritt
From "As the mist-blurred light..." – H. P. Lovecraft
From "From that final lap of senselessness..." – Robert E. Howard
From "Out of the tent..." – Frank Belknap Long

The Man in the Ambry

Gwendolyn Kiste

Dear Man in the Ambry:

I know you're there. I see your shape in the shadows every morning when I pick out my shoes. Nobody else believes me, but that's okay. In my sixteen years, I've found the best things are the ones you keep to yourself. The little truths about the world that everyone else thinks are crazy. Like when I told my aunt I could taste stars, and she made my parents take me to a doctor. I didn't tell anybody about the stars again, but that didn't make them any less real.

Can you read? I'll slip this letter under your door to find out. You can write back too if you want. I hope you do. I'm bored and could use a friend.

Sincerely,

Molly Jane Richards

***

Dear Man in the Ambry:

This morning, I checked the letter I left you. It was crumpled in the corner, so you must have read it. Or maybe you thought it was a piece of trash and you were trying to dispose of it.

I searched the whole ambry but couldn't find a letter back to me. Oh well. Maybe you don't think you're much of a Shakespeare and would rather not write back. That's okay. I'll keep leaving these letters so long as you notice them.

Molly Jane

P. S. While in the ambry, I did come across something small and white near the letter. It reminds me of a thin pillar of salt, but pointy too like a kid's pocketknife. Does it belong to you? I could leave it with my next letter if you want. Or you could come retrieve it yourself. It's in my jewelry box.

***

Dear Man in the Ambry:

I bet you're wondering what an ambry is. That's what my mom calls the place you live. "Molly Jane, stop hanging out all day in that ambry!" she'll say. But an ambry's just a fancy word for a cabinet or closet.

Do you ever leave there? Nobody's ever seen you in the rest of the house, and I've only caught you in the shadows or when the door's ajar. Are you shy?

I'm sure glad I chose the room next to yours for my bedroom. Otherwise, I don't know how I'd spend my time.

Curiously,
Molly Jane

***

Dear Man in the Ambry:

How many years have you lived in this house? We've been here a month, and it's already long enough. Our old place was better. Bigger and with neater windows (stained glass, the whole deal). But according to Mom and Dad, this one's in a better area. A historic neighborhood or something like that.

I'd hoped since it was so old, the house might be haunted, but no such luck. Unless you count. Are you a ghost? I don't think so. Not one chain has rattled in the ambry since we moved in.

Earlier this week, my parents did say they heard something between my bedroom and theirs. Was that you? And in lieu of chains, do you have an accessory you prefer?

More Curiously,
Molly Jane

P.S. I still have your little white trinket in my jewelry box. I'll give it back if you want. No member of the Richards family has ever been called a thief, and I won't start such an unscrupulous tradition now.

***

Dear Man in the Ambry:

Last night, my parents stayed up and listened to some distant scratching. They say it's coming from inside the walls. I didn't hear anything, but my cat Snappy sure did. She's been pawing at the ambry door ever since. And her hearing's not even very good (she's almost 25!), so you must have been pretty busy overnight.

We should play a game. That's what friends do, right? I don't really know for sure. My only friends have been my cousins, and none of them are very nice. They're like default friends, the ones you end up with by accident, not by choice.

But you're my friend by choice. You and Snappy.

I'm not sure what games you play there in the ambry. Checkers maybe?

Your Devoted Compatriot,
Molly Jane

***

Dear Man in the Ambry:

Sorry I made you scurry off last night! But you can't roll a soccer ball against my bed at half past two and not expect me to sneak a quick look at where it came from!

I always wanted to see your face. And now I have. Well, half your face anyhow. At least I know you're not a ghost.

And in case you were wondering, I never made the soccer team (thankfully). I only have that ball in there because my parents thought organized sports might be good for me. And what does that mean? Organized sports? As opposed to disorganized free-for-all sports?

Anyway, I think it's a good idea for a game. I'll crack the ambry door tonight and wait against the wall. From there, I can send the ball back to you. No peeking. I promise.

Your Athletically Challenged Teammate,
Molly Jane

***

Dear Man in the Ambry:
My parents are now convinced the house is haunted. "We hear strange rolling noises all night," they say.

Let's please continue our game.

Your Devious One,
Molly Jane

***

Dear Man in the Ambry:
I should give you a name. How about George? No, that's silly. That reminds me of Lenny and George in *Of Mice and Men*. We read that last year in English class, and I liked the part with the dead mouse. It made me laugh (and think of how Snappy never means to kill mice either), but the scene bothered the other kids. The dead girl was awful though. And everyone just called her "Curley's Wife" like she wasn't worth anything except her husband.

So George is out. Here are some other names I like. Let me know which one you prefer.

Luke   James   Andrew   Christopher

Your Friend in More than Name Only,
Molly Jane

***

Dear Andrew:
I found the last letter I wrote you, and Andrew was scratched out. The rest of the names were left alone, so I'm guessing you like Andrew best. Or maybe you like it least, and you were trying to tell me to name you anything other than Andrew. If that's the case, give me some kind of sign. Like rip this letter in half or something.

Eager to Hear from You,
Molly Jane

***

Dear Andrew:
Last night's letter was in pristine condition, so Andrew it is! I like that name best too. So distinguished.

This morning, my mom came into my room to discuss school – more about my friends (or lack thereof) than arithmetic homework or anything – and she noticed your white souvenir in my jewelry box. She turned it over and over again in her hand and demanded to know what it was. I said I didn't know. She got all angry and quiet. Then she told my dad. He marched up to my room and tossed your bauble in the trash. I don't know what harm it was doing just sitting in an old box.

So I'm sorry I can't give it back to you. But then again, you had plenty of time to salvage it, so you probably didn't want it anymore.

Apologetically,

Molly Jane

***

Dear Andrew:

Mom found my letters to you. She claims she was searching for laundry, but I think she was spying on me. That white trinket really bothered her. And judging from her screeching and screaming the moment I exited the school bus yesterday, she would have been happier if she'd discovered a spoon and syringe or a positive pregnancy test in my room. She made my dad pull everything out of the ambry to prove no one's there. (Sorry about the mess.)

Part of me thinks they were hoping for a secret passageway where some neighborhood creeper was living. At least then their little girl wouldn't be crazy. But there was nothing other than a normal old ambry.

I cried most of last night, which is why I didn't leave you a letter sooner. I tried to write a couple versions of this note, but my tears streaked up the pages and my handwriting was such a mess I don't think you can have read it anyhow.

The only way they'd let me keep my bedroom is if I promised not to write you anymore. So I'll leave this note overnight and burn it in the morning.

And don't worry about the fire. Mom will think I'm smoking a joint. Imagine how proud she'll be that her daughter has a normal adolescent vice.

Your Surreptitious Friend,

Molly Jane

***

Dear Andrew:

I graduate next week. I can't wait to get out of this house, so no one will read my letters except me and you.

College is less than three months away. Will you come visit? I'm going to study psychology. That sounds fun, right? Pedestrian but fun. I'd rather study ghosts and demons and worlds other than my own, but if I wanted that enough, I could move into the ambry with you. Is there available real estate?

No, psychology won't be so bad. My parents said I might finally figure out what's wrong with me. They thought it was funny. I didn't laugh.

Collegiate Bound,

Molly Jane

***

Dear Andrew:

I saw you again today. Just a glimpse of course, but a good glimpse. Mom was calling upstairs, and all her hollering was distracting me, which is how you must have thought you'd slip by. But when I looked at my mirror, your reflection was there in the fissure of the door. You're beautiful. Or handsome. I should say handsome, even though I mean beautiful.

Did you always look like that, or have you changed to please me?

Swooning (not really),

Molly Jane

***

Dear Andrew:

Two weeks until college!

I don't think my parents will notice, but you and Snappy will miss me. I'll leave the ambry door open, so you two can commiserate while I'm away.

Homesick Already,

Molly Jane

***

Dear Andrew:

It's my first Thanksgiving break, and I'm already not sure about school. I live with this girl named Heather. She's got a different idea of fun than me, but then most people don't spend their free time writing to guys who live in the walls of spare rooms.

I hoped you would visit me at college, but the nooks and crannies in the dorm must not be so comfortable.

If you could leave here, would you take the bus? Or would you walk? Or is there some arcane transportation where you're from? Like maybe you ride in the mouth of a dragon or use the fires of the underworld to power a steamship?

Or maybe you walk. You probably walk.

Your Forever Dreamer,

Molly Jane

***

Dear Andrew:

While I was away at school, my parents converted my bedroom into a guest room. They packed all my things and told me to take the boxes with me to school or else my stuff goes into storage. Welcome home, Molly Jane.

Sorry about them traipsing all over the ambry. But you have a lot more breathing room in there now. Do you breathe? If so, it can't be very comfortable in those stuffy walls.

My parents left my bed (for the benefit of all the elusive guests they must be expecting), so at least I can sleep next to the ambry. But if there wasn't a bed, I'd just sleep inside the ambry. Heck, you'd make a better roommate than Heather.

By the way, Snappy seems livelier than ever. Mom says she disappeared last week for a few days, but they could still hear her meowing. "Like she was in the walls," my mom said.

I knew the two of you would be the best of friends.
Your Faraway Comrade,
Molly Jane

***

Dear Andrew:

It's Christmas again. The holidays are all eggnog and misery.

Sometimes, my parents still hear strange scratching in the walls. And Snappy's gone. She's been missing for over a month now. But last night, I heard her purring, so it must not be so bad wherever she is. Wherever you are.

Do the stars taste like bliss there? Do you have stars at all?

Your Celestial Body,
Molly Jane

***

Dear Andrew:

Heather has this trick she taught me. If there's a guy she likes and he's hanging out in the dorm hallway (that's how it is at college, all communal and whatnot), she leaves the door to our room open a little while she changes for bed.

I must confess I tried her ploy last night when I got home for the semester. Sloughed off my academic garb and prepared for the summer all while giving the ambry a front row seat.

You never looked. Maybe you're too much of a gentleman. Or maybe you don't care.

And now I just feel embarrassed about the whole thing.

Your Discomfited Coquette,
Molly Jane

***

Dear Man in the Ambry:

It's been three semesters since I wrote to you. I guess I don't have much to say. Have you changed? I know I have.

I'm seeing this boy. Derek Adler. He's alright. He says he loves me. Do you think he does? My mom insists he'd make a good husband. We've only been seeing each other for two months, and she's already planning the wedding. A spring ceremony, she says, with pink and ivory as the colors. I don't like pink, and I hate every wretched permutation of white, but May or June is as good a month as any to surrender your freedom, don't you think?

Their Indentured Servant,
Molly Jane

P.S. I found another of those white pillars in the ambry. Mom says she's gathered up a couple dozen in the last year. She already discarded the others, but I'll keep this one in case you need it back.

***

Dear Man in the Ambry:

On Sunday, I graduated *summa cum laude* in psychology. With honors too. It would have been a good day if Derek hadn't proposed to me over dinner. And both his parents and mine were there, so what was I supposed to do?

Here Comes the Bride,

Molly Jane

***

Dear Man in the Ambry:

I got married today. People said it was a nice ceremony. They said I wore a beautiful dress.

Derek's waiting in the car while I pick up some things for the honeymoon. Will you be the something borrowed and come with me? I don't want to go alone.

A Brand New Mrs.,

Molly Jane ~~Richards~~ Adler

***

Dear Man in the Ambry:

Have you ever seen Niagara Falls? Even though it looks like the same Niagara Falls from last week or last year or some centuries-old tintype photograph of a daredevil on a tightrope, it's different. The water's always changing.

People are like that too. I've heard every seven years, we shed each individual cell.

If our entire body's changed, are we even the same person? Is Niagara Falls still Niagara Falls?

I don't have many reasons to visit my old bedroom anymore, especially now that I have a new bedroom everyone keeps reminding me about. You probably don't know this, but when you get married, people make it their business to ask about your love life. Like you're an incomparable letdown if there are no swaddling clothes in nine months or less.

Maternally,

Molly Jane

P.S. How's Snappy? Mom and Dad haven't heard her in a while.

***

Dear Man in the Ambry:

Good news at last! A counseling center hired me. I'll be talking to young kids with so-called behavioral issues (AKA parents like mine). I'm already counseling a girl named Carla. I don't know why her parents think she needs so much help. She seems swell to me.

Do they have jobs where you are? Maybe you work to earn those little white knives, so you can spend them on bigger white knives.

Putting my Degree to Use,

Molly Jane

***

Dear Man in the Ambry:

Remember the girl I told you about? Carla? Yesterday in our weekly session, she confided in me about someone she knew. Someone no one else could see. He lives in the family's garage. He's like you, only his hair's a different color and he's a little shorter. At least that's what it sounds like from her description.

I'll tell you more when I meet with her again next week. Maybe her friend's a cousin of yours!

Until then,

Molly Jane

***

Dear Man in the Ambry:

I'm not counseling Carla anymore. My boss pulled me aside and claimed I was feeding her delusions. Her mother must have complained. Now Carla's with another counselor.

As if anyone else can understand her like I can.

Cosmically Disappointed,

Molly Jane

***

Dear Man in the Ambry:

Do they downsize where you are?

Sometimes I've wondered if maybe I wasn't meant for this world. Maybe my job was to taste stars, but everyone got me off-track. I shouldn't complain though. Life's certainly a lot worse for most people. Like Carla's parents. Carla vanished last week, and they can't find her anywhere. I could tell them where she is, but nobody asks my opinion, of course, because they know they wouldn't like what I'd say.

Last night, my mom thought she heard Snappy. But that cat would be over 30 now and couldn't possibly be alive. Especially without any food and water in the walls.

Your Incurable Human,

Mrs. Adler

***

Dear Man in the Ambry:

Mom called me tonight and demanded I talk to my dad. When I got here, he was taking a sledgehammer to the wall in their bedroom. Something was behind there, and he said he was going to scare it off.

With all that pounding, I sure hope he didn't disturb your rest too much. But don't worry if he did. He's calmer now. "Mice," I told him. "It's only mice."

Are there any pests in the walls? I hope not. How unpleasant that would be for you!

The Not So Mousy,

Molly Jane

***

Dear Andrew:
After Sunday dinner, I found the gift you left me. It made me laugh. Laugh like a hopeless hysteric until my parents and Derek ran all the way upstairs to check on me. They didn't laugh. I guess a pile of dead mice doesn't have traditional comic appeal. I explained it was an inside joke, but they still didn't laugh. Not even a slight smile. And Derek was so mad he went home without me. Something about needing space. He says he'll pick me up in the morning, but I don't care if he does. What a curmudgeon.
Would you like any rat poison or mouse traps? I could leave some with the next letter.
Yours Truly,
Molly Jane

P.S. I'm still laughing and will be even after I put this letter in the ambry.

P.P.S. Did you like the gift I gave you in return?

***

Dear Man in the Ambry:
Derek has a plan. A plan he thinks will "even out my disposition".
"And you're not working right now," he said. "It's the perfect time."
I bet he thinks a mother could never giggle at a glut of dead rodents.
My parents are already nudging each other and smiling more than usual over meals. Like the three of them are colluding against me. Like they know something I don't.
Doubtfully,
Derek's Wife

***

Dear Man in the Ambry:
I found out what my parents were hiding. They bought a new place closer to me and Derek. Closer for when they have grandkids. As if the offspring are inevitable.
Their last day in this house is in less than two weeks.
I offered to stay and help them pack. But I don't care about packing. I care about writing to you as many times as I can before I never can again.
Your Friend,
Molly Jane

***

Dear Man in the Ambry:
Twelve days until we abandon the house.
I'm not feeling well this evening, so I'll leave it at that.
Hopelessly,
Molly Jane

***

Dear Man in the Ambry:
Ten days.

I'm still sick, but it comes and goes, so I doubt it's terminal.

My dad keeps saying he's happy we're leaving, especially since the scratching in the walls has started again. Mom wants to leave sooner to appease him, but I begged her to wait. I want every moment I can spend in the ambry.

Please visit me soon. I miss your face. I miss it so much.

Eagerly,
Molly Jane

***

Dear Man in the Ambry:
Thank you for coming overnight. It was nice to know someone was there, even if I could only hear you breathing.

Four days left. I'm nauseous. And tired. And out of things to tell you except I'm sorry. But I can't stop them. It's their house to sell.

Tenuously,
Molly Jane

***

Dear Man in the Ambry:
I know now why I've been sick. Turns out it is terminal. I'm pregnant.

I tried to be careful. I tried to avoid it. Whichever time damned me, I'll never know, but I'm damned nonetheless.

Desperately,
Molly Jane

***

Andrew:
This is the last night here. My parents and Derek are out to dinner. Celebrating the move. I stayed home, said I was sick. And I am sick. I need you to come to me one last time. Before it's too late.

They'll be back soon. I'll put this letter in the ambry, and I'll wait.

Maybe there aren't stars where you are. Maybe Snappy's not there either. Maybe the fires of the underworld will turn me to ash.

But I want the chance to discover that for myself.

For the Last Time,
Molly Jane

P.S. They don't know about me. And I never want them to find out.

***

To the Man Living in our Former Ambry:

I know you're there. I know because you took my daughter.

At first, we thought Molly Jane just wanted to scare us. We didn't even report it for the first few days because we figured she'd come back.

That was a year ago. The police conducted a search, a pretty exhaustive one I might add, but her father and I couldn't see the point. It was more for her husband's benefit. Did she tell you she was married?

We hired some men to look for you. They pulled out all the walls to see if she was in there. It was like we thought. There's no way in or out of the ambry except the door to her bedroom.

But then the men inspected the walling they'd removed. They all said it was the darndest thing. They said it looked like someone wrote on the back of that paneling. Not words any of us could read. Maybe not words at all. More like something trying to write. Something with claws. Claws like pillars of salt.

Please let her come home. Her husband and parents miss her. She belongs with us.

Sincerely,

A Distraught Mother

P.S. Please stop cooing at night. And stop giggling too. It's scaring the new tenants.

Start with Color

Bill Kte'pi

START WITH COLOR. A nimbus of blue at the base, a finger of black, a flicker of yellow and orange. Start with color, and then as soon as color turns into flame, forget the color: just leave the heat. Good. The mug starts to warm, from the base up through the cold coffee, and when the first wisps of steam appear – there we go. Now stop: send the flame away.

Take a sip. Now what was Carly saying?

"They really let you quit?"

I take another gulp of the coffee and tap my finger on the side of the mug. "The necessity of my work has diminished."

Her eyes narrow and she pushes her morning paper away, unread. Her dreams have been lazing at her elbows, small white elephants and green giraffes, grazing from invisible trees. They move aside, harrumphing at her as the paper interrupts their breakfast. "What does that mean, Will?"

I had started to dream my notepad into my hand from my study, but I stop. Vaguely, I sense the notepad, out there, half one place and half another, and as I stroke Carly's hand with my fingertips, I concentrate harder on its original position: sitting on my desk, slightly at an angle next to the computer keyboard, the better to read from while typing. The vagueness disappears. "It means I'll be home from now on, sweetheart. I promise."

"The Sops don't let anyone quit."

"Well, they've let me retire. And you know I don't like that term. It sounds too much like 'cops.'"

"And they may as well be. But fine, Soporifics then. No one retires from the Soporifics until they're too old to work. It's in the Tochko Amendment. You're as much a natural resource as you are a citizen." The elephants start to darken in color, from white to blue.

I shrug and begin to make breakfast, drawing on memories of my grandmother's flapjacks, fluffy and golden-brown, layered with pats of yellow-white butter and drizzled with maple syrup, the real stuff, Grade B —

"Will, stop daydreaming and pay attention to me."

I forget about breakfast for now. "What is it you want me to say?"

"I want you to look me in the eye and promise me that this is for real. That you're going to be home from now on. No more late nights or overnights at headquarters. No more running off to the west coast for a month to track down some death-dreamer. No more leaving for a year 'on loan' to some foreign government, when you can't even tell me which one. I want you to tell me they're not going to come for you. MacKenzie's six years old, he hardly knows his father. I barely know my husband anymore."

This is what it's always been like. These arguments, this argument. I tell myself I do the work for my family, not at their expense, but that argument has grown old even with me. I squeeze Carly's hand, so much younger than my own, untouched by wrinkles, free of blemish, and look straight into her green-blue eyes, fix on them, forgetting the coffee (which stops warming up when I drop my attention from it), forgetting the flapjacks, forgetting the notebook in my upstairs study. "I'm going to be home. I'm not going back. They don't need me anymore."

It gets through to her, and when her eyes widen my heart breaks a little bit. She's never known the effect that has on me, that little widening, that when we were young and she wasn't allowed in my office, it was because if I got trapped looking at those eyes I'd forget everything else and my work would disappear. It didn't always work that way: if you were disciplined enough, you could keep a dream "alive" indefinitely by keeping it at the back of your mind. But it had taken a long time for me to learn that discipline.

Ever since the experiment went horribly wrong in New Mexico, people's dreams have been coming alive. And there are a few of us, few but enough, who dream so strongly that we can make almost anything happen, make anything real. When we dream of fire, it burns, and when we stop dreaming of it, the things it burned don't come back. The Soporifics helped us control our talents: they trained us, taught us to focus, taught us concentration, withdrawal, guardedness.

"You did it." She doesn't have to ask; she knows. She knows that if I'm serious, there's only one explanation.

"Daddy, you're home!" MacKenzie comes into the breakfast room with that waddle-scurry only little children can manage. His eyes are dull with more than sleep, with the usual 30 ccs of morpheum the law mandates that he take every morning until he's old enough to join the Sops. I can see the reflection of his dreams in his eyes: Super Dragon Warriors again, that annoying cartoon I'd hoped he'd get over.

I give him a hug and scoop him into my lap, kissing the top of his head and resting my chin on it as I watch Carly give me the look I dread, the look I can't stand, a mixture of hope and aggravation and the hatred she's prepared to unleash on me if I leave again. I've seen her preparing for this, for the ultimatum. Stay or don't come back again. All or nothing. She wants to believe in my work, but she doesn't want to wait, isn't willing to give up her child for the sake of future generations. "Hey, Big Mac," I say. "Up for breakfast?"

He fiddles with the feet of his Super Dragon Warriors pyjamas, curling his legs up under him as he sniffs at my cold coffee. "That isn't my name, Daddy, I'm MacKenzie." His mother doesn't let him have fast food, and more power to her, but he never gets my jokes. "Can I have a chocolate banana blueberry pancake for breakfast? I think that's my favorite, but I have to try it again so I'm sure."

"Ask your Mom." I nudge him, and keep watching Carly. There's a flash of fear across her eyes, thin and fleeting like color on a soap bubble. She guards it, but she's not as good at secrecy as I am. Part of her, God bless her, will always be afraid of her son, because she knows what he can do, and what's in store for the rest of his life if his father fails. Or she thinks she does.

"Sure." Carly smiles. "But only one. And no syrup, not if there's chocolate in the pancake."

"Oh, Mom." MacKenzie shakes his head. "I can just make syrup that doesn't have any calories anyway."

"That's not the point, and you know it." That's one of those things Carly sticks to. Let the boy dream up his breakfast, since he's strong enough to dream up something with sustenance, but don't let him have anything that would be too unhealthy for him if it were real.

MacKenzie sighs dramatically and rolls his eyes up at me, and I shrug. He starts to stare at the table, and I can smell the rich chocolate and warm bananas and melting blueberries, in that moment of a moment before the oversized blue china plate appears, covered in a pancake the size of a place mat. He didn't bother dreaming of a fork, of course – what child dreams of silverware? – so I do it for him and he goes to work. I know Carly's annoyed he got around her 'just one' loophole, but it's not like the kid's actually going to be able to eat a pancake that size anyway, so what's the harm?

"MacKenzie, let your father get up so he and I can finish our grown-up talk, okay?"

Mac shakes his head and talks through a mouthful of fruit and chocolate. "Nope. Daddy's my booster seat."

"Donald MacKenzie Duquette –" Before she gets to Duquette, Mac sighs and everything spins vertigo around me as the ceiling becomes closer and the floor farther away, air warping around me, and I find myself standing at the other end of the table, with Mac sitting on a bright blue plastic booster seat instead of my lap. His position didn't even shift; the seat's just the right height to keep him in the same place.

I shift my feet and look straight ahead, trying to cover up the fact that he forgot to adjust my balance. No point in giving his mother something else to yell at him for, especially when it's really me she wants to yell at.

He's had his 30 ccs. He's not scheduled for a dosage increase until he turns eight. But there's no way he should have been able to move me without my cooperation, without even turning around to look at me, until the morpheum starts to wear off at noon.

He's getting stronger. Just like I knew he would. Just like he did before.

Carly grabs my hand and pulls me out the door, through the porch and onto the patch of grass between the house and the driveway. "You did it, Will. Didn't you? Why didn't you just tell me that? Why isn't it on the news?"

I shake my head. "It's not that simple, hon. I didn't want to get your hopes up. Look, it's not like I was the only Soporific on the project. I was group leader, but only of one group. There are others, too, and if our plan doesn't work – then maybe one of the other groups will come up with something."

"So you didn't fix it."

"I might have. I think I did. All of my work led up to this – if I'm wrong, I have no idea where to start over."

"And that's why they let you retire?"

"Yeah. Either way, they don't need me anymore. Either way, it's all over for me."

"Were you going to tell me?"

No. I wasn't. "Of course I was! I was just waiting – I didn't want MacKenzie to walk in. I mean, who knows how he'll take it. It's not like with me."

Her eyes widen again, and dammit, another part of me breaks. She turns and looks at the house, at our reflections in the porch's picture windows. "It's like telling Mozart there's no such thing as pianos anymore, isn't it? Or no such thing as music?"

"I don't know. Maybe."

"What do you mean, you don't know? How do you feel?"

"Carly, it's not the same with me. When New Mexico happened, I was Mac's age. I remember what it was like when dreams weren't real, when everything was just in our heads. I didn't grow up with imaginary friends who really could get into the cookie jar – I had to make them up."

"So you feel good about it?"

I watch the back of her head, glad I can't see her eyes, don't have to look at them. "Whatever . . . awkwardness I might feel as a result of it, it's what needs to be done. The world can't continue like this. It just can't." Where dreams come to life, where nightmares crawl through the shadows to kill and feast, where parents worry their kids don't understand how sex can be anything but casual because they've been having it with their dreams for as long as their hormones have told them to, where whole cities have been wiped out by sleep disorders. Where whole new arts have been invented, where nearly every neurological disease is now curable or treatable as a side effect of the research done in the wake of New Mexico, where psychotherapy has literally been given a new life.

"Awkwardness." She turns around to look at me and I look away, watch the sun yellow the sky, watch the clouds move, listen to the sparrows and the ravens. "You don't . . ." Her eyes narrow again as they meet mine, and she crosses her arms, shifts her weight to one foot, cocks her head, breaks my heart. "You don't want it to work."

"Carly —"

"You don't. I can hear it in your voice. I can see it in your eyes. I can see your goddamned dreams." I'd forgotten, become distracted, released one of the birds I dream of when I don't remember not to, a glossy black raven of regret chirping, "Nevermore!"

"I have mixed feelings, it's true, but —"

"Mixed feelings! You son of a bitch. You go in there and have breakfast with your son. Have a pancake the size of a fucking house with your son, and tell me the Soporifics wouldn't take him away in three years, and that he'd grow up normal, without having to be drugged up all the time to keep from killing someone. Go sit down with the son you never see, the one I have to watch slowly turn into something I'm not even sure is human anymore – and tell me what the fuck you have mixed feelings about." She storms past me, almost shoving me aside with her shoulders.

"Where are you going?" I ask.

"Out. I'm going for a drive."

And she leaves me there, watching the sky. I could bring her back. I could dream her to me the way Mac dreamed me out of the chair. There was a time I would have thought that was the solution, but I let her go.

Somewhere out there, the machines are working, reversing what was done in New Mexico. If it works, it'll happen all at once or nearly so: when New Mexico went to hell, it was like blowing the lid off of a box. It's been my job to build a new lid, and by the end of the day, the box will be closed. If I've done my job right, this is the last platter-sized chocolate banana blueberry pancake my son will have.

So I go back inside and have breakfast with him. I listen to him tell me about the Super Dragon Warriors and let him watch television after he cleans his plate – by hand, the way his mother would want. He sits in my lap on the couch, and we watch morning cartoons and order a pizza for lunch. I let him keep his pyjamas on, and we watch the Super Dragon Warriors movie for what must be the hundredth time, sharing a sausage and pepper pizza, slice by slice.

"You know I love you, MacKenzie."

"Of course you do, Daddy. Now be quiet, this is the best part."

I make a call to work after putting Mac down for his nap, just to check in. The machines are running fine. The European team reports the figures we were hoping for in their dream activity. It's working.

God help me. It's working.

Carly comes home while Mac is still asleep. Her hair is disheveled – she was driving with the top down, probably along the coast, something she does when she's very upset. She looks up at me through the fog of her hair and I grab her wrists and hug her.

"You're right," I say. "Look, I'm not saying that to avoid a fight. If you want to yell at me, if you want me to sleep on the couch, if you want to go to your mother's, fine. But you're right. It isn't fair for me to have mixed feelings. But you have to understand that, for a little while, I'm going to have them – but then they'll go away. I know I'm doing the right thing."

She rests her head on my shoulder, tilted away from me, and sighs. "I know. I know you do. I'm just scared, Will. Like you said, I don't want to get my hopes up. You don't know what it's like, with Mac – the other day, he almost set the house on fire." God, Carly, don't say it. We've talked about it before. There was nothing I could do about it, I wasn't home, and you weren't strong enough to undo his dreams. "If you had been home –"

"And I will be, if anything like that happens again. But it won't, sweetheart. Okay? Let's just do today, and take it one step at a time from here." Ever since we'd realized the strength of Mac's dreams, she'd hated for me to be gone: when I was there, she knew she was safe, she knew I'd feel it if Mac started to dream anything dangerous.

I remember the last time Mac dreamed of fire, the looks of first fear and then pity from the firemen. "I'm going to go see how —" Carly starts to say, and I kiss her before she can finish.

"No," I say. "You're not. Dance with me."

"What?"

I forget about everything except the things I'm never able to, and raise my hands. Music fills the air: no radio, no television, no orchestra, but music all the same, her favorite waltz, the one we danced to at the wedding. "Dance with me. Celebrate. It's all going to be over."

I rest my hand beneath her shoulder blade and wait for her to give in, because I know she will, if for no other reason than that she's my wife and she can see that I need her to. The music rises, and I daydream dampers up the stairs so MacKenzie doesn't wake up, and we dance.

Dreaming of fire is one of the easiest things to do, which is why it's so dangerous. Fire grows, fire feeds, and you only need to dream a spark to dream an inferno.

Left foot forward.

Fire is the leading factor in dream-related deaths. The first thing the Soporifics teach you, one of the few things I've tried teaching Mac, is how to control your fire dreams. Even the cadets who never make it through training leave with that much. We estimate that this training has accounted for a seventy percent reduction in dream-related deaths, since the formation of the Soporifics.

Right foot side.

We never knew Mac was going to be so strong, so difficult to control. Carly's dreams are normal, even weaker than normal, the giraffes and elephants about the limit of what she can come up with except under the most extreme conditions. Dreams are always strongest during times of emotional intensity – fights, sex, imminent jeopardy, grief.

Left foot close.

Somewhere out there, the machines are working, and it's all going to be okay. No more fire dreams. The layoffs in the fire departments will be immense, but the Soporifics will be out of work, too. I can feel it already, the intensity dimming, control becoming easier as the box starts to close.

Right foot forward.

I lean into Carly's hair and kiss her earlobe, whispering, "I love you, baby." She nods, still uncertain of me, still breaking my heart, still following my lead.

Left foot side.

You start with color because it gives you something to see. Start with color, and as soon as it turns into flame, forget it. As soon as you feel the heat, send the flame away.

Right foot close.

The last time Mac dreamed of fire was the last time. The firemen were scared of me because I came home straight from work, still in my Sop uniform. Fear melted into pity in front of the blazing glow of the house, as I watched the ambulance drive away, with the sirens off. When it's a DOA, they don't turn the siren on. Not even when it's two bodies. Fourteen years as a Sop and I hadn't known that.

The dance is over because the music is gone and there's no one left to dance with. My feet keep moving, left foot forward, right foot side, because I don't know what else to do with myself. The dance is over, because the box is closed and the dreams are gone and it's beyond my power to make my house stand anymore, it's beyond my power to keep my family with me while I finish my work, and all I can do is keep waltzing through ashes that have been cold for a decade.

Left foot close. Right foot forward.

The Rocking-Horse Winner

D.H. Lawrence

THERE WAS A WOMAN who was beautiful, who started with all the advantages, yet she had no luck. She married for love, and the love turned to dust. She had bonny children, yet she felt they had been thrust upon her, and she could not love them. They looked at her coldly, as if they were finding fault with her. And hurriedly she felt she must cover up some fault in herself. Yet what it was that she must cover up she never knew.

Nevertheless, when her children were present, she always felt the centre of her heart go hard. This troubled her, and in her manner she was all the more gentle and anxious for her children, as if she loved them very much. Only she herself knew that at the centre of her heart was a hard little place that could not feel love, no, not for anybody. Everybody else said of her: "She is such a good mother. She adores her children." Only she herself, and her children themselves, knew it was not so. They read it in each other's eyes.

There were a boy and two little girls. They lived in a pleasant house, with a garden, and they had discreet servants, and felt themselves superior to anyone in the neighbourhood.

Although they lived in style, they felt always an anxiety in the house. There was never enough money. The mother had a small income, and the father had a small income, but not nearly enough for the social position which they had to keep up. The father went into town to some office. But though he had good prospects, these prospects never materialised. There was always the grinding sense of the shortage of money, though the style was always kept up.

At last the mother said: "I will see if I can't make something." But she did not know where to begin. She racked her brains, and tried this thing and the other, but could not find anything successful. The failure made deep lines come into her face. Her children were growing up, they would have to go to school. There must be more money, there must be more money. The father, who was always very handsome and expensive in his tastes, seemed as if he never would be able to do anything worth doing. And the mother, who had a great belief in herself, did not succeed any better, and her tastes were just as expensive.

And so the house came to be haunted by the unspoken phrase: There must be more money! There must be more money! The children could hear it all the time though nobody said it aloud. They heard it at Christmas, when the expensive and splendid toys filled the nursery. Behind the shining modern rocking-horse, behind the smart doll's house, a voice would start whispering: "There must be more money! There must be more money!" And the children would stop playing, to listen for a moment. They would look into each other's eyes, to see if they had all heard. And each one saw in the eyes of the other two that they too had heard. "There must be more money! There must be more money!"

It came whispering from the springs of the still-swaying rocking-horse, and even the horse, bending his wooden, champing head, heard it. The big doll, sitting so pink and smirking in her new pram, could hear it quite plainly, and seemed to be smirking all the more self-consciously because of it. The foolish puppy, too, that took the place of the teddy-bear, he was looking so extraordinarily foolish for no other reason but that he heard the secret whisper all over the house: "There must be more money!"

Yet nobody ever said it aloud. The whisper was everywhere, and therefore no one spoke it. Just as no one ever says: "We are breathing!" in spite of the fact that breath is coming and going all the time.

"Mother," said the boy Paul one day, "why don't we keep a car of our own? Why do we always use uncle's, or else a taxi?"

"Because we're the poor members of the family," said the mother.

"But why are we, mother?"

"Well – I suppose," she said slowly and bitterly, "it's because your father has no luck."

The boy was silent for some time.

"Is luck money, mother?" he asked, rather timidly.

"No, Paul. Not quite. It's what causes you to have money."

"Oh!" said Paul vaguely. "I thought when Uncle Oscar said filthy lucker, it meant money."

"Filthy lucre does mean money," said the mother. "But it's lucre, not luck."

"Oh!" said the boy. "Then what is luck, mother?"

"It's what causes you to have money. If you're lucky you have money. That's why it's better to be born lucky than rich. If you're rich, you may lose your money. But if you're lucky, you will always get more money."

"Oh! Will you? And is father not lucky?"

"Very unlucky, I should say," she said bitterly.

The boy watched her with unsure eyes.

"Why?" he asked.

"I don't know. Nobody ever knows why one person is lucky and another unlucky."

"Don't they? Nobody at all? Does nobody know?"

"Perhaps God. But He never tells."

"He ought to, then. And are'nt you lucky either, mother?"

"I can't be, it I married an unlucky husband."

"But by yourself, aren't you?"

"I used to think I was, before I married. Now I think I am very unlucky indeed."

"Why?"

"Well – never mind! Perhaps I'm not really," she said.

The child looked at her to see if she meant it. But he saw, by the lines of her mouth, that she was only trying to hide something from him.

"Well, anyhow," he said stoutly, "I'm a lucky person."

"Why?" said his mother, with a sudden laugh.

He stared at her. He didn't even know why he had said it.

"God told me," he asserted, brazening it out.

"I hope He did, dear!", she said, again with a laugh, but rather bitter.

"He did, mother!"

"Excellent!" said the mother, using one of her husband's exclamations.

The boy saw she did not believe him; or rather, that she paid no attention to his assertion. This angered him somewhere, and made him want to compel her attention.

He went off by himself, vaguely, in a childish way, seeking for the clue to 'luck'. Absorbed, taking no heed of other people, he went about with a sort of stealth, seeking inwardly for luck. He wanted luck, he wanted it, he wanted it. When the two girls were playing dolls in the nursery, he would sit on his big rocking-horse, charging madly into space, with a frenzy that made the little girls peer at him uneasily. Wildly the horse careered, the waving dark hair of the boy tossed, his eyes had a strange glare in them. The little girls dared not speak to him.

When he had ridden to the end of his mad little journey, he climbed down and stood in front of his rocking-horse, staring fixedly into its lowered face. Its red mouth was slightly open, its big eye was wide and glassy-bright.

"Now!" he would silently command the snorting steed. "Now take me to where there is luck! Now take me!"

And he would slash the horse on the neck with the little whip he had asked Uncle Oscar for. He knew the horse could take him to where there was luck, if only he forced it. So he would mount again and start on his furious ride, hoping at last to get there.

"You'll break your horse, Paul!" said the nurse.

"He's always riding like that! I wish he'd leave off!" said his elder sister Joan.

But he only glared down on them in silence. Nurse gave him up. She could make nothing of him. Anyhow, he was growing beyond her.

One day his mother and his Uncle Oscar came in when he was on one of his furious rides. He did not speak to them.

"Hallo, you young jockey! Riding a winner?" said his uncle.

"Aren't you growing too big for a rocking-horse? You're not a very little boy any longer, you know," said his mother.

But Paul only gave a blue glare from his big, rather close-set eyes. He would speak to nobody when he was in full tilt. His mother watched him with an anxious expression on her face.

At last he suddenly stopped forcing his horse into the mechanical gallop and slid down.

"Well, I got there!" he announced fiercely, his blue eyes still flaring, and his sturdy long legs straddling apart.

"Where did you get to?" asked his mother.

"Where I wanted to go," he flared back at her.

"That's right, son!" said Uncle Oscar. "Don't you stop till you get there. What's the horse's name?"

"He doesn't have a name," said the boy.

"Get's on without all right?" asked the uncle.

"Well, he has different names. He was called Sansovino last week."

"Sansovino, eh? Won the Ascot. How did you know this name?"

"He always talks about horse-races with Bassett," said Joan.

The uncle was delighted to find that his small nephew was posted with all the racing news. Bassett, the young gardener, who had been wounded in the left foot in the war and had got his present job through Oscar Cresswell, whose batman he had been, was a perfect blade of the 'turf'. He lived in the racing events, and the small boy lived with him.

Oscar Cresswell got it all from Bassett.

"Master Paul comes and asks me, so I can't do more than tell him, sir," said Bassett, his face terribly serious, as if he were speaking of religious matters.

"And does he ever put anything on a horse he fancies?"

"Well – I don't want to give him away – he's a young sport, a fine sport, sir. Would you mind asking him himself? He sort of takes a pleasure in it, and perhaps he'd feel I was giving him away, sir, if you don't mind.

Bassett was serious as a church.

The uncle went back to his nephew and took him off for a ride in the car.

"Say, Paul, old man, do you ever put anything on a horse?" the uncle asked.

The boy watched the handsome man closely.

"Why, do you think I oughtn't to?" he parried.

"Not a bit of it! I thought perhaps you might give me a tip for the Lincoln."

The car sped on into the country, going down to Uncle Oscar's place in Hampshire.

"Honour bright?" said the nephew.

"Honour bright, son!" said the uncle.

"Well, then, Daffodil."

"Daffodil! I doubt it, sonny. What about Mirza?"

"I only know the winner," said the boy. "That's Daffodil."

"Daffodil, eh?"

There was a pause. Daffodil was an obscure horse comparatively.

"Uncle!"

"Yes, son?"

"You won't let it go any further, will you? I promised Bassett."

"Bassett be damned, old man! What's he got to do with it?"

"We're partners. We've been partners from the first. Uncle, he lent me my first five shillings, which I lost. I promised him, honour bright, it was only between me and him; only you gave me that ten-shilling note I started winning with, so I thought you were lucky. You won't let it go any further, will you?"

The boy gazed at his uncle from those big, hot, blue eyes, set rather close together. The uncle stirred and laughed uneasily.

"Right you are, son! I'll keep your tip private. How much are you putting on him?"

"All except twenty pounds," said the boy. "I keep that in reserve."

The uncle thought it a good joke.

"You keep twenty pounds in reserve, do you, you young romancer? What are you betting, then?"

"I'm betting three hundred," said the boy gravely. "But it's between you and me, Uncle Oscar! Honour bright?"

"It's between you and me all right, you young Nat Gould," he said, laughing. "But where's your three hundred?"

"Bassett keeps it for me. We're partners."

"You are, are you! And what is Bassett putting on Daffodil?"

"He won't go quite as high as I do, I expect. Perhaps he'll go a hundred and fifty."

"What, pennies?" laughed the uncle.

"Pounds," said the child, with a surprised look at his uncle. "Bassett keeps a bigger reserve than I do."

Between wonder and amusement Uncle Oscar was silent. He pursued the matter no further, but he determined to take his nephew with him to the Lincoln races.

"Now, son," he said, "I'm putting twenty on Mirza, and I'll put five on for you on any horse you fancy. What's your pick?"

"Daffodil, uncle."

"No, not the fiver on Daffodil!"

"I should if it was my own fiver," said the child.

"Good! Good! Right you are! A fiver for me and a fiver for you on Daffodil."

The child had never been to a race-meeting before, and his eyes were blue fire. He pursed his mouth tight and watched. A Frenchman just in front had put his money on Lancelot. Wild with excitement, he flayed his arms up and down, yelling "Lancelot!, Lancelot!" in his French accent.

Daffodil came in first, Lancelot second, Mirza third. The child, flushed and with eyes blazing, was curiously serene. His uncle brought him four five-pound notes, four to one.

"What am I to do with these?" he cried, waving them before the boys eyes.

"I suppose we'll talk to Bassett," said the boy. "I expect I have fifteen hundred now; and twenty in reserve; and this twenty."

His uncle studied him for some moments.

"Look here, son!" he said. "You're not serious about Bassett and that fifteen hundred, are you?"

"Yes, I am. But it's between you and me, uncle. Honour bright?"

"Honour bright all right, son! But I must talk to Bassett."

"If you'd like to be a partner, uncle, with Bassett and me, we could all be partners. Only, you'd have to promise, honour bright, uncle, not to let it go beyond us three. Bassett and I are lucky, and you must be lucky, because it was your ten shillings I started winning with …"

Uncle Oscar took both Bassett and Paul into Richmond Park for an afternoon, and there they talked.

"It's like this, you see, sir," Bassett said. "Master Paul would get me talking about racing events, spinning yarns, you know, sir. And he was always keen on knowing if I'd made or if I'd lost. It's about a year since, now, that I put five shillings on Blush of Dawn for him: and we lost. Then the luck turned, with that ten shillings he had from you: that we put on Singhalese. And since that time, it's been pretty steady, all things considering. What do you say, Master Paul?"

"We're all right when we're sure," said Paul. "It's when we're not quite sure that we go down."

"Oh, but we're careful then," said Bassett.

"But when are you sure?" smiled Uncle Oscar.

"It's Master Paul, sir," said Bassett in a secret, religious voice. "It's as if he had it from heaven. Like Daffodil, now, for the Lincoln. That was as sure as eggs."

"Did you put anything on Daffodil?" asked Oscar Cresswell.

"Yes, sir, I made my bit."

"And my nephew?"

Bassett was obstinately silent, looking at Paul.

"I made twelve hundred, didn't I, Bassett? I told uncle I was putting three hundred on Daffodil."

"That's right," said Bassett, nodding.

"But where's the money?" asked the uncle.

"I keep it safe locked up, sir. Master Paul he can have it any minute he likes to ask for it."

"What, fifteen hundred pounds?"

"And twenty! And forty, that is, with the twenty he made on the course."

"It's amazing!" said the uncle.

"If Master Paul offers you to be partners, sir, I would, if I were you: if you'll excuse me," said Bassett.

Oscar Cresswell thought about it.

"I'll see the money," he said.

They drove home again, and, sure enough, Bassett came round to the garden-house with fifteen hundred pounds in notes. The twenty pounds reserve was left with Joe Glee, in the Turf Commission deposit.

"You see, it's all right, uncle, when I'm sure! Then we go strong, for all we're worth, don't we, Bassett?"

"We do that, Master Paul."

"And when are you sure?" said the uncle, laughing.

"Oh, well, sometimes I'm absolutely sure, like about Daffodil," said the boy; "and sometimes I have an idea; and sometimes I haven't even an idea, have I, Bassett? Then we're careful, because we mostly go down."

"You do, do you! And when you're sure, like about Daffodil, what makes you sure, sonny?"

"Oh, well, I don't know," said the boy uneasily. "I'm sure, you know, uncle; that's all."

"It's as if he had it from heaven, sir," Bassett reiterated.

"I should say so!" said the uncle.

But he became a partner. And when the Leger was coming on Paul was 'sure' about Lively Spark, which was a quite inconsiderable horse. The boy insisted on putting a thousand on the horse, Bassett went for five hundred, and Oscar Cresswell two hundred. Lively Spark came in first, and the betting had been ten to one against him. Paul had made ten thousand.

"You see," he said. "I was absolutely sure of him."

Even Oscar Cresswell had cleared two thousand.

"Look here, son," he said, "this sort of thing makes me nervous."

"It needn't, uncle! Perhaps I shan't be sure again for a long time."

"But what are you going to do with your money?" asked the uncle.

"Of course," said the boy, "I started it for mother. She said she had no luck, because father is unlucky, so I thought if I was lucky, it might stop whispering."

"What might stop whispering?"

"Our house. I hate our house for whispering."

"What does it whisper?"

"Why – why" – the boy fidgeted – "why, I don't know. But it's always short of money, you know, uncle."

"I know it, son, I know it."

"You know people send mother writs, don't you, uncle?"

"I'm afraid I do," said the uncle.

"And then the house whispers, like people laughing at you behind your back. It's awful, that is! I thought if I was lucky –"

"You might stop it," added the uncle.

The boy watched him with big blue eyes, that had an uncanny cold fire in them, and he said never a word.

"Well, then!" said the uncle. "What are we doing?"

"I shouldn't like mother to know I was lucky," said the boy.

"Why not, son?"

"She'd stop me."

"I don't think she would."

"Oh!" – and the boy writhed in an odd way – "I don't want her to know, uncle."

"All right, son! We'll manage it without her knowing."

They managed it very easily. Paul, at the other's suggestion, handed over five thousand pounds to his uncle, who deposited it with the family lawyer, who was then to inform Paul's mother that a relative had put five thousand pounds into his hands, which sum was to be paid out a thousand pounds at a time, on the mother's birthday, for the next five years.

"So she'll have a birthday present of a thousand pounds for five successive years," said Uncle Oscar. "I hope it won't make it all the harder for her later."

Paul's mother had her birthday in November. The house had been 'whispering' worse than ever lately, and, even in spite of his luck, Paul could not bear up against it. He was very anxious to see the effect of the birthday letter, telling his mother about the thousand pounds.

When there were no visitors, Paul now took his meals with his parents, as he was beyond the nursery control. His mother went into town nearly every day. She had discovered that she had an odd knack of sketching furs and dress materials, so she worked secretly in the studio of a friend who was the chief 'artist' for the leading drapers. She drew the figures of ladies in furs and ladies in silk and sequins for the newspaper advertisements. This young woman artist earned several thousand pounds a year, but Paul's mother only made several hundreds, and she was again dissatisfied. She so wanted to be first in something, and she did not succeed, even in making sketches for drapery advertisements.

She was down to breakfast on the morning of her birthday. Paul watched her face as she read her letters. He knew the lawyer's letter. As his mother read it, her face hardened and became more expressionless. Then a cold, determined look came on her mouth. She hid the letter under the pile of others, and said not a word about it.

"Didn't you have anything nice in the post for your birthday, mother?" said Paul.

"Quite moderately nice," she said, her voice cold and hard and absent.

She went away to town without saying more.

But in the afternoon Uncle Oscar appeared. He said Paul's mother had had a long interview with the lawyer, asking if the whole five thousand could not be advanced at once, as she was in debt.

"What do you think, uncle?" said the boy.

"I leave it to you, son."

"Oh, let her have it, then! We can get some more with the other," said the boy.

"A bird in the hand is worth two in the bush, laddie!" said Uncle Oscar.

"But I'm sure to know for the Grand National; or the Lincolnshire; or else the Derby. I'm sure to know for one of them," said Paul.

So Uncle Oscar signed the agreement, and Paul's mother touched the whole five thousand. Then something very curious happened. The voices in the house suddenly went mad, like a chorus of frogs on a spring evening. There were certain new furnishings, and Paul had a tutor. He was really going to Eton, his father's school, in the following autumn. There were flowers in the winter, and a blossoming of the luxury Paul's mother had been used to.

And yet the voices in the house, behind the sprays of mimosa and almond-blossom, and from under the piles of iridescent cushions, simply trilled and screamed in a sort of ecstasy: "There must be more money! Oh-h-h; there must be more money. Oh, now, now-w! Now-w-w – there must be more money! – More than ever! More than ever!"

It frightened Paul terribly. He studied away at his Latin and Greek with his tutor. But his intense hours were spent with Bassett. The Grand National had gone by: he had not 'known', and had lost a hundred pounds. Summer was at hand. He was in agony for the Lincoln. But even for the Lincoln he didn't 'know', and he lost fifty pounds. He became wild-eyed and strange, as if something were going to explode in him.

"Let it alone, son! Don't you bother about it!" urged Uncle Oscar. But it was as if the boy couldn't really hear what his uncle was saying.

"I've got to know for the Derby! I've got to know for the Derby!" the child reiterated, his big blue eyes blazing with a sort of madness.

His mother noticed how overwrought he was.

"You'd better go to the seaside. Wouldn't you like to go now to the seaside, instead of waiting? I think you'd better," she said, looking down at him anxiously, her heart curiously heavy because of him.

But the child lifted his uncanny blue eyes.

"I couldn't possibly go before the Derby, mother!" he said. "I couldn't possibly!"

"Why not?" she said, her voice becoming heavy when she was opposed. "Why not? You can still go from the seaside to see the Derby with your Uncle Oscar, if that's what you wish. No need for you to wait here. Besides, I think you care too much about these races. It's a bad sign. My family has been a gambling family, and you won't know till you grow up how much damage it has done. But it has done damage. I shall have to send Bassett away, and ask Uncle Oscar not to talk racing to you, unless you promise to be reasonable about it: go away to the seaside and forget it. You're all nerves!"

"I'll do what you like, mother, so long as you don't send me away till after the Derby," the boy said.

"Send you away from where? Just from this house?"

"Yes," he said, gazing at her.

"Why, you curious child, what makes you care about this house so much, suddenly? I never knew you loved it."

He gazed at her without speaking. He had a secret within a secret, something he had not divulged, even to Bassett or to his Uncle Oscar.

But his mother, after standing undecided and a little bit sullen for some moments, said: "Very well, then! Don't go to the seaside till after the Derby, if you don't wish it. But promise me you won't think so much about horse-racing and events as you call them!"

"Oh no," said the boy casually. "I won't think much about them, mother. You needn't worry. I wouldn't worry, mother, if I were you."

"If you were me and I were you," said his mother, "I wonder what we should do!"

"But you know you needn't worry, mother, don't you?" the boy repeated.

"I should be awfully glad to know it," she said wearily.

"Oh, well, you can, you know. I mean, you ought to know you needn't worry," he insisted.

"Ought I? Then I'll see about it," she said.

Paul's secret of secrets was his wooden horse, that which had no name. Since he was emancipated from a nurse and a nursery-governess, he had had his rocking-horse removed to his own bedroom at the top of the house.

"Surely you're too big for a rocking-horse!" his mother had remonstrated.

"Well, you see, mother, till I can have a real horse, I like to have some sort of animal about," had been his quaint answer.

"Do you feel he keeps you company?" she laughed.

"Oh yes! He's very good, he always keeps me company, when I'm there," said Paul.

So the horse, rather shabby, stood in an arrested prance in the boy's bedroom.

The Derby was drawing near, and the boy grew more and more tense. He hardly heard what was spoken to him, he was very frail, and his eyes were really uncanny. His mother had sudden strange seizures of uneasiness about him. Sometimes, for half an hour, she would feel a sudden anxiety about him that was almost anguish. She wanted to rush to him at once, and know he was safe.

Two nights before the Derby, she was at a big party in town, when one of her rushes of anxiety about her boy, her first-born, gripped her heart till she could hardly speak. She fought with the feeling, might and main, for she believed in common sense. But it was too strong. She had to leave the dance and go downstairs to telephone to the country. The children's nursery-governess was terribly surprised and startled at being rung up in the night.

"Are the children all right, Miss Wilmot?"

"Oh yes, they are quite all right."

"Master Paul? Is he all right?"

"He went to bed as right as a trivet. Shall I run up and look at him?"

"No," said Paul's mother reluctantly. "No! Don't trouble. It's all right. Don't sit up. We shall be home fairly soon." She did not want her son's privacy intruded upon.

"Very good," said the governess.

It was about one o'clock when Paul's mother and father drove up to their house. All was still. Paul's mother went to her room and slipped off her white fur cloak. She had told her maid not to wait up for her. She heard her husband downstairs, mixing a whisky and soda.

And then, because of the strange anxiety at her heart, she stole upstairs to her son's room. Noiselessly she went along the upper corridor. Was there a faint noise? What was it?

She stood, with arrested muscles, outside his door, listening. There was a strange, heavy, and yet not loud noise. Her heart stood still. It was a soundless noise, yet rushing and powerful. Something huge, in violent, hushed motion. What was it? What in God's name was it? She ought to know. She felt that she knew the noise. She knew what it was.

Yet she could not place it. She couldn't say what it was. And on and on it went, like a madness.

Softly, frozen with anxiety and fear, she turned the door-handle.

The room was dark. Yet in the space near the window, she heard and saw something plunging to and fro. She gazed in fear and amazement.

Then suddenly she switched on the light, and saw her son, in his green pyjamas, madly surging on the rocking-horse. The blaze of light suddenly lit him up, as he urged the wooden horse, and lit her up, as she stood, blonde, in her dress of pale green and crystal, in the doorway.

"Paul!" she cried. "Whatever are you doing?"

"It's Malabar!" he screamed in a powerful, strange voice. "It's Malabar!"

His eyes blazed at her for one strange and senseless second, as he ceased urging his wooden horse. Then he fell with a crash to the ground, and she, all her tormented motherhood flooding upon her, rushed to gather him up.

But he was unconscious, and unconscious he remained, with some brain-fever. He talked and tossed, and his mother sat stonily by his side.

"Malabar! It's Malabar! Bassett, Bassett, I know! It's Malabar!"

So the child cried, trying to get up and urge the rocking-horse that gave him his inspiration.

"What does he mean by Malabar?" asked the heart-frozen mother.

"I don't know," said the father stonily.

"What does he mean by Malabar?" she asked her brother Oscar.

"It's one of the horses running for the Derby," was the answer.

And, in spite of himself, Oscar Cresswell spoke to Bassett, and himself put a thousand on Malabar: at fourteen to one.

The third day of the illness was critical: they were waiting for a change. The boy, with his rather long, curly hair, was tossing ceaselessly on the pillow. He neither slept nor regained consciousness, and his eyes were like blue stones. His mother sat, feeling her heart had gone, turned actually into a stone.

In the evening Oscar Cresswell did not come, but Bassett sent a message, saying could he come up for one moment, just one moment? Paul's mother was very angry at the intrusion, but on second thoughts she agreed. The boy was the same. Perhaps Bassett might bring him to consciousness.

The gardener, a shortish fellow with a little brown moustache and sharp little brown eyes, tiptoed into the room, touched his imaginary cap to Paul's mother, and stole to the bedside, staring with glittering, smallish eyes at the tossing, dying child.

"Master Paul!" he whispered. "Master Paul! Malabar came in first all right, a clean win. I did as you told me. You've made over seventy thousand pounds, you have; you've got over eighty thousand. Malabar came in all right, Master Paul."

"Malabar! Malabar! Did I say Malabar, mother? Did I say Malabar? Do you think I'm lucky, mother? I knew Malabar, didn't I? Over eighty thousand pounds! I call that lucky, don't you, mother? Over eighty thousand pounds! I knew, didn't I know I knew? Malabar came in all right. If I ride my horse till I'm sure, then I tell you, Bassett, you can go as high as you like. Did you go for all you were worth, Bassett?"

"I went a thousand on it, Master Paul."

"I never told you, mother, that if I can ride my horse, and get there, then I'm absolutely sure – oh, absolutely! Mother, did I ever tell you? I am lucky!"

"No, you never did," said his mother.

But the boy died in the night.

And even as he lay dead, his mother heard her brother's voice saying to her, "My God, Hester, you're eighty-odd thousand to the good, and a poor devil of a son to the bad. But, poor devil, poor devil, he's best gone out of a life where he rides his rocking-horse to find a winner."

The Magnificat of Devils

James Lecky

THREE DAYS HAVE PASSED, the longest and most fear-filled I have ever known. I cannot eat, I cannot sleep; the slightest creak upon the stairway causes me to cry out and clutch the battered bible against my chest.

The door of the room is locked and barred, the windows shuttered, even though I know the gesture is futile; she has journeyed too far for such things to stand in her way.

I was a fool to accept Stahl's invitation, yet the request seemed a simple one and the money he promised too tempting.

"Sing for me, Vitelli,"

I should have refused him, kept my pride – and my soul – intact. But pride and hunger are never good bedfellows and I saw in his request a chance to recapture old glories I had thought long since lost.

I have exhausted all my prayers.

There is nothing more to be done.

Except wait.

***

The singer stood in the centre of the room, peering into the darkness beyond a row of guttering candles.

Dancing light accentuated his gaunt features, throwing shadows into the hollows of his cheeks, the dark pits of his eyes. Even a liberal application of powder and rouge could not fully disguise the pallor of his skin, like old wax mixed with ash. His limbs were long and gangling, his chest broad. The clothes he wore – a red velvet coat and grey leather breeches – may have been magnificent once, but now were as worn as their owner.

A soft sound broke the silence, a door opening and closing, followed by hesitant footsteps. The crooked shadow of an old man cast itself upon the floor.

"You are as punctual as ever, Vitelli."

The singer nodded and then said:

"Tonight is the last night. You will pay me as promised?"

"When the recital is over." The old man sat, just outside the yellow circle of light, his face a blurred oval in the gloom.

A long silence, broken only by Vitelli's nervous shuffling and the ragged breathing of the old man. Bruno Stahl was dying, eaten away by a malignant tumour, his wealth unable to save him, and Vitelli could smell the corruption that rose from him, a debased perfume that drifted across the room.

At last, a distant clock boomed midnight, the sound muffled but audible.

With a great effort, Stahl stood and crossed into the circle of candlelight.

The sight of him was a shock. In the past five days, since Vitelli had begun his midnight recitals, Stahl had visibly worsened. His body, hidden beneath a voluminous black suit, was wasted, his face skeletal – yellow skin stretched across his skull – eyes burning with a feverish intensity, and each time he drew a breath the air rattled in his lungs.

He held out a yellowed manuscript, the fingers that clutched it twiglike, the nails black and chipped.

"The final aria," he said. "You will sing it exactly – no deviation."

Vitelli nodded and took the manuscript. The paper felt rough, like parchment, and a quick glance at the spider-like notes, in faded brown ink that seemed more etched than written – told him that this final piece would be more complex, more unfathomable, than any of the others.

The music that Stahl had insisted upon was unlike any he had seen or heard before – a random collection of notes and rhythms that, to him, seemed without form or structure. He had sang as instructed for the past five nights, unsure of what purpose the cacophonous music served but, despite himself, drawn by inches into its embrace. It was though the music had escaped from some higher sphere, the outpourings of eternal harmony and discordance, the voices of angels and devils, the magnificat of saints and demons.

It was the work of a genius. Or a madman.

***

"You are Gregori Vitelli, the castrati."

Vitelli did not look up from his meal. It was the first hot food he had eaten in days.

"And if I am, what concern is that of yours?"

"My master wishes to employ you."

"Then your master is an idiot."

The clink of coins against wood was lost in the general noise of the taverna. No one paid attention to it except Gregori Vitelli.

"My master is a rich man, Signor Vitelli."

Vitelli reached across the table and gathered the coins with an elegant sweep.

"What does your master wish?"

"That you sing for him. Come to this address tonight." A scrap of paper was placed on the table before him. "You will be expected."

Vitelli did not look up until the man had gone. He quickly counted the money he had been given – four silver tari. Not a fortune by any means but more than enough to ensure his appearance.

Once, it would have been a fraction of his fee. In the days when Gregori Vitelli had sung before the crowned heads of Europe, in the grand opera houses of Milan, Paris and Vienna, when strong men wept and women swooned as he sang.

But what was he now? A relic of a bygone age. A freak whose manhood had been sacrificed to preserve his beautiful, golden voice. A child who had never been allowed to grow up, his every wish pandered to as his fame grew, and who had been cast aside by a fickle public to wallow in obscurity and past glories.

Yes, four silver tari would be enough.

***

Stahl arranged the manuscript on a stand in front of the castrati, then turned and made his pain-wracked way back to his seat.

"I have waited a long time for this moment.," he said. "I have suffered much to reach it – more than I thought possible." He laughed softly, the sound a mixture of bubbling blood and mucus from somewhere in his depleted torso. "But everything will have been worthwhile – all the suffering and the pain – if she comes to me tonight."

Vitelli had no idea what Stahl meant, or even if the words had even been directed at him – the ranting of a man driven half insane by pain and the knowledge of his own impending death.

"Sing!" Stahl commanded, his voice surprisingly strong. "She will hear you and come."

"Who will come?" Some patron or other, he supposed, one as eccentric as the dying composer himself.

"Sing!" Stahl barked again.

Hesitantly, Vitelli drew a deep breath, sounding out the first notes of the strange composition in his mind.

Then he began to sing.

The melody was tangled but sweet, soft and slow. He could see Stahl, leaning forwards in his chair and listening intently, but it seemed that he was searching for something other than the music itself, something within it that went beyond mere sound.

The melody grew harsh and wild, disturbed and disturbing, slowed to a lament then quickened again to rush like flames.

The music changed so quickly and often that Vitelli could barely keep pace with it, each note snatched from his throat just in time and he hovered on the edge of panic, driven by, as much as driving, the arrangement.

"Exquisite," Stahl breathed, his voice low but still audible above the wild, untamed aria. "I knew I was right to use the castrati – what range, what mastery."

Vitelli's voice soared, conjuring alien sounds that no human voice had uttered before. The notes rebounded from the high ceiling, tangling into each other. The candlelight danced in time to the exotic rhythms, light forming itself into new and bizarre patterns.

And there were pictures in the fractured harmonies.

They were grainy and ill-formed at first but gaining substance with each passing beat. Stahl could see a twisted landscape – its geometry all wrong yet somehow natural – and the malformed creatures that wandered across its surface. He could hear their cries in the music: part of it yet detached at the same time.

And there, white robes billowing in an unfelt breeze, a beautiful woman making her way across the undulating hills, coming closer and closer in response to the music.

Her eyes were closed but her footsteps were assured, drawn by the melody from her world to this world.

"She comes!" Stahl shrieked. "She comes!"

Vitelli's voice soared He no longer needed to look at the manuscript – the music possessed him, filled his soul with a desire that drove him on even though every nerve in his body screamed for him to stop. He no longer sang the melody, the melody sang him, forcing each new cadence and resonance into the room. And into the grotesque world beyond.

The woman drew closer now, preparing to step into the room. Her eyes opened and he could see the void in them – black, impenetrable eyes that promised nothing but pain and despair.

"Vanith," Stahl whispered, the name both a blessing and a curse.

Vitelli screamed with every ounce of his fading strength and will. Screamed until his throat was raw and blood spewed from his lips.

But the song continued and each note brought fresh pain to his tortured larynx. Soaring and plummeting, harmony and discordance mingled together until he could not tell one from the other – then a crescendo that ended it with a single note, clear and perfect.

"Who has brought me to this place?" she said, her voice husky – as though the words emerged through a mouthful of wormwood and grave dirt.

"I brought you here," Stahl said. "You are mine to command."

She turned and looked at him, the movement smooth and sinuous as if there were no bones in her body.

"I know you Bruno Stahl, you were pledged to me long ago."

Stahl rose and took a step forward, his palms upraised to her. "Heal me," he said. "Take the corruption from my bones. Give me the eternal life which has been promised."

Vitelli stood there, spellbound, unable to move or to think, able only to watch her dark eyes as they twinkled with the knowledge of worlds beyond worlds.

Then she laughed, a high hard sound that grated against the soft matter of his soul.

"Eternal life, Stahl, is that what you hoped I would bring?" Vanith said. "I bring you nothing, old fool, you did not call me. The summoning was not yours."

"The manuscript was mine. The music was mine. The power was mine."

Vanith pointed a black-nailed finger towards Vitelli.

"His is the power. His is the summoning." She glided towards him, her smile glittering like steel. "Come with me," she said. "Let me show you delights the like of which your soul never dreamed and your flesh could not withstand. Let me show you the kiss of a razor and the passion of fire, the beauty of pain and the righteousness of suffering. Let me bring you an eternity of pain."

Vitelli took a step forward and reached for her outstretched hand – the void calling to him, to that blackest part of his soul.

And then the spell was broken, shattered by Stahl's outraged screech.

"No – the power is mine!" He reached out with clawed hands and she swatted him to one side with a casual gesture, crushing his ribs and spine with a sound like a gunshot, wrapping his disease-riddled flesh with cold white fire.

His senses returned and Vitelli ran, out through the door and into the fog-wreathed streets. He could feel the chill of the flames on his back and when he turned to look the house had already been engulfed in white flames that burned without heat or smoke, sending thin tendrils into the night sky.

And somewhere, the other-worldly laughter of the creature named Vanith.

***

She will find me. I have no doubt of that. She will find me and take me. The music brought her – a melody so ancient and powerful that it crossed the divide between the living world and the world beyond. Poor Stahl, the fool thought that he could command her. But no one commands Hell – Hell commands itself.

I am without hope, without salvation. Damned for what I have done and what I wish to do.

I hear her footsteps outside, soft as a whisper. I hear her breath my name and the words are filled with the promise of suffering and delight, of purity and corruption.

And when she next offers me her hand, I will take it.

The Dunwich Horror

H.P. Lovecraft

CHAPTER I

WHEN a traveler in north central Massachusetts takes the wrong fork at the junction of Aylesbury pike just beyond Dean's Corners he comes upon a lonely and curious country.

The ground gets higher, and the brier-bordered stone walls press closer and closer against the ruts of the dusty, curving road. The trees of the frequent forest belts seem too large, and the wild weeds, brambles and grasses attain a luxuriance not often found in settled regions. At the same time the planted fields appear singularly few and barren; while the sparsely scattered houses wear a surprisingly uniform aspect of age, squalor, and dilapidation.

Without knowing why, one hesitates to ask directions from the gnarled solitary figures spied now and then on crumbling doorsteps or on the sloping, rock-strewn meadows. Those figures are so silent and furtive that one feels somehow confronted by forbidden things, with which it would be better to have nothing to do. When a rise in the road brings the mountains in view above the deep woods, the feeling of strange uneasiness is increased. The summits are too rounded and symmetrical to give a sense of comfort and naturalness, and sometimes the sky silhouettes with especial clearness the queer circles of tall stone pillars with which most of them are crowned.

Gorges and ravines of problematical depth intersect the way, and the crude wooden bridges always seem of dubious safety. When the road dips again there are stretches of marshland that one instinctively dislikes, and indeed almost fears at evening when unseen whippoorwills chatter and the fireflies come out in abnormal profusion to dance to the raucous, creepily insistent rhythms of stridently piping bull-frogs. The thin, shining line of the Miskatonic's upper reaches has an oddly serpent-like suggestion as it winds close to the feet of the domed hills among which it rises.

As the hills draw nearer, one heeds their wooded sides more than their stone-crowned tops. Those sides loom up so darkly and precipitously that one wishes they would keep their distance, but there is no road by which to escape them. Across a covered bridge one sees a small village huddled between the stream and the vertical slope of Round Mountain, and wonders at the cluster of rotting gambrel roofs bespeaking an earlier architectural period than that of the neighboring region. It is not reassuring to see, on a closer glance, that most of the houses are deserted and falling to ruin, and that the broken-steepled church now harbors the one slovenly mercantile establishment of the hamlet. One dreads to trust the tenebrous tunnel of the bridge, yet there is no way to avoid it. Once across, it is hard to prevent the impression of a faint, malign odor about the village street, as of the massed mould and decay of centuries. It is always a relief to get clear of the place, and to follow the narrow road around the base of the hills and across the level country beyond till it rejoins the Aylesbury pike. Afterwards one sometimes learns that one has been through Dunwich.

Outsiders visit Dunwich as seldom as possible, and since a certain season of horror all the signboards pointing towards it have been taken down. The scenery, judged by an ordinary aesthetic canon, is more than commonly beautiful; yet there is no influx of artists or summer tourists. Two centuries ago, when talk of witch-blood, Satan-worship, and strange forest presences was not laughed at, it was the custom to give reasons for avoiding the locality. In our sensible age – since the Dunwich horror of 1928 was hushed up by those who had the town's and the world's welfare at heart – people shun it without knowing exactly why. Perhaps one reason – though it cannot apply to uninformed strangers – is that the natives are now repellently decadent, having gone far along that path of retrogression so common in many New England backwaters. They have come to form a race by themselves, with the well-defined mental and physical stigmata of degeneracy and inbreeding. The average of their intelligence is woefully low, whilst their annals reek of overt viciousness and of half-hidden murders, incests, and deeds of almost unnameable violence and perversity. The old gentry, representing the two or three armigerous families which came from Salem in 1692, have kept somewhat above the general level of decay; though many branches are sunk into the sordid populace so deeply that only their names remain as a key to the origin they disgrace. Some of the Whateleys and Bishops still send their eldest sons to Harvard and Miskatonic, though those sons seldom return to the mouldering gambrel roofs under which they and their ancestors were born.

No one, even those who have the facts concerning the recent horror, can say just what is the matter with Dunwich; though old legends speak of unhallowed rites and conclaves of the Indians, amidst which they called forbidden shapes of shadow out of the great rounded hills, and made wild orgiastic prayers that were answered by loud crackings and rumblings from the ground below. In 1747 the Reverend Abijah Hoadley, newly come to the Congregational Church at Dunwich Village, preached a memorable sermon on the close presence of Satan and his imps; in which he said:

> "It must be allow'd, that these Blasphemies of an infernall Train of Daemons are Matters of too common Knowledge to be deny'd; the cursed Voices of Azazel and Buzrael, of Beelzebub and Belial, being heard now from under Ground by above a Score of credible Witnesses now living. I myself did not more than a Fortnight ago catch a very plain Discourse of evill Powers in the Hill behind my House; wherein there were a Rattling and Rolling, Groaning, Screeching, and Hissing, such as no Things of this Earth could raise up, and which must needs have come from those Caves that only black Magick can discover, and only the Divell unlock."

Mr. Hoadley disappeared soon after delivering this sermon, but the text, printed in Springfield, is still extant. Noises in the hills continued to be reported from year to year, and still form a puzzle to geologists and physiographers.

Other traditions tell of foul odors near the hill-crowning circles of stone pillars, and of rushing airy presences to be heard faintly at certain hours from stated points at the bottom of the great ravines; while still others try to explain the Devil's Hop Yard – a bleak, blasted hillside where no tree, shrub, or grass-blade will grow. Then, too, the natives are mortally afraid of the numerous whippoorwills which grow vocal on warm nights. It is vowed that the birds are psychopomps lying in wait for the souls of the dying, and that they time their eerie cries in unison with the sufferer's struggling breath. If they can catch the fleeing soul when it leaves the body, they instantly flutter away chittering in daemoniac laughter; but if they fail, they subside gradually into a disappointed silence.

These tales, of course, are obsolete and ridiculous; because they come down from very old times. Dunwich is indeed ridiculously old – older by far than any of the communities within thirty miles of it. South of the village one may still spy the cellar walls and chimney of the ancient Bishop house, which was built before 1700; whilst the ruins of the mill at the falls, built in 1806, form the most modern piece of architecture to be seen. Industry did not flourish here, and the nineteenth-century factory movement proved short-lived. Oldest of all are the great rings of rough-hewn stone columns on the hilltops, but these are more generally attributed to the Indians than to the settlers. Deposits of skulls and bones, found within these circles and around the sizeable table-like rock on Sentinel Hill, sustain the popular belief that such spots were once the burial-places of the Pocumtucks; even though many ethnologists, disregarding the absurd improbability of such a theory, persist in believing the remains Caucasian.

CHAPTER II

IT WAS IN the township of Dunwich, in a large and partly inhabited farmhouse set against a hillside four miles from the village and a mile and a half from any other dwelling, that Wilbur Whateley was born at 5 a.m. on Sunday, the second of February, 1913. This date was recalled because it was Candlemas, which people in Dunwich curiously observe under another name; and because the noises in the hills had sounded, and all the dogs of the countryside had barked persistently, throughout the night before. Less worthy of notice was the fact that the mother was one of the decadent Whateleys, a somewhat deformed, unattractive albino woman of thirty-five, living with an aged and half-insane father about whom the most frightful tales of wizardry had been whispered in his youth. Lavinia Whateley had no known husband, but according to the custom of the region made no attempt to disavow the child; concerning the other side of whose ancestry the country folk might – and did – speculate as widely as they chose. On the contrary, she seemed strangely proud of the dark, goatish-looking infant who formed such a contrast to her own sickly and pink-eyed albinism, and was heard to mutter many curious prophecies about its unusual powers and tremendous future.

Lavinia was one who would be apt to mutter such things, for she was a lone creature given to wandering amidst thunderstorms in the hills and trying to read the great odorous books which her father had inherited through two centuries of Whateleys, and which were fast falling to pieces with age and wormholes. She had never been to school, but was filled with disjointed scraps of ancient lore that Old Whateley had taught her. The remote farmhouse had always been feared because of Old Whateley's reputation for black magic, and the unexplained death by violence of Mrs Whateley when Lavinia was twelve years old had not helped to make the place popular. Isolated among strange influences, Lavinia was fond of wild and grandiose day-dreams and singular occupations; nor was her leisure much taken up by household cares in a home from which all standards of order and cleanliness had long since disappeared.

There was a hideous screaming which echoed above even the hill noises and the dogs' barking on the night Wilbur was born, but no known doctor or midwife presided at his coming. Neighbors knew nothing of him till a week afterward, when Old Whateley drove his sleigh through the snow into Dunwich Village and discoursed incoherently to the group of loungers at Osborne's general store. There seemed to be a change in the old man – an added element of furtiveness in the clouded brain which subtly transformed him from an object to a subject of fear – though he was not one to be perturbed by any common family event. Amidst it all he showed some trace of the pride later noticed in his daughter, and what he said of the child's paternity was remembered by many of his hearers years afterward.

'I dun't keer what folks think – ef Lavinny's boy looked like his pa, he wouldn't look like nothin' ye expeck. Ye needn't think the only folks is the folks hereabouts. Lavinny's read some, an' has seed some things the most o' ye only tell abaout. I calc'late her man is as good a husban' as ye kin find this side of Aylesbury; an' ef ye knowed as much abaout the hills as I dew, ye wouldn't ast no better church weddin' nor her'n. Let me tell ye suthin –*some day yew folks'll hear a child o' Lavinny's a-callin' its father's name on the top o' Sentinel Hill!*'

The only person who saw Wilbur during the first month of his life were old Zechariah Whateley, of the undecayed Whateleys, and Earl Sawyer's common-law wife, Mamie Bishop. Mamie's visit was frankly one of curiosity, and her subsequent tales did justice to her observations; but Zechariah came to lead a pair of Alderney cows which Old Whateley had bought of his son Curtis. This marked the beginning of a course of cattle-buying on the part of small Wilbur's family which ended only in 1928, when the Dunwich horror came and went; yet at no time did the ramshackle Whateley barn seem overcrowded with livestock. There came a period when people were curious enough to steal up and count the herd that grazed precariously on the steep hillside above the old farm-house, and they could never find more than ten or twelve anemic, bloodless-looking specimens. Evidently some blight or distemper, perhaps sprung from the unwholesome pasturage or the diseased fungi and timbers of the filthy barn, caused a heavy mortality amongst the Whateley animals. Odd wounds or sores, having something of the aspect of incisions, seemed to afflict the visible cattle; and once or twice during the earlier months certain callers fancied they could discern similar sores about the throats of the grey, unshaven old man and his slatternly, crinkly-haired albino daughter.

In the spring after Wilbur's birth Lavinia resumed her customary rambles in the hills, bearing in her misproportioned arms the swarthy child. Public interest in the Whateleys subsided after most of the country folk had seen the baby, and no one bothered to comment on the swift development which that newcomer seemed every day to exhibit. Wilbur's growth was indeed phenomenal, for within three months of his birth he had attained a size and muscular power not usually found in infants under a full year of age. His motions and even his vocal sounds showed a restraint and deliberateness highly peculiar in an infant, and no one was really unprepared when, at seven months, he began to walk unassisted, with falterings which another month was sufficient to remove.

It was somewhat after this time – on Hallowe'en – that a great blaze was seen at midnight on the top of Sentinel Hill where the old table-like stone stands amidst its tumulus of ancient bones. Considerable talk was started when Silas Bishop – of the undecayed Bishops –mentioned having seen the boy running sturdily up that hill ahead of his mother about an hour before the blaze was remarked. Silas was rounding up a stray heifer, but he nearly forgot his mission when he fleetingly spied the two figures in the dim light of his lantern.

They darted almost noiselessly through the underbrush, and the astonished watcher seemed to think they were entirely unclothed. Afterwards he could not be sure about the boy, who may have had some kind of a fringed belt and a pair of dark trunks or trousers on. Wilbur was never subsequently seen alive and conscious without complete and tightly buttoned attire, the disarrangement or threatened disarrangement of which always seemed to fill him with anger and alarm. His contrast with his squalid mother and grandfather in this respect was thought very notable until the horror of 1928 suggested the most valid of reasons.

The next January gossips were mildly interested in the fact that 'Lavinny's black brat' had commenced to talk, and at the age of only eleven months. His speech was somewhat remarkable both because of its difference from the ordinary accents of the region, and because it displayed a freedom from infantile lisping of which many children of three or four might well be proud. The boy was not talkative, yet when he spoke he seemed to reflect some elusive element wholly unpossessed by Dunwich and its denizens. The strangeness did not reside in what he said, or even in the simple idioms he used; but seemed vaguely linked with his intonation or with the internal organs that produced the spoken sounds. His facial aspect, too, was remarkable for its maturity; for though he shared his mother's and grandfather's chinlessness, his firm and precociously shaped nose united with the expression of his large, dark, almost Latin eyes to give him an air of quasi-adulthood and well-nigh preternatural intelligence. He was, however, exceedingly ugly despite his appearance of brilliancy; there being something almost goatish or animalistic about his thick lips, large-pored, yellowish skin, coarse crinkly hair, and oddly elongated ears. He was soon disliked even more decidedly than his mother and grandsire, and all conjectures about him were spiced with references to the bygone magic of Old Whateley, and how the hills once shook when he shrieked the dreadful name of *Yog-Sothoth* in the midst of a circle of stones with a great book open in his arms before him. Dogs abhorred the boy, and he was always obliged to take various defensive measures against their barking menace.

CHAPTER III

MEANWHILE OLD WHATELEY continued to buy cattle without measurably increasing the size of his herd. He also cut timber and began to repair the unused parts of his house – a spacious, peak-roofed affair whose rear end was buried entirely in the rocky hillside, and whose three least-ruined ground-floor rooms had always been sufficient for himself and his daughter.

There must have been prodigious reserves of strength in the old man to enable him to accomplish so much hard labour; and though he still babbled dementedly at times, his carpentry seemed to show the effects of sound calculation. It had already begun as soon as Wilbur was born, when one of the many tool sheds had been put suddenly in order, clapboarded, and fitted with a stout fresh lock. Now, in restoring the abandoned upper storey of the house, he was a no less thorough craftsman. His mania showed itself only in his tight boarding-up of all the windows in the reclaimed section – though many declared that it was a crazy thing to bother with the reclamation at all.

Less inexplicable was his fitting up of another downstairs room for his new grandson – a room which several callers saw, though no one was ever admitted to the closely-boarded upper storey. This chamber he lined with tall, firm shelving, along which he began gradually to arrange, in apparently careful order, all the rotting ancient books and parts of books which during his own day had been heaped promiscuously in odd corners of the various rooms.

'I made some use of 'em,' he would say as he tried to mend a torn black- letter page with paste prepared on the rusty kitchen stove, 'but the boy's fitten to make better use of 'em. He'd orter hev 'em as well so as he kin, for they're goin' to be all of his larnin'.'

When Wilbur was a year and seven months old – in September of 1914– his size and accomplishments were almost alarming. He had grown as large as a child of four, and was a fluent and incredibly intelligent talker. He ran freely about the fields and hills, and accompanied his mother on all her wanderings. At home he would pore diligently over the queer pictures and charts in his grandfather's books, while Old Whateley would instruct and catechize him through long, hushed afternoons. By this time the restoration of the house was finished, and those who watched it wondered why one of the upper windows had been made into a solid plank door. It was a window in the rear of the east gable end, close against the hill; and no one could imagine why a cleated wooden runway was built up to it from the ground. About the period of this work's completion people noticed that the old tool-house, tightly locked and windowlessly clapboarded since Wilbur's birth, had been abandoned again. The door swung listlessly open, and when Earl Sawyer once stepped within after a cattle-selling call on Old Whateley he was quite discomposed by the singular odor he encountered – such a stench, he averred, as he had never before smelt in all his life except near the Indian circles on the hills, and which could not come from anything sane or of this earth. But then, the homes and sheds of Dunwich folk have never been remarkable for olfactory immaculateness.

The following months were void of visible events, save that everyone swore to a slow but steady increase in the mysterious hill noises. On May Eve of 1915 there were tremors which even the Aylesbury people felt, whilst the following Hallowe'en produced an underground rumbling queerly synchronized with bursts of flame – 'them witch Whateleys' doin's' – from the summit of Sentinel Hill. Wilbur was growing up uncannily, so that he looked like a boy of ten as he entered his fourth year. He read avidly by himself now; but talked much less than formerly. A settled taciturnity was absorbing him, and for the first time people began to speak specifically of the dawning look of evil in his goatish face. He would sometimes mutter an unfamiliar jargon, and chant in bizarre rhythms which chilled the listener with a sense of unexplainable terror. The aversion displayed towards him by dogs had now become a matter of wide remark, and he was obliged to carry a pistol in order to traverse the countryside in safety. His occasional use of the weapon did not enhance his popularity amongst the owners of canine guardians.

The few callers at the house would often find Lavinia alone on the ground floor, while odd cries and footsteps resounded in the boarded-up second storey. She would never tell what her father and the boy were doing up there, though once she turned pale and displayed an abnormal degree of fear when a jocose fish-peddler tried the locked door leading to the stairway. That peddler told the store loungers at Dunwich Village that he thought he heard a horse stamping on that floor above. The loungers reflected, thinking of the door and runway, and of the cattle that so swiftly disappeared. Then they shuddered as they recalled tales of Old Whateley's youth, and of the strange things that are called out of the earth when a bullock is sacrificed at the proper time to certain heathen gods. It had for some time been noticed that dogs had begun to hate and fear the whole Whateley place as violently as they hated and feared young Wilbur personally.

In 1917 the war came, and Squire Sawyer Whateley, as chairman of the local draft board, had hard work finding a quota of young Dunwich men fit even to be sent to development camp. The government, alarmed at such signs of wholesale regional decadence, sent several officers and medical experts to investigate; conducting a survey which New England newspaper readers may still recall. It was the publicity attending this investigation which set reporters on the track of the Whateleys, and caused the Boston Globe and Arkham Advertiser to print flamboyant Sunday stories of young Wilbur's precociousness, Old Whateley's black magic, and the shelves of strange books, the sealed second storey of the ancient farmhouse, and the weirdness of the whole region and its hill noises. Wilbur was four and a half then, and looked like a lad of fifteen. His lips and cheeks were fuzzy with a coarse dark down, and his voice had begun to break.

Earl Sawyer went out to the Whateley place with both sets of reporters and camera men, and called their attention to the queer stench which now seemed to trickle down from the sealed upper spaces. It was, he said, exactly like a smell he had found in the tool-shed abandoned when the house was finally repaired; and like the faint odors which he sometimes thought he caught near the stone circle on the mountains. Dunwich folk read the stories when they appeared, and grinned over the obvious mistakes. They wondered, too, why the writers made so much of the fact that Old Whateley always paid for his cattle in gold pieces of extremely ancient date. The Whateleys had received their visitors with ill-concealed distaste, though they did not dare court further publicity by a violent resistance or refusal to talk.

CHAPTER IV

FOR A DECADE the annals of the Whateleys sink indistinguishably into the general life of a morbid community used to their queer ways and hardened to their May Eve and All-Hallows orgies. Twice a year they would light fires on the top of Sentinel Hill, at which times the mountain rumblings would recur with greater and greater violence; while at all seasons there were strange and portentous doings at the lonely farm-house. In the course of time callers professed to hear sounds in the sealed upper storey even when all the family were downstairs, and they wondered how swiftly or how lingeringly a cow or bullock was usually sacrificed. There was talk of a complaint to the Society for the Prevention of Cruelty to Animals but nothing ever came of it, since Dunwich folk are never anxious to call the outside world's attention to themselves.

About 1923, when Wilbur was a boy of ten whose mind, voice, stature, and bearded face gave all the impressions of maturity, a second great siege of carpentry went on at the old house. It was all inside the sealed upper part, and from bits of discarded lumber people concluded that the youth and his grandfather had knocked out all the partitions and even removed the attic floor, leaving only one vast open void between the ground storey and the peaked roof. They had torn down the great central chimney, too, and fitted the rusty range with a flimsy outside tin stove-pipe.

In the spring after this event Old Whateley noticed the growing number of whippoorwills that would come out of Cold Spring Glen to chirp under his window at night. He seemed to regard the circumstance as one of great significance, and told the loungers at Osborn's that he thought his time had almost come.

'They whistle jest in tune with my breathin' naow,' he said, 'an' I guess they're gittin' ready to ketch my soul. They know it's a-goin' aout, an' dun't calc'late to miss it. Yew'll know, boys, arter I'm gone, whether they git me er not. Ef they dew, they'll keep up a-singin' an' laffin' till break o' day. Ef they dun't they'll kinder quiet daown like. I expeck them an' the souls they hunts fer hev some pretty tough tussles sometimes.'

On Lammas Night, 1924, Dr. Houghton of Aylesbury was hastily summoned by Wilbur Whateley, who had lashed his one remaining horse through the darkness and telephoned from Osborn's in the village. He found Old Whateley in a very grave state, with a cardiac action and stertorous breathing that told of an end not far off. The shapeless albino daughter and oddly bearded grandson stood by the bedside, whilst from the vacant abyss overhead there came a disquieting suggestion of rhythmical surging or lapping, as of the waves on some level beach. The doctor, though, was chiefly disturbed by the chattering night birds outside; a seemingly limitless legion of whippoorwills that cried their endless message in repetitions timed diabolically to the wheezing gasps of the dying man. It was uncanny and unnatural – too much, thought Dr. Houghton, like the whole of the region he had entered so reluctantly in response to the urgent call.

Towards one o'clock Old Whateley gained consciousness, and interrupted his wheezing to choke out a few words to his grandson.

'More space, Willy, more space soon. Yew grows – an' that grows faster. It'll be ready to serve ye soon, boy. Open up the gates to Yog-Sothoth with the long chant that ye'll find *on page 751 of the complete edition*, an' then put a match to the prison. Fire from airth can't burn it nohaow.'

He was obviously quite mad. After a pause, during which the flock of whippoorwills outside adjusted their cries to the altered tempo while some indications of the strange hill noises came from afar off, he added another sentence or two.

'Feed it reg'lar, Willy, an' mind the quantity; but dun't let it grow too fast fer the place, fer ef it busts quarters or gits aout afore ye opens to Yog-Sothoth, it's all over an' no use. Only them from beyont kin make it multiply an' work... Only them, the old uns as wants to come back...'

But speech gave place to gasps again, and Lavinia screamed at the way the whippoorwills followed the change. It was the same for more than an hour, when the final throaty rattle came. Dr. Houghton drew shrunken lids over the glazing grey eyes as the tumult of birds faded imperceptibly to silence. Lavinia sobbed, but Wilbur only chuckled whilst the hill noises rumbled faintly.

'They didn't git him,' he muttered in his heavy bass voice.

Wilbur was by this time a scholar of really tremendous erudition in his one-sided way, and was quietly known by correspondence to many librarians in distant places where rare and forbidden books of old days are kept. He was more and more hated and dreaded around Dunwich because of certain youthful disappearances which suspicion laid vaguely at his door; but was always able to silence inquiry through fear or through use of that fund of old-time gold which still, as in his grandfather's time, went forth regularly and increasingly for cattle-buying. He was now tremendously mature of aspect, and his height, having reached the normal adult limit, seemed inclined to wax beyond that figure. In 1925, when a scholarly correspondent from Miskatonic University called upon him one day and departed pale and puzzled, he was fully six and three-quarters feet tall.

Through all the years Wilbur had treated his half-deformed albino mother with a growing contempt, finally forbidding her to go to the hills with him on May Eve and Hallowmass; and in 1926 the poor creature complained to Mamie Bishop of being afraid of him.

'They's more abaout him as I knows than I kin tell ye, Mamie,' she said, 'an' naowadays they's more nor what I know myself. I vaow afur Gawd, I dun't know what he wants nor what he's a-tryin' to dew.'

That Hallowe'en the hill noises sounded louder than ever, and fire burned on Sentinel Hill as usual; but people paid more attention to the rhythmical screaming of vast flocks of unnaturally belated whippoorwills which seemed to be assembled near the unlighted Whateley farmhouse. After midnight their shrill notes burst into a kind of pandemoniac cachinnation which filled all the countryside, and not until dawn did they finally quiet down. Then they vanished, hurrying southward where they were fully a month overdue. What this meant, no one could quite be certain till later. None of the countryfolk seemed to have died – but poor Lavinia Whateley, the twisted albino, was never seen again.

In the summer of 1927 Wilbur repaired two sheds in the farmyard and began moving his books and effects out to them. Soon afterwards Earl Sawyer told the loungers at Osborn's that more carpentry was going on in the Whateley farmhouse. Wilbur was closing all the doors and windows on the ground floor, and seemed to be taking out partitions as he and his grandfather had done upstairs four years before. He was living in one of the sheds, and Sawyer thought he seemed unusually worried and tremulous. People generally suspected him of knowing something about his mother disappearance, and very few ever approached his neighborhood now. His height had increased to more than seven feet, and showed no signs of ceasing its development.

CHAPTER V

THE FOLLOWING WINTER brought an event no less strange than Wilbur's first trip outside the Dunwich region. Correspondence with the Widener Library at Harvard, the Bibliothèque Nationale in Paris, the British Museum, the University of Buenos Aires, and the Library of Miskatonic University at Arkham had failed to get him the loan of a book he desperately wanted; so at length he set out in person, shabby, dirty, bearded, and uncouth of dialect, to consult the copy at Miskatonic, which was the nearest to him geographically. Almost eight feet tall, and carrying a cheap new valise from Osborne's general store, this dark and goatish gargoyle appeared one day in Arkham in quest of the dreaded volume kept under lock and key at the college library – the hideous *Necronomicon* of the mad Arab Abdul Alhazred in Olaus Wormius' Latin version, as printed in Spain in the seventeenth century. He had never seen a city before, but had no thought save to find his way to the university grounds; where indeed, he passed heedlessly by the great white-fanged watchdog that barked with unnatural fury and enmity, and tugged frantically at its stout chain.

Wilbur had with him the priceless but imperfect copy of Dr. Dee's English version which his grandfather had bequeathed him, and upon receiving access to the Latin copy he at once began to collate the two texts with the aim of discovering a certain passage which would have come on the 751st page of his own defective volume. This much he could not civilly refrain from telling the librarian – the same erudite Henry Armitage (A.M. Miskatonic, Ph.D. Princeton, Litt.D. Johns Hopkins) who had once called at the farm, and who now politely plied him with questions. He was looking, he had to admit, for a kind of formula or incantation containing the frightful name *Yog-Sothoth*, and it puzzled him to find discrepancies, duplications, and ambiguities which made the matter of determination far from easy. As he copied the formula he finally chose, Dr. Armitage looked involuntarily over his shoulder at the open pages; the left-hand one of which, in the Latin version, contained such monstrous threats to the peace and sanity of the world.

Nor is it to be thought (ran the text as Armitage mentally translated it) that man is either the oldest or the last of earth's masters, or that the common bulk of life and substance walks alone. The Old Ones were, the Old Ones are, and the Old Ones shall be. Not in the spaces we know, but between them, they walk serene and primal, undimensioned and to us unseen. Yog-Sothoth knows the gate. Yog-Sothoth is the gate. Yog-Sothoth is the key and guardian of the gate. Past, present, future, all are one in Yog-Sothoth. He knows where the Old Ones broke through of old, and where They shall break through again. He knows where They had trod earth's fields, and where They still tread them, and why no one can behold Them as They tread. By Their smell can men sometimes know Them near, but of Their semblance can no man know, saving only in the features of those They have begotten on mankind; and of those are there many sorts, differing in likeness from man's truest eidolon to that shape without sight or substance which is Them. They walk unseen and foul in lonely places where the Words have been spoken and the Rites howled through at their Seasons. The wind gibbers with Their voices, and the earth mutters with Their consciousness. They bend the forest and crush the city, yet may not forest or city behold the hand that smites. Kadath in the cold waste hath known Them, and what man knows Kadath? The ice desert of the South and the sunken isles of Ocean hold stones whereon Their seal is engraver, but who hath seen the deep frozen city or the sealed tower long garlanded with seaweed and barnacles? Great Cthulhu is Their cousin, yet can he spy Them only dimly. Iä! Shub-Niggurath! As a foulness shall ye know Them. Their hand is at your throats, yet ye see Them not; and Their habitation is even one with your guarded threshold. Yog-Sothoth is the key to the gate, whereby the spheres meet. Man rules now where They ruled once; They shall soon rule where man rules now. After summer is winter, after winter summer. They wait patient and potent, for here shall They reign again.

Dr. Armitage, associating what he was reading with what he had heard of Dunwich and its brooding presences, and of Wilbur Whateley and his dim, hideous aura that stretched from a dubious birth to a cloud of probable matricide, felt a wave of fright as tangible as a draught of the tomb's cold clamminess. The bent, goatish giant before him seemed like the spawn of another planet or dimension; like something only partly of mankind, and linked to black gulfs of essence and entity that stretch like titan phantasms beyond all spheres of force and matter, space and time. Presently Wilbur raised his head and began speaking in that strange, resonant fashion which hinted at sound-producing organs unlike the run of mankind's.

'Mr Armitage,' he said, 'I calc'late I've got to take that book home. They's things in it I've got to try under sarten conditions that I can't git here, en' it 'ud be a mortal sin to let a red-tape rule hold me up. Let me take it along, Sir, an' I'll swar they wun't nobody know the difference. I dun't need to tell ye I'll take good keer of it. It wan't me that put this Dee copy in the shape it is...'

He stopped as he saw firm denial on the librarian's face, and his own goatish features grew crafty. Armitage, half-ready to tell him he might make a copy of what parts he needed, thought suddenly of the possible consequences and checked himself. There was too much responsibility in giving such a being the key to such blasphemous outer spheres. Whateley saw how things stood, and tried to answer lightly.

'Wal, all right, ef ye feel that way abaout it. Maybe Harvard won't be so fussy as yew be.' And without saying more he rose and strode out of the building, stooping at each doorway.

Armitage heard the savage yelping of the great watchdog, and studied Whateley's gorilla-like lope as he crossed the bit of campus visible from the window. He thought of the wild tales he had heard, and recalled the old Sunday stories in *the Advertiser*; these things, and the lore he had picked up from Dunwich rustics and villagers during his one visit there. Unseen things not of earth – or at least not of tridimensional earth – rushed fetid and horrible through New England's glens, and brooded obscenely on the mountain tops. Of this he had long felt certain. Now he seemed to sense the close presence of some terrible part of the intruding horror, and to glimpse a hellish advance in the black dominion of the ancient and once passive nightmare. He locked away *the Necronomicon* with a shudder of disgust, but the room still reeked with an unholy and unidentifiable stench. 'As a foulness shall ye know them,a he quoted. Yes – the odor was the same as that which had sickened him at the Whateley farmhouse less than three years before. He thought of Wilbur, goatish and ominous, once again, and laughed mockingly at the village rumors of his parentage.

'Inbreeding?' Armitage muttered half-aloud to himself. 'Great God, what simpletons! Show them Arthur Machen's Great God Pan and they'll think it a common Dunwich scandal! But what thing – what cursed shapeless influence on or off this three-dimensional earth – was Wilbur Whateley's father? Born on Candlemas – nine months after May Eve of 1912, when the talk about the queer earth noises reached clear to Arkham – what walked on the mountains that May night? What Roodmas horror fastened itself on the world in half-human flesh and blood?'

During the ensuing weeks Dr. Armitage set about to collect all possible data on Wilbur Whateley and the formless presences around Dunwich. He got in communication with Dr. Houghton of Aylesbury, who had attended Old Whateley in his last illness, and found much to ponder over in the grandfather's last words as quoted by the physician. A visit to Dunwich Village failed to bring out much that was new; but a close survey of *the Necronomicon*, in those parts which Wilbur had sought so avidly, seemed to supply new and terrible clues to the nature, methods, and desires of the strange evil so vaguely threatening this planet. Talks with several students of archaic lore in Boston, and letters to many others elsewhere, gave him a growing amazement which passed slowly through varied degrees of alarm to a state of really acute spiritual fear. As the summer drew on he felt dimly that something ought to be done about the lurking terrors of the upper Miskatonic valley, and about the monstrous being known to the human world as Wilbur Whateley.

CHAPTER VI

THE DUNWICH HORROR itself came between Lammas and the equinox in 1928, and Dr. Armitage was among those who witnessed its monstrous prologue. He had heard, meanwhile, of Whateley's grotesque trip to Cambridge, and of his frantic efforts to borrow or copy from *the Necronomicon* at the Widener Library. Those efforts had been in vain, since Armitage had issued warnings of the keenest intensity to all librarians having charge of the dreaded volume. Wilbur had been shockingly nervous at Cambridge; anxious for the book, yet almost equally anxious to get home again, as if he feared the results of being away long.

Early in August the half-expected outcome developed, and in the small hours of the third Dr. Armitage was awakened suddenly by the wild, fierce cries of the savage watchdog on the college campus. Deep and terrible, the snarling, half-mad growls and barks continued; always in mounting volume, but with hideously significant pauses. Then there rang out a scream from a wholly different throat – such a scream as roused half the sleepers of Arkham and haunted their dreams ever afterwards – such a scream as could come from no being born of earth, or wholly of earth.

Armitage, hastening into some clothing and rushing across the street and lawn to the college buildings, saw that others were ahead of him; and heard the echoes of a burglar-alarm still shrilling from the library. An open window showed black and gaping in the moonlight. What had come had indeed completed its entrance; for the barking and the screaming, now fast fading into a mixed low growling and moaning, proceeded unmistakably from within. Some instinct warned Armitage that what was taking place was not a thing for unfortified eyes to see, so he brushed back the crowd with authority as he unlocked the vestibule door. Among the others he saw Professor Warren Rice and Dr. Francis Morgan, men to whom he had told some of his conjectures and misgivings; and these two he motioned to accompany him inside. The inward sounds, except for a watchful, droning whine from the dog, had by this time quite subsided; but Armitage now perceived with a sudden start that a loud chorus of whippoorwills among the shrubbery had commenced a damnably rhythmical piping, as if in unison with the last breaths of a dying man.

The building was full of a frightful stench which Dr. Armitage knew too well, and the three men rushed across the hall to the small genealogical reading-room whence the low whining came. For a second nobody dared to turn on the light, then Armitage summoned up his courage and snapped the switch. One of the three – it is not certain which – shrieked aloud at what sprawled before them among disordered tables and overturned chairs. Professor Rice declares that he wholly lost consciousness for an instant, though he did not stumble or fall.

The thing that lay half-bent on its side in a fetid pool of greenish- yellow ichor and tarry stickiness was almost nine feet tall, and the dog had torn off all the clothing and some of the skin. It was not quite dead, but twitched silently and spasmodically while its chest heaved in monstrous unison with the mad piping of the expectant whippoorwills outside. Bits of shoe-leather and fragments of apparel were scattered about the room, and just inside the window an empty canvas sack lay where it had evidently been thrown. Near the central desk a revolver had fallen, a dented but undischarged cartridge later explaining why it had not been fired. The thing itself, however, crowded out all other images at the time. It would be trite and not wholly accurate to say that no human pen could describe it, but one may properly say that it could not be vividly visualized by anyone whose ideas of aspect and contour are too closely bound up with the common life-forms of this planet and of the three known dimensions. It was partly human, beyond a doubt, with very manlike hands and head, and the goatish, chinless face had the stamp of the Whateley's upon it. But the torso and lower parts of the body were teratologically fabulous, so that only generous clothing could ever have enabled it to walk on earth unchallenged or uneradicated.

Above the waist it was semi-anthropomorphic; though its chest, where the dog's rending paws still rested watchfully, had the leathery, reticulated hide of a crocodile or alligator. The back was piebald with yellow and black, and dimly suggested the squamous covering of certain snakes. Below the waist, though, it was the worst; for here all human resemblance left off and sheer phantasy began. The skin was thickly covered with coarse black fur, and from the abdomen a score of long greenish-grey tentacles with red sucking mouths protruded limply.

Their arrangement was odd, and seemed to follow the symmetries of some cosmic geometry unknown to earth or the solar system. On each of the hips, deep set in a kind of pinkish, ciliated orbit, was what seemed to be a rudimentary eye; whilst in lieu of a tail there depended a kind of trunk or feeler with purple annular markings, and with many evidences of being an undeveloped mouth or throat. The limbs, save for their black fur, roughly resembled the hind legs of prehistoric earth's giant saurians, and terminated in ridgy-veined pads that were neither hooves nor claws. When the thing breathed, its tail and tentacles rhythmically changed color, as if from some circulatory cause normal to the non-human greenish tinge, whilst in the tail it was manifest as a yellowish appearance which alternated with a sickly grayish-white in the spaces between the purple rings. Of genuine blood there was none; only the fetid greenish-yellow ichor which trickled along the painted floor beyond the radius of the stickiness, and left a curious discoloration behind it.

As the presence of the three men seemed to rouse the dying thing, it began to mumble without turning or raising its head. Dr. Armitage made no written record of its mouthings, but asserts confidently that nothing in English was uttered. At first the syllables defied all correlation with any speech of earth, but towards the last there came some disjointed fragments evidently taken from *the Necronomicon*, that monstrous blasphemy in quest of which the thing had perished. These fragments, as Armitage recalls them, ran something like '*N'gai, n'gha'ghaa, bugg-shoggog, y'hah: Yog-Sothoth, Yog- Sothoth...*' They trailed off into nothingness as the whippoorwills shrieked in rhythmical crescendos of unholy anticipation.

Then came a halt in the gasping, and the dog raised its head in a long, lugubrious howl. A change came over the yellow, goatish face of the prostrate thing, and the great black eyes fell in appallingly. Outside the window the shrilling of the whippoorwills had suddenly ceased, and above the murmurs of the gathering crowd there came the sound of a panic-struck whirring and fluttering. Against the moon vast clouds of feathery watchers rose and raced from sight, frantic at that which they had sought for prey.

All at once the dog started up abruptly, gave a frightened bark, and leaped nervously out of the window by which it had entered. A cry rose from the crowd, and Dr. Armitage shouted to the men outside that no one must be admitted till the police or medical examiner came. He was thankful that the windows were just too high to permit of peering in, and drew the dark curtains carefully down over each one. By this time two policemen had arrived; and Dr. Morgan, meeting them in the vestibule, was urging them for their own sakes to postpone entrance to the stench-filled reading-room till the examiner came and the prostrate thing could be covered up.

Meanwhile frightful changes were taking place on the floor. One need not describe the kind and rate of shrinkage and disintegration that occurred before the eyes of Dr. Armitage and Professor Rice; but it is permissible to say that, aside from the external appearance of face and hands, the really human element in Wilbur Whateley must have been very small. When the medical examiner came, there was only a sticky whitish mass on the painted boards, and the monstrous odor had nearly disappeared. Apparently Whateley had had no skull or bony skeleton; at least, in any true or stable sense. He had taken somewhat after his unknown father.

CHAPTER VII

YET ALL THIS was only the prologue of the actual Dunwich horror. Formalities were gone through by bewildered officials, abnormal details were duly kept from press and public, and men were sent to Dunwich and Aylesbury to look up property and notify any who might be heirs of the late Wilbur Whateley. They found the countryside in great agitation, both because of the growing rumblings beneath the domed hills, and because of the unwonted stench and the surging, lapping sounds which came increasingly from the great empty shell formed by Whateley's boarded-up farmhouse. Earl Sawyer, who tended the horse and cattle during Wilbur's absence, had developed a woefully acute case of nerves. The officials devised excuses not to enter the noisome boarded place; and were glad to confine their survey of the deceased's living quarters, the newly mended sheds, to a single visit. They filed a ponderous report at the courthouse in Aylesbury, and litigations concerning heirship are said to be still in progress amongst the innumerable Whateleys, decayed and undecayed, of the upper Miskatonic valley.

An almost interminable manuscript in strange characters, written in a huge ledger and adjudged a sort of diary because of the spacing and the variations in ink and penmanship, presented a baffling puzzle to those who found it on the old bureau which served as its owner's desk. After a week of debate it was sent to Miskatonic University, together with the deceased's collection of strange books, for study and possible translation; but even the best linguists soon saw that it was not likely to be unriddled with ease. No trace of the ancient gold with which Wilbur and Old Whateley had always paid their debts has yet been discovered.

It was in the dark of September ninth that the horror broke loose. The hill noises had been very pronounced during the evening, and dogs barked frantically all night. Early risers on the tenth noticed a peculiar stench in the air. About seven o'clock Luther Brown, the hired boy at George Corey's, between Cold Spring Glen and the village, rushed frenziedly back from his morning trip to Ten-Acre Meadow with the cows. He was almost convulsed with fright as he stumbled into the kitchen; and in the yard outside the no less frightened herd were pawing and lowing pitifully, having followed the boy back in the panic they shared with him. Between gasps Luther tried to stammer out his tale to Mrs Corey.

'Up thar in the rud beyont the glen, Mis' Corey – they's suthin' ben thar! It smells like thunder, an' all the bushes an' little trees is pushed back from the rud like they'd a haouse ben moved along of it. An' that ain't the wust, nuther. They's prints in the rud, Mis' Corey – great raound prints as big as barrel-heads, all sunk dawon deep like a elephant had ben along, only they's a sight more nor four feet could make! I looked at one or two afore I run, an' I see every one was covered with lines spreadin' aout from one place, like as if big palm-leaf fans – twice or three times as big as any they is – hed of ben paounded dawon into the rud. An' the smell was awful, like what it is around Wizard Whateley's ol' haouse...'

Here he faltered, and seemed to shiver afresh with the fright that had sent him flying home. Mrs Corey, unable to extract more information, began telephoning the neighbors; thus starting on its rounds the overture of panic that heralded the major terrors. When she got Sally Sawyer, housekeeper at Seth Bishop's, the nearest place to Whateley's, it became her turn to listen instead of transmit; for Sally's boy Chauncey, who slept poorly, had been up on the hill towards Whateley's, and had dashed back in terror after one look at the place, and at the pasturage where Mr Bishop's cows had been left out all night.

'Yes, Mis' Corey,' came Sally's tremulous voice over the party wire, 'Cha'ncey he just come back a-postin', and couldn't half talk fer bein' scairt! He says Ol' Whateley's house is all blowed up, with timbers scattered raound like they'd ben dynamite inside; only the bottom floor ain't through, but is all covered with a kind o' tar-like stuff that smells awful an' drips daown offen the aidges onto the graoun' whar the side timbers is blowed away. An' they's awful kinder marks in the yard, tew – great raound marks bigger raound than a hogshead, an' all sticky with stuff like is on the browed-up haouse. Cha'ncey he says they leads off into the medders, whar a great swath wider'n a barn is matted daown, an' all the stun walls tumbled every whichway wherever it goes.

'An' he says, says he, Mis' Corey, as haow he sot to look fer Seth's caows, frightened ez he was an' faound 'em in the upper pasture nigh the Devil's Hop Yard in an awful shape. Haff on 'em's clean gone, an' nigh haff o' them that's left is sucked most dry o' blood, with sores on 'em like they's ben on Whateleys cattle ever senct Lavinny's black brat was born. Seth hes gone aout naow to look at 'em, though I'll vaow he won't keer ter git very nigh Wizard Whateley's! Cha'ncey didn't look keerful ter see whar the big matted-daown swath led arter it leff the pasturage, but he says he thinks it p'inted towards the glen rud to the village.

'I tell ye, Mis' Corey, they's suthin' abroad as hadn't orter be abroad, an' I for one think that black Wilbur Whateley, as come to the bad end he deserved, is at the bottom of the breedin' of it. He wa'n't all human hisself, I allus says to everybody; an' I think he an' Ol' Whateley must a raised suthin' in that there nailed-up haouse as ain't even so human as he was. They's allus ben unseen things araound Dunwich – livin' things – as ain't human an' ain't good fer human folks.

'The graoun' was a-talkin' las' night, an' towards mornin' Cha'ncey he heered the whippoorwills so laoud in Col' Spring Glen he couldn't sleep nun. Then he thought he heered another faint-like saound over towards Wizard Whateley's – a kinder rippin' or tearin' o' wood, like some big box er crate was bein' opened fur off. What with this an' that, he didn't git to sleep at all till sunup, an' no sooner was he up this mornin', but he's got to go over to Whateley's an' see what's the matter. He see enough I tell ye, Mis' Corey! This dun't mean no good, an' I think as all the men-folks ought to git up a party an' do suthin'. I know suthin' awful's abaout, an' feel my time is nigh, though only Gawd knows jest what it is.

'Did your Luther take accaount o' whar them big tracks led tew? No? Wal, Mis' Corey, ef they was on the glen rud this side o' the glen, an' ain't got to your haouse yet, I calc'late they must go into the glen itself. They would do that. I allus says Col' Spring Glen ain't no healthy nor decent place. The whippoorwills an' fireflies there never did act like they was creaters o' Gawd, an' they's them as says ye kin hear strange things a-rushin' an' a-talkin' in the air dawon thar ef ye stand in the right place, atween the rock falls an' Bear's Den.'

By that noon fully three-quarters of the men and boys of Dunwich were trooping over the roads and meadows between the newmade Whateley ruins and Cold Spring Glen, examining in horror the vast, monstrous prints, the maimed Bishop cattle, the strange, noisome wreck of the farmhouse, and the bruised, matted vegetation of the fields and roadside. Whatever had burst loose upon the world had assuredly gone down into the great sinister ravine; for all the trees on the banks were bent and broken, and a great avenue had been gouged in the precipice-hanging underbrush. It was as though a house, launched by an avalanche, had slid down through the tangled growths of the almost vertical slope. From below no sound came, but only a distant, undefinable fetor; and it is not to be wondered at that the men preferred to stay on the edge and argue, rather than descend and beard the unknown Cyclopean horror in its lair. Three dogs that were with the party had barked furiously at first, but seemed cowed and reluctant when near the glen. Someone telephoned the news to the *Aylesbury Transcript*; but the editor, accustomed to wild tales from Dunwich, did no more than concoct a humorous paragraph about it; an item soon afterwards reproduced by the Associated Press.

That night everyone went home, and every house and barn was barricaded as stoutly as possible. Needless to say, no cattle were allowed to remain in open pasturage. About two in the morning a frightful stench and the savage barking of the dogs awakened the household at Elmer Frye's, on the eastern edge of Cold Spring Glen, and all agreed that they could hear a sort of muffled swishing or lapping sound from somewhere outside. Mrs Frye proposed telephoning the neighbors, and Elmer was about to agree when the noise of splintering wood burst in upon their deliberations. It came, apparently, from the barn; and was quickly followed by a hideous screaming and stamping amongst the cattle. The dogs slavered and crouched close to the feet of the fear-numbed family. Frye lit a lantern through force of habit, but knew it would be death to go out into that black farmyard. The children and the women-folk whimpered, kept from screaming by some obscure, vestigial instinct of defence which told them their lives depended on silence. At last the noise of the cattle subsided to a pitiful moaning, and a great snapping, crashing, and crackling ensued. The Fryes, huddled together in the sitting-room, did not dare to move until the last echoes died away far down in Cold Spring Glen. Then, amidst the dismal moans from the stable and the daemoniac piping of the late whippoorwills in the glen, Selina Frye tottered to the telephone and spread what news she could of the second phase of the horror.

The next day all the countryside was in a panic; and cowed, uncommunicative groups came and went where the fiendish thing had occurred. Two titan swaths of destruction stretched from the glen to the Frye farmyard, monstrous prints covered the bare patches of ground, and one side of the old red barn had completely caved in. Of the cattle, only a quarter could be found and identified. Some of these were in curious fragments, and all that survived had to be shot. Earl Sawyer suggested that help be asked from Aylesbury or Arkham, but others maintained it would be of no use. Old Zebulon Whateley, of a branch that hovered about halfway between soundness and decadence, made darkly wild suggestions about rites that ought to be practiced on the hill-tops. He came of a line where tradition ran strong, and his memories of chantings in the great stone circles were not altogether connected with Wilbur and his grandfather.

Darkness fell upon a stricken countryside too passive to organize for real defence. In a few cases closely related families would band together and watch in the gloom under one roof; but in general there was only a repetition of the barricading of the night before, and a futile, ineffective gesture of loading muskets and setting pitchforks handily about. Nothing, however, occurred except some hill noises; and when the day came there were many who hoped that the new horror had gone as swiftly as it had come. There were even bold souls who proposed an offensive expedition down in the glen, though they did not venture to set an actual example to the still reluctant majority.

When night came again the barricading was repeated, though there was less huddling together of families. In the morning both the Frye and the Seth Bishop households reported excitement among the dogs and vague sounds and stenches from afar, while early explorers noted with horror a fresh set of the monstrous tracks in the road skirting Sentinel Hill. As before, the sides of the road showed a bruising indicative of the blasphemously stupendous bulk of the horror; whilst the conformation of the tracks seemed to argue a passage in two directions, as if the moving mountain had come from Cold Spring Glen and returned to it along the same path. At the base of the hill a thirty-foot swath of crushed shrubbery saplings led steeply upwards, and the seekers gasped when they saw that even the most perpendicular places did not deflect the inexorable trail. Whatever the horror was, it could scale a sheer stony cliff of almost complete verticality; and as the investigators climbed round to the hill's summit by safer routes they saw that the trail ended – or rather, reversed – there.

It was here that the Whateleys used to build their hellish fires and chant their hellish rituals by the table-like stone on May Eve and Hallowmass. Now that very stone formed the center of a vast space thrashed around by the mountainous horror, whilst upon its slightly concave surface was a thick and fetid deposit of the same tarry stickiness observed on the floor of the ruined Whateley farmhouse when the horror escaped. Men looked at one another and muttered. Then they looked down the hill. Apparently the horror had descended by a route much the same as that of its ascent. To speculate was futile. Reason, logic, and normal ideas of motivation stood confounded. Only old Zebulon, who was not with the group, could have done justice to the situation or suggested a plausible explanation.

Thursday night began much like the others, but it ended less happily. The whippoorwills in the glen had screamed with such unusual persistence that many could not sleep, and about 3 A.M. all the party telephones rang tremulously. Those who took down their receivers heard a fright-mad voice shriek out, 'Help, oh, my Gawd!...' and some thought a crashing sound followed the breaking off of the exclamation. There was nothing more. No one dared do anything, and no one knew till morning whence the call came. Then those who had heard it called everyone on the line, and found that only the Fryes did not reply. The truth appeared an hour later, when a hastily assembled group of armed men trudged out to the Frye place at the head of the glen. It was horrible, yet hardly a surprise. There were more swaths and monstrous prints, but there was no longer any house. It had caved in like an egg-shell, and amongst the ruins nothing living or dead could be discovered. Only a stench and a tarry stickiness. The Elmer Fryes had been erased from Dunwich.

CHAPTER VIII

IN THE MEANTIME a quieter yet even more spiritually poignant phase of the horror had been blackly unwinding itself behind the closed door of a shelf- lined room in Arkham. The curious manuscript record or diary of Wilbur Whateley, delivered to Miskatonic University for translation had caused much worry and bafflement among the experts in language both ancient and modern; its very alphabet, notwithstanding a general resemblance to the heavily-shaded Arabic used in Mesopotamia, being absolutely unknown to any available authority. The final conclusion of the linguists was that the text represented an artificial alphabet, giving the effect of a cipher; though none of the usual methods of cryptographic solution seemed to furnish any clue, even when applied on the basis of every tongue the writer might conceivably have used. The ancient books taken from Whateley's quarters, while absorbingly interesting and in several cases promising to open up new and terrible lines of research among philosophers and men of science, were of no assistance whatever in this matter. One of them, a heavy tome with an iron clasp, was in another unknown alphabet– this one of a very different cast, and resembling Sanskrit more than anything else. The old ledger was at length given wholly into the charge of Dr. Armitage, both because of his peculiar interest in the Whateley matter, and because of his wide linguistic learning and skill in the mystical formulae of antiquity and the middle ages.

Armitage had an idea that the alphabet might be something esoterically used by certain forbidden cults which have come down from old times, and which have inherited many forms and traditions from the wizards of the Saracenic world. That question, however, he did not deem vital; since it would be unnecessary to know the origin of the symbols if, as he suspected, they were used as a cipher in a modern language. It was his belief that, considering the great amount of text involved, the writer would scarcely have wished the trouble of using another speech than his own, save perhaps in certain special formulae and incantations. Accordingly he attacked the manuscript with the preliminary assumption that the bulk of it was in English.

Dr. Armitage knew, from the repeated failures of his colleagues, that the riddle was a deep and complex one; and that no simple mode of solution could merit even a trial. All through late August he fortified himself with the mass lore of cryptography; drawing upon the fullest resources of his own library, and wading night after night amidst the arcana of Trithemius' *Poligraphia*, Giambattista Porta's *De Furtivis Literarum Notis*, De Vigenere's *Traite des Chiffres*, Falconer's *Cryptomenysis Patefacta*, Davys' and Thicknesse's eighteenth-century treatises, and such fairly modern authorities as Blair, van Marten and Kluber's script itself, and in time became convinced that he had to deal with one of those subtlest and most ingenious of cryptograms, in which many separate lists of corresponding letters are arranged like the multiplication table, and the message built up with arbitrary key-words known only to the initiated. The older authorities seemed rather more helpful than the newer ones, and Armitage concluded that the code of the manuscript was one of great antiquity, no doubt handed down through a long line of mystical experimenters. Several times he seemed near daylight, only to be set back by some unforeseen obstacle. Then, as September approached, the clouds began to clear. Certain letters, as used in certain parts of the manuscript, emerged definitely and unmistakably; and it became obvious that the text was indeed in English.

On the evening of September second the last major barrier gave way, and Dr. Armitage read for the first time a continuous passage of Wilbur Whateley's annals. It was in truth a diary, as all had thought; and it was couched in a style clearly showing the mixed occult erudition and general illiteracy of the strange being who wrote it. Almost the first long passage that Armitage deciphered, an entry dated November 26, 1916, proved highly startling and disquieting. It was written,he remembered, by a child of three and a half who looked like a lad of twelve or thirteen.

Today learned the Aklo for the Sabaoth (it ran), which did not like, it being answerable from the hill and not from the air. That upstairs more ahead of me than I had thought it would be, and is not like to have much earth brain. Shot Elam Hutchins's collie Jack when he went to bite me, and Elam says he would kill me if he dast. I guess he won't. Grandfather kept me saying the Dho formula last night, and I think I saw the inner city at the 2 magnetic poles. I shall go to those poles when the earth is cleared off, if I can't break through with the Dho-Hna formula when I commit it. They from the air told me at Sabbat that it will be years before I can clear off the earth, and I guess grandfather will be dead then, so I shall have to learn all the angles of the planes and all the formulas between the Yr and the Nhhngr. They from outside will help, but they cannot take body without human blood. That upstairs looks it will have the right cast. I can see it a little when I make the Voorish sign or blow the powder of Ibn Ghazi at it, and it is near like them at May Eve on the Hill. The other face may wear off some. I wonder how I shall look when the earth is cleared and there are no earth beings on it. He that came with the Aklo Sabaoth said I may be transfigured there being much of outside to work on.

Morning found Dr. Armitage in a cold sweat of terror and a frenzy of wakeful concentration. He had not left the manuscript all night, but sat at his table under the electric light turning page after page with shaking hands as fast as he could decipher the cryptic text. He had nervously telephoned his wife he would not be home, and when she brought him a breakfast from the house he could scarcely dispose of a mouthful. All that day he read on, now and then halted maddeningly as a reapplication of the complex key became necessary. Lunch and dinner were brought him, but he ate only the smallest fraction of either. Toward the middle of the next night he drowsed off in his chair, but soon woke out of a tangle of nightmares almost as hideous as the truths and menaces to man's existence that he had uncovered.

On the morning of September fourth Professor Rice and Dr. Morgan insisted on seeing him for a while, and departed trembling and ashen-grey. That evening he went to bed, but slept only fitfully. Wednesday – the next day –he was back at the manuscript, and began to take copious notes both from the current sections and from those he had already deciphered. In the small hours of that night he slept a little in a easy chair in his office, but was at the manuscript again before dawn. Some time before noon his physician, Dr. Hartwell, called to see him and insisted that he cease work. He refused; intimating that it was of the most vital importance for him to complete the reading of the diary and promising an explanation in due course of time. That evening, just as twilight fell, he finished his terrible perusal and sank back exhausted. His wife, bringing his dinner, found him in a half-comatose state; but he was conscious enough to warn her off with a sharp cry when he saw her eyes wander toward the notes he had taken. Weakly rising, he gathered up the scribbled papers and sealed them all in a great envelope, which he immediately placed in his inside coat pocket. He had sufficient strength to get home, but was so clearly in need of medical aid that Dr. Hartwell was summoned at once. As the doctor put him to bed he could only mutter over and over again, *'But what, in God's name, can we do?'*

Dr. Armitage slept, but was partly delirious the next day. He made no explanations to Hartwell, but in his calmer moments' spoke of the imperative need of a long conference with Rice and Morgan. His wilder wanderings were very startling indeed, including frantic appeals that something in a boarded-up farmhouse be destroyed, and fantastic references to some plan for the extirpation of the entire human race and all animal and vegetable life from the earth by some terrible elder race of beings from another dimension. He would shout that the world was in danger, since the Elder Things wished to strip it and drag it away from the solar system and cosmos of matter into some other plane or phase of entity from which it had once fallen, vigintillions of aeons ago. At other times he would call for the dreaded *Necronomicon* and the *Daemonolatreia* of Remigius, in which he seemed hopeful of finding some formula to check the peril he conjured up.

'Stop them, stop them!' he would shout. 'Those Whateleys meant to let them in, and the worst of all is left! Tell Rice and Morgan we must do something – it's a blind business, but I know how to make the powder... It hasn't been fed since the second of August, when Wilbur came here to his death, and at that rate...'

But Armitage had a sound physique despite his seventy-three years, and slept off his disorder that night without developing any real fever. He woke late Friday, clear of head, though sober with a gnawing fear and tremendous sense of responsibility. Saturday afternoon he felt able to go over to the library and summon Rice and Morgan for a conference, and the rest of that day and evening the three men tortured their brains in the wildest speculation and the most desperate debate. Strange and terrible books were drawn voluminously from the stack shelves and from secure places of storage; and diagrams and formulae were copied with feverish haste and in bewildering abundance. Of skepticism there was none. All three had seen the body of Wilbur Whateley as it lay on the floor in a room of that very building, and after that not one of them could feel even slightly inclined to treat the diary as a madman's raving.

Opinions were divided as to notifying the Massachusetts State Police, and the negative finally won. There were things involved which simply could not be believed by those who had not seen a sample, as indeed was made clear during certain subsequent investigations. Late at night the conference disbanded without having developed a definite plan, but all day Sunday Armitage was busy comparing formulae and mixing chemicals obtained from the college laboratory. The more he reflected on the hellish diary, the more he was inclined to doubt the efficacy of any material agent in stamping out the entity which Wilbur Whateley had left behind him – the earth threatening entity which, unknown to him, was to burst forth in a few hours and become the memorable Dunwich horror.

Monday was a repetition of Sunday with Dr. Armitage, for the task in hand required an infinity of research and experiment. Further consultations of the monstrous diary brought about various changes of plan, and he knew that even in the end a large amount of uncertainty must remain. By Tuesday he had a definite line of action mapped out, and believed he would try a trip to Dunwich within a week. Then, on Wednesday, the great shock came. Tucked obscurely away in a corner of the *Arkham Advertiser* was a facetious little item from the Associated Press, telling what a record-breaking monster the bootleg whisky of Dunwich had raised up. Armitage, half stunned, could only telephone for Rice and Morgan. Far into the night they discussed, and the next day was a whirlwind of preparation on the part of them all. Armitage knew he would be meddling with terrible powers, yet saw that there was no other way to annul the deeper and more malign meddling which others had done before him.

CHAPTER IX

FRIDAY MORNING Armitage, Rice, and Morgan set out by motor for Dunwich, arriving at the village about one in the afternoon. The day was pleasant, but even in the brightest sunlight a kind of quiet dread and portent seemed to hover about the strangely domed hills and the deep, shadowy ravines of the stricken region. Now and then on some mountain top a gaunt circle of stones could be glimpsed against the sky. From the air of hushed fright at Osborn's store they knew something hideous had happened, and soon learned of the annihilation of the Elmer Frye house and family. Throughout that afternoon they rode around Dunwich, questioning the natives concerning all that had occurred, and seeing for themselves with rising pangs of horror the drear Frye ruins with their lingering traces of the tarry stickiness, the blasphemous tracks in the Frye yard, the wounded Seth Bishop cattle, and the enormous swaths of disturbed vegetation in various places. The trail up and down Sentinel Hill seemed to Armitage of almost cataclysmic significance, and he looked long at the sinister altar-like stone on the summit.

At length the visitors, apprised of a party of State Police which had come from Aylesbury that morning in response to the first telephone reports of the Frye tragedy, decided to seek out the officers and compare notes as far as practicable. This, however, they found more easily planned than performed; since no sign of the party could be found in any direction. There had been five of them in a car, but now the car stood empty near the ruins in the Frye yard. The natives, all of whom had talked with the policemen, seemed at first as perplexed as Armitage and his companions. Then old Sam Hutchins thought of something and turned pale, nudging Fred Farr and pointing to the dank, deep hollow that yawned close by.

'Gawd,' he gasped, 'I telled 'em not ter go daown into the glen, an' I never thought nobody'd dew it with them tracks an' that smell an' the whippoorwills a-screechin' daown thar in the dark o' noonday...'

A cold shudder ran through natives and visitors alike, and every ear seemed strained in a kind of instinctive, unconscious listening. Armitage, now that he had actually come upon the horror and its monstrous work, trembled with the responsibility he felt to be his. Night would soon fall, and it was then that the mountainous blasphemy lumbered upon its eldritch course. *Negotium perambulans in tenebris...* The old librarian rehearsed the formulae he had memorized, and clutched the paper containing the alternative one he had not memorized. He saw that his electric flashlight was in working order. Rice, beside him, took from a valise a metal sprayer of the sort used in combating insects; whilst Morgan uncased the big-game rifle on which he relied despite his colleague's warnings that no material weapon would be of help.

Armitage, having read the hideous diary, knew painfully well what kind of a manifestation to expect; but he did not add to the fright of the Dunwich people by giving any hints or clues. He hoped that it might be conquered without any revelation to the world of the monstrous thing it had escaped. As the shadows gathered, the natives commenced to disperse homeward, anxious to bar themselves indoors despite the present evidence that all human locks and bolts were useless before a force that could bend trees and crush houses when it chose. They shook their heads at the visitors' plan to stand guard at the Frye ruins near the glen; and, as they left, had little expectancy of ever seeing the watchers again.

There were rumblings under the hills that night, and the whippoorwills piped threateningly. Once in a while a wind, sweeping up out of Cold Spring Glen, would bring a touch of ineffable fetor to the heavy night air; such a fetor as all three of the watchers had smelled once before, when they stood above a dying thing that had passed for fifteen years and a half as a human being. But the looked-for terror did not appear. Whatever was down there in the glen was biding its time, and Armitage told his colleagues it would be suicidal to try to attack it in the dark.

Morning came wanly, and the night-sounds ceased. It was a grey, bleak day, with now and then a drizzle of rain; and heavier and heavier clouds seemed to be piling themselves up beyond the hills to the north-west. The men from Arkham were undecided what to do. Seeking shelter from the increasing rainfall beneath one of the few undestroyed Frye outbuildings, they debated the wisdom of waiting, or of taking the aggressive and going down into the glen in quest of their nameless, monstrous quarry. The downpour waxed in heaviness, and distant peals of thunder sounded from far horizons. Sheet lightning shimmered, and then a forky bolt flashed near at hand, as if descending into the accursed glen itself. The sky grew very dark, and the watchers hoped that the storm would prove a short, sharp one followed by clear weather.

It was still gruesomely dark when, not much over an hour later, a confused babel of voices sounded down the road. Another moment brought to view a frightened group of more than a dozen men, running, shouting, and even whimpering hysterically. Someone in the lead began sobbing out words, and the Arkham men started violently when those words developed a coherent form.

'Oh, my Gawd, my Gawd,' the voice choked out. 'It's a-goin' agin, an' this time by day! It's aout – it's aout an' a-movin' this very minute, an' only the Lord knows when it'll be on us all!'

The speaker panted into silence, but another took up his message.

'Nigh on a haour ago Zeb Whateley here heered the 'phone a-ringin', an' it was Mis' Corey, George's wife, that lives daown by the junction. She says the hired boy Luther was aout drivin' in the caows from the storm arter the big bolt, when he see all the trees a-bendin' at the maouth o' the glen –opposite side ter this – an' smelt the same awful smell like he smelt when he faound the big tracks las' Monday mornin'. An' she says he says they was a swishin' lappin' saound, more nor what the bendin' trees an' bushes could make, an' all on a suddent the trees along the rud begun ter git pushed one side, an' they was a awful stompin' an' splashin' in the mud. But mind ye, Luther he didn't see nothin' at all, only just the bendin' trees an' underbrush.

'Then fur ahead where Bishop's Brook goes under the rud he heerd a awful creakin' an' strainin' on the bridge, an' says he could tell the saound o' wood a-startin' to crack an' split. An' all the whiles he never see a thing, only them trees an' bushes a-bendin'. An' when the swishin' saound got very fur off– on the rud towards Wizard Whateley's an' Sentinel Hill – Luther he had the guts ter step up whar he'd heerd it fust an' look at the graound. It was all mud an' water, an' the sky was dark, an' the rain was wipin' aout all tracks abaout as fast as could be; but beginnin' at the glen maouth, whar the trees hed moved, they was still some o' them awful prints big as bar'ls like he seen Monday.'

At this point the first excited speaker interrupted.

'But that ain't the trouble naow – that was only the start. Zeb here was callin' folks up an' everybody was a-listenin' in when a call from Seth Bishop's cut in. His haousekeeper Sally was carryin' on fit to kill– she'd jest seed the trees a-bendin' beside the rud, an' says they was a kind o' mushy saound, like a elephant puffin' an' treadin', a-headin' fer the haouse. Then she up an' spoke suddent of a fearful smell, an' says her boy Cha'ncey was a-screamin' as haow it was jest like what he smelt up to the Whateley rewins Monday mornin'. An' the dogs was barkin' an' whinin' awful.

'An' then she let aout a turrible yell, an' says the shed daown the rud had jest caved in like the storm bed blowed it over, only the wind w'an't strong enough to dew that. Everybody was a-listenin', an' we could hear lots o' folks on the wire a-gaspin'. All to onct Sally she yelled again, an' says the front yard picket fence hed just crumbled up, though they wa'n't no sign o' what done it. Then everybody on the line could hear Cha'ncey an' old Seth Bishop a-yellin' tew, an' Sally was shriekin' aout that suthin' heavy hed struck the haouse – not lightnin' nor nothin', but suthin' heavy again' the front, that kep' a-launchin' itself agin an' agin, though ye couldn't see nothin' aout the front winders. An' then... an' then...'

Lines of fright deepened on every face; and Armitage, shaken as he was, had barely poise enough to prompt the speaker.

'An' then... Sally she yelled aout, "O help, the haouse is a-cavin' in ... an' on the wire we could hear a turrible crashin' an' a hull flock o' screaming... jes like when Elmer Frye's place was took, only wuss..."'

The man paused, and another of the crowd spoke.

'That's all – not a sound nor squeak over the 'phone arter that. Jest still-like. We that heerd it got aout Fords an' wagons an' rounded up as many able-bodied men-folks as we could git, at Corey's place, an' come up here ter see what yew thought best ter dew. Not but what I think it's the Lord's jedgment fer our iniquities, that no mortal kin ever set aside.'

Armitage saw that the time for positive action had come, and spoke decisively to the faltering group of frightened rustics.

'We must follow it, boys.' He made his voice as reassuring as possible. 'I believe there's a chance of putting it out of business. You men know that those Whateleys were wizards

– well, this thing is a thing of wizardry, and must be put down by the same means. I've seen Wilbur Whateley's diary and read some of the strange old books he used to read; and I think I know the right kind of spell to recite to make the thing fade away. Of course, one can't be sure, but we can always take a chance. It's invisible – I knew it would be – but there's powder in this long-distance sprayer that might make it show up for a second. Later on we'll try it. It's a frightful thing to have alive, but it isn't as bad as what Wilbur would have let in if he'd lived longer. You'll never know what the world escaped. Now we've only this one thing to fight, and it can't multiply. It can, though, do a lot of harm; so we mustn't hesitate to rid the community of it.

'We must follow it – and the way to begin is to go to the place that has just been wrecked. Let somebody lead the way – I don't know your roads very well, but I've an idea there might be a shorter cut across lots. How about it?'

The men shuffled about a moment, and then Earl Sawyer spoke softly, pointing with a grimy finger through the steadily lessening rain.

'I guess ye kin git to Seth Bishop's quickest by cuttin' across the lower medder here, wadin' the brook at the low place, an' climbin' through Carrier's mowin' an' the timber-lot beyont. That comes aout on the upper rud mighty nigh Seth's – a leetle t'other side.'

Armitage, with Rice and Morgan, started to walk in the direction indicated; and most of the natives followed slowly. The sky was growing lighter, and there were signs that the storm had worn itself away. When Armitage inadvertently took a wrong direction, Joe Osborn warned him and walked ahead to show the right one. Courage and confidence were mounting, though the twilight of the almost perpendicular wooded hill which lay towards the end of their short cut, and among whose fantastic ancient trees they had to scramble as if up a ladder, put these qualities to a severe test.

At length they emerged on a muddy road to find the sun coming out. They were a little beyond the Seth Bishop place, but bent trees and hideously unmistakable tracks showed what had passed by. Only a few moments were consumed in surveying the ruins just round the bend. It was the Frye incident all over again, and nothing dead or living was found in either of the collapsed shells which had been the Bishop house and barn. No one cared to remain there amidst the stench and tarry stickiness, but all turned instinctively to the line of horrible prints leading on towards the wrecked Whateley farmhouse and the altar-crowned slopes of Sentinel Hill.

As the men passed the site of Wilbur Whateley's abode they shuddered visibly, and seemed again to mix hesitancy with their zeal. It was no joke tracking down something as big as a house that one could not see, but that had all the vicious malevolence of a daemon. Opposite the base of Sentinel Hill the tracks left the road, and there was a fresh bending and matting visible along the broad swath marking the monster's former route to and from the summit.

Armitage produced a pocket telescope of considerable power and scanned the steep green side of the hill. Then he handed the instrument to Morgan, whose sight was keener. After a moment of gazing Morgan cried out sharply, passing the glass to Earl Sawyer and indicating a certain spot on the slope with his finger. Sawyer, as clumsy as most non-users of optical devices are, fumbled a while; but eventually focused the lenses with Armitage's aid. When he did so his cry was less restrained than Morgan's had been.

'Gawd almighty, the grass an' bushes is a'movin'! It's a-goin' up –slow-like – creepin' – up ter the top this minute, heaven only knows what fur!'

Then the germ of panic seemed to spread among the seekers. It was one thing to chase the nameless entity, but quite another to find it. Spells might be all right – but suppose they weren't? Voices began questioning Armitage about what he knew of the thing, and no reply seemed quite to satisfy. Everyone seemed to feel himself in close proximity to phases of Nature and of being utterly forbidden and wholly outside the sane experience of mankind.

CHAPTER X

IN THE END the three men from Arkham – old, white-bearded Dr. Armitage, stocky, iron-grey Professor Rice, and lean, youngish Dr. Morgan, ascended the mountain alone. After much patient instruction regarding its focusing and use, they left the telescope with the frightened group that remained in the road; and as they climbed they were watched closely by those among whom the glass was passed round. It was hard going, and Armitage had to be helped more than once. High above the toiling group the great swath trembled as its hellish maker repassed with snail-like deliberateness. Then it was obvious that the pursuers were gaining.

Curtis Whateley – of the undecayed branch – was holding the telescope when the Arkham party detoured radically from the swath. He told the crowd that the men were evidently trying to get to a subordinate peak which overlooked the swath at a point considerably ahead of where the shrubbery was now bending. This, indeed, proved to be true; and the party were seen to gain the minor elevation only a short time after the invisible blasphemy had passed it.

Then Wesley Corey, who had taken the glass, cried out that Armitage was adjusting the sprayer which Rice held, and that something must be about to happen. The crowd stirred uneasily, recalling that his sprayer was expected to give the unseen horror a moment of visibility. Two or three men shut their eyes, but Curtis Whateley snatched back the telescope and strained his vision to the utmost. He saw that Rice, from the party's point of advantage above and behind the entity, had an excellent chance of spreading the potent powder with marvelous effect.

Those without the telescope saw only an instant's flash of grey cloud– a cloud about the size of a moderately large building – near the top of the mountain. Curtis, who held the instrument, dropped it with a piercing shriek into the ankle-deep mud of the road. He reeled, and would have crumbled to the ground had not two or three others seized and steadied him. All he could do was moan half-inaudibly.

'Oh, oh, great Gawd... that... that...'

There was a pandemonium of questioning, and only Henry Wheeler thought to rescue the fallen telescope and wipe it clean of mud. Curtis was past all coherence, and even isolated replies were almost too much for him.

'Bigger'n a barn... all made o' squirmin' ropes... hull thing sort o' shaped like a hen's egg bigger'n anything with dozens o' legs like hogs-heads that haff shut up when they step... nothin' solid abaout it – all like jelly, an' made o' sep'rit wrigglin' ropes pushed clost together... great bulgin' eyes all over it... ten or twenty maouths or trunks a-stickin' aout all along the sides, big as stove-pipes an all a-tossin' an' an openin' an' shuttin'... all grey, with kinder blue or purple rings... an' Gawd it Heaven– that haff face on top...'

This final memory, whatever it was, proved too much for poor Curtis; and he collapsed completely before he could say more. Fred Farr and Will Hutchins carried him to the roadside and laid him on the damp grass. Henry Wheeler, trembling, turned the rescued telescope on the mountain to see what he might. Through the lenses were discernible three tiny figures, apparently running towards the summit as fast as the steep incline allowed. Only these –nothing more. Then everyone noticed a strangely unseasonable noise in the deep valley behind, and even in the underbrush of Sentinel Hill itself. It was the piping of unnumbered whippoorwills, and in their shrill chorus there seemed to lurk a note of tense and evil expectancy.

Earl Sawyer now took the telescope and reported the three figures as standing on the topmost ridge, virtually level with the altar-stone but at a considerable distance from it. One figure, he said, seemed to be raising its hands above its head at rhythmic intervals; and as Sawyer mentioned the circumstance the crowd seemed to hear a faint, half-musical sound from the distance, as if a loud chant were accompanying the gestures. The weird silhouette on that remote peak must have been a spectacle of infinite grotesqueness and impressiveness, but no observer was in a mood for aesthetic appreciation. 'I guess he's sayin' the spell,' whispered Wheeler as he snatched back the telescope. The whippoorwills were piping wildly, and in a singularly curious irregular rhythm quite unlike that of the visible ritual.

Suddenly the sunshine seemed to lessen without the intervention of any discernible cloud. It was a very peculiar phenomenon, and was plainly marked by all. A rumbling sound seemed brewing beneath the hills, mixed strangely with a concordant rumbling which clearly came from the sky. Lightning flashed aloft, and the wondering crowd looked in vain for the portents of storm. The chanting of the men from Arkham now became unmistakable, and Wheeler saw through the glass that they were all raising their arms in the rhythmic incantation. From some farmhouse far away came the frantic barking of dogs.

The change in the quality of the daylight increased, and the crowd gazed about the horizon in wonder. A purplish darkness, born of nothing more than a spectral deepening of the sky's blue, pressed down upon the rumbling hills. Then the lightning flashed again, somewhat brighter than before, and the crowd fancied that it had showed a certain mistiness around the altar-stone on the distant height. No one, however, had been using the telescope at that instant. The whippoorwills continued their irregular pulsation, and the men of Dunwich braced themselves tensely against some imponderable menace with which the atmosphere seemed surcharged.

Without warning came those deep, cracked, raucous vocal sounds which will never leave the memory of the stricken group who heard them. Not from any human throat were they born, for the organs of man can yield no such acoustic perversions. Rather would one have said they came from the pit itself, had not their source been so unmistakably the altar-stone on the peak. It is almost erroneous to call them sounds at all, since so much of their ghastly, infra-bass timbre spoke to dim seats of consciousness and terror far subtler than the ear; yet one must do so, since their form was indisputably though vaguely that of half-articulate words. They were loud – loud as the rumblings and the thunder above which they echoed – yet did they come from no visible being. And because imagination might suggest a conjectural source in the world of non-visible beings, the huddled crowd at the mountain's base huddled still closer, and winced as if in expectation of a blow.

'Ygnailh... ygnaiih... thflthkh'ngha... Yog-Sothoth...' rang the hideous croaking out of space. 'Y'bthnk... h'ehye – n'grkdl'lh...'

The speaking impulse seemed to falter here, as if some frightful psychic struggle were going on. Henry Wheeler strained his eye at the telescope, but saw only the three grotesquely silhouetted human figures on the peak, all moving their arms furiously in strange gestures as their incantation drew near its culmination. From what black wells of Acherontic fear or feeling, from what unplumbed gulfs of extra-cosmic consciousness or obscure, long-latent heredity, were those half-articulate thunder-croakings drawn? Presently they began to gather renewed force and coherence as they grew in stark, utter, ultimate frenzy.

'Eh-y-ya-ya-yahaah – e'yayayaaaa... ngh'aaaaa... ngh'aaa... h'yuh ... h'yuh... HELP! HELP!... ff – ff – ff – FATHER! FATHER! YOG-SOTHOTH!...'

But that was all. The pallid group in the road, still reeling at the indisputably English syllables that had poured thickly and thunderously down from the frantic vacancy beside that shocking altar-stone, were never to hear such syllables again. Instead, they jumped violently at the terrific report which seemed to rend the hills; the deafening, cataclysmic peal whose source, be it inner earth or sky, no hearer was ever able to place. A single lightning bolt shot from the purple zenith to the altar-stone, and a great tidal wave of viewless force and indescribable stench swept down from the hill to all the countryside. Trees, grass, and under-brush were whipped into a fury; and the frightened crowd at the mountain's base, weakened by the lethal fetor that seemed about to asphyxiate them, were almost hurled off their feet. Dogs howled from the distance, green grass and foliage wilted to a curious, sickly yellow-grey, and over field and forest were scattered the bodies of dead whippoorwills.

The stench left quickly, but the vegetation never came right again. To this day there is something queer and unholy about the growths on and around that fearsome hill Curtis Whateley was only just regaining consciousness when the Arkham men came slowly down the mountain in the beams of a sunlight once more brilliant and untainted. They were grave and quiet, and seemed shaken by memories and reflections even more terrible than those which had reduced the group of natives to a state of cowed quivering. In reply to a jumble of questions they only shook their heads and reaffirmed one vital fact.

'The thing has gone for ever,' Armitage said. 'It has been split up into what it was originally made of, and can never exist again. It was an impossibility in a normal world. Only the least fraction was really matter in any sense we know. It was like its father – and most of it has gone back to him in some vague realm or dimension outside our material universe; some vague abyss out of which only the most accursed rites of human blasphemy could ever have called him for a moment on the hills.'

There was a brief silence, and in that pause the scattered senses of poor Curtis Whateley began to knit back into a sort of continuity; so that he put his hands to his head with a moan. Memory seemed to pick itself up where it had left off, and the horror of the sight that had prostrated him burst in upon him again.

'Oh, oh, my Gawd, that haff face – that haff face on top of it... that face with the red eyes an' crinkly albino hair, an' no chin, like the Whateleys... It was a octopus, centipede, spider kind o' thing, but they was a haff-shaped man's face on top of it, an' it looked like Wizard Whateley's, only it was yards an' yards acrost...'

He paused exhausted, as the whole group of natives stared in a bewilderment not quite crystallized into fresh terror. Only old Zebulon Whateley, who wanderingly remembered ancient things but who had been silent heretofore, spoke aloud.

'Fifteen year' gone,' he rambled, 'I heered Ol' Whateley say as haow some day we'd hear a child o' Lavinny's a-callin' its father's name on the top o' Sentinel Hill...'

But Joe Osborn interrupted him to question the Arkham men anew.

'What was it, anyhaow, an' haowever did young Wizard Whateley call it aout o' the air it come from?'

Armitage chose his words very carefully.

'It was – well, it was mostly a kind of force that doesn't belong in our part of space; a kind of force that acts and grows and shapes itself by other laws than those of our sort of Nature. We have no business calling in such things from outside, and only very wicked people and very wicked cults ever try to. There was some of it in Wilbur Whateley himself – enough to make a devil and a precocious monster of him, and to make his passing out a pretty terrible sight. I'm going to burn his accursed diary, and if you men are wise you'll dynamite that altar-stone up there, and pull down all the rings of standing stones on the other hills. Things like that brought down the beings those Whateleys were so fond of – the beings they were going to let in tangibly to wipe out the human race and drag the earth off to some nameless place for some nameless purpose.

'But as to this thing we've just sent back – the Whateleys raised it for a terrible part in the doings that were to come. It grew fast and big from the same reason that Wilbur grew fast and big – but it beat him because it had a greater share of the outsideness in it. You needn't ask how Wilbur called it out of the air. He didn't call it out. It was his twin brother, but it looked more like the father than he did.'

The Call of Cthulhu

H.P. Lovecraft

(Found Among the Papers of the Late Francis Wayland Thurston, of Boston)

Of such great powers or beings there may be conceivably a survival... a survival of a hugely remote period when... consciousness was manifested, perhaps, in shapes and forms long since withdrawn before the tide of advancing humanity... forms of which poetry and legend alone have caught a flying memory and called them gods, monsters, mythical beings of all sorts and kinds...
Algernon Blackwood

I: The Horror in Clay

THE MOST MERCIFUL thing in the world, I think, is the inability of the human mind to correlate all its contents. We live on a placid island of ignorance in the midst of black seas of infinity, and it was not meant that we should voyage far. The sciences, each straining in its own direction, have hitherto harmed us little; but some day the piecing together of dissociated knowledge will open up such terrifying vistas of reality, and of our frightful position therein, that we shall either go mad from the revelation or flee from the deadly light into the peace and safety of a new dark age.

Theosophists have guessed at the awesome grandeur of the cosmic cycle wherein our world and human race form transient incidents. They have hinted at strange survival in terms which would freeze the blood if not masked by a bland optimism. But it is not from them that there came the single glimpse of forbidden aeons which chills me when I think of it and maddens me when I dream of it. That glimpse, like all dread glimpses of truth, flashed out from an accidental piecing together of separated things – in this case an old newspaper item and the notes of a dead professor. I hope that no one else will accomplish this piecing out; certainly, if I live, I shall never knowingly supply a link in so hideous a chain. I think that the professor, too, intended to keep silent regarding the part he knew, and that he would have destroyed his notes had not sudden death seized him.

My knowledge of the thing began in the winter of 1926-27 with the death of my great-uncle, George Gammell Angell, Professor Emeritus of Semitic Languages in Brown University, Providence, Rhode Island. Professor Angell was widely known as an authority on ancient inscriptions, and had frequently been resorted to by the heads of prominent museums; so that his passing at the age of ninety-two may be recalled by many. Locally, interest was intensified by the obscurity of the cause of death. The professor had been stricken whilst returning from the Newport boat; falling suddenly, as witnesses said, after having been jostled by a nautical-looking negro who had come from one of the queer dark courts on the precipitous hillside which formed a short cut from the waterfront to the deceased's home in Williams Street. Physicians were unable to find any visible disorder, but concluded after perplexed debate that some obscure lesion of the heart, induced by the brisk ascent of so steep a hill by so elderly a man, was responsible for the end. At the time I saw no reason to dissent from this dictum, but latterly I am inclined to wonder – and more than wonder.

As my great-uncle's heir and executor, for he died a childless widower, I was expected to go over his papers with some thoroughness; and for that purpose moved his entire set of files and boxes to my quarters in Boston. Much of the material which I correlated will be later published by the American Archaeological Society, but there was one box which I found exceedingly puzzling, and which I felt much averse from showing to other eyes. It had been locked, and I did not find the key till it occurred to me to examine the personal ring which the professor carried always in his pocket. Then, indeed, I succeeded in opening it, but when I did so seemed only to be confronted by a greater and more closely locked barrier. For what could be the meaning of the queer clay bas-relief and the disjointed jottings, ramblings and cuttings which I found? Had my uncle, in his latter years, become credulous of the most superficial impostures? I resolved to search out the eccentric sculptor responsible for this apparent disturbance of an old man's peace of mind.

The bas-relief was a rough rectangle less than an inch thick and about five by six inches in area; obviously of modern origin. Its designs, however, were far from modern in atmosphere and suggestion; for, although the vagaries of cubism and futurism are many and wild, they do not often reproduce that cryptic regularity which lurks in prehistoric writing. And writing of some kind the bulk of these designs seemed certainly to be; though my memory, despite much familiarity with the papers and collections of my uncle, failed in any way to identify this particular species, or even hint at its remotest affiliations.

Above these apparent hieroglyphics was a figure of evidently pictorial intent, though its impressionistic execution forbade a very clear idea of its nature. It seemed to be a sort of monster, or symbol representing a monster, of a form which only a diseased fancy could conceive. If I say that my somewhat extravagant imagination yielded simultaneous pictures of an octopus, a dragon, and a human caricature, I shall not be unfaithful to the spirit of the thing. A pulpy, tentacled head surmounted a grotesque and scaly body with rudimentary wings; but it was the general outline of the whole which made it most shockingly frightful. Behind the figure was a vague suggestion of a Cyclopean architectural background.

The writing accompanying this oddity was, aside from a stack of press cuttings, in Professor Angell's most recent hand; and made no pretension to literary style. What seemed to be the main document was headed "CTHULHU CULT" in characters painstakingly printed to avoid the erroneous reading of a word so unheard-of. This manuscript was divided into two sections, the first of which was headed "1925 – Dream and Dream Work of H. A. Wilcox, 7 Thomas St., Providence, R. I.", and the second, "Narrative of Inspector John R. Legrasse, 121 Bienville St., New Orleans, La., at 1908 A. A. S. Mtg. – Notes on Same, & Prof. Webb's Acct." The other manuscript papers were all brief notes, some of them accounts of the queer dreams of different persons, some of them citations from theosophical books and magazines (notably W. Scott-Elliot's Atlantis and the Lost Lemuria), and the rest comments on long-surviving secret societies and hidden cults, with references to passages in such mythological and anthropological source-books as Frazer's Golden Bough and Miss Murray's Witch-Cult in Western Europe. The cuttings largely alluded to outré mental illness and outbreaks of group folly or mania in the spring of 1925.

The first half of the principal manuscript told a very peculiar tale. It appears that on 1 March 1925, a thin, dark young man of neurotic and excited aspect had called upon Professor Angell bearing the singular clay bas-relief, which was then exceedingly damp and fresh. His card bore the name of Henry Anthony Wilcox, and my uncle had recognized him as the youngest son of an excellent family slightly known to him, who had latterly been studying sculpture at the Rhode Island School of Design and living alone at the Fleur-de-Lys

Building near that institution. Wilcox was a precocious youth of known genius but great eccentricity, and had from childhood excited attention through the strange stories and odd dreams he was in the habit of relating. He called himself "psychically hypersensitive", but the staid folk of the ancient commercial city dismissed him as merely "queer". Never mingling much with his kind, he had dropped gradually from social visibility, and was now known only to a small group of aesthetes from other towns. Even the Providence Art Club, anxious to preserve its conservatism, had found him quite hopeless.

On the occasion of the visit, ran the professor's manuscript, the sculptor abruptly asked for the benefit of his host's archaeological knowledge in identifying the hieroglyphics on the bas-relief. He spoke in a dreamy, stilted manner which suggested pose and alienated sympathy; and my uncle showed some sharpness in replying, for the conspicuous freshness of the tablet implied kinship with anything but archaeology. Young Wilcox's rejoinder, which impressed my uncle enough to make him recall and record it verbatim, was of a fantastically poetic cast which must have typified his whole conversation, and which I have since found highly characteristic of him. He said, "It is new, indeed, for I made it last night in a dream of strange cities; and dreams are older than brooding Tyre, or the contemplative Sphinx, or garden-girdled Babylon."

It was then that he began that rambling tale which suddenly played upon a sleeping memory and won the fevered interest of my uncle. There had been a slight earthquake tremor the night before, the most considerable felt in New England for some years; and Wilcox's imaginations had been keenly affected. Upon retiring, he had had an unprecedented dream of great Cyclopean cities of Titan blocks and sky-flung monoliths, all dripping with green ooze and sinister with latent horror. Hieroglyphics had covered the walls and pillars, and from some undetermined point below had come a voice that was not a voice; a chaotic sensation which only fancy could transmute into sound, but which he attempted to render by the almost unpronounceable jumble of letters, "Cthulhu fhtagn".

This verbal jumble was the key to the recollection which excited and disturbed Professor Angell. He questioned the sculptor with scientific minuteness; and studied with almost frantic intensity the bas-relief on which the youth had found himself working, chilled and clad only in his nightclothes, when waking had stolen bewilderingly over him. My uncle blamed his old age, Wilcox afterward said, for his slowness in recognizing both hieroglyphics and pictorial design. Many of his questions seemed highly out of place to his visitor, especially those which tried to connect the latter with strange cults or societies; and Wilcox could not understand the repeated promises of silence which he was offered in exchange for an admission of membership in some widespread mystical or paganly religious body. When Professor Angell became convinced that the sculptor was indeed ignorant of any cult or system of cryptic lore, he besieged his visitor with demands for future reports of dreams. This bore regular fruit, for after the first interview the manuscript records daily calls of the young man, during which he related startling fragments of nocturnal imagery whose burden was always some terrible Cyclopean vista of dark and dripping stone, with a subterrene voice or intelligence shouting monotonously in enigmatical sense-impacts uninscribable save as gibberish. The two sounds most frequently repeated are those rendered by the letters "Cthulhu" and "R'lyeh".

On 23 March, the manuscript continued, Wilcox failed to appear; and inquiries at his quarters revealed that he had been stricken with an obscure sort of fever and taken to the home of his family in Waterman Street. He had cried out in the night, arousing several other artists in the building, and had manifested since then only alternations of unconsciousness and delirium. My uncle at once telephoned the family, and from that time forward kept close watch of the case; calling often at the Thayer Street office of Dr. Tobey, whom he learned to be in charge. The youth's febrile mind, apparently, was dwelling on strange things; and the doctor shuddered now and then as he spoke of them. They included not only a repetition of what he had formerly dreamed, but touched wildly on a gigantic thing "miles high" which walked or lumbered about. He at no time fully described this object but occasional frantic words, as repeated by Dr. Tobey, convinced the professor that it must be identical with the nameless monstrosity he had sought to depict in his dream-sculpture. Reference to this object, the doctor added, was invariably a prelude to the young man's subsidence into lethargy. His temperature, oddly enough, was not greatly above normal; but the whole condition was otherwise such as to suggest true fever rather than mental disorder.

On 2 April at about 3 P.M. every trace of Wilcox's malady suddenly ceased. He sat upright in bed, astonished to find himself at home and completely ignorant of what had happened in dream or reality since the night of 22 March. Pronounced well by his physician, he returned to his quarters in three days; but to Professor Angell he was of no further assistance. All traces of strange dreaming had vanished with his recovery, and my uncle kept no record of his night-thoughts after a week of pointless and irrelevant accounts of thoroughly usual visions.

Here the first part of the manuscript ended, but references to certain of the scattered notes gave me much material for thought – so much, in fact, that only the ingrained skepticism then forming my philosophy can account for my continued distrust of the artist. The notes in question were those descriptive of the dreams of various persons covering the same period as that in which young Wilcox had had his strange visitations. My uncle, it seems, had quickly instituted a prodigiously far-flung body of inquiries amongst nearly all the friends whom he could question without impertinence, asking for nightly reports of their dreams, and the dates of any notable visions for some time past. The reception of his request seems to have been varied; but he must, at the very least, have received more responses than any ordinary man could have handled without a secretary. This original correspondence was not preserved, but his notes formed a thorough and really significant digest. Average people in society and business – New England's traditional "salt of the earth" – gave an almost completely negative result, though scattered cases of uneasy but formless nocturnal impressions appear here and there, always between 23 March and 2 April – the period of young Wilcox's delirium. Scientific men were little more affected, though four cases of vague description suggest fugitive glimpses of strange landscapes, and in one case there is mentioned a dread of something abnormal.

It was from the artists and poets that the pertinent answers came, and I know that panic would have broken loose had they been able to compare notes. As it was, lacking their original letters, I half suspected the compiler of having asked leading questions, or of having edited the correspondence in corroboration of what he had latently resolved to see. That is why I continued to feel that Wilcox, somehow cognizant of the old data which my uncle had possessed, had been imposing on the veteran scientist. These responses from aesthetes told a disturbing tale. From 28 February to 2 April a large proportion of them had dreamed very bizarre things, the intensity of the dreams being immeasurably the stronger during the period of the sculptor's delirium. Over a fourth of those who reported anything, reported scenes and half-sounds not unlike those which Wilcox had described; and some of the dreamers confessed acute fear of the gigantic nameless thing visible towards the last. One case, which the note describes with emphasis, was very sad. The subject, a widely known architect with leanings towards theosophy and occultism, went violently insane on the date of young Wilcox's seizure, and expired several months later after incessant screamings to be saved from some escaped denizen of hell. Had my uncle referred to these cases by name instead of merely by number, I should have attempted some corroboration and personal investigation; but as it was, I succeeded in tracing down only a few. All of these, however, bore out the notes in full. I have often wondered if all the objects of the professor's questioning felt as puzzled as did this fraction. It is well that no explanation shall ever reach them.

The press cuttings, as I have intimated, touched on cases of panic, mania, and eccentricity during the given period. Professor Angell must have employed a cutting bureau, for the number of extracts was tremendous, and the sources scattered throughout the globe. Here was a nocturnal suicide in London, where a lone sleeper had leaped from a window after a shocking cry. Here likewise a rambling letter to the editor of a paper in South America, where a fanatic deduces a dire future from visions he has seen. A dispatch from California describes a theosophist colony as donning white robes en masse for some "glorious fulfilment" which never arrives, whilst items from India speak guardedly of serious native unrest towards the end of March. Voodoo orgies multiply in Haiti, and African outposts report ominous mutterings. American officers in the Philippines find certain tribes bothersome about this time, and New York policemen are mobbed by hysterical Levantines on the night of 22-23 March. The west of Ireland, too, is full of wild rumour and legendry, and a fantastic painter named Ardois-Bonnot hangs a blasphemous Dream Landscape in the Paris spring salon of 1926. And so numerous are the recorded troubles in insane asylums that only a miracle can have stopped the medical fraternity from noting strange parallelisms and drawing mystified conclusions. A weird bunch of cuttings, all told; and I can at this date scarcely envisage the callous rationalism with which I set them aside. But I was then convinced that young Wilcox had known of the older matters mentioned by the professor.

II: The Tale of Inspector Legrasse

THE OLDER MATTERS which had made the sculptor's vision and bas-relief so significant to my uncle formed the subject of the second half of his long manuscript. Once before, it appears, Professor Angell had seen the hellish outlines of the nameless monstrosity, puzzled over the unknown hieroglyphics, and heard the ominous syllables which can be rendered only as "Cthulhu"; and all this in so stirring and horrible a connection that it is small wonder he pursued young Wilcox with queries and demands for data.

This earlier experience had come in 1908, seventeen years before, when the American Archaeological Society held its annual meeting in St Louis. Professor Angell, as befitted one of his authority and attainments, had had a prominent part in all the deliberations, and was one of the first to be approached by the several outsiders who took advantage of the convocation to offer questions for correct answering and problems for expert solution.

The chief of these outsiders, and in a short time the focus of interest for the entire meeting, was a commonplace-looking middle-aged man who had travelled all the way from New Orleans for certain special information unobtainable from any local source. His name was John Raymond Legrasse, and he was by profession an inspector of police. With him he bore the subject of his visit, a grotesque, repulsive, and apparently very ancient stone statuette whose origin he was at a loss to determine.

It must not be fancied that Inspector Legrasse had the least interest in archaeology. On the contrary, his wish for enlightenment was prompted by purely professional considerations. The statuette, idol, fetish, or whatever it was, had been captured some months before in the wooden swamps south of New Orleans during a raid on a supposed voodoo meeting; and so singular and hideous were the rites connected with it, that the police could not but realize that they had stumbled on a dark cult totally unknown to them, and infinitely more diabolic than even the blackest of the African voodoo circles. Of its origin, apart from the erratic and unbelievable tales extorted from the captured members, absolutely nothing was to be discovered; hence the anxiety of the police for any antiquarian lore which might help them to place the frightful symbol, and through it track down the cult to its fountain-head.

Inspector Legrasse was scarcely prepared for the sensation which his offering created. One sight of the thing had been enough to throw the assembled men of science into a state of tense excitement, and they lost no time in crowding around him to gaze at the diminutive figure whose utter strangeness and air of genuinely abysmal antiquity hinted so potently at unopened and archaic vistas. No recognized school of sculpture had animated this terrible object, yet centuries and even thousands of years seemed recorded in its dim and greenish surface of unplaceable stone.

The figure, which was finally passed slowly from man to man for close and careful study, was between seven and eight inches in height, and of exquisitely artistic workmanship. It represented a monster of vaguely anthropoid outline, but with an octopus-like head whose face was a mass of feelers, a scaly, rubbery-looking body, prodigious claws on hind and fore feet, and long, narrow wings behind. This thing, which seemed instinct with a fearsome and unnatural malignancy, was of a somewhat bloated corpulence, and squatted evilly on a rectangular block or pedestal covered with undecipherable characters. The tips of the wings touched the back edge of the block, the seat occupied the centre, whilst the long, curved claws of the doubled-up, crouching hind legs gripped the front edge and extended a quarter of the way down towards the bottom of the pedestal. The cephalopod head was bent forward, so that the ends of the facial feelers brushed the backs of huge fore-paws which clasped the croucher's elevated knees. The aspect of the whole was abnormally lifelike, and the more subtly fearful because its source was so totally unknown. Its vast, awesome, and incalculable age was unmistakable; yet not one link did it show with any known type of art belonging to civilization's youth – or indeed to any other time.

Totally separate and apart, its very material was a mystery; for the soapy, greenish-black stone with its golden or iridescent flecks and striations resembled nothing familiar to geology or mineralogy. The characters along the base were equally baffling; and no member present, despite a representation of half the world's expert learning in this field, could form the least notion of even their remotest linguistic kinship. They, like the subject and material, belonged to something horribly remote and distinct from mankind as we know it; something frightfully suggestive of old and unhallowed cycles of life in which our world and our conceptions have no part.

And yet, as the members severally shook their heads and confessed defeat at the inspector's problem, there was one man in that gathering who suspected a touch of bizarre familiarity in the monstrous shape and writing, and who presently told with some diffidence of the odd trifle he knew. This person was the late William Channing Webb, professor of anthropology in Princeton University, and an explorer of no slight note.

Professor Webb had been engaged, forty-eight years before, in a tour of Greenland and Iceland in search of some Runic inscriptions which he failed to unearth; and whilst high up on the West Greenland coast had encountered a singular tribe or cult of degenerate Eskimos whose religion, a curious form of devil-worship, chilled him with its deliberate bloodthirstiness and repulsiveness. It was a faith of which other Eskimos knew little, and which they mentioned only with shudders, saying that it had come down from horribly ancient aeons before ever the world was made. Besides nameless rites and human sacrifices there were certain queer hereditary rituals addressed to a supreme elder devil or tornasuk; and of this Professor Webb had taken a careful phonetic copy from an aged angekok or wizard-priest, expressing the sounds in Roman letters as best he knew how. But just now of prime significance was the fetish which this cult had cherished, and around which they danced when the aurora leaped high over the ice cliffs. It was, the professor stated, a very crude bas-relief of stone, comprising a hideous picture and some cryptic writing. And as far as he could tell, it was a rough parallel in all essential features of the bestial thing now lying before the meeting.

These data, received with suspense and astonishment by the assembled members, proved doubly exciting to Inspector Legrasse; and he began at once to ply his informant with questions. Having noted and copied an oral ritual among the swamp cult-worshippers his men had arrested, he besought the professor to remember as best he might the syllables taken down amongst the diabolist Eskimos. There then followed an exhaustive comparison of details, and a moment of really awed silence when both detective and scientist agreed on the virtual identity of the phrase common to two hellish rituals so many worlds of distance apart. What, in substance, both the Eskimo wizards and the Louisiana swamp-priests had chanted to their kindred idols was something very like this – the word-divisions being guessed at from traditional breaks in the phrase as chanted aloud:

"Ph'nglui mglw'nafh Cthulhu R'lyeh wgah'nagl fhtagn."

Legrasse had one point in advance of Professor Webb, for several among his mongrel prisoners had repeated to him what older celebrants had told them the words meant. This text, as given, ran something like this:

"In his house at R'lyeh dead Cthulhu waits dreaming."

And now, in response to a general and urgent demand, Inspector Legrasse related as fully as possible his experience with the swamp worshippers; telling a story to which I could see my uncle attached profound significance. It savoured of the wildest dreams of myth-maker and theosophist, and disclosed an astonishing degree of cosmic imagination among such half-castes and pariahs as might be least expected to possess it.

On 1 November 1907, there had come to New Orleans police a frantic summons from the swamp and lagoon country to the south. The squatters there, mostly primitive but good-natured descendants of Lafitte's men, were in the grip of stark terror from an unknown thing which had stolen upon them in the night. It was voodoo, apparently, but voodoo of a more terrible sort than they had ever known; and some of their women and children had disappeared since the malevolent tom-tom had begun its incessant beating far within the black haunted woods where no dweller ventured. There were insane shouts and harrowing screams, soul-chilling chants and dancing devil-flames; and, the frightened messenger added, the people could stand it no more.

So a body of twenty police, filling two carriages and an automobile, had set out in the late afternoon with the shivering squatter as a guide. At the end of the passable road they alighted, and for miles splashed on in silence through the terrible cypress woods where day never came. Ugly roots and malignant hanging nooses of Spanish moss beset them, and now and then a pile of dank stones or fragments of a rotting wall intensified by its hint of morbid habitation a depression which every malformed tree and every fungous islet combined to create. At length the squatter settlement, a miserable huddle of huts, hove in sight; and hysterical dwellers ran out to cluster around the group of bobbing lanterns. The muffled beat of tom-toms was now faintly audible far, far ahead; and a curdling shriek came at infrequent intervals when the wind shifted. A reddish glare, too, seemed to filter through the pale undergrowth beyond endless avenues of forest night. Reluctant even to be left alone again, each one of the cowed squatters refused point-blank to advance another inch towards the scene of unholy worship, so Inspector Legrasse and his nineteen colleagues plunged on unguided into black arcades of horror that none of them had ever trod before.

The region now entered by the police was one of traditionally evil repute, substantially unknown and untraversed by white men. There were legends of a hidden lake unglimpsed by mortal sight, in which dwelt a huge, formless white polypus thing with luminous eyes; and squatters whispered that bat-winged devils flew up out of caverns in inner earth to worship it at midnight. They said it had been there before D'Iberville, before La Salle, before the Indians, and before even the wholesome beasts and birds of the woods. It was nightmare itself, and to see it was to die. But it made men dream, and so they knew enough to keep away. The present voodoo orgy was, indeed, on the merest fringe of this abhorred area, but that location was bad enough; hence perhaps the very place of the worship had terrified the squatters more than the shocking sounds and incidents.

Only poetry or madness could do justice to the noises heard by Legrasse's men as they ploughed on through the black morass towards the red glare and the muffled tom-toms. There are vocal qualities peculiar to men, and vocal qualities peculiar to beasts; and it is terrible to hear the one when the source should yield the other. Animal fury and orgiastic licence here whipped themselves to demoniac heights by howls and squawking ecstasies that tore and reverberated through those nighted woods like pestilential tempests from the gulfs of hell. Now and then the less organized ululations would cease, and from what seemed a well-drilled chorus of hoarse voices would rise in singsong chant that hideous phrase or ritual:

"Ph'nglui mglw'nafh Cthulhu R'lyeh wgah'nagl fhtagn."

Then the men, having reached a spot where the trees were thinner, came suddenly in sight of the spectacle itself. Four of them reeled, one fainted, and two were shaken into a frantic cry which the mad cacophony of the orgy fortunately deadened. Legrasse dashed swamp water on the face of the fainting man, and all stood trembling and nearly hypnotized with horror.

In a natural glade of the swamp stood a grassy island of perhaps an acre's extent, clear of trees and tolerably dry. On this now leaped and twisted a more indescribable horde of human abnormality than any but a Sime or an Angarola could paint. Void of clothing, this hybrid spawn were braying, bellowing and writhing about a monstrous ringshaped bonfire; in the centre of which, revealed by occasional rifts in the curtain of flame, stood a great granite monolith some eight feet in height; on top of which, incongruous in its diminutiveness, rested the noxious carven statuette. From a wide circle of ten scaffolds set up at regular intervals with the flame-girt monolith as a centre hung, head downward, the oddly marred bodies of the helpless squatters who had disappeared. It was inside this circle that the ring of worshippers jumped and roared, the general direction of the mass motion being from left to right in endless bacchanale between the ring of bodies and the ring of fire.

It may have been only imagination and it may have been only echoes which induced one of the men, an excitable Spaniard, to fancy he heard antiphonal responses to the ritual from some far and unillumined spot deeper within the wood of ancient legendry and horror. This man, Joseph D. Galvez, I later met and questioned; and he proved distractingly imaginative. He indeed went so far as to hint of the faint beating of great wings, and of a glimpse of shining eyes and a mountainous white bulk beyond the remotest trees – but I suppose he had been hearing too much native superstition.

Actually, the horrified pause of the men was of comparatively brief duration. Duty came first; and although there must have been nearly a hundred mongrel celebrants in the throng, the police relied on their firearms and plunged determinedly into the nauseous rout. For five minutes the resultant din and chaos were beyond description. Wild blows were struck, shots were fired, and escapes were made; but in the end Legrasse was able to count some forty-seven sullen prisoners, whom he forced to dress in haste and fall into line between two rows of policemen. Five of the worshippers lay dead, and two severely wounded ones were carried away on improvised stretchers by their fellow-prisoners. The image on the monolith, of course, was carefully removed and carried back by Legrasse.

Examined at headquarters after a trip of intense strain and weariness, the prisoners all proved to be men of a very low, mixed-blooded, and mentally aberrant type. Most were seamen, and a sprinkling of negroes and mulattos, largely West Indians or Brava Portuguese from the Cape Verde Islands, gave a colouring of voodooism to the heterogeneous cult. But before many questions were asked, it became manifest that something far deeper and older than negro fetishism was involved. Degraded and ignorant as they were, the creatures held with surprising consistency to the central idea of their loathsome faith.

They worshipped, so they said, the Great Old Ones who lived ages before there were any men, and who came to the young world out of the sky. These Old Ones were gone now, inside the earth and under the sea; but their dead bodies had told their secrets in dreams to the first men, who formed a cult which had never died. This was that cult, and the prisoners said it had always existed and always would exist, hidden in distant wastes and dark places all over the world until the time when the great priest Cthulhu, from his dark house in the mighty city of R'lyeh under the waters, should rise and bring the earth again beneath his sway. Some day he would call, when the stars were ready, and the secret cult would always be waiting to liberate him.

Meanwhile no more must be told. There was a secret which even torture could not extract. Mankind was not absolutely alone among the conscious things of earth, for shapes came out of the dark to visit the faithful few. But these were not the Great Old Ones. No man had ever seen the Old Ones. The carven idol was great Cthulhu, but none might say whether or not the others were precisely like him. No one could read the old writing now, but things were told by word of mouth. The chanted ritual was not the secret – that was never spoken aloud, only whispered. The chant meant only this: "In his house at R'lyeh dead Cthulhu waits dreaming."

Only two of the prisoners were found sane enough to be hanged, and the rest were committed to various institutions. All denied a part in the ritual murders, and averred that the killing had been done by Black-winged Ones which had come to them from their immemorial meeting-place in the haunted wood. But of those mysterious allies no coherent account could ever be gained. What the police did extract came mainly from an immensely aged mestizo named Castro, who claimed to have sailed to strange ports and talked with undying leaders of the cult in the mountains of China.

Old Castro remembered bits of hideous legend that paled the speculations of theosophists and made man and the world seem recent and transient indeed. There had been aeons when other Things ruled on the earth, and They had had great cities. Remains of Them, he said the deathless Chinamen had told him, were still to be found as Cyclopean stones on islands in the Pacific. They all died vast epochs of time before men came, but there were arts which could revive Them when the stars had come round again to the right positions in the cycle of eternity. They had, indeed, come themselves from the stars, and brought Their images with Them.

These Great Old Ones, Castro continued, were not composed altogether of flesh and blood. They had shape – for did not this star-fashioned image prove it? – but that shape was not made of matter. When the stars were right, They could plunge from world to world through the sky; but when the stars were wrong, They could not live. But although They no longer lived, They would never really die. They all lay in stone houses in Their great city of R'lyeh, preserved by the spells of mighty Cthulhu for a glorious resurrection when the stars and the earth might once more be ready for Them. But at that time some force from outside must serve to liberate Their bodies. The spells that preserved them intact likewise prevented Them from making an initial move, and They could only lie awake in the dark and think whilst uncounted millions of years rolled by. They knew all that was occurring in the universe, for Their mode of speech was transmitted thought. Even now They talked in Their tombs. When, after infinities of chaos, the first men came, the Great Old Ones spoke to the sensitive among them by moulding their dreams; for only thus could Their language reach the fleshy minds of mammals.

Then, whispered Castro, those first men formed the cult around small idols which the Great Ones showed them; idols brought in dim eras from dark stars. That cult would never die till the stars came right again, and the secret priests would take great Cthulhu from His tomb to revive His subjects and resume His rule of earth. The time would be easy to know, for then mankind would have become as the Great Old Ones; free and wild and beyond good and evil, with laws and morals thrown aside and all men shouting and killing and revelling in joy. Then the liberated Old Ones would teach them new ways to shout and kill and revel and enjoy themselves, and all the earth would flame with a holocaust of ecstasy and freedom. Meanwhile the cult, by appropriate rites, must keep alive the memory of those ancient ways and shadow forth the prophecy of their return.

In the elder time chosen men had talked with the entombed Old Ones in dreams, but then something had happened. The great stone city R'lyeh, with its monoliths and sepulchres, had sunk beneath the waves; and the deep waters, full of the one primal mystery through which not even thought can pass, had cut off the spectral intercourse. But memory never died, and high priests said that the city would rise again when the stars were right. Then came out of the earth the black spirits of earth, mouldy and shadowy, and full of dim rumours picked up in caverns beneath forgotten sea-bottoms. But of them old Castro dared not speak much. He cut himself off hurriedly, and no amount of persuasion or subtlety could elicit more in this direction. The size of the Old Ones, too, he curiously declined to mention. Of the cult, he said that he thought the centre lay amid the pathless deserts of Arabia, where Irem, the City of Pillars, dreams hidden and untouched. It was not allied to the European witch-cult, and was virtually unknown beyond its members. No book had ever really hinted of it, though the deathless Chinamen said that there were double meanings in the Necronomicon of the mad Arab Abdul Alhazred which the initiated might read as they chose, especially the much-discussed couplet:

> *That is not dead which can eternal lie,*
> *And with strange aeons even death may die.*

Legrasse, deeply impressed and not a little bewildered, had inquired in vain concerning the historic affiliations of the cult. Castro, apparently, had told the truth when he said that it was wholly secret. The authorities at Tulane University could shed no light upon either cult or image, and now the detective had come to the highest authorities in the country and met with no more than the Greenland tale of Professor Webb.

The feverish interest aroused at the meeting by Legrasse's tale, corroborated as it was by the statuette, is echoed in the subsequent correspondence of those who attended; although scant mention occurs in the formal publication of the society. Caution is the first care of those accustomed to face occasional charlatanry and imposture. Legrasse for some time lent the image to Professor Webb, but at the latter's death it was returned to him and remains in his possession, where I viewed it not long ago. It is truly a terrible thing, and unmistakably akin to the dream-sculpture of young Wilcox.

That my uncle was excited by the tale of the sculptor I did not wonder, for what thoughts must arise upon hearing, after a knowledge of what Legrasse had learned of the cult, of a sensitive young man, who had dreamed not only the figure and exact hieroglyphics of the swamp-found image and the Greenland devil tablet, but had come in his dreams upon at least three of the precise words of the formula uttered alike by Eskimo diabolists and mongrel Louisianans? Professor Angell's instant start on an investigation of the utmost thoroughness was eminently natural; though privately I suspected young Wilcox of having heard of the cult in some indirect way, and of having invented a series of dreams to heighten and continue the mystery at my uncle's expense. The dream-narratives and cuttings collected by the professor were, of course, strong corroboration; but the rationalism of my mind and the extravagance of the whole subject led me to adopt what I thought the most sensible conclusions. So, after thoroughly studying the manuscript again and correlating the theosophical and anthropological notes with the cult narrative of Legrasse, I made a trip to Providence to see the sculptor and give him the rebuke I thought proper for so boldly imposing upon a learned and aged man.

Wilcox still lived alone in the Fleur-de-Lys Building in Thomas Street, a hideous Victorian imitation of seventeenth century Breton architecture which flaunts its stuccoed front amidst the lovely Colonial houses on the ancient hill, and under the very shadow of the finest Georgian steeple in America. I found him at work in his rooms, and at once conceded from the specimens scattered about that his genius is indeed profound and authentic. He will, I believe, be heard from some time as one of the great decadents; for he has crystallized in clay and will one day mirror in marble those nightmares and phantasies which Arthur Machen evokes in prose, and Clark Ashton Smith makes visible in verse and in painting.

Dark, frail, and somewhat unkempt in aspect, he turned languidly at my knock and asked me my business without rising. When I told him who I was, he displayed some interest; for my uncle had excited his curiosity in probing his strange dreams, yet had never explained the reason for the study. I did not enlarge his knowledge in this regard, but sought with some subtlety to draw him out.

In a short time I became convinced of his absolute sincerity for he spoke of the dreams in a manner none could mistake. They and their subconscious residuum had influenced his art profoundly, and he showed me a morbid statue whose contours almost made me shake with the potency of its black suggestion. He could not recall having seen the original of this thing except in his own dream bas-relief, but the outlines had formed themselves insensibly under his hands. It was, no doubt, the giant shape he had raved of in delirium. That he really knew nothing of the hidden cult, save from what my uncle's relentless catechism had let fall, he soon made clear; and again I strove to think of some way in which he could possibly have received the weird impressions.

He talked of his dreams in a strangely poetic fashion; making me see with terrible vividness the damp Cyclopean city of slimy green stone – whose geometry, he oddly said, was all wrong – and hear with frightened expectancy the ceaseless, half-mental calling from underground: "Cthulhu fhtagn, Cthulhu fhtagn."

These words had formed part of that dread ritual which told of dead Cthulhu's dream-vigil in his stone vault at R'lyeh, and I felt deeply moved despite my rational beliefs. Wilcox, I was sure, had heard of the cult in some casual way, and had soon forgotten it amidst the mass of his equally weird reading and imagining. Later, by virtue of its sheer impressiveness, it had found subconscious expression in dreams, in the bas-relief, and in the terrible statue I now beheld; so that his imposture upon my uncle had been a very innocent one. The youth was of a type, at once slightly affected and slightly ill-mannered, which I could never like; but I was willing enough now to admit both his genius and his honesty. I took leave of him amicably, and wish him all the success his talent promises.

The matter of the cult still remained to fascinate me, and at times I had visions of personal fame from researches into its origin and connections. I visited New Orleans, talked with Legrasse and others of that old-time raiding-party, saw the frightful image, and even questioned such of the mongrel prisoners as still survived. Old Castro, unfortunately, had been dead for some years. What I now heard so graphically at first hand, though it was really no more than a detailed confirmation of what my uncle had written, excited me afresh; for I felt sure that I was on the track of a very real, very secret, and very ancient religion whose discovery would make me an anthropologist of note. My attitude was still one of absolute materialism as I wish it still were, and I discounted with a most inexplicable perversity the coincidence of the dream notes and odd cuttings collected by Professor Angell.

One thing which I began to suspect, and which I now fear I know, is that my uncle's death was far from natural. He fell on a narrow hill street leading up from an ancient waterfront swarming with foreign mongrels, after a careless push from a negro sailor. I did not forget the mixed blood and marine pursuits of the cult-members in Louisiana, and would not be surprised to learn of secret methods and poison needles as ruthless and as anciently known as the cryptic rites and beliefs. Legrasse and his men, it is true, have been let alone; but in Norway a certain seaman who saw things is dead. Might not the deeper inquiries of my uncle after encountering the sculptor's data have come to sinister ears? I think Professor Angell died because he knew too much, or because he was likely to learn too much. Whether I shall go as he did remains to be seen, for I have learned much now.

III The Madness from the Sea

IF HEAVEN ever wishes to grant me a boon, it will be a total effacing of the results of a mere chance which fixed my eye on a certain stray piece of shelf-paper. It was nothing on which I would naturally have stumbled in the course of my daily round, for it was an old number of an Australian journal, the Sydney Bulletin for April 18, 1925. It had escaped even the cutting bureau which had at the time of its issuance been avidly collecting material for my uncle's research.

I had largely given over my inquiries into what Professor Angell called the "Cthulhu Cult", and was visiting a learned friend in Paterson, New Jersey; the curator of a local museum and a mineralogist of note. Examining one day the reserve specimens roughly set on the storage shelves in a rear room of the museum, my eye was caught by an odd picture in one of the old papers spread beneath the stones. It was the Sydney Bulletin I have mentioned, for my friend had wide affiliations in all conceivable foreign parts; and the picture was a half-tone cut of a hideous stone image almost identical with that which Legrasse had found in the swamp.

Eagerly clearing the sheet of its precious contents, I scanned the item in detail; and was disappointed to find it of only moderate length. What it suggested, however, was of portentous significance to my flagging quest; and I carefully tore it out for immediate action. It read as follows:

Mystery Derelict Found at Sea

Vigilant Arrives With Helpless Armed New Zealand Yacht in Tow. One Survivor and Dead Man Found Aboard. Tale of Desperate Battle and Deaths at Sea. Rescued Seaman Refuses Particulars of Strange Experience. Odd Idol Found in His Possession. Inquiry to Follow.

The Morrison Co.'s freighter Vigilant, bound from Valparaiso, arrived this morning at its wharf in Darling Harbour, having in tow the battled and disabled but heavily armed steam yacht Alert of Dunedin, N.Z., which was sighted April 12th in S. Latitude 34°21', W. Longitude 152°17', with one living and one dead man aboard.

The Vigilant left Valparaiso March 25th, and on April 2nd was driven considerably south of her course by exceptionally heavy storms and monster waves. On April 12th the derelict was sighted; and though apparently deserted, was found upon boarding to contain one survivor in a half-delirious condition and one man who had evidently been dead for more than a week. The living man was clutching a horrible stone idol of unknown origin, about one foot in height, regarding whose nature authorities at Sydney University, the Royal Society, and the Museum in College Street all profess complete bafflement, and which the survivor says he found in the cabin of the yacht, in a small carved shrine of common pattern.

This man, after recovering his senses, told an exceedingly strange story of piracy and slaughter. He is Gustaf Johansen, a Norwegian of some intelligence, and had been second mate of the two-masted schooner Emma of Auckland, which sailed for Callao February 20th with a complement of eleven men. The Emma, he says, was delayed and thrown widely south of her course by the great storm of March 1st, and on March 22nd, in S. Latitude 49°51' W. Longitude 128°34', encountered the Alert, manned by a queer and evil-looking crew of Kanakas and half-castes. Being ordered peremptorily to turn back, Capt. Collins refused; whereupon the strange crew began to fire savagely and without warning upon the schooner with a peculiarly heavy battery of brass cannon forming part of the yacht's equipment. The Emma's men showed fight, says the survivor, and though the schooner began to sink from shots beneath the water-line they managed to heave alongside their enemy and board her, grappling with the savage crew on the yacht's deck, and being forced to kill them all, the number being slightly superior, because of their particularly abhorrent and desperate though rather clumsy mode of fighting.

Three of the Emma's men, including Capt. Collins and First Mate Green, were killed; and the remaining eight under Second Mate Johansen proceeded to navigate the captured yacht, going ahead in their original direction to see if any reason for their ordering back had existed. The next day, it appears, they raised and landed on a small island, although none is known to exist in that part of the ocean; and six of the men somehow died ashore, though Johansen is queerly reticent about this part of his story, and speaks only of their falling into a rock chasm. Later, it seems, he and one companion boarded the yacht and tried to manage her, but were beaten about by the storm of April 2nd, From that time till his rescue on the 12th the man remembers little, and he does not even recall when William Briden, his companion, died. Briden's death reveals no apparent cause, and was probably due to excitement or exposure. Cable advices from Dunedin report that the Alert was well known there as an island trader, and bore an evil reputation along the waterfront, It was owned by a curious group of half-castes whose frequent meetings and night trips to the woods attracted no little curiosity; and it had set sail in great haste just after the storm and earth tremors of March 1st. Our Auckland correspondent gives the Emma and her crew an excellent reputation, and Johansen is described as a sober and worthy man. The admiralty will institute an inquiry on the whole matter beginning tomorrow, at which every effort will be made to induce Johansen to speak more freely than he has done hitherto.

This was all, together with the picture of the hellish image; but what a train of ideas it started in my mind! Here were new treasuries of data on the Cthulhu Cult, and evidence that it had strange interests at sea as well as on land. What motive prompted the hybrid crew to order back the Emma as they sailed about with their hideous idol? What was the unknown island on which six of the Emma's crew had died, and about which the mate Johansen was so secretive? What had the vice-admiralty's investigation brought out, and what was known of the noxious cult in Dunedin? And most marvelous of all, what deep and more than natural linkage of dates was this which gave a malign and now undeniable significance to the various turns of events so carefully noted by my uncle?

March 1st – or February 28th according to the International Date Line – the earthquake and storm had come. From Dunedin the Alert and her noisome crew had darted eagerly forth as if imperiously summoned, and on the other side of the earth poets and artists had begun to dream of a strange, dank Cyclopean city whilst a young sculptor had moulded in his sleep the form of the dreaded Cthulhu. March 23rd the crew of the Emma landed on an unknown island and left six men dead; and on that date the dreams of sensitive men assumed a heightened vividness and darkened with dread of a giant monster's malign pursuit, whilst an architect had gone mad and a sculptor had lapsed suddenly into delirium! And what of this storm of April 2nd – the date on which all dreams of the dank city ceased, and Wilcox emerged unharmed from the bondage of strange fever? What of all this – and of those hints of old Castro about the sunken, star-born Old Ones and their coming reign; their faithful cult and their mastery of dreams? Was I tottering on the brink of cosmic horrors beyond man's power to bear? If so, they must be horrors of the mind alone, for in some way the second of April had put a stop to whatever monstrous menace had begun its siege of mankind's soul.

That evening, after a day of hurried cabling and arranging, I bade my host adieu and took a train for San Francisco. In less than a month I was in Dunedin; where, however, I found that little was known of the strange cult-members who had lingered in the old sea-taverns. Waterfront scum was far too common for special mention; though there was vague talk about one inland trip these mongrels had made, during which faint drumming and red flame were noted on the distant hills. In Auckland I learned that Johansen had returned with yellow hair turned white after a perfunctory and inconclusive questioning at Sydney, and had thereafter sold his cottage in West Street and sailed with his wife to his old home in Oslo. Of his stirring experience he would tell his friends no more than he had told the admiralty officials, and all they could do was to give me his Oslo address.

After that I went to Sydney and talked profitlessly with seamen and members of the vice-admiralty court. I saw the Alert, now sold and in commercial use, at Circular Quay in Sydney Cove, but gained nothing from its non-committal bulk. The crouching image with its cuttlefish head, dragon body, scaly wings, and hieroglyphed pedestal, was preserved in the Museum at Hyde Park; and I studied it long and well, finding it a thing of balefully exquisite workmanship, and with the same utter mystery, terrible antiquity, and unearthly strangeness of material which I had noted in Legrasse's smaller specimen. Geologists, the curator told me, had found it a monstrous puzzle; for they vowed that the world held no rock like it. Then I thought with a shudder of what Old Castro had told Legrasse about the Old Ones; "They had come from the stars, and had brought Their images with Them."

Shaken with such a mental resolution as I had never before known, I now resolved to visit Mate Johansen in Oslo. Sailing for London, I reembarked at once for the Norwegian capital; and one autumn day landed at the trim wharves in the shadow of the Egeberg. Johansen's address, I discovered, lay in the Old Town of King Harold Haardrada, which kept alive the name of Oslo during all the centuries that the greater city masqueraded as "Christiana." I made the brief trip by taxicab, and knocked with palpitant heart at the door of a neat and ancient building with plastered front. A sad-faced woman in black answered my summons, and I was stung with disappointment when she told me in halting English that Gustaf Johansen was no more.

He had not long survived his return, said his wife, for the doings at sea in 1925 had broken him. He had told her no more than he told the public, but had left a long manuscript – of "technical matters" as he said – written in English, evidently in order to guard her from the peril of casual perusal. During a walk through a narrow lane near the Gothenburg dock, a bundle of papers falling from an attic window had knocked him down. Two Lascar sailors at once helped him to his feet, but before the ambulance could reach him he was dead. Physicians found no adequate cause the end, and laid it to heart trouble and a weakened constitution. I now felt gnawing at my vitals that dark terror which will never leave me till I, too, am at rest; "accidentally" or otherwise. Persuading the widow that my connection with her husband's "technical matters" was sufficient to entitle me to his manuscript, I bore the document away and began to read it on the London boat.

It was a simple, rambling thing – a naive sailor's effort at a post-facto diary – and strove to recall day by day that last awful voyage. I cannot attempt to transcribe it verbatim in all its cloudiness and redundance, but I will tell its gist enough to show why the sound of the water against the vessel's sides became so unendurable to me that I stopped my ears with cotton.

Johansen, thank God, did not know quite all, even though he saw the city and the Thing, but I shall never sleep calmly again when I think of the horrors that lurk ceaselessly behind life in time and in space, and of those unhallowed blasphemies from elder stars which dream beneath the sea, known and favoured by a nightmare cult ready and eager to loose them upon the world whenever another earthquake shall heave their monstrous stone city again to the sun and air.

Johansen's voyage had begun just as he told it to the vice-admiralty. The Emma, in ballast, had cleared Auckland on February 20th, and had felt the full force of that earthquake-born tempest which must have heaved up from the sea-bottom the horrors that filled men's dreams. Once more under control, the ship was making good progress when held up by the Alert on March 22nd, and I could feel the mate's regret as he wrote of her bombardment and sinking. Of the swarthy cult-fiends on the Alert he speaks with significant horror. There was some peculiarly abominable quality about them which made their destruction seem almost a duty, and Johansen shows ingenuous wonder at the charge of ruthlessness brought against his party during the proceedings of the court of inquiry. Then, driven ahead by curiosity in their captured yacht under Johansen's command, the men sight a great stone pillar sticking out of the sea, and in S. Latitude 47°9', W. Longitude 126°43', come upon a coastline of mingled mud, ooze, and weedy Cyclopean masonry which can be nothing less than the tangible substance of earth's supreme terror – the nightmare corpse-city of R'lyeh, that was built in measureless aeons behind history by the vast, loathsome shapes that seeped down from the dark stars. There lay great Cthulhu and his hordes, hidden in green slimy vaults and sending out at last, after cycles incalculable, the thoughts that spread fear to the dreams of the sensitive and called imperiously to the faithful to come on a pilgrimage of liberation and restoration. All this Johansen did not suspect, but God knows he soon saw enough!

I suppose that only a single mountain-top, the hideous monolith-crowned citadel whereon great Cthulhu was buried, actually emerged from the waters. When I think of the extent of all that may be brooding down there I almost wish to kill myself forthwith. Johansen and his men were awed by the cosmic majesty of this dripping Babylon of elder daemons, and must have guessed without guidance that it was nothing of this or of any sane planet. Awe at the unbelievable size of the greenish stone blocks, at the dizzying height of the great carven monolith, and at the stupefying identity of the colossal statues and bas-reliefs with the queer image found in the shrine on the Alert, is poignantly visible in every line of the mate's frightened description.

Without knowing what futurism is like, Johansen achieved something very close to it when he spoke of the city; for instead of describing any definite structure or building, he dwells only on broad impressions of vast angles and stone surfaces – surfaces too great to belong to anything right or proper for this earth, and impious with horrible images and hieroglyphs. I mention his talk about angles because it suggests something Wilcox had told me of his awful dreams. He said that the geometry of the dream-place he saw was abnormal, non-Euclidean, and loathsomely redolent of spheres and dimensions apart from ours. Now an unlettered seaman felt the same thing whilst gazing at the terrible reality.

Johansen and his men landed at a sloping mud-bank on this monstrous Acropolis, and clambered slipperily up over titan oozy blocks which could have been no mortal staircase. The very sun of heaven seemed distorted when viewed through the polarising miasma welling out from this sea-soaked perversion, and twisted menace and suspense lurked leeringly in those crazily elusive angles of carven rock where a second glance showed concavity after the first showed convexity.

Something very like fright had come over all the explorers before anything more definite than rock and ooze and weed was seen. Each would have fled had he not feared the scorn of the others, and it was only half-heartedly that they searched – vainly, as it proved – for some portable souvenir to bear away.

It was Rodriguez the Portuguese who climbed up the foot of the monolith and shouted of what he had found. The rest followed him, and looked curiously at the immense carved door with the now familiar squid-dragon bas-relief. It was, Johansen said, like a great barn-door; and they all felt that it was a door because of the ornate lintel, threshold, and jambs around it, though they could not decide whether it lay flat like a trap-door or slantwise like an outside cellar-door. As Wilcox would have said, the geometry of the place was all wrong. One could not be sure that the sea and the ground were horizontal, hence the relative position of everything else seemed phantasmally variable.

Briden pushed at the stone in several places without result. Then Donovan felt over it delicately around the edge, pressing each point separately as he went. He climbed interminably along the grotesque stone moulding – that is, one would call it climbing if the thing was not after all horizontal – and the men wondered how any door in the universe could be so vast. Then, very softly and slowly, the acre-great lintel began to give inward at the top; and they saw that it was balanced.

Donovan slid or somehow propelled himself down or along the jamb and rejoined his fellows, and everyone watched the queer recession of the monstrously carven portal. In this phantasy of prismatic distortion it moved anomalously in a diagonal way, so that all the rules of matter and perspective seemed upset.

The aperture was black with a darkness almost material. That tenebrousness was indeed a positive quality; for it obscured such parts of the inner walls as ought to have been revealed, and actually burst forth like smoke from its aeon-long imprisonment, visibly darkening the sun as it slunk away into the shrunken and gibbous sky on flapping membraneous wings. The odour rising from the newly opened depths was intolerable, and at length the quick-eared Hawkins thought he heard a nasty, slopping sound down there. Everyone listened, and everyone was listening still when It lumbered slobberingly into sight and gropingly squeezed Its gelatinous green immensity through the black doorway into the tainted outside air of that poison city of madness.

Poor Johansen's handwriting almost gave out when he wrote of this. Of the six men who never reached the ship, he thinks two perished of pure fright in that accursed instant. The Thing cannot be described – there is no language for such abysms of shrieking and immemorial lunacy, such eldritch contradictions of all matter, force, and cosmic order. A mountain walked or stumbled. God! What wonder that across the earth a great architect went mad, and poor Wilcox raved with fever in that telepathic instant? The Thing of the idols, the green, sticky spawn of the stars, had awaked to claim his own. The stars were right again, and what an age-old cult had failed to do by design, a band of innocent sailors had done by accident. After vigintillions of years great Cthulhu was loose again, and ravening for delight.

Three men were swept up by the flabby claws before anybody turned. God rest them, if there be any rest in the universe. They were Donovan, Guerrera, and Angstrom. Parker slipped as the other three were plunging frenziedly over endless vistas of green-crusted rock to the boat, and Johansen swears he was swallowed up by an angle of masonry which shouldn't have been there; an angle which was acute, but behaved as if it were obtuse. So only Briden and Johansen reached the boat, and pulled desperately for the Alert as the mountainous monstrosity flopped down the slimy stones and hesitated, floundering at the edge of the water.

Steam had not been suffered to go down entirely, despite the departure of all hands for the shore; and it was the work of only a few moments of feverish rushing up and down between wheel and engines to get the Alert under way. Slowly, amidst the distorted horrors of that indescribable scene, she began to churn the lethal waters; whilst on the masonry of that charnel shore that was not of earth the titan Thing from the stars slavered and gibbered like Polypheme cursing the fleeing ship of Odysseus. Then, bolder than the storied Cyclops, great Cthulhu slid greasily into the water and began to pursue with vast wave-raising strokes of cosmic potency. Briden looked back and went mad, laughing shrilly as he kept on laughing at intervals till death found him one night in the cabin whilst Johansen was wandering deliriously.

But Johansen had not given out yet. Knowing that the Thing could surely overtake the Alert until steam was fully up, he resolved on a desperate chance; and, setting the engine for full speed, ran lightning-like on deck and reversed the wheel. There was a mighty eddying and foaming in the noisome brine, and as the steam mounted higher and higher the brave Norwegian drove his vessel head on against the pursuing jelly which rose above the unclean froth like the stern of a daemon galleon. The awful squid-head with writhing feelers came nearly up to the bowsprit of the sturdy yacht, but Johansen drove on relentlessly. There was a bursting as of an exploding bladder, a slushy nastiness as of a cloven sunfish, a stench as of a thousand opened graves, and a sound that the chronicler could not put on paper. For an instant the ship was befouled by an acrid and blinding green cloud, and then there was only a venomous seething astern; where – God in heaven! – the scattered plasticity of that nameless sky-spawn was nebulously recombining in its hateful original form, whilst its distance widened every second as the Alert gained impetus from its mounting steam.

That was all. After that Johansen only brooded over the idol in the cabin and attended to a few matters of food for himself and the laughing maniac by his side. He did not try to navigate after the first bold flight, for the reaction had taken something out of his soul. Then came the storm of April 2nd, and a gathering of the clouds about his consciousness. There is a sense of spectral whirling through liquid gulfs of infinity, of dizzying rides through reeling universes on a comets tail, and of hysterical plunges from the pit to the moon and from the moon back again to the pit, all livened by a cachinnating chorus of the distorted, hilarious elder gods and the green, bat-winged mocking imps of Tartarus.

Out of that dream came rescue – the Vigilant, the vice-admiralty court, the streets of Dunedin, and the long voyage back home to the old house by the Egeberg. He could not tell – they would think him mad. He would write of what he knew before death came, but his wife must not guess. Death would be a boon if only it could blot out the memories.

That was the document I read, and now I have placed it in the tin box beside the bas-relief and the papers of Professor Angell. With it shall go this record of mine – this test of my own sanity, wherein is pieced together that which I hope may never be pieced together again. I have looked upon all that the universe has to hold of horror, and even the skies of spring and the flowers of summer must ever afterward be poison to me. But I do not think my life will be long. As my uncle went, as poor Johansen went, so I shall go. I know too much, and the cult still lives.

Cthulhu still lives, too, I suppose, again in that chasm of stone which has shielded him since the sun was young. His accursed city is sunken once more, for the Vigilant sailed over the spot after the April storm; but his ministers on earth still bellow and prance and slay around idol-capped monoliths in lonely places. He must have been trapped by the sinking whilst within his black abyss, or else the world would by now be screaming with fright and frenzy. Who knows the end? What has risen may sink, and what has sunk may rise. Loathsomeness waits and dreams in the deep, and decay spreads over the tottering cities of men. A time will come – but I must not and cannot think! Let me pray that, if I do not survive this manuscript, my executors may put caution before audacity and see that it meets no other eye.

The Horla

Guy de Maupassant

MAY 8. What a lovely day! I have spent all the morning lying on the grass in front of my house, under the enormous plantain tree which covers and shades and shelters the whole of it. I like this part of the country; I am fond of living here because I am attached to it by deep roots, the profound and delicate roots which attach a man to the soil on which his ancestors were born and died, to their traditions, their usages, their food, the local expressions, the peculiar language of the peasants, the smell of the soil, the hamlets, and to the atmosphere itself.

I love the house in which I grew up. From my windows I can see the Seine, which flows by the side of my garden, on the other side of the road, almost through my grounds, the great and wide Seine, which goes to Rouen and Havre, and which is covered with boats passing to and fro.

On the left, down yonder, lies Rouen, populous Rouen with its blue roofs massing under pointed, Gothic towers. Innumerable are they, delicate or broad, dominated by the spire of the cathedral, full of bells which sound through the blue air on fine mornings, sending their sweet and distant iron clang to me, their metallic sounds, now stronger and now weaker, according as the wind is strong or light.

What a delicious morning it was! About eleven o'clock, a long line of boats drawn by a steam-tug, as big a fly, and which scarcely puffed while emitting its thick smoke, passed my gate.

After two English schooners, whose red flags fluttered toward the sky, there came a magnificent Brazilian three-master; it was perfectly white and wonderfully clean and shining. I saluted it, I hardly know why, except that the sight of the vessel gave me great pleasure.

May 12. I have had a slight feverish attack for the last few days, and I feel ill, or rather I feel low-spirited.

Whence come those mysterious influences which change our happiness into discouragement, and our self-confidence into diffidence? One might almost say that the air, the invisible air, is full of unknowable Forces, whose mysterious presence we have to endure. I wake up in the best of spirits, with an inclination to sing in my heart. Why? I go down by the side of the water, and suddenly, after walking a short distance, I return home wretched, as if some misfortune were awaiting me there. Why? Is it a cold shiver which, passing over my skin, has upset my nerves and given me a fit of low spirits? Is it the form of the clouds, or the tints of the sky, or the colors of the surrounding objects which are so changeable, which have troubled my thoughts as they passed before my eyes? Who can tell? Everything that surrounds us, everything that we see without looking at it, everything that we touch without knowing it, everything that we handle without feeling it, everything that we meet without clearly distinguishing it, has a rapid, surprising, and inexplicable effect upon us and upon our organs, and through them on our ideas and on our being itself.

How profound that mystery of the Invisible is! We cannot fathom it with our miserable senses: our eyes are unable to perceive what is either too small or too great, too near to or too far from us; we can see neither the inhabitants of a star nor of a drop of water; our ears deceive us, for they transmit to us the vibrations of the air in sonorous notes. Our senses are fairies who work the miracle of changing that movement into noise, and by that metamorphosis give birth to music, which makes the mute agitation of nature a harmony. So with our sense of smell, which is weaker than that of a dog, and so with our sense of taste, which can scarcely distinguish the age of a wine!

Oh! If we only had other organs which could work other miracles in our favor, what a number of fresh things we might discover around us!

May 16. I am ill, decidedly! I was so well last month! I am feverish, horribly feverish, or rather I am in a state of feverish enervation, which makes my mind suffer as much as my body. I have without ceasing the horrible sensation of some danger threatening me, the apprehension of some coming misfortune or of approaching death, a presentiment which is no doubt, an attack of some illness still unnamed, which germinates in the flesh and in the blood.

May 18. I have just come from consulting my medical man, for I can no longer get any sleep. He found that my pulse was high, my eyes dilated, my nerves highly strung, but no alarming symptoms. I must have a course of shower baths and of bromide of potassium.

May 25. No change! My state is really very peculiar. As the evening comes on, an incomprehensible feeling of disquietude seizes me, just as if night concealed some terrible menace toward me. I dine quickly, and then try to read, but I do not understand the words, and can scarcely distinguish the letters. Then I walk up and down my drawing-room, oppressed by a feeling of confused and irresistible fear, a fear of sleep and a fear of my bed.

About ten o'clock I go up to my room. As soon as I have entered I lock and bolt the door. I am frightened – of what? Up till the present time I have been frightened of nothing. I open my cupboards, and look under my bed; I listen – I listen – to what? How strange it is that a simple feeling of discomfort, of impeded or heightened circulation, perhaps the irritation of a nervous center, a slight congestion, a small disturbance in the imperfect and delicate functions of our living machinery, can turn the most light-hearted of men into a melancholy one, and make a coward of the bravest? Then, I go to bed, and I wait for sleep as a man might wait for the executioner. I wait for its coming with dread, and my heart beats and my legs tremble, while my whole body shivers beneath the warmth of the bedclothes, until the moment when I suddenly fall asleep, as a man throws himself into a pool of stagnant water in order to drown. I do not feel this perfidious sleep coming over me as I used to, but a sleep which is close to me and watching me, which is going to seize me by the head, to close my eyes and annihilate me.

I sleep – a long time – two or three hours perhaps – then a dream – no – a nightmare lays hold on me. I feel that I am in bed and asleep – I feel it and I know it – and I feel also that somebody is coming close to me, is looking at me, touching me, is getting on to my bed, is kneeling on my chest, is taking my neck between his hands and squeezing it – squeezing it with all his might in order to strangle me.

I struggle, bound by that terrible powerlessness which paralyzes us in our dreams; I try to cry out – but I cannot; I want to move – I cannot; I try, with the most violent efforts and out of breath, to turn over and throw off this being which is crushing and suffocating me – I cannot!

And then suddenly I wake up, shaken and bathed in perspiration; I light a candle and find that I am alone, and after that crisis, which occurs every night, I at length fall asleep and slumber tranquilly till morning.

June 2. My state has grown worse. What is the matter with me? The bromide does me no good, and the shower-baths have no effect whatever. Sometimes, in order to tire myself out, though I am fatigued enough already, I go for a walk in the forest of Roumare. I used to think at first that the fresh light and soft air, impregnated with the odor of herbs and leaves, would instill new life into my veins and impart fresh energy to my heart. One day I turned into a broad ride in the wood, and then I diverged toward La Bouille, through a narrow path, between two rows of exceedingly tall trees, which placed a thick, green, almost black roof between the sky and me.

A sudden shiver ran through me, not a cold shiver, but a shiver of agony, and so I hastened my steps, uneasy at being alone in the wood, frightened stupidly and without reason, at the profound solitude. Suddenly it seemed as if I were being followed, that somebody was walking at my heels, close, quite close to me, near enough to touch me.

I turned round suddenly, but I was alone. I saw nothing behind me except the straight, broad ride, empty and bordered by high trees, horribly empty; on the other side also it extended until it was lost in the distance, and looked just the same – terrible.

I closed my eyes. Why? And then I began to turn round on one heel very quickly, just like a top. I nearly fell down, and opened my eyes; the trees were dancing round me and the earth heaved; I was obliged to sit down. Then, ah! I no longer remembered how I had come! What a strange idea! What a strange, strange idea! I did not the least know. I started off to the right, and got back into the avenue which had led me into the middle of the forest.

June 3. I have had a terrible night. I shall go away for a few weeks, for no doubt a journey will set me up again.

July 2. I have come back, quite cured, and have had a most delightful trip into the bargain. I have been to Mont Saint-Michel, which I had not seen before.

What a sight, when one arrives as I did, at Avranches toward the end of the day! The town stands on a hill, and I was taken into the public garden at the extremity of the town. I uttered a cry of astonishment. An extraordinarily large bay lay extended before me, as far as my eyes could reach, between two hills which were lost to sight in the mist; and in the middle of this immense yellow bay, under a clear, golden sky, a peculiar hill rose up, somber and pointed in the midst of the sand. The sun had just disappeared, and under the still flaming sky stood out the outline of that fantastic rock which bears on its summit a picturesque monument.

At daybreak I went to it. The tide was low, as it had been the night before, and I saw that wonderful abbey rise up before me as I approached it. After several hours' walking, I reached the enormous mass of rock which supports the little town, dominated by the great church. Having climbed the steep and narrow street, I entered the most wonderful Gothic building that has ever been erected to God on earth, large as a town, and full of low rooms which seem buried beneath vaulted roofs, and of lofty galleries supported by delicate columns.

I entered this gigantic granite jewel, which is as light in its effect as a bit of lace and is covered with towers, with slender belfries to which spiral staircases ascend. The flying buttresses raise strange heads that bristle with chimeras. with devils, with fantastic animals, with monstrous flowers, are joined together by finely carved arches, to the blue sky by day, and to the black sky by night.

When I had reached the summit. I said to the monk who accompanied me: "Father, how happy you must be here!" And he replied: "It is very windy, Monsieur"; and so we began to talk while watching the rising tide, which ran over the sand and covered it with a steel cuirass.

And then the monk told me stories, all the old stories belonging to the place – legends, nothing but legends.

One of them struck me forcibly. The country people, those belonging to the Mornet, declare that at night one can hear talking going on in the sand, and also that two goats bleat, one with a strong, the other with a weak voice. Incredulous people declare that it is nothing but the screaming of the sea birds, which occasionally resembles bleatings, and occasionally human lamentations; but belated fishermen swear that they have met an old shepherd, whose cloak covered head they can never see, wandering on the sand, between two tides, round the little town placed so far out of the world. They declare he is guiding and walking before a he-goat with a man's face and a she-goat with a woman's face, both with white hair, who talk incessantly, quarreling in a strange language, and then suddenly cease talking in order to bleat with all their might.

"Do you believe it?" I asked the monk. "I scarcely know," he replied; and I continued: "If there are other beings besides ourselves on this earth, how comes it that we have not known it for so long a time, or why have you not seen them? How is it that I have not seen them?"

He replied: "Do we see the hundred-thousandth part of what exists? Look here; there is the wind, which is the strongest force in nature. It knocks down men, and blows down buildings, uproots trees, raises the sea into mountains of water, destroys cliffs and casts great ships on to the breakers; it kills, it whistles, it sighs, it roars. But have you ever seen it, and can you see it? Yet it exists for all that."

I was silent before this simple reasoning. That man was a philosopher, or perhaps a fool; I could not say which exactly, so I held my tongue. What he had said had often been in my own thoughts.

July 3. I have slept badly; certainly there is some feverish influence here, for my coachman is suffering in the same way as I am. When I went back home yesterday, I noticed his singular paleness, and I asked him: "What is the matter with you, Jean?"

"The matter is that I never get any rest, and my nights devour my days. Since your departure, Monsieur, there has been a spell over me."

However, the other servants are all well, but I am very frightened of having another attack, myself.

July 4. I am decidedly taken again; for my old nightmares have returned. Last night I felt somebody leaning on me who was sucking my life from between my lips with his mouth. Yes, he was sucking it out of my neck like a leech would have done. Then he got up, satiated, and I woke up, so beaten, crushed, and annihilated that I could not move. If this continues for a few days, I shall certainly go away again.

July 5. Have I lost my reason? What has happened? What I saw last night is so strange that my head wanders when I think of it!

As I do now every evening, I had locked my door; then, being thirsty, I drank half a glass of water, and I accidentally noticed that the water-bottle was full up to the cut-glass stopper.

Then I went to bed and fell into one of my terrible sleeps, from which I was aroused in about two hours by a still more terrible shock.

Picture to yourself a sleeping man who is being murdered, who wakes up with a knife in his chest, a gurgling in his throat, is covered with blood, can no longer breathe, is going to die and does not understand anything at all about it – there you have it.

Having recovered my senses, I was thirsty again, so I lighted a candle and went to the table on which my water-bottle was. I lifted it up and tilted it over my glass, but nothing came out. It was empty! It was completely empty! At first I could not understand it at all; then suddenly I was seized by such a terrible feeling that I had to sit down, or rather fall into a chair! Then I sprang up with a bound to look about me; then I sat down again, overcome by astonishment and fear, in front of the transparent crystal bottle! I looked at it with fixed eyes, trying to solve the puzzle, and my hands trembled! Some body had drunk the water, but who? I? I without any doubt. It could surely only be I? In that case I was a somnambulist – was living, without knowing it, that double, mysterious life which makes us doubt whether there are not two beings in us – whether a strange, unknowable, and invisible being does not, during our moments of mental and physical torpor, animate the inert body, forcing it to a more willing obedience than it yields to ourselves.

Oh! Who will understand my horrible agony? Who will understand the emotion of a man sound in mind, wide-awake, full of sense, who looks in horror at the disappearance of a little water while he was asleep, through the glass of a water-bottle! And I remained sitting until it was daylight, without venturing to go to bed again.

July 6. I am going mad. Again all the contents of my water-bottle have been drunk during the night; or rather I have drunk it!

But is it I? Is it I? Who could it be? Who? Oh! God! Am I going mad? Who will save me?

July 10. I have just been through some surprising ordeals. Undoubtedly I must be mad! And yet!

On July 6, before going to bed, I put some wine, milk, water, bread, and strawberries on my table. Somebody drank – I drank – all the water and a little of the milk, but neither the wine, nor the bread, nor the strawberries were touched.

On the seventh of July I renewed the same experiment, with the same results, and on July 8 I left out the water and the milk and nothing was touched.

Lastly, on July 9 I put only water and milk on my table, taking care to wrap up the bottles in white muslin and to tie down the stoppers. Then I rubbed my lips, my beard, and my hands with pencil lead, and went to bed.

Deep slumber seized me, soon followed by a terrible awakening. I had not moved, and my sheets were not marked. I rushed to the table. The muslin round the bottles remained intact; I undid the string, trembling with fear. All the water had been drunk, and so had the milk! Ah! Great God! I must start for Paris immediately.

July 12. Paris. I must have lost my head during the last few days! I must be the plaything of my enervated imagination, unless I am really a somnambulist, or I have been brought under the power of one of those influences – hypnotic suggestion, for example – which are known to exist, but have hitherto been inexplicable. In any case, my mental state bordered on madness, and twenty-four hours of Paris sufficed to restore me to my equilibrium.

Yesterday after doing some business and paying some visits, which instilled fresh and invigorating mental air into me, I wound up my evening at the Theatre Francais. A drama by Alexander Dumas the Younger was being acted, and his brilliant and powerful play completed my cure. Certainly solitude is dangerous for active minds. We need men who can think and can talk, around us. When we are alone for a long time, we people space with phantoms.

I returned along the boulevards to my hotel in excellent spirits. Amid the jostling of the crowd I thought, not without irony, of my terrors and surmises of the previous week, because I believed, yes, I believed, that an invisible being lived beneath my roof. How weak our mind is; how quickly it is terrified and unbalanced as soon as we are confronted with a small, incomprehensible fact. Instead of dismissing the problem with: "We do not understand because we cannot find the cause," we immediately imagine terrible mysteries and supernatural powers.

July 14. Fete of the Republic. I walked through the streets, and the crackers and flags amused me like a child. Still, it is very foolish to make merry on a set date, by Government decree. People are like a flock of sheep, now steadily patient, now in ferocious revolt. Say to it: "Amuse yourself," and it amuses itself. Say to it: "Go and fight with your neighbor," and it goes and fights. Say to it: "Vote for the Emperor," and it votes for the Emperor; then say to it: "Vote for the Republic," and it votes for the Republic.

Those who direct it are stupid, too; but instead of obeying men they obey principles, a course which can only be foolish, ineffective, and false, for the very reason that principles are ideas which are considered as certain and unchangeable, whereas in this world one is certain of nothing, since light is an illusion and noise is deception.

July 16. I saw some things yesterday that troubled me very much. I was dining at my cousin's, Madame Sable, whose husband is colonel of the Seventy-sixth Chasseurs at Limoges. There were two young women there, one of whom had married a medical man, Dr. Parent, who devotes himself a great deal to nervous diseases and to the extraordinary manifestations which just now experiments in hypnotism and suggestion are producing.

He related to us at some length the enormous results obtained by English scientists and the doctors of the medical school at Nancy, and the facts which he adduced appeared to me so strange, that I declared that I was altogether incredulous.

"We are," he declared, "on the point of discovering one of the most important secrets of nature, I mean to say, one of its most important secrets on this earth, for assuredly there are some up in the stars, yonder, of a different kind of importance. Ever since man has thought, since he has been able to express and write down his thoughts, he has felt himself close to a mystery which is impenetrable to his coarse and imperfect senses, and he endeavors to supplement the feeble penetration of his organs by the efforts of his intellect. As long as that intellect remained in its elementary stage, this intercourse with invisible spirits assumed forms which were commonplace though terrifying. Thence sprang the popular belief in the supernatural, the legends of wandering spirits, of fairies, of gnomes, of ghosts, I might even say the conception of God, for our ideas of the Workman-Creator, from whatever religion they may have come down to us, are certainly the most mediocre, the stupidest, and the most unacceptable inventions that ever sprang from the frightened brain of any human creature. Nothing is truer than what Voltaire says: 'If God made man in His own image, man has certainly paid Him back again.'

"But for rather more than a century, men seem to have had a presentiment of something new. Mesmer and some others have put us on an unexpected track, and within the last two or three years especially, we have arrived at results really surprising."

My cousin, who is also very incredulous, smiled, and Dr. Parent said to her: "Would you like me to try and send you to sleep, Madame?"

"Yes, certainly."

She sat down in an easy-chair, and he began to look at her fixedly, as if to fascinate her. I suddenly felt myself somewhat discomposed; my heart beat rapidly and I had a choking feeling in my throat. I saw that Madame Sable's eyes were growing heavy, her mouth twitched, and her bosom heaved, and at the end of ten minutes she was asleep.

"Go behind her," the doctor said to me; so I took a seat behind her. He put a visiting-card into her hands, and said to her: "This is a looking-glass; what do you see in it?"

She replied: "I see my cousin."

"What is he doing?"

"He is twisting his mustache."

"And now?"

"He is taking a photograph out of his pocket."

"Whose photograph is it?"

"His own."

That was true, for the photograph had been given me that same evening at the hotel.

"What is his attitude in this portrait?"

"He is standing up with his hat in his hand."

She saw these things in that card, in that piece of white pasteboard, as if she had seen them in a looking-glass.

The young women were frightened, and exclaimed: "That is quite enough! Quite, quite enough!"

But the doctor said to her authoritatively: "You will get up at eight o'clock tomorrow morning; then you will go and call on your cousin at his hotel and ask him to lend you the five thousand francs which your husband asks of you, and which he will ask for when he sets out on his coming journey."

Then he woke her up.

On returning to my hotel, I thought over this curious seance and I was assailed by doubts, not as to my cousin's absolute and undoubted good faith, for I had known her as well as if she had been my own sister ever since she was a child, but as to a possible trick on the doctor's part. Had not he, perhaps, kept a glass hidden in his hand, which he showed to the young woman in her sleep at the same time as he did the card? Professional conjurers do things which are just as singular.

However, I went to bed, and this morning, at about half past eight, I was awakened by my footman, who said to me: "Madame Sable has asked to see you immediately, Monsieur." I dressed hastily and went to her.

She sat down in some agitation, with her eyes on the floor, and without raising her veil said to me: "My dear cousin, I am going to ask a great favor of you."

"What is it, cousin?"

"I do not like to tell you, and yet I must. I am in absolute want of five thousand francs."

"What, you?"

"Yes, I, or rather my husband, who has asked me to procure them for him."

I was so stupefied that I hesitated to answer. I asked myself whether she had not really been making fun of me with Dr. Parent, if it were not merely a very well-acted farce which had been got up beforehand. On looking at her attentively, however, my doubts disappeared. She was trembling with grief, so painful was this step to her, and I was sure that her throat was full of sobs.

I knew that she was very rich and so I continued: "What! Has not your husband five thousand francs at his disposal? Come, think. Are you sure that he commissioned you to ask me for them?"

She hesitated for a few seconds, as if she were making a great effort to search her memory, and then she replied: "Yes – yes, I am quite sure of it."

"He has written to you?"

She hesitated again and reflected, and I guessed the torture of her thoughts. She did not know. She only knew that she was to borrow five thousand francs of me for her husband. So she told a lie.

"Yes, he has written to me."

"When, pray? You did not mention it to me yesterday."

"I received his letter this morning."

"Can you show it to me?"

"No; no – no – it contained private matters, things too personal to ourselves. I burned it."

"So your husband runs into debt?"

She hesitated again, and then murmured: "I do not know."

Thereupon I said bluntly: "I have not five thousand francs at my disposal at this moment, my dear cousin."

She uttered a cry, as if she were in pair; and said: "Oh! oh! I beseech you, I beseech you to get them for me."

She got excited and clasped her hands as if she were praying to me! I heard her voice change its tone; she wept and sobbed, harassed and dominated by the irresistible order that she had received.

"Oh! oh! I beg you to – if you knew what I am suffering – I want them today."

I had pity on her: "You shall have them by and by, I swear to you."

"Oh! thank you! thank you! How kind you are."

I continued: "Do you remember what took place at your house last night?"

"Yes."

"Do you remember that Dr. Parent sent you to sleep?"

"Yes."

"Oh! Very well then; he ordered you to come to me this morning to borrow five thousand francs, and at this moment you are obeying that suggestion."

She considered for a few moments, and then replied: "But as it is my husband who wants them —"

For a whole hour I tried to convince her, but could not succeed, and when she had gone I went to the doctor. He was just going out, and he listened to me with a smile, and said: "Do you believe now?"

"Yes, I cannot help it."

"Let us go to your cousin's."

She was already resting on a couch, overcome with fatigue. The doctor felt her pulse, looked at her for some time with one hand raised toward her eyes, which she closed by degrees under the irresistible power of this magnetic influence. When she was asleep, he said:

"Your husband does not require the five thousand francs any longer! You must, therefore, forget that you asked your cousin to lend them to you, and, if he speaks to you about it, you will not understand him."

Then he woke her up, and I took out a pocket-book and said: "Here is what you asked me for this morning, my dear cousin." But she was so surprised, that I did not venture to persist; nevertheless, I tried to recall the circumstance to her, but she denied it vigorously, thought that I was making fun of her, and in the end, very nearly lost her temper.

There! I have just come back, and I have not been able to eat any lunch, for this experiment has altogether upset me.

July 19. Many people to whom I have told the adventure have laughed at me. I no longer know what to think. The wise man says: Perhaps?

July 21. I dined at Bougival, and then I spent the evening at a boatmen's ball. Decidedly everything depends on place and surroundings. It would be the height of folly to believe in the supernatural on the Ile de la Grenouilliere. But on the top of Mont Saint-Michel or in India, we are terribly under the influence of our surroundings. I shall return home next week.

July 30. I came back to my own house yesterday. Everything is going on well.

August 2. Nothing fresh; it is splendid weather, and I spend my days in watching the Seine flow past.

August 4. Quarrels among my servants. They declare that the glasses are broken in the cupboards at night. The footman accuses the cook, she accuses the needlewoman, and the latter accuses the other two. Who is the culprit? It would take a clever person to tell.

August 6. This time, I am not mad. I have seen – I have seen – I have seen! – I can doubt no longer – I have seen it!

I was walking at two o'clock among my rose-trees, in the full sunlight – in the walk bordered by autumn roses which are beginning to fall. As I stopped to look at a Geant de Bataille, which had three splendid blooms, I distinctly saw the stalk of one of the roses bend close to me, as if an invisible hand had bent it, and then break, as if that hand had picked it! Then the flower raised itself, following the curve which a hand would have described in carrying it toward a mouth, and remained suspended in the transparent air, alone and motionless, a terrible red spot, three yards from my eyes. In desperation I rushed at it to take it! I found nothing; it had disappeared. Then I was seized with furious rage against myself, for it is not wholesome for a reasonable and serious man to have such hallucinations.

But was it a hallucination? I turned to look for the stalk, and I found it immediately under the bush, freshly broken, between the two other roses which remained on the branch. I returned home, then, with a much disturbed mind; for I am certain now, certain as I am of the alternation of day and night, that there exists close to me an invisible being who lives on milk and on water, who can touch objects, take them and change their places; who is, consequently, endowed with a material nature, although imperceptible to sense, and who lives as I do, under my roof -

August 7. I slept tranquilly. He drank the water out of my decanter, but did not disturb my sleep.

I ask myself whether I am mad. As I was walking just now in the sun by the riverside, doubts as to my own sanity arose in me; not vague doubts such as I have had hitherto, but precise and absolute doubts. I have seen mad people, and I have known some who were quite intelligent, lucid, even clear-sighted in every concern of life, except on one point. They could speak clearly, readily, profoundly on everything; till their thoughts were caught in the breakers of their delusions and went to pieces there, were dispersed and swamped in that furious and terrible sea of fogs and squalls which is called *madness*.

I certainly should think that I was mad, absolutely mad, if I were not conscious that I knew my state, if I could not fathom it and analyze it with the most complete lucidity. I should, in fact, be a reasonable man laboring under a hallucination. Some unknown disturbance must have been excited in my brain, one of those disturbances which physiologists of the present day try to note and to fix precisely, and that disturbance must have caused a profound gulf in my mind and in the order and logic of my ideas. Similar phenomena occur in dreams, and lead us through the most unlikely phantasmagoria, without causing us any surprise, because our verifying apparatus and our sense of control have gone to sleep, while our imaginative faculty wakes and works. Was it not possible that one of the imperceptible keys of the cerebral finger-board had been paralyzed in me? Some men lose the recollection of proper names, or of verbs, or of numbers, or merely of dates, in consequence of an accident. The localization of all the avenues of thought has been accomplished nowadays; what, then, would there be surprising in the fact that my faculty of controlling the unreality of certain hallucinations should be destroyed for the time being?

I thought of all this as I walked by the side of the water. The sun was shining brightly on the river and made earth delightful, while it filled me with love for life, for the swallows, whose swift agility is always delightful in my eyes, for the plants by the riverside, whose rustling is a pleasure to my ears.

By degrees, however, an inexplicable feeling of discomfort seized me. It seemed to me as if some unknown force were numbing and stopping me, were preventing me from going further and were calling me back. I felt that painful wish to return which comes on you when you have left a beloved invalid at home, and are seized by a presentiment that he is worse.

I, therefore, returned despite of myself, feeling certain that I should find some bad news awaiting me, a letter or a telegram. There was nothing, however, and I was surprised and uneasy, more so than if I had had another fantastic vision.

August 8. I spent a terrible evening, yesterday. He does not show himself any more, but I feel that He is near me, watching me, looking at me, penetrating me, dominating me, and more terrible to me when He hides himself thus than if He were to manifest his constant and invisible presence by supernatural phenomena. However, I slept.

August 9. Nothing, but I am afraid.

August 10. Nothing; but what will happen tomorrow?

August 11. Still nothing. I cannot stop at home with this fear hanging over me and these thoughts in my mind; I shall go away.

August 12. Ten o'clock at night. All day long I have been trying to get away, and have not been able. I contemplated a simple and easy act of liberty, a carriage ride to Rouen – and I have not been able to do it. What is the reason?

August 13. When one is attacked by certain maladies, the springs of our physical being seem broken, our energies destroyed, our muscles relaxed, our bones to be as soft as our flesh, and our blood as liquid as water. I am experiencing the same in my moral being, in a strange and distressing manner. I have no longer any strength, any courage, any self-control, nor even any power to set my own will in motion. I have no power left to WILL anything, but some one does it for me and I obey.

August 14. I am lost! Somebody possesses my soul and governs it! Somebody orders all my acts, all my movements, all my thoughts. I am no longer master of myself, nothing except an enslaved and terrified spectator of the things which I do. I wish to go out; I cannot. *He* does not wish to; and so I remain, trembling and distracted in the armchair in which he keeps me sitting. I merely wish to get up and to rouse myself, so as to think that I am still master of myself: I cannot! I am riveted to my chair, and my chair adheres to the floor in such a manner that no force of mine can move us.

Then suddenly, I must, I *must* go to the foot of my garden to pick some strawberries and eat them – and I go there. I pick the strawberries and I eat them! Oh! my God! my God! Is there a God? If there be one, deliver me! save me! succor me! Pardon! Pity! Mercy! Save me! Oh! what sufferings! what torture! what horror!

August 15. Certainly this is the way in which my poor cousin was possessed and swayed, when she came to borrow five thousand francs of me. She was under the power of a strange will which had entered into her, like another soul, a parasitic and ruling soul. Is the world coming to an end?

But who is he, this invisible being that rules me, this unknowable being, this rover of a supernatural race?

Invisible beings exist, then! how is it, then, that since the beginning of the world they have never manifested themselves in such a manner as they do to me? I have never read anything that resembles what goes on in my house. Oh! If I could only leave it, if I could only go away and flee, and never return, I should be saved; but I cannot.

August 16. I managed to escape today for two hours, like a prisoner who finds the door of his dungeon accidentally open. I suddenly felt that I was free and that He was far away, and so I gave orders to put the horses in as quickly as possible, and I drove to Rouen. Oh! how delightful to be able to say to my coachman: "Go to Rouen!"

I made him pull up before the library, and I begged them to lend me Dr. Herrmann Herestauss's treatise on the unknown inhabitants of the ancient and modern world.

Then, as I was getting into my carriage, I intended to say: "To the railway station!" but instead of this I shouted – I did not speak; but I shouted – in such a loud voice that all the passers-by turned round: "Home!" and I fell back on to the cushion of my carriage, overcome by mental agony. He had found me out and regained possession of me.

August 17. Oh! What a night! what a night! And yet it seems to me that I ought to rejoice. I read until one o'clock in the morning! Herestauss, Doctor of Philosophy and Theogony, wrote the history and the manifestation of all those invisible beings which hover around man, or of whom he dreams. He describes their origin, their domains, their power; but none of them resembles the one which haunts me. One might say that man, ever since he has thought, has had a foreboding and a fear of a new being, stronger than himself, his successor in this world, and that, feeling him near, and not being able to foretell the nature of the unseen one, he has, in his terror, created the whole race of hidden beings, vague phantoms born of fear.

Having, therefore, read until one o'clock in the morning, I went and sat down at the open window, in order to cool my forehead and my thoughts in the calm night air. It was very pleasant and warm! How I should have enjoyed such a night formerly!

There was no moon, but the stars darted out their rays in the dark heavens. Who inhabits those worlds? What forms, what living beings, what animals are there yonder? Do those who are thinkers in those distant worlds know more than we do? What can they do more than we? What do they see which we do not? Will not one of them, some day or other, traversing space, appear on our earth to conquer it, just as formerly the Norsemen crossed the sea in order to subjugate nations feebler than themselves?

We are so weak, so powerless, so ignorant, so small – we who live on this particle of mud which revolves in liquid air.

I fell asleep, dreaming thus in the cool night air, and then, having slept for about three quarters of an hour, I opened my eyes without moving, awakened by an indescribably confused and strange sensation. At first I saw nothing, and then suddenly it appeared to me as if a page of the book, which had remained open on my table, turned over of its own accord. Not a breath of air had come in at my window, and I was surprised and waited. In about four minutes, I saw, I saw – yes I saw with my own eyes – another page lift itself up and fall down on the others, as if a finger had turned it over. My armchair was empty, appeared empty, but I knew that He was there, He, and sitting in my place, and that He was reading. With a furious bound, the bound of an enraged wild beast that wishes to disembowel its tamer, I crossed my room to seize him, to strangle him, to kill him! But before I could reach it, my chair fell over as if somebody had run away from me. My table rocked, my lamp fell and went out, and my window closed as if some thief had been surprised and had fled out into the night, shutting it behind him.

So He had run away; He had been afraid; He, afraid of me!

So tomorrow, or later – some day or other, I should be able to hold him in my clutches and crush him against the ground! Do not dogs occasionally bite and strangle their masters?

August 18. I have been thinking the whole day long. Oh! yes, I will obey Him, follow His impulses, fulfill all His wishes, show myself humble, submissive, a coward. He is the stronger; but an hour will come.

August 19. I know, I know, I know all! I have just read the following in the "Revue du Monde Scientifique": "A curious piece of news comes to us from Rio de Janeiro. Madness, an epidemic of madness, which may be compared to that contagious madness which attacked the people of Europe in the Middle Ages, is at this moment raging in the Province of San-Paulo. The frightened inhabitants are leaving their houses, deserting their villages, abandoning their land, saying that they are pursued, possessed, governed like human cattle by invisible, though tangible beings, by a species of vampire, which feeds on their life while they are asleep, and which, besides, drinks water and milk without appearing to touch any other nourishment.

"Professor Don Pedro Henriques, accompanied by several medical savants, has gone to the Province of San-Paulo, in order to study the origin and the manifestations of this surprising madness on the spot, and to propose such measures to the Emperor as may appear to him to be most fitted to restore the mad population to reason."

Ah! Ah! I remember now that fine Brazilian three-master which passed in front of my windows as it was going up the Seine, on the eighth of last May! I thought it looked so pretty, so white and bright! That Being was on board of her, coming from there, where its race sprang from. And it saw me! It saw my house, which was also white, and He sprang from the ship on to the land. Oh! Good heavens!

Now I know, I can divine. The reign of man is over, and he has come. He whom disquieted priests exorcised, whom sorcerers evoked on dark nights, without seeing him appear, He to whom the imaginations of the transient masters of the world lent all the monstrous or graceful forms of gnomes, spirits, genii, fairies, and familiar spirits. After the coarse conceptions of primitive fear, men more enlightened gave him a truer form. Mesmer divined him, and ten years ago physicians accurately discovered the nature of his power, even before He exercised it himself. They played with that weapon of their new Lord, the sway of a mysterious will over the human soul, which had become enslaved. They called it mesmerism, hypnotism, suggestion, I know not what? I have seen them diverting themselves like rash children with this horrible power! Woe to us! Woe to man! He has come, the – the – what does He call himself – the – I fancy that he is shouting out his name to me and I do not hear him – the – yes – He is shouting it out – I am listening – I cannot – repeat – it – Horla – I have heard – the Horla – it is He – the Horla – He has come! -

Ah! the vulture has eaten the pigeon, the wolf has eaten the lamb; the lion has devoured the sharp-horned buffalo; man has killed the lion with an arrow, with a spear, with gunpowder; but the Horla will make of man what man has made of the horse and of the ox: his chattel, his slave, and his food, by the mere power of his will. Woe to us!

But, nevertheless, sometimes the animal rebels and kills the man who has subjugated it. I should also like – I shall be able to – but I must know Him, touch Him, see Him! Learned men say that eyes of animals, as they differ from ours, do not distinguish as ours do. And my eye cannot distinguish this newcomer who is oppressing me.

Why? Oh! Now I remember the words of the monk at Mont Saint-Michel: "Can we see the hundred-thousandth part of what exists? Listen; there is the wind which is the strongest force in nature; it knocks men down, blows down buildings, uproots trees, raises the sea into mountains of water, destroys cliffs, and casts great ships on to the breakers; it kills, it whistles, it sighs, it roars, – have you ever seen it, and can you see it? It exists for all that, however!"

And I went on thinking: my eyes are so weak, so imperfect, that they do not even distinguish hard bodies, if they are as transparent as glass! If a glass without quicksilver behind it were to bar my way, I should run into it, just like a bird which has flown into a room breaks its head against the windowpanes. A thousand things, moreover, deceive a man and lead him astray. How then is it surprising that he cannot perceive a new body which is penetrated and pervaded by the light?

A new being! Why not? It was assuredly bound to come! Why should we be the last? We do not distinguish it, like all the others created before us? The reason is, that its nature is more delicate, its body finer and more finished than ours. Our makeup is so weak, so awkwardly conceived; our body is encumbered with organs that are always tired, always being strained like locks that are too complicated; it lives like a plant and like an animal nourishing itself with difficulty on air, herbs, and flesh; it is a brute machine which is a prey to maladies, to malformations, to decay; it is broken-winded, badly regulated, simple and eccentric, ingeniously yet badly made, a coarse and yet a delicate mechanism, in brief, the outline of a being which might become intelligent and great.

There are only a few – so few – stages of development in this world, from the oyster up to man. Why should there not be one more, when once that period is accomplished which separates the successive products one from the other?

Why not one more? Why not, also, other trees with immense, splendid flowers, perfuming whole regions? Why not other elements beside fire, air, earth, and water? There are four, only four, nursing fathers of various beings! What a pity! Why should not there be forty, four hundred, four thousand! How poor everything is, how mean and wretched – grudgingly given, poorly invented, clumsily made! Ah! the elephant and the hippopotamus, what power! And the camel, what suppleness!

But the butterfly, you will say, a flying flower! I dream of one that should be as large as a hundred worlds, with wings whose shape, beauty, colors, and motion I cannot even express. But I see it – it flutters from star to star, refreshing them and perfuming them with the light and harmonious breath of its flight! And the people up there gaze at it as it passes in an ecstasy of delight!

What is the matter with me? It is He, the Horla who haunts me, and who makes me think of these foolish things! He is within me, He is becoming my soul; I shall kill him!

August 20. I shall kill Him. I have seen Him! Yesterday I sat down at my table and pretended to write very assiduously. I knew quite well that He would come prowling round me, quite close to me, so close that I might perhaps be able to touch him, to seize him. And then – then I should have the strength of desperation; I should have my hands, my knees, my chest, my forehead, my teeth to strangle him, to crush him, to bite him, to tear him to pieces. And I watched for him with all my overexcited nerves.

I had lighted my two lamps and the eight wax candles on my mantelpiece, as if, by this light I should discover Him.

My bed, my old oak bed with its columns, was opposite to me; on my right was the fireplace; on my left the door, which was carefully closed, after I had left it open for some time, in order to attract Him; behind me was a very high wardrobe with a looking-glass in it, which served me to dress by every day, and in which I was in the habit of inspecting myself from head to foot every time I passed it.

So I pretended to be writing in order to deceive Him, for He also was watching me, and suddenly I felt, I was certain, that He was reading over my shoulder, that He was there, almost touching my ear.

I got up so quickly, with my hands extended, that I almost fell. Horror! It was as bright as at midday, but I did not see myself in the glass! It was empty, clear, profound, full of light! But my figure was not reflected in it – and I, I was opposite to it! I saw the large, clear glass from top to bottom, and I looked at it with unsteady eyes. I did not dare advance; I did not venture to make a movement; feeling certain, nevertheless, that He was there, but that He would escape me again, He whose imperceptible body had absorbed my reflection.

How frightened I was! And then suddenly I began to see myself through a mist in the depths of the looking-glass, in a mist as it were, or through a veil of water; and it seemed to me as if this water were flowing slowly from left to right, and making my figure clearer every moment. It was like the end of an eclipse. Whatever hid me did not appear to possess any clearly defined outlines, but was a sort of opaque transparency, which gradually grew clearer.

At last I was able to distinguish myself completely, as I do every day when I look at myself.

I had seen Him! And the horror of it remained with me, and makes me shudder even now.

August 21. How could I kill Him, since I could not get hold of Him? Poison? But He would see me mix it with the water; and then, would our poisons have any effect on His impalpable body? No – no – no doubt about the matter. Then? – then?

August 22. I sent for a blacksmith from Rouen and ordered iron shutters of him for my room, such as some private hotels in Paris have on the ground floor, for fear of thieves, and he is going to make me a similar door as well. I have made myself out a coward, but I do not care about that!

September 10. Rouen, Hotel Continental. It is done; it is done – but is He dead? My mind is thoroughly upset by what I have seen.

Well then, yesterday, the locksmith having put on the iron shutters and door, I left everything open until midnight, although it was getting cold.

Suddenly I felt that He was there, and joy, mad joy took possession of me. I got up softly, and I walked to the right and left for some time, so that He might not guess anything; then I took off my boots and put on my slippers carelessly; then I fastened the iron shutters and going back to the door quickly I double-locked it with a padlock, putting the key into my pocket.

Suddenly I noticed that He was moving restlessly round me, that in his turn He was frightened and was ordering me to let Him out. I nearly yielded, though I did not quite, but putting my back to the door, I half opened it, just enough to allow me to go out backward, and as I am very tall, my head touched the lintel. I was sure that He had not been able to escape, and I shut Him up quite alone, quite alone. What happiness! I had Him fast. Then I ran downstairs into the drawing-room which was under my bedroom. I took the two lamps and poured all the oil on to the carpet, the furniture, everywhere; then I set fire to it and made my escape, after having carefully double locked the door.

I went and hid myself at the bottom of the garden, in a clump of laurel bushes. How long it was! how long it was! Everything was dark, silent, motionless, not a breath of air and not a star, but heavy banks of clouds which one could not see, but which weighed, oh! so heavily on my soul.

I looked at my house and waited. How long it was! I already began to think that the fire had gone out of its own accord, or that He had extinguished it, when one of the lower windows gave way under the violence of the flames, and a long, soft, caressing sheet of red flame mounted up the white wall, and kissed it as high as the roof. The light fell on to the trees, the branches, and the leaves, and a shiver of fear pervaded them also! The birds awoke; a dog began to howl, and it seemed to me as if the day were breaking! Almost immediately two other windows flew into fragments, and I saw that the whole of the lower part of my house was nothing but a terrible furnace. But a cry, a horrible, shrill, heart-rending cry, a woman's cry, sounded through the night, and two garret windows were opened! I had forgotten the servants! I saw the terror-struck faces, and the frantic waving of their arms!

Then, overwhelmed with horror, I ran off to the village, shouting: "Help! help! fire! fire!" Meeting some people who were already coming on to the scene, I went back with them to see!

By this time the house was nothing but a horrible and magnificent funeral pile, a monstrous pyre which lit up the whole country, a pyre where men were burning, and where He was burning also, He, He, my prisoner, that new Being, the new Master, the Horla!

Suddenly the whole roof fell in between the walls, and a volcano of flames darted up to the sky. Through all the windows which opened on to that furnace, I saw the flames darting, and I reflected that He was there, in that kiln, dead.

Dead? Perhaps? His body? Was not his body, which was transparent, indestructible by such means as would kill ours?

If He were not dead? Perhaps time alone has power over that Invisible and Redoubtable Being. Why this transparent, unrecognizable body, this body belonging to a spirit, if it also had to fear ills, infirmities, and premature destruction?

Premature destruction? All human terror springs from that! After man the Horla. After him who can die every day, at any hour, at any moment, by any accident, He came, He who was only to die at his own proper hour and minute, because He had touched the limits of his existence!

No – no – there is no doubt about it – He is not dead. Then – then – I suppose I must kill myself!

The Woman of the Wood

A. Merritt

MCKAY sat on the balcony of the little inn that squatted like a brown gnome among the pines on the eastern shore of the lake.

It was a small and lonely lake high up in the Vosges; and yet, lonely is not just the word with which to tag its spirit; rather was it aloof, withdrawn. The mountains came down on every side, making a great tree-lined bowl that seemed, when McKay first saw it, to be filled with the still wine of peace.

McKay had worn the wings in the world war with honor, flying first with the French and later with his own country's forces. And as a bird loves the trees, so did McKay love them. To him they were not merely trunks and roots, branches and leaves; to him they were personalities. He was acutely aware of differences in character even among the same species – that pine was benevolent and jolly; that one austere and monkish; there stood a swaggering bravo, and there dwelt a sage wrapped in green meditation; that birch was a wanton – the birch near her was virginal, still a dream.

The war had sapped him, nerve and brain and soul. Through all the years that had passed since then the wound had kept open. But now, as he slid his car down the vast green bowl, he felt its spirit reach out to him; reach out to him and caress and quiet him, promising him healing. He seemed to drift like a falling leaf through the clustered woods; to be cradled by gentle hands of the trees.

He had stopped at the little gnome of an inn, and there he had lingered, day after day, week after week.

The trees had nursed him; soft whisperings of leaves, slow chant of the needled pines, had first deadened, then driven from him the re-echoing clamor of the war and its sorrow. The open wound of his spirit had closed under their green healing; had closed and become scar; and even the scar had been covered and buried, as the scars on Earth's breast are covered and buried beneath the falling leaves of Autumn. The trees had laid green healing hands on his eyes, banishing the pictures of war. He had sucked strength from the green breasts of the hills.

Yet as strength flowed back to him and mind and spirit healed, McKay had grown steadily aware that the place was troubled; that its tranquillity was not perfect; that there was ferment of fear within it.

It was as though the trees had waited until he himself had become whole before they made their own unrest known to him. Now they were trying to tell him something; there was a shrillness as of apprehension, of anger, in the whispering of the leaves, the needled chanting of the pines.

And it was this that had kept McKay at the inn – a definite consciousness of appeal, consciousness of something wrong – something wrong that he was being asked to right. He strained his ears to catch words in the rustling branches, words that trembled on the brink of his human understanding.

Never did they cross that brink.

Gradually he had orientated himself, had focused himself, so he believed, to the point of the valley's unease.

On all the shores of the lake there were but two dwellings. One was the inn, and around the inn the trees clustered protectively, confiding; friendly. It was as though they had not only accepted it, but had made it part of themselves.

Not so was it of the other habitation. Once it had been the hunting lodge of long dead lords; now it was half ruined, forlorn. It stood across the lake almost exactly opposite the inn and back upon the slope a half mile from the shore. Once there had been fat fields around it and a fair orchard.

The forest had marched down upon them. Here and there in the fields, scattered pines and poplars stood like soldiers guarding some outpost; scouting parties of saplings lurked among the gaunt and broken fruit trees. But the forest had not had its way unchecked; ragged stumps showed where those who dwelt in the old lodge had cut down the invaders, blackened patches of the woodland showed where they had fired the woods.

Here was the conflict he had sensed. Here the green folk of the forest were both menaced and menacing; at war. The lodge was a fortress beleaguered by the woods, a fortress whose garrison sallied forth with axe and torch to take their toll of the besiegers.

Yet McKay sensed the inexorable pressing-in of the forest; he saw it as a green army ever filling the gaps in its enclosing ranks, shooting its seeds into the cleared places, sending its roots out to sap them; and armed always with a crushing patience, a patience drawn from the stone breasts of the eternal hills.

He had the impression of constant regard of watchfulness, as though night and day the forest kept its myriads of eyes upon the lodge; inexorably, not to be swerved from its purpose. He had spoken of this impression to the inn keeper and his wife, and they had looked at him oddly.

"Old Polleau does not love the trees, no," the old man had said. "No, nor do his two sons. They do not love the trees – and very certainly the trees do not love them."

Between the lodge and the shore, marching down to the verge of the lake was a singularly beautiful little coppice of silver birches and firs. The coppice stretched for perhaps a quarter of a mile, was not more than a hundred feet or two in depth, and it was not alone the beauty of its trees but their curious grouping that aroused McKay's interest so vividly. At each end of the coppice were a dozen or more of the glistening needled firs, not clustered but spread out as though in open marching order; at widely spaced intervals along its other two sides paced single firs. The birches, slender and delicate, grew within the guard of these sturdier trees, yet not so thickly as to crowd each other.

To McKay the silver birches were for all the world like some gay caravan of lovely demoiselles under the protection of debonair knights. With that odd other sense of his he saw the birches as delectable damsels, merry and laughing – the pines as lovers, troubadours in their green needled mail. And when the winds blew and the crests of the trees bent under them, it was as though dainty demoiselles picked up fluttering, leafy skirts, bent leafy hoods and danced while the knights of the firs drew closer round them, locked arms with theirs and danced with them to the roaring horns of the winds. At such times he almost heard sweet laughter from the birches, shoutings from the firs.

Of all the trees in that place McKay loved best this little wood; had rowed across and rested in its shade, had dreamed there and, dreaming, had heard again elfin echoes of the sweet laughter; eyes closed, had heard mysterious whisperings and the sound of dancing feet light as falling leaves; had taken dream draught of that gaiety which was the soul of the little wood.

And two days ago he had seen Polleau and his two sons. McKay had been dreaming in the coppice all that afternoon. As dusk began to fall he had reluctantly arisen and begun the row back to the inn. When he had been a few hundred feet from shore three men had come out from the trees and had stood watching him – three grim, powerful men taller than the average French peasant.

He had called a friendly greeting to them, but they had not answered it; stood there, scowling. Then as he bent again to his oars, one of the sons had raised a hatchet and had driven it savagely into the trunk of a slim birch beside him. He thought he heard a thin wailing cry from the stricken tree, a sigh from all the little wood.

McKay had felt as though the keen edge had bitten into his own flesh.

"Stop that!" he had cried, "Stop it, damn you!"

For answer the son had struck again – and never had McKay seen hate etched so deep as on his face as he struck. Cursing, a killing rage in heart, had swung the boat around, raced back to shore. He had heard the hatchet strike again and again and, close now to shore, had heard a crackling and over it once more the thin, high wailing. He had turned to look.

The birch was tottering, was falling. But as it had fallen he had seen a curious thing. Close beside it grew one of the firs, and, as the smaller tree crashed over, it dropped upon the fir like a fainting maid in the arms of a lover. And as it lay and trembled there, one of the great branches of the fir slipped from under it, whipped out and smote the hatchet wielder a crushing blow upon the head, sending him to earth.

It had been, of course, only the chance blow of a bough, bent by pressure of the fallen tree and then released as that tree slipped down. But there had been such suggestion of conscious action in the branch's recoil, so much of bitter anger in it, so much, in truth, had it been like the vengeful blow of a man that McKay had felt an eerie prickling of his scalp, his heart had missed its beat.

For a moment Polleau and the standing son had stared at the sturdy fir with the silvery birch lying on its green breast and folded in, shielded by, its needled boughs as though – again the swift impression came to McKay– as though it were a wounded maid stretched on breast, in arms, of knightly lover. For a long moment father and son had stared.

Then, still wordless but with that same bitter hatred on both their faces, they had stopped and picked up the other and with his arms around the neck of each had borne him limply away.

McKay, sitting on the balcony of the inn that morning, went over and over that scene; realized more and more clearly the human aspect of fallen birch and clasping fir, and the conscious deliberateness of the fir's blow. And during the two days that had elapsed since then, he had felt the unease of the trees increase, their whispering appeal became more urgent.

What were they trying to tell him? What did they want him to do?

Troubled, he stared across the lake, trying to pierce the mists that hung over it and hid the opposite shore. And suddenly it seemed that he heard the coppice calling him, felt it pull the point of his attention toward it irresistibly, as the lodestone swings and holds the compass needle.

The coppice called him, bade him come to it.

Instantly McKay obeyed the command; he arose and walked down to the boat landing; he stepped into his skiff and began to row across the lake. As his oars touched the water his trouble fell from him. In its place flowed peace and a curious exaltation.

The mist was thick upon the lake. There was no breath of wind, yet the mist billowed and drifted, shook and curtained under the touch of unfelt airy hands.

They were alive – the mists; they formed themselves into fantastic palaces past whose opalescent facades he flew; they built themselves into hills and valleys and circled plains whose floors were rippling silk. Tiny rainbows gleamed out among them, and upon the water prismatic patches shone and spread like spilled wine of opals. He had the illusion of vast distances– the hills of mist were real mountains, the valleys between them were not illusory. He was a colossus cleaving through some elfin world. A trout broke, and it was like leviathan leaping from the fathomless deep. Around the arc of its body rainbows interlaced and then dissolved into rain of softly gleaming gems – diamonds in dance with sapphires, flame hearted rubies and pearls with shimmering souls of rose. The fish vanished, diving cleanly without sound; the jeweled bows vanished with it; a tiny irised whirlpool swirled for an instant where trout and flashing arcs had been.

Nowhere was there sound. He let his oars drop and leaned forward, drifting. In the silence, before him and around him, he felt opening the gateways of an unknown world.

And suddenly he heard the sound of voices, many voices; faint at first and murmurous; louder they became, swiftly; women's voices sweet and lilting and mingled with them the deeper tones of men. Voices that lifted and fell in a wild, gay chanting through whose joyousness ran undertones both of sorrow and of rage – as though faery weavers threaded through silk spun of sunbeams sombre strands dipped in the black of graves and crimson strands stained in the red of wrathful sunsets.

He drifted on, scarce daring to breathe lest even that faint sound break the elfin song. Closer it rang and clearer; and now he became aware that the speed of his boat was increasing, that it was no longer drifting; that it was as though the little waves on each side were pushing him ahead with soft and noiseless palms. His boat grounded and as it rustled along over the smooth pebbles of the beach the song ceased.

McKay half arose and peered before him. The mists were thicker here but he could see the outlines of the coppice. It was like looking at it through many curtains of fine gauze; its trees seemed shifting, ethereal, unreal. And moving among the trees were figures that threaded the boles and flitted in rhythmic measures like the shadows of leafy boughs swaying to some cadenced wind.

He stepped ashore and made his way slowly toward them. The mists dropped behind him, shutting off all sight of shore.

The rhythmic flittings ceased; there was now no movement as there was no sound among the trees – yet he felt the little woods abrim with watching life. McKay tried to speak; there was a spell of silence on his mouth.

"You called me. I have come to listen to you – to help you if I can."

The words formed within his mind, but utter them he could not. Over and over he tried, desperately; the words seemed to die before his lips could give them life.

A pillar of mist whirled forward and halted, eddying half an arm length away. And suddenly out of it peered a woman's face, eyes level with his own. A woman's face – yes; but McKay, staring into those strange eyes probing his, knew that face though it seemed it was that of no woman of human breed. They were without pupils, the irises deer-like and of the soft green of deep forest dells; within them sparkled tiny star points of light like motes in a moon beam. The eyes were wide and set far apart beneath a broad, low brow over which was piled braid upon braid of hair of palest gold, braids that seemed spun of shining ashes of gold. Her nose was small and straight, her mouth scarlet and exquisite. The face was oval, tapering to a delicately pointed chin.

Beautiful was that face, but its beauty was an alien one; elfin. For long moments the strange eyes thrust their gaze deep into his. Then out of the mist two slender white arms stole, the hands long, fingers tapering. The tapering fingers touched his ears.

"He shall hear," whispered the red lips.

Immediately from all about him a cry arose; in it was the whispering and rustling of the leaves beneath the breath of the winds, the shrilling of the harp strings of the boughs, the laughter of hidden brooks, the shoutings of waters flinging themselves down to deep and rocky pools – the voices of the woods made articulate.

"He shall hear!" they cried.

The long white fingers rested on his lips, and their touch was cool as bark of birch on cheek after some long upward climb through forest; cool and subtly sweet.

"He shall speak," whispered the scarlet lips.

"He shall speak!" answered the wood voices again, as though in litany.

"He shall see," whispered the woman and the cool fingers touched his eyes.

"He shall see!" echoed the wood voices.

The mists that had hidden the coppice from McKay wavered, thinned and were gone. In their place was a limpid, translucent, palely green ether, faintly luminous – as though he stood within some clear wan emerald. His feet pressed a golden moss spangled with tiny starry bluets. Fully revealed before him was the woman of the strange eyes and the face of elfin beauty. He dwelt for a moment upon the slender shoulders, the firm small tip-tilted breasts, the willow litheness of her body. From neck to knees a smock covered her, sheer and silken and delicate as though spun of cobwebs; through it her body gleamed as though fire of the young Spring moon ran in her veins.

Beyond her, upon the golden moss were other women like her, many of them; they stared at him with the same wide set green eyes in which danced the clouds of sparkling moonbeam motes; like her they were crowned with glistening, pallidly golden hair; like hers too were their oval faces with the pointed chins and perilous elfin beauty. Only where she stared at him gravely, measuring him, weighing him – there were those of these her sisters whose eyes were mocking; and those whose eyes called to him with a weirdly tingling allure, their mouths athirst; those whose eyes looked upon him with curiosity alone and those whose great eyes pleaded with him, prayed to him.

Within that pellucid, greenly luminous air McKay was abruptly aware that the trees of the coppice still had a place. Only now they were spectral indeed; they were like white shadows cast athwart a glaucous screen; trunk and bough, twig and leaf they arose around him and they were as though etched in air by phantom craftsmen – thin, unsubstantial; they were ghost trees rooted in another space.

Suddenly he was aware that there were men among the women; men whose eyes were set wide apart as were theirs, as strange and pupilless as were theirs but with irises of brown and blue; men with pointed chins and oval faces, broad shouldered and clad in kirtles of darkest green; swarthy-skinned men muscular and strong, with that same lithe grace of the women – and like them of a beauty alien and elfin.

McKay heard a little wailing cry. He turned. Close beside him lay a girl clasped in the arms of one of the swarthy, green clad men. She lay upon his breast. His eyes were filled with a black flame of wrath, and hers were misted, anguished. For an instant McKay had a glimpse of the birch old Polleau's son had sent crashing down into the boughs of the fir. He saw birch and fir as immaterial outlines around the man and girl. For an instant girl and man and birch and fir seemed one and the same. The scarlet lipped woman touched his shoulder, and the confusion cleared.

"She withers," sighed the woman, and in her voice McKay heard a faint rustling as of mournful leaves. "Now is it not pitiful that she withers– our sister who was so young, so slender and so lovely?"

McKay looked again at the girl. The white skin seemed shrunken; the moon radiance that gleamed through the bodies of the others in hers was dim and pallid; her slim arms hung listlessly; her body drooped. The mouth too was wan and parched, the long and misted green eyes dull. The palely golden hair lusterless, and dry. He looked on slow death – a withering death.

"May the arm that struck her down wither!" the green clad man who held her shouted, and in his voice McKay heard a savage strumming as of winter winds through bleak boughs: "May his heart wither and the sun blast him! May the rain and the waters deny him and the winds scourge him!"

"I thirst," whispered the girl.

There was a stirring among the watching women. One came forward holding a chalice that was like thin leaves turned to green crystal. She paused beside the trunk of one of the spectral trees, reached up and drew down to her a branch. A slim girl with half-frightened, half-resentful eyes glided to her side and threw her arms around the ghostly bole. The woman with the chalice bent the branch and cut it deep with what seemed an arrow-shaped flake of jade. From the wound a faintly opalescent liquid slowly filled the cup. When it was filled the woman beside McKay stepped forward and pressed her own long hands around the bleeding branch. She stepped away and McKay saw that the stream had ceased to flow. She touched the trembling girl and unclasped her arms.

"It is healed," said the woman gently. "And it was your turn little sister. The wound is healed. Soon, you will have forgotten."

The woman with the chalice knelt and set it to the wan, dry lips of her who was – withering. She drank of it, thirstily, to the last drop. The misty eyes cleared, they sparkled; the lips that had been so parched and pale grew red, the white body gleamed as though the waning light had been fed with new.

"Sing, sisters," she cried, and shrilly. "Dance for me, sisters!"

Again burst out that chant McKay had heard as he had floated through the mists upon the lake. Now, as then, despite his opened ears, he could distinguish no words, but clearly he understood its mingled themes –the joy of Spring's awakening, rebirth, with the green life streaming singing up through every bough, swelling the buds, burgeoning with tender leaves the branches; the dance of the trees in the scented winds of Spring; the drums of the jubilant rain on leafy hoods; passion of Summer sun pouring its golden flood down upon the trees; the moon passing with stately step and slow and green hands stretching up to her and drawing from her breast milk of silver fire; riot of wild gay winds with their mad pipings and strummings; – soft interlacing of boughs, the kiss of amorous leaves – all these and more, much more that McKay could not understand since it dealt with hidden, secret things for which man has no images, were in that chanting.

And all these and more were in the measures, the rhythms of the dancing of those strange, green eyed women and brown skinned men; something incredibly ancient yet young as the speeding moment, something of a world before and beyond man.

McKay listened, McKay watched, lost in wonder; his own world more than half forgotten; his mind meshed in web of green sorcery.

The woman beside him touched his arm. She pointed to the girl.

"Yet she withers," she said. "And not all our life, if we poured it through her lips, could save her."

He looked; he saw that the red was draining slowly from the girl's lips, the luminous life tides waning; the eyes that had been so bright were misting and growing dull once more, suddenly a great pity and a great rage shook him. He knelt beside her, took her hands in his.

"Take them away! Take away your hands! They burn me!" she moaned.

"He tries to help you," whispered the green clad man, gently. But he reached over and drew McKay's hands away.

"Not so can you help her," said the woman.

"What can I do?" McKay arose, looked helplessly from one to the other. "What can I do to help?"

The chanting died, the dance stopped. A silence fell and he felt upon him the eyes of all. They were tense – waiting. The woman took his hands. Their touch was cool and sent a strange sweetness sweeping through his veins.

"There are three men yonder," she said. "They hate us. Soon we shall be as she is there – withering. They have sworn it, and as they have sworn so will they do. Unless—"

She paused; and McKay felt the stirrings of a curious unease. The moonbeam-dancing motes in her eyes had changed to tiny sparklings of red. In a way, deep down, they terrified him – those red sparklings.

"Three men?" – in his clouded mind was the memory of Polleau and his two strong sons. "Three men," he repeated, stupidly – "But what are three men to you who are so many? What could three men do against those stalwart gallants of yours?"

"No," she shook her head. "No – there is nothing our – men– can do; nothing that we can do. Once, night and day, we were gay. Now we fear – night and day. They mean to destroy us. Our kin have warned us. And our kin cannot help us. Those three are masters of blade and flame. Against blade and flame we are helpless."

"Blade and flame!" echoed the listeners. "Against blade and flame we are helpless."

"Surely will they destroy us," murmured the woman. "We shall wither all of us. Like her there, or burn – unless—"

Suddenly she threw white arms around McKay's neck. She pressed her lithe body close to him. Her scarlet mouth sought and found his lips and clung to them. Through all McKay's body ran swift, sweet flames, green fire of desire. His own arms went round her, crushed her to him.

"You shall not die!" he cried. "No – by God, you shall not!"

She drew back her head, looked deep into his eyes.

"They have sworn to destroy us," she said, "and soon. With blade and flame they will destroy us – these three – unless—"

"Unless?" he asked, fiercely.

"Unless you – slay them first!" she answered.

A cold shock ran through McKay, chilling the green sweet fires of his desire. He dropped his arm from around the woman; thrust her from him. For an instant she trembled before him.

"Slay!" he heard her whisper – and she was gone. The spectral trees wavered; their outlines thickened out of immateriality into substance. The green translucence darkened. He had a swift vertiginous moment as though he swung between two worlds. He closed his eyes. The vertigo passed and he opened them, looked around him.

McKay stood on the lakeward skirts of the little coppice. There were no shadows flitting, no sign of the white women and the swarthy, green clad men. His feet were on green moss; gone was the soft golden carpet with its blue starlets. Birches and firs clustered solidly before him. At his left was a sturdy fir in whose needled arms a broken birch tree lay withering. It was the birch that Polleau's men had so wantonly slashed down. For an instant he saw within the fir and birch the immaterial outlines of the green clad man and the slim girl who withered. For that instant birch and fir and girl and man seemed one and the same. He stepped back, and his hands touched the smooth, cool bark of another birch that rose close at his right.

Upon his hands the touch of that bark was like – was like? –yes, curiously was it like the touch of the long slim hands of the woman of the scarlet lips. But it gave him none of that alien rapture, that pulse of green life her touch had brought. Yet, now as then, the touch steadied him. The outlines of girl and man were gone.

He looked upon nothing but a sturdy fir with a withering birch fallen into its branches.

McKay stood there, staring, wondering, like a man who has but half awakened from dream. And suddenly a little wind stirred the leaves of the rounded birch beside him. The leaves murmured, sighed. The wind grew stronger and the leaves whispered.

"Slay!" he heard them whisper – and again: "Slay! Help us! Slay!"

And the whisper was the voice of the woman of the scarlet lips!

Rage, swift and unreasoning, sprang up in McKay. He began to run up through the coppice, up to where he knew was the old lodge in which dwelt Polleau and his sons. And as he ran the wind blew stronger, and louder and louder grew the whisperings of the trees.

"Slay!" they whispered. "Slay them! Save us! Slay!"

"I will slay! I will save you!" McKay, panting, hammer pulse beating in his ears, rushing through the woods heard himself answering that ever louder, ever more insistent command. And in his mind was but one desire – to clutch the throats of Polleau and his sons, to crack their necks; to stand by them then and watch them wither; wither like that slim girl in the arms of the green clad man.

So crying, he came to the edge of the coppice and burst from it out into a flood of sunshine. For a hundred feet he ran, and then he was aware that the whispering command was stilled; that he heard no more that maddening rustling of wrathful leaves. A spell seemed to have been loosed from him; it was as though he had broken through some web of sorcery. McKay stopped, dropped upon the ground, buried his face in the grasses.

He lay there, marshaling his thoughts into some order of sanity. What had he been about to do? To rush berserk upon those three who lived in the old lodge and – kill them! And for what? Because that elfin, scarlet lipped woman whose kisses he still could feel upon his mouth had bade him! Because the whispering trees of the little wood had maddened him with that same command!

And for this he had been about to kill three men!

What were that woman and her sisters and the green clad swarthy gallants of theirs? Illusions of some waking dream – phantoms born of the hypnosis of the swirling mists through which he had rowed and floated across the lake? Such things were not uncommon. McKay knew of those who by watching the shifting clouds could create and dwell for a time with wide open eyes within some similar land of fantasy; knew others who needed but to stare at smoothly falling water to set themselves within a world of waking dream; there were those who could summon dreams by gazing into a ball of crystal, others found their phantoms in saucers of shining ebon ink.

Might not the moving mists have laid those same hypnotic fingers upon his own mind – and his love for the trees the sense of appeal that he had felt so long and his memory of the wanton slaughter of the slim birch have all combined to paint upon his drugged consciousness the phantasms he had beheld?

Then in the flood of sunshine the spell had melted, his consciousness leaped awake?

McKay arose to his feet, shakily enough. He looked back at the coppice. There was no wind now, the leaves were silent, motionless. Again he saw it as the caravan of demoiselles with their marching knights and troubadours. But no longer was it gay. The words of the scarlet lipped woman came back to him– that gaiety had fled and fear had taken its place. Dream phantom or– dryad, whatever she was, half of that at least was truth.

He turned, a plan forming in his mind. Reason with himself as he might, something deep within him stubbornly asserted the reality of his experience. At any rate, he told himself, the little wood was far too beautiful to be despoiled. He would put aside the experience as dream – but he would save the little wood for the essence of beauty that it held in its green cup.

The old lodge was about a quarter of a mile away. A path led up to it through the ragged fields. McKay walked up the path, climbed rickety steps and paused, listening. He heard voices and knocked. The door was flung open and old Polleau stood there, peering at him through half shut, suspicious eyes. One of the sons stood close behind him. They stared at McKay with grim, hostile faces.

He thought he heard a faint, far off despairing whisper from the distant wood. And it was as though the pair in the doorway heard it too, for their gaze shifted from him to the coppice, and he saw hatred nicker swiftly across their grim faces; their gaze swept back to him.

"What do you want?" demanded Polleau, curtly.

"I am a neighbor of yours, stopping at the inn—" began McKay, courteously.

"I know who you are," Polleau interrupted brusquely, "But what is it that you want?"

"I find the air of this place good for me," McKay stifled a rising anger. "I am thinking of staying for a year or more until my health is fully recovered. I would like to buy some of your land and build me a lodge upon it."

"Yes, M'sieu?" there was acid politeness now in the powerful old man's voice. "But is it permitted to ask why you do not remain at the inn? Its fare is excellent and you are well liked there."

"I have desire to be alone," replied McKay. "I do not like people too close to me. I would have my own land, and sleep under my own roof."

"But why come to me?" asked Polleau. "There are many places upon the far side of the lake that you could secure. It is happy there, and this side is not happy, M'sieu. But tell me, what part of my land is it that you desire?"

"That little wood yonder," answered McKay, and pointed to the coppice.

"Ah! I thought so!" whispered Polleau, and between him and his sons passed a look of bitter understanding. He looked at McKay, somberly.

"That wood is not for sale, M'sieu," he said at last. "I can afford to pay well for what I want," said McKay. "Name your price."

"It is not for sale," repeated Polleau, stolidly, "at any price."

"Oh, come," laughed McKay, although his heart sank at the finality in that answer. "You have many acres and what is it but a few trees? I can afford to gratify my fancies. I will give you all the worth of your other land for it."

"You have asked what that place that you so desire is, and you have answered that it is but a few trees," said Polleau, slowly, and the tall son behind him laughed, abruptly, maliciously. "But it is more than that, M'sieu– Oh, much more than that. And you know it, else why would you pay such price? Yes, you know it – since you know also that we are ready to destroy it, and you would save it. And who told you all that, M'sieu?" he snarled.

There was such malignance in the face thrust suddenly close to McKay's, teeth bared by uplifted lip, that involuntarily he recoiled.

"But a few trees!" snarled old Polleau. "Then who told him what we mean to do – eh, Pierre?"

Again the son laughed. And at that laughter McKay felt within him resurgence of his own blind hatred as he had fled through the whispering wood. He mastered himself, turned away, there was nothing he could do –now. Polleau halted him.

"M'sieu," he said, "Wait. Enter. There is something I would tell you; something too I would show you. Something, perhaps, that I would ask you."

He stood aside, bowing with a rough courtesy. McKay walked through the doorway. Polleau with his son followed him. He entered a large, dim room whose ceiling was spanned with smoke blackened beams. From these beams hung onion strings and herbs and smoke cured meats. On one side was a wide fireplace. Huddled beside it sat Polleau's other son. He glanced up as they entered and McKay saw that a bandage covered one side of his head, hiding his left eye. McKay recognized him as the one who had cut down the slim birch. The blow of the fir, he reflected with a certain satisfaction, had been no futile one.

Old Polleau strode over to that son.

"Look, M'sieu," he said and lifted the bandage.

McKay with a faint tremor of horror, saw a gaping blackened socket, red rimmed and eyeless.

"Good God, Polleau!" he cried. "But this man needs medical attention. I know something of wounds. Let me go across the lake and bring back my kit. I will attend him."

Old Polleau shook his head, although his grim face for the first time softened. He drew the bandages back in place.

"It heals," he said. "We have some skill in such things. You saw what did it. You watched from your boat as the cursed tree struck him. The eye was crushed and lay upon his cheek. I cut it away. Now he heals. We do not need your aid, M'sieu."

"Yet he ought not have cut the birch," muttered McKay, more to himself than to be heard.

"Why not?" asked old Polleau, fiercely, "Since it hated him."

McKay stared at him. What did this old peasant know? The words strengthened that deep stubborn conviction that what he had seen and heard in the coppice had been actuality – no dream. And still more did Polleau's next words strengthen that conviction.

"M'sieu," he said, "you come here as ambassador – of a sort. The wood has spoken to you. Well, as ambassador I shall speak to you. Four centuries my people have lived in this place. A century we have owned this land. M'sieu, in all those years there has been no moment that the trees have not hated us – nor we the trees.

"For all those hundred years there have been hatred and battle between us and the forest. My father, M'sieu, was crushed by a tree; my elder brother crippled by another. My father's father, woodsman that he was, was lost in the forest – he came back to us with mind gone, raving of wood women who had bewitched and mocked him, luring him into swamp and fen and tangled thicket, tormenting him. In every generation the trees have taken their toll of us – women as well as men – maiming or killing us."

"Accidents," interrupted McKay. "This is childish, Polleau. You cannot blame the trees."

"In your heart you do not believe so," said Polleau. "Listen, the feud is an ancient one. Centuries ago it began when we were serfs, slaves of the nobles. To cook, to keep us warm in winter, they let us pick up the fagots, the dead branches and twigs that dropped from the trees. But if we cut down a tree to keep us warm, to keep our women and our children warm, yes, if we but tore down a branch – they hanged us, or they threw us into dungeons to rot, or whipped us till our backs were red lattices.

"They had their broad fields, the nobles – but we must raise our food in the patches where the trees disdained to grow. And if they did thrust themselves into our poor patches, then, M'sieu, we must let them have their way – or be flogged, or be thrown into the dungeons or be hanged.

"They pressed us in – the trees," the old man's voice grew sharp with fanatic hatred. "They stole our fields and they took the food from the mouths of our children; they dropped their fagots to us like dole to beggars; they tempted us to warmth when the cold struck our bones – and they bore us as fruit a-swing at the end of the foresters' ropes if we yielded to their tempting.

"Yes, M'sieu – we died of cold that they might live! Our children died of hunger that their young might find root space! They despised us– the trees! We died that they might live – and we were men!

"Then, M'sieu came the Revolution and the freedom. Ah, M'sieu, then we took our toll! Great logs roaring in the winter cold – no more huddling over the alms of fagots. Fields where the trees had been – no more starving of our children that theirs might live. Now the trees were the slaves and we the masters.

"And the trees knew and they hated us!

"But blow for blow, a hundred of their lives for each life of ours – we have returned their hatred. With axe and torch we have fought them—

"The trees!" shrieked Polleau, suddenly, eyes blazing red rage, face writhing, foam at the corners of his mouth and gray hair clutched in rigid hands – "The cursed trees! Armies of the trees creeping –creeping – closer, ever closer – crushing us in! Stealing our fields as they did of old! Building their dungeon round us as they built of old the dungeons of stone! Creeping – creeping! Armies of trees! Legions of trees! The trees! The cursed trees!"

McKay listened, appalled. Here was crimson heart of hate. Madness! But what was at the root of it? Some deep inherited instinct, coming down from forefathers who had hated the forest as the symbol of their masters. Forefathers whose tides of hatred had overflowed to the green life on which the nobles had laid their tabu – as one neglected child will hate the favorite on whom love and gifts are lavished? In such warped minds the crushing fall of a tree, the maiming sweep of a branch, might well appear as deliberate, the natural growth of the forest seem the implacable advance of an enemy.

And yet – the blow of the fir as the cut birch fell had been deliberate! and there had been those women of the wood—

"Patience," the standing son touched the old man's shoulder. "Patience! Soon we strike our blow."

Some of the frenzy died out of Polleau's face.

"Though we cut down a hundred," he whispered, "By the hundred they return! But one of us, when they strike – he does not return. No! They have numbers and they have – time. We are now but three, and we have little time. They watch us as we go through the forest, alert to trip, to strike, to crush!

"But M'sieu," he turned blood-shot eyes to McKay. "We strike our blow, even as Pierre has said. We strike at the coppice that you so desire. We strike there because it is the very heart of the forest. There the secret life of the forest runs at full tide. We know – and you know! Something that, destroyed, will take the heart out of the forest – will make it know us for its masters."

"The women!" the standing son's eyes glittered, "I have seen the women there! The fair women with the shining skins who invite – and mock and vanish before hands can seize them."

"The fair women who peer into our windows in the night – and mock us!" muttered the eyeless son.

"They shall mock no more!" shouted Polleau, the frenzy again taking him. "Soon they shall lie, dying! All of them – all of them! They die!"

He caught McKay by the shoulders, shook him like a child.

"Go tell them that!" he shouted. "Say to them that this very day we destroy them. Say to them it is we who will laugh when winter comes and we watch their round white bodies blaze in this hearth of ours and warm us! Go– tell them that!"

He spun McKay around, pushed him to the door, opened it and flung him staggering down the steps. He heard the tall son laugh, the door close. Blind with rage he rushed up the steps and hurled himself against the door. Again the tall son laughed. McKay beat at the door with clenched fists, cursing. The three within paid no heed. Despair began to dull his rage. Could the trees help him – counsel him? He turned and walked slowly down the field path to the little wood.

Slowly and ever more slowly he went as he neared it. He had failed. He was a messenger bearing a warrant of death. The birches were motionless; their leaves hung listlessly. It was as though they knew he had failed. He paused at the edge of the coppice. He looked at his watch, noted with faint surprise that already it was high noon. Short shrift enough had the little wood. The work of destruction would not be long delayed.

McKay squared his shoulders and passed in between the trees. It was strangely silent in the coppice. And it was mournful. He had a sense of life brooding around him, withdrawn into itself; sorrowing. He passed through the silent, mournful wood until he reached the spot where the rounded, gleaming barked tree stood close to the fir that held the withering birch. Still there was no sound, no movement. He laid his hands upon the cool bark of the rounded tree.

"Let me see again!" he whispered. "Let me hear! Speak to me!"

There was no answer. Again and again he called. The coppice was silent. He wandered through it, whispering, calling. The slim birches stood, passive with limbs and leaves adroop like listless arms and hands of captive maids awaiting with dull woe the will of conquerors. The firs seemed to crouch like hopeless men with heads in hands. His heart ached to the woe that filled the little wood, this hopeless submission of the trees.

When, he wondered, would Polleau strike. He looked at his watch again; an hour had gone by. How long would Polleau wait? He dropped to the moss, back against a smooth bole.

And suddenly it seemed to McKay that he was a madman – as mad as Polleau and his sons. Calmly, he went over the old peasant's indictment of the forest; recalled the face and eyes filled with the fanatic hate. Madness! After all, the trees were – only trees. Polleau and his sons – so he reasoned – had transferred to them the bitter hatred their forefathers had felt for those old lords who had enslaved them; had laid upon them too all the bitterness of their own struggle to exist in this high forest land. When they struck at the trees, it was the ghosts of these forefathers striking at the nobles who had oppressed them; it was themselves striking against their own destiny. The trees were but symbols. It was the warped minds of Polleau and his sons that clothed them in false semblance of conscious life in blind striving to wreak vengeance against the ancient masters and the destiny that had made their lives hard and unceasing battle against Nature. The nobles were long dead; destiny can be brought to grips by no man. But the trees were here and alive. Clothed in mirage, through them the driving lust for vengeance could be sated.

And he, McKay, was it not his own deep love and sympathy for the trees that similarly had clothed them in that false semblance of conscious life? Had he not built his own mirage? The trees did not really mourn, could not suffer, could not – know. It was his own sorrow that he had transferred to them; only his own sorrow that he felt echoing back to him from them.

The trees were – only trees.

Instantly, upon the heels of that thought, as though it were an answer, he was aware that the trunk against which he leaned was trembling; that the whole coppice was trembling; that all the little leaves were shaking, tremulously.

McKay, bewildered, leaped to his feet. Reason told him that it was the wind – yet there was no wind!

And as he stood there, a sighing arose as though a mournful breeze were blowing through the trees – and again there was no wind!

Louder grew the sighing and within it now faint wailings.

"They come! They come! Farewell sisters! Sisters – farewell!"

Clearly he heard the mournful whispers.

McKay began to run through the trees to the trail that led out to the fields of the old lodge. And as he ran the wood darkened as though clear shadows gathered in it, as though vast unseen wings hovered over it. The trembling of the coppice increased; bough touched bough, clung to each other; and louder became the sorrowful crying:

"Farewell sister! Sister – farewell!"

McKay burst out into the open. Halfway between him and the lodge were Polleau and his sons. They saw him; they pointed and lifted mockingly to him bright axes. He crouched, waiting for them to come, all fine spun theories gone and rising within him that same rage that hours before had sent him out to slay.

So crouching, he heard from the forested hills a roaring clamor. From every quarter it came, wrathful, menacing; like the voices of legions of great trees bellowing through the horns of tempest. The clamor maddened McKay; fanned the flame of rage to white heat.

If the three men heard it, they gave no sign. They came on steadily, jeering at him, waving their keen blades. He ran to meet them.

"Go back!" he shouted. "Go back, Polleau! I warn you!"

"He warns us!" jeered Polleau. "He – Pierre, Jean – he warns us!"

The old peasant's arm shot out and his hand caught McKay's shoulder with a grip that pinched to the bone. The arm flexed and hurled him against the unmaimed son. The son caught him, twisted him about and whirled him headlong a dozen yards, crashing him through the brush at the skirt of the wood.

McKay sprang to his feet howling like a wolf. The clamor of the forest had grown stronger. "Kill!" it roared. "Kill!"

The unmaimed son had raised his axe. He brought it down upon the trunk of a birch, half splitting it with one blow. McKay heard a wail go up from the little wood. Before the axe could be withdrawn he had crashed a fist in the axe wielder's face. The head of Polleau's son rocked back; he yelped, and before McKay could strike again had wrapped strong arms around him, crushing breath from him. McKay relaxed, went limp, and the son loosened his grip. Instantly McKay slipped out of it and struck again, springing aside to avoid the rib breaking clasp. Polleau's son was quicker than he, the long arms caught him. But as the arms tightened, there was the sound of sharp splintering and the birch into which the axe had bitten toppled. It struck the ground directly behind the wrestling men. Its branches seemed to reach out and clutch at the feet of Polleau's son.

He tripped and fell backward, McKay upon him. The shock of the fall broke his grip and again McKay writhed free. Again he was upon his feet, and again Polleau's strong son, quick as he, faced him. Twice McKay's blows found their mark beneath his heart before once more the long arms trapped him. But their grip was weaker; McKay felt that now his strength was equal.

Round and round they rocked, McKay straining to break away. They fell, and over they rolled and over, arms and legs locked, each striving to free a hand to grip the other's throat. Around them ran Polleau and the one-eyed son, shouting encouragement to Pierre, yet neither daring to strike at McKay lest the blow miss and be taken by the other.

And all that time McKay heard the little wood shouting. Gone from it now was all mournfulness, all passive resignation. The wood was alive and raging. He saw the trees shake and bend as though torn by a tempest. Dimly he realized that the others must hear none of this, see none of it; as dimly wondered why this should be.

"Kill!" shouted the coppice – and over its tumult he heard the roar of the great forest: "Kill! Kill!"

He became aware of two shadowy shapes, shadowy shapes of swarthy green clad men, that pressed close to him as he rolled and fought.

"Kill!" they whispered. "Let his blood flow! Kill! Let his blood flow!"

He tore a wrist free from the son's clutch. Instantly he felt within his hand the hilt of a knife.

"Kill!" whispered the shadowy men.

"Kill!" shrieked the coppice.

"Kill!" roared the forest.

McKay's free arm swept up and plunged the knife into the throat of Polleau's son! He heard a choking sob; heard Polleau shriek; felt the hot blood spurt in face and over hand; smelt its salt and faintly acrid odor. The encircling arms dropped from him; he reeled to his feet.

As though the blood had been a bridge, the shadowy men leaped from immateriality into substances. One threw himself upon the man McKay had stabbed; the other hurled upon old Polleau. The maimed son turned and fled, howling with terror. A white woman sprang out from the shadow, threw herself at his feet, clutched them and brought him down. Another woman and another dropped upon him. The note of his shrieking changed from fear to agony; then died abruptly into silence.

And now McKay could see none of the three, neither old Polleau or his sons, for the green clad men and the white women covered them!

McKay stood stupidly, staring at his red hands. The roar of the forest had changed to a deep triumphal chanting. The coppice was mad with joy. The trees had become thin phantoms etched in emerald translucent air as they had been when first the green sorcery had enmeshed him. And all around him wove and danced the slim, gleaming women of the wood.

They ringed him, their song bird-sweet and shrill; jubilant. Beyond them he saw gliding toward him the woman of the misty pillars whose kisses had poured the sweet green fire into his veins. Her arms were outstretched to him, her strange wide eyes were rapt on his, her white body gleamed with the moon radiance, her red lips were parted and smiling – a scarlet chalice filled with the promise of undreamed ecstasies. The dancing circle, chanting, broke to let her through.

Abruptly, a horror filled McKay. Not of this fair woman, not of her jubilant sisters – but of himself.

He had killed! And the wound the war had left in his soul, the wound he thought had healed, had opened.

He rushed through the broken circle, thrust the shining woman aside with his blood stained hands and ran, weeping, toward the lake shore. The singing ceased. He heard little cries, tender, appealing; little cries of pity; soft voices calling on him to stop, to return. Behind him was the sound of little racing feet, light as the fall of leaves upon the moss.

McKay ran on. The coppice lightened, the beach was before him. He heard the fair woman call him, felt the touch of her hand upon his shoulder. He did not heed her. He ran across the narrow strip of beach, thrust his boat out into the water and wading through the shallows threw himself into it.

He lay there for a moment, sobbing; then drew himself up, caught at the oars. He looked back at the shore now a score of feet away. At the edge of the coppice stood the woman, staring at him with pitying, wise eyes. Behind her clustered the white faces of her sisters, the swarthy faces of the green clad men.

"Come back!" the woman whispered, and held out to him slender arms.

McKay hesitated, his horror lessening in that clear, wise, pitying gaze. He half swung the boat around. His gaze dropped upon his blood-stained hands and again the hysteria gripped him. One thought only was in his mind –to get far away from where Polleau's son lay with his throat ripped open, to put the lake between that body and him.

Head bent low, McKay bowed to the oars, skimming swiftly outward. When he looked up a curtain of mist had fallen between him and the shore. It hid the coppice and from beyond it there came to him no sound. He glanced behind him, back toward the inn. The mists swung there, too, concealing it.

McKay gave silent thanks for these vaporous curtains that hid him from both the dead and the alive. He slipped limply under the thwarts. After a while he leaned over the side of the boat and, shuddering, washed the blood from his hands. He scrubbed the oar blades where his hands had left red patches. He ripped the lining out of his coat and drenching it in the lake he cleansed his face. He took off the stained coat, wrapped it with the lining round the anchor stone in the skiff and sunk it in the lake. There were other stains upon his shirt; but these he would have to let be.

For a time he rowed aimlessly, finding in the exertion a lessening of his soul sickness. His numbed mind began to function, analyzing his plight, planning how to meet the future – how to save him.

What ought he do? Confess that he had killed Polleau's son? What reason could he give? Only that he had killed because the man had been about to cut down some trees – trees that were his father's to do with as he willed!

And if he told of the wood woman, the wood women, the shadowy shapes of their green gallants who had helped him – who would believe?

They would think him mad – mad as he half believed himself to be.

No, none would believe him. None! Nor would confession bring back life to him he had slain. No; he would not confess.

But stay – another thought came! Might he not be – accused? What actually had happened to old Polleau and his other son? He had taken it for granted that they were dead; that they had died under those bodies white and swarthy. But had they? While the green sorcery had meshed him he had held no doubt of this – else why the jubilance of the little wood, the triumphant chanting of the forest?

Were they dead – Polleau and the one-eyed son? Clearly it came to him that they had not heard as he had, had not seen as he had. To them McKay and his enemy had been but two men battling, in a woodland glade; nothing more than that – until the last! Until the last? Had they seen more than that even then?

No, all that he could depend upon as real was that he had ripped out the throat of one of old Polleau's sons. That was the one unassailable verity. He had washed the blood of that man from his hands and his face.

All else might have been mirage – but one thing was true. He had murdered Polleau's son!

Remorse? He had thought that he had felt it. He knew now that he did not; that he had no shadow of remorse for what he had done. It had been panic that had shaken him, panic realization of the strangenesses, reaction from the battle lust, echoes of the war. He had been justified in that –execution. What right had those men to destroy the little wood; to wipe wantonly its beauty away?

None! He was glad that he had killed!

At that moment McKay would gladly have turned his boat and raced away to drink of the crimson chalice of the wood woman's lips. But the mists were raising, He saw that he was close to the landing of the inn.

There was no one about. Now was his time to remove the last of those accusing stains. After that —

Quickly he drew up, fastened the skiff, slipped unseen to his room. He locked the door, started to undress. Then sudden sleep swept over him like a wave, drew him helplessly down into ocean depths of sleep.

A knocking at the door awakened McKay, and the innkeeper's voice summoned him to dinner. Sleepily, he answered, and as the old man's footsteps died away, he roused himself. His eyes fell upon his shirt and the great stains now rusty brown. Puzzled, he stared at them for a moment, then full memory clicked back in place.

He walked to the window. It was dusk. A wind was blowing and the trees were singing, all the little leaves dancing; the forest hummed a cheerful vespers. Gone was all the unease, all the inarticulate trouble and the fear. The forest was tranquil and it was happy.

He sought the coppice through the gathering twilight. Its demoiselles were dancing lightly in the wind, leafy hoods dipping, leafy skirts ablow. Beside them marched the green troubadours, carefree, waving their needled arms. Gay was the little wood, gay as when its beauty had first drawn him to it.

McKay undressed, hid the stained shirt in his traveling trunk, bathed and put on a fresh outfit, sauntered down to dinner. He ate excellently. Wonder now and then crossed his mind that he felt no regret, no sorrow even, for the man he had killed. Half he was inclined to believe it all a dream – so little of any emotion did he feel. He had even ceased to think of what discovery might mean.

His mind was quiet; he heard the forest chanting to him that there was nothing he need fear; and when he sat for a time that night upon the balcony a peace that was half an ecstasy stole in upon him from the murmuring woods and enfolded him. Cradled by it he slept dreamlessly.

McKay did not go far from the inn that next day. The little wood danced gaily and beckoned him, but he paid no heed. Something whispered to wait, to keep the lake between him and it until word came of what lay or had lain there. And the peace still was on him.

Only the old innkeeper seemed to grow uneasy as the hours went by. He went often to the landing, scanning the further shore.

"It is strange," he said at last to McKay as the sun was dipping behind the summits. "Polleau was to see me here today. He never breaks his word. If he could not come he would have sent one of his sons."

McKay nodded, carelessly.

"There is another thing I do not understand," went on the old man. "I have seen no smoke from the lodge all day. It is as though they were not there."

"Where could they be?" asked McKay, indifferently.

"I do not know," the voice was more perturbed. "It all troubles me, M'sieu. Polleau is hard, yes; but he is my neighbor. Perhaps an accident—"

"They would let you know soon enough if there was anything wrong," McKay said.

"Perhaps, but—" the old man hesitated. "If he does not come tomorrow and again I see no smoke I will go to him," he ended.

McKay felt a little shock run through him – tomorrow then he would know, definitely know, what it was that had happened in the little wood.

"I would if I were you," he said. "I'd not wait too long either. After all– well, accidents do happen."

"Will you go with me, M'sieu," asked the old man.

"No!" whispered the warning voice within McKay. "No! Do not go!"

"Sorry," he said, aloud. "But I've some writing to do. If you should need me send back your man. I'll come."

And all that night he slept, again dreamlessly, while the crooning forest cradled him.

The morning passed without sign from the opposite shore. An hour after noon he watched the old innkeeper and his man row across the lake. And suddenly McKay's composure was shaken, his serene certainty wavered. He unstrapped his field glasses and kept them on the pair until they had beached the boat and entered the coppice. His heart was beating uncomfortably, his hands felt hot and his lips dry. He scanned the shore. How long had they been in the wood? It must have been an hour! What were they doing there? What had they found? He looked at his watch, incredulously. Less than fifteen minutes had passed.

Slowly the seconds ticked by. And it was all of an hour indeed before he saw them come out upon the shore and drag their boat into the water. McKay, throat curiously dry, a deafening pulse within his ears, steadied himself; forced himself to stroll leisurely down to the landing.

"Everything all right?" he called as they were near. They did not answer; but as the skiff warped against the landing they looked up at him and on their faces were stamped horror and a great wonder.

"They are dead, M'sieu," whispered the innkeeper. "Polleau and his two sons – all dead!"

McKay's heart gave a great leap, a swift faintness took him.

"Dead!" he cried. "What killed them?"

"What but the trees, M'sieu?" answered the old man, and McKay thought his gaze dwelt upon him strangely. "The trees killed them. See – we went up the little path through the wood, and close to its end we found it blocked by fallen trees. The flies buzzed round those trees, M'sieu, so we searched there. They were under them, Polleau and his sons. A fir had fallen upon Polleau and had crushed in his chest. Another son we found beneath a fir and upturned birches. They had broken his back, and an eye had been torn out – but that was no new wound, the latter." He paused.

"It must have been a sudden wind," said his man. "Yet I never knew of a wind like that must have been. There were no trees down except those that lay upon them. And of those it was as though they had leaped out of the ground! Yes, as though they had leaped out of the ground upon them. Or it was as though giants had torn them out for clubs. They were not broken – their roots were bare—"

"But the other son – Polleau had two?" – try as he might, McKay could not keep the tremor out of his voice.

"Pierre," said the old man, and again McKay felt that strange quality in his gaze. "He lay beneath a fir. His throat was torn out!"

"His throat torn out!" whispered McKay, His knife! The knife that had been slipped into his hand by the shadowy shapes!

"His throat was torn out," repeated the innkeeper. "And in it still was the broken branch that had done it. A broken branch, M'sieu, pointed as a knife. It must have caught Pierre as the fir fell and ripping through his throat – been broken off as the tree crashed."

McKay stood, mind whirling in wild conjecture. "You said – a broken branch?" McKay asked through lips gone white.

"A broken branch, M'sieu," the innkeeper's eyes searched him. "It was very plain – what it was that happened. Jacques," he turned to his man. "Go up to the house."

He watched until the man shuffled out of sight. "Yet not all plain, M'sieu," he spoke low to McKay. "For in Pierre's hand I found – this."

He reached into a pocket and drew out a button from which hung a strip of cloth. Cloth and button had once been part of that blood-stained coat which McKay had sunk within the lake; torn away no doubt when death had struck Polleau's son!

McKay strove to speak. The old man raised his hand. Button and cloth fell from it, into the water. A wave took it and floated it away; another and another. They watched it silently until it had vanished.

"Tell me nothing, M'sieu," the old innkeeper turned to him, "Polleau was hard and hard men, too, were his sons. The trees hated them. The trees killed them. And now the trees are happy. That is all. And the – souvenir– is gone. I have forgotten I saw it. Only M'sieu would better also – go."

That night McKay packed. When dawn had broken he stood at his window, looked long at the little wood. It was awakening, stirring sleepily like drowsy delicate demoiselles. He drank in its beauty – for the last time; waved it farewell.

McKay breakfasted well. He dropped into the driver's seat; set the engine humming.

The old innkeeper and his wife, solicitous as ever for his welfare, bade him Godspeed. On both their faces was full friendliness – and in the old man's eyes somewhat of puzzled awe.

His road lay through the thick forest. Soon inn and lake were far behind him.

And singing went McKay, soft whisperings of leaves following him, glad chanting of needled pines; the voice of the forest tender, friendly, caressing – the forest pouring into him as farewell gift its peace, its happiness, its strength.

The Vampire

Jan Neruda

THE EXCURSION STEAMER brought us from Constantinople to the shore of the island of Prinkipo and we disembarked. The number of passengers was not large. There was one Polish family, a father, a mother, a daughter and her bridegroom, and then we two. Oh, yes, I must not forget that when we were already on the wooden bridge which crosses the Golden Horn to Constantinople, a Greek, a rather youthful man, joined us. He was probably an artist, judging by the portfolio he carried under his arm. Long black locks floated to his shoulders, his face was pale, and his black eyes were deeply set in their sockets. From the first moment he interested me, especially for his obligingness and for his knowledge of local conditions. But he talked too much, and I then turned away from him.

All the more agreeable was the Polish family. The father and mother were good-natured, fine people, the lover a handsome young fellow, of direct and refined manners. They had come to Prinkipo to spend the summer months for the sake of the daughter, who was slightly ailing. The beautiful pale girl was either just recovering from a severe illness or else a serious disease was just fastening its hold upon her. She leaned upon her lover when she walked and very often sat down to rest, while a frequent dry little cough interrupted her whispers. Whenever she coughed, her escort would considerately pause in their walk. He always cast upon her a glance of sympathetic suffering and she would look back at him as if she would say: "It is nothing. I am happy!" They believed in health and happiness.

On the recommendation of the Greek, who departed from us immediately at the pier, the family secured quarters in the hotel on the hill. The hotel-keeper was a Frenchman and his entire building was equipped comfortably and artistically, according to the French style.

We breakfasted together and when the noon heat had abated somewhat we all betook ourselves to the heights, where in the grove of Siberian stone-pines we could refresh ourselves with the view. Hardly had we found a suitable spot and settled ourselves when the Greek appeared again. He greeted us lightly, looked about and seated himself only a few steps from us. He opened his portfolio and began to sketch.

"I think he purposely sits with his back to the rocks so that we can't look at his sketch," I said.

"We don't have to," said the young Pole. "We have enough before us to look at." After a while he added, "It seems to me he's sketching us in as a sort of background. Well – let him!"

We truly did have enough to gaze at. There is not a more beautiful or more happy corner in the world than that very Prinkipo! The political martyr, Irene, contemporary of Charles the Great, lived there for a month as an exile. If I could live a month of my life there I would be happy for the memory of it for the rest of my days! I shall never forget even that one day spent at Prinkipo.

The air was as clear as a diamond, so soft, so caressing, that one's whole soul swung out upon it into the distance. At the right beyond the sea projected the brown Asiatic summits; to the left in the distance purpled the steep coasts of Europe. The neighboring Chalki, one of the nine islands of the "Prince's Archipelago," rose with its cypress forests into the peaceful heights like a sorrowful dream, crowned by a great structure – an asylum for those whose minds are sick.

The Sea of Marmora was but slightly ruffled and played in all colors like a sparkling opal. In the distance the sea was as white as milk, then rosy, between the two islands a glowing orange and below us it was beautifully greenish blue, like a transparent sapphire. It was resplendent in its own beauty. Nowhere were there any large ships – only two small craft flying the English flag sped along the shore. One was a steamboat as big as a watchman's booth, the second had about twelve oarsmen, and when their oars rose simultaneously molten silver dripped from them. Trustful dolphins darted in and out among them and dove with long, arching flights above the surface of the water. Through the blue heavens now and then calm eagles winged their way, measuring the space between two continents.

The entire slope below us was covered with blossoming roses whose fragrance filled the air. From the coffee-house near the sea music was carried up to us through the clear air, hushed somewhat by the distance.

The effect was enchanting. We all sat silent and steeped our souls completely in the picture of paradise. The young Polish girl lay on the grass with her head supported on the bosom of her lover. The pale oval of her delicate face was slightly tinged with soft color, and from her blue eyes tears suddenly gushed forth. The lover understood, bent down and kissed tear after tear. Her mother also was moved to tears, and I – even I – felt a strange twinge.

"Here mind and body both must get well," whispered the girl. "How happy a land this is!"

"God knows I haven't any enemies, but if I had I would forgive them here!" said the father in a trembling voice.

And again we became silent. We were all in such a wonderful mood – so unspeakably sweet it all was! Each felt for himself a whole world of happiness and each one would have shared his happiness with the whole world. All felt the same – and so no one disturbed another. We had scarcely even noticed the Greek, after an hour or so, had arisen, folded his portfolio and with a slight nod had taken his departure. We remained.

Finally after several hours, when the distance was becoming overspread with a darker violet, so magically beautiful in the south, the mother reminded us it was time to depart. We arose and walked down towards the hotel with the easy, elastic steps that characterize carefree children. We sat down in the hotel under the handsome veranda.

Hardly had we been seated when we heard below the sounds of quarreling and oaths. Our Greek was wrangling the hotelkeeper, and for the entertainment of it we listened.

The amusement did not last long. "If I didn't have other guests," growled the hotel-keeper, and ascended the steps towards us.

"I beg you to tell me, sir," asked the young Pole of the approaching hotel-keeper, "who is that gentleman? What's his name?"

"Eh – who knows what the fellow's name is?" grumbled the hotel-keeper, and he gazed venomously downwards. "We call him the Vampire."

"An artist?"

"Fine trade! He sketches only corpses. Just as soon as someone in Constantinople or here in the neighborhood dies, that very day he has a picture of the dead one completed.

That fellow paints them beforehand – and he never makes a mistake–just like a vulture!"

The old Polish woman shrieked affrightedly. In her arms lay her daughter pale as chalk. She had fainted.

In one bound the lover had leaped down the steps. With one hand he seized the Greek and with the other reached for the portfolio.

We ran down after him. Both men were rolling in the sand. The contents of the portfolio were scattered all about. On one sheet, sketched with a crayon, was the head of the young Polish girl, her eyes closed and a wreath of myrtle on her brow.

The Masque of the Red Death

Edgar Allan Poe

THE 'RED DEATH' had long devastated the country. No pestilence had ever been so fatal, or so hideous. Blood was its Avator and its seal – the redness and the horror of blood. There were sharp pains, and sudden dizziness, and then profuse bleeding at the pores, with dissolution. The scarlet stains upon the body and especially upon the face of the victim, were the pest ban which shut him out from the aid and from the sympathy of his fellow-men. And the whole seizure, progress, and termination of the disease, were the incidents of half an hour.

But the Prince Prospero was happy and dauntless and sagacious. When his dominions were half depopulated, he summoned to his presence a thousand hale and light-hearted friends from among the knights and dames of his court, and with these retired to the deep seclusion of one of his castellated abbeys. This was an extensive and magnificent structure, the creation of the prince's own eccentric yet august taste. A strong and lofty wall girdled it in. This wall had gates of iron. The courtiers, having entered, brought furnaces and massy hammers and welded the bolts. They resolved to leave means neither of ingress or egress to the sudden impulses of despair or of frenzy from within. The abbey was amply provisioned. With such precautions the courtiers might bid defiance to contagion. The external world could take care of itself. In the meantime it was folly to grieve, or to think. The prince had provided all the appliances of pleasure. There were buffoons, there were improvisatori, there were ballet-dancers, there were musicians, there was Beauty, there was wine. All these and security were within. Without was the 'Red Death'.

It was toward the close of the fifth or sixth month of his seclusion, and while the pestilence raged most furiously abroad, that the Prince Prospero entertained his thousand friends at a masked ball of the most unusual magnificence.

It was a voluptuous scene, that masquerade. But first let me tell of the rooms in which it was held. There were seven – an imperial suite. In many palaces, however, such suites form a long and straight vista, while the folding doors slide back nearly to the walls on either hand, so that the view of the whole extent is scarcely impeded. Here the case was very different; as might have been expected from the duke's love of the bizarre. The apartments were so irregularly disposed that the vision embraced but little more than one at a time. There was a sharp turn at every twenty or thirty yards, and at each turn a novel effect. To the right and left, in the middle of each wall, a tall and narrow Gothic window looked out upon a closed corridor which pursued the windings of the suite. These windows were of stained glass whose color varied in accordance with the prevailing hue of the decorations of the chamber into which it opened.

That at the eastern extremity was hung, for example in blue – and vividly blue were its windows. The second chamber was purple in its ornaments and tapestries, and here the panes were purple. The third was green throughout, and so were the casements. The fourth was furnished and lighted with orange – the fifth with white – the sixth with violet. The seventh apartment was closely shrouded in black velvet tapestries that hung all over the ceiling and down the walls, falling in heavy folds upon a carpet of the same material and hue. But in this chamber only, the color of the windows failed to correspond with the decorations. The panes here were scarlet – a deep blood color. Now in no one of the seven apartments was there any lamp or candelabrum, amid the profusion of golden ornaments that lay scattered to and fro or depended from the roof. There was no light of any kind emanating from lamp or candle within the suite of chambers. But in the corridors that followed the suite, there stood, opposite to each window, a heavy tripod, bearing a brazier of fire, that projected its rays through the tinted glass and so glaringly illumined the room. And thus were produced a multitude of gaudy and fantastic appearances. But in the western or black chamber the effect of the fire-light that streamed upon the dark hangings through the blood-tinted panes, was ghastly in the extreme, and produced so wild a look upon the countenances of those who entered, that there were few of the company bold enough to set foot within its precincts at all.

It was in this apartment, also, that there stood against the western wall, a gigantic clock of ebony. Its pendulum swung to and fro with a dull, heavy, monotonous clang; and when the minute-hand made the circuit of the face, and the hour was to be stricken, there came from the brazen lungs of the clock a sound which was clear and loud and deep and exceedingly musical, but of so peculiar a note and emphasis that, at each lapse of an hour, the musicians of the orchestra were constrained to pause, momentarily, in their performance, to harken to the sound; and thus the waltzers perforce ceased their evolutions; and there was a brief disconcert of the whole gay company; and, while the chimes of the clock yet rang, it was observed that the giddiest grew pale, and the more aged and sedate passed their hands over their brows as if in confused revery or meditation.

But when the echoes had fully ceased, a light laughter at once pervaded the assembly; the musicians looked at each other and smiled as if at their own nervousness and folly, and made whispering vows, each to the other, that the next chiming of the clock should produce in them no similar emotion; and then, after the lapse of sixty minutes, (which embrace three thousand and six hundred seconds of the Time that flies,) there came yet another chiming of the clock, and then were the same disconcert and tremulousness and meditation as before.

But, in spite of these things, it was a gay and magnificent revel. The tastes of the duke were peculiar. He had a fine eye for colors and effects. He disregarded the decora of mere fashion. His plans were bold and fiery, and his conceptions glowed with barbaric lustre. There are some who would have thought him mad. His followers felt that he was not. It was necessary to hear and see and touch him to be sure that he was not.

He had directed, in great part, the moveable embellishments of the seven chambers, upon occasion of this great fete; and it was his own guiding taste which had given character to the masqueraders. Be sure they were grotesque. There were much glare and glitter and piquancy and phantasm – much of what has been since seen in Hernani. There were arabesque figures with unsuited limbs and appointments. There were delirious fancies such as the madman fashions. There were much of the beautiful, much of the wanton, much of the bizarre, something of the terrible, and not a little of that which might have excited disgust. To and fro in the seven chambers there stalked, in fact, a multitude of dreams. And these – the dreams – writhed in and about, taking hue from the rooms, and causing the wild music of the orchestra to seem as the echo of their steps.

And, anon, there strikes the ebony clock which stands in the hall of the velvet. And then, for a moment, all is still, and all is silent save the voice of the clock. The dreams are stiff-frozen as they stand. But the echoes of the chime die away – they have endured but an instant – and a light, half-subdued laughter floats after them as they depart. And now again the music swells, and the dreams live, and writhe to and fro more merrily than ever, taking hue from the many tinted windows through which stream the rays from the tripods. But to the chamber which lies most westwardly of the seven, there are now none of the maskers who venture; for the night is waning away; and there flows a ruddier light through the blood-colored panes; and the blackness of the sable drapery appals; and to him whose foot falls upon the sable carpet, there comes from the near clock of ebony a muffled peal more solemnly emphatic than any which reaches their ears who indulge in the more remote gaieties of the other apartments.

But these other apartments were densely crowded, and in them beat feverishly the heart of life. And the revel went whirlingly on, until at length there commenced the sounding of midnight upon the clock. And then the music ceased, as I have told; and the evolutions of the waltzers were quieted; and there was an uneasy cessation of all things as before. But now there were twelve strokes to be sounded by the bell of the clock; and thus it happened, perhaps that more of thought crept, with more of time, into the meditations of the thoughtful among those who revelled. And thus too, it happened, perhaps, that before the last echoes of the last chime had utterly sunk into silence, there were many individuals in the crowd who had found leisure to become aware of the presence of a masked figure which had arrested the attention of no single individual before. And the rumor of this new presence having spread itself whisperingly around, there arose at length from the whole company a buzz, or murmur, expressive of disapprobation and surprise – then, finally, of terror, of horror, and of disgust.

In an assembly of phantasms such as I have painted, it may well be supposed that no ordinary appearance could have excited such sensation. In truth the masquerade license of the night was nearly unlimited; but the figure in question had out-Heroded Herod, and gone beyond the bounds of even the prince's indefinite decorum. There are chords in the hearts of the most reckless which cannot be touched without emotion. Even with the utterly lost, to whom life and death are equally jests, there are matters of which no jest can be made.

The whole company, indeed, seemed now deeply to feel that in the costume and bearing of the stranger neither wit nor propriety existed. The figure was tall and gaunt, and shrouded from head to foot in the habiliments of the grave. The mask which concealed the visage was made so nearly to resemble the countenance of a stiffened corpse that the closest scrutiny must have had difficulty in detecting the cheat. And yet all this might have been endured, if not approved, by the mad revellers around. But the mummer had gone so far as to assume the type of the Red Death. His vesture was dabbled in blood – and his broad brow, with all the features of the face, was besprinkled with the scarlet horror.

When the eyes of Prince Prospero fell upon this spectral image (which with a slow and solemn movement, as if more fully to sustain its role, stalked to and fro among the waltzers) he was seen to be convulsed, in the first moment with a strong shudder either of terror or distaste; but, in the next, his brow reddened with rage.

"Who dares?" he demanded hoarsely of the courtiers who stood near him – "who dares insult us with this blasphemous mockery? Seize him and unmask him – that we may know whom we have to hang at sunrise, from the battlements!"

It was in the eastern or blue chamber in which stood the Prince Prospero as he uttered these words. They rang throughout the seven rooms loudly and clearly – for the prince was a bold and robust man, and the music had become hushed at the waving of his hand.

It was in the blue room where stood the prince, with a group of pale courtiers by his side. At first, as he spoke, there was a slight rushing movement of this group in the direction of the intruder, who, at the moment was also near at hand, and now, with deliberate and stately step, made closer approach to the speaker. But from a certain nameless awe with which the mad assumptions of the mummer had inspired the whole party, there were found none who put forth hand to seize him; so that, unimpeded, he passed within a yard of the prince's person; and, while the vast assembly, as if with one impulse, shrank from the centres of the rooms to the walls, he made his way uninterruptedly, but with the same solemn and measured step which had distinguished him from the first, through the blue chamber to the purple – through the purple to the green – through the green to the orange – through this again to the white – and even thence to the violet, ere a decided movement had been made to arrest him.

It was then, however, that the Prince Prospero, maddening with rage and the shame of his own momentary cowardice, rushed hurriedly through the six chambers, while none followed him on account of a deadly terror that had seized upon all. He bore aloft a drawn dagger, and had approached, in rapid impetuosity, to within three or four feet of the retreating figure, when the latter, having attained the extremity of the velvet apartment, turned suddenly and confronted his pursuer.

There was a sharp cry – and the dagger dropped gleaming upon the sable carpet, upon which, instantly afterwards, fell prostrate in death the Prince Prospero. Then, summoning the wild courage of despair, a throng of the revellers at once threw themselves into the black apartment, and, seizing the mummer, whose tall figure stood erect and motionless within the shadow of the ebony clock, gasped in unutterable horror at finding the grave cerements and corpse-like mask which they handled with so violent a rudeness, untenanted by any tangible form.

And now was acknowledged the presence of the Red Death. He had come like a thief in the night. And one by one dropped the revellers in the blood-bedewed halls of their revel, and died each in the despairing posture of his fall. And the life of the ebony clock went out with that of the last of the gay. And the flames of the tripods expired. And Darkness and Decay and the Red Death held illimitable dominion over all.

The Premature Burial

Edgar Allan Poe

THERE ARE CERTAIN THEMES of which the interest is all-absorbing, but which are too entirely horrible for the purposes of legitimate fiction. These the mere romanticist must eschew, if he do not wish to offend or to disgust. They are with propriety handled only when the severity and majesty of Truth sanctify and sustain them. We thrill, for example, with the most intense of 'pleasurable pain' over the accounts of the Passage of the Beresina, of the Earthquake at Lisbon, of the Plague at London, of the Massacre of St. Bartholomew, or of the stifling of the hundred and twenty-three prisoners in the Black Hole at Calcutta. But in these accounts it is the fact – it is the reality – it is the history which excites. As inventions, we should regard them with simple abhorrence.

I have mentioned some few of the more prominent and august calamities on record; but in these it is the extent, not less than the character of the calamity, which so vividly impresses the fancy. I need not remind the reader that, from the long and weird catalogue of human miseries, I might have selected many individual instances more replete with essential suffering than any of these vast generalities of disaster. The true wretchedness, indeed – the ultimate woe – is particular, not diffuse. That the ghastly extremes of agony are endured by man the unit, and never by man the mass – for this let us thank a merciful God!

To be buried while alive is, beyond question, the most terrific of these extremes which has ever fallen to the lot of mere mortality. That it has frequently, very frequently, so fallen will scarcely be denied by those who think. The boundaries which divide Life from Death are at best shadowy and vague. Who shall say where the one ends, and where the other begins? We know that there are diseases in which occur total cessations of all the apparent functions of vitality, and yet in which these cessations are merely suspensions, properly so called. They are only temporary pauses in the incomprehensible mechanism. A certain period elapses, and some unseen mysterious principle again sets in motion the magic pinions and the wizard wheels. The silver cord was not for ever loosed, nor the golden bowl irreparably broken. But where, meantime, was the soul?

Apart, however, from the inevitable conclusion, a priori that such causes must produce such effects – that the well-known occurrence of such cases of suspended animation must naturally give rise, now and then, to premature interments – apart from this consideration, we have the direct testimony of medical and ordinary experience to prove that a vast number of such interments have actually taken place. I might refer at once, if necessary to a hundred well authenticated instances. One of very remarkable character, and of which the circumstances may be fresh in the memory of some of my readers, occurred, not very long ago, in the neighboring city of Baltimore, where it occasioned a painful, intense, and widely-extended excitement. The wife of one of the most respectable citizens – a lawyer of eminence and a member of Congress – was seized with a sudden and unaccountable illness, which completely baffled the skill of her physicians. After much suffering she died, or was supposed to die. No one suspected, indeed, or had reason to suspect, that she was not actually dead. She presented all the ordinary appearances of death. The face assumed the usual pinched and sunken outline. The lips were of the usual marble pallor. The eyes were lustreless. There was no warmth. Pulsation had ceased. For three days the body was preserved unburied, during which it had acquired a stony rigidity. The funeral, in short, was hastened, on account of the rapid advance of what was supposed to be decomposition.

The lady was deposited in her family vault, which, for three subsequent years, was undisturbed. At the expiration of this term it was opened for the reception of a sarcophagus; – but, alas! how fearful a shock awaited the husband, who, personally, threw open the door! As its portals swung outwardly back, some white-apparelled object fell rattling within his arms. It was the skeleton of his wife in her yet unmoulded shroud.

A careful investigation rendered it evident that she had revived within two days after her entombment; that her struggles within the coffin had caused it to fall from a ledge, or shelf to the floor, where it was so broken as to permit her escape. A lamp which had been accidentally left, full of oil, within the tomb, was found empty; it might have been exhausted, however, by evaporation. On the uttermost of the steps which led down into the dread chamber was a large fragment of the coffin, with which, it seemed, that she had endeavored to arrest attention by striking the iron door. While thus occupied, she probably swooned, or possibly died, through sheer terror; and, in failing, her shroud became entangled in some iron-work which projected interiorly. Thus she remained, and thus she rotted, erect.

In the year 1810, a case of living inhumation happened in France, attended with circumstances which go far to warrant the assertion that truth is, indeed, stranger than fiction. The heroine of the story was a Mademoiselle Victorine Lafourcade, a young girl of illustrious family, of wealth, and of great personal beauty. Among her numerous suitors was Julien Bossuet, a poor litterateur, or journalist of Paris. His talents and general amiability had recommended him to the notice of the heiress, by whom he seems to have been truly beloved; but her pride of birth decided her, finally, to reject him, and to wed a Monsieur Renelle, a banker and a diplomatist of some eminence. After marriage, however, this gentleman neglected, and, perhaps, even more positively ill-treated her. Having passed with him some wretched years, she died, – at least her condition so closely resembled death as to deceive every one who saw her. She was buried – not in a vault, but in an ordinary grave in the village of her nativity. Filled with despair, and still inflamed by the memory of a profound attachment, the lover journeys from the capital to the remote province in which the village lies, with the romantic purpose of disinterring the corpse, and possessing himself of its luxuriant tresses. He reaches the grave. At midnight he unearths the coffin, opens it, and is in the act of detaching the hair, when he is arrested by the unclosing of the beloved eyes. In fact, the lady had been buried alive. Vitality had not altogether departed, and she was aroused by the caresses of her lover from the lethargy which had been mistaken for death. He bore her frantically to his lodgings in the village. He employed certain powerful restoratives suggested by no little medical learning. In fine, she revived. She recognized her preserver. She remained with him until, by slow degrees, she fully recovered her original health. Her woman's heart was not adamant, and this last lesson of love sufficed to soften it. She bestowed it upon Bossuet. She returned no more to her husband, but, concealing from him her resurrection, fled with her lover to America. Twenty years afterward, the two returned to France, in the persuasion that time had so greatly altered the lady's appearance that her friends would be unable to recognize her. They were mistaken, however, for, at the first meeting, Monsieur Renelle did actually recognize and make claim to his wife. This claim she resisted, and a judicial tribunal sustained her in her resistance, deciding that the peculiar circumstances, with the long lapse of years, had extinguished, not only equitably, but legally, the authority of the husband.

The "Chirurgical Journal" of Leipsic – a periodical of high authority and merit, which some American bookseller would do well to translate and republish, records in a late number a very distressing event of the character in question.

An officer of artillery, a man of gigantic stature and of robust health, being thrown from an unmanageable horse, received a very severe contusion upon the head, which rendered him insensible at once; the skull was slightly fractured, but no immediate danger was apprehended. Trepanning was accomplished successfully. He was bled, and many other of the ordinary means of relief were adopted. Gradually, however, he fell into a more and more hopeless state of stupor, and, finally, it was thought that he died.

The weather was warm, and he was buried with indecent haste in one of the public cemeteries. His funeral took place on Thursday. On the Sunday following, the grounds of the cemetery were, as usual, much thronged with visiters, and about noon an intense excitement was created by the declaration of a peasant that, while sitting upon the grave of the officer, he had distinctly felt a commotion of the earth, as if occasioned by some one struggling beneath. At first little attention was paid to the man's asseveration; but his evident terror, and the dogged obstinacy with which he persisted in his story, had at length their natural effect upon the crowd. Spades were hurriedly procured, and the grave, which was shamefully shallow, was in a few minutes so far thrown open that the head of its occupant appeared. He was then seemingly dead; but he sat nearly erect within his coffin, the lid of which, in his furious struggles, he had partially uplifted.

He was forthwith conveyed to the nearest hospital, and there pronounced to be still living, although in an asphytic condition. After some hours he revived, recognized individuals of his acquaintance, and, in broken sentences spoke of his agonies in the grave.

From what he related, it was clear that he must have been conscious of life for more than an hour, while inhumed, before lapsing into insensibility. The grave was carelessly and loosely filled with an exceedingly porous soil; and thus some air was necessarily admitted. He heard the footsteps of the crowd overhead, and endeavored to make himself heard in turn. It was the tumult within the grounds of the cemetery, he said, which appeared to awaken him from a deep sleep, but no sooner was he awake than he became fully aware of the awful horrors of his position.

This patient, it is recorded, was doing well and seemed to be in a fair way of ultimate recovery, but fell a victim to the quackeries of medical experiment. The galvanic battery was applied, and he suddenly expired in one of those ecstatic paroxysms which, occasionally, it superinduces.

The mention of the galvanic battery, nevertheless, recalls to my memory a well known and very extraordinary case in point, where its action proved the means of restoring to animation a young attorney of London, who had been interred for two days. This occurred in 1831, and created, at the time, a very profound sensation wherever it was made the subject of converse.

The patient, Mr. Edward Stapleton, had died, apparently of typhus fever, accompanied with some anomalous symptoms which had excited the curiosity of his medical attendants. Upon his seeming decease, his friends were requested to sanction a post-mortem examination, but declined to permit it. As often happens, when such refusals are made, the practitioners resolved to disinter the body and dissect it at leisure, in private. Arrangements were easily effected with some of the numerous corps of body-snatchers, with which London abounds; and, upon the third night after the funeral, the supposed corpse was unearthed from a grave eight feet deep, and deposited in the opening chamber of one of the private hospitals.

An incision of some extent had been actually made in the abdomen, when the fresh and undecayed appearance of the subject suggested an application of the battery. One experiment succeeded another, and the customary effects supervened, with nothing to characterize them in any respect, except, upon one or two occasions, a more than ordinary degree of life-likeness in the convulsive action.

It grew late. The day was about to dawn; and it was thought expedient, at length, to proceed at once to the dissection. A student, however, was especially desirous of testing a theory of his own, and insisted upon applying the battery to one of the pectoral muscles. A rough gash was made, and a wire hastily brought in contact, when the patient, with a hurried but quite unconvulsive movement, arose from the table, stepped into the middle of the floor, gazed about him uneasily for a few seconds, and then – spoke. What he said was unintelligible, but words were uttered; the syllabification was distinct. Having spoken, he fell heavily to the floor.

For some moments all were paralyzed with awe – but the urgency of the case soon restored them their presence of mind. It was seen that Mr. Stapleton was alive, although in a swoon. Upon exhibition of ether he revived and was rapidly restored to health, and to the society of his friends – from whom, however, all knowledge of his resuscitation was withheld, until a relapse was no longer to be apprehended. Their wonder – their rapturous astonishment – may be conceived.

The most thrilling peculiarity of this incident, nevertheless, is involved in what Mr. S. himself asserts. He declares that at no period was he altogether insensible – that, dully and confusedly, he was aware of everything which happened to him, from the moment in which he was pronounced dead by his physicians, to that in which he fell swooning to the floor of the hospital. "I am alive," were the uncomprehended words which, upon recognizing the locality of the dissecting-room, he had endeavored, in his extremity, to utter.

It were an easy matter to multiply such histories as these – but I forbear – for, indeed, we have no need of such to establish the fact that premature interments occur. When we reflect how very rarely, from the nature of the case, we have it in our power to detect them, we must admit that they may frequently occur without our cognizance. Scarcely, in truth, is a graveyard ever encroached upon, for any purpose, to any great extent, that skeletons are not found in postures which suggest the most fearful of suspicions.

Fearful indeed the suspicion – but more fearful the doom! It may be asserted, without hesitation, that no event is so terribly well adapted to inspire the supremeness of bodily and of mental distress, as is burial before death. The unendurable oppression of the lungs – the stifling fumes from the damp earth – the clinging to the death garments – the rigid embrace of the narrow house – the blackness of the absolute Night – the silence like a sea that overwhelms – the unseen but palpable presence of the Conqueror Worm – these things, with the thoughts of the air and grass above, with memory of dear friends who would fly to save us if but informed of our fate, and with consciousness that of this fate they can never be informed – that our hopeless portion is that of the really dead – these considerations, I say, carry into the heart, which still palpitates, a degree of appalling and intolerable horror from which the most daring imagination must recoil. We know of nothing so agonizing upon Earth – we can dream of nothing half so hideous in the realms of the nethermost Hell. And thus all narratives upon this topic have an interest profound; an interest, nevertheless, which, through the sacred awe of the topic itself, very properly and very peculiarly depends upon our conviction of the truth of the matter narrated. What I have now to tell is of my own actual knowledge – of my own positive and personal experience.

For several years I had been subject to attacks of the singular disorder which physicians have agreed to term catalepsy, in default of a more definitive title. Although both the immediate and the predisposing causes, and even the actual diagnosis, of this disease are still mysterious, its obvious and apparent character is sufficiently well understood. Its variations seem to be chiefly of degree. Sometimes the patient lies, for a day only, or even for a shorter period, in a species of exaggerated lethargy. He is senseless and externally motionless; but the pulsation of the heart is still faintly perceptible; some traces of warmth remain; a slight color lingers within the centre of the cheek; and, upon application of a mirror to the lips, we can detect a torpid, unequal, and vacillating action of the lungs. Then again the duration of the trance is for weeks – even for months; while the closest scrutiny, and the most rigorous medical tests, fail to establish any material distinction between the state of the sufferer and what we conceive of absolute death. Very usually he is saved from premature interment solely by the knowledge of his friends that he has been previously subject to catalepsy, by the consequent suspicion excited, and, above all, by the non-appearance of decay. The advances of the malady are, luckily, gradual. The first manifestations, although marked, are unequivocal. The fits grow successively more and more distinctive, and endure each for a longer term than the preceding. In this lies the principal security from inhumation. The unfortunate whose first attack should be of the extreme character which is occasionally seen, would almost inevitably be consigned alive to the tomb.

My own case differed in no important particular from those mentioned in medical books. Sometimes, without any apparent cause, I sank, little by little, into a condition of hemi-syncope, or half swoon; and, in this condition, without pain, without ability to stir, or, strictly speaking, to think, but with a dull lethargic consciousness of life and of the presence of those who surrounded my bed, I remained, until the crisis of the disease restored me, suddenly, to perfect sensation. At other times I was quickly and impetuously smitten. I grew sick, and numb, and chilly, and dizzy, and so fell prostrate at once. Then, for weeks, all was void, and black, and silent, and Nothing became the universe. Total annihilation could be no more. From these latter attacks I awoke, however, with a gradation slow in proportion to the suddenness of the seizure. Just as the day dawns to the friendless and houseless beggar who roams the streets throughout the long desolate winter night – just so tardily – just so wearily – just so cheerily came back the light of the Soul to me.

Apart from the tendency to trance, however, my general health appeared to be good; nor could I perceive that it was at all affected by the one prevalent malady – unless, indeed, an idiosyncrasy in my ordinary sleep may be looked upon as superinduced. Upon awaking from slumber, I could never gain, at once, thorough possession of my senses, and always remained, for many minutes, in much bewilderment and perplexity; – the mental faculties in general, but the memory in especial, being in a condition of absolute abeyance.

In all that I endured there was no physical suffering but of moral distress an infinitude. My fancy grew charnel, I talked "of worms, of tombs, and epitaphs." I was lost in reveries of death, and the idea of premature burial held continual possession of my brain. The ghastly

Danger to which I was subjected haunted me day and night. In the former, the torture of meditation was excessive – in the latter, supreme. When the grim Darkness overspread the Earth, then, with every horror of thought, I shook – shook as the quivering plumes upon the hearse. When Nature could endure wakefulness no longer, it was with a struggle that I consented to sleep – for I shuddered to reflect that, upon awaking, I might find myself the tenant of a grave. And when, finally, I sank into slumber, it was only to rush at once into a world of phantasms, above which, with vast, sable, overshadowing wing, hovered, predominant, the one sepulchral Idea.

From the innumerable images of gloom which thus oppressed me in dreams, I select for record but a solitary vision. Methought I was immersed in a cataleptic trance of more than usual duration and profundity. Suddenly there came an icy hand upon my forehead, and an impatient, gibbering voice whispered the word "Arise!" within my ear.

I sat erect. The darkness was total. I could not see the figure of him who had aroused me. I could call to mind neither the period at which I had fallen into the trance, nor the locality in which I then lay. While I remained motionless, and busied in endeavors to collect my thought, the cold hand grasped me fiercely by the wrist, shaking it petulantly, while the gibbering voice said again:

"Arise! did I not bid thee arise?"

"And who," I demanded, "art thou?"

"I have no name in the regions which I inhabit," replied the voice, mournfully; "I was mortal, but am fiend. I was merciless, but am pitiful. Thou dost feel that I shudder. My teeth chatter as I speak, yet it is not with the chilliness of the night – of the night without end. But this hideousness is insufferable. How canst thou tranquilly sleep? I cannot rest for the cry of these great agonies. These sights are more than I can bear. Get thee up! Come with me into the outer Night, and let me unfold to thee the graves. Is not this a spectacle of woe? – Behold!"

I looked; and the unseen figure, which still grasped me by the wrist, had caused to be thrown open the graves of all mankind, and from each issued the faint phosphoric radiance of decay, so that I could see into the innermost recesses, and there view the shrouded bodies in their sad and solemn slumbers with the worm. But alas! the real sleepers were fewer, by many millions, than those who slumbered not at all; and there was a feeble struggling; and there was a general sad unrest; and from out the depths of the countless pits there came a melancholy rustling from the garments of the buried. And of those who seemed tranquilly to repose, I saw that a vast number had changed, in a greater or less degree, the rigid and uneasy position in which they had originally been entombed. And the voice again said to me as I gazed:

"Is it not – oh! is it not a pitiful sight?" – but, before I could find words to reply, the figure had ceased to grasp my wrist, the phosphoric lights expired, and the graves were closed with a sudden violence, while from out them arose a tumult of despairing cries, saying again: "Is it not – O, God, is it not a very pitiful sight?"

Phantasies such as these, presenting themselves at night, extended their terrific influence far into my waking hours. My nerves became thoroughly unstrung, and I fell a prey to perpetual horror. I hesitated to ride, or to walk, or to indulge in any exercise that would carry me from home. In fact, I no longer dared trust myself out of the immediate presence of those who were aware of my proneness to catalepsy, lest, falling into one of my usual fits, I should be buried before my real condition could be ascertained. I doubted the care, the fidelity of my dearest friends. I dreaded that, in some trance of more than customary duration, they might be prevailed upon to regard me as irrecoverable. I even went so far as to fear that, as I occasioned much trouble, they might be glad to consider any very protracted attack as sufficient excuse for getting rid of me altogether. It was in vain they endeavored to reassure me by the most solemn promises. I exacted the most sacred oaths, that under no circumstances they would bury me until decomposition had so materially advanced as to render farther preservation impossible. And, even then, my mortal terrors would listen to no reason – would accept no consolation. I entered into a series of elaborate precautions. Among other things, I had the family vault so remodelled as to admit of being readily opened from within. The slightest pressure upon a long lever that extended far into the tomb would cause the iron portal to fly back. There were arrangements also for the free admission of air and light, and convenient receptacles for food and water, within immediate reach of the coffin intended for my reception. This coffin was warmly and softly padded, and was provided with a lid, fashioned upon the principle of the vault-door, with the addition of springs so contrived that the feeblest movement of the body would be sufficient to set it at liberty. Besides all this, there was suspended from the roof of the tomb, a large bell, the rope of which, it was designed, should extend through a hole in the coffin, and so be fastened to one of the hands of the corpse. But, alas? what avails the vigilance against the Destiny of man? Not even these well-contrived securities sufficed to save from the uttermost agonies of living inhumation, a wretch to these agonies foredoomed!

There arrived an epoch – as often before there had arrived – in which I found myself emerging from total unconsciousness into the first feeble and indefinite sense of existence. Slowly – with a tortoise gradation – approached the faint gray dawn of the psychal day. A torpid uneasiness. An apathetic endurance of dull pain. No care – no hope – no effort. Then, after a long interval, a ringing in the ears; then, after a lapse still longer, a prickling or tingling sensation in the extremities; then a seemingly eternal period of pleasurable quiescence, during which the awakening feelings are struggling into thought; then a brief re-sinking into non-entity; then a sudden recovery. At length the slight quivering of an eyelid, and immediately thereupon, an electric shock of a terror, deadly and indefinite, which sends the blood in torrents from the temples to the heart. And now the first positive effort to think. And now the first endeavor to remember. And now a partial and evanescent success. And now the memory has so far regained its dominion, that, in some measure, I am cognizant of my state. I feel that I am not awaking from ordinary sleep. I recollect that I have been subject to catalepsy. And now, at last, as if by the rush of an ocean, my shuddering spirit is overwhelmed by the one grim Danger – by the one spectral and ever-prevalent idea.

For some minutes after this fancy possessed me, I remained without motion. And why? I could not summon courage to move. I dared not make the effort which was to satisfy me of my fate – and yet there was something at my heart which whispered me it was sure. Despair – such as no other species of wretchedness ever calls into being – despair alone urged me, after long irresolution, to uplift the heavy lids of my eyes. I uplifted them. It was dark – all dark. I knew that the fit was over. I knew that the crisis of my disorder had long passed. I knew that I had now fully recovered the use of my visual faculties – and yet it was dark – all dark – the intense and utter raylessness of the Night that endureth for evermore.

I endeavored to shriek, and my lips and my parched tongue moved convulsively together in the attempt – but no voice issued from the cavernous lungs, which oppressed as if by the weight of some incumbent mountain, gasped and palpitated, with the heart, at every elaborate and struggling inspiration.

The movement of the jaws, in this effort to cry aloud, showed me that they were bound up, as is usual with the dead. I felt, too, that I lay upon some hard substance, and by something similar my sides were, also, closely compressed. So far, I had not ventured to stir any of my limbs – but now I violently threw up my arms, which had been lying at length, with the wrists crossed. They struck a solid wooden substance, which extended above my person at an elevation of not more than six inches from my face. I could no longer doubt that I reposed within a coffin at last.

And now, amid all my infinite miseries, came sweetly the cherub Hope – for I thought of my precautions. I writhed, and made spasmodic exertions to force open the lid: it would not move. I felt my wrists for the bell-rope: it was not to be found. And now the Comforter fled for ever, and a still sterner Despair reigned triumphant; for I could not help perceiving the absence of the paddings which I had so carefully prepared – and then, too, there came suddenly to my nostrils the strong peculiar odor of moist earth. The conclusion was irresistible. I was not within the vault. I had fallen into a trance while absent from home – while among strangers – when, or how, I could not remember – and it was they who had buried me as a dog – nailed up in some common coffin – and thrust deep, deep, and for ever, into some ordinary and nameless grave.

As this awful conviction forced itself, thus, into the innermost chambers of my soul, I once again struggled to cry aloud. And in this second endeavor I succeeded. A long, wild, and continuous shriek, or yell of agony, resounded through the realms of the subterranean Night.

"Hillo! hillo, there!" said a gruff voice, in reply.

"What the devil's the matter now!" said a second.

"Get out o' that!" said a third.

"What do you mean by yowling in that ere kind of style, like a cattymount?" said a fourth; and hereupon I was seized and shaken without ceremony, for several minutes, by a junto of very rough-looking individuals. They did not arouse me from my slumber – for I was wide awake when I screamed – but they restored me to the full possession of my memory.

This adventure occurred near Richmond, in Virginia. Accompanied by a friend, I had proceeded, upon a gunning expedition, some miles down the banks of the James River. Night approached, and we were overtaken by a storm. The cabin of a small sloop lying at anchor in the stream, and laden with garden mould, afforded us the only available shelter. We made the best of it, and passed the night on board. I slept in one of the only two berths in the vessel – and the berths of a sloop of sixty or twenty tons need scarcely be described. That which I occupied had no bedding of any kind. Its extreme width was eighteen inches. The distance of its bottom from the deck overhead was precisely the same. I found it a matter of exceeding difficulty to squeeze myself in. Nevertheless, I slept soundly, and the whole of my vision – for it was no dream, and no nightmare – arose naturally from the circumstances of my position – from my ordinary bias of thought – and from the difficulty, to which I have alluded, of collecting my senses, and especially of regaining my memory, for a long time after awaking from slumber. The men who shook me were the crew of the sloop, and some laborers engaged to unload it. From the load itself came the earthly smell. The bandage about the jaws was a silk handkerchief in which I had bound up my head, in default of my customary nightcap.

The tortures endured, however, were indubitably quite equal for the time, to those of actual sepulture. They were fearfully – they were inconceivably hideous; but out of Evil proceeded Good; for their very excess wrought in my spirit an inevitable revulsion. My soul acquired tone – acquired temper. I went abroad. I took vigorous exercise. I breathed the free air of Heaven. I thought upon other subjects than Death. I discarded my medical books. "Buchan" I burned. I read no "Night Thoughts" – no fustian about churchyards – no bugaboo tales – such as this. In short, I became a new man, and lived a man's life. From that memorable night, I dismissed forever my charnel apprehensions, and with them vanished the cataleptic disorder, of which, perhaps, they had been less the consequence than the cause.

There are moments when, even to the sober eye of Reason, the world of our sad Humanity may assume the semblance of a Hell – but the imagination of man is no Carathis, to explore with impunity its every cavern. Alas! the grim legion of sepulchral terrors cannot be regarded as altogether fanciful – but, like the Demons in whose company Afrasiab made his voyage down the Oxus, they must sleep, or they will devour us – they must be suffered to slumber, or we perish.

Trial And Error

Frank Roger

I

ALL COMMUNICATION CHANNELS with the outside world are still down. I'm totally isolated, after what happened to Dr. Swann. My cell phone and computer have been disabled. The exit is blocked. Does anyone out there know what's going on here? What is the situation out there for that matter? There is no way for me to know.

All I can do is write these notes, and hope they will be useful to whomever may stumble upon them.

II

I joined the project when it was already underway. I applied because I found the basic idea appealing and was hired promptly.

I recall an early TV interview with Dr. Swann in which he presented the project thus: "Our basic question is: will intelligence arise among a species if it's the only option for survival? This is what we'll try to achieve here, by guiding our ants colony step after step towards intelligence. Whether this will prove possible with a species of insects remains to be seen."

The interviewer asked if the experiment was supposed to provide evidence for the theory of evolution and to detract creationism.

Dr. Swann replied that as far as he was concerned there was sufficient evidence for the theory of evolution already. "I assume creationists and many religious people will disclaim our findings if we prove successful. So be it. We're doing science here."

Someone from the audience said: "I fail to see how you're going to make an ant smarter."

Dr. Swann explained: "This is not about making an ant smarter, but about raising intelligence in a species through natural selection. We're talking about a long-term breeding project here covering a number of generations of ants." He was unable to elaborate because a commercial break was coming up. Such is the nature of TV, even when covering scientific projects.

III

The strategy was thus: the ants colony would be faced with obstacles in its daily routines. This might involve their hunt for food, the maintenance of their nest, the safety of their queen, and so on. The problem could only be solved through intelligence: the ants had to grasp the nature of the obstacle and work towards a way around it.

Only those ants that managed to overcome the obstacles and deal efficiently with the problems they encountered were allowed to continue. All the others were 'removed from the experiment', as Dr. Swann put it euphemistically. They were wiped out and reprocessed as ant food for their more clever brothers.

In the early stages little progress was made, to the point that Dr. Swann grew pessimistic about the project's outcome. It was only after the twelfth generation that things started to move, and problems and obstacles were dealt with more quickly and more efficiently.

Dr. Swann felt he was heading in the right direction and responded by raising the stakes: he concocted increasingly more complex problems for the ants, and 'removed' (killed) those who failed to deliver with barely concealed glee. With intelligence having substantial survival value, and supposing it was a hereditary characteristic, this trait should rise to prominence in the gene pool, ultimately resulting in the project's stated goal.

IV

From that point onwards quick progress was made. Dr. Swann grew quite obsessed with the experiment, spending an incredible amount of time at the lab (of course he was single – no wife and kids clamouring for his presence) and only talking about "his creatures". He wrote papers about the project to be published in scientific journals, but preferred to avoid media attention, as "those guys were only after sensationalist nonsense and supported creationism anyway".

As funding was no problem (I understood Dr. Swann knew people in the right places), there was no need for media attention as a fundraising means. The lab had a rather limited staff anyway.

V

The sixtieth generation of ants marked a watershed. It was obvious from the efficiency with which the ants cleared all Dr. Swann's obstacles that the creatures had a firm grasp of their situation and knew how to deal with it. I recall Dr. Swann saying: "It's getting hard to match their progress. Rather than solving each problem they're faced with, they seem to anticipate my moves. In a sense that's good news, because that means they're heading where I wanted them all along. But I'm getting the feeling that the reins are slipping from my hands."

"Are they about to take over?" I asked, none too seriously.

"That's my main fear now," he replied. At that point I didn't know if he was joking or not. How could a bunch of insects outwit us? The very idea was ludicrous.

VI

Some generations later the ants started to restructure their nest in a very elaborate way. Dr. Swann had no idea what drove them, and studied the video footage from the scores of cameras recording non-stop for hours on end, without finding the answers he wanted.

To me it was clear the ants had something up their sleeves – the kind of expression Dr. Swann frowned upon. "You shouldn't use metaphors suitable for man but not for my creatures," he would say. Note that he always talked about "my creatures", never about ants. He did consider them – and perhaps rightly so – his own personal creation.

At first he tried to undo their 'renovations', but then he decided to let them have their way. "It's our only chance to find out what they're trying to achieve," he explained. "We'll monitor and analyse their every move and their motives will become clear."

We stared in awe as the nest grew into an intricately layered system of corridors, rooms and structures of unclear purpose of a truly gigantic size. As a matter of fact, it barely fitted within the confines of their part of the laboratory. Fortunately only transparent material had been used for the construction, allowing us an unobstructed view from any angle. Nothing could remain hidden from sight, none of the cameras could be blocked.

Dr. Swann gazed at the footage of the "construction work" with starry eyes, clearly proud about "what my creatures can do." I knew he was not open to any critical remarks, so I let it pass, even though I was tempted to think that perhaps other feelings than pride were called for.

Even when the "renovation" was finished, we still didn't have a clue about the ants' intention. "Don't worry," Dr. Swann said, "we'll find out soon enough."

Those were truly prophetic words.

VII

It happened at the time of the eighty-fifth generation, when Dr. Swann and I were the only ones present at the lab, late at night. I had night duty, Dr. Swann was merely staying late because he could not leave his project alone. "My creatures need me at their side," he used to say.

At one point he remarked: "We seem to have a computer problem. E-mail and internet are down. Could you check that, Kevin?"

So I did and I discovered that all our communications lines were down, including our cell phones. All exits from the lab were sealed too. Who had done this? And how? And why? The ants? Surely this went beyond their admittedly enhanced capabilities. But who else could be responsible?

We hadn't solved this mystery yet as we did another stunning discovery. To our dismay I noticed that the ants had found a way to penetrate our "ant-proof" security wall and had apparently gained access to the outside world. We had taken all precautions to prevent this. How had they managed to circumvent our safety measures?

When I mentioned this to Dr. Swann, he replied: "What interests me is not so much how they pulled it off, but why they did it. Were they aware of the existence of the outside world? Were they eager to explore it? Did they consider this lab to be a prison they wanted to escape from?"

"We should alert the authorities," I urged him. "This outbreak may pose a threat."

"That is probably why they cut all our communication lines," he said. "They found a way out and made sure we would not interfere with their plans. So they locked us in here and severed all our ties with the outside world. All we can hope for is that the authorities realise what's going on and do whatever it takes to contain the problem."

"How can they find out we're trapped in here?"

"I suppose that when the other staff members show up and find they can't get in, they'll take action. And certainly some people out there will miss us. Surely they'll understand something is wrong. We should count on them."

I assumed indeed that my girlfriend would grow worried when I failed to return from work and when she proved unable to call me. She was my only hope, my ticket back to the world. But how long would we have to wait?

Some time later I remarked: "This cannot be a coincidence. There's a strategy behind it. These creatures are intelligent after all."

"That was the point of the project," Dr. Swann replied irately, as if I had stated the obvious merely to annoy him. "What bothers me most now is that we'll be unable to monitor their progress. What will my creatures do with their newfound freedom? How will they respond to the unlimited lebensraum after the confines of this lab? How will they deal with other ants and insects they encounter out there, and with other people? So far their only contact with other species has been this project's staff. I must admit I can't anticipate their next move. Too bad I'm locked in here. Now that the project takes a quantum leap and veers into uncharted territory I sadly won't be able to keep track of everything. Still, this is a fascinating turn of events. Don't you think there should be a way to regain control? I'm sure there is."

This was so typical. He did not look worried in the least. He would do whatever it took to continue the project. He focussed on his creatures' plans and ambitions rather than on the potential threat their escape posed. Anyway, there was little we could do. We talked about the problem at length, but failed to come up with a solution. I thought about my girlfriend, who should be really worried by now and have taken some action already – but when would we see any results?

A few uneasy hours later Dr. Swann told me he had an idea. "Let me deal with this," he said, without going into the details.

I never saw him back alive. Well, that's not quite true. Allow me to elaborate.

VIII

At first I thought Dr. Swann had gone. But it was totally unimaginable that he would have found a way out and left the lab, leaving me stranded here. He would never leave "his creatures", and certainly would not let me down in such an uncompassionate way. But where was he then? He couldn't have gone far. The lab wasn't all that big. There were no dark corners where he could hide.

I grew restless and worried sick, and decided to go and look for him. I had this nagging fear that he might have left the lab's safe zone and ventured into the ants' territory, a move that was strictly prohibited by the project's regulations. Still, this was an emergency situation and maybe Dr. Swann had decided that any workable solution should be considered. I assumed he'd had an idea and felt like giving it a try. The same trial and error method that had led the ants down the path to intelligence.

So I set out, preparing myself for the worst: finding Dr. Swann's lifeless body, the victim of his own creatures.

I'll never forget the moment I saw him. My jaw dropped and I almost fainted. I was right, I thought. He joined his creatures. And they killed him. The damned critters had ripped him apart. What a horrible way to die.

I turned my eyes away in disgust and wanted to leave, knowing very well that the image of Dr. Swann's mutilated body would remain etched in my mind. Why had he done this, I thought. Why had he tried to establish direct contact with the ants? Had he hoped to start negotiations? Had he counted on respect and understanding from creatures whose very existence they owed to him? How could he have been so naïve? What had been his intention? Of course I would never know.

I cast one more look at Dr. Swann. Ants were crawling all over his body, or what was left of it. Were they eating him? I edged a bit closer to have a better view, without venturing too deep into the ants' territory. I'd rather not suffer the same fate as my boss.

Did I see that correctly? Was that blood flowing through Dr. Swann's veins, all clearly visible under his transparent skin? I fought the urge to run away and examined what was in front of my eyes. I had been right. Dr. Swann was not dead. And the ants didn't seem to be feasting on his flesh. Could it be they were… caring for him?

It began to dawn on me what had happened. The ants must have decided to incorporate Dr. Swann in their nest. As his body was too big and unwieldy for the maze of corridors and cavities that was their home, they had somehow 'adapted' it to make it suitable. How exactly they had done this without killing him was completely beyond me. Of course those creatures were intelligent and worked together in great numbers – and I had to admit they had been efficient.

Dr. Swann's body had undergone a nightmarish metamorphosis. It was suspended from the ceiling of a series of corridors and 'rooms', prepared for their esteemed guest. You might say he had been stripped down to his bare essentials: all clothes, hair and other material considered superfluous had been removed, his torso was unnaturally thin and streamlined, his legs and arms appeared stretched beyond endurance – in fact, he looked barely human, an elongated figure from an El Greco painting revised by H.R. Giger. His body was warped, to the point that I wondered what had happened to his bones – removed as well, or merely softened so as to allow remodelling? His skin was almost transparent, his veins throbbing with a semblance of life.

His face was expressionless, as if he didn't know or care about what had happened to him. His eyes struck me the most: they were open, unblinking, unfocussed, neither dead nor alive. Did Dr. Swann see me? Was his mind still intact? Could he have lived through all this without going stark raving mad? Did he know he had been ushered into his own private hell? Or was his consciousness floating in an everlasting twilight zone, mercifully oblivious of his surroundings?

Ants were crisscrossing all over his body, disappearing in and reappearing from all body orifices, perhaps checking whether their guest (their prey?) was all right, feeding him, monitoring his vital functions. Their knowledge of human physiology must be fabulous in order to have pulled off this trick. Perhaps they had gained that knowledge while 'working' on their first ever patient, their creator? I shuddered to think what they might do with this newly acquired wisdom.

As I was gazing at this horribly disfigured man, a huge number of ants spilled out of his mouth and his anus and I turned away in disgust, overcome by nausea. I didn't want to know what mission the creatures had accomplished in there, and I feared this image would haunt me for the rest of my days.

I retreated to the relative safety of my office, trying to regain control over my thoughts and emotions, wondering what fate was in store for me. There was little I could do but wait and hope for the best.

IX

A few days have gone by. I wonder what the ants will do to me. If they wanted to get rid of me, they could have killed me easily. Maybe I'm of no importance to them and they'll just ignore me. So I wait here, hoping to survive on my limited food supply until someone out there will come to the rescue.

I have a theory about Dr. Swann's fate. I think the ants knew very well who he was and what he was responsible for. When he entered their territory they felt the need to welcome their Creator and worship him in their midst. They disassembled him and refitted his body so that he was harmoniously integrated in their nest, without disrupting any vital functions – an amazing feat, and irrefutable evidence of their intelligence.

He is still alive, but probably not conscious – I can only hope he is not aware of his condition. Now suppose a rescue team gets here in time, would it be possible to restore Dr. Swann to his original condition? It seems hardly likely. Maybe all they could do would be to put an end to his suffering.

X

A few more days have passed. Dr. Swann's situation has not changed. He is lovingly cared for by his creatures.

And so am I. My limited food supply has dwindled, but the ants must have noticed and they feed me. I have no idea what the brownish stuff is they give me, but it's edible and digestible and I don't get sick from it and appear well-nourished, even if it's not exactly gourmet food and offers no variety at all. It's the best deal I could have hoped for – next to being allowed to get the hell out of here.

I have no idea what's going on outside. I just can't believe no one out there has been able to force their way into the lab and release me.

So I'm left wondering what the explanation for that mystery might be.

What are these highly intelligent ants doing out there? Exploring the world? Have they run into mankind and decided that it's in their best interest to wipe out this dangerous species before they might suffer that fate themselves?

Is that why there's nothing but silence from the outside world? Because the ants are wreaking havoc on a major scale and mankind is teetering on the brink of extinction? Can those creatures really have been that quick and efficient?

In that case there's no hope for me and these notes will prove useless. I'll eat my daily portion of food and wait until it becomes clear what Dr. Swann's minions have in mind for me.

I console myself by thinking that I could hardly face a worse fate than their Creator. And I think of my girlfriend and what may have become of her. And of everyone else out there.

XI

A thought occurred to me.

Maybe the ants want to keep me here alive as a sort of curiosity.

Maybe the lab, of which Dr. Swann is now an inextricable part, will one day attract ants on a pilgrimage, eager to visit the holy place where they gained intelligence and became what they are now, and where their Creator can be worshipped.

And so maybe it would be nice to have a small zoo next to it, where the last representative of mankind is put on display for educational purposes.

XII

My situation is unchanged. These are my final notes. All this may have been pointless.

Is there anyone still out there? What are the ants doing with the knowledge they gained from their in-depth examination of Dr. Swann's body? What happens to the human beings and all other living creatures they run into? Are they all wiped out mercilessly? Or do they suffer the same fate as Dr. Swann, which seems hardly likely? Are they perhaps turning all other life forms into a gigantic food farm, thus ensuring their own survival, hegemony and expansion?

I can't think of any other explanation for the lack of reaction from the outside world after all this time. In this case no news can't possibly be good news.

And where does all this leave me?

I guess it's no use to write any more notes.

The Mortal Immortal

Mary Shelley

July 16, 1833.

THIS IS a memorable anniversary for me; on it I complete my three hundred and twenty-third year!

The Wandering Jew? – certainly not. More than eighteen centuries have passed over his head. In comparison with him, I am a very young Immortal.

Am I, then, immortal? This is a question which I have asked myself, by day and night, for now three hundred and three years, and yet cannot answer it. I detected a gray hair amidst my brown locks this very day – that surely signifies decay. Yet it may have remained concealed there for three hundred years – for some persons have become entirely white headed before twenty years of age.

I will tell my story, and my reader shall judge for me. I will tell my story, and so contrive to pass some few hours of a long eternity, become so wearisome to me. For ever! Can it be? to live for ever! I have heard of enchantments, in which the victims were plunged into a deep sleep, to wake, after a hundred years, as fresh as ever: I have heard of the Seven Sleepers – thus to be immortal would not be so burthensome: but, oh! the weight of never-ending time – the tedious passage of the still-succeeding hours! How happy was the fabled Nourjahad! But to my task.

All the world has heard of Cornelius Agrippa. His memory is as immortal as his arts have made me. All the world has also heard of his scholar, who, unawares, raised the foul fiend during his master's absence, and was destroyed by him. The report, true or false, of this accident, was attended with many inconveniences to the renowned philosopher. All his scholars at once deserted him – his servants disappeared. He had no one near him to put coals on his ever-burning fires while he slept, or to attend to the changeful colours of his medicines while he studied. Experiment after experiment failed, because one pair of hands was insufficient to complete them: the dark spirits laughed at him for not being able to retain a single mortal in his service.

I was then very young – very poor – and very much. in love. I had been for about a year the pupil of Cornelius, though I was absent when this accident took place. On my return, my friends implored me not to return to the alchymist's abode. I trembled as I listened to the dire tale they told; I required no second warning; and when Cornelius came and offered me a purse of gold if I would remain under his roof, I felt as if Satan himself tempted me. My teeth chattered – my hair stood on end: – I ran off as fast as my trembling knees would permit.

My failing steps were directed whither for two years they had every evening been attracted, – a gently bubbling spring of pure living waters, beside which lingered a dark-haired girl, whose beaming eyes were fixed on the path I was accustomed each night to tread. I cannot remember the hour when I did not love Bertha; we had been neighbours and playmates from infancy – her parents, like mine, were of humble life, yet respectable – our attachment had been a source of pleasure to them. In an evil hour, a malignant fever carried off both her father and mother, and Bertha became an orphan. She would have found a home beneath my paternal roof, but, unfortunately, the old lady of the near castle, rich, childless, and solitary, declared her intention to adopt her. Henceforth Bertha was clad in silk – inhabited a marble palace – and was looked on as being highly favoured by fortune. But in her new situation among her new associates, Bertha remained true to the friend of her humbler days; she often visited the cottage of my father, and when forbidden to go thither, she would stray towards the neighbouring wood, and meet me beside its shady fountain.

She often declared that she owed no duty to her new protectress equal in sanctity to that which bound us. Yet still I was too poor to marry, and she grew weary of being tormented on my account. She had a haughty but an impatient spirit, and grew angry at the obstacles that prevented our union. We met now after an absence, and she had been sorely beset while I was away; she complained bitterly, and almost reproached me for being poor. I replied hastily:

"I am honest, if I am poor! – were I not, I might soon become rich!"

This exclamation produced a thousand questions. I feared to shock her by owning the truth, but she drew it from me; and then, casting a look of disdain on me, she said –

"You pretend to love, and you fear to face the Devil for my sake!"

I protested that I had only dreaded to offend her; – while she dwelt on the magnitude of the reward that I should receive. Thus encouraged –shamed by her – led on by love and hope, laughing at my late fears, with quick steps and a light heart, I returned to accept the offers of the alchymist, and was instantly installed in my office.

A year passed away. I became possessed of no insignificant sum of money. Custom had banished my fears. In spite of the most painful vigilance, I had never detected the trace of a cloven foot; nor was the studious silence of our abode ever disturbed by demoniac howls. I still continued my stolen interviews with Bertha, and Hope dawned on me – Hope – but not perfect joy; for Bertha fancied that love and security were enemies, and her pleasure was to divide them in my bosom. Though true of heart, she was somewhat of a coquette in manner; and I was jealous as a Turk. She slighted me in a thousand ways, yet would never acknowledge herself to be in the wrong. She would drive me mad with anger, and then force me to beg her pardon. Sometimes she fancied that I was not sufficiently submissive, and then she had some story of a rival, favoured by her protectress. She was surrounded by silk-clad youths – the rich and gay – What chance had the sad-robed scholar of Cornelius compared with these?

On one occasion, the philosopher made such large demands upon my time, that I was unable to meet her as I was wont. He was engaged in some mighty work, and I was forced to remain, day and night, feeding his furnaces and watching his chemical preparations. Bertha waited for me in vain at the fountain. Her haughty spirit fired at this neglect; and when at last I stole out during the few short minutes allotted to me for slumber, and hoped to be consoled by her, she received me with disdain, dismissed me in scorn, and vowed that any man should possess her hand rather than he who could not be in two places at once for her sake. She would be revenged! – And truly she was. In my dingy retreat I heard that she had been hunting, attended by Albert Hoffer. Albert Hoffer was favoured by her protectress, and the three passed in cavalcade before my smoky window. Methought that they mentioned my name – it was followed by a laugh of derision, as her dark eyes glanced contemptuously towards my abode.

Jealousy, with all its venom, and all its misery, entered my breast. Now I shed a torrent of tears, to think that I should never call her mine; and, anon, I imprecated a thousand curses on her inconstancy. Yet, still I must stir the fires of the alchymist, still attend on the changes of his unintelligible medicines.

Cornelius had watched for three days and nights, nor closed his eyes. The progress of his alembics was slower than he expected: in spite of his anxiety, sleep weighed upon his eyelids. Again and again he threw off drowsiness with more than human energy; again and again it stole away his senses. He eyed his crucibles wistfully. "Not ready yet," he murmured; "will another night pass before the work is accomplished? Winzy, you are vigilant – you are faithful – you have slept, my boy – you slept last night. Look at that glass vessel. The liquid it contains is of a soft rose-colour: the moment it begins to change its hue, awaken me – till then I may close my eyes. First, it will turn white, and then emit golden flashes; but wait not till then; when the rose-colour fades, rouse me." I scarcely heard the last words, muttered, as they were, in sleep. Even then he did not quite yield to nature. "Winzy, my boy," he again said, "do not touch the vessel – do not put it to your lips; it is a philter – a philter to cure love; you would not cease to love your Bertha – beware to drink!"

And he slept. His venerable head sunk on his breast, and I scarce heard his regular breathing. For a few minutes I watched the vessel – the rosy hue of the liquid remained unchanged. Then my thoughts wandered– they visited the fountain, and dwelt on a thousand charming scenes never to be renewed – never! Serpents and adders were in my heart as the word "Never!" half formed itself on my lips. False girl! – false and cruel! Never more would she smile on me as that evening she smiled on Albert. Worthless, detested woman! I would not remain unrevenged – she should see Albert expire at her feet – she should die beneath my vengeance. She had smiled in disdain and triumph – she knew my wretchedness and her power. Yet what power had she? – the power of exciting my hate – my utter scorn – my – oh, all but indifference! Could I attain that – could I regard her with careless eyes, transferring my rejected love to one fairer and more true, that were indeed a victory!

A bright flash darted before my eyes. I had forgotten the medicine of the adept; I gazed on it with wonder: flashes of admirable beauty, more bright than those which the diamond emits when the sun's rays are on it, glanced from the surface of the liquid; an odour the most fragrant and grateful stole over my sense; the vessel seemed one globe of living radiance, lovely to the eye, and most inviting to the taste. The first thought, instinctively inspired by the grosser sense, was, I will – I must drink. I raised the vessel to my lips. "It will cure me of love – of torture!" Already I had quaffed half of the most delicious liquor ever tasted by the palate of man, when the philosopher stirred. I started – I dropped the glass – the fluid flamed and glanced along the floor, while I felt Cornelius's gripe at my throat, as he shrieked aloud, "Wretch! you have destroyed the labour of my life!"

The philosopher was totally unaware that I had drunk any portion of his drug. His idea was, and I gave a tacit assent to it, that I had raised the vessel from curiosity, and that, frighted at its brightness, and the flashes of intense light it gave forth, I had let it fall. I never undeceived him. The fire of the medicine was quenched – the fragrance died away – he grew calm, as a philosopher should under the heaviest trials, and dismissed me to rest.

I will not attempt to describe the sleep of glory and bliss which bathed my soul in paradise during the remaining hours of that memorable night. Words would be faint and shallow types of my enjoyment, or of the gladness that possessed my bosom when I woke. I trod air – my thoughts were in heaven. Earth appeared heaven, and my inheritance upon it was to be one trance of delight. "This it is to be cured of love," I thought; "I will see Bertha this day, and she will find her lover cold and regardless: too happy to be disdainful, yet how utterly indifferent to her!"

The hours danced away. The philosopher, secure that he had once succeeded, and believing that he might again, began to concoct the same medicine once more. He was shut up with his books and drugs, and I had a holiday. I dressed myself with care; I looked in an old but polished shield, which served me for a mirror; methought my good looks had wonderfully improved. I hurried beyond the precincts of the town, joy in my soul, the beauty of heaven and earth around me. I turned my steps towards the castle – I could look on its lofty turrets with lightness of heart, for I was cured of love. My Bertha saw me afar off, as I came up the avenue. I know not what sudden impulse animated her bosom, but at the sight, she sprung with a light fawn-like bound down the marble steps, and was hastening towards me. But I had been perceived by another person. The old high-born hag, who called herself her protectress, and was her tyrant, had seen me, also; she hobbled, panting, up the terrace; a page, as ugly as herself, held up her train, and fanned her as she hurried along, and stopped my fair girl with a "How, now, my bold mistress? whither so fast? Back to your cage – hawks are abroad!"

Bertha clasped her hands – her eyes were still bent on my approaching figure. I saw the contest. How I abhorred the old crone who checked the kind impulses of my Bertha's softening heart. Hitherto, respect for her rank had caused me to avoid the lady of the castle; now I disdained such trivial considerations. I was cured of love, and lifted above all human fears; I hastened forwards, and soon reached the terrace. How lovely Bertha looked! her eyes flashing fire, her cheeks glowing with impatience and anger, she was a thousand times more graceful and charming than ever – I no longer loved – Oh! no, I adored – worshipped – idolized her!

She had that morning been persecuted, with more than usual vehemence, to consent to an immediate marriage with my rival. She was reproached with the encouragement that she had shown him – she was threatened with being turned out of doors with disgrace and shame. Her proud spirit rose in arms at the threat; but when she remembered the scorn that she had heaped upon me, and how, perhaps, she had thus lost one whom she now regarded as her only friend, she wept with remorse and rage. At that moment I appeared. "O, Winzy!" she exclaimed, "take me to your mother's cot; swiftly let me leave the detested luxuries and wretchedness of this noble dwelling – take me to poverty and happiness."

I clasped her in my arms with transport. The old lady was speechless with fury, and broke forth into invective only when we were far on our road to my natal cottage. My mother received the fair fugitive, escaped from a gilt cage to nature and liberty, with tenderness and joy; my father, who loved her, welcomed her heartily; it was a day of rejoicing, which did not need the addition of the celestial potion of the alchymist to steep me in delight.

Soon after this eventful day, I became the husband of Bertha. I ceased to be the scholar of Cornelius, but I continued his friend. I always felt grateful to him for having, unawares, procured me that delicious draught of a divine elixir, which, instead of curing me of love (sad cure! solitary and joyless remedy for evils which seem blessings to the memory), had inspired me with courage and resolution, thus winning for me an inestimable treasure in my Bertha.

I often called to mind that period of trance-like inebriation with wonder. The drink of

Cornelius had not fulfilled the task for which he affirmed that it had been prepared, but its effects were more potent and blissful than words can express.

They had faded by degrees, yet they lingered long – and painted life in hues of splendour. Bertha often wondered at my lightness of heart and unaccustomed gaiety; for, before, I had been rather serious, or even sad, in my disposition. She loved me the better for my cheerful temper, and our days were winged by joy.

Five years afterwards I was suddenly summoned to the bedside of the dying Cornelius. He had sent for me in haste, conjuring my instant presence. I found him stretched on his pallet, enfeebled even to death; all of life that yet remained animated his piercing eyes, and they were fixed on a glass vessel, full of a roseate liquid.

"Behold," he said, in a broken and inward voice, "the vanity of human wishes! a second time my hopes are about to be crowned, a second time they are destroyed. Look at that liquor – you remember five years ago I had prepared the same, with the same success; – then, as now, my thirsting lips expected to taste the immortal elixir – you dashed it from me! and at present it is too late."

He spoke with difficulty, and fell back on his pillow. I could not help saying, –

"How, revered master, can a cure for love restore you to life?"

A faint smile gleamed across his face as I listened earnestly to his scarcely intelligible answer. "A cure for love and for all things – the Elixir of Immortality. Ah! If now I might drink, I should live for ever!"

As he spoke, a golden flash gleamed from the fluid; a well-remembered fragrance stole over the air; he raised himself, all weak as he was – strength seemed miraculously to re-enter his frame – he stretched forth his hand – a loud explosion startled me – a ray of fire shot up from the elixir, and the glass vessel which contained it was shivered to atoms! I turned my eyes towards the philosopher; he had fallen back – his eyes were glassy – his features rigid – he was dead!

But I lived, and was to live for ever! So said the unfortunate alchymist, and for a few days I believed his words. I remembered the glorious drunkenness that had followed my stolen draught. I reflected on the change I had felt in my frame – in my soul. The bounding elasticity of the one – the buoyant lightness of the other. I surveyed myself in a mirror, and could perceive no change in my features during the space of the five years which had elapsed. I remembered the radiant hues and grateful scent of that delicious beverage – worthy the gift it was capable of bestowing – I was, then, immortal!

A few days after I laughed at my credulity. The old proverb, that "a prophet is least regarded in his own country," was true with respect to me and my defunct master. I loved him as a man – I respected him as a sage – but I derided the notion that he could command the powers of darkness, and laughed at the superstitious fears with which he was regarded by the vulgar. He was a wise philosopher, but had no acquaintance with any spirits but those clad in flesh and blood. His science was simply human; and human science, I soon persuaded myself, could never conquer nature's laws so far as to imprison the soul for ever within its carnal habitation. Cornelius had brewed a soul-refreshing drink – more inebriating than wine – sweeter and more fragrant than any fruit: it possessed probably strong medicinal powers, imparting gladness to the heart and vigor to the limbs; but its effects would wear out; already were they diminished in my frame. I was a lucky fellow to have quaffed health and joyous spirits, and perhaps long life, at my master's hands; but my good fortune ended there: longevity was far different from immortality.

I continued to entertain this belief for many years. Sometimes a thought stole across me

– Was the alchymist indeed deceived? But my habitual credence was, that I should meet the fate of all the children of Adam at my appointed time – a little late, but still at a natural age. Yet it was certain that I retained a wonderfully youthful look. I was laughed at for my vanity in consulting the mirror so often, but I consulted it in vain – my brow was untrenched – my cheeks – my eyes – my whole person continued as untarnished as in my twentieth year.

I was troubled. I looked at the faded beauty of Bertha – I seemed more like her son. By degrees our neighbours began to make similar observations, and I found at last that I went by the name of the Scholar bewitched. Bertha herself grew uneasy. She became jealous and peevish, and at length she began to question me. We had no children; we were all in all to each other; and though, as she grew older, her vivacious spirit became a little allied to ill-temper, and her beauty sadly diminished, I cherished her in my heart as the mistress I had idolized, the wife I had sought and won with such perfect love.

At last our situation became intolerable: Bertha was fifty – I twenty years of age. I had, in very shame, in some measure adopted the habits of a more advanced age; I no longer mingled in the dance among the young and gay, but my heart bounded along with them while I restrained my feet; and a sorry figure I cut among the Nestors of our village. But before the time I mention, things were altered – we were universally shunned; we were – at least, I was – reported to have kept up an iniquitous acquaintance with some of my former master's supposed friends. Poor Bertha was pitied, but deserted. I was regarded with horror and detestation.

What was to be done? we sat by our winter fire – poverty had made itself felt, for none would buy the produce of my farm; and often I had been forced to journey twenty miles, to some place where I was not known, to dispose of our property. It is true we had saved something for an evil day – that day was come.

We sat by our lone fireside – the old-hearted youth and his antiquated wife. Again Bertha insisted on knowing the truth; she recapitulated all she had ever heard said about me, and added her own observations. She conjured me to cast off the spell; she described how much more comely grey hairs were than my chestnut locks; she descanted on the reverence and respect due to age – how preferable to the slight regard paid to mere children: could I imagine that the despicable gifts of youth and good looks outweighed disgrace, hatred, and scorn? Nay, in the end I should be burnt as a dealer in the black art, while she, to whom I had not deigned to communicate any portion of my good fortune, might be stoned as my accomplice. At length she insinuated that I must share my secret with her, and bestow on her like benefits to those I myself enjoyed, or she would denounce me – and then she burst into tears.

Thus beset, methought it was the best way to tell the truth. I revealed it as tenderly as I could, and spoke only of a very long life, not of immortality – which representation, indeed, coincided best with my own ideas. When I ended, I rose and said,

"And now, my Bertha, will you denounce the lover of your youth? – You will not, I know. But it is too hard, my poor wife, that you should suffer from my ill-luck and the accursed arts of Cornelius. I will leave you – you have wealth enough, and friends will return in my absence. I will go; young as I seem, and strong as I am, I can work and gain my bread among strangers, unsuspected and unknown. I loved you in youth; God is my witness that I would not desert you in age, but that your safety and happiness require it."

I took my cap and moved towards the door; in a moment Bertha's arms were round my neck, and her lips were pressed to mine. "No, my husband, my Winzy," she said, "you shall not go alone – take me with you; we will remove from this place, and, as you say, among strangers we shall be unsuspected and safe. I am not so very old as quite to shame you, my Winzy; and I dare say the charm will soon wear off, and, with the blessing of God, you will become more elderly-looking, as is fitting; you shall not leave me."

I returned the good soul's embrace heartily. "I will not, my Bertha; but for your sake I had not thought of such a thing. I will be your true, faithful husband while you are spared to me, and do my duty by you to the last."

The next day we prepared secretly for our emigration. We were obliged to make great pecuniary sacrifices – it could not be helped. We realised a sum sufficient, at least, to maintain us while Bertha lived; and, without saying adieu to any one, quitted our native country to take refuge in a remote part of western France.

It was a cruel thing to transport poor Bertha from her native village, and the friends of her youth, to a new country, new language, new customs. The strange secret of my destiny rendered this removal immaterial to me; but I compassionated her deeply, and was glad to perceive that she found compensation for her misfortunes in a variety of little ridiculous circumstances. Away from all tell-tale chroniclers, she sought to decrease the apparent disparity of our ages by a thousand feminine arts – rouge, youthful dress, and assumed juvenility of manner. I could not be angry – Did not I myself wear a mask? Why quarrel with hers, because it was less successful? I grieved deeply when I remembered that this was my Bertha, whom I had loved so fondly, and won with such transport – the dark eyed, dark-haired girl, with smiles of enchanting archness and a step like a fawn – this mincing, simpering, jealous old woman. I should have revered her gray locks and withered cheeks; but thus! – It was my, work, I knew; but I did not the less deplore this type of human weakness.

Her jealousy never slept. Her chief occupation was to discover that, in spite of outward appearances, I was myself growing old. I verily believe that the poor soul loved me truly in her heart, but never had woman so tormenting a mode of displaying fondness. She would discern wrinkles in my face and decrepitude in my walk, while I bounded along in youthful vigour, the youngest looking of twenty youths. I never dared address another woman: on one occasion, fancying that the belle of the village regarded me with favouring eyes, she bought me a gray wig. Her constant discourse among her acquaintances was, that though I looked so young, there was ruin at work within my frame; and she affirmed that the worst symptom about me was my apparent health. My youth was a disease, she said, and I ought at all times to prepare, if not for a sudden and awful death, at least to awake some morning white-headed, and bowed down with all the marks of advanced years. I let her talk – I often joined in her conjectures. Her warnings chimed in with my never-ceasing speculations concerning my state, and I took an earnest, though painful, interest in listening to all that her quick wit and excited imagination could say on the subject.

Why dwell on these minute circumstances? We lived on for many long years. Bertha became bed-rid and paralytic: I nursed her as mother might a child. She grew peevish, and still harped upon one string – of how long I should survive her. It has ever been a source of consolation to me, that I performed my duty scrupulously towards her. She had been mine in youth, she was mine in age, and at last, when I heaped the sod over her corpse, I wept to feel that I had lost all that really bound me to humanity.

Since then how many have been my cares and woes, how few and empty my enjoyments! I pause here in my history – I will pursue it no further. A sailor without rudder or compass, tossed on a stormy sea – a traveller lost on a wide-spread heath, without landmark or star to him – such have I been: more lost, more hopeless than either. A nearing ship, a gleam from some far cot, may save them; but I have no beacon except the hope of death.

Death! mysterious, ill-visaged friend of weak humanity! Why alone of all mortals have you cast me from your sheltering fold? O, for the peace of the grave! the deep silence of the iron-bound tomb! that thought would cease to work in my brain, and my heart beat no more with emotions varied only by new forms of sadness!

Am I immortal? I return to my first question. In the first place, is it not more probable that the beverage of the alchymist was fraught rather with longevity than eternal life? Such is my hope. And then be it remembered that I only drank half of the potion prepared by him. Was not the whole necessary to complete the charm? To have drained half the Elixir of Immortality is but to be half immortal – my Forever is thus truncated and null.

But again, who shall number the years of the half of eternity? I often try to imagine by what rule the infinite may be divided. Sometimes I fancy age advancing upon me. One gray hair I have found. Fool! Do I lament? Yes, the fear of age and death often creeps coldly into my heart; and the more I live, the more I dread death, even while I abhor life. Such an enigma is man – born to perish – when he wars, as I do, against the established laws of his nature.

But for this anomaly of feeling surely I might die: the medicine of the alchymist would not be proof against fire – sword – and the strangling waters. I have gazed upon the blue depths of many a placid lake, and the tumultuous rushing of many a mighty river, and have said, peace inhabits those waters; yet I have turned my steps away, to live yet another day. I have asked myself, whether suicide would be a crime in one to whom thus only the portals of the other world could be opened. I have done all, except presenting myself as a soldier or duellist, an object of destruction to my – no, not my fellow-mortals, and therefore I have shrunk away. They are not my fellows. The inextinguishable power of life in my frame, and their ephemeral existence, place us wide as the poles asunder. I could not raise a hand against the meanest or the most powerful among them.

Thus I have lived on for many a year – alone, and weary of myself – desirous of death, yet never dying – a mortal immortal. Neither ambition nor avarice can enter my mind, and the ardent love that gnaws at my heart, never to be returned – never to find an equal on which to expend itself – lives there only to torment me.

This very day I conceived a design by which I may end all – without self-slaughter, without making another man a Cain – an expedition, which mortal frame can never survive, even endued with the youth and strength that inhabits mine. Thus I shall put my immortality to the test, and rest for ever – or return, the wonder and benefactor of the human species.

Before I go, a miserable vanity has caused me to pen these pages. I would not die, and leave no name behind. Three centuries have passed since I quaffed the fatal beverage: another year shall not elapse before, encountering gigantic dangers – warring with the powers of frost in their home – beset by famine, toil, and tempest – I yield this body, too tenacious a cage for a soul which thirsts for freedom, to the destructive elements of air and water – or, if I survive, my name shall be recorded as one of the most famous among the sons of men; and, my task achieved, I shall adopt more resolute means, and, by scattering and annihilating the atoms that compose my frame, set at liberty the life imprisoned within, and so cruelly prevented from soaring from this dim earth to a sphere more congenial to its immortal essence.

The Body Snatcher

Robert Louis Stevenson

EVERY NIGHT in the year, four of us sat in the small parlour of the George at Debenham – the undertaker, and the landlord, and Fettes, and myself. Sometimes there would be more; but blow high, blow low, come rain or snow or frost, we four would be each planted in his own particular arm-chair. Fettes was an old drunken Scotchman, a man of education obviously, and a man of some property, since he lived in idleness. He had come to Debenham years ago, while still young, and by a mere continuance of living had grown to be an adopted townsman. His blue camlet cloak was a local antiquity, like the church-spire.

His place in the parlour at the George, his absence from church, his old, crapulous, disreputable vices, were all things of course in Debenham. He had some vague Radical opinions and some fleeting infidelities, which he would now and again set forth and emphasise with tottering slaps upon the table. He drank rum – five glasses regularly every evening; and for the greater portion of his nightly visit to the George sat, with his glass in his right hand, in a state of melancholy alcoholic saturation. We called him the Doctor, for he was supposed to have some special knowledge of medicine, and had been known, upon a pinch, to set a fracture or reduce a dislocation; but beyond these slight particulars, we had no knowledge of his character and antecedents.

One dark winter night – it had struck nine some time before the landlord joined us – there was a sick man in the George, a great neighbouring proprietor suddenly struck down with apoplexy on his way to Parliament; and the great man's still greater London doctor had been telegraphed to his bedside. It was the first time that such a thing had happened in Debenham, for the railway was but newly open, and we were all proportionately moved by the occurrence.

"He's come," said the landlord, after he had filled and lighted his pipe.

"He?" said I. "Who? – not the doctor?"

"Himself," replied our host.

"What is his name?"

"Doctor Macfarlane," said the landlord.

Fettes was far through his third tumbler, stupidly fuddled, now nodding over, now staring mazily around him; but at the last word he seemed to awaken, and repeated the name "Macfarlane" twice, quietly enough the first time, but with sudden emotion at the second.

"Yes," said the landlord, "that's his name, Doctor Wolfe Macfarlane."

Fettes became instantly sober; his eyes awoke, his voice became clear, loud, and steady, his language forcible and earnest. We were all startled by the transformation, as if a man had risen from the dead.

"I beg your pardon," he said, "I am afraid I have not been paying much attention to your talk. Who is this Wolfe Macfarlane?" And then, when he had heard the landlord out, "It cannot be, it cannot be," he added; "and yet I would like well to see him face to face."

"Do you know him, Doctor?" asked the undertaker, with a gasp.

"God forbid!" was the reply. "And yet the name is a strange one; it were too much to fancy two. Tell me, landlord, is he old?"

"Well," said the host, "he's not a young man, to be sure, and his hair is white; but he looks younger than you."

"He is older, though; years older. But," with a slap upon the table, "it's the rum you see in my face – rum and sin. This man, perhaps, may have an easy conscience and a good digestion. Conscience! Hear me speak. You would think I was some good, old, decent Christian, would you not? But no, not I; I never canted. Voltaire might have canted if he'd stood in my shoes; but the brains" – with a rattling fillip on his bald head – "the brains were clear and active, and I saw and made no deductions."

"If you know this doctor," I ventured to remark, after a somewhat awful pause, "I should gather that you do not share the landlord's good opinion."

Fettes paid no regard to me.

"Yes," he said, with sudden decision, "I must see him face to face."

There was another pause, and then a door was closed rather sharply on the first floor, and a step was heard upon the stair.

"That's the doctor," cried the landlord. "Look sharp, and you can catch him."

It was but two steps from the small parlour to the door of the old George Inn; the wide oak staircase landed almost in the street; there was room for a Turkey rug and nothing more between the threshold and the last round of the descent; but this little space was every evening brilliantly lit up, not only by the light upon the stair and the great signal-lamp below the sign, but by the warm radiance of the bar-room window. The George thus brightly advertised itself to passers-by in the cold street. Fettes walked steadily to the spot, and we, who were hanging behind, beheld the two men meet, as one of them had phrased it, face to face.

Dr. Macfarlane was alert and vigorous. His white hair set off his pale and placid, although energetic, countenance. He was richly dressed in the finest of broadcloth and the whitest of linen, with a great gold watch-chain, and studs and spectacles of the same precious material. He wore a broad- folded tie, white and speckled with lilac, and he carried on his arm a comfortable driving-coat of fur. There was no doubt but he became his years, breathing, as he did, of wealth and consideration; and it was a surprising contrast to see our parlour sot – bald, dirty, pimpled, and robed in his old camlet cloak – confront him at the bottom of the stairs.

"Macfarlane!" he said somewhat loudly, more like a herald than a friend.

The great doctor pulled up short on the fourth step, as though the familiarity of the address surprised and somewhat shocked his dignity.

"Toddy Macfarlane!" repeated Fettes.

The London man almost staggered. He stared for the swiftest of seconds at the man before him, glanced behind him with a sort of scare, and then in a startled whisper, "Fettes!" he said, "You!"

"Ay," said the other, "me! Did you think I was dead too? We are not so easy shut of our acquaintance."

"Hush, hush!" exclaimed the doctor. "Hush, hush! this meeting is so unexpected – I can see you are unmanned. I hardly knew you, I confess, at first; but I am overjoyed – overjoyed to have this opportunity. For the present it must be how-d'ye-do and goodbye in one, for my fly is waiting, and I must not fail the train; but you shall – let me see – yes – you shall give me your address, and you can count on early news of me. We must do something for you, Fettes. I fear you are out at elbows; but we must see to that for auld lang syne, as once we sang at suppers."

"Money!" cried Fettes; "money from you! The money that I had from you is lying where I cast it in the rain."

Dr. Macfarlane had talked himself into some measure of superiority and confidence, but the uncommon energy of this refusal cast him back into his first confusion.

A horrible, ugly look came and went across his almost venerable countenance. "My dear fellow," he said, "be it as you please; my last thought is to offend you. I would intrude on none. I will leave you my address, however – "

"I do not wish it – I do not wish to know the roof that shelters you," interrupted the other. "I heard your name; I feared it might be you; I wished to know if, after all, there were a God; I know now that there is none. Begone!"

He still stood in the middle of the rug, between the stair and doorway; and the great London physician, in order to escape, would be forced to step to one side. It was plain that he hesitated before the thought of this humiliation. White as he was, there was a dangerous glitter in his spectacles; but while he still paused uncertain, he became aware that the driver of his fly was peering in from the street at this unusual scene and caught a glimpse at the same time of our little body from the parlour, huddled by the corner of the bar. The presence of so many witnesses decided him at once to flee. He crouched together, brushing on the wainscot, and made a dart like a serpent, striking for the door. But his tribulation was not yet entirely at an end, for even as he was passing Fettes clutched him by the arm and these words came in a whisper, and yet painfully distinct, "Have you seen it again?"

The great rich London doctor cried out aloud with a sharp, throttling cry; he dashed his questioner across the open space, and, with his hands over his head, fled out of the door like a detected thief. Before it had occurred to one of us to make a movement the fly was already rattling toward the station. The scene was over like a dream, but the dream had left proofs and traces of its passage. Next day the servant found the fine gold spectacles broken on the threshold, and that very night we were all standing breathless by the bar-room window, and Fettes at our side, sober, pale, and resolute in look.

"God protect us, Mr. Fettes!" said the landlord, coming first into possession of his customary senses. "What in the universe is all this? These are strange things you have been saying."

Fettes turned toward us; he looked us each in succession in the face. "See if you can hold your tongues," said he. "That man Macfarlane is not safe to cross; those that have done so already have repented it too late."

And then, without so much as finishing his third glass, far less waiting for the other two, he bade us goodbye and went forth, under the lamp of the hotel, into the black night.

We three turned to our places in the parlour, with the big red fire and four clear candles; and as we recapitulated what had passed, the first chill of our surprise soon changed into a glow of curiosity. We sat late; it was the latest session I have known in the old George. Each man, before we parted, had his theory that he was bound to prove; and none of us had any nearer business in this world than to track out the past of our condemned companion, and surprise the secret that he shared with the great London doctor. It is no great boast, but I believe I was a better hand at worming out a story than either of my fellows at the George;

and perhaps there is now no other man alive who could narrate to you the following foul and unnatural events.

In his young days Fettes studied medicine in the schools of Edinburgh. He had talent of a kind, the talent that picks up swiftly what it hears and readily retails it for its own. He worked little at home; but he was civil, attentive, and intelligent in the presence of his masters. They soon picked him out as a lad who listened closely and remembered well; nay, strange as it seemed to me when I first heard it, he was in those days well favoured, and pleased by his exterior. There was, at that period, a certain extramural teacher of anatomy, whom I shall here designate by the letter K. His name was subsequently too well known. The man who bore it skulked through the streets of Edinburgh in disguise, while the mob that applauded at the execution of Burke called loudly for the blood of his employer.

But Mr. K- was then at the top of his vogue; he enjoyed a popularity due partly to his own talent and address, partly to the incapacity of his rival, the university professor. The students, at least, swore by his name, and Fettes believed himself, and was believed by others, to have laid the foundations of success when he had acquired the favour of this meteorically famous man. Mr. K- was a bon vivant as well as an accomplished teacher; he liked a sly illusion no less than a careful preparation. In both capacities Fettes enjoyed and deserved his notice, and by the second year of his attendance he held the half-regular position of second demonstrator or sub-assistant in his class.

In this capacity the charge of the theatre and lecture-room devolved in particular upon his shoulders. He had to answer for the cleanliness of the premises and the conduct of the other students, and it was a part of his duty to supply, receive, and divide the various subjects. It was with a view to this last – at that time very delicate – affair that he was lodged by Mr. K- in the same wynd, and at last in the same building, with the dissecting-rooms. Here, after a night of turbulent pleasures, his hand still tottering, his sight still misty and confused, he would be called out of bed in the black hours before the winter dawn by the unclean and desperate interlopers who supplied the table. He would open the door to these men, since infamous throughout the land. He would help them with their tragic burden, pay them their sordid price, and remain alone, when they were gone, with the unfriendly relics of humanity. From such a scene he would return to snatch another hour or two of slumber, to repair the abuses of the night, and refresh himself for the labours of the day.

Few lads could have been more insensible to the impressions of a life thus passed among the ensigns of mortality. His mind was closed against all general considerations. He was incapable of interest in the fate and fortunes of another, the slave of his own desires and low ambitions. Cold, light, and selfish in the last resort, he had that modicum of prudence, miscalled morality, which keeps a man from inconvenient drunkenness or punishable theft. He coveted, besides, a measure of consideration from his masters and his fellow-pupils, and he had no desire to fail conspicuously in the external parts of life. Thus he made it his pleasure to gain some distinction in his studies, and day after day rendered unimpeachable eye-service to his employer, Mr. K-. For his day of work he indemnified himself by nights of roaring, blackguardly enjoyment; and when that balance had been struck, the organ that he called his conscience declared itself content.

The supply of subjects was a continual trouble to him as well as to his master. In that large and busy class, the raw material of the anatomists kept perpetually running out; and the business thus rendered necessary was not only unpleasant in itself, but threatened dangerous consequences to all who were concerned. It was the policy of Mr. K- to ask no questions in his dealings with the trade. "They bring the body, and we pay the price," he used to say, dwelling on the alliteration – "quid pro quo." And, again, and somewhat profanely, "Ask no questions," he would tell his assistants, "for conscience sake." There was no understanding that the subjects were provided by the crime of murder. Had that idea been broached to him in words, he would have recoiled in horror; but the lightness of his speech upon so grave a matter was, in itself, an offence against good manners, and a temptation to the men with whom he dealt. Fettes, for instance, had often remarked to himself upon the singular freshness of the bodies. He had been struck again and again by the hang-dog, abominable looks of the ruffians who came to him before the dawn; and putting things together clearly in his private thoughts, he perhaps attributed a meaning too immoral and too categorical to the unguarded counsels of his master. He understood his duty, in short, to have three branches: to take what was brought, to pay the price, and to avert the eye from any evidence of crime.

One November morning this policy of silence was put sharply to the test. He had been awake all night with a racking toothache – pacing his room like a caged beast or throwing himself in fury on his bed – and had fallen at last into that profound, uneasy slumber that so often follows on a night of pain, when he was awakened by the third or fourth angry repetition of the concerted signal. There was a thin, bright moonshine; it was bitter cold, windy, and frosty; the town had not yet awakened, but an indefinable stir already preluded the noise and business of the day. The ghouls had come later than usual, and they seemed more than usually eager to be gone. Fettes, sick with sleep, lighted them upstairs. He heard their grumbling Irish voices through a dream; and as they stripped the sack from their sad merchandise he leaned dozing, with his shoulder propped against the wall; he had to shake himself to find the men their money. As he did so his eyes lighted on the dead face. He started; he took two steps nearer, with the candle raised.

"God Almighty!" he cried. "That is Jane Galbraith!"

The men answered nothing, but they shuffled nearer the door.

"I know her, I tell you," he continued. "She was alive and hearty yesterday. It's impossible she can be dead; it's impossible you should have got this body fairly."

"Sure, sir, you're mistaken entirely," said one of the men.

But the other looked Fettes darkly in the eyes, and demanded the money on the spot.

It was impossible to misconceive the threat or to exaggerate the danger. The lad's heart failed him. He stammered some excuses, counted out the sum, and saw his hateful visitors depart. No sooner were they gone than he hastened to confirm his doubts. By a dozen unquestionable marks he identified the girl he had jested with the day before. He saw, with horror, marks upon her body that might well betoken violence. A panic seized him, and he took refuge in his room. There he reflected at length over the discovery that he had made; considered soberly the bearing of Mr. K-'s instructions and the danger to himself of interference in so serious a business, and at last, in sore perplexity, determined to wait for the advice of his immediate superior, the class assistant.

This was a young doctor, Wolfe Macfarlane, a high favourite among all the reckless students, clever, dissipated, and unscrupulous to the last degree. He had travelled and studied abroad. His manners were agreeable and a little forward. He was an authority on the stage, skilful on the ice or the links with skate or golf-club; he dressed with nice audacity, and, to put the finishing touch upon his glory, he kept a gig and a strong trotting-horse. With Fettes he was on terms of intimacy; indeed, their relative positions called for some community of life; and when subjects were scarce the pair would drive far into the country in Macfarlane's gig, visit and desecrate some lonely graveyard, and return before dawn with their booty to the door of the dissecting-room.

On that particular morning Macfarlane arrived somewhat earlier than his wont. Fettes heard him, and met him on the stairs, told him his story, and showed him the cause of his alarm. Macfarlane examined the marks on her body.

"Yes," he said with a nod, "it looks fishy."

"Well, what should I do?" asked Fettes.

"Do?" repeated the other. "Do you want to do anything? Least said soonest mended, I should say."

"Some one else might recognise her," objected Fettes. "She was as well known as the Castle Rock."

"We'll hope not," said Macfarlane, "and if anybody does – well, you didn't, don't you see, and there's an end. The fact is, this has been going on too long. Stir up the mud, and you'll get K- into the most unholy trouble; you'll be in a shocking box yourself. So will I, if you come to that. I should like to know how any one of us would look, or what the devil we should have to say for ourselves, in any Christian witness-box. For me, you know there's one thing certain – that, practically speaking, all our subjects have been murdered."

"Macfarlane!" cried Fettes.

"Come now!" sneered the other. "As if you hadn't suspected it yourself!"

"Suspecting is one thing – "

"And proof another. Yes, I know; and I'm as sorry as you are this should have come here," tapping the body with his cane. "The next best thing for me is not to recognise it; and," he added coolly, "I don't. You may, if you please. I don't dictate, but I think a man of the world would do as I do; and I may add, I fancy that is what K- would look for at our hands. The question is, Why did he choose us two for his assistants? And I answer, because he didn't want old wives."

This was the tone of all others to affect the mind of a lad like Fettes. He agreed to imitate Macfarlane. The body of the unfortunate girl was duly dissected, and no one remarked or appeared to recognise her.

One afternoon, when his day's work was over, Fettes dropped into a popular tavern and found Macfarlane sitting with a stranger. This was a small man, very pale and dark, with coal-black eyes. The cut of his features gave a promise of intellect and refinement which was but feebly realised in his manners, for he proved, upon a nearer acquaintance, coarse, vulgar, and stupid. He exercised, however, a very remarkable control over Macfarlane; issued orders like the Great Bashaw; became inflamed at the least discussion or delay, and commented rudely on the servility with which he was obeyed. This most offensive person took a fancy to Fettes on the spot, plied him with drinks, and honoured him with unusual confidences on his past career. If a tenth part of what he confessed were true, he was a very loathsome rogue; and the lad's vanity was tickled by the attention of so experienced a man.

"I'm a pretty bad fellow myself," the stranger remarked, "but Macfarlane is the boy – Toddy Macfarlane I call him. Toddy, order your friend another glass." Or it might be, "Toddy, you jump up and shut the door." "Toddy hates me," he said again. "Oh yes, Toddy, you do!"

"Don't you call me that confounded name," growled Macfarlane.

"Hear him! Did you ever see the lads play knife? He would like to do that all over my body," remarked the stranger.

"We medicals have a better way than that," said Fettes. "When we dislike a dead friend of ours, we dissect him."

Macfarlane looked up sharply, as though this jest were scarcely to his mind.

The afternoon passed. Gray, for that was the stranger's name, invited Fettes to join them at dinner, ordered a feast so sumptuous that the tavern was thrown into commotion, and when all was done commanded Macfarlane to settle the bill. It was late before they separated; the man Gray was incapably drunk. Macfarlane, sobered by his fury, chewed the cud of the money he had been forced to squander and the slights he had been obliged to swallow. Fettes, with various liquors singing in his head, returned home with devious footsteps and a mind entirely in abeyance. Next day Macfarlane was absent from the class, and Fettes smiled to himself as he imagined him still squiring the intolerable Gray from tavern to tavern. As soon as the hour of liberty had struck he posted from place to place in quest of his last night's companions. He could find them, however, nowhere; so returned early to his rooms, went early to bed, and slept the sleep of the just.

At four in the morning he was awakened by the well-known signal. Descending to the door, he was filled with astonishment to find Macfarlane with his gig, and in the gig one of those long and ghastly packages with which he was so well acquainted.

"What?" he cried. "Have you been out alone? How did you manage?"

But Macfarlane silenced him roughly, bidding him turn to business. When they had got the body upstairs and laid it on the table, Macfarlane made at first as if he were going away. Then he paused and seemed to hesitate; and then, "You had better look at the face," said he, in tones of some constraint. "You had better," he repeated, as Fettes only stared at him in wonder.

"But where, and how, and when did you come by it?" cried the other.

"Look at the face," was the only answer.

Fettes was staggered; strange doubts assailed him. He looked from the young doctor to the body, and then back again. At last, with a start, he did as he was bidden. He had almost expected the sight that met his eyes, and yet the shock was cruel. To see, fixed in the rigidity of death and naked on that coarse layer of sackcloth, the man whom he had left well clad and full of meat and sin upon the threshold of a tavern, awoke, even in the thoughtless Fettes, some of the terrors of the conscience. It was a *cras tibi* which re-echoed in his soul, that two whom he had known should have come to lie upon these icy tables. Yet these were only secondary thoughts. His first concern regarded Wolfe. Unprepared for a challenge so momentous, he knew not how to look his comrade in the face. He durst not meet his eye, and he had neither words nor voice at his command.

It was Macfarlane himself who made the first advance. He came up quietly behind and laid his hand gently but firmly on the other's shoulder.

"Richardson," said he, "may have the head."

Now Richardson was a student who had long been anxious for that portion of the human subject to dissect. There was no answer, and the murderer resumed: "Talking of business, you must pay me; your accounts, you see, must tally."

Fettes found a voice, the ghost of his own: "Pay you!" he cried. "Pay you for that?"

"Why, yes, of course you must. By all means and on every possible account, you must," returned the other. "I dare not give it for nothing, you dare not take it for nothing; it would compromise us both. This is another case like Jane Galbraith's. The more things are wrong the more we must act as if all were right. Where does old K- keep his money?"

"There," answered Fettes hoarsely, pointing to a cupboard in the corner.

"Give me the key, then," said the other, calmly, holding out his hand.

There was an instant's hesitation, and the die was cast. Macfarlane could not suppress a nervous twitch, the infinitesimal mark of an immense relief, as he felt the key between his fingers. He opened the cupboard, brought out pen and ink and a paper-book that stood in one compartment, and separated from the funds in a drawer a sum suitable to the occasion.

"Now, look here," he said, "there is the payment made – first proof of your good faith: first step to your security. You have now to clinch it by a second. Enter the payment in your book, and then you for your part may defy the devil."

The next few seconds were for Fettes an agony of thought; but in balancing his terrors it was the most immediate that triumphed. Any future difficulty seemed almost welcome if he could avoid a present quarrel with Macfarlane. He set down the candle which he had been carrying all this time, and with a steady hand entered the date, the nature, and the amount of the transaction.

"And now," said Macfarlane, "it's only fair that you should pocket the lucre. I've had my share already. By the·bye, when a man of the world falls into a bit of luck, has a few shillings extra in his pocket – I'm ashamed to speak of it, but there's a rule of conduct in the case. No treating, no purchase of expensive class-books, no squaring of old debts; borrow, don't lend."

"Macfarlane," began Fettes, still somewhat hoarsely, "I have put my neck in a halter to oblige you."

"To oblige me?" cried Wolfe. "Oh, come! You did, as near as I can see the matter, what you downright had to do in self-defence. Suppose I got into trouble, where would you be? This second little matter flows clearly from the first. Mr. Gray is the continuation of Miss Galbraith. You can't begin and then stop. If you begin, you must keep on beginning; that's the truth. No rest for the wicked."

A horrible sense of blackness and the treachery of fate seized hold upon the soul of the unhappy student.

"My God!" he cried, "but what have I done? and when did I begin? To be made a class assistant – in the name of reason, where's the harm in that? Service wanted the position; Service might have got it. Would he have been where I am now?"

"My dear fellow," said Macfarlane, "what a boy you are! What harm *has* come to you? What harm can come to you if you hold your tongue? Why, man, do you know what this life is? There are two squads of us – the lions and the lambs. If you're a lamb, you'll come to lie upon these tables like Gray or Jane Galbraith; if you're a lion, you'll live and drive a horse like me, like K—, like all the world with any wit or courage. You're staggered at the first. But look at K—! My dear fellow, you're clever, you have pluck. I like you, and K- likes you. You were born to lead the hunt; and I tell you, on my honour and my experience of life, three days from now you'll laugh at all these scarecrows like a High School boy at a farce."

And with that Macfarlane took his departure and drove off up the wynd in his gig to get under cover before daylight. Fettes was thus left alone with his regrets. He saw the miserable peril in which he stood involved. He saw, with inexpressible dismay, that there was no limit to his weakness, and that, from concession to concession, he had fallen from the arbiter of Macfarlane's destiny to his paid and helpless accomplice. He would have given the world to have been a little braver at the time, but it did not occur to him that he might still be brave. The secret of Jane Galbraith and the cursed entry in the day-book closed his mouth.

Hours passed; the class began to arrive; the members of the unhappy Gray were dealt out to one and to another, and received without remark. Richardson was made happy with the head; and before the hour of freedom rang Fettes trembled with exultation to perceive how far they had already gone toward safety.

For two days he continued to watch, with increasing joy, the dreadful process of disguise.

On the third day Macfarlane made his appearance. He had been ill, he said; but he made up for lost time by the energy with which he directed the students. To Richardson in particular he extended the most valuable assistance and advice, and that student, encouraged by the praise of the demonstrator, burned high with ambitious hopes, and saw the medal already in his grasp.

Before the week was out Macfarlane's prophecy had been fulfilled. Fettes had outlived his terrors and had forgotten his baseness. He began to plume himself upon his courage, and had so arranged the story in his mind that he could look back on these events with an unhealthy pride. Of his accomplice he saw but little. They met, of course, in the business of the class; they received their orders together from Mr. K-. At times they had a word or two in private, and Macfarlane was from first to last particularly kind and jovial. But it was plain that he avoided any reference to their common secret; and even when Fettes whispered to him that he had cast in his lot with the lions and foresworn the lambs, he only signed to him smilingly to hold his peace.

At length an occasion arose which threw the pair once more into a closer union. Mr. K- was again short of subjects; pupils were eager, and it was a part of this teacher's pretensions to be always well supplied. At the same time there came the news of a burial in the rustic graveyard of Glencorse. Time has little changed the place in question. It stood then, as now, upon a cross road, out of call of human habitations, and buried fathom deep in the foliage of six cedar trees. The cries of the sheep upon the neighbouring hills, the streamlets upon either hand, one loudly singing among pebbles, the other dripping furtively from pond to pond, the stir of the wind in mountainous old flowering chestnuts, and once in seven days the voice of the bell and the old tunes of the precentor, were the only sounds that disturbed the silence around the rural church. The Resurrection Man – to use a byname of the period – was not to be deterred by any of the sanctities of customary piety. It was part of his trade to despise and desecrate the scrolls and trumpets of old tombs, the paths worn by the feet of worshippers and mourners, and the offerings and the inscriptions of bereaved affection.

To rustic neighbourhoods, where love is more than commonly tenacious, and where some bonds of blood or fellowship unite the entire society of a parish, the body-snatcher, far from being repelled by natural respect, was attracted by the ease and safety of the task. To bodies that had been laid in earth, in joyful expectation of a far different awakening, there came that hasty, lamp-lit, terror-haunted resurrection of the spade and mattock. The coffin was forced, the cerements torn, and the melancholy relics, clad in sackcloth, after being rattled for hours on moonless byways, were at length exposed to uttermost indignities before a class of gaping boys.

Somewhat as two vultures may swoop upon a dying lamb, Fettes and Macfarlane were to be let loose upon a grave in that green and quiet resting-place. The wife of a farmer, a woman who had lived for sixty years, and been known for nothing but good butter and a godly conversation, was to be rooted from her grave at midnight and carried, dead and naked, to that far-away city that she had always honoured with her Sunday's best; the place beside her family was to be empty till the crack of doom; her innocent and almost venerable members to be exposed to that last curiosity of the anatomist.

Late one afternoon the pair set forth, well wrapped in cloaks and furnished with a formidable bottle. It rained without remission – a cold, dense, lashing rain. Now and again there blew a puff of wind, but these sheets of falling water kept it down. Bottle and all, it was a sad and silent drive as far as Penicuik, where they were to spend the evening. They stopped once, to hide their implements in a thick bush not far from the churchyard, and once again at the Fisher's Tryst, to have a toast before the kitchen fire and vary their nips of whisky with a glass of ale. When they reached their journey's end the gig was housed, the horse was fed and comforted, and the two young doctors in a private room sat down to the best dinner and the best wine the house afforded. The lights, the fire, the beating rain upon the window, the cold, incongruous work that lay before them, added zest to their enjoyment of the meal. With every glass their cordiality increased. Soon Macfarlane handed a little pile of gold to his companion.

"A compliment," he said. "Between friends these little d-d accommodations ought to fly like pipe-lights."

Fettes pocketed the money, and applauded the sentiment to the echo. "You are a philosopher," he cried. "I was an ass till I knew you. You and K- between you, by the Lord Harry! but you'll make a man of me."

"Of course we shall," applauded Macfarlane. "A man? I tell you, it required a man to back me up the other morning. There are some big, brawling, forty-year-old cowards who would have turned sick at the look of the d-d thing; but not you – you kept your head. I watched you."

"Well, and why not?" Fettes thus vaunted himself. "It was no affair of mine. There was nothing to gain on the one side but disturbance, and on the other I could count on your gratitude, don't you see?" And he slapped his pocket till the gold pieces rang.

Macfarlane somehow felt a certain touch of alarm at these unpleasant words. He may have regretted that he had taught his young companion so successfully, but he had no time to interfere, for the other noisily continued in this boastful strain:–

"The great thing is not to be afraid. Now, between you and me, I don't want to hang – that's practical; but for all cant, Macfarlane, I was born with a contempt. Hell, God, Devil, right, wrong, sin, crime, and all the old gallery of curiosities – they may frighten boys, but men of the world, like you and me, despise them. Here's to the memory of Gray!"

It was by this time growing somewhat late. The gig, according to order, was brought round to the door with both lamps brightly shining, and the young men had to pay their bill and take the road. They announced that they were bound for Peebles, and drove in that direction till they were clear of the last houses of the town; then, extinguishing the lamps, returned upon their course, and followed a by-road toward Glencorse. There was no sound but that of their own passage, and the incessant, strident pouring of the rain. It was pitch dark; here and there a white gate or a white stone in the wall guided them for a short space across the night; but for the most part it was at a foot pace, and almost groping, that they picked their way through that resonant blackness to their solemn and isolated destination. In the sunken woods that traverse the neighbourhood of the burying-ground the last glimmer failed them, and it became necessary to kindle a match and re-illumine one of the lanterns of the gig. Thus, under the dripping trees, and environed by huge and moving shadows, they reached the scene of their unhallowed labours.

They were both experienced in such affairs, and powerful with the spade; and they had scarce been twenty minutes at their task before they were rewarded by a dull rattle on the coffin lid. At the same moment Macfarlane, having hurt his hand upon a stone, flung it carelessly above his head. The grave, in which they now stood almost to the shoulders, was close to the edge of the plateau of the graveyard; and the gig lamp had been propped, the better to illuminate their labours, against a tree, and on the immediate verge of the steep bank descending to the stream. Chance had taken a sure aim with the stone.

Then came a clang of broken glass; night fell upon them; sounds alternately dull and ringing announced the bounding of the lantern down the bank, and its occasional collision with the trees. A stone or two, which it had dislodged in its descent, rattled behind it into the profundities of the glen; and then silence, like night, resumed its sway; and they might bend their hearing to its utmost pitch, but naught was to be heard except the rain, now marching to the wind, now steadily falling over miles of open country.

They were so nearly at an end of their abhorred task that they judged it wisest to complete it in the dark. The coffin was exhumed and broken open; the body inserted in the dripping sack and carried between them to the gig; one mounted to keep it in its place, and the other, taking the horse by the mouth, groped along by wall and bush until they reached the wider road by the Fisher's Tryst. Here was a faint, diffused radiancy, which they hailed like daylight; by that they pushed the horse to a good pace and began to rattle along merrily in the direction of the town.

They had both been wetted to the skin during their operations, and now, as the gig jumped among the deep ruts, the thing that stood propped between them fell now upon one and now upon the other. At every repetition of the horrid contact each instinctively repelled it with the greater haste; and the process, natural although it was, began to tell upon the nerves of the companions. Macfarlane made some ill-favoured jest about the farmer's wife, but it came hollowly from his lips, and was allowed to drop in silence. Still their unnatural burden bumped from side to side; and now the head would be laid, as if in confidence, upon their shoulders, and now the drenching sack-cloth would flap icily about their faces. A creeping chill began to possess the soul of Fettes. He peered at the bundle, and it seemed somehow larger than at first. All over the country-side, and from every degree of distance, the farm dogs accompanied their passage with tragic ululations; and it grew and grew upon his mind that some unnatural miracle had been accomplished, that some nameless change had befallen the dead body, and that it was in fear of their unholy burden that the dogs were howling.

"For God's sake," said he, making a great effort to arrive at speech, "for God's sake, let's have a light!"

Seemingly Macfarlane was affected in the same direction; for, though he made no reply, he stopped the horse, passed the reins to his companion, got down, and proceeded to kindle the remaining lamp. They had by that time got no farther than the cross-road down to Auchenclinny. The rain still poured as though the deluge were returning, and it was no easy matter to make a light in such a world of wet and darkness. When at last the flickering blue flame had been transferred to the wick and began to expand and clarify, and shed a wide circle of misty brightness round the gig, it became possible for the two young men to see each other and the thing they had along with them. The rain had moulded the rough sacking to the outlines of the body underneath; the head was distinct from the trunk, the shoulders plainly modelled; something at once spectral and human riveted their eyes upon the ghastly comrade of their drive.

For some time Macfarlane stood motionless, holding up the lamp. A nameless dread was swathed, like a wet sheet, about the body, and tightened the white skin upon the face of Fettes; a fear that was meaningless, a horror of what could not be, kept mounting to his brain. Another beat of the watch, and he had spoken. But his comrade forestalled him.

"That is not a woman," said Macfarlane, in a hushed voice.

"It was a woman when we put her in," whispered Fettes.

"Hold that lamp," said the other. "I must see her face."

And as Fettes took the lamp his companion untied the fastenings of the sack and drew down the cover from the head. The light fell very clear upon the dark, well-moulded features and smooth-shaven cheeks of a too familiar countenance, often beheld in dreams of both of these young men. A wild yell rang up into the night; each leaped from his own side into the roadway: the lamp fell, broke, and was extinguished; and the horse, terrified by this unusual commotion, bounded and went off toward Edinburgh at a gallop, bearing along with it, sole occupant of the gig, the body of the dead and long-dissected Gray.

Dracula's Guest

Bram Stoker

WHEN WE STARTED for our drive the sun was shining brightly on Munich, and the air was full of the joyousness of early summer. Just as we were about to depart, Herr Delbruck (the maitre d'hotel of the Quatre Saisons, where I was staying) came down bareheaded to the carriage and, after wishing me a pleasant drive, said to the coachman, still holding his hand on the handle of the carriage door, "Remember you are back by nightfall. The sky looks bright but there is a shiver in the north wind that says there may be a sudden storm. But I am sure you will not be late." Here he smiled and added,"for you know what night it is."

Johann answered with an emphatic, *"Ja, mein Herr,"* and, touching his hat, drove off quickly. When we had cleared the town, I said, after signalling to him to stop:

"Tell me, Johann, what is tonight?"

He crossed himself, as he answered laconically: "Walpurgis nacht." Then he took out his watch, a great, old-fashioned German silver thing as big as a turnip and looked at it, with his eyebrows gathered together and a little impatient shrug of his shoulders. I realized that this was his way of respectfully protesting against the unnecessary delay and sank back in the carriage, merely motioning him to proceed. He started off rapidly, as if to make up for lost time. Every now and then the horses seemed to throw up their heads and sniff the air suspiciously. On such occasions I often looked round in alarm. The road was pretty bleak, for we were traversing a sort of high windswept plateau. As we drove, I saw a road that looked but little used and which seemed to dip through a little winding valley. It looked so inviting that, even at the risk of offending him, I called Johann to stop – and when he had pulled up, I told him I would like to drive down that road. He made all sorts of excuses and frequently crossed himself as he spoke. This somewhat piqued my curiosity, so I asked him various questions. He answered fencingly and repeatedly looked at his watch in protest.

Finally I said, "Well, Johann, I want to go down this road. I shall not ask you to come unless you like; but tell me why you do not like to go, that is all I ask." For answer he seemed to throw himself off the box, so quickly did he reach the ground. Then he stretched out his hands appealingly to me and implored me not to go. There was just enough of English mixed with the German for me to understand the drift of his talk. He seemed always just about to tell me something – the very idea of which evidently frightened him; but each time he pulled himself up saying, "Walpurgis nacht!"

I tried to argue with him, but it was difficult to argue with a man when I did not know his language. The advantage certainly rested with him, for although he began to speak in English, of a very crude and broken kind, he always got excited and broke into his native tongue – and every time he did so, he looked at his watch. Then the horses became restless and sniffed the air. At this he grew very pale, and, looking around in a frightened way, he suddenly jumped forward, took them by the bridles, and led them on some twenty feet. I followed and asked why he had done this. For an answer he crossed himself, pointed to the spot we had left, and drew his carriage in the direction of the other road, indicating a cross, and said, first in German, then in English, "Buried him – him what killed themselves."

I remembered the old custom of burying suicides at cross roads: "Ah! I see, a suicide. How interesting!" But for the life of me I could not make out why the horses were frightened.

Whilst we were talking, we heard a sort of sound between a yelp and a bark. It was far away; but the horses got very restless, and it took Johann all his time to quiet them. He was pale and said, "It sounds like a wolf – but yet there are no wolves here now."

"No?" I said, questioning him. "Isn't it long since the wolves were so near the city?"

"Long, long," he answered, "in the spring and summer; but with the snow the wolves have been here not so long."

Whilst he was petting the horses and trying to quiet them, dark clouds drifted rapidly across the sky. The sunshine passed away, and a breath of cold wind seemed to drift over us. It was only a breath, however, and more of a warning than a fact, for the sun came out brightly again.

Johann looked under his lifted hand at the horizon and said, "The storm of snow, he comes before long time." Then he looked at his watch again, and, straightway holding his reins firmly – for the horses were still pawing the ground restlessly and shaking their heads – he climbed to his box as though the time had come for proceeding on our journey.

I felt a little obstinate and did not at once get into the carriage.

"Tell me," I said, "about this place where the road leads," and I pointed down.

Again he crossed himself and mumbled a prayer before he answered, "It is unholy."

"What is unholy?" I enquired.

"The village."

"Then there is a village?"

"No, no. No one lives there hundreds of years."

My curiosity was piqued, "But you said there was a village."

"There was."

"Where is it now?"

Whereupon he burst out into a long story in German and English, so mixed up that I could not quite understand exactly what he said. Roughly I gathered that long ago, hundreds of years, men had died there and been buried in their graves; but sounds were heard under the clay, and when the graves were opened, men and women were found rosy with life and their mouths red with blood. And so, in haste to save their lives (aye, and their souls! – and here he crossed himself) those who were left fled away to other places, where the living lived and the dead were dead and not – not something. He was evidently afraid to speak the last words. As he proceeded with his narration, he grew more and more excited. It seemed as if his imagination had got hold of him, and he ended in a perfect paroxysm of fear – white-faced, perspiring, trembling, and looking round him as if expecting that some dreadful presence would manifest itself there in the bright sunshine on the open plain.

Finally, in an agony of desperation, he cried, "Walpurgis nacht!" and pointed to the carriage for me to get in.

All my English blood rose at this, and standing back I said, "You are afraid, Johann – you are afraid. Go home, I shall return alone, the walk will do me good." The carriage door was open. I took from the seat my oak walking stick – which I always carry on my holiday excursions – and closed the door, pointing back to Munich, and said, "Go home,Johann – Walpurgis nacht doesn't concern Englishmen."

The horses were now more restive than ever, and Johann was trying to hold them in, while excitedly imploring me not to do anything so foolish. I pitied the poor fellow, he was so deeply in earnest; but all the same I could not help laughing. His English was quite gone now. In his anxiety he had forgotten that his only means of making me understand was to talk my language, so he jabbered away in his native German. It began to be a little tedious. After giving the direction, "Home!" I turned to go down the cross road into the valley.

With a despairing gesture,Johann turned his horses towards Munich. I leaned on my stick and looked after him. He went slowly along the road for a while, then there came over the crest of the hill a man tall and thin. I could see so much in the distance. When he drew near the horses,they began to jump and kick about, then to scream with terror. Johann could not hold them in; they bolted down the road, running away madly. I watched them out of sight, then looked for the stranger; but I found that he, too, was gone.

With a light heart I turned down the side road through the deepening valley to which Johann had objected. There was not the slightest reason,that I could see, for his objection; and I daresay I tramped for a couple of hours without thinking of time or distance and certainly without seeing a person or a house. So far as the place was concerned, it was desolation itself. But I did not notice this particularly till, on turning a bend in the road,I came upon a scattered fringe of wood; then I recognized that I had been impressed unconsciously by the desolation of the region through which I had passed.

I sat down to rest myself and began to look around. It struck me that it was considerably colder than it had been at the commencement of my walk – a sort of sighing sound seemed to be around me with, now and then, high overhead, a sort of muffled roar. Looking upwards I noticed that great thick clouds were drafting rapidly across the sky from north to south at a great height.There were signs of a coming storm in some lofty stratum of the air. I was a little chilly, and, thinking that it was the sitting still after the exercise of walking, I resumed my journey.

The ground I passed over was now much more picturesque. There were no striking objects that the eye might single out, but in all there was a charm of beauty.I took little heed of time, and it was only when the deepening twilight forced itself upon me that I began to think of how I should find my way home. The air was cold, and the drifting of clouds high overhead was more marked. They were accompanied by a sort of far away rushing sound, through which seemed to come at intervals that mysterious cry which the driver had said came from a wolf. For a while I hesitated. I had said I would see the deserted village, so on I went and presently came on a wide stretch of open country, shut in by hills all around. Their sides were covered with trees which spread down to the plain, dotting in clumps the gentler slopes and hollows which showed here and there.I followed with my eye the winding of the road and saw that it curved close to one of the densest of these clumps and was lost behind it.

As I looked there came a cold shiver in the air, and the snow began to fall. I thought of the miles and miles of bleak country I had passed, and then hurried on to seek shelter of the wood in front. Darker and darker grew the sky, and faster and heavier fell the snow, till the earth before and around me was a glistening white carpet the further edge of which was lost in misty vagueness. The road was here but crude, and when on the level its boundaries were not so marked as when it passed through the cuttings; and in a little while I found that I must have strayed from it, for I missed underfoot the hard surface, and my feet sank deeper in the grass and moss. Then the wind grew stronger and blew with ever increasing force, till I was fain to run before it. The air became icy-cold, and in spite of my exercise I began to suffer. The snow was now falling so thickly and whirling around me in such rapid eddies that I could hardly keep my eyes open. Every now and then the heavens were torn asunder by vivid lightning, and in the flashes I could see ahead of me a great mass of trees, chiefly yew and cypress all heavily coated with snow.

I was soon amongst the shelter of the trees, and there in comparative silence I could hear the rush of the wind high overhead. Presently the blackness of the storm had become merged in the darkness of the night. By-and-by the storm seemed to be passing away, it now only came in fierce puffs or blasts. At such moments the weird sound of the wolf appeared to be echoed by many similar sounds around me.

Now and again, through the black mass of drifting cloud, came a straggling ray of moonlight which lit up the expanse and showed me that I was at the edge of a dense mass of cypress and yew trees. As the snow had ceased to fall, I walked out from the shelter and began to investigate more closely. It appeared to me that, amongst so many old foundations as I had passed, there might be still standing a house in which, though in ruins, I could find some sort of shelter for a while. As I skirted the edge of the copse, I found that a low wall encircled it, and following this I presently found an opening. Here the cypresses formed an alley leading up to a square mass of some kind of building. Just as I caught sight of this, however, the drifting clouds obscured the moon, and I passed up the path in darkness. The wind must have grown colder, for I felt myself shiver as I walked; but there was hope of shelter, and I groped my way blindly on.

I stopped, for there was a sudden stillness. The storm had passed; and, perhaps in sympathy with nature's silence, my heart seemed to cease to beat. But this was only momentarily; for suddenly the moonlight broke through the clouds showing me that I was in a graveyard and that the square object before me was a great massive tomb of marble, as white as the snow that lay on and all around it. With the moonlight there came a fierce sigh of the storm which appeared to resume its course with a long, low howl, as of many dogs or wolves. I was awed and shocked, and I felt the cold perceptibly grow upon me till it seemed to grip me by the heart. Then while the flood of moonlight still fell on the marble tomb, the storm gave further evidence of renewing, as though it were returning on its track. Impelled by some sort of fascination, I approached the sepulchre to see what it was and why such a thing stood alone in such a place. I walked around it and read, over the Doric door, in German:

> *COUNTESS DOLINGEN OF GRATZ*
> *IN STYRIA*
> *SOUGHT AND FOUND DEATH*
> *1801*

On the top of the tomb, seemingly driven through the solid marble – for the structure was composed of a few vast blocks of stone – was a great iron spike or stake. On going to the back I saw, graven in great Russian letters: "The dead travel fast."

There was something so weird and uncanny about the whole thing that it gave me a turn and made me feel quite faint. I began to wish, for the first time, that I had taken Johann's advice. Here a thought struck me, which came under almost myssterious circumstances and with a terrible shock. This was Walpurgis Night!

Walpurgis Night was when, according to the belief of millions of people, the devil was abroad – when the graves were opened and the dead came forth and walked. When all evil things of earth and air and water held revel. This very place the driver had specially shunned. This was the depopulated village of centuries ago.This was where the suicide lay; and this was the place where I was alone – unmanned, shivering with cold in a shroud of snow with a wild storm gathering again upon me! It took all my philosophy, all the religion I had been taught,all my courage,not to collapse in a paroxysm of fright.

And now a perfect tornado burst upon me. The ground shook as though thousands of horses thundered across it; and this time the storm bore on its icy wings, not snow, but great hailstones which drove with such violence that they might have come from the thongs of Balearic slingers – hailstones that beat down leaf and branch and made the shelter of the cypresses of no more avail than though their stems were standing corn. At the first I had rushed to the nearest tree;but I was soon fain to leave it and seek the only spot that seemed to afford refuge, the deep Doric doorway of the marble tomb. There, crouching against the massive bronze door, I gained a certain amount of protection from the beating of the hailstones, for now they only drove against me as they ricochetted from the ground and the side of the marble.

As I leaned against the door, it moved slightly and opened inwards. The shelter of even a tomb was welcome in that pitiless tempest and I was about to enter it when there came a flash of forked lightning that lit up the whole expanse of the heavens. In the instant, as I am a living man, I saw, as my my eyes turned into the darkness of the tomb, a beautiful woman with rounded cheeks and red lips, seemingly sleeping on a bier. As the thunder broke overhead, I was grasped as by the hand of a giant and hurled out into the storm. The whole thing was so sudden that, before I could realize the shock, moral as well as physical, I found the hailstones beating me down. At the same time I had a strange, dominating feeling that I was not alone. I looked towards the tomb. Just then there came another blinding flash which seemed to strike the iron stake that surmounted the tomb and to pour through to the earth, blasting and crumbling the marble, as in a burst of flame. The dead woman rose for a moment of agony while she was lapped in the flame, and her bitter scream of pain was drowned in the thunder-crash. The last thing I heard was this mingling of dreadful sound,as again I was seized in the giant grasp and dragged away, while the hailstones beat on me and the air around seemed reverberant with the howling of wolves. The last sight that I remembered was a vague, white, moving mass,as if all the graves around me had sent out the phantoms of their sheeted dead, and that they were closing in on me through the white cloudiness of the driving hail.

Gradually there came a sort of vague beginning of consciousness, then a sense of weariness that was dreadful. For a time I remembered nothing, but slowly my senses returned. My feet seemed positively racked with pain, yet I could not move them. They seemed to be numbed. There was an icy feeling at the back of my neck and all down my spine, and my ears, like my feet, were dead yet in torment; but there was in my breast a sense of warmth which was by comparison delicious.It was as a nightmare – a physical nightmare, if one may use such an expression; for some heavy weight on my chest made it difficult for me to breathe.

This period of semilethargy seemed to remain a long time, and as it faded away I must have slept or swooned. Then came a sort of loathing, like the first stage of seasickness, and a wild desire to be free of something – I knew not what.A vast stillness enveloped me, as though all the world were asleep or dead – only broken by the low panting as of some animal close to me. I felt a warm rasping at my throat, then came a consciousness of the awful truth which chilled me to the heart and sent the blood surging up through my brain. Some great animal was lying on me and now licking my throat. I feared to stir, for some instinct of prudence bade me lie still; but the brute seemed to realize that there was now some change in me, for it raised its head. Through my eyelashes I saw above me the two great flaming eyes of a gigantic wolf. Its sharp white teeth gleamed in the gaping red mouth, and I could feel its hot breath fierce and acrid upon me.

For another spell of time I remembered no more. Then I became conscious of a low growl, followed by a yelp, renewed again and again. Then seemingly very far away, I heard a "Holloa! holloa!" as of many voices calling in unison. Cautiously I raised my head and looked in the direction whence the sound came, but the cemetery blocked my view. The wolf still continued to yelp in a strange way, and a red glare began to move round the grove of cypresses, as though following the sound. As the voices drew closer, the wolf yelped faster and louder. I feared to make either sound or motion. Nearer came the red glow over the white pall which stretched into the darkness around me. Then all at once from beyond the trees there came at a trot a troop of horsemen bearing torches. The wolf rose from my breast and made for the cemetery. I saw one of the horsemen (soldiers by their caps and their long military cloaks) raise his carbine and take aim. A companion knocked up his arm, and I heard the ball whiz over my head. He had evidently taken my body for that of the wolf. Another sighted the animal as it slunk away, and a shot followed. Then, at a gallop, the troop rode forward – some towards me, others following the wolf as it disappeared amongst the snow-clad cypresses.

As they drew nearer I tried to move but was powerless, although I could see and hear all that went on around me. Two or three of the soldiers jumped from their horses and knelt beside me. One of them raised my head and placed his hand over my heart.

"Good news, comrades!" he cried. "His heart still beats!"

Then some brandy was poured down my throat; it put vigor into me, and I was able to open my eyes fully and look around. Lights and shadows were moving among the trees, and I heard men call to one another. They drew together, uttering frightened exclamations; and the lights flashed as the others came pouring out of the cemetery pell-mell, like men possessed. When the further ones came close to us, those who were around me asked them eagerly, "Well, have you found him?"

The reply rang out hurriedly, "No! no! Come away quick-quick! This is no place to stay, and on this of all nights!"

"What was it?" was the question, asked in all manner of keys. The answer came variously and all indefinitely as though the men were moved by some common impulse to speak yet were restrained by some common fear from giving their thoughts.

"It – it – indeed!" gibbered one, whose wits had plainly given out for the moment.

"A wolf – and yet not a wolf!" another put in shudderingly.

"No use trying for him without the sacred bullet," a third remarked in a more ordinary manner.

"Serve us right for coming out on this night! Truly we have earned our thousand marks!" were the ejaculations of a fourth.

"There was blood on the broken marble," another said after a pause, "the lightning never brought that there. And for him–is he safe? Look at his throat! See comrades, the wolf has been lying on him and keeping his blood warm."

The officer looked at my throat and replied, "He is all right, the skin is not pierced. What does it all mean? We should never have found him but for the yelping of the wolf."

"What became of it?" asked the man who was holding up my head and who seemed the least panic-stricken of the party, for his hands were steady and without tremor. On his sleeve was the chevron of a petty officer.

"It went home," answered the man, whose long face was pallid and who actually shook with terror as he glanced around him fearfully. "There are graves enough there in which it may lie. Come, comrades – come quickly! Let us leave this cursed spot."

The officer raised me to a sitting posture, as he uttered a word of command; then several men placed me upon a horse.He sprang to the saddle behind me, took me in his arms, gave the word to advance; and, turning our faces away from the cypresses, we rode away in swift military order.

As yet my tongue refused its office, and I was perforce silent. I must have fallen asleep; for the next thing I remembered was finding myself standing up, supported by a soldier on each side of me. It was almost broad daylight, and to the north a red streak of sunlight was reflected like a path of blood over the waste of snow. The officer was telling the men to say nothing of what they had seen, except that they found an English stranger, guarded by a large dog.

"Dog! that was no dog," cut in the man who had exhibited such fear. "I think I know a wolf when I see one."

The young officer answered calmly, "I said a dog."

"Dog!" reiterated the other ironically.It was evident that his courage was rising with the sun; and, pointing to me, he said, "Look at his throat. Is that the work of a dog, master?"

Instinctively I raised my hand to my throat, and as I touched it I cried out in pain. The men crowded round to look, some stooping down from their saddles;and again there came the calm voice of the young officer, "A dog, as I said. If aught else were said we should only be laughed at."

I was then mounted behind a trooper, and we rode on into the suburbs of Munich. Here we came across a stray carriage into which I was lifted , and it was driven off to the Quatre Saisons – the young officer accompanying me, whilst a trooper followed with his horse, and the others rode off to their barracks.

When we arrived, Herr Delbruck rushed so quickly down the steps to meet me, that it was apparent he had been watching within. Taking me by both hands he solicitously led me in.The officer saluted me and was turning to withdraw, when I recognized his purpose and insisted that he should come to my rooms. Over a glass of wine I warmly thanked him and his brave comrades for saving me. He replied simply that he was more than glad, and that Herr Delbruck had at the first taken steps to make all the searching party pleased; at which ambiguous utterance the maitre d'hotel smiled, while the officer plead duty and withdrew.

"But Herr Delbruck," I enquired, "how and why was it that the soldiers searched for me?"

He shrugged his shoulders, as if in depreciation of his own deed, as he replied, "I was so fortunate as to obtain leave from the commander of the regiment in which I serve, to ask for volunteers."

"But how did you know I was lost?" I asked.

"The driver came hither with the remains of his carriage, which had been upset when the horses ran away."

"But surely you would not send a search party of soldiers merely on this account?"

"Oh, no!" he answered, "but even before the coachman arrived, I had this telegram from the Boyar whose guest you are," and he took from his pocket a telegram which he handed to me, and I read:

> *Bistritz. Be careful of my guest – his safety is most precious to me. Should aught happen to him, or if he be missed, spare nothing to find him and ensure his safety. He is English and therefore adventurous. There are often dangers from snow and wolves and night. Lose not a moment if you suspect harm to him. I answer your zeal with my fortune.– Dracula.*

As I held the telegram in my hand, the room seemed to whirl around me, and if the attentive maitre d'hotel had not caught me, I think I should have fallen. There was something so strange in all this, something so weird and impossible to imagine, that there grew on me a sense of my being in some way the sport of opposite forces – the mere vague idea of which seemed in a way to paralyze me. I was certainly under some form of mysterious protection. From a distant country had come, in the very nick of time, a message that took me out of the danger of the snow sleep and the jaws of the wolf.

Blessed Be the Bound

Lucy Taylor

THE BINDING takes place tomorrow at the Sisters of Solace Hospital outside Charlottesville, Virginia. From my bed, I can just see the peaks of the October hills, dappled maroon and scarlet.

If I could lift my head, I'd be able to glimpse the wing of what was once a dormitory at the University of Virginia and now serves as a Confinement Center for the most violent prisoners/ inmates, but gel compression restraints, deemed more humane by hospital staff than electro- loops, ensnare my wrists and ankles. Even if I braved the pain and wriggled free, shimmering vertical bands across the windows expose the presence of high voltage grids.

Today is Mother's last chance to see me before I am Bound to my brother.

My last hope for deliverance.

Acid rises in my throat at the bitter irony of hoping for rescue from Mother, since O'Dell and I have long suspected it was she who, in a fit of pique or spite, reported us for what the law calls fourth degree sexual deviancy. Especially galling if we're right, since we both shared unsanctioned intimacies with Mother for years before we explored activities, deviant or otherwise, with each other.

At the hearing, a venerable psychiatrist argued I was addicted to my sibling as surely as the psychonauts and ket-freaks in the floating colonies off the coast are in thrall to the black gusts of brain-burn, that having been kept homebound by Mother, I was both naive and eminently corruptible, a victim of my wicked brother's perverse desires.

"Enticed into his depravity," hissed the gerbil-faced little defense attorney while I sat meekly, head bowed, trying to convey with every breath my profound and scalding shame.

The performance failed; my carefully pantomimed remorse was judged a poor facsimile of penitence. I was the cunning, lustful one, the judge declared. My pretty brother, though condemned to the same fate as I, was merely susceptible and stupid.

Our sentence, to be Bound for life, is the penalty reserved for society's worst: murderers, traitors to the State, and second through fourth degree sex criminals.

Unlike O'Dell, who remains willfully ignorant of the details of Binding and still claims to fully expect a last minute reprieve, I've researched the procedure compulsively. I've read biographies and watched biopics of the Bound, conversed with holographic surgeons, and prior to my conviction, toured the Museum of the Bound on the Plaza in Washington D.C., where visitors must sign a waver holding the Museum blameless if they pass out, throw up, or suffer permanent trauma from viewing the exhibits.

The reality of it still stalls my mind: two bodies of the same or opposite sex, snipped and sliced and stitched together in a gruesome flesh-garment of jigsawed limbs, split bones, and sutured skin, afflicted with the vacant gaze and shuffling, stumbling gait peculiar to their maimed condition. Worst of all are the monstrous final hours of the partner who outlasts its mate, since Binding is forever, even when the so-called 'living' one is fused to a decaying, putrid corpse.

Although the physical abominations leave me reeling, still more soul-shattering is the utter forfeiture of privacy and solitude, an especially bitter hell for one whose preferred companionship has always been her own.

I reflect that the one thing not forfeited is the very act that led to this catastrophe in the first place. A jocular therapist even winkingly assured me that, since I am limber and O'Dell well-made, we will eventually learn to mate, or may even – unimaginably – decide to procreate.Nothing, after all, is forbidden to the Bound.They have paid for their crimes and are at liberty to indulge whatever indecencies or degradations they're disposed to. In more backward parts of the world, I'm told, people pay small fortunes to watch Bound couples making love. Or vaster sums to join them.

I can't imagine why anyone would wish either form of entertainment.

I remember, as a child of ten, going up the steps to the

Abbey of the Stoning with Mother and O'Dell, who was then nine.A Bound couple, one of the first to survive longer than a few weeks, was on display. Above the creature's heads, a gold plaque provided details of their crime, but I was too stunned to read anything beyond their name, which I still recall was Marcus-Angelina.

* * *

Incapable of standing, the poor off-kilter beast crouched on a specially constructed seat before the altar.From beneath its purple robes protruded two thick legs, hirsute and muscular, while the female's one remaining leg, tube-thin and flaccid, dangled at the side, an abutment of lab-grown flesh conjoining her legless hip to the male's intact one. Their three mismatched arms, two belonging to the female, one to the male, fidgeted and twitched in ceaseless, spastic agitation.

Their cloudy and dilated eyes were white and empty as eggs. I know now that the ministers had drugged it, but at the time I thought the enraptured gaze was the result of its unholy union, a kind of ghastly erotic trance.

I know better now.Poor maimed creature that it was, a waxy tear slid down the female's bloodless cheek.

"Touch it. Touch it for luck," urged Mother.

The thought of contact with that mutilated flesh revolted and appalled me, in part due to the fact that I knew those three legs extended upward to two groins, two sets of genitals, but unlike O'Dell, who looked like he might faint, I was also fascinated.

I pressed a single finger to the female's spongy thigh and watched, repulsed, as tremors rippled knee to ankle and a rash of gooseflesh spread across the skin like faded Braille upon an ashen parchment.

"The Lord has purified them," intoned Mother.She bowed, dragging O'Dell and me with her, and kissed the creature's three bare feet as was the custom among the more ostentatiously devout.

* * *

"Eugenia?"

The door revolves and a fax-bot with a smile like a surgical scar coos in a ludicrously come-hither voice, "Mama is here, Eugenia." She pronounces 'Mama' with a British accent, a ridiculous affectation that can only mean she is an elder-bot, programmed in the U.K. prior to the Euro-Sino conflict.

Swiveling toward the bed, she commands, "Deactivate restraints."

After a moment the gel clamps ungrip, allowing me to sit up and finally, unsteadily, to stand. The fax-bot, evidently programmed to feign consideration, diplomatically withdraws.

Mother minces gingerly into the room, stiff-legged as a deflowered child. Except for plumped lips dyed permanently scarlet, her face is leached of color, her eyes are kohl hollows scooped above the jutting cliffs of her implanted cheekbones.

Around the ivory column of her neck gleams a sunstone cross that glimmers softly as though lit from within; from her ears dangle pendulous pearls. Her numerous tattoos are raised and garishly colored, according to the fashion.

At the sight of her, adrenalin claws through my bloodstream and, astonishingly, tears of relief sprout copiously.

"I was afraid you wouldn't come." The admission shocks me; I hadn't understood the depth of my terror that, in my time of greatest need, I'd be abandoned by her.

But then, before I can ask for what she's brought me, she whispers gravely, "Terrible news. O'Dell bit his wrists open last night and almost bled to death. The sensors activated a warning just in time. When I saw him, he was hysterical, screaming that the Binding can't really be happening, that he can't go through with it."

"I'm glad he lived," I say in my best hypocrite's simper. "If O'Dell had died, I'd just be Bound to another criminal." Of course, once I'm dead, that's exactly what will happen to O'Dell, but I can't worry about that. Was he thinking about me with his face pressed to his own gore? Did it bother him, knowing that I'd be Bound to a stranger?

Mother's gaze darts about the room like a bottled fly. Her talon-sharp nails clamp onto my arm. For the first time in years, I tolerate her touch without recoiling.

"What we talked about, Eugenia...what you asked me to do..."

"Yes, yes, I'm ready. It's time."

She fingers the sunstone, which yields up rays of delicate, refracted light. "Sometimes people do terrible things, my darling. Sometimes love expresses itself in desperate ways."

Is this her way of saying O'Dell and I are forgiven? Or is she finally confessing that she betrayed us to the authorities?

She starts to tremble uncontrollably, a tic plucking so violently at her mouth that it drags her face askew. I guess that even she, though a vocal supporter of the idea of Binding, quails before the truth of it.

"I loved O'Dell," she says defiantly, as though someone has suggested otherwise, "but a daughter is different. A son goes out into the world and takes a bridemother. A first-born daughter, if she's virtuous, remains at home. A mother's love for her daughter – that's the unbreakable bond."

She slides her hand seductively along my forearm, gently and sensuously, as though her palm is a small boat gliding silently up a river of milky skin. "Your arms are so soft and shapely. I wonder which one they'll remove."

That breaks the spell. I seize her wrist and twist it until she cringes and cries out.

"Stop it! Give me what you brought!"

Her fingers stroke the sunstone again and I think: There! It's hidden there!, until she says, "I'm sorry, I can't do it. I can't kill you. The toxin I smuggled in for you, I gave it to O'Dell." Her voice soars recklessly and she directs her words toward the voice monitors disguised as air filter units in the wall. "He was so grateful when I put the poison on his tongue. His face was rapturous. He died thanking me."

The screams I've swallowed all my life tear past my teeth, an anguished howl that brings the fax-bot accelerating into the room so fast she bangs into the wall. A red oblivion-dot gleams wetly on her finger.

"Too noisy you," she chides, though not unkindly, and taps the dot with its cornucopia of hallucinogens directly in the center of my forehead. I have time only to gasp, "My brother –she murdered him", before the world incinerates, the drugs blitzing through synapses, resurrecting extinct galaxies and annihilating new ones inside my neo-cortex.

The fax-bot's face looms wide and globulous, an enormous amoeboid blob undulating in and out of my telescoping vision. Moles as big as barnacles, conceived for verisimilitude by some bot-designer comic, festoon her ill-made chin.

"We know she killed O'Dell," she says.

And that is all that matters.

* * *

When I wake up, I am riddled with razors, my bones a bed of nails, my lungs full of mucus and mud. At my slightest movement, unseen incisions rip and leak.

An avuncular and dour face hovers above me. I recognize the doctor, Montague Tritt, assigned to counsel O'Dell and me post-Binding.

But O'Dell is dead.

Tritt frowns and steeples his fingers, his whiskery mouth forming a mackerel-ish 'o'. "Dear me," he says.

Beside me, something thrashes feebly. It whimpers tremulously as it forms words.I must say "it", for I can't attribute to it any sex, any individuality, any name, but I can tell the stump of its left leg is Bound to my right hip and the stump of my right arm is fused to its left shoulder, each wound affixed by a few centimeters of artfully applied prosthetic meat.

"Eugenia," exults the thing that speaks like Mother, "we've been forgiven for our crime."

With my remaining arm, I tear at the graft on our mutual shoulder and hear my scream and hers scrape the upper ends of agony. Tritt thumbs an oblivion-dot against my temple. My skull brims with hissing lava that quickly cools to a gentle snowdrift of ash as I sink into the center of the dead volcano that is my core.

I pray that I can hide in here forever.

"Blessed," someone murmurs, "be the Bound."

Dead End

Kristopher Triana

WITH THE BODY securely locked in the trunk, all Jake had to do was shatter the mirrors and he would be ready to leave. It didn't matter where to. It never did. The only important thing was to keep moving.

Perpetual motion. Keep the body strong by pumping blood.

So much blood.

Some was even speckled across the high heel he now used to shatter the side mirrors of the car. Getting in, he broke the rear view in the same fashion, the cracks bursting like lightning across the reflection as he averted his gaze. He pulled his bandana from his jeans and used it to wipe the shoe of any prints before throwing it out the window. It landed in the gutter of the motel lot, swishing in the rain swill, adrift with so many cigarette butts and condom wrappers.

Old Vegas. A candy colored monument to wretchedness.

The motel was like so many on the outskirts of the city, shit-sandwiched between bail bond joints and discount wedding chapels. This was the side of Vegas they didn't advertise, far from the expensive glamour of the main strip. To Jake, that whole stretch was so soft-boiled you could sop it up with a biscuit. The true exploitive sleaze was to be found on Fremont and beyond, down where the buses stopped running. He'd drifted around here for a few months, pushing his own disciplined time limits because he'd been enjoying himself perhaps a little too much.

Don't stay in one place. Don't show a pattern. Don't allow yourself to have an M.O.

As the exhaust belched to life the car shuddered forward. The trunk gave a soft thud as the bar whore's corpse flopped about before settling. Jake wondered if when the whore had first gotten this car if she had thought *anyone* would have ever ended up in the trunk, let alone she herself. It was an uncommon stroke of luck for him that she had one at all. When he'd finished with her he'd rooted through her purse and found the keys. It had one of those beepers on it to unlock the car. He'd gone outside and hit the button and the Dodge honked, identifying itself. It made sense. From the lived-in look of the motel room it was obvious that she'd been living there. It was a foreign concept to Jake. Not living in a motel room, but living anywhere. He knew, just as surely as he knew he would kill again, that there was no such thing as home.

* * *

Jake was a misogynist, but that wasn't why he primarily murdered women. He chose them because the act of killing was so intimate and emotional. The methodical taking of a life was the one act that made him feel connected to the human race in any way. It almost felt homoerotic for him to kill a man unless it was out of blind rage, which had occurred on a few occasions in his wasted youth. He chose to kill women just as straight men would choose to sleep with women; it was an instinctual, sexual impulse as natural to him as eating or taking a piss.

Not that Jake could explain it or put it into words. The dollar-store education of a renegade orphan didn't get him much further cognitively than his bad genes and the mild brain damage he'd suffered in the womb from his mother's drug use.

The world had been cruel to Jake from the beginning.

He'd gone from the dumpster they'd found him in right into the hands of the state, allowing apathy and bureaucracy to further poison his future. He was shuffled through orphanages, never fitting in or getting along with even other abandoned children like himself. By thirteen his bad behavior and petty crimes led him to a reform school that was really nothing more than a juvenile detention hall; a sort of pre-prison.It was there that he learned to be a much better fighter and thief.

It was also where he'd learned to hate mirrors.

He'd always been uncomfortable with his own reflection because whom he felt he was never looked back at him in a mirror. His image haunted him, always looking so alien and never matching the image he felt was imposed upon the mirror. He was like a dog seeing its own reflection in a sliding glass door and barking, never seeing the image as itself. As he reached his teens the identity denial worsened, and so did the mirror image: pimples, uneven facial hair, and an awkward body struggling through growth spurts. The greasy hair never settled right, the skin always oily and inflamed, the chest birdlike and freckled. He didn't think of it as a body so much as an inescapable shell, a prison that had him bound in a manner far more debilitating than the bars of any jail.

He hated what he saw in the mirror.

But he hated what others saw in it more.

* * *

"You're looking kinda pretty there, boy," Larry had said from behind him.

Jake wore only a damp towel around his waist. He'd just finished in the shower room and was standing before the sink where the long mirror stretched from one end of the bathroom counter to the other. As usual, he had been avoiding looking into it, so he hadn't seen Larry walking up behind him.

Larry was one of the bigger bullies in juvie hall. At eighteen, he had a few years on Jake then to boot, years that packed on meanness as well as size. Jake had felt his hand on his shoulder before Larry spun him around. He'd watched Larry's nose crinkle in confusion as he looked at Jake, then at Jake's reflection, and then back again.

"How come you look so pretty in the mirror when you look so ugly in real life?" Larry had asked him.

Jake was silent. Larry got so close to him he could smell his morning cigarette breath. Fear made his legs tremble, and that just seemed to excite Larry. He'd spun Jake back around to make him face the mirror.

"Your reflection makes you look real pretty don't it?"

Larry had grabbed him by the jaw then and made him look at himself, but Jake only saw the same ugly boy who always greeted him. He couldn't see what Larry meant. But that hadn't stopped Larry from bending him over the sink.

The whole time, Larry had stared at Jake's reflection in the mirror.

* * *

He drove through the Nevada desert now, excited by what unseen curiosities might lurk within the tangerine haze beyond. Red sandstone formations were all that lined the sides of the state road now, the dilapidated ghetto of Vegas's outskirts far behind. The rocks were magnificent in color, bleeding orange and forming psychedelic swirls of lavender upon their jagged edges. On some of them Jake could see the rock art petroglyphs that an ancient race had left behind some three hundred years before Christ. While Jake didn't know or care much about history, he'd heard many whispered ghost stories during his time in Old Vegas; the tall tales of the old tribes of the valley that were said to practice ritual sacrifice so to be favored by the things that lurked in the core of the basin. Things that were said to make a man go mad at the sheer sight of them. Because of its haunted history, the locals regarded it as some sort of Bermuda Triangle where any kind of supernatural nightmare could become reality. Now the high walls of the desert told a similar story with their carved images of stick figures splitting one another in half, impaling each other, and even feeding each other to horned serpents. The engravings were ominous, titillating Jake's vicious psyche. They were images of a Hell on earth, etched into a landscape that looked as if it could be quite the happy home for Satan himself. He gnawed on his thumbnail as his blood throbbed beneath his sweaty flesh, the horrible summer heat making him and the desert boil together.

Gotta love a little Twilight Zone thrill.

But he didn't just want to explore these demonic stomping grounds. He also needed to dispose of the dead whore in the trunk. What better place than in the bowels of a devil's canyon?

He exited unto a side road and then another, winding through the plains, hoping for even further seclusion. He hadn't seen another car in a while but he wasn't careless enough to stop on a road that was adjacent to the interstate. He found a fork that had one path leading to a dead end. A rusted cattle gate blocked it off and a bullet-hole riddled road closed sign hung crookedly from one hinge. He pulled up close and got out, leaving the car running.

The dry heat was even more intense outside. He could feel himself baking in the blinding sun the moment he stepped out. It was more than just hot, it was downright blistering; a heat that bordered on otherworldly. He needed to use his bandana to open the trunk. It felt like a damn oven rack.

The comforter had held together fine, tied together using the whore's nylons. There was a bit of seepage from her head still. He'd drained her in the bathtub and had been meticulous about it, working her arms like pumps. But a few drops always remained.

No such thing as clean.

He hauled her out and let her drop upon the pot-holes with a wet thud. Upon impact the flap covering her face came loose and her lifeless eyes looked up at him, into him, through him. She wore mascara tears like graffiti. She looked even older now in the daylight. Her face bore the scars of many broken dreams and her dyed hair was matted with blood, sticking to the gash he'd made in her forehead.

"Love is a burnin' thing," he said, quoting the song that'd been playing when he'd taken her.

* * *

After a few bourbons in the casino, Jake had come with the whore back to her motel room. It had been several weeks since his last kill – a twenty-something runaway whose guard he'd lowered with fast food and cocaine. He'd felt the old itch burning inside him, the beast within howling and gargling blood. When the lust for murder flushed him it was impossible to ignore for long. Only his sensibility and desire to not return to prison kept him in control. Armed robbery had given him a long enough stint. He sure as Hell didn't want to go up on a murder rap and spend the rest of his days rotting on death row. He had to be careful, but he also had to give in. There was temptation and then there was need. The act of killing fell under the latter for Jake; it had since he'd strangled his girlfriend when he was nineteen.

In the motel room, Jake could feel the black murk of murder enveloping him as the whore began to do what she'd been paid for. It was like the same sinking feeling he'd always get in his gut when a rollercoaster dropped. It felt like that at first, and then the gooseflesh would hit him as his eyes glazed. It was almost like a meditative state. There were no voices in his head, no split personalities or any of the other horseshit he'd heard about in relation to serial killers. There was just the darkness, warm and sweet like molasses and just as thick. It was a high he'd never been able to top with drugs and booze, exhilaration far greater than sex, beyond religious and beyond transcendence.

He'd heard a weird word once that he felt summed it up right.

Euphoria.

That was the essence of creating death.

When he'd finished getting his money's worth out of the whore he'd slipped into his jeans and gone to the bathroom to freshen up. He could feel the hard bulk of the folded knife in his front pocket, nudging him more seductively than the whore's breasts when they'd pressed against his bare back. She had come up behind him. Her lips grazed his ear in a soft nibble.

"Fantastic, baby," she'd said.

"Yeah, right."

He hated when women played up how great the sex was, lying to him and every other man they met. *They're all whores,* he often told himself, *except the ones who say they aren't; they're lying whores.*

"Is there anything else I can do for you, sugar?" she'd asked.

"No. I'm broke now."

"Well, maybe after pay day then. Want me to pencil you in for sometime next week?"

"You won't have time."

"I can make time for you, baby."

She'd run her nails across his scalp and through his thinning hair.

That's when she'd caught his reflection in the mirror.

He had known then what was coming next. It had happened so many times before. Her head had cocked to one side, revealing her puzzlement. She'd peered closer into the stained mirror, looking at Jake's image.

"I must have had too much to drink," she said. "You look so different in the mirror."

He was glad she'd left the old country station going on the radio at such a high volume. It would drown out some of the noise. *I fell into a burning ring of fire, I went down, down, down, and the flames went higher.*

"You look pretty," she said and snorted a laugh, "why you almost look like a..."

Her words fell into a gasp as he'd forced her skull into the mirror. It exploded all about them as her head cracked. The sink became an instant blossom of blood. She had still been conscious as he threw her into the bathtub. He'd planned to use the knife, but a large sliver from the mirror felt right as he picked it up. She'd begun to stand on her wobbly legs, hyperventilating in her sudden thrall of fear as she reached out blindly, her own blood obscuring her vision.More of her blood misted the air as he'd plunged the shard into her for the first time, and then again and again in movements just as fluid.

He lived for this.

The frantic look in their eyes when they grasped what was happening, and the even more frantic look when they knew it would soon be over along with everything else they had ever experienced. They had eaten their last bite, had their last screw, spoken to their loved ones for the final time, all without knowing it. Animal-like, they would shudder and writhe against his embrace as he ravaged their torsos with his weapon. Anything that could enter and exit would do. He had evolved from strangulation, to rage killing, to sickly sensuous stabbing. He thought of it as sensuous not because of the penetrating nature of the stab. but because he knew he would be their last goodbye, and in that essence he claimed ownership. It was post-mortem husbandry to Jake, and each fresh kill left a notch on his heart like on a gunman's revolver.

The whore had slammed backward, breaking a tile. Her eyes had dilated with the twist of the shard in her stomach, and that old acidic stench hit Jake's nostrils making him bray like a horse. He'd let his jaw give in to his trembles, making his teeth chatter closer and closer to her as he inhaled her final breaths, savoring them.

They were always so beautiful in the end. They were open to him, without judgment of him. They were free of anxiety and self-consciousness, limp in their expired carcasses.

The dead never treated you like a creep for looking when they'd been taunting you with high heels and lipstick to begin with.

The dead never talked back,

The dead never said no.

* * *

With the whore's body tossed into a gorge of forgotten rock, Jake lit up a cigarette in a small toast and got back into her car. It was mid day now, the sun was merciless, and the a/c unit only wheezed out a little whiff. It was about as helpful as someone fanning an ice cream cone at him.

He'd thought he'd taken the fork right back, but he must have made a wrong turn somewhere. Perhaps he was getting snow-blind in the middle of all that red dust. The desert seemed to heave in the haze, the invisible heat lines distorting the alien world around him. He was having trouble finding his way back to the main road. The one he was on seemed endless but he pressed on, delving deeper into the canyon's heart.

He continued to hum Cash's *Ring of Fire*. It had been stuck in his head to the point of annoyance.

A good hour passed before he saw another sign of life.

There'd been nary a vulture in the sky or a lizard baking on the asphalt when the hitchhiker appeared.He hadn't even seen a road sign for the last thirty miles, just endless, unrelenting rock and sand. At first he mistook her for a cactus, the only green in this god-forsaken badland. But the swivel in her hips gave her away.

Well look what we have here.

She may as well have been a mirage out there in the haze. She was a busty brunette in a wife beater and a pair of tight jean shorts. A pair of cowboy boots completed her outfit. She had no backpack or water bottle. She didn't even have a purse.

She must be out of her mind. He laughed at the sight of her. *Maybe someone got sick of her and threw her out of the car.* Just passing her by and leaving her alone out there would be enough to kill her. It was an interesting death sentence, but not one that satisfied him the way a personal tango of violence would.

She turned around to wave him down and he slowed. There wasn't a nearby rock that an accomplice could be hiding behind and if she had a gun on her he didn't know where she could possibly be hiding it, except in one of those boots. Being that he had just come from Vegas, he was still in a gambling mood. He pulled up next to her and got a better ogling. Sweat had made her clothes cling to her and her nipples pushed through her top like she was in a dirty magazine. She leaned down to greet him.

"Thanks for stopping," she said.

She had smooth features and smoother skin that was flushed in the cheeks. Her good looks were only slightly spoiled by the crazed and frantic look in her eyes.Even her eyelids twitched as if struggling to contain them. She was like a centerfold with a Manson family stare.

"Get in good lookin'," Jake said, and she did.

He knew the vinyl of the seat must have felt like lava, but it didn't seem to bother those long, tan legs of hers. She closed the door and they took off.

"What's a pretty thing like you doing all alone out here?" he asked.

Her stare was locked on the road ahead even as she replied.

"Car broke down."

He nodded and there was an awkward silence.

"Where you headed?" he asked, not caring.

"Just had to get out of Vegas, I guess."

He looked at her face more closely now, sizing her up. Her left eye had a hint of a bruise and he wondered if she was running from an abusive boyfriend. He'd been so focused on her body before that he hadn't looked at her face as much. On top of being beautiful, there was something familiar about her. Something he couldn't place. But she wasn't much for conversation, even though she seemed like she had something to get off her chest. She was twitchy and seemed anxious, squirming slightly in her seat. She picked at her cuticles while still staring out at the endless desert.

"I'm headed west," he said. "Following the sun."

He was trying to joke based on how hot it was outside, but she didn't seem amused. Instead she seemed deep in crazed contemplation, as if she was struggling for words that just wouldn't come.

"What is it?" he finally asked. "What's going on?"

She looked at him now. Her eyes were not only frantic, he saw, but bloodshot and dilated.

Probably stoned out of her mind. Probably came out here to trip out on the colors of the rocks.

"I'm okay," she said. "I'm just not sure what to say to you."

She turned her head away again and began to make little noises under her breath. At first he thought she was sighing. But as she continued, he realized she was humming a song.

She was humming *Ring of Fire.*

Something cold moved inside of him despite the heat.

"How about a little music?" he asked, trying to shake off the creeps.

He flicked on the radio, half expecting dead air. He didn't expect to hear screaming and the sounds of breaking glass. He wondered if it was some sort of radio play like *War of the Worlds*, but then he recognized the bar whore's whimpers from the night before, the soft cries of a woman in the throes of dying. He switched the station in a sudden panic and the next one had similar sounds. These screams were of the runaway he'd slain after they shared a night of cocaine and rough sex. Her recognized her repeated cries of "*no*". He switched the dial once more and heard another woman, gasping and gagging. It was the girlfriend he'd choked to death all those years ago.

He turned the radio off and looked at the hitchhiker. Her eyes were crazed but they had been that way since he'd picked her up. She seemed unfazed. She was still humming Johnny Cash.

Had she even heard any of that?

He wondered if he was cracking up, starting to hear voices like all those other serial killers he'd read about. He shook his head as if to get the memory of the noise out of his skull. He hoped it was just the heat fucking with him. But if he was going nuts he wasn't alone. He noticed the hitchhiker wasn't just picking at her nails. Now she was peeling one off. Blood had pooled around the rim of the nail as she picked it, making a clicking percussion for her humming. He watched her tug with each flick of the nail, seeing the connecting flesh begin to shred.

I'll be doing this pretty mess a favor.

He didn't want to admit that he was lost, but when the check engine light popped on he began to worry. He didn't want to be one hundred miles from the nearest gas station with nothing but this sexy voodoo zombie for help.He figured the car was just overheating, but that didn't improve his situation. He was getting frustrated; with the car, his own mind, the hitchhiker's odd behavior, and the whole goddamned desert that just stretched out before him in a horrible infinity.

"Do you know how to get back to the highway from here?" he asked her.

"There's only one way out."

He waited for her to go on but she went all crazy mute again.

"Well," he asked, losing patience, "how the Hell do I get out?"

"That's what I've been having trouble telling you. I'm not sure what to say. I want you to take it right."

He didn't understand but tried to act as if he did.

"I'll take it right," he told her.

"You didn't last time."

"What?" he asked. He wasn't just losing his patience now. He was losing his temper. "Look, you psycho bitch, do you know the way out or don't you?"

Her mad eyes left the desert and fell upon him.

"The only way out," she said, "is to not kill me."

Jake spun the wheel and rode the brake, sending the car hurtling off the road and into the plains. He was overcome with fury and paranoia, and he vented by riding deeper into the desert, pumping the gas again, shaking the car about to rattle his passenger. He sneered with sadism as her body thrashed about the interior, knocking into the dash and back. He then slammed on the brakes and the hitchhiker went face first into the dashboard. Her nose exploded in a burst of dark blood, broken in an instant.

He put the car in park and got out. He reached in and dragged her out too.

"Who the fuck are you?" he demanded.

He threw her against the car and hit her in the stomach. She flopped about like a wet doll.

"You'll never believe me," she said, spitting blood.

He put his hands in her armpits and threw her up on the hood. He could actually hear her exposed flesh sizzle like an egg in a skillet when she touched it.He pushed her all the way down and realized their crotches were grinding together.It excited him and she must have felt it.

"Do it if you want," she said, "just don't kill me. Otherwise we'll never get out of this Hell."

He drew the pocketknife from his jeans and flicked it open.

"You stupid son of a bitch," she hissed.

He saw that her eyes had dilated further somehow, the blackness taking up more space than the whites. She bore her bloodied teeth like a mad beast, rage flushing her face.

"You moron!" she screamed, "it will never end because of you!"

She lunged at him, punching him in the eye before he got the knife in her. Even then she kicked and bucked, furious and surprisingly strong. Her madness seemed to give her the strength of a man. He snatched her by the throat and held her up, silhouetting her against the white sun as he slid the blade in and out of her in quick, hot thrusts.Jets of red splashed across his cheeks in little gore geysers. He could feel her shudder into dying. He could smell the gutting and taste the kill sweat bubbling on his upper lip. But there was no euphoria in it, hardly even a thrill. It felt filthy to him somehow, off kilter and unnatural, unlike all of the others. It was suddenly alien and repulsive, something about it feeling like a form of incest.

He let her bleed out.

Disgusted, he pushed her limp body off of him and let it fall into the sand.

The car quaked as it stalled out. In his rage he'd just left it running and now it had finally farted out one last puff of exhaust before croaking.He turned to it grimacing.

Ah, man, I am screwed.

He took his bandana out of his pocket and wiped off his knife. He held it in the light to make sure he'd gotten all of the blood off and he caught a glimpse of himself reflected in the blade.

Only it wasn't him.

He peered closer, finally seeing what so many others had seen in his mirror image.

He had smooth features and smoother skin that was flushed in the cheeks from where the blood had sprayed. His good looks were only slightly spoiled by the crazed and frantic look in his eyes, one of which had a small bruise from where she'd hit him. His lips were fuller and his hair wasn't just longer, *it was still growing.*

He gasped and dropped the blade, turning to his bigger reflection in the windshield of the car. Breasts and curves greeted him with effeminate menace. For a moment he'd been so focused on his body that he hadn't looked at his face as much. On top of being beautiful, his new face was all too familiar. He could place it now.

He stumbled backward in crazed shock and stumbled over the hitchhiker's body.

It was now his own.

His old male face stared up at him, into him, through him.

* * *

The road was what he stuck to, having no other destination.

His clothes were lighter now but the desert heat was wicked. That was one of the reasons he was sweating rain barrels. The other reason was the terror that boiled in his veins, for he was throttled now in the unrelenting stranglehold of insanity.

He walked on, trying not to look up at the engravings in the nearby rocks. The petroglyphs were no longer just morbid depictions of ancient bloodshed. They were fresher now, updated. Each of his own murders was depicted in stunning detail, the gruesome slayings illustrated with macabre artistry upon the crimson walls of the devil's canyon. He avoided them as if they were mirrors and waited for the stolen Dodge to appear on the horizon. When it did, he waved it down, wondering how he was going to approach things from this end.

The car slowed to a stop and he leaned down to see the driver, knowing who it would be, wishing there was some other way out.

"Get in good lookin'," his old self said, and she did.

Justified

DJ Tyrer

I AM WRITING THIS to explain why I did what I did, to justify my killing of my lover and former school friend, to put down my reasons for what I did. I will be dead soon. I am certain that the autopsies of the bodies will confirm my suspicions, justifying my killing of her, even if the authorities assume that I was insane, as doubtless they will, unable to accept the veracity of what I have discovered; or, they will concoct a halfway-plausible narrative of deceit to satisfy their need to reject the horrific truths gnawing at the fringes of reason.

Mary came into my life just over a year ago, contacting me online. I hadn't seen her in over a decade and, the last time I had seen her, she had been a he; Martin. Martin and I had been at school together and quite good friends. Not best friends, but we had shared interests in philosophy, psychology and the occult. We had gone our separate ways when University beckoned and lost contact. The last I heard of him, a mutual friend said he had dropped out and joined some cult or commune; I hadn't been too surprised at that news. It was a shock when he got back in touch and told me about the sex change. I suppose, looking back, there were clues, but not so as it had seemed a likely outcome. Still, it was no big deal.

We messaged one another for a few weeks and it was clear that Mary had retained Martin's fascination with the occult. Of course, that should have been a warning flag; I had recently purchased the only privately-owned copy of the Krypticon of Silander; with hindsight, it is clear that Mary only wanted to get her hands upon it, but I didn't see that then; she was very careful in drip-feeding hints as to her interest, neither too keen nor too slow, so as to arouse my suspicion. Instead, she aroused me in an entirely different manner.

We had out past connection, of course, but Mary was also almost the perfect woman to me: a pretty, fine-boned brunette with a pale complexion and lovely blue-grey eyes. In fact, I was pleasantly surprised at just how beautiful she was. Too often, none but the earliest transitions get such a perfectly-feminine outcome; my assumption was that she must have spent a fortune on cosmetic surgery to get things so perfect. As I remembered him, Martin had not been so delicate, even if a little fey; the transformation seemed almost miraculous. Another red flag I never spotted.

Naturally, doubtless as she planned, I fell in love with Mary. Her looks, personality and interests all served to entice me in. Our reborn friendship blossomed as we messaged and texted all the more often, began to phone and video call, until we finally agreed to meet in person, arranging a lunch date. By this point, she must have known that she had hooked me.

There was no talk, then, of the occult and musty old tomes, just casual conversation over sautéed chicken breasts and white wine in an upmarket bistro-pub near my office, culminating in our agreeing to see one another again. Not even a kiss; she knew just how to reel me in.

After that, we began to date regularly; lunches, dinners, nightclubs, theatres, exhibitions, all the usual things a couple might enjoy. Few mentions of our past preoccupations, a single philosophy lecture, no more. Naturally, she did not wish to tip her hand until she had guaranteed that I would give her what she wanted. Act too eagerly and I might become suspicious about her reasons for renewing contact after such a long time and in such unusual circumstances.

She did not mention the Krypticon of Silander until I finally could no longer holdout against her charms and asked, somewhat shyly, if she would come home with me; in fact, she never did mention it, I did. Doubtless, this was what Mary had planned all along, or something like it. Like any would-be paramour, I needed to impress the object of my desire and, given the subtle nudging to recall past interests, what better way than to display my rarity to her?

"Look at this," I said to her, taking her into my library, where the medieval manuscript, illuminated in Bari a millennium ago from a Greek original rescued from Muslim hands, sat in a climatically-controlled glass case.

"Can I take it out?" she had asked, clearly fascinated.

I laughed at the suggestion. The pages were so old and fragile that handling them was asking for trouble. However, I had a reply: "But, I do have a digital copy, if you would like to see it?"

She did. I retrieved a tablet from a shelf beneath the case and switched it on. I had had every page of the manuscript scanned to catalogue the beautiful illuminated volume. I passed the tablet to her and allowed her to examine several of the pages. However, I intended the night to be something other than a book club, so soon asked her to put the tablet down. Mary did so with barely the slightest hint of irritation and I promised her that she would soon have the chance to view the volume in detail.

We made love for the first time that night, with a frantic urgency as if we truly had waited all our lives for this moment. Had I paused to savour our passion, I might have noticed what was to become apparent later. But, I did not; I was enjoying myself too much at the time. I suppose it may be considered unmanly to admit it, but it wounds me, now, to realise that Mary was just using me; using sex to get what she wanted from me. It surprises me that the realisation hurts so much, given all that I have learnt since; there are worse things than the realisation that sex was being dangled as a lure, not offered out of any genuine feeling. Yet, it is that sense of betrayal that hurts the most.

That night, I awoke to discover Mary cradled serenely in my arms. Gently, I stroked her hair. Never when I had known Martin would I ever have imagined us lying together like this, yet, at that moment, it seemed so right, as if it were meant to be. Lying there, Mary betrayed no hint of the horrors that she concealed in her soul. At that moment, I could never have imagined any of what was to follow, what was to bring me to this place of horrendous doom when I must, must, cast my life aside in order, in some perverse paradox, to save it.

That moment of perfection ended with a sudden, yet slight, movement of Mary, the barest twitch as she slept, and the murmur of a word, a sound that was like "shasta" or "saster". The word – somehow, I knew it was a word, if perhaps only half formed, not the mere sound of her breath – niggled at my memory, unpleasant, if too nebulous to place. In the end, I assumed she must be dreaming of Mount Shasta, axis mundi of the New Age, and set the thought aside, even if I wasn't entirely pleased with that deduction; it was only later that I placed the word, realised what it was she was invoking in her sleep. If only I had realised sooner... instead, I drifted back off to sleep, still cradling Mary in my arms. It seems like a bad joke to recall it, now.

When I next awoke, the early light of a new day was filtering in through the curtains. Mary stirred as I did, waking in my arms. She tilted her head to gaze into my eyes with a look that I took to be love, as her words to me proclaimed. I responded in kind and kissed her forehead. How could I be such a fool?

As we lay there in the still of the morning, Mary talked to me of our childhood together. It was peculiar, lying there in the embrace of a gorgeous woman discussing our boyhood together. Naturally, she spoke of our shared interests, adolescent speculations, and, at last, turned the conversation round to the Krypticon. I could not help but crow over my coup in gaining possession of the volume. Who wouldn't? It was the crowning glory of my collection. If it would further impress my lover, well, who wouldn't take advantage?

It is a rarity, little studied by even the most erudite of scholars, seldom referenced in other works, and obscure to those who did read it, the Greek of Silander being a rather obtuse dialect, and the wording enigmatic and strange. I had once gained access to a copy of the infamous Necronomicon of the mad Arab, but even that's strange couplets were as nothing compared to the ramblings of the mysterious Greek philosopher who had penned this most marvellous of tomes. I was happy to expound upon all I had learnt of it. There can be little doubt that she was humouring me as she smiled and nodded and gasped as I talked; Mary already knew what the Krypticon contained, that was why she sought it.

We continued to see one another, our relationship crystallising into one publicly acknowledged. That did, of course, lead to the awkward question of whether to acknowledge our past. On her part, there was no problem as Mary told me that she was estranged from her family. ("They refused to accept my transition," she told me. I have no idea if Martin's family know of Mary or not.) Most of my friends and business acquaintances had not known me back when Mary had been Martin, so they could safely be kept in the dark; the remainder were of little importance. It was my family that posed the problem. How do you tell your parents that the woman you are sleeping with was born a boy and that they met him when you were at school? Could they accept it? Some maybe, but mine were very traditional; they found my hobby of collecting mouldy old texts of dubious provenance embarrassing enough without my adding such a transgression to the list. "What will people think?" was their constant refrain. I wanted to tell them that 'people' could go fuck themselves, but I dared not. It seemed as if silence must be our watchword; not that it matters any more – they will likely read this or hear of it, and decide that their son was a dangerous lunatic. Is that better or worse than a transsexual lover? "What will people think?" What, indeed!

Such issues side, our relationship was excellent, with amazing sex and plenty of it. I couldn't get enough of Mary and she couldn't get enough of me – or, what I could do for her. In-between bouts of lovemaking, I allowed her access to my scans of the Krypticon and she always seemed most passionate, invigorated, in her attentions after examining it; I, in turn, frequently found myself feeling drained after our most vigorous sessions; I doubt my exhaustion was due merely to the exertions of our energetic sex life.

But, even as I was beginning to entertain thoughts of proposing to her, asking her to become my wife, I was beginning to have doubts about Mary. I was beginning to wonder if she really had been Martin after all.

It is difficult to explain; I suppose it was the cumulation of a myriad of minor doubts, each so negligible, so insignificant, as to be unnoticeable on its own, but building up to an inescapable, if unbelievable, conclusion in the same manner as every grain of sand, each almost too small to see, makes up a vast desert. I was beginning to believe that Mary was an impostor.

It made no sense. Mary knew everything about my friendship with Martin, even those little details it seemed so unlikely for an impostor to learn. Still, such an imposture would not be impossible; had Mary been, perhaps, a girlfriend of Martin's or a stalker of his, it might have been possible to wheedle the information our of him or read it in a diary. But, there were certain mannerisms, little tics, barely noticeable yet integral to my memory of Martin, that she possessed; quirks of thought, turns of phrase. No matter how carefully observed, it seemed impossible that she could not only have memorised every little tic, but managed to deploy them, naturally, unconsciously, even in the frantic heights of our lovemaking. There is not way that an actor could be that good.

Yet, I found it impossible to believe that she could really be Martin: she seemed far too perfect a woman. I admit that I have had little experience of transsexuals, and I know that modern medical procedures can achieve miracles of transformation in the right circumstances, but what I do know is women and Mary just seemed too perfect a woman to have once been a man. As I grew to know her body intimately, it seemed impossible that she was anything but a born woman; I even noticed a monthly pattern to the periods in which she was not amenable for sex. And, looking at old photos of Martin, it seemed our relative heights and certain features didn't tally with the woman who so often shared my bed. Had I not had such evidence of her identity as my old school friend, I would have had no doubt that she truly was a woman all her life.

Of course, no matter how great my doubts at that point, I just couldn't believe the conclusion to which my reasoning had led me; probably lust played its part in blinding me to my doubts for so long, for I wanted nothing more than to have her; Mary had successfully ensnared me, and it was a miracle that I ever escaped her clutches. I rationalised my doubts as evidence of just how successful her transition had been and how dedicated she was to truly becoming a woman, not merely playacting at it, but fully embracing her true nature. I suppose, in a sense, that my rationalisation was correct.

Had our relationship been a genuine one, that is most likely where such concerns would have ended, but it was the Krypticon that Mary wanted, not me, and it was Silander's book that was to prove her undoing.

No matter how much time she spent in my company – and a significant amount of our time together was spent in bed – Mary continued to live in her own apartment, to which she never invited me, always visiting me, which meant that her opportunities for reading the book were limited and frequently supervised by me, limiting her progress in deciphering its contents; already a slow labour as her Greek was poor.

"Oh, honestly," she would say, "it isn't as if I am handling the real thing; you needn't babysit me..."

Eventually, I submitted to her wheedling pleas and agreed that she could take the tablet home with her and examine the scans at her leisure. She was delighted and rewarded me handsomely, as was her way.

I shouldn't have been surprised, yet was, and emotionally devastated, too, that she ceased all contact with me the moment that she left with the tablet. At first, she responded to my calls and texts by telling me that she was ill; at first, I believed her. But, as I grew more doubtful, she just ceased to respond at all, leaving me desperately wondering what I might have said or done to drive her away until, finally, my earlier doubts resurfaced and I was struck by the very real possibility that I had been set up, that the entirety of our romance had been nothing more than a ploy to gain access to the Krypticon.

Except, that made no sense. The Krypticon was worth a fortune, it was true, but, whilst the scans of its pages were not publicly available, they had little value in comparison. Yes, a collector would have paid good money for what was on the tablet, but they would have paid far more for the tome itself. If Mary had been duping me all along, why take the tablet when she might have taken advantage of me to steal the real book – hell, it was even plausible to imagine that she might have been able to seduce me into gifting it to her, allowing her to vanish with it. Then, there was the way in which she had shown such an interest in it. Thinking back to it, her approach to the Krypticon had been almost reverent. This was no theft for a collector, of that I was certain; Mary had wanted the volume for herself – not as a collectible, a relic of the past, but as a source of knowledge. Martin had always taken the occult more seriously than me; whatever Mary's connection with him, it seemed that that was a trait which they shared.

I wasn't sure how to proceed, although I knew that I didn't want to involve the police, nor any others, such as private detectives. Although I told myself that I wanted to protect Mary, that escalating the issue would only harm her, my real reason for wanting to keep things between us private was a fear of being made to look the fool. "What would people say?" A great deal if I was exposed as the victim of sexual enticement by a transwoman, real or ersatz. People would find it a real joke and I had my pride. Not that any of that matters, now.

So, I resolved to retrieve the volume myself. Although I had never been into Mary's apartment, I knew where it was, having seen her to her door and picked her up from there several times during our time together. Watching the place, I confirmed that she had not left; clearly she imagined me fooled by her charms or, perhaps, she just didn't believe I would act against her to recover the tablet (I suppose I could easily have written it off, but I was offended at being used). Whatever the case, I knew that she had not left and laid my plans to retrieve my property, waiting until she went out before bribing the concierge to allow me access to her home under the pretence of arranging a romantic surprise for her at which I would 'pop the question', taking with me flowers, chocolates and balloons as if that really were my purpose.

Once inside, I dumped the items I had carried in with me on the floor by the door and began to search methodically. I had no idea which room lay behind which door and, so, had to open each in turn, even when doing so disappointingly and time-wastingly revealed a cupboard of her bathroom. It was in that latter that I found evidence that convinced me that, no matter what the indications to the contrary, Mary was not Martin: tossed casually into a bin was a used sanitary towel. I had once seen an episode of a crime drama in which a transwoman faked her period to fool her fiancée that she was a born woman, but I could see no scenario in which Mary, if she had been Martin, would want to give that impression; after all, she had identified herself as him right from the moment she contacted me and had made little effort to hide her alleged status from the world, and she had never invited me in nor had I seen any signs of her having other visitors to her home, rendering any fakery utterly pointless. Of course, the confirmation of my suspicions raised a whole new series of questions about her method and motivation, but I pushed these aside in favour of concentrating on the task in hand. I had to work fast: my observations indicated she would be gone no more than an hour, probably less.

There was no sign of the tablet and I was running out of time; maybe she had hidden it, perhaps she had taken it with her, I had no clue. I knew I was going to have to abandon my attempt – and that raised the question of the stuff I had brought with me; take it or leave it? I decided to leave it, scribbling a quick note in the oversized novelty card telling her just how much I missed her, hoping Mary might be prompted to resume contact, leaving it on her desk. It was then that I noticed a swipecard in a desk tidy, marked with the name of a storage company. It seemed unlikely that the tablet was there – she would have had less access than at mine – but, I couldn't help but wonder what she had stored there, whether it might offer me some clue to her true identity, just what her plot was.

I took the swipecard and left.

About an hour later, she phoned me, complaining: "You were in my apartment!"

I told her I had intended it to be romantic and hung-up as she began to rant about boundaries; I had arrived at my destination.

The card let me through the outer door of the storage depot and that presented me with a quandary: the card lacked a door number. That left me trying each door in turn and thanking my lucky stars that the starkly-lit place was empty at that time of night. Luckily, it was eighth try successful and I had it, the light on the door lock blinking from red to green.

I rolled the door-shutter up to reveal an almost empty storage space. I didn't see my tablet, but hadn't expected to. However, there was a large chest freezer up against the far wall. I approached it with an unpleasant feeling in my stomach, half-expecting what I might find within.

I found it. A body. Martin's body.

Although I hadn't seen him in years, I recognised Martin immediately; I had studied his picture enough times when comparing his face to Mary's. It was a hideous sight: frozen stiff and rimed with frost, his head lolled at an unpleasant angle suggestive of a broken neck and the face was wide-eyed with horror. Even having expected to find his corpse, I was revolted and had to look away. Perhaps what I found most horrific, even more than the hideous, shocked look in the eyes, was the way in which the corpse had been mutilated, brutally and with obvious loathing. The shirt had been pulled open and a livid symbol carved in the pallid flesh, something like a three-legged swastika. But, worse than that, his trousers had been opened and his penis cut off. No, not cut, hacked away. When you see the corpse, you will know what I mean. Mary had castrated Martin with an unconstrained loathing for the man. Then, she had impersonated him. I imagined she had tortured information out of him. I had no idea then what was going on in her mind, but she was clearly crazy!

I'm not entirely certain what happened next. I had to look away, too disgusted by what the freezer contained. I think every man must understand the feelings that churned inside me as I looked down upon Martin's mutilated corpse. I think I shut the place up before stumbling outside. I remember brief flashes as I drove back to Mary's apartment; it is a miracle I wasn't stopped for speeding. If I had been, things would have been very different: I wouldn't be planning to kill myself and I surely would've been damned...

Somehow, I reached her apartment block and got inside – I don't recall if she buzzed me in, if I somehow seemed rational enough to convince the concierge, or just smashed my way in. The next thing I clearly remember is hammering on her door, shouting. For some reason, she chose to open the door, perhaps thinking I was upset over her behaviour, perhaps hoping to reason with me, maybe just attempting to avoid 'a scene'; I barged in past her.

I heard the door slam behind me and she chased after me as I stormed into her lounge and tossed the keycard onto her desk.

"You lost something," I spat, turning to confront her.

Mary had been shrieking something about me overstepping the bounds, but the sight of the keycard silenced her.

"I don't know who you are – but, I know that you killed Martin."

To my surprise, Mary didn't seem concerned. There was a wry sort of smile on her lips that was uniquely Martin. I shivered – whether from the smile or the realisation that she would surely kill me as she had killed my old friend, I'm not sure. Had he been alive when she sliced it off and carved that symbol into his chest? I didn't want to contemplate it.

Someone once wrote that knowing that you will shortly die helps concentrate the mind; I think that may be true. As horrible as it all was, something clicked into place in the back of my mind.

The symbol that had been so brutally engraved into Martin's flesh appeared in the text of the Krypticon. It was the Kitrino Simvolo, the Yellow Symbol or Pale Sign, the emblem of a nebulous, chthonic deity, Khasteer or, maybe, Hasteer; to someone like Mary, whose Greek was atrocious, it might be mispronounced as if it were 'Xastur'; Zaster or similar – the word she had mumbled in her sleep. A deity whose name was close to 'khaos' in the Greek. I recalled that Silander wrote of this Khasteer as a tripartite God, a trinity similar to that of the Christian deity: Father, Mother and Son; or, King, Queen and Heir. A God that could shift gender with ease and whose feminine form was described, in one passage, as a 'wild Lamia, feasting upon the sceptre of man, devouring her mate.' Mary had clearly adopted 'Xastur' as her own feminist deity, sacrificing my schoolfriend to Her.

I confronted her with my insight.

"Oh, so, I had the pronunciation wrong?" was her immediate reaction to my accusation: no denial, no attempt to justify herself. "Still, it is with the heart and soul that we glorify God, not our voice." There was a certain irony that her error had made me much slower in putting together the clues.

I think I must have uttered some affronted response as she chuckled, then said, "I think you misunderstand..."

"What? That you're a psycho-bitch? You killed Martin!"

If only it had been that simple. "Well, bodily, perhaps," she smirked. "Oh, don't worry, I won't kill you... well, not your body..."

"What are you gibbering about?"

"I am Martin. Well, this body is the vessel for my soul and my soul is his. Just as yours will be. I want the Krypticon and this will guarantee your silence."

"I don't understand..."

"Oh, I think you do," she told me, "I can see it in your eyes...." She was right. She was Martin, in mind and soul. I understood the truth, even if I didn't understand how or why.

She explained – if talk of magic and demons can be called an explanation. Somehow, she had translated her – his – mind into the body of a woman he had seduced especially for the task, imprisoning her mind in the body that had been his, murdering her whilst she was too shocked and confused to react. So, what she had told me, of a sex change, was true in a bizarre sense.

"It is disorientating," she said.

I understood, now, that she planned to do the same thing to me – slip her soul from the vessel that currently held it into my body and send mine into hers. With a horrific sense of irony, I saw how she would excuse her murder of me in her guise – I had discovered that Mary was a sadistic murderer – she, as me, would kill the 'psycho-bitch' in 'self-defence' and the killing would be vindicated. Perfect.

But, there was one thing that didn't ring true. After she had killed the body that had, once, hosted her mind, the one in which Martin's essence had been born, why mutilate it as she had; and why masquerade as Martin?

"Oh, I always wanted to be a woman. The choice of this body was quite deliberate, I assure you. So much more convenient, and far less painful, than surgery and trying to pass."

"But, then, why take my body?" I was slowly moving closer to her as we spoke.

"Convenience. As much as I have enjoyed sleeping with you, I have no particular desire to own your body. Once I have made use of you, I will find another woman whose body to seize and live my life in comfort; you will commit suicide or die in a 'tragic accident'..."

"No respect..." I muttered, a grim amusement insinuating its way into me as I, literally, stared death in the face.

She opened her mouth to say something caustic and I swung my fist. Her jaw shattered and she fell to the floor, eyes wide with surprise, her lower face a bloody, pulpy mess. I turned away and found a statuette of some squat, toad-like being; I drove the heavy object down onto her head, killing her.

Of course, my hope was that I could use her own plan to justify my killing of her: a misandrist killer slain by her intended victim; I could live with the embarrassment of our relationship. But then the words of Silander came back to me: "Even the dead may act from beyond the grave." I began to search through her shelves to see what I could discover about her spell; I was unsuccessful, but still had my fears confirmed as I felt something reminiscent of an oil slick glide across the surface of my mind. If I am right, and I know in my heart I am, the mind that is Martin is seeking a way into my body and it is only a matter of time before my defences fail and Martin seizes my body and casts my soul out into that corpse.

So, I sit here at her desk, mere feet from her bloodied body, writing this to explain why I did what I did, and to justify my killing of my lover and former school friend. It will prove to be true, even if the metaphysical aspects are doubted, and I will be vindicated in killing her.

Even as I write this, I feel my hand twitch outside of my control and my sense of presence dim. If I do not act now, I will be dead and she will be free to kill again in the name of her misandrist deity. I cannot allow that to happen. I would rather die first. And, I will...

Afterward

Edith Wharton

I

"**OH, THERE IS** one, of course, but you'll never know it."

The assertion, laughingly flung out six months earlier in a bright June garden, came back to Mary Boyne with a sharp perception of its latent significance as she stood, in the December dusk, waiting for the lamps to be brought into the library.

The words had been spoken by their friend Alida Stair, as they sat at tea on her lawn at Pangbourne, in reference to the very house of which the library in question was the central, the pivotal 'feature'. Mary Boyne and her husband, in quest of a country place in one of the southern or southwestern counties, had, on their arrival in England, carried their problem straight to Alida Stair, who had successfully solved it in her own case; but it was not until they had rejected, almost capriciously, several practical and judicious suggestions that she threw it out: "Well, there's Lyng, in Dorsetshire. It belongs to Hugo's cousins, and you can get it for a song."

The reasons she gave for its being obtainable on these terms – its remoteness from a station, its lack of electric light, hot-water pipes, and other vulgar necessities – were exactly those pleading in its favor with two romantic Americans perversely in search of the economic drawbacks which were associated, in their tradition, with unusual architectural felicities.

"I should never believe I was living in an old house unless I was thoroughly uncomfortable," Ned Boyne, the more extravagant of the two, had jocosely insisted; "the least hint of ‹convenience› would make me think it had been bought out of an exhibition, with the pieces numbered, and set up again." And they had proceeded to enumerate, with humorous precision, their various suspicions and exactions, refusing to believe that the house their cousin recommended was really Tudor till they learned it had no heating system, or that the village church was literally in the grounds till she assured them of the deplorable uncertainty of the watersupply.

"It's too uncomfortable to be true!" Edward Boyne had continued to exult as the avowal of each disadvantage was successively wrung from her; but he had cut short his rhapsody to ask, with a sudden relapse to distrust: "And the ghost? You've been concealing from us the fact that there is no ghost!"

Mary, at the moment, had laughed with him, yet almost with her laugh, being possessed of several sets of independent perceptions, had noted a sudden flatness of tone in Alida's answering hilarity.

"Oh, Dorsetshire's full of ghosts, you know."

"Yes, yes; but that won't do. I don't want to have to drive ten miles to see somebody else's ghost. I want one of my own on the premises. Is there a ghost at Lyng?"

His rejoinder had made Alida laugh again, and it was then that she had flung back tantalizingly: "Oh, there is one, of course, but you'll never know it."

"Never know it?" Boyne pulled her up. "But what in the world constitutes a ghost except the fact of its being known for one?"

"I can't say. But that's the story."

"That there's a ghost, but that nobody knows it's a ghost?"

"Well – not till afterward, at any rate."

"Till afterward?"

"Not till long, long afterward."

"But if it's once been identified as an unearthly visitant, why hasn't its signalement been handed down in the family? How has it managed to preserve its incognito?"

Alida could only shake her head. "Don't ask me. But it has."

"And then suddenly –" Mary spoke up as if from some cavernous depth of divination – "suddenly, long afterward, one says to one's self, 'That was it?'"

She was oddly startled at the sepulchral sound with which her question fell on the banter of the other two, and she saw the shadow of the same surprise flit across Alida's clear pupils. "I suppose so. One just has to wait."

"Oh, hang waiting!" Ned broke in. "Life's too short for a ghost who can only be enjoyed in retrospect. Can't we do better than that, Mary?"

But it turned out that in the event they were not destined to, for within three months of their conversation with Mrs. Stair they were established at Lyng, and the life they had yearned for to the point of planning it out in all its daily details had actually begun for them.

It was to sit, in the thick December dusk, by just such a widehooded fireplace, under just such black oak rafters, with the sense that beyond the mullioned panes the downs were darkening to a deeper solitude: it was for the ultimate indulgence in such sensations that Mary Boyne had endured for nearly fourteen years the soul-deadening ugliness of the Middle West, and that Boyne had ground on doggedly at his engineering till, with a suddenness that still made her blink, the prodigious windfall of the Blue Star Mine had put them at a stroke in possession of life and the leisure to taste it. They had never for a moment meant their new state to be one of idleness; but they meant to give themselves only to harmonious activities. She had her vision of painting and gardening (against a background of gray walls), he dreamed of the production of his long-planned book on the "Economic Basis of Culture"; and with such absorbing work ahead no existence could be too sequestered; they could not get far enough from the world, or plunge deep enough into the past.

Dorsetshire had attracted them from the first by a semblance of remoteness out of all proportion to its geographical position. But to the Boynes it was one of the ever-recurring wonders of the whole incredibly compressed island – a nest of counties, as they put it – that for the production of its effects so little of a given quality went so far: that so few miles made a distance, and so short a distance a difference.

"It's that," Ned had once enthusiastically explained, "that gives such depth to their effects, such relief to their least contrasts. They've been able to lay the butter so thick on every exquisite mouthful."

The butter had certainly been laid on thick at Lyng: the old gray house, hidden under a shoulder of the downs, had almost all the finer marks of commerce with a protracted past. The mere fact that it was neither large nor exceptional made it, to the Boynes, abound the more richly in its special sense – the sense of having been for centuries a deep, dim reservoir of life. The life had probably not been of the most vivid order: for long periods, no doubt, it had fallen as noiselessly into the past as the quiet drizzle of autumn fell, hour after hour, into the green fish-pond between the yews; but these back-waters of existence sometimes breed, in their sluggish depths, strange acuities of emotion, and Mary Boyne had felt from the first the occasional brush of an intenser memory.

The feeling had never been stronger than on the December afternoon when, waiting in the library for the belated lamps, she rose from her seat and stood among the shadows of the hearth. Her husband had gone off, after luncheon, for one of his long tramps on the downs. She had noticed of late that he preferred to be unaccompanied on these occasions; and, in the tried security of their personal relations, had been driven to conclude that his book was bothering him, and that he needed the afternoons to turn over in solitude the problems left from the morning's work. Certainly the book was not going as smoothly as she had imagined it would, and the lines of perplexity between his eyes had never been there in his engineering days. Then he had often looked fagged to the verge of illness, but the native demon of "worry" had never branded his brow. Yet the few pages he had so far read to her – the introduction, and a synopsis of the opening chapter – gave evidences of a firm possession of his subject, and a deepening confidence in his powers.

The fact threw her into deeper perplexity, since, now that he had done with "business" and its disturbing contingencies, the one other possible element of anxiety was eliminated. Unless it were his health, then? But physically he had gained since they had come to Dorsetshire, grown robuster, ruddier, and fresher-eyed. It was only within a week that she had felt in him the undefinable change that made her restless in his absence, and as tongue-tied in his presence as though it were she who had a secret to keep from him!

The thought that there was a secret somewhere between them struck her with a sudden smart rap of wonder, and she looked about her down the dim, long room.

"Can it be the house?" she mused.

The room itself might have been full of secrets. They seemed to be piling themselves up, as evening fell, like the layers and layers of velvet shadow dropping from the low ceiling, the dusky walls of books, the smoke-blurred sculpture of the hooded hearth.

"Why, of course – the house is haunted!" she reflected.

The ghost – Alida's imperceptible ghost – after figuring largely in the banter of their first month or two at Lyng, had been gradually discarded as too ineffectual for imaginative use. Mary had, indeed, as became the tenant of a haunted house, made the customary inquiries among her few rural neighbors, but, beyond a vague, "They du say so, Ma'am," the villagers had nothing to impart. The elusive specter had apparently never had sufficient identity for a legend to crystallize about it, and after a time the Boynes had laughingly set the matter down to their profit and-loss account, agreeing that Lyng was one of the few houses good enough in itself to dispense with supernatural enhancements.

"And I suppose, poor, ineffectual demon, that's why it beats its beautiful wings in vain in the void," Mary had laughingly concluded.

"Or, rather," Ned answered, in the same strain, "why, amid so much that's ghostly, it can never affirm its separate existence as the ghost." And thereupon their invisible housemate had finally dropped out of their references, which were numerous enough to make them promptly unaware of the loss.

Now, as she stood on the hearth, the subject of their earlier curiosity revived in her with a new sense of its meaning – a sense gradually acquired through close daily contact with the scene of the lurking mystery. It was the house itself, of course, that possessed the ghost-seeing faculty, that communed visually but secretly with its own past; and if one could only get into close enough communion with the house, one might surprise its secret, and acquire the ghost-sight on one's own account. Perhaps, in his long solitary hours in this very room, where she never trespassed till the afternoon, her husband had acquired it already, and was silently carrying the dread weight of whatever it had revealed to him. Mary was too well-versed in the code of the spectral world not to know that one could not talk about the ghosts one saw: to do so was almost as great a breach of goodbreeding as to name a lady in a club. But this explanation did not really satisfy her. "What, after all, except for the fun of the frisson," she reflected, "would he really care for any of their old ghosts?" And thence she was thrown back once more on the fundamental dilemma: the fact that one's greater or less susceptibility to spectral influences had no particular bearing on the case, since, when one did see a ghost at Lyng, one did not know it.

"Not till long afterward," Alida Stair had said. Well, supposing Ned had seen one when they first came, and had known only within the last week what had happened to him? More and more under the spell of the hour, she threw back her searching thoughts to the early days of their tenancy, but at first only to recall a gay confusion of unpacking, settling, arranging of books, and calling to each other from remote corners of the house as treasure after treasure of their habitation revealed itself to them. It was in this particular connection that she presently recalled a certain soft afternoon of the previous October, when, passing from the first rapturous flurry of exploration to a detailed inspection of the old house, she had pressed (like a novel heroine) a panel that opened at her touch, on a narrow flight of stairs leading to an unsuspected flat ledge of the roof – the roof which, from below, seemed to slope away on all sides too abruptly for any but practised feet to scale.

The view from this hidden coign was enchanting, and she had flown down to snatch Ned from his papers and give him the freedom of her discovery. She remembered still how, standing on the narrow ledge, he had passed his arm about her while their gaze flew to the long, tossed horizon-line of the downs, and then dropped contentedly back to trace the arabesque of yew hedges about the fish-pond, and the shadow of the cedar on the lawn.

"And now the other way," he had said, gently turning her about within his arm; and closely pressed to him, she had absorbed, like some long, satisfying draft, the picture of the gray-walled court, the squat lions on the gates, and the lime-avenue reaching up to the highroad under the downs.

It was just then, while they gazed and held each other, that she had felt his arm relax, and heard a sharp "Hullo!" that made her turn to glance at him.

Distinctly, yes, she now recalled she had seen, as she glanced, a shadow of anxiety, of perplexity, rather, fall across his face; and, following his eyes, had beheld the figure of a man – a man in loose, grayish clothes, as it appeared to her – who was sauntering down the lime-avenue to the court with the tentative gait of a stranger seeking his way. Her short-sighted eyes had given her but a blurred impression of slightness and grayness, with something foreign, or at least unlocal, in the cut of the figure or its garb; but her husband had apparently seen more – seen enough to make him push past her with a sharp "Wait!" and dash down the twisting stairs without pausing to give her a hand for the descent.

A slight tendency to dizziness obliged her, after a provisional clutch at the chimney against which they had been leaning, to follow him down more cautiously; and when she had reached the attic landing she paused again for a less definite reason, leaning over the oak banister to strain her eyes through the silence of the brown, sun-flecked depths below. She lingered there till, somewhere in those depths, she heard the closing of a door; then, mechanically impelled, she went down the shallow flights of steps till she reached the lower hall.

The front door stood open on the mild sunlight of the court, and hall and court were empty. The library door was open, too, and after listening in vain for any sound of voices within, she quickly crossed the threshold, and found her husband alone, vaguely fingering the papers on his desk.

He looked up, as if surprised at her precipitate entrance, but the shadow of anxiety had passed from his face, leaving it even, as she fancied, a little brighter and clearer than usual.

"What was it? Who was it?" she asked.

"Who?" he repeated, with the surprise still all on his side.

"The man we saw coming toward the house."

He seemed honestly to reflect. "The man? Why, I thought I saw Peters; I dashed after him to say a word about the stable-drains, but he had disappeared before I could get down."

"Disappeared? Why, he seemed to be walking so slowly when we saw him."

Boyne shrugged his shoulders. "So I thought; but he must have got up steam in the interval. What do you say to our trying a scramble up Meldon Steep before sunset?"

That was all. At the time the occurrence had been less than nothing, had, indeed, been immediately obliterated by the magic of their first vision from Meldon Steep, a height which they had dreamed of climbing ever since they had first seen its bare spine heaving itself above the low roof of Lyng. Doubtless it was the mere fact of the other incident's having occurred on the very day of their ascent to Meldon that had kept it stored away in the unconscious fold of association from which it now emerged; for in itself it had no mark of the portentous. At the moment there could have been nothing more natural than that Ned should dash himself from the roof in the pursuit of dilatory tradesmen. It was the period when they were always on the watch for one or the other of the specialists employed about the place; always lying in wait for them, and dashing out at them with questions, reproaches, or reminders. And certainly in the distance the gray figure had looked like Peters.

Yet now, as she reviewed the rapid scene, she felt her husband's explanation of it to have been invalidated by the look of anxiety on his face. Why had the familiar appearance of Peters made him anxious? Why, above all, if it was of such prime necessity to confer with that authority on the subject of the stable-drains, had the failure to find him produced such a look of relief? Mary could not say that any one of these considerations had occurred to her at the time, yet, from the promptness with which they now marshaled themselves at her summons, she had a sudden sense that they must all along have been there, waiting their hour.

II

WEARY WITH her thoughts, she moved toward the window. The library was now completely dark, and she was surprised to see how much faint light the outer world still held.

As she peered out into it across the court, a figure shaped itself in the tapering perspective of bare lines: it looked a mere blot of deeper gray in the grayness, and for an instant, as it moved toward her, her heart thumped to the thought, "It's the ghost!"

She had time, in that long instant, to feel suddenly that the man of whom, two months earlier, she had a brief distant vision from the roof was now, at his predestined hour, about to reveal himself as not having been Peters; and her spirit sank under the impending fear of the disclosure. But almost with the next tick of the clock the ambiguous figure, gaining substance and character, showed itself even to her weak sight as her husband's; and she turned away to meet him, as he entered, with the confession of her folly.

"It's really too absurd," she laughed out from the threshold, "but I never can remember!"

"Remember what?" Boyne questioned as they drew together.

"That when one sees the Lyng ghost one never knows it."

Her hand was on his sleeve, and he kept it there, but with no response in his gesture or in the lines of his fagged, preoccupied face.

"Did you think you'd seen it?" he asked, after an appreciable interval.

"Why, I actually took you for it, my dear, in my mad determination to spot it!"

"Me – just now?" His arm dropped away, and he turned from her with a faint echo of her laugh. "Really, dearest, you'd better give it up, if that's the best you can do."

"Yes, I give it up – I give it up. Have you?" she asked, turning round on him abruptly.

The parlor-maid had entered with letters and a lamp, and the light struck up into Boyne's face as he bent above the tray she presented.

"Have you?" Mary perversely insisted, when the servant had disappeared on her errand of illumination.

"Have I what?" he rejoined absently, the light bringing out the sharp stamp of worry between his brows as he turned over the letters.

"Given up trying to see the ghost." Her heart beat a little at the experiment she was making.

Her husband, laying his letters aside, moved away into the shadow of the hearth.

"I never tried," he said, tearing open the wrapper of a newspaper.

"Well, of course," Mary persisted, "the exasperating thing is that there's no use trying, since one can't be sure till so long afterward."

He was unfolding the paper as if he had hardly heard her; but after a pause, during which the sheets rustled spasmodically between his hands, he lifted his head to say abruptly, "Have you any idea how long?"

Mary had sunk into a low chair beside the fireplace. From her seat she looked up, startled, at her husband's profile, which was darkly projected against the circle of lamplight.

"No; none. Have YOU?" she retorted, repeating her former phrase with an added keenness of intention.

Boyne crumpled the paper into a bunch, and then inconsequently turned back with it toward the lamp.

"Lord, no! I only meant," he explained, with a faint tinge of impatience, "is there any legend, any tradition, as to that?"

"Not that I know of," she answered; but the impulse to add, "What makes you ask?" was checked by the reappearance of the parlormaid with tea and a second lamp.

With the dispersal of shadows, and the repetition of the daily domestic office, Mary Boyne felt herself less oppressed by that sense of something mutely imminent which had darkened her solitary afternoon. For a few moments she gave herself silently to the details of her task, and when she looked up from it she was struck to the point of bewilderment by the change in her husband's face. He had seated himself near the farther lamp, and was absorbed in the perusal of his letters; but was it something he had found in them, or merely the shifting of her own point of view, that had restored his features to their normal aspect? The longer she looked, the more definitely the change affirmed itself. The lines of painful tension had vanished, and such traces of fatigue as lingered were of the kind easily attributable to steady mental effort. He glanced up, as if drawn by her gaze, and met her eyes with a smile.

"I'm dying for my tea, you know; and here's a letter for you," he said.

She took the letter he held out in exchange for the cup she proffered him, and, returning to her seat, broke the seal with the languid gesture of the reader whose interests are all inclosed in the circle of one cherished presence.

Her next conscious motion was that of starting to her feet, the letter falling to them as she rose, while she held out to her husband a long newspaper clipping.

"Ned! What's this? What does it mean?"

He had risen at the same instant, almost as if hearing her cry before she uttered it; and for a perceptible space of time he and she studied each other, like adversaries watching for an advantage, across the space between her chair and his desk.

"What's what? You fairly made me jump!" Boyne said at length, moving toward her with a sudden, half-exasperated laugh. The shadow of apprehension was on his face again, not now a look of fixed foreboding, but a shifting vigilance of lips and eyes that gave her the sense of his feeling himself invisibly surrounded.

Her hand shook so that she could hardly give him the clipping.

"This article – from the 'Waukesha Sentinel' – that a man named Elwell has brought suit against you – that there was something wrong about the Blue Star Mine. I can't understand more than half."

They continued to face each other as she spoke, and to her astonishment, she saw that her words had the almost immediate effect of dissipating the strained watchfulness of his look.

"Oh, that!" He glanced down the printed slip, and then folded it with the gesture of one who handles something harmless and familiar. "What's the matter with you this afternoon, Mary? I thought you'd got bad news."

She stood before him with her undefinable terror subsiding slowly under the reassuring touch of his composure.

"You knew about this, then – it's all right?"

"Certainly I knew about it; and it's all right."

"But what is it? I don't understand. What does this man accuse you of?"

"Oh, pretty nearly every crime in the calendar." Boyne had tossed the clipping down, and thrown himself comfortably into an arm-chair near the fire. "Do you want to hear the story? It's not particularly interesting – just a squabble over interests in the Blue Star."

"But who is this Elwell? I don't know the name."

"Oh, he's a fellow I put into it – gave him a hand up. I told you all about him at the time."

"I daresay. I must have forgotten." Vainly she strained back among her memories. "But if you helped him, why does he make this return?"

"Oh, probably some shyster lawyer got hold of him and talked him over. It's all rather technical and complicated. I thought that kind of thing bored you."

His wife felt a sting of compunction. Theoretically, she deprecated the American wife's detachment from her husband's professional interests, but in practice she had always found it difficult to fix her attention on Boyne's report of the transactions in which his varied interests involved him. Besides, she had felt from the first that, in a community where the amenities of living could be obtained only at the cost of efforts as arduous as her husband's professional labors, such brief leisure as they could command should be used as an escape from immediate preoccupations, a flight to the life they always dreamed of living. Once or twice, now that this new life had actually drawn its magic circle about them, she had asked herself if she had done right; but hitherto such conjectures had been no more than the retrospective excursions of an active fancy. Now, for the first time, it startled her a little to find how little she knew of the material foundation on which her happiness was built.

She glanced again at her husband, and was reassured by the composure of his face; yet she felt the need of more definite grounds for her reassurance.

"But doesn't this suit worry you? Why have you never spoken to me about it?"

He answered both questions at once: "I didn't speak of it at first because it did worry me – annoyed me, rather. But it's all ancient history now. Your correspondent must have got hold of a back number of the 'Sentinel.'"

She felt a quick thrill of relief. "You mean it's over? He's lost his case?"

There was a just perceptible delay in Boyne's reply. "The suit's been withdrawn – that's all."

But she persisted, as if to exonerate herself from the inward charge of being too easily put off. "Withdrawn because he saw he had no chance?"

"Oh, he had no chance," Boyne answered.

She was still struggling with a dimly felt perplexity at the back of her thoughts.

"How long ago was it withdrawn?"

He paused, as if with a slight return of his former uncertainty. "I've just had the news now; but I've been expecting it."

"Just now – in one of your letters?"

"Yes; in one of my letters."

She made no answer, and was aware only, after a short interval of waiting, that he had risen, and strolling across the room, had placed himself on the sofa at her side. She felt him, as he did so, pass an arm about her, she felt his hand seek hers and clasp it, and turning slowly, drawn by the warmth of his cheek, she met the smiling clearness of his eyes.

"It's all right – it's all right?" she questioned, through the flood of her dissolving doubts; and "I give you my word it never was righter!" he laughed back at her, holding her close.

III

ONE OF THE strangest things she was afterward to recall out of all the next day's incredible strangeness was the sudden and complete recovery of her sense of security.

It was in the air when she woke in her low-ceilinged, dusky room; it accompanied her down-stairs to the breakfast-table, flashed out at her from the fire, and re-duplicated itself brightly from the flanks of the urn and the sturdy flutings of the Georgian teapot. It was as if, in some roundabout way, all her diffused apprehensions of the previous day, with their moment of sharp concentration about the newspaper article, – as if this dim questioning of the future, and startled return upon the past,-had between them liquidated the arrears of some haunting moral obligation. If she had indeed been careless of her husband's affairs, it was, her new state seemed to prove, because her faith in him instinctively justified such carelessness; and his right to her faith had overwhelmingly affirmed itself in the very face of menace and suspicion. She had never seen him more untroubled, more naturally and unconsciously in possession of himself, than after the cross-examination to which she had subjected him: it was almost as if he had been aware of her lurking doubts, and had wanted the air cleared as much as she did.

It was as clear, thank Heaven! as the bright outer light that surprised her almost with a touch of summer when she issued from the house for her daily round of the gardens. She had left Boyne at his desk, indulging herself, as she passed the library door, by a last peep at his quiet face, where he bent, pipe in his mouth, above his papers, and now she had her own morning's task to perform. The task involved on such charmed winter days almost as much delighted loitering about the different quarters of her demesne as if spring were already at work on shrubs and borders. There were such inexhaustible possibilities still before her, such opportunities to bring out the latent graces of the old place, without a single irreverent touch of alteration, that the winter months were all too short to plan what spring and autumn executed. And her recovered sense of safety gave, on this particular morning, a peculiar zest to her progress through the sweet, still place. She went first to the kitchen-garden, where the espaliered pear-trees drew complicated patterns on the walls, and pigeons were fluttering and preening about the silvery-slated roof of their cot. There was something wrong about the piping of the hothouse, and she was expecting an authority from Dorchester, who was to drive out between trains and make a diagnosis of the boiler. But when she dipped into the damp heat of the greenhouses, among the spiced scents and waxy pinks and reds of old-fashioned exotics, – even the flora of Lyng was in the note!-she learned that the great man had not arrived, and the day being too rare to waste in an artificial atmosphere, she came out again and paced slowly along the springy turf of the bowling-green to the gardens behind the house. At their farther end rose a grass terrace, commanding, over the fish-pond and the yew hedges, a view of the long house-front, with its twisted chimney-stacks and the blue shadows of its roof angles, all drenched in the pale gold moisture of the air.

Seen thus, across the level tracery of the yews, under the suffused, mild light, it sent her, from its open windows and hospitably smoking chimneys, the look of some warm human presence, of a mind slowly ripened on a sunny wall of experience. She had never before had so deep a sense of her intimacy with it, such a conviction that its secrets were all beneficent, kept, as they said to children, "for one's good," so complete a trust in its power to gather up her life and Ned's into the harmonious pattern of the long, long story it sat there weaving in the sun.

She heard steps behind her, and turned, expecting to see the gardener, accompanied by the engineer from Dorchester. But only one figure was in sight, that of a youngish, slightly built man, who, for reasons she could not on the spot have specified, did not remotely resemble her preconceived notion of an authority on hot-house boilers. The new-comer, on seeing her, lifted his hat, and paused with the air of a gentleman – perhaps a traveler-desirous of having it immediately known that his intrusion is involuntary. The local fame of Lyng occasionally attracted the more intelligent sight-seer, and Mary half-expected to see the stranger dissemble a camera, or justify his presence by producing it. But he made no gesture of any sort, and after a moment she asked, in a tone responding to the courteous deprecation of his attitude: "Is there any one you wish to see?"

"I came to see Mr. Boyne," he replied. His intonation, rather than his accent, was faintly American, and Mary, at the familiar note, looked at him more closely. The brim of his soft felt hat cast a shade on his face, which, thus obscured, wore to her short-sighted gaze a look of seriousness, as of a person arriving "on business," and civilly but firmly aware of his rights.

Past experience had made Mary equally sensible to such claims; but she was jealous of her husband's morning hours, and doubtful of his having given any one the right to intrude on them.

"Have you an appointment with Mr. Boyne?" she asked.

He hesitated, as if unprepared for the question.

"Not exactly an appointment," he replied.

"Then I'm afraid, this being his working-time, that he can't receive you now. Will you give me a message, or come back later?"

The visitor, again lifting his hat, briefly replied that he would come back later, and walked away, as if to regain the front of the house. As his figure receded down the walk between the yew hedges, Mary saw him pause and look up an instant at the peaceful house-front bathed in faint winter sunshine; and it struck her, with a tardy touch of compunction, that it would have been more humane to ask if he had come from a distance, and to offer, in that case, to inquire if her husband could receive him. But as the thought occurred to her he passed out of sight behind a pyramidal yew, and at the same moment her attention was distracted by the approach of the gardener, attended by the bearded pepper-and-salt figure of the boiler-maker from Dorchester.

The encounter with this authority led to such far-reaching issues that they resulted in his finding it expedient to ignore his train, and beguiled Mary into spending the remainder of the morning in absorbed confabulation among the greenhouses. She was startled to find, when the colloquy ended, that it was nearly luncheon-time, and she half expected, as she hurried back to the house, to see her husband coming out to meet her. But she found no one in the court but an under-gardener raking the gravel, and the hall, when she entered it, was so silent that she guessed Boyne to be still at work behind the closed door of the library.

Not wishing to disturb him, she turned into the drawing-room, and there, at her writing-table, lost herself in renewed calculations of the outlay to which the morning's conference had committed her. The knowledge that she could permit herself such follies had not yet lost its novelty; and somehow, in contrast to the vague apprehensions of the previous days, it now seemed an element of her recovered security, of the sense that, as Ned had said, things in general had never been "righter."

She was still luxuriating in a lavish play of figures when the parlor-maid, from the threshold, roused her with a dubiously worded inquiry as to the expediency of serving luncheon. It was one of their jokes that Trimmle announced luncheon as if she were divulging a state secret, and Mary, intent upon her papers, merely murmured an absent-minded assent.

She felt Trimmle wavering expressively on the threshold as if in rebuke of such offhand acquiescence; then her retreating steps sounded down the passage, and Mary, pushing away her papers, crossed the hall, and went to the library door. It was still closed, and she wavered in her turn, disliking to disturb her husband, yet anxious that he should not exceed his normal measure of work. As she stood there, balancing her impulses, the esoteric Trimmle returned with the announcement of luncheon, and Mary, thus impelled, opened the door and went into the library.

Boyne was not at his desk, and she peered about her, expecting to discover him at the book-shelves, somewhere down the length of the room; but her call brought no response, and gradually it became clear to her that he was not in the library.

She turned back to the parlor-maid.

"Mr. Boyne must be up-stairs. Please tell him that luncheon is ready."

The parlor-maid appeared to hesitate between the obvious duty of obeying orders and an equally obvious conviction of the foolishness of the injunction laid upon her. The struggle resulted in her saying doubtfully, "If you please, Madam, Mr. Boyne's not up-stairs."

"Not in his room? Are you sure?"

"I'm sure, Madam."

Mary consulted the clock. "Where is he, then?"

"He's gone out," Trimmle announced, with the superior air of one who has respectfully waited for the question that a well-ordered mind would have first propounded.

Mary's previous conjecture had been right, then. Boyne must have gone to the gardens to meet her, and since she had missed him, it was clear that he had taken the shorter way by the south door, instead of going round to the court. She crossed the hall to the glass portal opening directly on the yew garden, but the parlormaid, after another moment of inner conflict, decided to bring out recklessly, "Please, Madam, Mr. Boyne didn't go that way."

Mary turned back. "Where did he go? And when?"

"He went out of the front door, up the drive, Madam." It was a matter of principle with Trimmle never to answer more than one question at a time.

"Up the drive? At this hour?" Mary went to the door herself, and glanced across the court through the long tunnel of bare limes. But its perspective was as empty as when she had scanned it on entering the house.

"Did Mr. Boyne leave no message?" she asked.

Trimmle seemed to surrender herself to a last struggle with the forces of chaos.

"No, Madam. He just went out with the gentleman."

"The gentleman? What gentleman?" Mary wheeled about, as if to front this new factor.

"The gentleman who called, Madam," said Trimmle, resignedly.

"When did a gentleman call? Do explain yourself, Trimmle!"

Only the fact that Mary was very hungry, and that she wanted to consult her husband about the greenhouses, would have caused her to lay so unusual an injunction on her attendant; and even now she was detached enough to note in Trimmle's eye the dawning defiance of the respectful subordinate who has been pressed too hard.

"I couldn't exactly say the hour, Madam, because I didn't let the gentleman in," she replied, with the air of magnanimously ignoring the irregularity of her mistress's course.

"You didn't let him in?"

"No, Madam. When the bell rang I was dressing, and Agnes –"

"Go and ask Agnes, then," Mary interjected. Trimmle still wore her look of patient magnanimity. "Agnes would not know, Madam, for she had unfortunately burnt her hand in trying the wick of the new lamp from town –" Trimmle, as Mary was aware, had always been opposed to the new lamp –"and so Mrs. Dockett sent the kitchen-maid instead."

Mary looked again at the clock. "It's after two! Go and ask the kitchen-maid if Mr. Boyne left any word."

She went into luncheon without waiting, and Trimmle presently brought her there the kitchen-maid's statement that the gentleman had called about one o'clock, that Mr. Boyne had gone out with him without leaving any message. The kitchen-maid did not even know the caller's name, for he had written it on a slip of paper, which he had folded and handed to her, with the injunction to deliver it at once to Mr. Boyne.

Mary finished her luncheon, still wondering, and when it was over, and Trimmle had brought the coffee to the drawing-room, her wonder had deepened to a first faint tinge of disquietude. It was unlike Boyne to absent himself without explanation at so unwonted an hour, and the difficulty of identifying the visitor whose summons he had apparently obeyed made his disappearance the more unaccountable. Mary Boyne's experience as the wife of a busy engineer, subject to sudden calls and compelled to keep irregular hours, had trained her to the philosophic acceptance of surprises; but since Boyne's withdrawal from business he had adopted a Benedictine regularity of life. As if to make up for the dispersed and agitated years, with their "stand-up" lunches and dinners rattled down to the joltings of the dining-car, he cultivated the last refinements of punctuality and monotony, discouraging his wife's fancy for the unexpected; and declaring that to a delicate taste there were infinite gradations of pleasure in the fixed recurrences of habit.

Still, since no life can completely defend itself from the unforeseen, it was evident that all Boyne's precautions would sooner or later prove unavailable, and Mary concluded that he had cut short a tiresome visit by walking with his caller to the station, or at least accompanying him for part of the way.

This conclusion relieved her from farther preoccupation, and she went out herself to take up her conference with the gardener. Thence she walked to the village post-office, a mile or so away; and when she turned toward home, the early twilight was setting in.

She had taken a foot-path across the downs, and as Boyne, meanwhile, had probably returned from the station by the highroad, there was little likelihood of their meeting on the way. She felt sure, however, of his having reached the house before her; so sure that, when she entered it herself, without even pausing to inquire of Trimmle, she made directly for the library. But the library was still empty, and with an unwonted precision of visual memory she immediately observed that the papers on her husband's desk lay precisely as they had lain when she had gone in to call him to luncheon.

Then of a sudden she was seized by a vague dread of the unknown. She had closed the door behind her on entering, and as she stood alone in the long, silent, shadowy room, her dread seemed to take shape and sound, to be there audibly breathing and lurking among the shadows. Her short-sighted eyes strained through them, halfdiscerning an actual presence, something aloof, that watched and knew; and in the recoil from that intangible propinquity she threw herself suddenly on the bell-rope and gave it a desperate pull.

The long, quavering summons brought Trimmle in precipitately with a lamp, and Mary breathed again at this sobering reappearance of the usual.

"You may bring tea if Mr. Boyne is in," she said, to justify her ring.

"Very well, Madam. But Mr. Boyne is not in," said Trimmle, putting down the lamp.

"Not in? You mean he's come back and gone out again?"

"No, Madam. He's never been back."

The dread stirred again, and Mary knew that now it had her fast.

"Not since he went out with – the gentleman?"

"Not since he went out with the gentleman."

"But who was the gentleman?" Mary gasped out, with the sharp note of some one trying to be heard through a confusion of meaningless noises.

"That I couldn't say, Madam." Trimmle, standing there by the lamp, seemed suddenly to grow less round and rosy, as though eclipsed by the same creeping shade of apprehension.

"But the kitchen-maid knows – wasn't it the kitchen-maid who let him in?"

"She doesn't know either, Madam, for he wrote his name on a folded paper."

Mary, through her agitation, was aware that they were both designating the unknown visitor by a vague pronoun, instead of the conventional formula which, till then, had kept their allusions within the bounds of custom. And at the same moment her mind caught at the suggestion of the folded paper.

"But he must have a name! Where is the paper?"

She moved to the desk, and began to turn over the scattered documents that littered it. The first that caught her eye was an unfinished letter in her husband's hand, with his pen lying across it, as though dropped there at a sudden summons.

"My dear Parvis," – who was Parvis? –"I have just received your letter announcing Elwell's death, and while I suppose there is now no farther risk of trouble, it might be safer –"

She tossed the sheet aside, and continued her search; but no folded paper was discoverable among the letters and pages of manuscript which had been swept together in a promiscuous heap, as if by a hurried or a startled gesture.

"But the kitchen-maid saw him. Send her here," she commanded, wondering at her dullness in not thinking sooner of so simple a solution.

Trimmle, at the behest, vanished in a flash, as if thankful to be out of the room, and when she reappeared, conducting the agitated underling, Mary had regained her self-possession, and had her questions pat.

The gentleman was a stranger, yes – that she understood. But what had he said? And, above all, what had he looked like? The first question was easily enough answered, for the disconcerting reason that he had said so little – had merely asked for Mr. Boyne, and, scribbling something on a bit of paper, had requested that it should at once be carried in to him.

"Then you don't know what he wrote? You're not sure it was his name?"

The kitchen-maid was not sure, but supposed it was, since he had written it in answer to her inquiry as to whom she should announce.

"And when you carried the paper in to Mr. Boyne, what did he say?"

The kitchen-maid did not think that Mr. Boyne had said anything, but she could not be sure, for just as she had handed him the paper and he was opening it, she had become aware that the visitor had followed her into the library, and she had slipped out, leaving the two gentlemen together.

"But then, if you left them in the library, how do you know that they went out of the house?"

This question plunged the witness into momentary inarticulateness, from which she was rescued by Trimmle, who, by means of ingenious circumlocutions, elicited the statement that before she could cross the hall to the back passage she had heard the gentlemen behind her, and had seen them go out of the front door together.

"Then, if you saw the gentleman twice, you must be able to tell me what he looked like."

But with this final challenge to her powers of expression it became clear that the limit of the kitchen-maid's endurance had been reached. The obligation of going to the front door to "show in" a visitor was in itself so subversive of the fundamental order of things that it had thrown her faculties into hopeless disarray, and she could only stammer out, after various panting efforts at evocation, "His hat, mum, was different-like, as you might say –"

"Different? How different?" Mary flashed out at her, her own mind, in the same instant, leaping back to an image left on it that morning, but temporarily lost under layers of subsequent impressions.

"His hat had a wide brim, you mean? and his face was pale – a youngish face?" Mary pressed her, with a white-lipped intensity of interrogation. But if the kitchen-maid found any adequate answer to this challenge, it was swept away for her listener down the rushing current of her own convictions. The stranger – the stranger in the garden! Why had Mary not thought of him before? She needed no one now to tell her that it was he who had called for her husband and gone away with him. But who was he, and why had Boyne obeyed his call?

IV

IT LEAPED OUT at her suddenly, like a grin out of the dark, that they had often called England so little – "such a confoundedly hard place to get lost in."

A confoundedly hard place to get lost in! That had been her husband's phrase. And now, with the whole machinery of official investigation sweeping its flash-lights from shore to shore, and across the dividing straits; now, with Boyne's name blazing from the walls of every town and village, his portrait (how that wrung her!) hawked up and down the country like the image of a hunted criminal; now the little compact, populous island, so policed, surveyed, and administered, revealed itself as a Sphinx-like guardian of abysmal mysteries, staring back into his wife's anguished eyes as if with the malicious joy of knowing something they would never know!

In the fortnight since Boyne's disappearance there had been no word of him, no trace of his movements. Even the usual misleading reports that raise expectancy in tortured bosoms had been few and fleeting. No one but the bewildered kitchen-maid had seen him leave the house, and no one else had seen "the gentleman" who accompanied him. All inquiries in the neighborhood failed to elicit the memory of a stranger's presence that day in the neighborhood of Lyng. And no one had met Edward Boyne, either alone or in company, in any of the neighboring villages, or on the road across the downs, or at either of the local railway-stations. The sunny English noon had swallowed him as completely as if he had gone out into Cimmerian night.

Mary, while every external means of investigation was working at its highest pressure, had ransacked her husband's papers for any trace of antecedent complications, of entanglements or obligations unknown to her, that might throw a faint ray into the darkness. But if any such had existed in the background of Boyne's life, they had disappeared as completely as the slip of paper on which the visitor had written his name. There remained no possible thread of guidance except – if it were indeed an exception – the letter which Boyne had apparently been in the act of writing when he received his mysterious summons. That letter, read and reread by his wife, and submitted by her to the police, yielded little enough for conjecture to feed on.

"I have just heard of Elwell's death, and while I suppose there is now no farther risk of trouble, it might be safer –" That was all. The "risk of trouble" was easily explained by the newspaper clipping which had apprised Mary of the suit brought against her husband by one of his associates in the Blue Star enterprise. The only new information conveyed in the letter was the fact of its showing Boyne, when he wrote it, to be still apprehensive of the results of the suit, though he had assured his wife that it had been withdrawn, and though the letter itself declared that the plaintiff was dead. It took several weeks of exhaustive cabling to fix the identity of the 'Parvis' to whom the fragmentary communication was addressed, but even after these inquiries had shown him to be a Waukesha lawyer, no new facts concerning the Elwell suit were elicited. He appeared to have had no direct concern in it, but to have been conversant with the facts merely as an acquaintance, and possible intermediary; and he declared himself unable to divine with what object Boyne intended to seek his assistance.

This negative information, sole fruit of the first fortnight's feverish search, was not increased by a jot during the slow weeks that followed. Mary knew that the investigations were still being carried on, but she had a vague sense of their gradually slackening, as the actual march of time seemed to slacken. It was as though the days, flying horror-struck from the shrouded image of the one inscrutable day, gained assurance as the distance lengthened, till at last they fell back into their normal gait. And so with the human imaginations at work on the dark event. No doubt it occupied them still, but week by week and hour by hour it grew less absorbing, took up less space, was slowly but inevitably crowded out of the foreground of consciousness by the new problems perpetually bubbling up from the vaporous caldron of human experience.

Even Mary Boyne's consciousness gradually felt the same lowering of velocity. It still swayed with the incessant oscillations of conjecture; but they were slower, more rhythmical in their beat. There were moments of overwhelming lassitude when, like the victim of some poison which leaves the brain clear, but holds the body motionless, she saw herself domesticated with the Horror, accepting its perpetual presence as one of the fixed conditions of life.

These moments lengthened into hours and days, till she passed into a phase of stolid acquiescence. She watched the familiar routine of life with the incurious eye of a savage on whom the meaningless processes of civilization make but the faintest impression. She had come to regard herself as part of the routine, a spoke of the wheel, revolving with its motion; she felt almost like the furniture of the room in which she sat, an insensate object to be dusted and pushed about with the chairs and tables. And this deepening apathy held her fast at Lyng, in spite of the urgent entreaties of friends and the usual medical recommendation of "change." Her friends supposed that her refusal to move was inspired by the belief that her husband would one day return to the spot from which he had vanished, and a beautiful legend grew up about this imaginary state of waiting. But in reality she had no such belief: the depths of anguish inclosing her were no longer lighted by flashes of hope. She was sure that Boyne would never come back, that he had gone out of her sight as completely as if Death itself had waited that day on the threshold. She had even renounced, one by one, the various theories as to his disappearance which had been advanced by the press, the police, and her own agonized imagination. In sheer lassitude her mind turned from these alternatives of horror, and sank back into the blank fact that he was gone.

No, she would never know what had become of him – no one would ever know. But the house knew; the library in which she spent her long, lonely evenings knew. For it was here that the last scene had been enacted, here that the stranger had come, and spoken the word which had caused Boyne to rise and follow him. The floor she trod had felt his tread; the books on the shelves had seen his face; and there were moments when the intense consciousness of the old, dusky walls seemed about to break out into some audible revelation of their secret. But the revelation never came, and she knew it would never come. Lyng was not one of the garrulous old houses that betray the secrets intrusted to them. Its very legend proved that it had always been the mute accomplice, the incorruptible custodian of the mysteries it had surprised. And Mary Boyne, sitting face to face with its portentous silence, felt the futility of seeking to break it by any human means.

V

"I DON'T SAY it wasn't straight, yet don't say it was straight. It was business."

Mary, at the words, lifted her head with a start, and looked intently at the speaker.

When, half an hour before, a card with "Mr. Parvis" on it had been brought up to her, she had been immediately aware that the name had been a part of her consciousness ever since she had read it at the head of Boyne's unfinished letter. In the library she had found awaiting her a small neutral-tinted man with a bald head and gold eye-glasses, and it sent a strange tremor through her to know that this was the person to whom her husband's last known thought had been directed.

Parvis, civilly, but without vain preamble – in the manner of a man who has his watch in his hand, – had set forth the object of his visit. He had "run over" to England on business, and finding himself in the neighborhood of Dorchester, had not wished to leave it without paying his respects to Mrs. Boyne; without asking her, if the occasion offered, what she meant to do about Bob Elwell's family.

The words touched the spring of some obscure dread in Mary's bosom. Did her visitor, after all, know what Boyne had meant by his unfinished phrase? She asked for an elucidation of his question, and noticed at once that he seemed surprised at her continued ignorance of the subject. Was it possible that she really knew as little as she said?

"I know nothing – you must tell me," she faltered out; and her visitor thereupon proceeded to unfold his story. It threw, even to her confused perceptions, and imperfectly initiated vision, a lurid glare on the whole hazy episode of the Blue Star Mine. Her husband had made his money in that brilliant speculation at the cost of "getting ahead" of some one less alert to seize the chance; the victim of his ingenuity was young Robert Elwell, who had "put him on" to the Blue Star scheme.

Parvis, at Mary's first startled cry, had thrown her a sobering glance through his impartial glasses.

"Bob Elwell wasn't smart enough, that's all; if he had been, he might have turned round and served Boyne the same way. It's the kind of thing that happens every day in business. I guess it's what the scientists call the survival of the fittest," said Mr. Parvis, evidently pleased with the aptness of his analogy.

Mary felt a physical shrinking from the next question she tried to frame; it was as though the words on her lips had a taste that nauseated her.

"But then – you accuse my husband of doing something dishonorable?"

Mr. Parvis surveyed the question dispassionately. "Oh, no, I don't. I don't even say it wasn't straight." He glanced up and down the long lines of books, as if one of them might have supplied him with the definition he sought. "I don't say it wasn't straight, and yet I don't say it was straight. It was business." After all, no definition in his category could be more comprehensive than that.

Mary sat staring at him with a look of terror. He seemed to her like the indifferent, implacable emissary of some dark, formless power.

"But Mr. Elwell's lawyers apparently did not take your view, since I suppose the suit was withdrawn by their advice."

"Oh, yes, they knew he hadn't a leg to stand on, technically. It was when they advised him to withdraw the suit that he got desperate. You see, he'd borrowed most of the money he lost in the Blue Star, and he was up a tree. That's why he shot himself when they told him he had no show."

The horror was sweeping over Mary in great, deafening waves.

"He shot himself? He killed himself because of that? "

"Well, he didn't kill himself, exactly. He dragged on two months before he died." Parvis emitted the statement as unemotionally as a gramophone grinding out its "record."

"You mean that he tried to kill himself, and failed? And tried again?"

"Oh, he didn't have to try again," said Parvis, grimly.

They sat opposite each other in silence, he swinging his eyeglass thoughtfully about his finger, she, motionless, her arms stretched along her knees in an attitude of rigid tension.

"But if you knew all this," she began at length, hardly able to force her voice above a whisper, "how is it that when I wrote you at the time of my husband's disappearance you said you didn't understand his letter?"

Parvis received this without perceptible discomfiture. "Why, I didn't understand it – strictly speaking. And it wasn't the time to talk about it, if I had. The Elwell business was settled when the suit was withdrawn. Nothing I could have told you would have helped you to find your husband."

Mary continued to scrutinize him. "Then why are you telling me now?"

Still Parvis did not hesitate. "Well, to begin with, I supposed you knew more than you appear to – I mean about the circumstances of Elwell's death. And then people are talking of it now; the whole matter's been raked up again. And I thought, if you didn't know, you ought to."

She remained silent, and he continued: "You see, it's only come out lately what a bad state Elwell's affairs were in. His wife's a proud woman, and she fought on as long as she could, going out to work, and taking sewing at home, when she got too sick-something with the heart, I believe. But she had his bedridden mother to look after, and the children, and she broke down under it, and finally had to ask for help. That attracted attention to the case, and the papers took it up, and a subscription was started. Everybody out there liked Bob Elwell, and most of the prominent names in the place are down on the list, and people began to wonder why –"

Parvis broke off to fumble in an inner pocket. "Here," he continued, "here's an account of the whole thing from the 'Sentinel' – a little sensational, of course. But I guess you'd better look it over."

He held out a newspaper to Mary, who unfolded it slowly, remembering, as she did so, the evening when, in that same room, the perusal of a clipping from the "Sentinel" had first shaken the depths of her security.

As she opened the paper, her eyes, shrinking from the glaring head-lines, "Widow of Boyne's Victim Forced to Appeal for Aid," ran down the column of text to two portraits inserted in it. The first was her husband's, taken from a photograph made the year they had come to England. It was the picture of him that she liked best, the one that stood on the writing-table up-stairs in her bedroom. As the eyes in the photograph met hers, she felt it would be impossible to read what was said of him, and closed her lids with the sharpness of the pain.

"I thought if you felt disposed to put your name down –" she heard Parvis continue.

She opened her eyes with an effort, and they fell on the other portrait. It was that of a youngish man, slightly built, in rough clothes, with features somewhat blurred by the shadow of a projecting hat-brim. Where had she seen that outline before? She stared at it confusedly, her heart hammering in her throat and ears. Then she gave a cry.

"This is the man – the man who came for my husband!"

She heard Parvis start to his feet, and was dimly aware that she had slipped backward into the corner of the sofa, and that he was bending above her in alarm. With an intense effort she straightened herself, and reached out for the paper, which she had dropped.

"It's the man! I should know him anywhere!" she cried in a voice that sounded in her own ears like a scream.

Parvis's voice seemed to come to her from far off, down endless, fog-muffled windings.

"Mrs. Boyne, you're not very well. Shall I call somebody? Shall I get a glass of water?"

"No, no, no!" She threw herself toward him, her hand frantically clenching the newspaper. "I tell you, it's the man! I know him! He spoke to me in the garden!"

Parvis took the journal from her, directing his glasses to the portrait. "It can't be, Mrs. Boyne. It's Robert Elwell."

"Robert Elwell?" Her white stare seemed to travel into space. "Then it was Robert Elwell who came for him."

"Came for Boyne? The day he went away?" Parvis's voice dropped as hers rose. He bent over, laying a fraternal hand on her, as if to coax her gently back into her seat. "Why, Elwell was dead! Don't you remember?"

Mary sat with her eyes fixed on the picture, unconscious of what he was saying.

"Don't you remember Boyne's unfinished letter to me – the one you found on his desk that day? It was written just after he'd heard of Elwell's death." She noticed an odd shake in Parvis's unemotional voice. "Surely you remember that!" he urged her.

Yes, she remembered: that was the profoundest horror of it. Elwell had died the day before her husband's disappearance; and this was Elwell's portrait; and it was the portrait of the man who had spoken to her in the garden. She lifted her head and looked slowly about the library. The library could have borne witness that it was also the portrait of the man who had come in that day to call Boyne from his unfinished letter. Through the misty surgings of her brain she heard the faint boom of halfforgotten words – words spoken by Alida Stair on the lawn at Pangbourne before Boyne and his wife had ever seen the house at Lyng, or had imagined that they might one day live there.

"This was the man who spoke to me," she repeated.

She looked again at Parvis. He was trying to conceal his disturbance under what he imagined to be an expression of indulgent commiseration; but the edges of his lips were blue. "He thinks me mad; but I'm not mad," she reflected; and suddenly there flashed upon her a way of justifying her strange affirmation.

She sat quiet, controlling the quiver of her lips, and waiting till she could trust her voice to keep its habitual level; then she said, looking straight at Parvis: "Will you answer me one question, please? When was it that Robert Elwell tried to kill himself?"

"When – when?" Parvis stammered.

"Yes; the date. Please try to remember."

She saw that he was growing still more afraid of her. "I have a reason," she insisted gently.

"Yes, yes. Only I can't remember. About two months before, I should say."

"I want the date," she repeated.

Parvis picked up the newspaper. "We might see here," he said, still humoring her. He ran his eyes down the page. "Here it is. Last October – the –"

She caught the words from him. "The 20th, wasn't it?" With a sharp look at her, he verified. "Yes, the 20th. Then you did know?"

"I know now." Her white stare continued to travel past him. "Sunday, the 20th – that was the day he came first."

Parvis's voice was almost inaudible. "Came here first?"

"Yes."

"You saw him twice, then?"

"Yes, twice." She breathed it at him with dilated eyes. "He came first on the 20th of October. I remember the date because it was the day we went up Meldon Steep for the first time." She felt a faint gasp of inward laughter at the thought that but for that she might have forgotten.

Parvis continued to scrutinize her, as if trying to intercept her gaze.

"We saw him from the roof," she went on. "He came down the limeavenue toward the house. He was dressed just as he is in that picture. My husband saw him first. He was frightened, and ran down ahead of me; but there was no one there. He had vanished."

"Elwell had vanished?" Parvis faltered.

"Yes." Their two whispers seemed to grope for each other. "I couldn't think what had happened. I see now. He tried to come then; but he wasn't dead enough – he couldn't reach us. He had to wait for two months; and then he came back again – and Ned went with him."

She nodded at Parvis with the look of triumph of a child who has successfully worked out a difficult puzzle. But suddenly she lifted her hands with a desperate gesture, pressing them to her bursting temples.

"Oh, my God! I sent him to Ned – I told him where to go! I sent him to this room!" she screamed out.

She felt the walls of the room rush toward her, like inward falling ruins; and she heard Parvis, a long way off, as if through the ruins, crying to her, and struggling to get at her. But she was numb to his touch, she did not know what he was saying. Through the tumult she heard but one clear note, the voice of Alida Stair, speaking on the lawn at Pangbourne.

"You won't know till afterward," it said. "You won't know till long, long afterward."

Deep-Sixed Without a Depth Gauge

Andrew J. Wilson

"**ONE OF THE FEW** advantages of having a false eye," Stark said, "is that you can fill it with nitroglycerine."

The flight attendant clapped beautifully manicured fingers over her gaping mouth as the big Scotsman slipped his little insurance policy out of its socket. The eye glistened damply in Stark's hand as he waved it under her nose. The stewardess backed away, frantically scanning the cabin for help.

"Don't waste your time looking for air marshals," Stark told her, kicking the body at his feet. "This bastard would never have taken the flight if there were any on board."

Then he stepped purposefully over the Mafia bagman he'd punched senseless and picked up the all-important briefcase. The puckered red hole on the left side of Stark's face leaked tears down his cheek, but he was grinning like a lottery winner. After all, the black leather attaché case did contain fifteen million dollars in high-denomination bills.

The Mafia had been trying to slip the money out of the States to launder it in central Europe. Unfortunately for the mob, word gets around. Fortunately for Stark, he heard the news. Unfortunately for the informers, they got to take turns swallowing the business end of a .44 Magnum.

"And now, sweetheart," Stark said gently, rolling the "r" like a purring cat, "we're going to walk quietly up to the cockpit and have a nice wee chat with the captain."

Actually, he had to have a long argument with the pilot. There was the matter of explaining that the airliner was going to cut its speed, drop to five thousand feet and circle an exact set of coordinates in the North Atlantic. While the crew were taking the 747 on this little detour, Stark was going to be collecting a few items from the pressurized luggage bay. He would be needing the parachute and survival suit that his blackmail victim in the airline baggage crew had smuggled on board for him.

The captain told him what he thought of the plan: he thought it was insane; he thought Stark would never get away with it. The Scot smiled calmly and winked at the pilot with his good eye.

"I'll be straight with you," Stark told him, "I really couldn't give a monkey's what you reckon. I'm going to get away with this because you don't want me to blow a hole in the side of your jumbo jet. Now, get with the programme, flyboy – I'm a criminal, not a terrorist, so you know you can deal with me. It's not your money anyway – in fact, it belongs to people you wouldn't stop to piss on if they were on fire. It's drug money and the outfit will never find me."

The captain pointed out that this was because the skyjacker was going to end up at the bottom of the Atlantic.

"Maybe, maybe not, but that's my problem, pal – your problem is keeping everybody else alive..."

As the plane descended into the clouds, red rain splattered across the windows. It was the kind of thing that happened all the time these days. The media blamed algal overgrowth in the world's oceans. Stark put it down to Mother Nature suffering from PMT.

He slipped his false eye back in place and the trembling stewardess led him down to the luggage bay. His survival suit and parachute were hidden in a fake diplomatic bag. Stark pulled them on and handcuffed the briefcase to his wrist.

The stewardess led him back to the cabin, and the passengers in tourist class watched in awe as he forced open the outer door and prepared to jump. Stark couldn't resist taking advantage of the moment.

"Ladies and gentlemen," he screamed above the roar of the slipstream, "Elvis has left the building!"

As he kicked himself backwards out of the door, Stark caught a last glimpse of his audience. The idiots were actually applauding.

* * *

The North Atlantic was wrapped in fog that night. Stark plunged into the ocean and unbuckled his 'chute. As he bobbed to the surface, he saw the silk sheet ripple away into the icy water like an enormous jellyfish. The briefcase weighed him down, but the suit helped to maintain his buoyancy.

Stark pulled out one of his flares and tugged the cord to ignite it. The red stick coughed and the phosphorus beacon rocketed into the night sky. The fog obscured much of the glow, but the flare was still visible as it fell back towards the sea, suspended from its little parachute.

Stark trod water, getting colder, wetter and more furious as he realized that his so-called survival suit had sprung a leak. He wouldn't have much time in the ocean before he began to suffer from exposure, and dying in the middle of the Atlantic with fifteen million dollars chained to his wrist was definitely not part of the plan. What was more, the fog smelled rancid. There was an acrid, chemical flavour to it which caught at the back of his throat.

Then the wind began to strip away shreds of fog and Stark saw the boat. It was the *Peerie Quine* out of Aberdeen, all right, and she was only thirty feet away. The deep-sea trawler was his ticket home, but she was floating dead in the water and drifting off into the mist again.

Stark struck out towards the boat, using a crippled kind of dog paddle since he was hampered by the briefcase and weighed down by his cumbersome protective clothing. The cold from the ocean was sinking into his bones and he was beginning to lose his strength even as he tried to close the distance. Lights were burning in the wheelhouse, but no one was visible on the deck of the sixty-foot boat.

"Rab!" he yelled at the top of his voice. "Where are you, you useless waste of space?"

Nobody replied. This was also very much not part of the plan. Stark was a hard man to ignore, standing six feet, three and a half inches in his socks, but adding another yet more to his height with his combat boots and wiry military flat-top. He had been trained to kill in the army and had taught himself how to survive in the glasshouse. The big man had also learned the importance of discipline during his time in the service and now rigorously adhered to a code of self-control in his life of crime. The only time he allowed himself the liberty of losing control was when other people failed to follow orders. Stark was going to be very, very peevish when he got his hands on whoever was responsible for this predicament.

The *Peerie Quine* stood fifteen feet out of the water. Even as Stark dragged himself towards her, he realized that his associates had failed to drop the rope ladder over the side. At the last moment, he saw that one of the huge tractor tyres that made up the boat's fenders had been lowered to the water level on its chain. Stark grabbed the clammy rubber and pulled himself on to the tyre as something big cut through the black water beneath him.

For a few moments, Stark stared at the great ripples slapping the peeling hull of the boat and tried to get his breath back. Now there was nothing in the ocean but salty water. Soon he wouldn't be able to see anything because the foul-smelling fog was coming in again.

Stark clambered on top of the tractor tyre. He unlocked the handcuffs and lobbed the briefcase onto the deck. Then he hauled himself up the chain, fighting cramps which made his muscles spasm. At last, Stark clutched at the rail and wriggled on board the trawler. He couldn't stand up any more, so he crawled towards the shelter deck on all fours.

The boat was empty. Stark decided that the *Peerie Quine* needed to be renamed the Marie Celeste and then sent to a watery grave. If he was given the choice, the crew would go down with the ship, but only after he'd given them their heads to play with.

Stark slid down the ladder and held his shaky footing on the rusty steel. His vision was blackening at the edges now, but as far as he could see, the briefcase wasn't there. He dragged himself under the covered shelter and made for the galley, but the deck vanished beneath his numbed feet when something snuffed out his consciousness as if it were a spark in the wind.

* * *

Simon Stark's friends called him 'Cyclops'. His enemies would have done the same, but Stark didn't follow the Old Testament philosophy of an eye for an eye. He firmly believed in hunting down his opponents and giving them a one-way ticket to the morgue.

The only person who had called him by his first name had been Hope.

"Why don't you quit, Simon?" she had asked him after they had made love for the last time. "For Christ's sake, get out while you're ahead and play the stock market – you're smart enough to make a killing, you know."

Stark had smiled sardonically, relaxed into the hotel bed and shaken his head.

"It's too risky, Hope. The whole world's going to fall apart soon – you know that. The market is going to crash any time, there's wars erupting in places we've never even heard of, and the papers say that superbugs are going to wipe out anybody who dodges those bullets. If I'm going to gamble, I want to play a game where the odds are stacked in my **favour** – a game where I can make the rules."

She had massaged the knots in the corded muscles of his shoulders and sworn gently behind his back.

"You're such a bloody pessimist, Simon. What's the point of doing anything, then?"

"You know what I've always said – plan your getaway. I'm lining up the job that's going to let us buy our own island and leave the rest of the world to go to hell..."

"But what if you get killed?" she murmured as her fingers kneaded his scarred flesh. "Where does that leave me?"

"Don't worry, sweetheart, we'll pull through," Stark had told her dreamily as he fell asleep.

Hope didn't call him anything now because she was dead, cut to pieces by the mob as a warning to Stark to keep out of their business. You would have thought the Mafia of all people would have understood the meaning of vendetta. It's been said that there are few more impressive sights in the world than a Scotsman on the make. Talk is cheap: there's nothing more frightening than any kind of man with nothing left to lose.

* * *

Stark came to in the fish room. His fall had been broken by a squid – a giant squid. There was no need for hyperbole: the creature was at least forty feet long. The monster had eyes as big as portholes and suckers the size of hub-caps. Its beak could have swallowed a man whole.

The giant squid was also very dead. There was a hole in its head that Stark could have put his size-twelve boot through. He studied the wound with his professional eye. At first, he wondered if someone had shot the creature, but that didn't make much sense. Anyway, the gaping cavity had been punched outwards through the cartilage and flesh.

The mystery lost his interest when Stark saw a lurching figure appear in silhouette at the top of the ladder leading down into the locker. The man was wrapped in oilskins. He was also carrying the large spanner that must have been used to knock him out. The fisherman began to climb down into the fish room.

Stark slid off the mountain of squid flesh and pulled another flare from his survival suit. Then he played dead. It was an Oscar-winning performance. The fisherman didn't suspect a thing until he leaned over Stark's body and the flare went off.

The crewman jerked back as the rocket shot into his mouth. The little parachute had wrapped itself across his face, but Stark could see the fisherman's eyes flash brightly through the silk as the flare exploded inside his brain. The man was blown backwards into the ice store, and his skull popped and splintered as the intense heat of the phosphorus met the freezing cold.

Stark picked up the spanner, ready for trouble, then dragged himself up the ladder and on to the shelter deck again. It was a double-cross, he was sure of it. There was still no one to be seen. Stark's legs began to wobble with pain and exhaustion. He realized that he had to pull himself together before anyone else took him apart.

The door to the galley swung open on its groaning hinges and he heard distorted voices, but the room was empty. The radio was playing, but the tuning had drifted off station. Stark swept up a handful of grubby towels and wrenched open the cupboards until he found a bottle of Grouse. He threw the top away and necked a fifth in less than a minute as he began to dry himself off. The alcohol ignited his throat and the fire swept through his body deliciously. It was a great deal better than a poke in the eye with a sharp stick, he decided. He should know: that was how he had ended up with his nickname.

Stark twisted the radio tuner until he found the World Service.

"...still erupting in the Atlantic. The fumaroles have violently disturbed the ocean floor and volcanic gasses have caused widespread fog banks which constitute a shipping hazard..."

Fortified by the drink, Stark climbed the steps to the wheelhouse. This was deserted too. Then there was a sound from below as a door was opened in the galley. Stark crushed himself into the corner beside the top of the stairs.

The blue-black barrel of a pump-action shotgun slowly appeared out of the stairwell. Stark waited until the hands holding the Remington twelve-gauge came into his line of sight and then brought the spanner down as hard as he could on the tense fingers clutching the barrel. There was a shriek and he jerked the Remington away from its owner before using the stock to club the figure back down the steps. Then Stark shouldered the shotgun and carefully stepped round to the head of the stairs.

"Don't, Si! It's Rab! It's me!" howled the little man lying spread-eagled over the galley table. Stark cycled the pump.

"You little shit," he hissed, "I am not a happy bunny. What the fuck is going on here?"

* * *

Rab Nixon was a fixer and the two men had worked together several times before. They had both been born and brought up in Edinburgh. Rab and Stark had moved in the same underworld circles since their teens, and the trajectories of their careers had intersected on many jobs in the past. Stark didn't like the scrawny dock rat very much, but the creep had always been a professional: that was why he had brought Rab in on the biggest operation of their criminal careers.

"What happened?" Stark asked. "Did you and your fish-molesting pals decide you were going to split the take between yourselves? Did you think I was going to do the dirty work and then let you sail off into the sunset with the haul?"

Rab was now sitting in one of the chairs massaging his bruised hands and watching the barrel of the shotgun as Stark swung it across his chest.

"Listen, Si – for God's sake – it's not like that at all! We have to get off this boat right now!"

Stark swigged at the whisky again and then began to towel himself down again.

"OK, Rab... I'll bite. What's the story?"

"Everything was just tickety-boo until they brought up some kind of bloody octopus in the net —"

"I know – it was a giant squid. I saw it."

"Well, I told them to forget about it. I said, we've got to get to the rendezvous or Si's going to kill us" – Stark smiled with merciless satisfaction – "but the skipper says this thing's going to tear the net to pieces if they don't get it in on the boat. I told them to just get on with it and came up here to take the wheel. Anyway, they dump the beast in the fish room and then there's this God-awful racket and the lads start screaming. So I went on to the deck to take a look and they're all down there, tearing each other apart. I think the octopus-thingy was infected with something and the crew caught it. They've gone radge, Si, absolutely radio rental. I just legged it to the cabin, got the shooter and then locked myself in the bog. I only came out because I knew I had to help you on to the boat..."

Stark laughed in his face. "That has got to be the most pathetic excuse I've ever heard, Rab. It's worse than the dog ate my homework. You should have tried that one instead. Still, there's one way to get to the bottom of it."

He brought the shotgun up and pulled the trigger.

The little man squealed and dived under the table, but the blast was aimed over his head. Stark walked to the door and kicked something that sounded wet. Rab scuttled after him. Stark had shot one of the crew in the chest. A fat man was writhing on the shelter deck and clawing at the bloody hole in his ribcage. The cap on the victim's head was crusted with dried blood and quivered with movement underneath the filthy wool.

"Who is it, Rab?"

"It's the cook, Si."

"He doesn't look too good, does he? Pull his hat off."

"What? You've got to be kidding!"

"Do as you're told, you prick!"

Rab lunged forward and whipped of the cook's **woollen** cap away as quickly as he could. The fisherman groaned and felt for his skull, but Stark stamped on his hand. The cook's balding cranium had been had been cracked all the way round the hair-line like a boiled egg. The top of his skull was now a grey-green **colour** and there was a strong smell of brine coming off it. The flesh seemed to be flaking into plates and pulsing slightly.

"What do you make of that?" Stark asked. "Check it out."

Rab made a noise like a boiling kettle, but he jabbed the cook's crown and recoiled.

What had looked like the top of the cook's skull reared up and showed itself. "Oh, Christ," Rab whined, "it's a slater – it's a giant fucking woodlouse and it's chewed his brains out!"

The little man doubled over and vomited onto the deck.

The cook was still moving long after he should have been dead. Stark bent closer. The huge crustacean had displaced most of the grey matter and rooted itself into the base of the skull with its seven pairs of jointed legs. The creature was also very much alive.

Stark jerked back as the thing turned purposefully towards him. Its antennae waved lazily like two probing fingers. He cycled the Remington and blew the cook's skull to pieces at point-blank range. The fisherman's oilskins heaved and more of the creatures spilled out from underneath the clothing. Stark got one with the heel of his boot, but the rest scuttled into the shadows too quickly for him.

The sound of the radio interrupted their silence: "...among the species being brought to the surface by the undersea eruptions are ribbonfish, cephalopods and the voracious giant isopod..."

The ruined shell of the dead crustacean pulsed as the broken plates were forced apart from the inside. Stark crouched down and plunged his gloved hand into the shattered carapace. His fingers wrenched out a mass of parasitic worms that had infested the soft tissue of the larger creature. Stark cast most of the writhing handful back on the deck and stamped on the helminths. Then he held one faintly phosphorescent worm under the light from the galley and teased its body apart. The creature burst under the pressure and his gloves were covered in the translucent lice which had given the worm its eerie glow.

"OK, Rab, you were right," Stark told his cringing accomplice. "We're in really deep shit now."

* * *

Stark covered them until they got to the cabin. It was empty. He gave the shotgun to Rab, then stripped off his wet clothes and got into dry gear. The engines started up while he was changing.

"What's going on, Rab?"

"They're hauling the net in again. Jesus, we've got to get out of here."

"Not without the money."

"But those fucking creepy-crawlies —"

"Isopods, Rab – that's what the radio called them – giant isopods..."

"Whatever they're called, Si, they're chewing into people's heads and taking them over.

This stuff is way out of our league..."

"Speak for yourself."

Stark took back the shotgun and they moved forward again, climbing onto the fore deck. The rank volcanic fog was beginning to lift as the wind freshened from the east. Rab went straight for the lifeboat. He began to tug at the seals on the orange plastic drum that would unfold into a dinghy when it was released into the water.

"I don't think we want to do that," Stark told him. "I say we find the others and waste them. Then we take this tub back to dry land on our own. How many are left?"

"Just three, Si, but I can't hack this any more. We've got to get off the *Peerie Quine* or we're going to end up like the cook... We should cut our losses and save our own necks."

"I want my money, OK? I'll see you all in hell before I run away from fifteen million."

Rab shook his head. Stark didn't continue the argument. He knew that the little man was more frightened of the forces loose on the trawler than the shotgun or his fists.

"Right, you do what ever you want. I'm off to sort this out."

Stark was on the steps when he heard the lifeboat hit the water. Then Rab started screaming like a lobster in a pot of boiling water. One of the crew had been hiding in the locker. The fisherman had hooked Stark's accomplice with a gaff. The metal barb on the end of the pole was sunk into Rab's shattered skull and he was being dragged along the deck.

For a moment, Stark hesitated, then he ran back. The fisherman was cramming another of the giant isopods into the jagged hole in Rab's head. The little man stopped shrieking and began to convulse.

Three shots from the pump blasted the crewman into a bloody smear on the deck. Several dying crustaceans wriggled around the corpse. Stark dropped the gun and hauled Rab off the deck to shake him, but he could see the deep-sea parasite chewing its way into his accomplice's brain.

"Sorry, mate," he said as he wrenched the little man's head through one hundred and eighty degrees, snapping his neck. Stark threw the corpse over the side and watched as it slapped into the lifeboat below.

"Well, you got what you wanted, after all..."

Stark picked up the gun and headed for the wheelhouse. He fired up the engines, turned the boat in the direction of the far-distant Scottish mainland and locked the wheel. Then he went back down to the shelter deck for the last time.

The two remaining members of the crew had finally appeared. They were operating the winch to haul the net out of the water. The fishermen turned towards Stark in unison. They were both wearing blood-encrusted woollen hats and their oilskins were splattered with vomit. The briefcase was lying behind them.

"Hello, boys." said Stark. "Are you ready to rock and roll?"

He shouldered the gun and squeezed the trigger. Nothing happened. One of the crewmen stumbled forward, while the other stayed on the winch.

Stark charged the attacker, swinging the jammed shotgun like a club. The fisherman caught the weapon and wrenched it out of Stark's hands with inhuman strength. Stark stumbled and rolled out of the way as the gun was smashed down on the deck beside him. He could hear the muscles tearing in his opponent's arms, but the thing driving what was left of the fisherman was immune to the agony it must have been causing its host.

The loaded net burst out of the water and the man at the winch swung it over the deck.

"Give me a fucking break!" Stark croaked as he staggered to his feet.

The plastic web held a thrashing pilot whale. There was a huge grey-green bump on its cranium which made it resemble a 747 jet. The lump arched and a parasitic crustacean as large as a man reared its ugly head. The whale must have weighed more than a ton, and as it was swung down onto the deck, the suffering beast ripped open the taught and whining warps with its powerful flukes.

The pilot whale slid out of the net, fixing Stark with its tortured gaze, and let out a ghastly ululating whine. Then the mammal was choked as it spewed a tide of parasites over the deck. Stark kicked frantically as the things scuttled around him.

Two tendrils lashed out from the gigantic crustacean buried in the whale and these glowing filaments sank into the skulls of the fishermen, connecting with the parasites inside. For a moment, the two creatures which had once been trawlermen and the gigantic beast riding the pilot whale froze in a dark epiphany.

Stark took his chance. He pulled his false eye out of its socket and lobbed it into the engine room. Then he ran for the side and jumped.

The nitroglycerine blew the aft of the *Peerie Quine* into matchwood. The diesel tanks exploded seconds later and the trawler was swamped in burning fuel. Stark didn't look back. He was swimming for the lifeboat, and watching fifteen million dollars rain down in a burning shower around him.

It took Stark twelve minutes to reach the lifeboat and by then he was nearly done. He clutched at the side of the dinghy and tried to get his breath back before climbing in. Then the broken-necked thing which had once been called Rab Nixon gave him a helping hand.

The Dew of Heaven, Like Ashes

William R.D. Wood

BREE DIDN'T FEEL SAD necessarily, but the tears came just the same, smearing the black soot coating her cheeks. All she truly felt was tired and thirsty. Everything else lacked certainty.

She'd been on foot for hours. The VW was dead in a ditch somewhere far behind on a stretch of unfamiliar country road just like this one. The black dust that hung in the air everywhere was thicker here, drifting in clouds like fog. Her arms ached from swinging the bat, but she waved the length of polished wood in the swirl ahead, shaking it as the dust clung in each gouge and chip. A signature ran down one side of the bat. Someone famous from when her dad was a boy. He'd been so proud. The name was illegible but the words beneath were not.

Serenity. Courage. Wisdom.

Now the bat was crusty with the dried blood and guts of the abominations that came for her time and again.

Her body tensed at the thought, the muscles between her shoulder blades cramping. Her face was tight and hot. When she brushed at the dust, the skin on her cheek tingled beneath her touch. The unforgiving July sun was partially blocked by the airborne dust but enough UV was getting through that her cheeks stung. A chemical burn, maybe. It had been bothering her since the first day.

The first day.

The thought lingered in her head.

How many days? Had it been only days?

To the left an old farmhouse crouched on the ground, streaks of white siding peeking through smears of the dust. Across the dirt road from the farmhouse stood stalks of maize, swaying oddly out of sync with the breeze. A bird swooped down, skimming alongside the closest row. Bree flinched as an ear of maize snapped open, silky tendrils snatching the creature from the air, sinking into the feathers as kernels, like tiny teeth, took it apart. Black smoke drifted away from the stalk as blood seeped between the leaves. Her grip tightened on the bat, then slackened as she turned away, unsure if the squeal came from the bird or the maize.

Serenity to accept the things I cannot change, she thought.

She just needed rest. Not to think. Not to run. Not to fight.

"How's that working out for you?" she mumbled to herself.

Bree shuffled down the dirt drive toward the old farmhouse with its white picket fence and clapboard shutters. She took shallow breaths hoping to minimise the amount of dust getting into her lungs. She knew the attempt was ultimately futile and, honestly, the stuff didn't have a smell. A hint of must, maybe. Mostly it just felt wet in your nose.

It couldn't possibly be healthy.

She smiled. That was just the sort of observation her father would make. People always said she inherited her father's smile. That man could be happy in the middle of anything. Her smile now, tugging at skin drawn tight over her cheeks, was just a reminder her sunburn was going to be a major problem by morning.

No cars sat in the drive or along the sides of the house. They could have escaped the farm, of course. Hell, maybe they didn't even have a vehicle. But then, how can anyone living on a farm survive without a vehicle? No, they either fled the farm or they had parked around back. The ruts in the gravel drive extended around the left side of the house so that could be it.

The prospect of a working vehicle quickened her pace.

The screen door of the house swung wide, the twang of the return spring loud and sharp in the still air. A woman in a yellowed nightgown and unlaced boots stepped into view, the shade from the low-slung wooden roof casting her face in shadow.

Holding the bat at her side, Bree raised her free hand in a wave, her throat too parched to call out.

The ground to her right exploded, thunder booming across the yard. Dirt and specks of rock showered her as she staggered to the left.

"Get off my land," shouted the woman, her voice old and shrill. The sleek black muzzle of a shotgun poked out of the shadow, glinting in a stray swath of sunlight. "Don't much care if I kill you or not."

The ground to Bree's left erupted. She stumbled back a step uncertain if the woman was that bad of a shot or that good. Glancing over her shoulder toward the dirt road, Bree tried to remain focused as she moved slowly back the way she'd come. The sweltering heat and her exhaustion made it difficult to remain calm but she seemed to be pulling on reserves she'd have denied she had a week ago.

She turned back to the crazy old woman. Didn't she realise how dangerous making noise could be? Of course, maybe living way out here, she didn't. She wasn't sure, but a distant buzz seemed to ride on the rustling of the maize stalks.

Courage to change the things I can.

The world had gone insane, but still she should warn the woman. "Ma'am, you've got to be quiet —"

Thunder blasted outward again from the porch and Bree felt the wind from a mass of buckshot whizz by her, several tiny pieces striking her right shoulder. Fire lanced through her arm and neck and she dropped the bat as she dashed toward the end of the drive.

Once safely out of range of the shotgun she looked back at the bat, lying in the dirt.

She'd find something else to defend herself with. Still she hated losing the only thing she had from *before*.

This wasn't worth it. If she stayed the woman would kill her, and if not, the blasts from the shotgun were sure to attract unwanted attention from something more mobile than the maize. Either way, she would be dead if she didn't hurry away from this place.

A hum like a tiny engine filled the air, as a shadow flitted overhead. An instant later Bree dropped to her knees.

Gaze snapping from the flying creatures to the old woman to her bat, Bree dared a glance down the road. A heavy cloud like ink in water swirled in the distance, the hum in the air growing to a muted roar. Like a distant storm.

Scrambling to her feet, she bolted for the farmhouse, slowing just enough to snatch the bat from the ground. Thunder cracked once, then twice, sending Bree dodging to one side. But the shots were not directed at her. The old woman swung the shotgun at a bug as it swooped in, drawing closer with each pass.

The woman lost her balance and toppled down the stairs. Her cry of pain was punctuated by a hollow snap as the force of her fall busted a wooden step. Still, even as she came to rest on the ground, she whipped the shotgun out at the attacking bug. The bugs were only centimetres long, about the size of a small bird, but they moved fast. At least the old woman was a fighter.

The second bug, hovering clear of the fight must have noticed Bree. With a dip in the air, it moved in her direction.

Still running, pain radiating from her shoulder, Bree swung the bat, connecting with a crunch. The bug hurtled back toward the house. Momentum carrying her forward, she saw the woman crawling up the stairs as the other bug's stinger planted in her neck. The old woman convulsed, one arm outstretched toward the doorway as if the house offered some sort of protection. The unscreened windows to each side were propped open. After all, it should have been a relaxing, if breezeless, summer scorcher.

The hum behind her was a rumble. She'd never be able to lock the place down before the swarm hit. She'd seen the things come crashing through windowpanes before, their chitinous heads tucked against their bodies as they shattered the glass.

She veered left, toward the back of the house. There could be a vehicle there. Just because Granny had been home didn't mean she *couldn't* leave. And where would she go that was more remote, *more* safe? Where could she go to get away from nature?

Bree skidded to a halt.

A rusty old pickup rested in the middle of the back yard, wheel-less rims atop stacked cinder blocks. One door hung ajar from a single hinge. Beyond the truck leaned a rickety wooden shed, some of the planks fallen away. Twenty metres farther on, the sea of maize.

Her shoulders slumped and tears formed in the corners of her eyes. The dust really must be an irritant. She wasn't the weepy sort but she'd been crying on and off since –

You come out here to me, little girl, her father had said on the phone before the line went dead. *Come on right away and we'll figure this thing out.*

Her father had overcome his weakness the day she was born, dropping the bottle in the trash for good. He'd always known what to say, what to do, every time she'd come to him as she was growing up.

"What do I do now, Daddy?" The dust swirled madly all around. The beat of the approaching swarm rose to a din, a vibration she could feel as much as hear. A shadow fell across the yard as the black cloud rose over the house. The ground beneath her feet began to shake.

The back of the house was a blank wall, broken only by a pair of small windows; both open and too far off the ground to reach even with a running start. Two sun-bleached stacks of wood lay propped against the back wall on top of a pile of concrete blocks. A lump formed in her throat and her stomach felt as if she were falling. She wasn't going to make it this time. Her fingers grasped the bat.

Serenity. Courage. Wisdom.

Taking a deep breath, she turned to face the cloud rising over the house. The shadow slid across the two wooden doors. They weren't just discarded boards leaning against the wall. They were doors.

Bree raced for the storm cellar. Instantly grateful the old woman hadn't seen fit to padlock the doors, she whipped one side open and jumped inside, just as one of the bugs struck the other door, rattling its hinges. Fighting for balance on the wobbly old set of stairs, she snatched the door closed, sliding a two-by-four latch into place.

Easing backwards down the stairs, she watched the wavering beams of light slip through gaps in the heavy boards. The double doors shook with impacts like hammer blows. A step gave way beneath her foot and she pitched forward, catching herself with her hands as her foot sent something made of glass skidding across the floor and ploughing noisily into empty cans.

Long seconds passed as the assault continued. Bree squinted into the shadowy cellar. No windows. The only light in the room came through the cracks in the cellar doors, affording her fleeting glimpses of glass jars filled with peppers and mushrooms. An entire shelf next to a set of stairs leading up into the house was loaded with gallon jugs of water. There were other shelves but she couldn't make out what they held.

The dank smell of the place clung in her nose as if it had a life of its own. She shuddered. Not her first choice of shelter, but as long as the bugs didn't get in, she'd be able to hole up here for a while.

Moving cautiously through the dark, she waded through more bottles which clinked against one another in her wake. A fan of light winked and shifted from beneath the door leading into the house. The scratching and buzzing from the other side was message enough that she should stay put.

Eyes growing used to the darkness, Bree noticed a small amber light at the base of the stairs. She pulled the combination nightlight/flashlight from the outlet and switched it on. Might as well have a quick look around. The beam was weak. Power must have gone out and let the nightlight function drain the battery.

The basement was bigger than she'd thought. Hard-packed dirt formed the floor, uneven in places, but smooth. The shelves she hadn't been able to see before held boxes marked clothes, mostly. A couple she couldn't see must be torn open judging by the clothing scattered on the floor. The canned goods were many and varied, though, and her mind wandered for an instant on how she might go about opening one.

The drone of thousands of wings outside swallowed up the sound of her footsteps, but not the growing buzz rising in the air behind her. Bree whipped the bat up and spun. The bug was a big one, the same perverted version as the ones outside. Must have made it through the cellar door when she had.

Guess you guys don't see so well in the dark either.

Bree tossed the flashlight to one side, hearing the buzz shift as the creature went after the light. It dropped onto the flashlight, disturbing the motes of black dust drifting in the beam. Birdlike claws dug into the cylinder as its scorpion-like tail stabbed repeatedly at the plastic.

Her bat connected on the first swing, crumpling the bug's body in a splatter of pus and blood. She stared at the thing. This was the first time she'd taken a good look. The body was small and feathered, hummingbird-like, but the tail was long and thin and ended in a bob sporting a serrated stinger. The head she wasn't sure about, but it was a bony version of a bird, only with a coiled proboscis like a butterfly instead of a beak.

She wretched, at once glad she hadn't eaten lately and doubly that she retained enough sanity to react at all.

The thing was an abomination. How did it even know how to fly? And how did those dogs on the campus sprout tentacles from their mouths and turn on their owners. How did they know how to ... use them? But they did just the same. Just like all the affected animals and plants. As if something deep in their genetic code had been coiled and waiting to pounce.

Using a cloth from a shelf, she wiped the flashlight down and panned it around looking for other intruders as the hum from outside quieted. Another yellow pinpoint of light glowed in the corner of the cellar farthest from both sets of stairs.

Bree tiptoed toward the light. A second flashlight she could hold in reserve. A few metres from the light, the floor squished. She jerked her foot back, tested the surface gingerly. Her flashlight was all but useless now, but the ground seemed firm enough, so she continued on, only slower. The dirt had become spongy, like moss or a freshly tilled garden.

Crouching in front of her target, she realised the tiny light was coming from the floor not the wall. If it were an LED on a charging flashlight, the light wasn't plugged into an outlet. Bree played the rapidly failing beam across the floor toward the yellow light. Lumps formed a miniature alien landscape ending in a mushroom the size of her thumbnail. The sickly yellow light coming from the mutant fungus pulsed like a beating heart.

Bree shivered.

Fungus. That was the dank, musty smell she'd recoiled from when she first entered the cellar. Not unlike the scent of the black dust that had become a part of everything these last few days. Poking at the yellow glow with her toe, she watched the light intensify. She clenched her jaw and brought her heel down sharply on the fungus, grinding it into the soft earth. In two strides she was clear of the mushroom garden.

The sounds from outside were fading, the spokes of light poking through the storm cellar doors growing brighter. Fewer and fewer thumps shook the doors, so she moved close enough to see a sliver of the yard through a gap. The ground was black with the undulating mass of bug ... birds.

They'd give up and move on soon. She hoped.

A series of soft clicks from behind startled Bree and she spun, bat at the ready. A ray of light speared across the cellar, framing the dead bug perfectly. Tugging at the carcass was a mouse with too many legs, all spindly and multi-jointed. Large black eyes in the middle of a red hourglass skull fixed on her. Its mouth spread wide in a hiss exposing two large flat teeth.

When she came to herself, Bree was standing over a smear of fur and legs, her grip relaxing on the bat, her heart hammering in her chest.

She nodded to herself. The fatigue was getting to her. Sooner or later she was going to have to sleep.

Slumping onto the bottom of the inside stairs, she leaned the bat against the handrail and kicked away a mouldy old boot on the floor to make room so she could spread out.

Just a few minutes. She didn't need long.

Placing her face in one palm she brushed at the dust on one leg of her jeans. Something heavy shifted in her pocket and she remembered her phone. She didn't know why she even kept the thing – it had been dead since yesterday. Every extra ounce she carried was an ounce slower she'd be able to run.

But she did know why.

How long ago had she spoken to her Dad? She'd been in the dorm lounge overlooking the Bio Building when the first report came in. Live from the National Zoo a news crew had been there covering the president's visit with his children. Something off camera caused the children to scream and the network cut away.

Bree woke, a stair step cutting into her already aching back. The cellar was darker than before, no light spilling in through the cracks in the outside doors.

Pushing to her feet, she stumbled, her right foot completely numb. She must have pinched off the blood supply the way she'd fallen asleep. She shifted her weight back and forth waiting for the pins and needles of restored circulation.

The outline of her shoe stood out against the blackness, a faint yellow glow like a cheap glow stick becoming brighter as she watched.

She looked toward the mushroom garden. A pinpoint of light pulsed in the corner illuminating a second boot like the one by the stairs. Beyond that a pair of crusty coveralls stretched out flat. Several sets of clothes lay strewn about the spongy section of floor. A choked sob escaped her lips. Bree snatched the old boot from the floor, hurling it toward the glow.

Two steps toward the stairs leading to the outside world and her hand tingled. Numbness spread up her arm from where she'd touched the boot. Her feet tangled in something in the dark, the sound of ripping cloth filling her ears as she fell. Cold crept along her skin as dampness flooded her nostrils. Her skull throbbed, pressure pushing the inside of her forehead, threatening to crack the bone.

No, God, please...

With her good leg and working hand, she scrabbled up the stairs. Balanced on one foot, Bree smacked at the latch. The board moved but only a centimetre, if that. Drawing back she put every bit of strength she had left into the second blow.

The swat connected and the board flew free but she'd sacrificed what little balance she had. For an instant she wondered why the doors were getting farther away, then she realised she was falling, toppling backwards.

She spun as she fell, landing flat on her back, her head striking the floor with a crack she was sure meant a fractured skull. White-hot pain burned behind her eyes and she wavered somewhere at the edge of the darkness, screaming inside her head not to pass out.

She had to keep moving. She had to get out.

Or did she?

Serenity to accept the things I cannot change. Courage to change the things I can. Wisdom to know the difference.

Her fight had been a long one. Now was the time to make the wise decision. The world was dead, or dying. Nothing would be left unchanged. She'd seen the animals, the plants. Surely whatever was changing them would also be destroying whatever remained of –

She choked at the thought.

– people.

Nothing would ever be the same.

She could hardly feel her body at all. Every twitch of her muscles seemed a hundred kilometres away. Faintly she sensed something moving along her neck, then her chin, across her lips. She was reminded of a snail, creeping along a viscous trail. Her arm twitched at her side, but did not move enough to brush the thing away. A tiny yellow light rose up onto the tip of her nose, blinking in sync with her beating heart.

Tendrils probed the edges of her nostrils and mouth, snaking in.

She considered screaming, but didn't.

Wisdom to know the difference.

Light exploded in her eyes, purple and gold. The smells of childhood flooded from forgotten memories. Air brushed against her skin like a summer breeze and she heard the crack of a baseball game in the distance. Daddy laughed, standing nearby in the sunlight. He leaned on a bat, a smile on his face.

The bat. His, then hers. Because he loved her.

Warmth flooded through her body, fear ebbing away as her dad waited patiently, just as he always had. The sunlight caught his face just right and his skin seemed to glow.

Bree reached out. Her arm was sluggish, bumping against her body as she stretched. Darkness flickered at the edges of her vision.

Tears ran backwards along the sides of her face. She knew she was standing in the field with her dad but the wetness flowed along the sides of her face as though she were lying flat on her back. But that wasn't possible. She opened her mouth to speak but her lips seemed frozen in the moment. Just as well. She didn't need to speak. She never had because he always knew just what to say and just when to say it.

And any moment she knew just what he'd say.

Serenity, Bree. Courage and ... wisdom.

Wisdom to know the difference.

The summer day grew dark, the breeze chill. Bree's arm flopped into view, fingers pinching at a light on her face. Threads tugged at her lips and nose, at the corners of her eyes, as she whipped the tiny mushroom away. Pin-pricks tickled her face, hints of pain but far away. The swirling lights faded taking with them the fondest of memories.

Numb and clumsy, arms and legs flailing, Bree heaved herself up one step. Then another. Pain tested the edge of her senses as she clenched her jaw, crushing rubbery tendrils between her teeth. Her thoughts grew crisper with each exertion. Endless moments strung together as she struggled up the few stairs until finally she rolled onto the dirt beneath the starry sky.

Her fingers ached as she loosened her grip on the wooden shaft of the bat she somehow managed to retrieve without conscious effort. The world beyond was dark, the shadows swaying in an odd rhythm.

Somewhere out beyond those fields her dad was waiting.

Using the bat to steady herself, Bree pushed to her feet, pins and needles dancing along her toes and fingers. She glanced into the pit where she'd left her serenity and spat.

She didn't know about wisdom, but she was damned sure she had some courage left.

Biographies & Sources

Rebecca J. Allred
Ecdysis
(First Publication)
Rebecca lives in Salt Lake City, Utah, working by day as a doctor of pathology, but after-hours she transforms into a practitioner of macabre fiction, infecting readers with her malign prose. Her work has been featured on Hellnotes.com, Freeze Frame Fiction, *Sirens Call* eZine and *Vignettes from the End of the World*. When she isn't busy rendering diagnoses or writing, Rebecca enjoys reading, drawing, laughing at RiffTrax, and spending time with her husband, Zach, and their kitty, Bug. You can keep up with Rebecca at diagnosisdiabolique.wordpress.com or follow her on Twitter @LadyHazmat.

Ambrose Bierce
The Damned Thing
(Originally Published in *Town Topics (New York)*, 1893)
Beyond the Wall
(Originally Published in *Cosmopolitan*, 1907)
Ambrose Bierce (1824–c. 1914) was born in Meigs County, Ohio. He was a famous journalist and author known for writing *The Devil's Dictionary*. After fighting in the American Civil War, Bierce used his combat experience to write stories based on the war, such as in *An Occurrence at Owl Creek Bridge*. Following the separate deaths of his ex-wife and two of his three children he gained a sardonic view of human nature and earned the name 'Bitter Bierce'. His disappearance at the age of 71 on a trip to Mexico remains a great mystery and continues to spark speculation.

Michael Bondies
Mirror's Keeper
(Originally Published in *Black Static*, 2011)
Michael Bondies is a native of Dallas, Texas, and a graduate of the University of Colorado Denver music program. He has work appearing or forthcoming in several different venues including *Bards and Sages Quarterly, Blood Moon Rising, Tales of the Undead: Suffer Eternal Anthology Volume III*, and the anthology *Little Stories for the Smallest Room*. He currently lives on the West Coast, and when he's not writing you will usually find him playing guitar. Visit him at: www.MichaelBondies.com.

John Buchan
The Watcher by the Threshold
(Originally Published in *Blackwood's Magazine*, 1900)
John Buchan (1875–1940) was born in Perth, Scotland. During his time as Commander-in-Chief of the Dominion of Canada, Buchan published his most famous work, *The Thirty-Nine Steps*. He was Governor General of Canada from 1935 until his death, and wrote many books pertaining to Canadian culture. Most of his horror stories – such as *No-Man's-Land*, *Fullcircle* and *The Wind in the Portico* – are influenced by the wild and strange places he experienced during his time as a government administrator in South Africa.

Glen Damien Campbell
The Dying Art
(Originally Published in *The Boneyard*, 2014)
Glen Damien Campbell lives and works in London. His horror fiction has appeared in a variety of anthologies and magazines, including *Something Wicked Vol. One*, *100 Doors to Madness*, *Tales of the Undead: Suffer Eternal*, *Tales from the Blue Gonk Café* and *Miseria's Chorale*. Besides writing, his interests are music, painting and horror movies. For more information about Glen, or to read his jottings on various things horror and heavy-metal related, visit his blog at gdcampbell. wordpress.com.

Robert W. Chambers
The Yellow Sign
(Originally Published in *The King in Yellow*, F. Tennyson Neely, 1895)
Robert William Chambers (1865–1933) was born in Brooklyn, New York. He was a successful writer in many genres: fantasy, historical fiction, horror, romance, supernatural and science fiction. His best-known works come from his short story collection *The King in Yellow*. Everett Franklin Bleiler, a respected scholar of science fiction and fantasy literature, described *The King in Yellow* as one of the most important works of American supernatural fiction.

Justin Coates
Breach
(First Publication)
Justin Coates is a citizen of Detroit, Michigan. His formative years of reading involved copious amounts of Lovecraft and King, and in recent years he has read every grim tale set in the 'Warhammer: 40K' universe he can get his hands on. A veteran with two tours in Afghanistan, Justin also draws on his combat experience when writing, and finds the process immensely useful in his spiritual recovery from war. This is his first publication, an opportunity for which he is extremely grateful.

F. Marion Crawford
The Dead Smile
(Originally Published in *Ainslee's*, 1899)
The Screaming Skull
(Originally Published in *Collier's Magazine*, 1908)
Francis Marion Crawford (1854–1909) was born in Bagni di Lucca, Italy. He is well known for his classically weird and fantastical stories. Travelling to and from Italy, England, Germany and the United States, Crawford became an extraordinary linguist and his first novel *Mr. Isaacs: A Tale of Modern India* was an instant success. His body of work in the horror genre is immense, including such short stories as *The Dead Smile* and *The Screaming Skull*.

Charles Dickens
The Child's Story
(Originally Published in *Household Words*, 1852)
The iconic and much-loved Charles Dickens (1812–70) was born in Portsmouth, though he spent much of his life in Kent and London. At the age of 12 Charles was forced into

working in a factory for a couple of months to support his family. He never forgot his harrowing experience there, and his stories always reflected the plight of the working class. He gave a view of contemporary England with a strong sense of realism, yet also incorporated occasional ghost and horror elements. He continued to work hard until his death in 1870.

Arthur Conan Doyle

The Leather Funnel

(Originally Published in *Tales of Terror and Mystery*, John Murray, 1922)

Arthur Conan Doyle (1859–1930) was born in Edinburgh, Scotland. As a medical student he was so impressed by his professor's powers of deduction that he was inspired to create the illustrious and much-loved figure Sherlock Holmes. However, Doyle became increasingly interested in spiritualism, leaving him keen to explore fantastical elements in his stories. Doyle's vibrant and remarkable characters have breathed life into all of his stories, engaging readers throughout the decades.

John H. Dromey

In Search of a New Wilhelm

(First Publication)

John H. Dromey was born in Northeast Missouri. He grew up on a farm, but likes the conveniences of city life. Once upon a time he had bylines for brief, humorous items (daffynitions, one-liners, light verse) in over 150 different newspapers and magazines, including *Reader's Digest* and *The Wall Street Journal*. He's had short fiction published in *Alfred Hitchcock's Mystery Magazine*, *Black Denim Lit #7*, *Gumshoe Review*, *Stupefying Stories Showcase*, and elsewhere, as well as in a number of anthologies.

Elise Forier Edie

Leonora

(Originally Published in *Penumbra Magazine*, 2013)

Elise Forier Edie lives in Los Angeles, California, with her husband and two dogs. Her works of horror and speculative fiction have been published by Tartarus Press and World Weaver Press. Before becoming a fiction writer, Elise worked for many years as a playwright, and still continues to work in the theatre as an actress and director. Her first novella, a paranormal romance called *The Devil in Midwinter*, was released in April 2014. She is a member of the Horror Writers Association and the Authors Guild.

David A. Elsensohn

A Game of Conquest

(Originally Published with Ether Books App, 2011)

David Elsensohn is usually busy being distracted by such language-coaxers as Tolkien, Howard, Leiber, Gaiman and Lovecraft, or by well-crafted batches of single malt whisky. He has works published in the *Northridge Review*, *Crack the Spine*, *The Golden Key*, Kazka Press's *California Cantata*, *Grim Corps II*, and Literary Underground's *Unearthed* Anthology. A native of Los Angeles, he lives with an inspirational wife and a curmudgeonly black cat.

Eric Esser
Thing in the Bucket
(Originally Published in *Fictionvale*, 2013)
Eric Esser lives and writes in San Francisco with his love Courtney and the ghost of their black cat Mina. When he was small he used to wander the perimeter of his elementary school soccer field every recess imagining stories set in other worlds, and for some reason no one made fun of him for it. He suspects they discussed him secretly. He is a graduate of the 2012 Clarion Writers Workshop. His fiction has appeared or is forthcoming in *Schoolbooks and Sorcery, Pseudopod*, and the *Awkward Robots* anthology series. Visit him at ericesser.net or follow him on Twitter (@ericdesser).

Sheridan Le Fanu
The Murdered Cousin
(Originally Published in *Ghost Stories and Tales of Mystery*, James McGlashan, 1851)
The remarkable father of Victorian ghost stories Joseph Thomas Sheridan Le Fanu (1814–73) was born in Dublin, Ireland. His gothic tales and mystery novels led to him becoming a leading ghost story writer of the nineteenth century. Three oft-cited works of his are *Uncle Silas, Carmilla* and *The House by the Churchyard,* which all are assumed to have influenced Bram Stoker's *Dracula.* Le Fanu wrote his most successful and productive works after his wife's tragic death and he remained a relatively strong writer up until his own death.

Elizabeth Gaskell
The Grey Woman
(Originally Published in *The Grey Woman and Other Tales*, Smith, Elder and Co., 1865)
Victorian novelist Elizabeth Gaskell (1810–65) was born in Chelsea, London, and is widely known for her biography of her friend Charlotte Brontë. In a family of eight children, only Elizabeth and her brother John survived past childhood. Her mother's early death caused her to be raised by her aunt in Knutsford, a place that inspired her to later write her most famous work, *Cranford.* Tragedy struck again when Gaskell's only son died, and it was then that she began to write. All the misfortune in her life led her to write many gothic and horror tales including *Lois the Witch.*

Michael Paul Gonzalez
Worth the Having
(Originally Published in *Halloween Tales*, Omnium Gatherum Books, 2014)
Michael Paul Gonzalez is the author of the novels *Angel Falls* and *Miss Massacre's Guide to Murder and Vengeance.* A member of the Horror Writer's Association, his short stories have appeared in print and online, including the *Booked* podcast anthology, FCJR, HeavyMetal. com, and the *Appalachian Undead* anthology. He resides in Los Angeles, a place full of wonders and monsters far stranger than any that live in the imagination. You can visit him online at MichaelPaulGonzalez.com

Ed Grabianowski
Extraneus Invokat
(Originally Published in *Black Static*, 2011)
Ed Grabianowski's stories have appeared in *Black Static*, the *Geek Love* anthology, and David Wellington's *Fear Project*. You'll find his non-fiction work at sites like io9

and HowStuffWorks. His influences include pulp horror and sword & sorcery like H.P. Lovecraft, Robert E. Howard and C.L. Moore, *The Twilight Zone* and *Friday the 13th Part VI: Jason Lives*. A native of Buffalo, New York, Ed likes zombies, welding, dogs and pizza.

Thomas Hardy
The Three Strangers
(Originally Published in *Longman's Magazine* and *Harper's Weekly*, 1883)
Thomas Hardy (1840–1928), one of the most renowned poets and novelists in English literary history, was born in Dorset, England. Influenced by Romanticism and Charles Dickens, he wrote critically about the Victorian society. He quickly gained fame for his dedication to Naturalism, made evident through his novels *Far from the Madding Crowd, Jude the Obscure* and *The Mayor of Casterbridge*. Most of his stories contain tragic characters, which developed into the characters that feature in his horror novels.

Nathaniel Hawthorne
Young Goodman Brown
(Originally Published in *The New-England Magazine*, 1835)
The prominent American writer Nathaniel Hawthorne (1804–64) was born in Salem, Massachusetts. His most famous novel *The Scarlet Letter* helped him become established as a writer in the 1850s. Most of his works were influenced by his friends Ralph Waldo Emerson and Herman Melville, as well as by his extended financial struggles. Hawthorne's works often incorporated a dark romanticism that focused on the evil and sin of humanity. Some of his most famous works detailed supernatural presences or occurrences, as in his *The House of the Seven Gables* and the short story collection *Twice Told Tales*.

William Hope Hodgson
The Gateway of the Monster
(Originally Published in *The Idler*, 1910)
William Hope Hodgson (1877–1918) was born in Essex, England but moved several times with his family, including living for some time in County Galway, Ireland – a setting that would later inspire *The House on the Borderland*. Hodgson made several unsuccessful attempts to run away to sea, until his uncle secured him some work in the Merchant Marine. This association with the ocean would unfold later in his many sea stories. After some initial rejections of his writing, Hodgson managed to become a full-time writer of both novels and short stories, which form a fantastic legacy of adventure, mystery and horror fiction.

Robert E. Howard
The Challenge from Beyond (as collaborator)
(Originally pubished in *Fantasy Magazine*, 1935)
Robert Ervin Howard (1906–36) was born in Peaster, Texas. He is responsible for forming the subgenre within fantasy known as 'Sword and Sorcery', establishing him as a pulp fiction writer. Being a very intellectual and athletic man, Howard wrote within the genres of westerns, boxing, historical and horror fiction as well. His novel *Pigeons from Hell*, which Stephen King quoted as the one of the finest horror stories of the century, exemplifies his dark yet realistic style. Howard will possibly always be known best for his association with the pulp magazine *Weird Tales*, in which he published many tales of a horror and fantasy nature.

Gwendolyn Kiste

The Man in the Ambry

(Originally Published in *Typehouse Literary Magazine*, 2015)

With parents who married on Halloween and read her Ray Bradbury and Edgar Allan Poe stories long before she started kindergarten, Gwendolyn Kiste considers horror, fantasy, and all things strange to be her birthright. Her speculative fiction has appeared or is forthcoming in *LampLight*, *Sanitarium Magazine*, and *Nightmare* among other outlets. An Ohio native, she currently resides on an abandoned horse farm in Pennsylvania. You can find her online at www.gwendolynkiste.com and on Twitter @GwendolynKiste.

Bill Kte'pi

Start with Color

(Originally Published in *Strange Horizons*, 2003)

Bill Kte'pi is the author of two horror novels, *Low Country* and *Frankie Teardrop*, the latter of which was published in 2015 by Fey Publishing. He has been publishing short stories for 25 years, with links to available online work at ktepi.com. *Start With Color* shares a setting with *The Minotaur*, originally published in *Strange Horizons*. Bill and his girlfriend live in New England and are planning a move to the Southern U.S.

D.H. Lawrence

The Rocking-Horse Winner

(Originally Published in *Harper's Bazaar*, 1926)

David Herbert Lawrence (1885–1930) was born in Nottinghamshire, England. Lawrence, best-known for his sexually explicit novel *Lady Chatterley's Lover*, was an audacious author, journalist, poet and playwright. Being one of the most influential writers in the twentieth century, he published an extreme variety of works detailing a vast range of emotional themes. His unique childhood influenced him to write his haunting and creative tales.

James Lecky

The Magnificat of Devils

(Originally Published in *Oktobyr*, 1997)

James Lecky is a writer, actor and (occasional) stand-up comedian from Derry, N. Ireland. His short fiction has appeared in a number of publications both in print and online including *Beneath Ceaseless Skies*, *Heroic Fantasy Quarterly*, *The Phantom Queen Awakes*, *Arcane*, *Jupiter SF* and *Emerald Eye: The Best Irish Imaginative Fiction*. His influences are many and varied including (but not limited to) Clark Ashton Smith, Jack Vance, Philip K. Dick, J.G. Ballard and Lord Dunsany.

Frank Belknap Long

The Challenge from Beyond (as collaborator)

(Originally pubished in *Fantasy Magazine*, 1935)

Prolific American writer of horror, Frank Belknap Long (1901–94) was born in Manhattan, New York, and was best known for writing *The Hounds of Tindalos*. Stories by H.G. Wells and Edgar Allan Poe filled his childhood, and after he came close to dying in the 1920s, Long decided to drop out of college and become a freelance writer. Writing an enormous amount of science fiction and horror novels, Ray Bradbury stated Long 'has helped shape the field' of American science fiction history.

H.P. Lovecraft

The Dunwich Horror
(Originally Published in *Weird Tales*, 1929)
The Call of Cthulhu
(Originally Published in *Weird Tales*, 1928)
The Challenge from Beyond (as collaborator)
(Originally pubished in *Fantasy Magazine*, 1935)
Howard Philips Lovecraft (1890–1937) was born in Providence, Rhode Island. Now one of the most significant American authors in the genre of horror fiction, Lovecraft did not receive much of his highly deserved recognition until after his death. His inspiration came predominantly from various astronomers and the writings of Edgar Allan Poe. Having nightmares repeatedly throughout his adulthood, he was inspired to write his dark and strange fantasy tales. Lovecraft's most famous story 'The Call of Cthulhu' went on to inspire many authors, as well as movies, art and games.

Guy de Maupassant

The Horla
(Originally Published in *Gil Blas*, 1886)
Henri René Albert Guy de Maupassant (1850–93) was born at the Château de Miromesnil in France, and is considered the father of the modern short story. He is perhaps known best for *The Necklace*, though his most stunning success is possibly his first published novel *Boule de Suif*, which was inspired by his time serving during the Franco-Prussian War. Maupassant developed syphilis early on in his life, causing him to develop a mental disorder coupled with nightmarish visions. These visions enabled Maupassant to write his most convincing works of horror fiction.

A. Merritt

The Woman of the Wood
(Originally Published in *Weird Tales*, 1926)
The Challenge from Beyond (as collaborator)
(Originally pubished in *Fantasy Magazine*, 1935)
Abraham Merritt (1884–1943) was born in Beverly, New Jersey. A writer of science fiction as well as an inductee to the Science Fiction and Fantasy Hall of Fame, Merritt wrote characteristic pulp fiction themes of lost civilization, monsters and treacherous villains. Many of his short stories and novels were published in *Argosy All-Story Weekly*. His most famous novels are perhaps *Burn Witch Burn* and *The Ship of Ishtar and Dwellers in the Mirage*.

C.L. Moore

The Challenge from Beyond (as collaborator)
(Originally pubished in *Fantasy Magazine*, 1935)
Catherine Lucille Moore (1911–87) worked as a writer in the weird, sf and fantasy genres, mainly in the magazines of the Golden Era of the pulps. Her forté was character development and scintillating plotlines, and she was much admired by many of her contemporaries including H.P. Lovecraft and Henry Kuttner, the latter of whom she married in 1940. She collaborated with Kuttner from then on, also producing a novel and a number of TV scripts in the 1950s. She was honoured with a World Fantasy Award in 1961, for lifetime achievement.

Jan Neruda
The Vampire
(Originally Published in *Czechoslovak Stories*, Duffield & Co., 1920)
The prominent Czech Realist Jan Neruda (1834–91) was born in Prague, Bohemia. He was a teacher before embarking on a career as a journalist and writer. His most notable sardonic work *Povídky Malostranské* assisted in the advancement of the idea to renew Czech patriotism. Neruda was known for his mocking representation of the bourgeois of Prague as he gained much fame for his prose style. It wasn't until mystery writer Ellis Peters translated Neruda's works into English that he became a worldwide phenomenon.

Edgar Allan Poe
The Masque of the Red Death
(Originally Published in *Graham's Magazine*, 1842)
The Premature Burial
(Originally Published in the *Philadelphia Dollar Newspaper*, 1844)
Versatile writer Edgar Allan Poe (1809–49) was born in Boston, Massachusetts. Poe is well known for being an author, poet, editor and literary critic during the American Romantic Movement. Poe is generally considered the inventor of the detective fiction genre, and his works are famously filled with terror, mystery, death and haunting. His better known works include *The Tell Tale Heart, The Raven* and *The Fall of the House of Usher*. The dark, mystifying characters from his tales have captured the public's imagination and reflect the struggling, poverty-stricken lifestyle he lived his whole life.

Frank Roger
Trial and Error
(Originally Published in *Portulaan*, 2013)
Frank Roger was born in 1957 in Ghent, Belgium. His first story appeared in 1975. He now has a few hundred short stories to his credit, published in more than 40 languages. In 2012 a story collection in English (*The Burning Woman and Other Stories*) was published in Ireland by Evertype (*www.evertype.com*). Apart from fiction, he also produces collages and graphic work in a surrealist and satirical tradition. They have appeared in various magazines and books. Find out more at www.frankroger.be .

Mary Shelley
The Mortal Immortal
(Originally Published in *The Keepsake for 1834*, Longman, Rees, Orme, Brown, 1833)
Mary Shelley (1797–1851) was born in Somers Town, London. Encouraged to write at a young age by her father, William Godwin, who was a journalist, philosopher and novelist, Shelley became an essayist, biographer, short story writer and novelist. She is famous for her horror novel *Frankenstein: or The Modern Prometheus*, and for being married to the poet Percy Bysshe Shelley. Suffering many traumatic events and widowed early on in her life, she worked hard to support herself and her son through several novels, such as *The Last Man*.

Robert Louis Stevenson
The Body Snatcher
(Originally Published in the *Pall Mall Christmas 'Extra'*, 1884)
Robert Louis Stevenson (1850–94) was born in Edinburgh, Scotland. He became a well-known

novelist, poet and travel writer, writing such famous works as *Treasure Island, Kidnapped* and *The Strange Case of Dr Jekyll and Mr Hyde*. His works were highly admired by many other artists, as he was a widely known literary celebrity. Travelling a lot for health reasons and because of his family's business, Stevenson ended up writing a lot of his journeys into his stories and wrote works mainly related to children's literature and the horror genre.

Bram Stoker
Dracula's Guest
(Originally Published in *Dracula's Guest and Other Weird Stories*, George Routledge and Sons, 1914)
Abraham 'Bram' Stoker (1847–1912) was born in Dublin, Ireland. Often ill during his childhood, he spent a lot of time in bed listening to his mother's grim stories, sparking his imagination. Striking up a friendship as an adult with the actor Henry Irving, Stoker eventually came to work and live in London, meeting notable authors such as Arthur Conan Doyle and Oscar Wilde. Stoker wrote several stories based on supernatural horror, such as the gothic masterpiece *Dracula* which has left an enduring and powerful impact on the genre, creating one of the most iconic figures that horror fiction has ever seen.

Lucy Taylor
Blessed Be the Bound
(Originally Published in *Guignoir*, 1991)
Lucy Taylor is the Stoker-winning author of *The Safety of Unknown Cities, Spree, Unnatural Acts and Other Stories* and eleven other horror/suspense novels and collections. Her most recent work includes the short story collection *Fatal Journeys* and the novelette *A Respite for the Dead*. Upcoming publications include the short story *In the Cave of the Delicate Singers* (Tor.com; August 2015), *Wingless Beasts* ('Best Horror of the Year #7'; Night Shade Books), and *Moth Frenzy* ('Peeling Back the Skin'; Grey Matter Press). She lives in Santa Fe, New Mexico: a land full of mystery, romance, and the macabre. Visit her website at: www. lucytaylor.us.

Dr Dale Townshend
Foreword: Chilling Horror Short Stories
Dale Townshend is Senior Lecturer in Gothic and Romantic Literature at the University of Stirling, Scotland, and Director of the MLitt in The Gothic Imagination. In the field of Gothic studies, his most recent publications include *The Gothic World*; *Ann Radcliffe, Romanticism and the Gothic*; and *Terror and Wonder: The Gothic Imagination*.

Kristopher Triana
Dead End
(First Publication)
Kristopher Triana is an American author of southern gothic, horror, western and crime fiction. He is the author of *Growing Dark* and he has two new novels, *The Ruin Season* and *Body Art*, which will both be released in 2016. His short stories have appeared in many magazines and anthologies, including *D.O.A. II*, *The Ghost is the Machine*, *Spinetingler Magazine*, *Zombie Jesus and Other True Stories*, and *Halloween Forevermore*. In addition, some of his work has also been translated into Russian. He works as a professional dog trainer and lives in North Carolina with his wife.

DJ Tyrer
Justified
(Originally Published in *Surreal Grotesque*, 2013)
DJ Tyrer lives in Southend-on-Sea, and is the person behind Atlantean Publishing. He has been published in anthologies and magazines in the UK, USA and elsewhere, including *A Grimoire of Eldritch Inquests, Volume I* (Emby Press), *State of Horror: Illinois* (Charon Coin Press), *Steampunk Cthulhu* (Chaosium), *Tales of the Dark Arts* (Hazardous Press), *Cosmic Horror* (Dark Hall Press) and *Sorcery & Sanctity: A Homage to Arthur Machen* (Hieroglyphics Press). In addition, he has a novella available in paperback and on the Kindle: *The Yellow House* (Dunhams Manor). DJ Tyrer's website is: djtyrer.blogspot.co.uk.

Edith Wharton
Afterward
(Originally Published in *The Century Magazine*, 1910)
Edith Wharton (1862–1937), the Pulitzer Prize-winning writer of *The Age of Innocence*, was born in New York. As well as her talent as an American novelist, Wharton was also known for her short stories and designer career. She was born into a controlled society where women were discouraged from achieving anything beyond a proper marriage. Defeating the norms, Wharton became one of America's greatest writers. Writing numerous ghost stories and murderous tales such as *The Lady's Maid's Bell*, *The Eyes* and *Afterward*, Wharton is widely known for the ghost tours at her old home, The Mount.

Andrew J. Wilson
Deep-sixed Without a Depth Gauge
(Originally Published with Ghostwriter Publications, 2009)
Andrew J. Wilson lives in Edinburgh with his wife and two sons. His short stories, poetry and journalism have appeared all over the world, sometimes in the most unlikely places. *The Terminal Zone*, his play about Rod Serling, has been performed several times, and was restaged under his direction at the 2014 World Science Fiction Convention in London. With Neil Williamson he co-edited *Nova Scotia: New Scottish Speculative Fiction*, a critically acclaimed original anthology that was nominated for a World Fantasy Award.

William R.D. Wood
The Dew of Heaven, Like Ashes
(Originally Published in *Tomorrow: Apocalyptic Short Stories*, Kayelle Press, 2013)
William R.D. Wood lives with his wife and children in Virginia's Shenandoah Valley in an old farmhouse turned backwards to the road. He enjoys exploring this world and creating new ones of his own. His work has appeared in *Omni Reboot*, the *Lovecraft eZine* and in titles from Emby Press, Morpheus Press and Apokrupha. Far, far too much greatness exists in the realms of speculative fiction to pick favorite influences, but William's ideal would be to write Lovecraftian fiction like Stephen King in an Arthur C. Clarke universe interpreted by H. R. Giger. Check out www.williamRDwood. com for more.